EAST OF EDEN

and

THE WAYWARD BUS

JOHN STEINBECK

East of Eden

AND

The Wayward Bus

THE VIKING PRESS · NEW YORK

East of Eden

East of Eden

PASCAL COVICI

Dear Pat,

You came upon me carving some kind of little figure out of wood and you said, "Why don't you make something for me?"

I asked you what you wanted, and you said, "A box."

"What for?"

"To put things in."

"What things?"

"Whatever you have," you said.

Well, here's your box. Nearly everything I have is in it, and it is not full. Pain and excitement are in it, and feeling good or bad and evil thoughts and good thoughts—the pleasure of design and some despair and the indescribable joy of creation.

And on top of these are all the gratitude and love I have for you.

And still the box is not full.

JOHN

PART ONE

PART ONE

ONE

The Salinas Valley is in Northern California. It is a long narrow swale between two ranges of mountains, and the Salinas River winds and twists up the center until it falls at last into Monterey Bay.

I remember my childhood names for grasses and secret flowers. I remember where a toad may live and what time the birds awaken in the summer—and what trees and seasons smelled like—how people looked and walked and smelled even. The memory of odors is very rich.

I remember that the Gabilan Mountains to the east of the valley were light gay mountains full of sun and loveliness and a kind of invitation, so that you wanted to climb into their warm foothills almost as you want to climb into the lap of a beloved mother. They were beckoning mountains with a brown grass love. The Santa Lucias stood up against the sky to the west and kept the valley from the open sea, and they were dark and brooding —unfriendly and dangerous. I always found in myself a dread of west and a love of east. Where I ever got such an idea I cannot say, unless it could be that the morning came over the peaks of the Gabilans and the night drifted back from the ridges of the Santa Lucias. It may be that the birth and death of the day had some part in my feeling about the two ranges of mountains.

From both sides of the valley little streams slipped out of the hill canyons and fell into the bed of the Salinas River. In the winter of wet years the streams ran full-freshet, and they swelled the river until sometimes it raged and boiled, bank full, and then it was a destroyer. The river tore the edges of the farm lands and washed whole acres down; it toppled barns and houses into itself, to go floating and bobbing away. It trapped cows and pigs and sheep and drowned them in its muddy brown water and carried them to the sea. Then when the late spring came, the river drew in from its edges and the sand banks appeared. And in the summer the river didn't run at all above ground. Some pools would be left in the deep swirl places under a high bank. The tules and grasses grew back, and willows straightened up with the flood debris in their upper branches. The Salinas was only a part-time river. The summer sun drove it underground. It was not a fine river at all, but it was the only one we had and so we boasted about it—how dangerous it was in a wet winter and how dry it was in a dry summer. You can boast about anything if it's all you have. Maybe the less you have, the more you are required to boast.

The floor of the Salinas Valley, between the ranges and below the foothills, is level because this valley used to be the bottom of a hundred-mile inlet from the sea. The river mouth at Moss Landing was centuries ago the entrance to this long inland water. Once, fifty miles down the valley, my father bored a well. The drill came up first with topsoil and then with gravel and then with white sea sand full of shells and even pieces of whalebone. There were twenty feet of sand and then black earth again, and even a piece of redwood, that imperishable wood that does not rot. Before the inland sea the valley must have been a forest. And those things had happened right under our feet. And it seemed to me sometimes at night that I could feel both the sea and the redwood forest before it.

On the wide level acres of the valley the topsoil lay deep and fertile. It required only a rich winter of rain to make it break forth in grass and flowers. The spring flowers in a wet year were unbelievable. The whole valley floor, and the foothills too, would be carpeted with lupins and poppies. Once a woman told me that colored flowers would seem more bright if you added a few white flowers to give the colors definition. Every petal of blue lupin is edged with white, so that a field of lupins is more blue than you can imagine. And mixed with these were splashes of California poppies. These too are of a burning color—not orange, not gold, but if pure gold were liquid and could raise a cream, that golden cream might be like the color of the poppies. When their season was over the yellow mustard came up and grew to a great height. When my grandfather came into the valley the mustard was so tall that a man on horseback showed only his head above the yellow flowers. On the uplands the grass would be strewn with buttercups, with hen-and-chickens, with black-centered yellow violets. And a little later in the season there would be red and yellow stands of Indian paintbrush. These were the flowers of the open places exposed to the sun.

Under the live oaks, shaded and dusky, the maidenhair flourished and gave a good smell, and under the mossy banks of the water courses whole clumps of five-fingered ferns and goldy-backs hung down. Then there were harebells, tiny lanterns, cream white and almost sinful looking, and these were so rare and magical that a child, finding one, felt singled out and special all day long.

When June came the grasses headed out and turned brown, and the hills turned a brown which was not brown but a gold and saffron and red—an indescribable color. And from then on until the next rains the earth dried and the streams stopped. Cracks appeared on the level ground. The Salinas River sank under its sand. The wind blew down the valley, picking up dust and straws, and grew stronger and harsher as it went south. It stopped in the evening. It was a rasping nervous wind, and the dust particles cut into a

man's skin and burned his eyes. Men working in the fields wore goggles and
tied handkerchiefs around their noses to keep the dirt out.

The valley land was deep and rich, but the foothills wore only a skin of
topsoil no deeper than the grass roots; and the farther up the hills you went,
the thinner grew the soil, with flints sticking through, until at the brush line
it was a kind of dry flinty gravel that reflected the hot sun blindingly.

I have spoken of the rich years when the rainfall was plentiful. But there
were dry years too, and they put a terror on the valley. The water came in a
thirty-year cycle. There would be five or six wet and wonderful years when
there might be nineteen to twenty-five inches of rain, and the land would
shout with grass. Then would come six or seven pretty good years of twelve
to sixteen inches of rain. And then the dry years would come, and sometimes there would be only seven or eight inches of rain. The land dried up
and the grasses headed out miserably a few inches high and great bare
scabby places appeared in the valley. The live oaks got a crusty look and
the sagebrush was gray. The land cracked and the springs dried up and the
cattle listlessly nibbled dry twigs. Then the farmers and the ranchers would
be filled with disgust for the Salinas Valley. The cows would grow thin and
sometimes starve to death. People would have to haul water in barrels to
their farms just for drinking. Some families would sell out for nearly nothing
and move away. And it never failed that during the dry years the people
forgot about the rich years, and during the wet years they lost all memory of
the dry years. It was always that way.

2

And that was the long Salinas Valley. Its history was like that of the rest of
the state. First there were Indians, an inferior breed without energy, in-
ventiveness, or culture, a people that lived on grubs and grasshoppers and
shellfish, too lazy to hunt or fish. They ate what they could pick up and
planted nothing. They pounded bitter acorns for flour. Even their warfare
was a weary pantomime.

Then the hard, dry Spaniards came exploring through, greedy and realistic,
and their greed was for gold or God. They collected souls as they collected
jewels. They gathered mountains and valleys, rivers and whole horizons,
the way a man might now gain title to building lots. These tough, dried-up
men moved restlessly up the coast and down. Some of them stayed on grants
as large as principalities, given to them by Spanish kings who had not the
faintest idea of the gift. These first owners lived in poor feudal settlements,
and their cattle ranged freely and multiplied. Periodically the owners killed
the cattle for their hides and tallow and left the meat to the vultures and
coyotes.

When the Spaniards came they had to give everything they saw a name.

This is the first duty of any explorer—a duty and a privilege. You must name a thing before you can note it on your hand-drawn map. Of course they were religious people, and the men who could read and write, who kept the records and drew the maps, were the tough untiring priests who traveled with the soldiers. Thus the first names of places were saints' names or religious holidays celebrated at stopping places. There are many saints, but they are not inexhaustible, so that we find repetitions in the first namings. We have San Miguel, St. Michael, San Ardo, San Bernardo, San Benito, San Lorenzo, San Carlos, San Francisquito. And then the holidays—Natividad, the Nativity; Nacimiente, the Birth; Soledad, the Solitude. But places were also named from the way the expedition felt at the time: Buena Esperenza, good hope; Buena Vista because the view was beautiful; and Chualar because it was pretty. The descriptive names followed: Paso de los Robles because of the oak trees; Los Laureles for the laurels; Tularcitos because of the reeds in the swamp; and Salinas for the alkali which was white as salt.

Then places were named for animals and birds seen—Gabilanes for the hawks which flew in those mountains; Topo for the mole; Los Gatos for the wild cats. The suggestions sometimes came from the nature of the place itself: Tassajara, a cup and saucer; Laguna Seca, a dry lake; Corral de Tierra for a fence of earth; Paraiso because it was like Heaven.

Then the Americans came—more greedy because there were more of them. They took the lands, remade the laws to make their titles good. And farmholds spread over the land, first in the valleys and then up the foothill slopes, small wooden houses roofed with redwood shakes, corrals of split poles. Wherever a trickle of water came out of the ground a house sprang up and a family began to grow and multiply. Cuttings of red geraniums and rosebushes were planted in the dooryards. Wheel tracks of buckboards replaced the trails, and fields of corn and barley and wheat squared out of the yellow mustard. Every ten miles along the traveled routes a general store and blacksmith shop happened, and these became the nuclei of little towns, Bradley, King City, Greenfield.

The Americans had a greater tendency to name places for people than had the Spanish. After the valleys were settled the names of places refer more to things which happened there, and these to me are the most fascinating of all names because each name suggests a story that has been forgotten. I think of Bolsa Nueva, a new purse; Morocojo, a lame Moor (who was he and how did he get there?); Wild Horse Canyon and Mustang Grade and Shirt Tail Canyon. The names of places carry a charge of the people who named them, reverent or irreverent, descriptive, either poetic or disparaging. You can name anything San Lorenzo, but Shirt Tail Canyon or the Lame Moor is something quite different.

The wind whistled over the settlements in the afternoon, and the farmers began to set out mile-long windbreaks of eucalyptus to keep the plowed topsoil from blowing away. And this is about the way the Salinas Valley was when my grandfather brought his wife and settled in the foothills to the east of King City.

TWO

I must depend on hearsay, on old photographs, on stories told, and on memories which are hazy and mixed with fable in trying to tell you about the Hamiltons. They were not eminent people, and there are few records concerning them except for the usual papers on birth, marriage, land ownership, and death.

Young Samuel Hamilton came from the north of Ireland and so did his wife. He was the son of small farmers, neither rich nor poor, who had lived on one landhold and in one stone house for many hundreds of years. The Hamiltons managed to be remarkably well educated and well read; and, as is so often true in that green country, they were connected and related to very great people and very small people, so that one cousin might be a baronet and another cousin a beggar. And of course they were descended from the ancient kings of Ireland, as every Irishman is.

Why Samuel left the stone house and the green acres of his ancestors I do not know. He was never a political man, so it is not likely a charge of rebellion drove him out, and he was scrupulously honest, which eliminates the police as prime movers. There was a whisper—not even a rumor but rather an unsaid feeling—in my family that it was love drove him out, and not love of the wife he married. But whether it was too successful love or whether he left in pique at unsuccessful love, I do not know. We always preferred to think it was the former. Samuel had good looks and charm and gaiety. It is hard to imagine that any country Irish girl refused him.

He came to the Salinas Valley full-blown and hearty, full of inventions and energy. His eyes were very blue, and when he was tired one of them wandered outward a little. He was a big man but delicate in a way. In the dusty business of ranching he seemed always immaculate. His hands were clever. He was a good blacksmith and carpenter and woodcarver, and he could improvise anything with bits of wood and metal. He was forever inventing a new way of doing an old thing and doing it better and quicker, but he never in his whole life had any talent for making money. Other men who had the talent took Samuel's tricks and sold them and grew rich, but Samuel barely made wages all his life.

I don't know what directed his steps toward the Salinas Valley. It was an unlikely place for a man from a green country to come to, but he came about thirty years before the turn of the century and he brought with him his

tiny Irish wife, a tight hard little woman humorless as a chicken. She had a
dour Presbyterian mind and a code of morals that pinned down and beat
the brains out of nearly everything that was pleasant to do.

I do not know where Samuel met her, how he wooed her, married. I
think there must have been some other girl printed somewhere in his heart,
for he was a man of love and his wife was not a woman to show her feelings.
And in spite of this, in all the years from his youth to his death in the
Salinas Valley, there was no hint that Samuel ever went to any other woman.

When Samuel and Liza came to the Salinas Valley all the level land was
taken, the rich bottoms, the little fertile creases in the hills, the forests, but
there was still marginal land to be homesteaded, and in the barren hills, to
the east of what is now King City, Samuel Hamilton homesteaded.

He followed the usual practice. He took a quarter-section for himself and
a quarter-section for his wife, and since she was pregnant he took a quarter-
section for the child. Over the years nine children were born, four boys and
five girls, and with each birth another quarter-section was added to the
ranch, and that makes eleven quarter-sections, or seventeen hundred and
sixty acres.

If the land had been any good the Hamiltons would have been rich people. But the acres were harsh and dry. There were no springs, and the crust
of topsoil was so thin that the flinty bones stuck through. Even the sagebrush struggled to exist, and the oaks were dwarfed from lack of moisture.
Even in reasonably good years there was so little feed that the cattle kept
thin running about looking for enough to eat. From their barren hills the
Hamiltons could look down to the west and see the richness of the bottom
land and the greenness around the Salinas River.

Samuel built his house with his own hands, and he built a barn and a
blacksmith shop. He found quite soon that even if he had ten thousand
acres of hill country he could not make a living on the bony soil without
water. His clever hands built a well-boring rig, and he bored wells on the
lands of luckier men. He invented and built a threshing machine and moved
through the bottom farms in harvest time, threshing the grain his own farm
would not raise. And in his shop he sharpened plows and mended harrows
and welded broken axles and shod horses. Men from all over the district
brought him tools to mend and to improve. Besides, they loved to hear
Samuel talk of the world and its thinking, of the poetry and philosophy
that were going on outside the Salinas Valley. He had a rich deep voice,
good both in song and in speech, and while he had no brogue there was a
rise and a lilt and a cadence to his talk that made it sound sweet in the ears
of the taciturn farmers from the valley bottom. They brought whisky too,
and out of sight of the kitchen window and the disapproving eye of Mrs.
Hamilton they took hot nips from the bottle and nibbled cuds of green wild
anise to cover the whisky breath. It was a bad day when three or four men
were not standing around the forge, listening to Samuel's hammer and his

talk. They called him a comical genius and carried his stories carefully home, and they wondered at how the stories spilled out on the way, for they never sounded the same repeated in their own kitchens.

Samuel should have been rich from his well rig and his threshing machine and his shop, but he had no gift for business. His customers, always pressed for money, promised payment after harvest, and then after Christmas, and then after—until at last they forgot it. Samuel had no gift for reminding them. And so the Hamiltons stayed poor.

The children came along as regularly as the years. The few overworked doctors of the county did not often get to the ranches for a birth unless the joy turned nightmare and went on for several days. Samuel Hamilton delivered all his own children and tied the cords neatly, spanked the bottoms and cleaned up the mess. When his youngest was born with some small obstruction and began to turn black, Samuel put his mouth against the baby's mouth and blew air in and sucked it out until the baby could take over for himself. Samuel's hands were so good and gentle that neighbors from twenty miles away would call on him to help with a birth. And he was equally good with mare, cow, or woman.

Samuel had a great black book on an available shelf and it had gold letters on the cover—*Dr. Gunn's Family Medicine*. Some pages were bent and beat up from use, and others were never opened to the light. To look through *Dr. Gunn* is to know the Hamiltons' medical history. These are the used sections—broken bones, cuts, bruises, mumps, measles, backache, scarlet fever, diphtheria, rheumatism, female complaints, hernia, and of course everything to do with pregnancy and the birth of children. The Hamiltons must have been either lucky or moral for the sections on gonorrhea and syphilis were never opened.

Samuel had no equal for soothing hysteria and bringing quiet to a frightened child. It was the sweetness of his tongue and the tenderness of his soul. And just as there was a cleanness about his body, so there was a cleanness in his thinking. Men coming to his blacksmith shop to talk and listen dropped their cursing for a while, not from any kind of restraint but automatically, as though this were not the place for it.

Samuel kept always a forcignness. Perhaps it was in the cadence of his speech, and this had the effect of making men, and women too, tell him things they would not tell to relatives or close friends. His slight strangeness set him apart and made him safe as a repository.

Liza Hamilton was a very different kettle of Irish. Her head was small and round and it held small round convictions. She had a button nose and a hard little set-back chin, a gripping jaw set on its course even though the angels of God argued against it.

Liza was a good plain cook, and her house—it was always her house—was brushed and pummeled and washed. Bearing her children did not hold her back very much—two weeks at the most she had to be careful. She must have had a pelvic arch of whalebone, for she had big children one after the other.

Liza had a finely developed sense of sin. Idleness was a sin, and card playing, which was a kind of idleness to her. She was suspicious of fun whether it involved dancing or singing or even laughter. She felt that people having a good time were wide open to the devil. And this was a shame, for Samuel was a laughing man, but I guess Samuel was wide open to the devil. His wife protected him whenever she could.

She wore her hair always pulled tight back and bunned behind in a hard knot. And since I can't remember how she dressed, it must have been that she wore clothes that matched herself exactly. She had no spark of humor and only occasionally a blade of cutting wit. She frightened her grandchildren because she had no weakness. She suffered bravely and uncomplainingly through life, convinced that that was the way her God wanted everyone to live. She felt that rewards came later.

2

When people first came to the West, particularly from the owned and fought-over farmlets of Europe, and saw so much land to be had for the signing of a paper and the building of a foundation, an itching land-greed seemed to come over them. They wanted more and more land—good land if possible, but land anyway. Perhaps they had filaments of memory of feudal Europe where great families became and remained great because they owned things. The early settlers took up land they didn't need and couldn't use; they took up worthless land just to own it. And all proportions changed. A man who might have been well-to-do on ten acres in Europe was rat-poor on two thousand in California.

It wasn't very long until all the land in the barren hills near King City and San Ardo was taken up, and ragged families were scattered through the hills, trying their best to scratch a living from the thin flinty soil. They and the coyotes lived clever, despairing, submarginal lives. They landed with no money, no equipment, no tools, no credit, and particularly with no knowledge of the new country and no technique for using it. I don't know whether it was a divine stupidity or a great faith that let them do it. Surely such venture is nearly gone from the world. And the families did survive and grow. They had a tool or a weapon that is also nearly gone, or perhaps it is only dormant for a while. It is argued that because they believed thoroughly in a just, moral God they could put their faith there and let the smaller securities take care of themselves. But I think that because they trusted themselves and respected themselves as individuals, because they knew beyond doubt that they were valuable and potentially moral units—because of this they could give God their own courage and dignity and then receive it back. Such things have disappeared perhaps because men do not trust themselves any more, and when that happens there is nothing left except perhaps to find some strong sure man, even though he may be wrong, and to dangle from his coattails.

While many people came to the Salinas Valley penniless, there were others who, having sold out somewhere else, arrived with money to start a new life. These usually bought land, but good land, and built their houses of planed lumber and had carpets and colored-glass diamond panes in their windows. There were numbers of these families and they got the good land of the valley and cleared the yellow mustard away and planted wheat.

Such a man was Adam Trask.

THREE

Adam Trask was born on a farm on the outskirts of a little town which was not far from a big town in Connecticut. He was an only son, and he was born six months after his father was mustered into a Connecticut regiment in 1862. Adam's mother ran the farm, bore Adam, and still had time to embrace a primitive theosophy. She felt that her husband would surely be killed by the wild and barbarous rebels, and she prepared herself to get in touch with him in what she called the beyond. He came home six weeks after Adam was born. His right leg was off at the knee. He stumped in on a crude wooden leg he himself had carved out of beechwood. And already it was splitting. He had in his pocket and placed on the parlor table the lead bullet they had given him to bite while they cut off his frayed leg.

Adam's father Cyrus was something of a devil—had always been wild—drove a two-wheeled cart too fast, and managed to make his wooden leg seem jaunty and desirable. He had enjoyed his military career, what there was of it. Being wild by nature, he had liked his brief period of training and the drinking and gambling and whoring that went with it. Then he marched south with a group of replacements, and he enjoyed that too—seeing the country and stealing chickens and chasing rebel girls up into the haystacks. The gray, despairing weariness of protracted maneuvers and combat did not touch him. The first time he saw the enemy was at eight o'clock one spring morning, and at eight-thirty he was hit in the right leg by a heavy slug that mashed and splintered the bones beyond repair. Even then he was lucky, for the rebels retreated and the field surgeons moved up immediately. Cyrus Trask did have his five minutes of horror while they cut the shreds away and sawed the bone off square and burned the open flesh. The toothmarks in the bullet proved that. And there was considerable pain while the wound healed under the unusually septic conditions in the hospitals of that day. But Cyrus had vitality and swagger. While he was carving his beechwood leg and hobbling about on a crutch, he contracted a particularly virulent dose of the

clap from a Negro girl who whistled at him from under a pile of lumber
and charged him ten cents. When he had his new leg, and painfully knew his
condition, he hobbled about for days, looking for the girl. He told his bunk-
mates what he was going to do when he found her. He planned to cut off her
ears and her nose with his pocketknife and get his money back. Carving on
his wooden leg, he showed his friends how he would cut her. "When I finish
her she'll be a funny-looking bitch," he said. "I'll make her so a drunk
Indian won't take out after her." His light of love must have sensed his intentions, for he never found her. By the time Cyrus was released from the
hospital and the army, his gonorrhea was dried up. When he got home to
Connecticut there remained only enough of it for his wife.

Mrs. Trask was a pale, inside-herself woman. No heat of sun ever reddened her cheeks, and no open laughter raised the corners of her mouth.
She used religion as a therapy for the ills of the world and of herself, and
she changed the religion to fit the ill. When she found that the theosophy
she had developed for communication with a dead husband was not necessary, she cast about for some new unhappiness. Her search was quickly rewarded by the infection Cyrus brought home from the war. And as soon as
she was aware that a condition existed, she devised a new theology. Her god
of communication became a god of vengeance—to her the most satisfactory
deity she had devised so far—and, as it turned out, the last. It was quite
easy for her to attribute her condition to certain dreams she had experienced
while her husband was away. But the disease was not punishment enough
for her nocturnal philandering. Her new god was an expert in punishment.
He demanded of her a sacrifice. She searched her mind for some proper
egotistical humility and almost happily arrived at the sacrifice—herself. It
took her two weeks to write her last letter with revisions and corrected
spelling. In it she confessed to crimes she could not possibly have committed
and admitted faults far beyond her capacity. And then, dressed in a secretly
made shroud, she went out on a moonlight night and drowned herself in a
pond so shallow that she had to get down on her knees in the mud and hold
her head under water. This required great will power. As the warm unconsciousness finally crept over her, she was thinking with some irritation of
how her white lawn shroud would have mud down the front when they
pulled her out in the morning. And it did.

Cyrus Trask mourned for his wife with a keg of whisky and three old army
friends who had dropped in on their way home to Maine. Baby Adam cried
a good deal at the beginning of the wake, for the mourners, not knowing
about babies, had neglected to feed him. Cyrus soon solved the problem. He
dipped a rag in whisky and gave it to the baby to suck, and after three or
four dippings young Adam went to sleep. Several times during the mourning
period he awakened and complained and got the dipped rag again and went
to sleep. The baby was drunk for two days and a half. Whatever may have
happened in his developing brain, it proved beneficial to his metabolism:

from that two and a half days he gained an iron health. And when at the end of three days his father finally went out and bought a goat, Adam drank the milk greedily, vomited, drank more, and was on his way. His father did not find the reaction alarming, since he was doing the same thing.

Within a month Cyrus Trask's choice fell on the seventeen-year-old daughter of a neighboring farmer. The courtship was quick and realistic. There was no doubt in anybody's mind about his intentions. They were honorable and reasonable. Her father abetted the courtship. He had two younger daughters, and Alice, the eldest, was seventeen. This was her first proposal.

Cyrus wanted a woman to take care of Adam. He needed someone to keep house and cook, and a servant cost money. He was a vigorous man and needed the body of a woman, and that too cost money—unless you were married to it. Within two weeks Cyrus had wooed, wedded, bedded, and impregnated her. His neighbors did not find his action hasty. It was quite normal in that day for a man to use up three or four wives in a normal lifetime.

Alice Trask had a number of admirable qualities. She was a deep scrubber and a corner-cleaner in the house. She was not very pretty, so there was no need to watch her. Her eyes were pale, her complexion sallow, and her teeth crooked, but she was extremely healthy and never complained during her pregnancy. Whether she liked children or not no one ever knew. She was not asked, and she never said anything unless she was asked. From Cyrus's point of view this was possibly the greatest of her virtues. She never offered any opinion or statement, and when a man was talking she gave a vague impression of listening while she went about doing the housework.

The youth, inexperience, and taciturnity of Alice Trask all turned out to be assets for Cyrus. While he continued to operate his farm as such farms were operated in the neighborhood, he entered on a new career—that of the old soldier. And that energy which had made him wild now made him thoughtful. No one now outside of the War Department knew the quality and duration of his service. His wooden leg was at once a certificate of proof of his soldiering and a guarantee that he wouldn't ever have to do it again. Timidly he began to tell Alice about his campaigns, but as his technique grew so did his battles. At the very first he knew he was lying, but it was not long before he was equally sure that every one of his stories was true. Before he had entered the service he had not been much interested in warfare; now he bought every book about war, read every report, subscribed to the New York papers, studied maps. His knowledge of geography had been shaky and his information about the fighting nonexistent; now he became an authority. He knew not only the battles, movements, campaigns, but also the units involved, down to the regiments, their colonels, and where they originated. And from telling he became convinced that he had been there.

All of this was a gradual development, and it took place while Adam was growing to boyhood and his young half-brother behind him. Adam and little Charles would sit silent and respectful while their father explained how every general thought and planned and where they had made their mistakes and what they should have done. And then—he had known it at the time—he had told Grant and McClellan where they were wrong and had begged them to take his analysis of the situation. Invariably they refused his advice and only afterward was he proved right.

There was one thing Cyrus did not do, and perhaps it was clever of him. He never once promoted himself to noncommissioned rank. Private Trask he began, and Private Trask he remained. In the total telling, it made him at once the most mobile and ubiquitous private in the history of warfare. It made it necessary for him to be in as many as four places at once. But perhaps instinctively he did not tell those stories close to each other. Alice and the boys had a complete picture of him: a private soldier, and proud of it, who not only happened to be where every spectacular and important action was taking place but who wandered freely into staff meetings and joined or dissented in the decisions of general officers.

The death of Lincoln caught Cyrus in the pit of the stomach. Always he remembered how he felt when he first heard the news. And he could never mention it or hear of it without quick tears in his eyes. And while he never actually said it, you got the indestructible impression that Private Cyrus Trask was one of Lincoln's closest, warmest, and most trusted friends. When Mr. Lincoln wanted to know about the army, the real army, not those prancing dummies in gold braid, he turned to Private Trask. How Cyrus managed to make this understood without saying it was a triumph of insinuation. No one could call him a liar. And this was mainly because the lie was in his head, and any truth coming from his mouth carried the color of the lie.

Quite early he began to write letters and then articles about the conduct of the war, and his conclusions were intelligent and convincing. Indeed, Cyrus developed an excellent military mind. His criticisms both of the war as it had been conducted and of the army organization as it persisted were irresistibly penetrating. His articles in various magazines attracted attention. His letters to the War Department, printed simultaneously in the newspapers, began to have a sharp effect in decisions on the army. Perhaps if the Grand Army of the Republic had not assumed political force and direction his voice might not have been heard so clearly in Washington, but the spokesman for a block of nearly a million men was not to be ignored. And such a voice in military matters Cyrus Trask became. It came about that he was consulted in matters of army organization, in officer relationships, in personnel and equipment. His expertness was apparent to everyone who heard him. He had a genius for the military. More than that, he was one of those responsible for the organization of the G.A.R. as a cohesive and potent force in the national life. After several unpaid offices in that organization, he took a paid secretaryship which he kept for the rest of his life. He traveled from one end of the country to the other, attending conventions, meetings, and encampments. So much for his public life.

His private life was also laced through with his new profession. He was a man devoted. His house and farm he organized on a military basis. He demanded and got reports on the conduct of his private economy. It is probable that Alice preferred it this way. She was not a talker. A terse report was easiest for her. She was busy with the growing boys and with keeping the house clean and the clothes washed. Also, she had to conserve her energy, though she did not mention this in any of her reports. Without warning her energy would leave her, and she would have to sit down and wait until it came back. In the night she would be drenched with perspiration. She knew perfectly well that she had what was called consumption, would have known even if she was not reminded by a hard, exhausting cough. And she did not know how long she would live. Some people wasted on for quite a few years. There wasn't any rule about it. Perhaps she didn't dare to mention it to her husband. He had devised a method for dealing with sickness which resembled punishment. A stomach ache was treated with a purge so violent that it was a wonder anyone survived it. If she had mentioned her condition, Cyrus might have started a treatment which would have killed her off before her consumption could have done it. Besides, as Cyrus became more military, his wife learned the only technique through which a soldier can survive. She never made herself noticeable, never spoke unless spoken to, performed what was expected and no more, and tried for no promotions. She became a rear rank private. It was much easier that way. Alice retired to the background until she was barely visible at all.

It was the little boys who really caught it. Cyrus had decided that even though the army was not perfect, it was still the only honorable profession for a man. He mourned the fact that he could not be a permanent soldier because of his wooden leg, but he could not imagine any career for his sons except the army. He felt a man should learn soldiering from the ranks, as he had. Then he would know what it was about from experience, not from charts and textbooks. He taught them the manual of arms when they could barely walk. By the time they were in grade school, close-order drill was as natural as breathing and as hateful as hell. He kept them hard with exercises, beating out the rhythm with a stick on his wooden leg. He made them walk for miles, carrying knapsacks loaded with stones to make their shoulders strong. He worked constantly on their marksmanship in the woodlot behind the house.

2

When a child first catches adults out—when it first walks into his grave little head that adults do not have divine intelligence, that their judgments are not always wise, their thinking true, their sentences just—his world falls into panic desolation. The gods are fallen and all safety gone. And there is one sure thing about the fall of gods: they do not fall a little; they crash and shatter or sink deeply into green muck. It is a tedious job to build them up again; they never quite shine. And the child's world is never quite whole again. It is an aching kind of growing.

Adam found his father out. It wasn't that his father changed but that some new quality came to Adam. He had always hated the discipline, as every normal animal does, but it was just and true and inevitable as measles, not to be denied or cursed, only to be hated. And then—it was very fast, almost a click in the brain—Adam knew that, for him at least, his father's methods had no reference to anything in the world but his father. The techniques and training were not designed for the boys at all but only to make Cyrus a great man. And the same click in the brain told Adam that his father was not a great man, that he was, indeed, a very strong-willed and concentrated little man wearing a huge busby. Who knows what causes this— a look in the eye, a lie found out, a moment of hesitation?—then god comes crashing down in a child's brain.

Young Adam was always an obedient child. Something in him shrank from violence, from contention, from the silent shrieking tensions that can rip at a house. He contributed to the quiet he wished for by offering no violence, no contention, and to do this he had to retire into secretness, since there is some violence in everyone. He covered his life with a veil of vagueness, while behind his quiet eyes a rich full life went on. This did not protect him from assault but it allowed him an immunity.

His half-brother Charles, only a little over a year younger, grew up with his father's assertiveness. Charles was a natural athlete, with instinctive timing and coordination and the competitor's will to win over others, which makes for success in the world.

Young Charles won all contests with Adam whether they involved skill, or strength, or quick intelligence, and won them so easily that quite early he lost interest and had to find his competition among other children. Thus it came about that a kind of affection grew up between the two boys, but it was more like an association between brother and sister than between brothers. Charles fought any boy who challenged or slurred Adam and usually won. He protected Adam from his father's harshness with lies and even with blame-taking. Charles felt for his brother the affection one has for helpless things, for blind puppies and new babies.

Adam looked out of his covered brain—out the long tunnels of his eyes— at the people of his world: His father, a one-legged natural force at first, installed justly to make little boys feel littler and stupid boys aware of their stupidity; and then—after god had crashed—he saw his father as the policeman laid on by birth, the officer who might be circumvented, or fooled, but never challenged. And out of the long tunnels of his eyes Adam saw his half-brother Charles as a bright being of another species, gifted with muscle and bone, speed and alertness, quite on a different plane, to be admired as one admires the sleek lazy danger of a black leopard, not by any chance to be compared with one's self. And it would no more have occurred to Adam to confide in his brother—to tell him the hunger, the gray dreams, the plans and silent pleasures that lay at the back of the tunneled eyes—than to share his thoughts with a lovely tree or a pheasant in flight. Adam was glad of Charles the way a woman is glad of a fat diamond, and he depended on his brother in the way that same woman depends on the diamond's glitter and the self-security tied up in its worth; but love, affection, empathy, were beyond conception.

Toward Alice Trask, Adam concealed a feeling that was akin to a warm shame. She was not his mother—that he knew because he had been told many times. Not from things said but from the tone in which other things were said, he knew that he had once had a mother and that she had done some shameful thing, such as forgetting the chickens or missing the target on the range in the woodlot. And as a result of her fault she was not here. Adam thought sometimes that if he could only find out what sin it was she had committed, why, he would sin it too—and not be here.

Alice treated the boys equally, washed them and fed them, and left everything else to their father, who had let it be known clearly and with finality that training the boys physically and mentally was his exclusive province. Even praise and reprimand he would not delegate. Alice never complained, quarreled, laughed, or cried. Her mouth was trained to a line that concealed nothing and offered nothing too. But once when Adam was quite small he wandered silently into the kitchen. Alice did not see him. She was darning socks and she was smiling. Adam retired secretly and walked out of the house and into the woodlot to a sheltered place behind a stump that he knew well. He settled deep between the protecting roots. Adam was as shocked as though he had come upon her naked. He breathed excitedly, high against his throat. For Alice had been naked—she had been smiling. He wondered how she had dared such wantonness. And he ached toward her with a longing that was passionate and hot. He did not know what it was about, but all the long lack of holding, of rocking, of caressing, the hunger for breast and nipple, and the softness of a lap, and the voice-tone of love and compassion, and the sweet feeling of anxiety—all of these were in his passion, and he did not know it because he did not know that such things existed, so how could he miss them?

Of course it occurred to him that he might be wrong, that some mis-begotten shadow had fallen across his face and warped his seeing. And so he cast back to the sharp picture in his head and knew that the eyes were smiling too. Twisted light could do one or the other but not both.

He stalked her then, game-wise, as he had the woodchucks on the knoll when day after day he had lain lifeless as a young stone and watched the old wary chucks bring their children out to sun. He spied on Alice, hidden, and from unsuspected eye-corner, and it was true. Sometimes when she was alone, and knew she was alone, she permitted her mind to play in a garden,

and she smiled. And it was wonderful to see how quickly she could drive
the smile to earth the way the woodchucks holed their children.

Adam concealed his treasure deep in his tunnels, but he was inclined to
pay for his pleasure with something. Alice began to find gifts—in her sewing
basket, in her worn-out purse, under her pillow—two cinnamon pinks, a
bluebird's tailfeather, half a stick of green sealing wax, a stolen handkerchief. At first Alice was startled, but then that passed, and when she found
some unsuspected present the garden smile flashed and disappeared the way
a trout crosses a knife of sunshine in a pool. She asked no questions and
made no comment.

Her coughing was very bad at night, so loud and disturbing that Cyrus
had at last to put her in another room or he would have got no sleep. But
he did visit her very often—hopping on his one bare foot, steadying himself
with hand on wall. The boys could hear and feel the jar of his body through
the house as he hopped to and from Alice's bed.

As Adam grew he feared one thing more than any other. He feared the
day he would be taken and enlisted in the army. His father never let him
forget that such a time would come. He spoke of it often. It was Adam who
needed the army to make a man of him. Charles was pretty near a man
already. And Charles was a man, and a dangerous man, even at fifteen, and
when Adam was sixteen.

3

The affection between the two boys had grown with the years. It may be
that part of Charles' feeling was contempt, but it was a protective contempt. It happened that one evening the boys were playing peewee, a new
game to them, in the dooryard. A small pointed stick was laid on the ground,
then struck near one end with a bat. The small stick flew into the air and
then was batted as far as possible.

Adam was not good at games. But by some accident of eye and timing he
beat his brother at peewee. Four times he drove the peewee farther than
Charles did. It was a new experience to him, and a wild flush came over
him, so that he did not watch and feel out his brother's mood as he usually
did. The fifth time he drove the peewee it flew humming like a bee far out
in the field. He turned happily to face Charles and suddenly he froze
deep in his chest. The hatred in Charles' face frightened him. "I guess it
was just an accident," he said lamely. "I bet I couldn't do it again."

Charles set his peewee, struck it, and, as it rose into the air, swung at it
and missed. Charles moved slowly toward Adam, his eyes cold and noncommittal. Adam edged away in terror. He did not dare to turn and run for
his brother could outrun him. He backed slowly away, his eyes frightened
and his throat dry. Charles moved close and struck him in the face with his
bat. Adam covered his bleeding nose with his hands, and Charles swung his

bat and hit him in the ribs, knocked the wind out of him, swung at his head and knocked him out. And as Adam lay unconscious on the ground Charles kicked him heavily in the stomach and walked away.

After a while Adam became conscious. He breathed shallowly because his chest hurt. He tried to sit up and fell back at the wrench of the torn muscles over his stomach. He saw Alice looking out, and there was something in her face that he had never seen before. He did not know what it was, but it was not soft or weak, and it might be hatred. She saw that he was looking at her, dropped the curtains into place, and disappeared. When Adam finally got up from the ground and moved, bent over, into the kitchen, he found a basin of hot water standing ready for him and a clean towel beside it. He could hear his stepmother coughing in her room.

Charles had one great quality. He was never sorry—ever. He never mentioned the beating, apparently never thought of it again. But Adam made very sure that he didn't win again—at anything. He had always felt the danger in his brother, but now he understood that he must never win unless he was prepared to kill Charles. Charles was not sorry. He had very simply fulfilled himself.

Charles did not tell his father about the beating, and Adam did not, and surely Alice did not, and yet he seemed to know. In the months that followed he turned a gentleness on Adam. His speech became softer toward him. He did not punish him any more. Almost nightly he lectured him, but not violently. And Adam was more afraid of the gentleness than he had been at the violence, for it seemed to him that he was being trained as a sacrifice, almost as though he was being subjected to kindness before death, the way victims intended to the gods were cuddled and flattered so that they might go happily to the stone and not outrage the gods with unhappiness.

Cyrus explained softly to Adam the nature of a soldier. And though his knowledge came from research rather than experience, he knew and he was accurate. He told his son of the sad dignity that can belong to a soldier, how he is necessary in the light of all the failures of man—the penalty of our frailties. Perhaps Cyrus discovered these things in himself as he told them. It was very different from the flag-waving, shouting bellicosity of his younger days. The humilities are piled on a soldier, so Cyrus said, in order that he may, when the time comes, be not too resentful of the final humility —a meaningless and dirty death. And Cyrus talked to Adam alone and did not permit Charles to listen.

Cyrus took Adam to walk with him one late afternoon, and the black conclusions of all of his study and his thinking came out and flowed with a kind of thick terror over his son. He said, "I'll have you know that a soldier is the most holy of all humans because he is the most tested—most tested of all. I'll try to tell you. Look now—in all of history men have been taught that killing of men is an evil thing not to be countenanced. Any man who kills must be destroyed because this is a great sin, maybe the worst sin we know. And then we take a soldier and put murder in his hands and we say to him, 'Use it well, use it wisely.' We put no checks on him. Go out and kill as many of a certain kind or classification of your brothers as you can. And we will reward you for it because it is a violation of your early training."

Adam wet his dry lips and tried to ask and failed and tried again. "Why do they have to do it?" he said. "Why is it?"

Cyrus was deeply moved and he spoke as he had never spoken before. "I don't know," he said. "I've studied and maybe learned how things are, but I'm not even close to why they are. And you must not expect to find that people understand what they do. So many things are done instinctively, the way a bee makes honey or a fox dips his paws in a stream to fool dogs. A fox can't say why he does it, and what bee remembers winter or expects it to come again? When I knew you had to go I thought to leave the future open so you could dig out your own findings, and then it seemed better if I could protect you with the little I know. You'll go in soon now—you've come to the age."

"I don't want to," said Adam quickly.

"You'll go in soon," his father went on, not hearing. "And I want to tell you so you won't be surprised. They'll first strip off your clothes, but they'll go deeper than that. They'll shuck off any little dignity you have—you'll lose what you think of as your decent right to live and to be let alone to live. They'll make you live and eat and sleep and shit close to other men. And when they dress you up again you'll not be able to tell yourself from the others. You can't even wear a scrap or pin a note on your breast to say, 'This is me—separate from the rest.'"

"I don't want to do it," said Adam.

"After a while," said Cyrus, "you'll think no thought the others do not think. You'll know no word the others can't say. And you'll do things because the others do them. You'll feel the danger in any difference whatever —a danger to the whole crowd of like-thinking, like-acting men."

"What if I don't?" Adam demanded.

"Yes," said Cyrus, "sometimes that happens. Once in a while there is a man who won't do what is demanded of him, and do you know what happens? The whole machine devotes itself coldly to the destruction of his difference. They'll beat your spirit and your nerves, your body and your mind, with iron rods until the dangerous difference goes out of you. And if you can't finally give in, they'll vomit you up and leave you stinking outside—neither part of themselves nor yet free. It's better to fall in with them. They only do it to protect themselves. A thing so triumphantly illogical, so beautifully senseless as an army can't allow a question to weaken it. Within itself, if you do not hold it up to other things for comparison and derision, you'll find slowly, surely, a reason and a logic and a kind of dreadful beauty. A man who can accept it is not a worse man always, and sometimes is a much better man. Pay good heed to me for I have thought long about it. Some men there are who go down the dismal wrack of soldiering, surrender themselves, and become faceless. But these had not much face to start with. And maybe you're like that. But there are others who go down, submerge in the common slough, and then rise more themselves than they were, because—because they have lost a littleness of vanity and have gained all the gold of the company and the regiment. If you can go down so low, you will be able to rise higher than you can conceive, and you will know a holy joy, a companionship almost like that of a heavenly company of angels. Then you will know the quality of men even if they are inarticulate. But until you have gone way down you can never know this."

As they walked back toward the house Cyrus turned left and entered the woodlot among the trees, and it was dusk. Suddenly Adam said, "You see that stump there, sir? I used to hide between the roots on the far side. After you punished me I used to hide there, and sometimes I went there just because I felt bad."

"Let's go and see the place," his father said. Adam led him to it, and Cyrus looked down at the nestlike hole between the roots. "I knew about it long ago," he said. "Once when you were gone a long time I thought you must have such a place, and I found it because I felt the kind of a place you would need. See how the earth is tamped and the little grass is torn? And while you sat in there you stripped little pieces of bark to shreds. I knew it was the place when I came upon it."

Adam was staring at his father in wonder. "You never came here looking for me," he said.

"No," Cyrus replied. "I wouldn't do that. You can drive a human too far. I wouldn't do that. Always you must leave a man one escape before death. Remember that! I knew, I guess, how hard I was pressing you. I didn't want to push you over the edge."

They moved restlessly off through the trees. Cyrus said, "So many things I want to tell you. I'll forget most of them. I want to tell you that a soldier gives up so much to get something back. From the day of a child's birth he is taught by every circumstance, by every law and rule and right, to protect his own life. He starts with that great instinct, and everything confirms it. And then he is a soldier and he must learn to violate all of this—he must learn coldly to put himself in the way of losing his own life without going mad. And if you can do that—and, mind you, some can't—then you will have the greatest gift of all. Look, son," Cyrus said earnestly, "nearly all men are afraid, and they don't even know what causes their fear—shadows, perplexities, dangers without names or numbers, fear of a faceless death. But if you can bring yourself to face not shadows but real death, described and recognizable, by bullet or saber, arrow or lance, then you need never be afraid again, at least not in the same way you were before. Then you will be a man set apart from other men, safe where other men may cry in terror. This is the

great reward. Maybe this is the only reward. Maybe this is the final purity all
ringed with filth. It's nearly dark. I'll want to talk to you again tomorrow
night when both of us have thought about what I've told you."

But Adam said, "Why don't you talk to my brother? Charles will be
going. He'll be good at it, much better than I am."

"Charles won't be going," Cyrus said. "There'd be no point in it."

"But he would be a better soldier."

"Only outside on his skin," said Cyrus. "Not inside. Charles is not afraid
so he could never learn anything about courage. He does not know anything
outside himself so he could never gain the things I've tried to explain to
you. To put him in an army would be to let loose things which in Charles
must be chained down, not let loose. I would not dare to let him go."

Adam complained, "You never punished him, you let him live his life,
you praised him, you did not haze him, and now you let him stay out of
the army." He stopped, frightened at what he had said, afraid of the rage
or the contempt or the violence his words might let loose.

His father did not reply. He walked on out of the woodlot, and his head
hung down so that his chin rested on his chest, and the rise and fall of his
hip when his wooden leg struck the ground was monotonous. The wooden
leg made a side semicircle to get ahead when its turn came.

It was completely dark by now, and the golden light of the lamps shone
out from the open kitchen door. Alice came to the doorway and peered out,
looking for them, and then she heard the uneven footsteps approaching and
went back to the kitchen.

Cyrus walked to the kitchen stoop before he stopped and raised his head.
"Where are you?" he asked.

"Here—right behind you—right here."

"You asked a question. I guess I'll have to answer. Maybe it's good and
maybe it's bad to answer it. You're not clever. You don't know what you
want. You have no proper fierceness. You let other people walk over you.
Sometimes I think you're a weakling who will never amount to a dog turd.
Does that answer your question? I love you better. I always have. This may
be a bad thing to tell you, but it's true. I love you better. Else why would
I have given myself the trouble of hurting you? Now shut your mouth and
go to your supper. I'll talk to you tomorrow night. My leg aches."

4

There was no talk at supper. The quiet was disturbed only by the slup of
soup and gnash of chewing, and his father waved his hand to try to drive
the moths away from the chimney of the kerosene lamp. Adam thought
his brother watched him secretly. And he caught an eye flash from Alice
when he looked up suddenly. After he had finished eating Adam pushed
back his chair. "I think I'll go for a walk," he said.

Charles stood up. "I'll go with you."

Alice and Cyrus watched them go out the door, and then she asked one of her rare questions. She asked nervously, "What did you do?"

"Nothing," he said.

"Will you make him go?"

"Yes."

"Does he know?"

Cyrus stared bleakly out the open door into the darkness. "Yes, he knows."

"He won't like it. It's not right for him."

"It doesn't matter," Cyrus said, and he repeated loudly, "It doesn't matter," and his tone said, "Shut your mouth. This is not your affair." They were silent a moment, and then he said almost in a tone of apology, "It isn't as though he were your child."

Alice did not reply.

The boys walked down the dark rutty road. Ahead they could see a few pinched lights where the village was.

"Want to go in and see if anything's stirring at the inn?" Charles asked.

"I hadn't thought of it," said Adam.

"Then what the hell are you walking out at night for?"

"You didn't have to come," said Adam.

Charles moved close to him. "What did he say to you this afternoon? I saw you walking together. What did he say?"

"He just talked about the army—like always."

"Didn't look like that to me," Charles said suspiciously. "I saw him leaning close, talking the way he talks to men—not telling, talking."

"He was telling," Adam said patiently, and he had to control his breath, for a little fear had begun to press up against his stomach. He took as deep a gulp of air as he could and held it to push back at the fear.

"What did he tell you?" Charles demanded again.

"About the army and how it is to be a soldier."

"I don't believe you," said Charles. "I think you're a goddam mealy-mouthed liar. What're you trying to get away with?"

"Nothing," said Adam.

Charles said harshly, "Your crazy mother drowned herself. Maybe she took a look at you. That'd do it."

Adam let out his breath gently, pressing down the dismal fear. He was silent.

Charles cried, "You're trying to take him away! I don't know how you're going about it. What do you think you're doing?"

"Nothing," said Adam.

Charles jumped in front of him so that Adam had to stop, his chest almost against his brother's chest. Adam backed away, but carefully, as one backs away from a snake.

"Look at his birthday!" Charles shouted. "I took six bits and I bought him a knife made in Germany—three blades and a corkscrew, pearl-handled. Where's that knife? Do you ever see him use it? Did he give it to you? I never even saw him hone it. Have you got that knife in your pocket? What did he do with it? 'Thanks,' he said, like that. And that's the last I heard of a pearl-handled German knife that cost six bits."

Rage was in his voice, and Adam felt the creeping fear; but he knew also that he had a moment left. Too many times he had seen the destructive machine that chopped down anything standing in its way. Rage came first and then a coldness, a possession; noncommittal eyes and a pleased smile and no voice at all, only a whisper. When that happened murder was on the way, but cool, deft murder, and hands that worked precisely, delicately. Adam swallowed saliva to dampen his dry throat. He could think of nothing to say that would be heard, for once in rage his brother would not listen, would not even hear. He bulked darkly in front of Adam, shorter, wider, thicker, but still not crouched. In the starlight his lips shone with wetness, but there was no smile yet and his voice still raged.

"What did you do on his birthday? You think I didn't see? Did you spend six bits or even four bits? You brought him a mongrel pup you picked up in the woodlot. You laughed like a fool and said it would make a good bird dog. That dog sleeps in his room. He plays with it while he's reading. He's got it all trained. And where's the knife? 'Thanks,' he said, just 'Thanks.'" Charles spoke in a whisper, and his shoulders dropped.

Adam made one desperate jump backward and raised his hands to guard his face. His brother moved precisely, each foot planted firmly. One fist lanced delicately to get the range, and then the bitter-frozen work—a hard blow in the stomach, and Adam's hands dropped; then four punches to the head. Adam felt the bone and gristle of his nose crunch. He raised his hands again and Charles drove at his heart. And all this time Adam looked at his brother as the condemned look hopelessly and puzzled at the executioner.

Suddenly to his own surprise Adam launched a wild, overhand, harmless swing which had neither force nor direction. Charles ducked in and under it and the helpless arm went around his neck. Adam wrapped his arms around his brother and hung close to him, sobbing. He felt the square fists whipping nausea into his stomach and still he held on. Time was slowed to him. With his body he felt his brother move sideways to force his legs apart. And he felt the knee come up, past his knees, scraping his thighs, until it crashed against his testicles and flashing white pain ripped and echoed through his body. His arms let go. He bent over and vomited, while the cold killing went on.

Adam felt the punches on temples, cheeks, eyes. He felt his lip split and tatter over his teeth, but his skin seemed thickened and dull, as though he were encased in heavy rubber. Dully he wondered why his legs did not buckle, why he did not fall, why unconsciousness did not come to him. The punching continued eternally. He could hear his brother panting with the quick explosive breath of a sledgehammer man, and in the sick starlit dark he could see his brother through the tear-watered blood that flowed from his eyes. He saw the innocent, noncommittal eyes, the small smile on wet lips. And as he saw these things—a flash of light and darkness.

Charles stood over him, gulping air like a run-out dog. And then he turned and walked quickly back, toward the house, kneading his bruised knuckles as he went.

Consciousness came back quick and frightening to Adam. His mind rolled in a painful mist. His body was heavy and thick with hurt. But almost instantly he forgot his hurts. He heard quick footsteps on the road. The instinctive fear and fierceness of a rat came over him. He pushed himself up on his knees and dragged himself off the road to the ditch that kept it drained. There was a foot of water in the ditch, and the tall grass grew up from its sides. Adam crawled quietly into the water, being very careful to make no splash.

The footsteps came close, slowed, moved on a little, came back. From his hiding place Adam could see only a darkness in the dark. And then a sulphur match was struck and burned a tiny blue until the wood caught, lighting his brother's face grotesquely from below. Charles raised the match and peered around, and Adam could see the hatchet in his right hand.

When the match went out the night was blacker than before. Charles moved slowly on and struck another match, and on and struck another. He searched the road for signs. At last he gave it up. His right hand rose and he threw the hatchet far off into the field. He walked rapidly away toward the pinched lights of the village.

For a long time Adam lay in the cool water. He wondered how his brother felt, wondered whether now that his passion was chilling he would feel panic or sorrow or sick conscience or nothing. These things Adam felt for him. His conscience bridged him to his brother and did his pain for him the way at other times he had done his homework.

Adam crept out of the water and stood up. His hurts were stiffening and the blood was dried in a crust on his face. He thought he would stay outside in the darkness until his father and Alice went to bed. He felt that he could not answer any questions, because he did not know any answers, and trying to find one was harsh to his battered mind. Dizziness edged with blue lights came fringing his forehead, and he knew that he would be fainting soon.

He shuffled slowly up the road with wide-spread legs. At the stoop he paused, looked in. The lamp hanging by its chain from the ceiling cast a yellow circle and lighted Alice and her mending basket on the table in front of her. On the other side his father chewed a wooden pen and dipped it in an open ink bottle and made entries in his black record book.

Alice, glancing up, saw Adam's bloody face. Her hand rose to her mouth and her fingers hooked over her lower teeth.

Adam dragfooted up one step and then the other and supported himself in the doorway.

Then Cyrus raised his head. He looked with a distant curiosity. The identity of the distortion came to him slowly. He stood up, puzzled and wondering. He stuck the wooden pen in the ink bottle and wiped his fingers on his pants. "Why did he do it?" Cyrus asked softly.

Adam tried to answer, but his mouth was caked and dry. He licked his lips and started them bleeding again. "I don't know," he said.

Cyrus stumped over to him and grasped him by the arm so fiercely that he winced and tried to pull away. "Don't lie to me! Why did he do it? Did you have an argument?"

"No."

Cyrus wrenched at him. "Tell me! I want to know. Tell me! You'll have to tell me. I'll make you tell me! Goddam it, you're always protecting him! Don't you think I know that? Did you think you were fooling me? Now tell me, or by God I'll keep you standing there all night!"

Adam cast about for an answer. "He doesn't think you love him."

Cyrus released the arm and hobbled back to his chair and sat down. He rattled the pen in the ink bottle and looked blindly at his record book. "Alice," he said, "help Adam to bed. You'll have to cut his shirt off, I guess. Give him a hand." He got up again, went to the corner of the room where the coats hung on nails, and, reaching behind the garments, brought out his shotgun, broke it to verify its load, and clumped out of the door.

Alice raised her hand as though she would hold him back with a rope of air. And her rope broke and her face hid her thoughts. "Go in your room," she said. "I'll bring some water in a basin."

Adam lay on the bed, a sheet pulled up to his waist, and Alice patted the cuts with a linen handkerchief dipped in warm water. She was silent for a long time and then she continued Adam's sentence as though there had never been an interval, "He doesn't think his father loves him. But you love him—you always have."

Adam did not answer her.

She went on quietly, "He's a strange boy. You have to know him—all rough shell, all anger until you know." She paused to cough, leaned down and coughed, and when the spell was over her cheeks were flushed and she was exhausted. "You have to know him," she repeated. "For a long time he has given me little presents, pretty things you wouldn't think he'd even notice. But he doesn't give them right out. He hides them where he knows I'll find them. And you can look at him for hours and he won't ever give the slightest sign he did it. You have to know him."

She smiled at Adam and he closed his eyes.

FOUR

Charles stood at the bar in the village inn and Charles was laughing delightedly at the funny stories the night-stranded drummers were telling. He got out his tobacco sack with its meager jingle of silver and bought the men a drink to keep them talking. He stood and grinned and rubbed his split knuckles. And when the drummers, accepting his drink, raised their glasses and said, "Here's to you," Charles was delighted. He ordered another drink for his new friends, and then he joined them for some kind of deviltry in another place.

When Cyrus stumped out into the night he was filled with a kind of despairing anger at Charles. He looked on the road for his son, and he went to the inn to look for him, but Charles was gone. It is probable that if he had found him that night he would have killed him, or tried to. The direction of a big act will warp history, but probably all acts do the same in their degree, down to a stone stepped over in the path or a breath caught at sight of a pretty girl or a fingernail nicked in the garden soil.

Naturally it was not long before Charles was told that his father was looking for him with a shotgun. He hid out for two weeks, and when he finally did return, murder had sunk back to simple anger and he paid his penalty in overwork and a false theatrical humility.

Adam lay four days in bed, so stiff and aching that he could not move without a groan. On the third day his father gave evidence of his power with the military. He did it as a poultice to his own pride and also as a kind of prize for Adam. Into the house, into Adam's bedroom, came a captain of cavalry and two sergeants in dress uniform of blue. In the dooryard their horses were held by two privates. Lying in his bed, Adam was enlisted in the army as a private in the cavalry. He signed the Articles of War and took the oath while his father and Alice looked on. And his father's eyes glistened with tears.

After the soldiers had gone his father sat with him a long time. "I've put you in the cavalry for a reason," he said. "Barrack life is not a good life for long. But the cavalry has work to do. I made sure of that. You'll like going for the Indian country. There's action coming. I can't tell you how I know. There's fighting on the way."

"Yes, sir," Adam said.

2

It has always seemed strange to me that it is usually men like Adam who have to do the soldiering. He did not like fighting to start with, and far from learning to love it, as some men do, he felt an increasing revulsion for violence. Several times his officers looked closely at him for malingering, but no charge was brought. During these five years of soldiering Adam did more detail work than any man in the squadron, but if he killed any enemy it was an accident of ricochet. Being a marksman and sharpshooter, he was peculiarly fitted to miss. By this time the Indian fighting had become like dangerous cattle drives—the tribes were forced into revolt, driven and decimated, and the sad, sullen remnants settled on starvation lands. It was not nice work but, given the pattern of the country's development, it had to be done.

To Adam who was an instrument, who saw not the future farms but only the torn bellies of fine humans, it was revolting and useless. When he fired his carbine to miss he was committing treason against his unit, and he didn't care. The emotion of nonviolence was building in him until it became a prejudice like any other thought-stultifying prejudice. To inflict any hurt on anything for any purpose became inimical to him. He became obsessed with this emotion, for such it surely was, until it blotted out any possible thinking in its area. But never was there any hint of cowardice in Adam's army record. Indeed he was commended three times and then decorated for bravery.

As he revolted more and more from violence, his impulse took the opposite direction. He ventured his life a number of times to bring in wounded men. He volunteered for work in field hospitals even when he was exhausted from his regular duties. He was regarded by his comrades with contemptuous affection and the unspoken fear men have of impulses they do not understand.

Charles wrote to his brother regularly—of the farm and the village, of sick cows and a foaling mare, of the added pasture and the lightning-struck barn, of Alice's choking death from her consumption and his father's move to a permanent paid position in the G.A.R. in Washington. As with many people, Charles, who could not talk, wrote with fullness. He set down his loneliness and his perplexities, and he put on paper many things he did not know about himself.

During the time Adam was away he knew his brother better than ever before or afterward. In the exchange of letters there grew a closeness neither of them could have imagined.

Adam kept one letter from his brother, not because he understood it completely but because it seemed to have a covered meaning he could not get at. "Dear Brother Adam," the letter said, "I take my pen in hand to hope you are in good health"—he always started this way to ease himself gently into the task of writing. "I have not had your answer to my last letter but I presume you have other things to do—ha! ha! The rain came wrong and damned the apple blossoms. There won't be many to eat next winter but I will save what I can. Tonight I cleaned the house, and it is wet and soapy and maybe not any cleaner. How do you suppose Mother kept it the way she did? It does not look the same. Something settles down on it. I don't know what, but it will not scrub off. But I have spread the dirt around more evenly anyways. Ha! ha!

"Did Father write you anything about his trip? He's gone clean out to San Francisco in California for an encampment of the Grand Army. The Secty. of War is going to be there, and Father is to introduce him. But this is not any great shucks to Father. He has met the President three, four times and even been to supper to the White House. I would like to see the White House. Maybe you and me can go together when you come home. Father could put us up for a few days and he would be wanting to see you anyways.

"I think I better look around for a wife. This is a good farm, and even if I'm no bargain there's girls could do worse than this farm. What do you think? You did not say if you are going to come live home when you get out of the army. I hope so. I miss you."

The writing stopped there. There was a scratch on the page and a splash of ink, and then it went on in pencil, but the writing was different.

In pencil it said, "Later. Well, right there the pen give out. One of the points broke off. I'll have to buy another penpoint in the village—rusted right through."

The words began to flow more smoothly. "I guess I should wait for a new penpoint and not write with a pencil. Only I was sitting here in the kitchen with the lamp on and I guess I got to thinking and it come on late—after twelve, I guess, but I never looked. Old Black Joe started crowing out in the henhouse. Then Mother's rocking chair cricked for all the world like she was sitting in it. You know I don't take truck with that, but it set me minding backwards, you know how you do sometimes. I guess I'll tear this letter up maybe, because what's the good of writing stuff like this."

The words began to race now as though they couldn't get out fast enough. "If I'm to throw it away I'd just as well set it down," the letter said. "It's like the whole house was alive and had eyes everywhere, and like there was people behind the door just ready to come in if you looked away. It kind of makes my skin crawl. I want to say—I want to say—I mean, I never understood—well, why our father did it. I mean, why didn't he like that knife I bought for him on his birthday. Why didn't he? It was a good knife and he needed a good knife. If he had used it or even honed it, or took it out of his pocket and looked at it—that's all he had to do. If he'd liked it I wouldn't have took out after you. I had to take out after you. Seems like to me my mother's chair is rocking a little. It's just the light. I don't take any truck with that. Seems like to me there's something not finished. Seems like when you half finished a job and can't think what it was. Something didn't get done. I shouldn't be here. I ought to be wandering around the world instead of sitting here on a good farm looking for a wife. There is something wrong, like it didn't get finished, like it happened too soon and left something out. It's me should be where you are and you here. I never thought like this before. Maybe because it's late—it's later than that. I just looked out and it's first dawn. I don't think I fell off to sleep. How could the night go so fast? I can't go to bed now. I couldn't sleep anyways."

The letter was not signed. Maybe Charles forgot he had intended to destroy it and sent it along. But Adam saved it for a time, and whenever he read it again it gave him a chill and he didn't know why.

FIVE

On the ranch the little Hamiltons began to grow up, and every year there was a new one. George was a tall handsome boy, gentle and sweet, who had from the first a kind of courtliness. Even as a little boy he was polite and what they used to call "no trouble." From his father he inherited the neatness of clothing and body and hair, and he never seemed ill dressed even when he was. George was a sinless boy and grew to be a sinless man. No crime of commission was ever attributed to him, and his crimes of omission were only misdemeanors. In his middle life, at about the time such things were known about, it was discovered that he had pernicious anemia. It is possible that his virtue lived on a lack of energy.

Behind George, Will grew along, dumpy and stolid. Will had little imagination but he had great energy. From childhood on he was a hard worker, if anyone would tell him what to work at, and once told he was indefatigable. He was a conservative, not only in politics but in everything. Ideas he found revolutionary, and he avoided them with suspicion and distaste. Will liked to live so that no one could find fault with him, and to do that he had to live as nearly like other people as possible.

Maybe his father had something to do with Will's distaste for either change or variation. When Will was a growing boy, his father had not been long enough in the Salinas Valley to be thought of as an "old-timer." He was in fact a foreigner and an Irishman. At that time the Irish were much disliked in America. They were looked upon with contempt, particularly on the East Coast, but a little of it must have seeped out to the West. And Samuel had not only variability but was a man of ideas and innovations. In small cut-off communities such a man is always regarded with suspicion until he has proved he is no danger to the others. A shining man like Samuel could, and can, cause a lot of trouble. He might, for example, prove too attractive to the wives of men who knew they were dull. Then there were his education and his reading, the books he bought and borrowed, his knowledge of things that could not be eaten or worn or cohabited with, his interest in poetry and his respect for good writing. If Samuel had been a rich man like the Thornes or the Delmars, with their big houses and wide flat lands, he would have had a great library.

The Delmars had a library—nothing but books in it and paneled in oak. Samuel, by borrowing, had read many more of the Delmars' books than the Delmars had. In that day an educated rich man was acceptable. He might send his sons to college without comment, might wear a vest and white shirt and tie in the daytime of a weekday, might wear gloves and keep his nails clean. And since the lives and practices of rich men were mysterious, who knows what they could use or not use? But a poor man —what need had he for poetry or for painting or for music not fit for singing or dancing? Such things did not help him bring in a crop or keep a scrap of cloth on his children's backs. And if in spite of this he persisted, maybe he had reasons which would not stand the light of scrutiny.

Take Samuel, for instance. He made drawings of work he intended to do with iron or wood. That was good and understandable, even enviable. But on the edges of the plans he made other drawings, sometimes trees, sometimes faces or animals or bugs, sometimes just figures that you couldn't make out at all. And these caused men to laugh with embarrassed uneasiness. Then, too, you never knew in advance what Samuel would think or say or do—it might be anything.

The first few years after Samuel came to Salinas Valley there was a vague distrust of him. And perhaps Will as a little boy heard talk in the San Lucas store. Little boys don't want their fathers to be different from other men. Will might have picked up his conservatism right then. Later, as the other children came along and grew, Samuel belonged to the valley, and it was proud of him in the way a man who owns a peacock is proud. They weren't afraid of him any more, for he did not seduce their wives or lure them out of sweet mediocrity. The Salinas Valley grew fond of Samuel, but by that time Will was formed.

Certain individuals, not by any means always deserving, are truly beloved of the gods. Things come to them without their effort or planning. Will Hamilton was one of these. And the gifts he received were the ones he could appreciate. As a growing boy Will was lucky. Just as his father could not make money, Will could not help making it. When Will Hamilton raised chickens and his hens began to lay, the price of eggs went up. As a young man, when two of his friends who ran a little store came to the point of despondent bankruptcy, Will was asked to lend them a little money to tide them over the quarter's bills, and they gave him a one-third interest for a pittance. He was not niggardly. He gave them what they asked for. The store was on its feet within one year, expanding in two, opening branches in three, and its descendants, a great mercantile system, now dominate a large part of the area.

Will also took over a bicycle-and-tool shop for a bad debt. Then a few rich people of the valley bought automobiles, and his mechanic worked on them. Pressure was put on him by a determined poet whose dreams were brass, cast iron, and rubber. This man's name was Henry Ford, and his plans were ridiculous if not illegal. Will grumblingly accepted the southern half of the valley as his exclusive area, and within fifteen years the valley was two-deep in Fords and Will was a rich man driving a Marmon.

Tom, the third son, was most like his father. He was born in fury and he lived in lightning. Tom came headlong into life. He was a giant in joy and enthusiasms. He didn't discover the world and its people, he created them. When he read his father's books, he was the first. He lived in a world shining and fresh and as uninspected as Eden on the sixth day. His mind plunged like a colt in a happy pasture, and when later the world put up fences he plunged against the wire, and when the final stockade surrounded him, he plunged right through it and out. And as he was capable of giant joy, so did he harbor huge sorrow, so that when his dog died the world ended.

Tom was as inventive as his father but he was bolder. He would try things his father would not dare. Also, he had a large concupiscence to put the spurs in his flanks, and this Samuel did not have. Perhaps it was his driving sexual need that made him remain a bachelor. It was a very moral family he was born into. It might be that his dreams and his longing, and his outlets for that matter, made him feel unworthy, drove him sometimes whining into the hills. Tom was a nice mixture of savagery and gentleness. He worked inhumanly, only to lose in effort his crushing impulses.

The Irish do have a despairing quality of gaiety, but they have also a dour and brooding ghost that rides on their shoulders and peers in on their thoughts. Let them laugh too loudly, it sticks a long finger down their throats. They condemn themselves before they are charged, and this makes them defensive always.

When Tom was nine years old he worried because his pretty little sister Mollie had an impediment in her speech. He asked her to open her mouth wide and saw that a membrane under her tongue caused the trouble. "I can fix that," he said. He led her to a secret place far from the house, whetted his pocketknife on a stone, and cut the offending halter of speech. And then he ran away and was sick.

The Hamilton house grew as the family grew. It was designed to be unfinished, so that lean-tos could jut out as they were needed. The original room and kitchen soon disappeared in a welter of these lean-tos.

Meanwhile Samuel got no richer. He developed a very bad patent habit, a disease many men suffer from. He invented a part of a threshing machine, better, cheaper, and more efficient than any in existence. The patent attorney ate up his little profit for the year. Samuel sent his models to a manufacturer, who promptly rejected the plans and used the method. The next few years were kept lean by the suing, and the drain stopped only when he lost the suit. It was his first sharp experience with the rule that without money you cannot fight money. But he had caught the patent fever, and year after year the money made by threshing and by smithing was drained off in patents. The Hamilton children went barefoot, and their overalls were patched and food was sometimes scarce, to pay for the crisp blueprints with cogs and planes and elevations.

Some men think big and some think little. Samuel and his sons Tom and Joe thought big and George and Will thought little. Joseph was the fourth son—a kind of mooning boy, greatly beloved and protected by the whole family. He early discovered that a smiling helplessness was his best protection from work. His brothers were tough hard workers, all of them. It was easier to do Joe's work than to make him do it. His mother and father thought him a poet because he wasn't any good at anything else. And they so impressed him with this that he wrote glib verses to prove it. Joe was physically lazy, and probably mentally lazy too. He daydreamed out his life, and his mother loved him more than the others because she thought he was helpless. Actually he was the least helpless, because he got exactly what he wanted with a minimum of effort. Joe was the darling of the family.

In feudal times an ineptness with sword and spear headed a young man for the church: in the Hamilton family Joe's inability properly to function at farm and forge headed him for a higher education. He was not sickly or weak but he did not lift very well; he rode horses badly and detested them. The whole family laughed with affection when they thought of Joe trying to learn to plow; his tortuous first furrow wound about like a flatland stream, and his second furrow touched his first only once and then to cross it and wander off.

Gradually he eliminated himself from every farm duty. His mother explained that his mind was in the clouds, as though this were some singular virtue.

When Joe had failed at every job, his father in despair put him to herding sixty sheep. This was the least difficult job of all and the one classically requiring no skill. All he had to do was to stay with the sheep. And Joe lost them—lost sixty sheep and couldn't find them where they were huddled in the shade in a dry gulch. According to the family story, Samuel called the family together, girls and boys, and made them promise to take care of Joe after he was gone, for if they did not Joe would surely starve.

Interspersed with the Hamilton boys were five girls: Una the oldest, a thoughtful, studious, dark girl; Lizzie—I guess Lizzie must have been the oldest since she was named for her mother—I don't know much about Lizzie. She early seemed to find a shame for her family. She married young and went away and thereafter was seen only at funerals. Lizzie had a capacity for hatred and bitterness unique among the Hamiltons. She had a son, and when he grew up and married a girl Lizzie didn't like she did not speak to him for many years.

Then there was Dessie, whose laughter was so constant that everyone near her was glad to be there because it was more fun to be with Dessie than with anyone else.

The next sister was Olive, my mother. And last was Mollie, who was a little beauty with lovely blond hair and violet eyes.

These were the Hamiltons, and it was almost a miracle how Liza, skinny little biddy that she was, produced them year after year and fed them, baked bread, made their clothes, and clothed them with good manners and iron morals too.

It is amazing how Liza stamped her children. She was completely without experience in the world, she was unread and, except for the one long trip from Ireland, untraveled. She had no experience with men save only her husband, and that she looked upon as a tiresome and sometimes painful duty. A good part of her life was taken up with bearing and raising. Her total intellectual association was the Bible, except the talk of Samuel and her children, and to them she did not listen. In that one book she had her history and her poetry, her knowledge of peoples and things, her ethics, her morals, and her salvation. She never studied the Bible or inspected it; she just read it. The many places where it seems to refute itself did not confuse her in the least. And finally she came to a point where she knew it so well that she went right on reading it without listening.

Liza enjoyed universal respect because she was a good woman and raised good children. She could hold up her head anywhere. Her husband and her children and her grandchildren respected her. There was a nail-hard strength in her, a lack of any compromise, a rightness in the face of all opposing wrongness, which made you hold her in a kind of awe but not in warmth.

Liza hated alcoholic liquors with an iron zeal. Drinking alcohol in any form she regarded as a crime against a properly outraged deity. Not only would she not touch it herself, but she resisted its enjoyment by anyone else. The result naturally was that her husband Samuel and all her children had a good lusty love for a drink.

Once when he was very ill Samuel asked, "Liza, couldn't I have a glass of whisky to ease me?"

She set her little hard chin. "Would you go to the throne of God with liquor on your breath? You would not!" she said.

Samuel rolled over on his side and went about his illness without ease.

When Liza was about seventy her elimination slowed up and her doctor told her to take a tablespoon of port wine for medicine. She forced down the first spoonful, making a crooked face, but it was not so bad. And from that moment she never drew a completely sober breath. She always took the wine in a tablespoon, it was always medicine, but after a time she was doing over a quart a day and she was a much more relaxed and happy woman.

Samuel and Liza Hamilton got all of their children raised and well toward adulthood before the turn of the century. It was a whole clot of Hamiltons growing up on the ranch to the east of King City. And they were American children and young men and women. Samuel never went back to Ireland and gradually he forgot it entirely. He was a busy man. He had no time for nostalgia. The Salinas Valley was the world. A trip to Salinas sixty miles to the north at the head of the valley was event enough for a year, and the incessant work on the ranch, the care and feeding and clothing of his bountiful family, took most of his time—but not all. His energy was large.

His daughter Una had become a brooding student, tense and dark. He was proud of her wild, exploring mind. Olive was preparing to take county examinations after a stretch in the secondary school in Salinas. Olive was going to be a teacher, an honor like having a priest in the family in Ireland. Joe was to be sent to college because he was no damn good at anything else. Will was well along the way to accidental fortune. Tom bruised himself on the world and licked his cuts. Dessie was studying dressmaking, and Mollie, pretty Mollie, would obviously marry some well-to-do man.

There was no question of inheritance. Although the hill ranch was large it was abysmally poor. Samuel sunk well after well and could not find water on his own land. That would have made the difference. Water would have made them comparatively rich. The one poor pipe of water pumped up from deep near the house was the only source; sometimes it got dangerously low, and twice it went dry. The cattle had to come from the far fringe of the ranch to drink and then go out again to feed.

All in all it was a good firm-grounded family, permanent, and successfully planted in the Salinas Valley, not poorer than many and not richer than many either. It was a well-balanced family with its conservatives and its radicals, its dreamers and its realists. Samuel was well pleased with the fruit of his loins.

SIX

After Adam joined the army and Cyrus moved to Washington, Charles lived alone on the farm. He boasted about getting himself a wife, but he did not go about doing it by the usual process of meeting girls, taking them to dances, testing their virtues or otherwise, and finally slipping feebly into marriage. The truth of it was that Charles was abysmally timid of girls. And, like most shy men, he satisfied his normal needs in the anonymity of the prostitute. There is great safety for a shy man with a whore. Having been paid for, and in advance, she has become a commodity, and a shy man can be gay with her and even brutal to her. Also, there is none of the horror of the possible turndown which shrivels the guts of timid men.

The arrangement was simple and reasonably secret. The owner of the inn kept three rooms on his top floor for transients, which he rented to girls for two-week periods. At the end of two weeks a new set of girls took their place. Mr. Hallam, the innkeeper, had no part in the arrangement. He could almost say with truth that he didn't know anything about it. He simply collected five times the normal rent for his three rooms. The girls were assigned, procured, moved, disciplined, and robbed by a whoremaster named Edwards, who lived in Boston. His girls moved in a slow circuit among the small towns, never staying anywhere more than two weeks. It was an extremely workable system. A girl was not in town long enough to cause remark either by citizen or town marshal. They stayed pretty much in the rooms and avoided public places. They were forbidden on pain of beating to drink or make noise or to fall in love with anyone. Meals were served in their rooms, and the clients were carefully screened. No drunken man was permitted to go up to them. Every six months each girl was given one month of vacation to get drunk and raise hell. On the job, let a girl be disobedient to the rules, and Mr. Edwards personally stripped her, gagged her, and horsewhipped her within an inch of her life. If she did it again she found herself in jail, charged with vagrancy and public prostitution.

The two-week stands had another advantage. Many of the girls were diseased, and a girl had nearly always gone away by the time her gift had incubated in a client. There was no one for a man to get mad at. Mr. Hallam knew nothing about it, and Mr. Edwards never appeared publicly in his business capacity. He had a very good thing in his circuit.

The girls were all pretty much alike—big, healthy, lazy, and dull. A man could hardly tell there had been a change. Charles Trask made it a habit to go to the inn at least once every two weeks, to creep up to the top floor, do his quick business, and return to the bar to get mildly drunk.

The Trask house had never been gay, but lived in only by Charles it took on a gloomy, rustling decay. The lace curtains were gray, the floors, although swept, grew sticky and dank. The kitchen was lacquered—walls, windows, and ceiling—with grease from the frying pans.

The constant scrubbing by the wives who had lived there and the biannual deep-seated scourging had kept the dirt down. Charles rarely did more than sweep. He gave up sheets on his bed and slept between blankets. What good to clean the house when there was no one to see it? Only on the nights he went to the inn did he wash himself and put on clean clothes.

Charles developed a restlessness that got him out at dawn. He worked the farm mightily because he was lonely. Coming in from his work, he gorged himself on fried food and went to bed and to sleep in the resulting torpor.

His dark face took on the serious expressionlessness of a man who is nearly always alone. He missed his brother more than he missed his mother and father. He remembered quite inaccurately the time before Adam went away as the happy time, and he wanted it to come again.

During the years he was never sick, except of course for the chronic indigestion which was universal, and still is, with men who live alone, cook for themselves, and eat in solitude. For this he took a powerful purge called Father George's Elixir of Life.

One accident he did have in the third year of his aloneness. He was digging out rocks and sledding them to the stone wall. One large boulder was difficult to move. Charles pried at it with a long iron bar, and the rock bucked and rolled back again and again. Suddenly he lost his temper. The little smile came on his face, and he fought the stone as though it were a man, in silent fury. He drove his bar deep behind it and threw his whole weight back. The bar slipped and its upper end crashed against his forehead. For a few moments he lay unconscious in the field and then he rolled over and staggered, half-blinded, to the house. There was a long torn welt on his forehead from hairline to a point between his eyebrows. For a few weeks his head was bandaged over a draining infection, but that did not worry him. In that day pus was thought to be benign, a proof that a wound was healing properly. When the wound did heal, it left a long and crinkled scar, and while most scar tissue is lighter than the surrounding skin, Charles' scar turned dark brown. Perhaps the bar had forced iron rust under the skin and made a kind of tattoo.

The wound had not worried Charles, but the scar did. It looked like a long fingermark laid on his forehead. He inspected it often in the little mirror by the stove. He combed his hair down over his forehead to conceal as much of it as he could. He conceived a shame for his scar; he hated his scar. He became restless when anyone looked at it, and fury rose in him if any question was asked about it. In a letter to his brother he put down his feeling about it.

"It looks," he wrote, "like somebody marked me like a cow. The damn thing gets darker. By the time you get home it will maybe be black. All I need is one going the other way and I would look like a Papist on Ash Wednesday. I don't know why it bothers me. I got plenty other scars. It just seems like I was marked. And when I go into town, like to the inn, why, people are always looking at it. I can hear them talking about it when they don't know I can hear. I don't know why they're so damn curious about it. It gets so I don't feel like going in town at all."

2

Adam was discharged in 1885 and started to beat his way home. In appearance he had changed little. There was no military carriage about him. The cavalry didn't act that way. Indeed some units took pride in a sloppy posture.

Adam felt that he was sleepwalking. It is a hard thing to leave any

deeply routined life, even if you hate it. In the morning he awakened on
a split second and lay waiting for reveille. His calves missed the hug of
leggings and his throat felt naked without its tight collar. He arrived in
Chicago, and there, for no reason, rented a furnished room for a week,
stayed in it for two days, went to Buffalo, changed his mind, and moved to
Niagara Falls. He didn't want to go home and he put it off as long as possible.
Home was not a pleasant place in his mind. The kind of feelings he had
had there were dead in him, and he had a reluctance to bring them to life.
He watched the falls by the hour. Their roar stupefied and hypnotized
him.

One evening he felt a crippling loneliness for the close men in barracks
and tent. His impulse was to rush into a crowd for warmth, any crowd. The
first crowded public place he could find was a little bar, thronged and smoky.
He sighed with pleasure, almost nestled in the human clot the way a cat
nestles into a woodpile. He ordered whisky and drank it and felt warm and
good. He did not see or hear. He simply absorbed the contact.

As it grew late and the men began to drift away, he became fearful of the
time when he would have to go home. Soon he was alone with the bartender,
who was rubbing and rubbing the mahogany of the bar and trying with his
eyes and his manner to get Adam to go.

"I'll have one more," Adam said.

The bartender set the bottle out. Adam noticed him for the first time.
He had a strawberry mark on his forehead.

"I'm a stranger in these parts," said Adam.

"That's what we mostly get at the falls," the bartender said.

"I've been in the army. Cavalry."

"Yeah!" the bartender said.

Adam felt suddenly that he had to impress this man, had to get under
his skin some way. "Fighting Indians," he said. "Had some great times."

The man did not answer him.

"My brother has a mark on his head."

The bartender touched the strawberry mark with his fingers. "Birthmark,"
he said. "Gets bigger every year. Your brother got one?"

"His came from a cut. He wrote me about it."

"You notice this one of mine looks like a cat?"

"Sure it does."

"That's my nickname, Cat. Had it all my life. They say my old lady must
of been scared by a cat when she was having me."

"I'm on my way home. Been away a long time. Won't you have a drink?"

"Thanks. Where you staying?"

"Mrs. May's boarding house."

"I know her. What they tell is she fills you up with soup so you can't eat
much meat."

"I guess there are tricks to every trade," said Adam.

"I guess that's right. There's sure plenty in mine."

"I bet that's true," said Adam.

"But the one trick I need I haven't got. I wisht I knew that one."

"What is it?"

"How the hell to get you to go home and let me close up."

Adam stared at him, stared at him and did not speak.

"It's a joke," the bartender said uneasily.

"I guess I'll go home in the morning," said Adam. "I mean my real home."

"Good luck," the bartender said.

Adam walked through the dark town, increasing his speed as though his loneliness sniffed along behind him. The sagging front steps of his boarding house creaked a warning as he climbed them. The hall was gloomed with the dot of yellow light from an oil lamp turned down so low that it jerked expiringly.

The landlady stood in her open doorway and her nose made a shadow to the bottom of her chin. Her cold eyes followed Adam as do the eyes of a front-painted portrait, and she listened with her nose for the whisky that was in him.

"Good night," said Adam.

She did not answer him.

At the top of the first flight he looked back. Her head was raised, and now her chin made a shadow on her throat and her eyes had no pupils.

His room smelled of dust dampened and dried many times. He picked a match from his block and scratched it on the side of the block. He lighted the shank of candle in the japanned candlestick and regarded the bed—as spineless as a hammock and covered with a dirty patchwork quilt, the cotton batting spilling from the edges.

The porch steps complained again, and Adam knew the woman would be standing in her doorway ready to spray inhospitality on the new arrival.

Adam sat down in a straight chair and put his elbows on his knees and supported his chin in his hands. A roomer down the hall began a patient, continuing cough against the quiet night.

And Adam knew he could not go home. He had heard old soldiers tell of doing what he was going to do.

"I just couldn't stand it. Didn't have no place to go. Didn't know nobody. Wandered around and pretty soon I got in a panic like a kid, and first thing I knowed I'm begging the sergeant to let me back in—like he was doing me a favor."

Back in Chicago, Adam re-enlisted and asked to be assigned to his old regiment. On the train going west the men of his squadron seemed very dear and desirable.

While he waited to change trains in Kansas City, he heard his name called and a message was shoved into his hand—orders to report to Washington to the office of the Secretary of War. Adam in his five years had absorbed

rather than learned never to wonder about an order. To an enlisted man
the high far gods in Washington were crazy, and if a soldier wanted to
keep his sanity he thought about generals as little as possible.

In due course Adam gave his name to a clerk and went to sit in an ante-
room. His father found him there. It took Adam a moment to recognize
Cyrus, and much longer to get used to him. Cyrus had become a great man.
He dressed like a great man—black broadcloth coat and trousers, wide black
hat, overcoat with a velvet collar, ebony cane which he made to seem a
sword. And Cyrus conducted himself like a great man. His speech was slow
and mellow, measured and unexcited, his gestures were wide, and new
teeth gave him a vulpine smile out of all proportion to his emotion.

After Adam had realized that this was his father he was still puzzled.
Suddenly he looked down—no wooden leg. The leg was straight, bent at the
knee, and the foot was clad in a polished kid congress gaiter. When he
moved there was a limp, but not a clumping wooden-legged limp.

Cyrus saw the look. "Mechanical," he said. "Works on a hinge. Got a
spring. Don't even limp when I set my mind to it. I'll show it to you when
I take it off. Come along with me."

Adam said, "I'm under orders, sir. I'm to report to Colonel Wells."

"I know you are. I told Wells to issue the orders. Come along."

Adam said uneasily, "If you don't mind, sir, I think I'd better report to
Colonel Wells."

His father reversed himself. "I was testing you," he said grandly. "I
wanted to see whether the army has any discipline these days. Good boy. I
knew it would be good for you. You're a man and a soldier, my boy."

"I'm under orders, sir," said Adam. This man was a stranger to him. A
faint distaste arose in Adam. Something was not true. And the speed with
which doors opened straight to the Colonel, the obsequious respect of that
officer, the words, "The Secretary will see you now, sir," did not remove
Adam's feeling.

"This is my son, a private soldier, Mr. Secretary—just as I was—a private
soldier in the United States Army."

"I was discharged a corporal, sir," said Adam. He hardly heard the
exchange of compliments. He was thinking, This is the Secretary of War.
Can't he see that this isn't the way my father is? He's play-acting. What's
happened to him? It's funny the Secretary can't see it.

They walked to the small hotel where Cyrus lived, and on the way Cyrus
pointed out the sights, the buildings, the spots of history, with the expan-
siveness of a lecturer. "I live in a hotel," he said. "I've thought of getting a
house, but I'm on the move so much it wouldn't hardly pay. I'm all over
the country most of the time."

The hotel clerk couldn't see either. He bowed to Cyrus, called him
"Senator," and indicated that he would give Adam a room if he had to
throw someone out.

"Send a bottle of whisky to my room, please."

"I can send some chipped ice if you like."

"Ice!" said Cyrus. "My son is a soldier." He rapped his leg with his stick and it gave forth a hollow sound. "I have been a soldier—a private soldier. What do we want ice for?"

Adam was amazed at Cyrus's accommodations. He had not only a bedroom but a sitting room beside it, and the toilet was in a closet right in the bedroom.

Cyrus sat down in a deep chair and sighed. He pulled up his trouser leg, and Adam saw the contraption of iron and leather and hard wood. Cyrus unlaced the leather sheath that held it on his stump and stood the travesty-on-flesh beside his chair. "It gets to pinching pretty bad," he said.

With the leg off, his father became himself again, the self Adam remembered. He had experienced the beginning of contempt, but now the childhood fear and respect and animosity came back to him, so that he seemed a little boy testing his father's immediate mood to escape trouble.

Cyrus made his preparations, drank his whisky, and loosened his collar. He faced Adam. "Well?"

"Sir?"

"Why did you re-enlist?"

"I—I don't know, sir. I just wanted to."

"You don't like the army, Adam."

"No, sir."

"Why did you go back?"

"I didn't want to go home."

Cyrus sighed and rubbed the tips of his fingers on the arms of his chair. "Are you going to stay in the army?" he asked.

"I don't know, sir."

"I can get you into West Point. I have influence. I can get you discharged so you can enter West Point."

"I don't want to go there."

"Are you defying me?" Cyrus asked quietly.

Adam took a long time to answer, and his mind sought escape before he said, "Yes, sir."

Cyrus said, "Pour me some whisky, son," and when he had it he continued, "I wonder if you know how much influence I really have. I can throw the Grand Army at any candidate like a sock. Even the President likes to know what I think about public matters. I can get senators defeated and I can pick appointments like apples. I can make men and I can destroy men. Do you know that?"

Adam knew more than that. He knew that Cyrus was defending himself with threats. "Yes, sir. I've heard."

"I could get you assigned to Washington—assigned to me even—teach you your way about."

"I'd rather go back to my regiment, sir." He saw the shadow of loss darken his father's face.

"Maybe I made a mistake. You've learned the dumb resistance of a soldier." He sighed. "I'll get you ordered to your regiment. You'll rot in barracks."

"Thank you, sir." After a pause Adam asked, "Why don't you bring Charles here?"

"Because I— No, Charles is better where he is—better where he is."

Adam remembered his father's tone and how he looked. And he had plenty of time to remember, because he did rot in barracks. He remembered that Cyrus was lonely and alone—and knew it.

3

Charles had looked forward to Adam's return after five years. He had painted the house and the barn, and as the time approached he had a woman in to clean the house, to clean it to the bone.

She was a clean, mean old woman. She looked at the dust-gray rotting curtains, threw them out, and made new ones. She dug grease out of the stove that had been there since Charles' mother died. And she leached the walls of a brown shiny nastiness deposited by cooking fat and kerosene lamps. She pickled the floors with lye, soaked the blankets in sal soda, complaining the whole time to herself, "Men—dirty animals. Pigs is clean compared. Rot in their own juice. Don't see how no woman ever marries them. Stink like measles. Look at oven—pie juice from Methusaleh."

Charles had moved into a shed where his nostrils would not be assailed by the immaculate but painful smells of lye and soda and ammonia and yellow soap. He did, however, get the impression that she didn't approve of his housekeeping. When finally she grumbled away from the shining house Charles remained in the shed. He wanted to keep the house clean for Adam. In the shed where he slept were the tools of the farm and the tools for their repair and maintenance. Charles found that he could cook his fried and boiled meals more quickly and efficiently on the forge than he could on the kitchen stove. The bellows forced quick flaring heat from the coke. A man didn't have to wait for a stove to heat up. He wondered why he had never thought of it before.

Charles waited for Adam, and Adam did not come. Perhaps Adam was ashamed to write. It was Cyrus who told Charles in an angry letter about Adam's re-enlistment against his wishes. And Cyrus indicated that, in some future, Charles could visit him in Washington, but he never asked him again.

Charles moved back to the house and lived in a kind of savage filth, taking a satisfaction in overcoming the work of the grumbling woman.

It was over a year before Adam wrote to Charles—a letter of embarrassed newsiness building his courage to say, "I don't know why I signed again. It was like somebody else doing it. Write soon and tell me how you are."

Charles did not reply until he had received four anxious letters, and then he replied coolly, "I didn't hardly expect you anyway," and he went on with a detailed account of farm and animals.

Time had got in its work. After that Charles wrote right after New Year's and received a letter from Adam written right after New Year's. They had grown so apart that there was little mutual reference and no questions.

Charles began to keep one slovenly woman after another. When they got on his nerves he threw them out the way he would sell a pig. He didn't like them and had no interest in whether or not they liked him. He grew away from the village. His contacts were only with the inn and the postmaster. The village people might denounce his manner of life, but one thing he had which balanced his ugly life even in their eyes. The farm had never been so well run. Charles cleared land, built up his walls, improved his drainage, and added a hundred acres to the farm. More than that, he was planting tobacco, and a long new tobacco barn stood impressively behind the house. For these things he kept the respect of his neighbors. A farmer cannot think too much evil of a good farmer. Charles was spending most of his money and all of his energy on the farm.

SEVEN

Adam spent his next five years doing the things an army uses to keep its men from going insane—endless polishing of metal and leather, parade and drill and escort, ceremony of bugle and flag, a ballet of business for men who aren't doing anything. In 1886 the big packing-house strike broke out in Chicago and Adam's regiment entrained, but the strike was settled before they were needed. In 1888 the Seminoles, who had never signed a peace treaty, stirred restlessly, and the cavalry entrained again; but the Seminoles retired into their swamps and were quiet, and the dreamlike routine settled on the troops again.

Time interval is a strange and contradictory matter in the mind. It would be reasonable to suppose that a routine time or an eventless time would seem interminable. It should be so, but it is not. It is the dull eventless times that have no duration whatever. A time splashed with interest, wounded with tragedy, crevassed with joy—that's the time that seems long in the memory. And this is right when you think about it. Eventlessness has no posts to drape duration on. From nothing to nothing is no time at all.

Adam's second five years were up before he knew it. It was late in 1890, and he was discharged with sergeant's stripes in the Presidio in San Francisco. Letters between Charles and Adam had become great rarities, but Adam wrote his brother just before his discharge, "This time I'm coming home," and that was the last Charles heard of him for over three years.

Adam waited out the winter, wandering up the river to Sacramento, ranging in the valley of the San Joaquin, and when the spring came Adam had no money. He rolled a blanket and started slowly eastward, sometimes walking and sometimes with groups of men on the rods under slow-moving freight cars. At night he jungled up with wandering men in the camping places on the fringes of towns. He learned to beg, not for money but for food. And before he knew it he was a bindlestiff himself.

Such men are rare now, but in the nineties there were many of them, wandering men, lonely men, who wanted it that way. Some of them ran from responsibilities and some felt driven out of society by injustice. They worked a little, but not for long. They stole a little, but only food and occasionally needed garments from a wash line. They were all kinds of men —literate men and ignorant men, clean men and dirty men—but all of them had restlessness in common. They followed warmth and avoided great heat and great cold. As the spring advanced they tracked it eastward, and the first frost drove them west and south. They were brothers to the coyote which, being wild, lives close to man and his chickenyards: they were near towns but not in them. Associations with other men were for a week or for a day and then they drifted apart.

Around the little fires where communal stew bubbled there was all manner of talk and only the personal was unmentionable. Adam heard of the development of the I.W.W. with its angry angels. He listened to philosophic discussions, to metaphysics, to esthetics, to impersonal experience. His companions for the night might be a murderer, an unfrocked priest or one who had unfrocked himself, a professor forced from his warm berth by a dull faculty, a lone driven man running from memory, a fallen archangel and a devil in training, and each contributed bits of thought to the fire as each contributed carrots and potatoes and onions and meat to the stew. He learned the technique of shaving with broken glass, of judging a house before knocking to ask for a handout. He learned to avoid or get along with hostile police and to evaluate a woman for her warmth of heart.

Adam took pleasure in the new life. When autumn touched the trees he had got as far as Omaha, and without question or reason or thought he hurried west and south, fled through the mountains and arrived with relief in Southern California. He wandered by the sea from the border north as far as San Luis Obispo, and he learned to pilfer the tide pools for abalones and eels and mussels and perch, to dig the sandbars for clams, and to trap a rabbit in the dunes with a noose of fishline. And he lay in the sun-warmed sand, counting the waves.

Spring urged him east again, but more slowly than before. Summer was cool in the mountains, and the mountain people were kind as lonesome people are kind. Adam took a job on a widow's outfit near Denver and shared her table and her bed humbly until the frost drove him south again. He followed the Rio Grande past Albuquerque and El Paso through the Big Bend, through Laredo to Brownsville. He learned Spanish words for food and pleasure, and he learned that when people are very poor they still have something to give and the impulse to give it. He developed a love for poor people he could not have conceived if he had not been poor himself. And by now he was an expert tramp, using humility as a working principle. He was lean and sun-darkened, and he could withdraw his own personality until he made no stir of anger or jealousy. His voice had grown soft, and he had merged many accents and dialects into his own speech, so that his speech did not seem foreign anywhere. This was the great safety of the tramp, a protective veil. He rode the trains very infrequently, for there was a growing anger against tramps, based on the angry violence of the I.W.W. and aggravated by the fierce reprisals against them. Adam was picked up for vagrancy. The quick brutality of police and prisoners frightened him and drove him away from the gatherings of tramps. He traveled alone after that and made sure that he was shaven and clean.

When spring came again he started north. He felt that his time of rest and peace was over. He aimed north toward Charles and the weakening memories of his childhood.

Adam moved rapidly across interminable East Texas, through Louisiana and the butt ends of Mississippi and Alabama, and into the flank of Florida. He felt that he had to move quickly. The Negroes were poor enough to be kind, but they could not trust any white man no matter how poor, and the poor white men had a fear of strangers.

Near Tallahassee he was picked up by sheriff's men, judged vagrant, and put on a road gang. That's how the roads were built. His sentence was six months. He was released and instantly picked up again for a second six months. And now he learned how men can consider other men as beasts and that the easiest way to get along with such men was to be a beast. A clean face, an open face, an eye raised to meet an eye—these drew attention and attention drawn brought punishment. Adam thought how a man doing an ugly or a brutal thing has hurt himself and must punish someone for the hurt. To be guarded at work by men with shotguns, to be shackled by the ankle at night to a chain, were simple matters of precaution, but the savage whippings for the least stir of will, for the smallest shred of dignity or resistance, these seemed to indicate that guards were afraid of prisoners, and Adam knew from his years in the army that a man afraid is a dangerous animal. And Adam, like anyone in the world, feared what whipping would do to his body and his spirit. He drew a curtain around himself. He removed expression from his face, light from his eyes, and silenced his speech. Later he was not so much astonished that it had happened to him but that he had been able to take it and with a minimum of pain. It was much more horrible afterward than when it was happening. It is a triumph of self-control to see a man whipped until the muscles of his back show white and glistening through the cuts and to give no sign of pity or anger or interest. And Adam learned this.

People are felt rather than seen after the first few moments. During his second sentence on the roads of Florida, Adam reduced his personality to a minus. He caused no stir, put out no vibration, became as nearly invisible as it is possible to be. And when the guards could not feel him, they were not afraid of him. They gave him the jobs of cleaning the camps, of handing out the slops to the prisoners, of filling the water buckets.

Adam waited until three days before his second release. Right after noon that day he filled the water buckets and went back to the little river for more. He filled his buckets with stones and sank them, and then he eased himself into the water and swam a long way downstream, rested and swam farther down. He kept moving in the water until at dusk he found a place under a bank with bushes for cover. He did not get out of the water.

Late in the night he heard the hounds go by, covering both sides of the river. He had rubbed his hair hard with green leaves to cover human odor. He sat in the water with his nose and eyes clear. In the morning the hounds came back, disinterested, and the men were too tired to beat the banks properly. When they were gone Adam dug a piece of water-logged fried sawbelly out of his pocket and ate it.

He had schooled himself against hurry. Most men were caught bolting. It took Adam five days to cross the short distance into Georgia. He took no chances, held back his impatience with an iron control. He was astonished at his ability.

On the edge of Valdosta, Georgia, he lay hidden until long after midnight, and he entered the town like a shadow, crept to the rear of a cheap store, forced a window slowly so that the screws of the lock were pulled from the sun-rotted wood. Then he replaced the lock but left the window open. He had to work by moonlight drifting through dirty windows. He stole a pair of cheap trousers, a white shirt, black shoes, black hat, and an oilskin raincoat, and he tried on each article for fit. He forced himself to make sure nothing looked disturbed before he climbed out the window. He had taken nothing which was not heavily stocked. He had not even looked for the cash drawer. He lowered the window carefully and slipped from shadow to shadow in the moonlight.

He lay hidden during the day and went in search of food at night— turnips, a few ears of corn from a crib, a few windfall apples—nothing that would be missed. He broke the newness of the shoes with rubbed sand and kneaded the raincoat to destroy its newness. It was three days before he got the rain he needed, or in his extreme caution felt he needed.

The rain started late in the afternoon. Adam huddled under his oilskin, waiting for the dark to come, and when it did he walked through the dripping night into the town of Valdosta. His black hat was pulled down over his eyes and his yellow oilskin was strapped tight against his throat. He made his way to the station and peered through a rain-blurred window. The station agent, in green eyeshade and black alpaca worksleeves, leaned through the ticket window, talking to a friend. It was twenty minutes before the friend went away. Adam watched him off the platform. He took a deep breath to calm himself and went inside.

2

Charles received very few letters. Sometimes he did not inquire at the post office for weeks. In February of 1894 when a thick letter came from a firm of attorneys in Washington the postmaster thought it might be important. He walked out to the Trask farm, found Charles cutting wood, and gave him the letter. And since he had taken so much trouble, he waited around to hear what the letter said.

Charles let him wait. Very slowly he read all five pages, went back and read them again, moving his lips over the words. Then he folded it up and turned toward the house.

The postmaster called after him, "Anything wrong, Mr. Trask?"

"My father is dead," Charles said, and he walked into the house and closed the door.

"Took it hard," the postmaster reported in town. "Took it real hard. Quiet man. Don't talk much."

In the house Charles lighted the lamp although it was not dark yet. He laid the letter on the table, and he washed his hands before he sat down to read it again.

There hadn't been anyone to send him a telegram. The attorneys had found his address among his father's papers. They were sorry—offered their condolences. And they were pretty excited too. When they had made Trask's will they thought he might have a few hundred dollars to leave his sons. That is what he looked to be worth. When they inspected his bankbooks they found that he had over ninety-three thousand dollars in the bank and ten thousand dollars in good securities. They felt very different about Mr. Trask then. People with that much money were rich. They would never have to worry. It was enough to start a dynasty. The lawyers congratulated Charles and his brother Adam. Under the will, they said, it was to be shared equally. After the money they listed the personal effects left by the deceased: five ceremonial swords presented to Cyrus at various G.A.R. conventions, an olivewood gavel with a gold plate on it, a Masonic watch charm with a diamond set in the dividers, the gold caps from the teeth he had out when he got his plates, watch (silver), gold-headed stick, and so forth.

Charles read the letter twice more and cupped his forehead in his hands.
He wondered about Adam. He wanted Adam home.

Charles felt puzzled and dull. He built up the fire and put the frying pan
to heat and sliced thick pieces of salt pork into it. Then he went back to
stare at the letter. Suddenly he picked it up and put it in the drawer of the
kitchen table. He decided not to think of the matter at all for a while.

Of course he thought of little else, but it was a dull circular thinking that
came back to the starting point again and again: Where had he gotten it?

When two events have something in common, in their natures or in time
or place, we leap happily to the conclusion that they are similar and from
this tendency we create magics and store them for retelling. Charles had
never before had a letter delivered at the farm in his life. Some weeks later
a boy ran out to the farm with a telegram. Charles always connected the
letter and the telegram the way we group two deaths and anticipate a third.
He hurried to the village railroad station, carrying the telegram in his hand.

"Listen to this," he said to the operator.

"I already read it."

"You did?"

"It comes over the wire," said the operator. "I wrote it down."

"Oh! Yes, sure. 'Urgent need you telegraph me one hundred dollars.
Coming home. Adam.'"

"Came collect," the operator said. "You owe me sixty cents."

"Valdosta, Georgia—I never heard of it."

"Neither'd I, but it's there."

"Say, Carlton, how do you go about telegraphing money?"

"Well, you bring me a hundred and two dollars and sixty cents and I send
a wire telling the Valdosta operator to pay Adam one hundred dollars. You
owe me sixty cents too."

"I'll pay—say, how do I know it's Adam? What's to stop anybody from
collecting it?"

The operator permitted himself a smile of worldliness. "Way we go about
it, you give me a question couldn't nobody else know the answer. So I send
both the question and the answer. Operator asks this fella the question, and
if he can't answer he don't get the money."

"Say, that's pretty cute. I better think up a good one."

"You better get the hundred dollars while Old Breen still got the window
open."

Charles was delighted with the game. He came back with the money in
his hand. "I got the question," he said.

"I hope it ain't your mother's middle name. Lot of people don't remember."

"No, nothing like that. It's this. 'What did you give father on his birthday
just before you went in the army?'"

"It's a good question but it's long as hell. Can't you cut it down to ten words?"

"Who's paying for it? Answer is, 'A pup.'"

"Wouldn't nobody guess that," said Carlton. "Well, it's you paying, not me."

"Be funny if he forgot," said Charles. "He wouldn't ever get home."

3

Adam came walking out from the village. His shirt was dirty and the stolen clothes were wrinkled and soiled from having been slept in for a week. Between the house and the barn he stopped and listened for his brother, and in a moment he heard him hammering at something in the big new tobacco barn. "Oh, Charles!" Adam called.

The hammering stopped, and there was silence. Adam felt as though his brother were inspecting him through the cracks in the barn. Then Charles came out quickly and hurried to Adam and shook hands.

"How are you?"

"Fine," said Adam.

"Good God, you're thin!"

"I guess I am. And I'm years older too."

Charles inspected him from head to foot. "You don't look prosperous."

"I'm not."

"Where's your valise?"

"I haven't got one."

"Jesus Christ! Where've you been?"

"Mostly wandering around all over."

"Like a hobo?"

"Like a hobo."

After all the years and the life that had made creased leather out of Charles' skin and redness in his dark eyes, Adam knew from remembering that Charles was thinking of two things—the questions and something else.

"Why didn't you come home?"

"I just got to wandering. Couldn't stop. It gets into you. That's a real bad scar you've got there."

"That's the one I wrote you about. Gets worse all the time. Why didn't you write? Are you hungry?" Charles' hands itched into his pockets and out and touched his chin and scratched his head.

"It may go away. I saw a man once—bartender—he had one that looked like a cat. It was a birthmark. His nickname was Cat."

"Are you hungry?"

"Sure, I guess I am."

"Plan to stay home now?"

"I—I guess so. Do you want to get to it now?"

"I—I guess so," Charles echoed him. "Our father is dead."

"I know."

"How the hell do *you* know?"

"Station agent told me. How long ago did he die?"

" 'Bout a month."

"What of?"

"Pneumonia."

"Buried here?"

"No. In Washington. I got a letter and newspapers. Carried him on a caisson with a flag over it. The Vice-President was there and the President sent a wreath. All in the papers. Pictures too—I'll show you. I've got it all."

Adam studied his brother's face until Charles looked away. "Are you mad at something?" Adam asked.

"What should I be mad at?"

"It just sounded—"

"I've got nothing to be mad at. Come on, I'll get you something to eat."

"All right. Did he linger long?"

"No. It was galloping pneumonia. Went right out."

Charles was covering up something. He wanted to tell it but he didn't know how to go about it. He kept hiding in words. Adam fell silent. It might be a good thing to be quiet and let Charles sniff and circle until he came out with it.

"I don't take much stock in messages from the beyond," said Charles. "Still, how can you know? Some people claim they've had messages—old Sarah Whitburn. She swore. You just don't know what to think. You didn't get a message, did you? Say, what the hell's bit off your tongue?"

Adam said, "Just thinking." And he was thinking with amazement, Why, I'm not afraid of my brother! I used to be scared to death of him, and I'm not any more. Wonder why not? Could it be the army? Or the chain gang? Could it be Father's death? Maybe—but I don't understand it. With the lack of fear, he knew he could say anything he wanted to, whereas before he had picked over his words to avoid trouble. It was a good feeling he had, almost as though he himself had been dead and resurrected.

They walked into the kitchen he remembered and didn't remember. It seemed smaller and dingier. Adam said almost gaily, "Charles, I been listening. You want to tell me something and you're walking around it like a terrier around a bush. You better tell before it bites you."

Charles' eyes sparked up with anger. He raised his head. His force was gone. He thought with desolation, I can't lick him any more. I can't.

Adam chuckled. "Maybe it's wrong to feel good when our father's just died, but you know, Charles, I never felt better in my whole life. I never felt as good. Spill it, Charles. Don't let it chew on you."

Charles asked, "Did you love our father?"

"I won't answer you until I know what you're getting at."

"Did you or didn't you?"

"What's that got to do with you?"

"Tell me."

The creative free boldness was all through Adam's bones and brain. "All right, I'll tell you. No. I didn't. Sometimes he scared me. Sometimes—yes, sometimes I admired him, but most of the time I hated him. Now tell me why you want to know."

Charles was looking down at his hands. "I don't understand," he said. "I just can't get it through my head. He loved you more than anything in the world."

"I don't believe that."

"You don't have to. He liked everything you brought him. He didn't like me. He didn't like anything I gave him. Remember the present I gave him, the pocketknife? I cut and sold a load of wood to get that knife. Well, he didn't even take it to Washington with him. It's right in his bureau right now. And you gave him a pup. It didn't cost you a thing. Well, I'll show you a picture of that pup. It was at his funeral. A colonel was holding it—it was blind, couldn't walk. They shot it after the funeral."

Adam was puzzled at the fierceness of his brother's tone. "I don't see," he said. "I don't see what you're getting at."

"I loved him," said Charles. And for the first time that Adam could remember, Charles began to cry. He put his head down in his arms and cried.

Adam was about to go to him when a little of the old fear came back. No, he thought, if I touched him he would try to kill me. He went to the open doorway and stood looking out, and he could hear his brother's sniffling behind him.

It was not a pretty farm near the house—never had been. There was litter about it, an unkemptness, a rundownness, a lack of plan; no flowers, and bits of paper and scraps of wood scattered about on the ground. The house was not pretty either. It was a well-built shanty for shelter and cooking. It was a grim farm and a grim house, unloved and unloving. It was no home, no place to long for or to come back to. Suddenly Adam thought of his stepmother—as unloved as the farm, adequate, clean in her way, but no more wife than the farm was a home.

His brother's sobbing had stopped. Adam turned. Charles was looking blankly straight ahead. Adam said, "Tell me about Mother."

"She died. I wrote you."

"Tell me about her."

"I told you. She died. It's so long ago. She wasn't your Mother."

The smile Adam had once caught on her face flashed up in his mind. Her face was projected in front of him.

Charles' voice came through the image and exploded it. "Will you tell me one thing—not quick—think before you tell me, and maybe don't answer unless it's true, your answer."

Charles moved his lips to form the question in advance. "Do you think it would be possible for our father to be—dishonest?"

"What do you mean?"

"Isn't that plain enough? I said it plain. There's only one meaning to dishonest."

"I don't know," said Adam. "I don't know. No one ever said it. Look what he got to be. Stayed overnight in the White House. The Vice-President came to his funeral. Does that sound like a dishonest man? Come on, Charles," he begged, "tell me what you've been wanting to tell me from the minute I got here."

Charles wet his lips. The blood seemed to have gone out of him, and with it energy and all ferocity. His voice became a monotone. "Father made a will. Left everything equal to me and you."

Adam laughed. "Well, we can always live on the farm. I guess we won't starve."

"It's over a hundred thousand dollars," the dull voice went on.

"You're crazy. More like a hundred dollars. Where would he get it?"

"It's no mistake. His salary with the G.A.R. was a hundred and thirty-five dollars a month. He paid his own room and board. He got five cents a mile and hotel expenses when he traveled."

"Maybe he had it all the time and we never knew."

"No, he didn't have it all the time."

"Well, why don't we write to the G.A.R. and ask? Someone there might know."

"I wouldn't dare," said Charles.

"Now look! Don't go off half-cocked. There's such a thing as speculation. Lots of men struck it rich. He knew big men. Maybe he got in on a good thing. Think of the men who went to the gold rush in California and came back rich."

Charles' face was desolate. His voice dropped so that Adam had to lean close to hear. It was as toneless as a report. "Our father went into the Union Army in June 1862. He had three months' training here in this state. That makes it September. He marched south. October twelfth he was hit in the leg and sent to the hospital. He came home in January."

"I don't see what you're getting at."

Charles' words were thin and sallow. "He was not at Chancellorsville. He was not at Gettysburg or the Wilderness or Richmond or Appomattox."

"How do you know?"

"His discharge. It came down with his other papers."

Adam sighed deeply. In his chest, like beating fists, was a surge of joy. He shook his head almost in disbelief.

Charles said, "How did he get away with it? How in hell did he get away with it? Nobody ever questioned it. Did you? Did I? Did my mother? Nobody did. Not even in Washington."

Adam stood up. "What's in the house to eat? I'm going to warm up something."

"I killed a chicken last night. I'll fry it if you can wait."

"Anything quick?"

"Some salt pork and plenty of eggs."

"I'll have that," said Adam.

They left the question lying there, walked mentally around it, stepped over it. Their words ignored it but their minds never left it. They wanted to talk about it and could not. Charles fried salt pork, warmed up a skillet of beans, fried eggs.

"I plowed the pasture," he said. "Put it in rye."

"How did it do?"

"Just fine, once I got the rocks out." He touched his forehead. "I got this damn thing trying to pry out a stone."

"You wrote about that," Adam said. "Don't know whether I told you your letters meant a lot to me."

"You never wrote much what you were doing," said Charles.

"I guess I didn't want to think about it. It was pretty bad, most of it."

"I read about the campaigns in the papers. Did you go on those?"

"Yes. I didn't want to think about them. Still don't."

"Did you kill Injuns?"

"Yes, we killed Injuns."

"I guess they're real ornery."

"I guess so."

"You don't have to talk about it if you don't want to."

"I don't want to."

They ate their dinner under the kerosene lamp. "We'd get more light if I would only get around to washing that lampshade."

"I'll do it," said Adam. "It's hard to think of everything."

"It's going to be fine having you back. How would you like to go to the inn after supper?"

"Well, we'll see. Maybe I'd like just to sit awhile."

"I didn't write about it in a letter, but they've got girls at the inn. I didn't know but you'd like to go in with me. They change every two weeks. I didn't know but you'd like to look them over."

"Girls?"

"Yes, they're upstairs. Makes it pretty handy. And I thought you just coming home—"

"Not tonight. Maybe later. How much do they charge?"

"A dollar. Pretty nice girls mostly."

"Maybe later," said Adam. "I'm surprised they let them come in."

"I was too at first. But they worked out a system."

"You go often?"

"Every two or three weeks. It's pretty lonesome here, a man living alone."

"You wrote once you were thinking of getting married."

"Well, I was. Guess I didn't find the right girl."

All around the main subject the brothers beat. Now and then they would almost step into it, and quickly pull away, back into crops and local gossip and politics and health. They knew they would come back to it sooner or later. Charles was more anxious to strike in deep than Adam was, but then Charles had had the time to think of it, and to Adam it was a new field of thinking and feeling. He would have preferred to put it over until another day, and at the same time he knew his brother would not permit him to.

Once he said openly, "Let's sleep on that other thing."

"Sure, if you want to," said Charles.

Gradually they ran out of escape talk. Every acquaintance was covered and every local event. The talk lagged and the time went on.

"Feel like turning in?" Adam asked.

"In a little while."

They were silent, and the night moved restlessly about the house, nudging them and urging them.

"I sure would like to've seen that funeral," said Charles.

"Must have been pretty fancy."

"Would you care to see the clippings from the papers? I've got them all in my room."

"No. Not tonight."

Charles squared his chair around and put his elbows on the table. "We'll have to figure it out," he said nervously. "We can put it off all we want, but we goddam well got to figure what we're going to do."

"I know that," said Adam. "I guess I just wanted some time to think about it."

"Would that do any good? I've had time, lots of time, and I just went in circles. I tried not to think about it, and I still went in circles. You think time is going to help?"

"I guess not. I guess not. What do you want to talk about first? I guess we might as well get into it. We're not thinking about anything else."

"There's the money," said Charles. "Over a hundred thousand dollars—a fortune."

"What about the money?"

"Well, where did it come from?"

"How do I know? I told you he might have speculated. Somebody might have put him onto a good thing there in Washington."

"Do you believe that?"

"I don't believe anything," Adam said. "I don't know, so what can I believe?"

"It's a lot of money," said Charles. "It's a fortune left to us. We can live the rest of our lives on it, or we can buy a hell of a lot of land and make it pay. Maybe you didn't think about it, but we're rich. We're richer than anybody hereabouts."

Adam laughed. "You say it like it was a jail sentence."

"Where did it come from?"

"What do you care?" Adam asked. "Maybe we should just settle back and enjoy it."

"He wasn't at Gettysburg. He wasn't at any goddam battle in the whole war. He was hit in a skirmish. Everything he told was lies."

"What are you getting at?" said Adam.

"I think he stole the money," Charles said miserably. "You asked me and that's what I think."

"Do you know where he stole it?"

"No."

"Then why do you think he stole it?"

"He told lies about the war."

"What?"

"I mean, if he lied about the war—why, he could steal."

"How?"

"He held jobs in the G.A.R.—big jobs. He maybe could have got into the treasury, rigged the books."

Adam sighed. "Well, if that's what you think, why don't you write to them and tell them? Have them go over the books. If it's true we could give back the money."

Charles' face was twisted and the scar on his forehead showed dark. "The Vice-President came to his funeral. The President sent a wreath. There was a line of carriages half a mile long and hundreds of people on foot. And do you know who the pallbearers were?"

"What are you digging at?"

" 'Spose we found out he's a thief. Then it would come out how he never was at Gettysburg or anyplace else. Then everybody would know he was a liar too, and his whole life was a goddam lie. Then even if sometimes he did tell the truth, nobody would believe it was the truth."

Adam sat very still. His eyes were untroubled but he was watchful. "I thought you loved him," he said calmly. He felt released and free.

"I did. I do. That's why I hate this—his whole life gone—all gone. And his grave—they might even dig him up and throw him out." His words were ragged with emotion. "Didn't you love him at all?" he cried.

"I wasn't sure until now," said Adam. "I was all mixed up with how I was supposed to feel. No. I did not love him."

"Then you don't care if his life is spoiled and his poor body rooted up and—oh, my God almighty!"

Adam's brain raced, trying to find words for his feeling. "I don't have to care."

"No, you don't," Charles said bitterly. "Not if you didn't love him, you don't. You can help kick him in the face."

Adam knew that his brother was no longer dangerous. There was no jealousy to drive him. The whole weight of his father was on him, but it was his father and no one could take his father away from him.

"How will you feel, walking in town, after everyone knows?" Charles demanded. "How will you face anybody?"

"I told you I don't care. I don't have to care because I don't believe it."

"You don't believe what?"

"I don't believe he stole any money. I believe in the war he did just what he said he did and was just where he said he was."

"But the proof—how about the discharge?"

"You haven't any proof that he stole. You just made that up because you don't know where the money came from."

"His army papers—"

"They could be wrong," Adam said. "I believe they are wrong. I believe in my father."

"I don't see how you can."

Adam said, "Let me tell you. The proofs that God does not exist are very strong, but in lots of people they are not as strong as the feeling that He does."

"But you said you did not love our father. How can you have faith in him if you didn't love him?"

"Maybe that's the reason," Adam said slowly, feeling his way. "Maybe if I had loved him I would have been jealous of him. You were. Maybe—maybe love makes you suspicious and doubting. Is it true that when you love a woman you are never sure—never sure of her because you aren't sure of yourself? I can see it pretty clearly. I can see how you loved him and what it did to you. I did not love him. Maybe he loved me. He tested me and hurt me and punished me and finally he sent me out like a sacrifice, maybe to make up for something. But he did not love you, and so he had faith in you. Maybe—why, maybe it's a kind of reverse."

Charles stared at him. "I don't understand," he said.

"I'm trying to," said Adam. "It's a new thought to me. I feel good. I feel better maybe than I have ever felt in my whole life. I've got rid of something. Maybe sometime I'll get what you have, but I haven't got it now."

"I don't understand," Charles said again.

"Can you see that I don't think our father was a thief? I don't believe he was a liar."

"But the papers—"

"I won't look at the papers. Papers are no match at all for my faith in my father."

Charles was breathing heavily. "Then you would take the money?"

"Of course."

"Even if he stole it?"

"He did not steal it. He couldn't have stolen it."

"I don't understand," said Charles.

"You don't? Well, it does seem that maybe this might be the secret of the whole thing. Look, I've never mentioned this—do you remember when you beat me up just before I went away?"

"Yes."

"Do you remember later? You came back with a hatchet to kill me."

"I don't remember very well. I must have been crazy."

"I didn't know then, but I know now—you were fighting for your love."

"Love?"

"Yes," said Adam. "We'll use the money well. Maybe we'll stay here. Maybe we'll go away—maybe to California. We'll have to see what we'll do. And of course we must set up a monument to our father—a big one."

"I couldn't ever go away from here," said Charles.

"Well, let's see how it goes. There's no hurry. We'll feel it out."

EIGHT

I believe there are monsters born in the world to human parents. Some you can see, misshapen and horrible, with huge heads or tiny bodies; some are born with no arms, no legs, some with three arms, some with tails or mouths in odd places. They are accidents and no one's fault, as used to be thought. Once they were considered the visible punishments for concealed sins.

And just as there are physical monsters, can there not be mental or psychic monsters born? The face and body may be perfect, but if a twisted gene or a malformed egg can produce physical monsters, may not the same process produce a malformed soul?

Monsters are variations from the accepted normal to a greater or a less degree. As a child may be born without an arm, so one may be born without kindness or the potential of conscience. A man who loses his arms in an accident has a great struggle to adjust himself to the lack, but one born without arms suffers only from people who find him strange. Having never had arms, he cannot miss them. Sometimes when we are little we imagine how it would be to have wings, but there is no reason to suppose it is the same feeling birds have. No, to a monster the norm must seem monstrous, since everyone is normal to himself. To the inner monster it must be even more obscure, since he has no visible thing to compare with others. To a man born without conscience, a soul-stricken man must seem ridiculous. To a criminal, honesty is foolish. You must not forget that a monster is only a variation, and that to a monster the norm is monstrous.

It is my belief that Cathy Ames was born with the tendencies, or lack of them, which drove and forced her all of her life. Some balance wheel was misweighted, some gear out of ratio. She was not like other people, never was from birth. And just as a cripple may learn to utilize his lack so that he becomes more effective in a limited field than the uncrippled, so did Cathy, using her difference, make a painful and bewildering stir in her world.

There was a time when a girl like Cathy would have been called possessed by the devil. She would have been exorcised to cast out the evil spirit, and if after many trials that did not work, she would have been burned as a witch for the good of the community. The one thing that may not be forgiven a witch is her ability to distress people, to make them restless and uneasy and even envious.

As though nature concealed a trap, Cathy had from the first a face of innocence. Her hair was gold and lovely; wide-set hazel eyes with upper lids that drooped made her look mysteriously sleepy. Her nose was delicate and thin, and her cheekbones high and wide, sweeping down to a small chin so that her face was heart-shaped. Her mouth was well shaped and well lipped but abnormally small—what used to be called a rosebud. Her ears were very little, without lobes, and they pressed so close to her head that even with her hair combed up they made no silhouette. They were thin flaps sealed against her head.

Cathy always had a child's figure even after she was grown, slender, delicate arms and hands—tiny hands. Her breasts never developed very much. Before her puberty the nipples turned inward. Her mother had to manipulate them out when they became painful in Cathy's tenth year. Her body was a boy's body, narrow-hipped, straight-legged, but her ankles were thin and straight without being slender. Her feet were small and round and stubby, with fat insteps almost like little hoofs. She was a pretty child and she became a pretty woman. Her voice was huskily soft, and it could be so sweet as to be irresistible. But there must have been some steel cord in her throat, for Cathy's voice could cut like a file when she wished.

Even as a child she had some quality that made people look at her, then look away, then look back at her, troubled at something foreign. Something looked out of her eyes, and was never there when one looked again. She moved quietly and talked little, but she could enter no room without causing everyone to turn toward her.

She made people uneasy but not so that they wanted to go away from her. Men and women wanted to inspect her, to be close to her, to try to find what caused the disturbance she distributed so subtly. And since this had always been so, Cathy did not find it strange.

Cathy was different from other children in many ways, but one thing in particular set her apart. Most children abhor difference. They want to look, talk, dress, and act exactly like all of the others. If the style of dress is an absurdity, it is pain and sorrow to a child not to wear that absurdity. If necklaces of pork chops were accepted, it would be a sad child who could not wear pork chops. And this slavishness to the group normally extends into every game, every practice, social or otherwise. It is a protective coloration children utilize for their safety.

Cathy had none of this. She never conformed in dress or conduct. She wore whatever she wanted to. The result was that quite often other children imitated her.

As she grew older the group, the herd, which is any collection of children, began to sense what adults felt, that there was something foreign about Cathy. After a while only one person at a time associated with her. Groups of boys and girls avoided her as though she carried a nameless danger.

Cathy was a liar, but she did not lie the way most children do. Hers was no daydream lying, when the thing imagined is told and, to make it seem more real, told as real. That is just ordinary deviation from external reality. I think the difference between a lie and a story is that a story utilizes the trappings and appearance of truth for the interest of the listener as well as of the teller. A story has in it neither gain nor loss. But a lie is a device for profit or escape. I suppose if that definition is strictly held to, then a writer of stories is a liar—if he is financially fortunate.

Cathy's lies were never innocent. Their purpose was to escape punishment, or work, or responsibility, and they were used for profit. Most liars are tripped up either because they forget what they have told or because the lie is suddenly faced with an incontrovertible truth. But Cathy did not forget her lies, and she developed the most effective method of lying. She stayed close enough to the truth so that one could never be sure. She knew two other methods also—either to interlard her lies with truth or to tell a truth as though it were a lie. If one is accused of a lie and it turns out to be the truth, there is a backlog that will last a long time and protect a number of untruths.

Since Cathy was an only child her mother had no close contrast in the family. She thought all children were like her own. And since all parents are worriers she was convinced that all her friends had the same problems.

Cathy's father was not so sure. He operated a small tannery in a town in Massachusetts, which made a comfortable, careful living if he worked very hard. Mr. Ames came in contact with other children away from his home and he felt that Cathy was not like other children. It was a matter more felt than known. He was uneasy about his daughter but he could not have said why.

Nearly everyone in the world has appetites and impulses, trigger emotions, islands of selfishness, lusts just beneath the surface. And most people either hold such things in check or indulge them secretly. Cathy knew not only these impulses in others but how to use them for her own gain. It is quite possible that she did not believe in any other tendencies in humans, for while she was preternaturally alert in some directions she was completely blind in others.

Cathy learned when she was very young that sexuality with all its attendant yearnings and pains, jealousies and taboos, is the most disturbing impulse humans have. And in that day it was even more disturbing than it is now, because the subject was unmentionable and unmentioned. Everyone concealed that little hell in himself, while publicly pretending it did not exist—and when he was caught up in it he was completely helpless. Cathy learned that by the manipulation and use of this one part of people she could gain and keep power over nearly anyone. It was at once a weapon and a threat. It was irresistible. And since the blind helplessness seems never to have fallen on Cathy, it is probable that she had very little of the impulse herself and indeed felt a contempt for those who did. And when you think of it in one way, she was right.

What freedom men and women could have, were they not constantly tricked and trapped and enslaved and tortured by their sexuality! The only drawback in that freedom is that without it one would not be a human. One would be a monster.

At ten Cathy knew something of the power of the sex impulse and began coldly to experiment with it. She planned everything coldly, foreseeing difficulties and preparing for them.

The sex play of children has always gone on. Everyone, I guess, who is not abnormal has foregathered with little girls in some dim leafy place, in the bottom of a manger, under a willow, in a culvert under a road—or at least has dreamed of doing so. Nearly all parents are faced with the problem sooner or later, and then the child is lucky if the parent remembers his own childhood. In the time of Cathy's childhood, however, it was harder. The parents, denying it in themselves, were horrified to find it in their children.

2

On a spring morning when with late-surviving dew the young grass bristled under the sun, when the warmth crept into the ground and pushed the yellow dandelions up, Cathy's mother finished hanging the washed clothes on the line. The Ameses lived on the edge of town, and behind their house were barn and carriage house, vegetable garden and fenced paddock for two horses.

Mrs. Ames remembered having seen Cathy stroll away toward the barn. She called for her, and when there was no answer she thought she might have been mistaken. She was about to go into the house when she heard a giggle from the carriage house. "Cathy!" she called. There was no answer. An uneasiness came over her. She reached back in her mind for the sound of the giggle. It had not been Cathy's voice. Cathy was not a giggler.

There is no knowing how or why dread comes on a parent. Of course many times apprehension arises when there is no reason for it at all. And it comes most often to the parents of only children, parents who have indulged in black dreams of loss.

Mrs. Ames stood still, listening. She heard soft secret voices and moved quietly toward the carriage house. The double doors were closed. The murmur of voices came from inside, but she could not make out Cathy's voice. She made a quick stride and pulled the doors open and the bright sun crashed inside. She froze, mouth open, at what she saw. Cathy lay on the floor, her skirts pulled up. She was naked to the waist, and beside her two boys about fourteen were kneeling. The shock of the sudden light froze them too. Cathy's eyes were blank with terror. Mrs. Ames knew the boys, knew their parents.

Suddenly one of the boys leaped up, darted past Mrs. Ames, and ran around the corner of the house. The other boy helplessly edged away from the woman and with a cry rushed through the doorway. Mrs. Ames clutched at him, but her fingers slipped from his jacket and he was gone. She could hear his running footsteps outside.

Mrs. Ames tried to speak and her voice was a croaking whisper. "Get up!"

Cathy stared blankly up at her and made no move. Mrs. Ames saw that Cathy's wrists were tied with a heavy rope. She screamed and flung herself down and fumbled at the knots. She carried Cathy into the house and put her to bed.

The family doctor, after he had examined Cathy, could find no evidence that she had been mistreated. "You can just thank God you got there in time," he said over and over to Mrs. Ames.

Cathy did not speak for a long time. Shock, the doctor called it. And when she did come out of the shock Cathy refused to talk. When she was questioned her eyes widened until the whites showed all around the pupils and her breathing stopped and her body grew rigid and her cheeks reddened from holding her breath.

The conference with the parents of the boys was attended by Dr. Williams. Mr. Ames was silent most of the time. He carried the rope which had been around Cathy's wrists. His eyes were puzzled. There were things he did not understand, but he did not bring them up.

Mrs. Ames settled down to a steady hysteria. She had been there. She had seen. She was the final authority. And out of her hysteria a sadistic devil peered. She wanted blood. There was a kind of pleasure in her demands for punishment. The town, the country, must be protected. She put it on that basis. She had arrived on time, thank God. But maybe the next time she would not; and how would other mothers feel? And Cathy was only ten years old.

Punishments were more savage then than they are now. A man truly believed that the whip was an instrument of virtue. First singly and then together the boys were whipped, whipped to raw cuts.

Their crime was bad enough, but the lies proved an evil that not even the whip could remove. And their defense was from the beginning ridiculous. Cathy, they said, had started the whole thing, and they had each given her five cents. They had not tied her hands. They said they remembered that she was playing with a rope.

Mrs. Ames said it first and the whole town echoed it. "Do they mean to say she tied her own hands? A ten-year-old child?"

If the boys had owned up to the crime they might have escaped some of the punishment. Their refusal brought a torturing rage not only to their fathers, who did the whipping, but to the whole community. Both boys were sent to a house of correction with the approval of their parents.

"She's haunted by it," Mrs. Ames told the neighbors. "If she could only talk about it, maybe she would get better. But when I ask her about it—it's like it came right back to her and she goes into shock again."

The Ameses never spoke of it to her again. The subject was closed. Mr. Ames very soon forgot his haunting reservations. He would have felt bad if two boys were in the house of correction for something they did not do.

After Cathy had fully recovered from her shock, boys and girls watched her from a distance and then moved closer, fascinated by her. She had no girl crushes, as is usual at twelve and thirteen. Boys did not want to take the chance of being ragged by their friends for walking home from school with her. But she exercised a powerful effect on both boys and girls. And if any boy could come on her alone, he found himself drawn to her by a force he could neither understand nor overcome.

She was dainty and very sweet and her voice was low. She went for long walks by herself, and it was a rare walk when some boy did not blunder out of a woodlot and come on her by accident. And while whispers went scurrying about, there is no knowing what Cathy did. If anything happened, only vague whispers followed, and this in itself was unusual at an age when there are many secrets and none of them kept long enough to raise a cream.

Cathy developed a little smile, just a hint of a smile. She had a way of looking sideways and down that hinted to a lone boy of secrets he could share.

In her father's mind another question stirred, and he shoved it down deep and felt dishonest for thinking about it at all. Cathy had remarkable luck in finding things—a gold charm, money, a little silken purse, a silver cross with red stones said to be rubies. She found many things, and when her father advertised in the weekly *Courier* about the cross no one ever claimed it.

Mr. William Ames, Cathy's father, was a covered man. He rarely told the thoughts in his mind. He wouldn't have dared so far to expose himself to the gaze of his neighbors. He kept the little flame of suspicion to himself. It was better if he didn't know anything, safer, wiser, and much more comfortable. As for Cathy's mother, she was so bound and twisted in a cocoon of gauzy half-lies, warped truth, suggestions, all planted by Cathy, that she would not have known a true thing if it had come to her.

3

Cathy grew more lovely all the time. The delicate blooming skin, the golden hair, the wide-set, modest, and yet promising eyes, the little mouth full of sweetness, caught attention and held it. She finished the eight grades of grammar school with such a good record that her parents entered her in the small high school, although in that time it was not usual for a girl to go on with her studies. But Cathy said she wanted to be a teacher, which delighted her mother and father, for this was the one profession of dignity open to a girl of a good but not well-to-do family. Parents took honor from a daughter who was a teacher.

Cathy was fourteen when she entered high school. She had always been precious to her parents, but with her entrance into the rarities of algebra and Latin she climbed into clouds where her parents could not follow. They had lost her. They felt that she was translated to a higher order.

The teacher of Latin was a pale intense young man who had failed in divinity school and yet had enough education to teach the inevitable grammar, Caesar, Cicero. He was a quiet young man who warmed his sense of failure to his bosom. Deep in himself he felt that he had been rejected by God, and for cause.

For a time it was noticed that a flame leaped in James Grew and some force glowed in his eyes. He was never seen with Cathy and no relationship was even suspected.

James Grew became a man. He walked on his toes and sang to himself. He wrote letters so persuasive that the directors of his divinity school looked favorably on readmitting him.

And then the flame went out. His shoulders, held so high and square, folded dejectedly. His eyes grew feverish and his hands twitched. He was seen in church at night, on his knees, moving his lips over prayers. He missed school and sent word that he was ill when it was known that he was walking all alone in the hills beyond the town.

One night, late, he tapped on the door of the Ames house. Mr. Ames complained his way out of bed, lighted a candle, flung an overcoat over his nightgown, and went to the door. It was a wild and crazy-looking James Grew who stood before him, his eyes shining and his body one big shudder.

"I've got to see you," he said hoarsely to Mr. Ames.

"It's after midnight," Mr. Ames said sternly.

"I've got to see you alone. Put on some clothes and come outside. I've got to talk to you."

"Young man, I think you're drunk or sick. Go home and get some sleep. It's after midnight."

"I can't wait. I've got to talk to you."

"Come down to the tannery in the morning," said Mr. Ames, and he closed the door firmly on the reeling caller and stood inside, listening. He heard the wailing voice, "I can't wait. I can't wait," and then the feet dragged slowly down the steps.

Mr. Ames shielded the candlelight away from his eyes with his cupped hand and went back to bed. He thought he saw Cathy's door close very silently, but perhaps the leaping candlelight had fooled his eyes, for a portiere seemed to move too.

"What in the world?" his wife demanded when he came back to the bedside.

Mr. Ames didn't know why he answered as he did—perhaps to save discussion. "A drunken man," he said. "Got the wrong house."

"I don't know what the world is coming to," said Mrs. Ames.

As he lay in the darkness after the light was out he saw the green circle left in his eyes by the candle flame, and in its whirling, pulsing frame he saw the frantic, beseeching eyes of James Grew. He didn't go back to sleep for a long time.

In the morning a rumor ran through the town, distorted here and there, added to, but by afternoon the story clarified. The sexton had found James Grew stretched on the floor in front of the altar. The whole top of his head was blown off. Beside him lay a shotgun, and beside it the piece of stick with which he had pushed the trigger. Near him on the floor was a candlestick from the altar. One of the three candles was still burning. The other two had not been lighted. And on the floor were two books, the hymnal and the Book of Common Prayer, one on top of the other. The way the sexton figured it, James Grew had propped the gun barrel on the books to bring it in line with his temple. The recoil of the discharge had thrown the shotgun off the books.

A number of people remembered having heard an explosion early in the morning, before daylight. James Grew left no letter. No one could figure why he had done it.

Mr. Ames' first impulse was to go to the coroner with his story of the midnight call. Then he thought, What good would it do? If I knew anything it would be different. But I don't know a single thing. He had a sick feeling in his stomach. He told himself over and over that it was not his fault. How could I have helped it? I don't even know what he wanted. He felt guilty and miserable.

At dinner his wife talked about the suicide and he couldn't eat. Cathy sat silent, but no more silent than usual. She ate with little dainty nips and wiped her mouth often on her napkin.

Mrs. Ames went over the matter of the body and the gun in detail. "There's one thing I meant to speak of," she said. "That drunken man who came to the door last night—could that have been young Grew?"

"No," he said quickly.

"Are you sure? Could you see him in the dark?"

"I had a candle," he said sharply. "Didn't look anything like, had a big beard."

"No need to snap at me," she said. "I just wondered."

Cathy wiped her mouth, and when she laid the napkin on her lap she was smiling.

Mrs. Ames turned to her daughter. "You saw him every day in school, Cathy. Has he seemed sad lately? Did you notice anything that might mean—"

Cathy looked down at her plate and then up. "I thought he was sick," she said. "Yes, he has looked bad. Everybody was talking in school today. And somebody—I don't remember who—said that Mr. Grew was in some kind of trouble in Boston. I didn't hear what kind of trouble. We all liked Mr. Grew." She wiped her lips delicately.

That was Cathy's method. Before the next day was out everybody in town knew that James Grew had been in trouble in Boston, and no one could possibly imagine that Cathy had planted the story. Even Mrs. Ames had forgotten where she heard it.

4

Soon after her sixteenth birthday a change came over Cathy. One morning she did not get up for school. Her mother went into her room and found her in bed, staring at the ceiling. "Hurry, you'll be late. It's nearly nine."

"I'm not going." There was no emphasis in her voice.

"Are you sick?"

"No."

"Then hurry, get up."

"I'm not going."

"You must be sick. You've never missed a day."

"I'm not going to school," Cathy said calmly. "I'm never going to school again."

Her mother's mouth fell open. "What do you mean?"

"Not ever," said Cathy and continued to stare at the ceiling.

"Well, we'll just see what your father has to say about that! With all our work and expense, and two years before you get your certificate!" Then she came close and said softly, "You aren't thinking of getting married?"

"No."

"What's that book you're hiding?"

"Here! I'm not hiding it."

"Oh! *Alice in Wonderland*. You're too big for that."

Cathy said, "I can get to be so little you can't even see me."

"What in the world are you talking about?"

"Nobody can find me."

Her mother said angrily, "Stop making jokes. I don't know what you're thinking of. What does Miss Fancy think she is going to do?"

"I don't know yet," said Cathy. "I think I'll go away."

"Well, you just lie there, Miss Fancy, and when your father comes home he'll have a thing or two to say to you."

Cathy turned her head very slowly and looked at her mother. Her eyes were expressionless and cold. And suddenly Mrs. Ames was afraid of her daughter. She went out quietly and closed the door. In her kitchen she sat down and cupped her hands in her lap and stared out the window at the weathering carriage house.

Her daughter had become a stranger to her. She felt, as most parents do at one time or another, that she was losing control, that the bridle put in her hands for the governing of Cathy was slipping through her fingers. She did not know that she had never had any power over Cathy. She had been used for Cathy's purposes always. After a while Mrs. Ames put on a bonnet and went to the tannery. She wanted to talk to her husband away from the house.

In the afternoon Cathy rose listlessly from her bed and spent a long time in front of the mirror.

That evening Mr. Ames, hating what he had to do, delivered a lecture to his daughter. He spoke of her duty, her obligation, her natural love for her parents. Toward the end of his speech he was aware that she was not listening to him. This made him angry and he fell into threats. He spoke of the authority God had given him over his child and of how this natural authority had been armed by the state. He had her attention now. She looked him right in the eyes. Her mouth smiled a little, and her eyes did not seem to blink. Finally he had to look away, and this enraged him further. He ordered her to stop her nonsense. Vaguely he threatened her with whipping if she did not obey him.

He ended on a note of weakness. "I want you to promise me that you will go to school in the morning and stop your foolishness."

Her face was expressionless. The little mouth was straight. "All right," she said.

Later that night Mr. Ames said to his wife with an assurance he did not feel, "You see, it just needs a little authority. Maybe we've been too lax. But she has been a good child. I guess she just forgot who's boss. A little sternness never hurt anybody." He wished he were as confident as his words.

In the morning she was gone. Her straw traveling basket was gone and the best of her clothing. Her bed was neatly made. The room was impersonal —nothing to indicate that a girl had grown up in it. There were no pictures, no mementos, none of the normal clutter of growing. Cathy had never played with dolls. The room had no Cathy imprint.

In his way Mr. Ames was an intelligent man. He clapped on his derby hat and walked quickly to the railroad station. The station agent was certain. Cathy had taken the early morning train. She had bought a ticket for Boston. He helped Mr. Ames write a telegram to the Boston police. Mr. Ames bought a round-trip ticket and caught the nine-fifty train to Boston. He was a very good man in a crisis.

That night Mrs. Ames sat in the kitchen with the door closed. She was white and she gripped the table with her hands to control her shaking. The sound, first of the blows and then of the screaming, came clearly to her through the closed doors.

Mr. Ames was not good at whipping because he had never done it. He lashed at Cathy's legs with the buggy whip, and when she stood quietly staring at him with calm cold eyes he lost his temper. The first blows were tentative and timid, but when she did not cry he slashed at her sides and shoulders. The whip licked and cut. In his rage he missed her several times or got too close so that the whip wrapped around her body.

Cathy learned quickly. She found him out and knew him, and once she had learned she screamed, she writhed, she cried, she begged, and she had the satisfaction of feeling the blows instantly become lighter.

Mr. Ames was frightened at the noise and hurt he was creating. He stopped. Cathy dropped back on the bed, sobbing. And if he had looked, her father would have seen that there were no tears in her eyes, but rather the muscles of her neck were tight and there were lumps just under her temples where the jaw muscle knotted.

He said, "Now, will you ever do that again?"

"No, oh, no! Forgive me," Cathy said. She turned over on the bed so that her father could not see the coldness in her face.

"See you remember who you are. And don't forget what I am."

Cathy's voice caught. She produced a dry sob. "I won't forget," she said.

In the kitchen Mrs. Ames wrestled her hands. Her husband put his fingers on her shoulder.

"I hated to do it," he said. "I had to. And I think it did her good. She seems like a changed girl to me. Maybe we haven't bent the twig enough. We've spared the rod. Maybe we were wrong." And he knew that although his wife had insisted on the whipping, although she had forced him to whip Cathy, she hated him for doing it. Despair settled over him.

5

There seemed no doubt that it was what Cathy needed. As Mr. Ames said, "It kind of opened her up." She had always been tractable but now she became thoughtful too. In the weeks that followed she helped her mother in the kitchen and offered to help more than was needed. She started to knit an afghan for her mother, a large project that would take months. Mrs. Ames told the neighbors about it. "She has such a fine color sense—rust and yellow. She's finished three squares already."

For her father Cathy kept a ready smile. She hung up his hat when he came in and turned his chair properly under the light to make it easy for him to read.

Even in school she was changed. Always she had been a good student, but now she began to make plans for the future. She talked to the principal about examinations for her teaching certificate, perhaps a year early. And the principal looked over her record and thought she might well try it with hope of success. He called on Mr. Ames at the tannery to discuss it.

"She didn't tell us any of this," Mr. Ames said proudly.

"Well, maybe I shouldn't have told you. I hope I haven't ruined a surprise."

Mr. and Mrs. Ames felt that they had blundered on some magic which solved all of their problems. They put it down to an unconscious wisdom which comes only to parents. "I never saw such a change in a person in my life," Mr. Ames said.

"But she was always a good child," said his wife. "And have you noticed how pretty she's getting? Why, she's almost beautiful. Her cheeks have so much color."

"I don't think she'll be teaching school long with her looks," said Mr. Ames.

It was true that Cathy glowed. The childlike smile was constantly on her lips while she went about her preparations. She had all the time in the world. She cleaned the cellar and stuffed papers all around the edges of the foundation to block the draft. When the kitchen door squeaked she oiled the hinges and then the lock that turned too hard, and while she had the oil can out she oiled the front-door hinges too. She made it her duty to keep the lamps filled and their chimneys clean. She invented a way of dipping the chimneys in a big can of kerosene she had in the basement.

"You'd have to see it to believe it," her father said.

And it wasn't only at home either. She braved the smell of the tannery to visit her father. She was just past sixteen and of course he thought of her as a baby. He was amazed at her questions about business.

"She's smarter than some men I could name," he told his foreman. "She might be running the business someday."

She was interested not only in the tanning processes but in the business end too. Her father explained the loans, the payments, the billing, and the payroll. He showed her how to open the safe and was pleased that after the first try she remembered the combination.

"The way I look at it is this," he told his wife. "We've all of us got a little of the Old Nick in us. I wouldn't want a child that didn't have some gumption. The way I see it, that's just a kind of energy. If you just check it and keep it in control, why, it will go in the right direction."

Cathy mended all of her clothes and put her things in order.

One day in May she came home from school and went directly to her knitting needles. Her mother was dressed to go out. "I have to go to the Altar Guild," she said. "It's about the cake sale next week. I'm chairman. Your father wondered if you would go by the bank and pick up the money for the payroll and take it to the tannery. I told him about the cake sale so I can't do it."

"I'd like to," said Cathy.

"They'll have the money ready for you in a bag," said Mrs. Ames, and she hurried out.

Cathy worked quickly but without hurry. She put on an old apron to cover her clothes. In the basement she found a jelly jar with a top and carried it out to the carriage house where the tools were kept. In the chicken-yard she caught a little pullet, took it to the block and chopped its head off, and held the writhing neck over the jelly jar until it was half full of blood. Then she carried the quivering pullet to the manure pile and buried it deep. Back in the kitchen she took off the apron and put it in the stove and poked the coals until a flame sprang up on the cloth. She washed her hands and inspected her shoes and stockings and wiped a dark spot from the toe of her right shoe. She looked at her face in the mirror. Her cheeks were bright with color and her eyes shone and her mouth turned up in its small childlike smile. On her way out she hid the jelly jar under the lowest part of the kitchen steps. Her mother had not been gone even ten minutes.

Cathy walked lightly, almost dancingly around the house and into the street. The trees were breaking into leaf and a few early dandelions were in yellow flower on the lawns. Cathy walked gaily toward the center of the town where the bank was. And she was so fresh and pretty that people walking turned and looked after her when she had passed.

6

The fire broke out at about three o'clock in the morning. It rose, flared, roared, crashed, and crumbled in on itself almost before anyone noticed it. When the volunteers ran up, pulling their hose cart, there was nothing for them to do but wet down the roofs of the neighboring houses to keep them from catching fire.

The Ames house had gone up like a rocket. The volunteers and the ordinary audience fires attract looked around at the lighted faces, trying to see Mr. and Mrs. Ames and their daughter. It came to everyone at once that they were not there. People gazed at the broad ember-bed and saw themselves and their children in there, and hearts rose up and pumped against throats. The volunteers began to dump water on the fire almost as though they might even so late save some corporeal part of the family. The frightened talk ran through the town that the whole Ames family had burned.

By sunrise everyone in town was tight-packed about the smoking black pile. Those in front had to shield their faces against the heat. The volunteers continued to pump water to cool off the charred mess. By noon the coroner was able to throw wet planks down and probe with a crowbar among the sodden heaps of charcoal. Enough remained of Mr. and Mrs. Ames to make sure there were two bodies. Near neighbors pointed out the approximate place where Cathy's room had been, but although the coroner and any number of helpers worked over the debris with a garden rake they could find no tooth or bone.

The chief of the volunteers meanwhile had found the doorknobs and lock of the kitchen door. He looked at the blackened metal, puzzled, but not quite knowing what puzzled him. He borrowed the coroner's rake and worked furiously. He went to the place where the front door had been and raked until he found that lock, crooked and half melted. By now he had his own small crowd, who demanded, "What are you looking for, George?" And "What did you find, George?"

Finally the coroner came over to him. "What's on your mind, George?"

"No keys in the locks," the chief said uneasily.

"Maybe they fell out."

"How?"

"Maybe they melted."

"The locks didn't melt."

"Maybe Bill Ames took them out."

"On the inside?" He held up his trophies. Both bolts stuck out.

Since the owner's house was burned and the owner ostensibly burned with it, the employees of the tannery, out of respect, did not go to work. They hung around the burned house, offering to help in any way they could, feeling official and generally getting in the way.

It wasn't until afternoon that Joel Robinson, the foreman, went down to the tannery. He found the safe open and papers scattered all over the floor. A broken window showed how the thief had entered.

Now the whole complexion changed. So, it was not an accident. Fear took the place of excitement and sorrow, and anger, brother of fear, crept in. The crowd began to spread.

They had not far to go. In the carriage house there was what is called "signs of a struggle"—in this case a broken box, a shattered carriage lamp, scraped marks in the dust, and straw on the floor. The onlookers might not have known these as signs of a struggle had there not been a quantity of blood on the floor.

The constable took control. This was his province. He pushed and herded everyone out of the carriage house. "Want to gum up all the clues?" he shouted at them. "Now you all stay clear outside the door."

He searched the room, picked up something, and in a corner found something else. He came to the door, holding his discoveries in his hands—a

blood-splattered blue hair ribbon and a cross with red stones. "Anybody recognize these here?" he demanded.

In a small town where everyone knows everyone it is almost impossible
to believe that one of your acquaintance could murder anyone. For that
reason, if the signs are not pretty strong in a particular direction, it must be
some dark stranger, some wanderer from the outside world where such things
happen. Then the hobo camps are raided and vagrants brought in and hotel
registers scrutinized. Every man who is not known is automatically suspected.
It was May, remember, and the wandering men had only recently taken to
the roads, now that the warming months let them spread their blankets by
any water course. And the gypsies were out too—a whole caravan less than
five miles away. And what a turning out those poor gypsies got!

The ground for miles around was searched for new-turned earth, and likely
pools were dragged for Cathy's body. "She was so pretty," everyone said, and
they meant that in themselves they could see a reason for carrying Cathy off.
At length a bumbling hairy half-wit was brought in for questioning. He was
a fine candidate for hanging because not only did he have no alibis, he
could not remember what he had done at anytime in his life. His feeble mind
sensed that these questioners wanted something of him and, being a friendly
creature, he tried to give it to them. When a baited and set question was
offered to him, he walked happily into the trap and was glad when the constable looked happy. He tried manfully to please these superior beings.
There was something very nice about him. The only trouble with his confession was that he confessed too much in too many directions. Also, he had
constantly to be reminded of what he was supposed to have done. He was
really pleased when he was indicted by a stern and frightened jury. He felt
that at last he amounted to something.

There were, and are, some men who become judges whose love for the law
and for its intention of promoting justice has the quality of love for a woman.
Such a man presided at the examination before plea—a man so pure and
good that he canceled out a lot of wickedness with his life. Without the
prompting the culprit was used to, his confession was nonsense. The judge
questioned him and found out that although the suspect was trying to follow
instructions he simply could not remember what he did, whom he killed,
how or why. The judge sighed wearily and motioned him out of the court-
room and crooked his fingers at the constable.

"Now look here, Mike," he said, "you shouldn't do a thing like that. If that
poor fellow had been just a little smarter you might have got him hanged."

"He said he did it." The constable's feelings were hurt because he was a
conscientious man.

"He would have admitted climbing the golden stairs and cutting St. Peter's throat with a bowling ball," the judge said. "Be more careful, Mike.
The law was designed to save, not to destroy."

In all such local tragedies time works like a damp brush on water color.

The sharp edges blur, the ache goes out of it, the colors melt together, and from the many separated lines a solid gray emerges. Within a month it was not so necessary to hang someone, and within two months nearly everybody discovered that there wasn't any real evidence against anyone. If it had not been for Cathy's murder, fire and robbery might have been a coincidence. Then it occurred to people that without Cathy's body you couldn't prove anything even though you thought she was dead.

Cathy left a scent of sweetness behind her.

NINE

Mr. Edwards carried on his business of whoremaster in an orderly and un-emotional way. He maintained his wife and his two well-mannered children in a good house in a good neighborhood in Boston. The children, two boys, were entered on the books at Groton when they were infants.

Mrs. Edwards kept a dustless house and controlled her servants. There were of course many times when Mr. Edwards had to be away from home on business, but he managed to live an amazingly domestic life and to spend more evenings at home than you could imagine. He ran his business with a public accountant's neatness and accuracy. He was a large and powerful man, running a little to fat in his late forties, and yet in surprisingly good condition for a time when a man wanted to be fat if only to prove he was a success.

He had invented his business—the circuit route through the small towns, the short stay of each girl, the discipline, the percentages. He felt his way along and made few mistakes. He never sent his girls into the cities. He could handle the hungry constables of the villages, but he had respect for the experienced and voracious big city police. His ideal stand was a small town with a mortgaged hotel and no amusements, one where his only competition came from wives and an occasional wayward girl. At this time he had ten units. Before he died at sixty-seven of strangulation on a chicken bone, he had groups of four girls in each of thirty-three small towns in New England. He was better than well fixed—he was rich; and the manner of his death was in itself symbolic of success and well-being.

At the present time the institution of the whorehouse seems to a certain extent to be dying out. Scholars have various reasons to give. Some say that the decay of morality among girls has dealt the whorehouse its deathblow. Others, perhaps more idealistic, maintain that police supervision on an in-creased scale is driving the houses out of existence. In the late days of the last century and the early part of this one, the whorehouse was an accepted if not openly discussed institution. It was said that its existence protected decent women. An unmarried man could go to one of these houses and evacute the sexual energy which was making him uneasy and at the same time maintain the popular attitudes about the purity and loveliness of women. It was a mystery, but then there are many mysterious things in our social thinking.

These houses ranged from palaces filled with gold and velvet to the crumniest cribs where the stench would drive a pig away. Every once in a while a story would start about how young girls were stolen and enslaved by the controllers of the industry, and perhaps many of the stories were true. But the great majority of whores drifted into their profession through laziness and stupidity. In the houses they had no responsibility. They were fed and clothed and taken care of until they were too old, and then they were kicked out. This ending was no deterrent. No one who is young is ever going to be old.

Now and then a smart girl came into the profession, but she usually moved up to better things. She got a house of her own or worked successfully at blackmail or married a rich man. There was even a special name for the smart ones. They were grandly called courtesans.

Mr. Edwards had no trouble either in recruiting or in controlling his girls. If a girl was not properly stupid, he threw her out. He did not want very pretty girls either. Some local young man might fall in love with a pretty whore and there would be hell to pay. When any of his girls became pregnant they had the choice of leaving or of being aborted so brutally that a fair proportion died. In spite of this the girls usually chose abortion.

It was not always smooth sailing for Mr. Edwards. He did have his problems. At the time of which I am telling you he had been subjected to a series of misfortunes. A train wreck had killed off two units of four girls each. Another of his units he lost to conversion when a small-town preacher suddenly caught fire and began igniting the townsfolk with his sermons. The swelling congregation had to move out of the church and into the fields. Then, as happens so often, the preacher turned over his hole-card, the surefire card. He predicted the date of the end of the world, and the whole county moved bleating in on him. Mr. Edwards went to the town, took the heavy quirt from his suitcase, and whipped the girls unmercifully; instead of seeing the thing his way, the girls begged for more whipping to wipe out their fancied sins. He gave up in disgust, took their clothes, and went back to Boston. The girls achieved a certain prominence when they went naked to the camp meeting to confess and testify. That is how Mr. Edwards happened to be interviewing and recruiting numbers of girls instead of picking one up here and there. He had three units to rebuild from the ground.

I don't know how Cathy Ames heard about Mr. Edwards. Perhaps a hack driver told her. The word got around when a girl really wanted to know. Mr. Edwards had not had a good morning when she came into his office. The pain in his stomach he ascribed to a halibut chowder his wife had given him for supper the night before. He had been up all night. The chowder had blown both ways and he still felt weak and crampy.

For this reason he did not take in all at once the girl who called herself Catherine Amesbury. She was far too pretty for his business. Her voice was low and throaty, she was slight, almost delicate, and her skin was lovely. In a word she was not Mr. Edwards' kind of girl at all. If he had not been weak he would have rejected her instantly. But while he did not look at her very closely during the routine questioning, mostly about relatives who might cause trouble, something in Mr. Edwards' body began to feel her. Mr. Edwards was not a concupiscent man, and besides he never mixed his professional life with his private pleasures. His reaction startled him. He looked up, puzzled, at the girl, and her eyelids dipped sweetly and mysteriously, and there was just a suggestion of a sway on her lightly padded hips. Her little mouth wore a cat smile. Mr. Edwards leaned forward at his desk, breathing heavily. He realized that he wanted this one for his own.

"I can't understand why a girl like you—" he began, and fell right into the oldest conviction in the world—that the girl you are in love with can't possibly be anything but true and honest.

"My father is dead," Catherine said modestly. "Before he died he had let things go to pieces. We didn't know he had borrowed money on the farm. And I can't let the bank take it away from my mother. The shock would kill her." Catherine's eyes dimmed with tears. "I thought maybe I could make enough to keep up the interest."

If ever Mr. Edwards had a chance it was now. And indeed a little warning buzz did sound in his brain, but it was not loud enough. About eighty per cent of the girls who came to him needed money to pay off a mortgage. And Mr. Edwards made it an unvarying rule not to believe anything his girls said at any time, beyond what they had for breakfast, and they sometimes lied about that. And here he was, a big, fat, grown-up whoremaster, leaning his stomach against his desk while his cheeks darkened with blood and excited chills ran up his legs and thighs.

Mr. Edwards heard himself saying, "Well now, my dear, let's talk this over. Maybe we can figure some way for you to get the interest money." And this to a girl who had simply asked for a job as a whore—or had she?

2

Mrs. Edwards was persistently if not profoundly religious. She spent a great part of her time with the mechanics of her church, which did not leave her time for either its background or its effects. To her, Mr. Edwards was in the importing business, and even if she had known—which she probably did— what business he was really in, she would not have believed it. And this is another mystery. Her husband had always been to her a coldly thoughtful man who made few and dutiful physical demands on her. If he had never been warm, he had never been cruel either. Her dramas and her emotions had to do with the boys, with the vestry, and with food. She was content with her life and thankful. When her husband's disposition began to disintegrate, causing him to be restless and snappish, to sit staring and then to rush out of the house in a nervous rage, she ascribed it first to his stomach and then to business reverses. When by accident she came upon him in the bathroom, sitting on the toilet and crying softly to himself, she knew he was a sick man. He tried quickly to cover his red, brimming eyes from her scrutiny. When neither herb teas nor physics cured him she was helpless.

If in all the years Mr. Edwards had heard about anyone like himself he would have laughed. For Mr. Edwards, as coldblooded a whoremaster as ever lived, had fallen hopelessly, miserably in love with Catherine Amesbury. He rented a sweet little brick house for her and then gave it to her. He bought her every imaginable luxury, overdecorated the house, kept it overwarm. The carpeting was too deep and the walls were crowded with heavy framed pictures.

Mr. Edwards had never experienced such misery. As a matter of business he had learned so much about women that he did not trust one for a second. And since he deeply loved Catherine and love requires trust, he was torn to quivering fragments by his emotion. He had to trust her and at the same time he did not trust her. He tried to buy her loyalty with presents and with money. When he was away from her, he tortured himself with the thought of other men slipping into her house. He hated to leave Boston to check up on his units because this would leave Catherine alone. To a certain extent he began to neglect his business. It was his first experience with this kind of love and it nearly killed him.

One thing Mr. Edwards did not know, and could not know because Catherine would not permit it, was that she was faithful to him in the sense that she did not receive or visit other men. To Catherine, Mr. Edwards was as cold a business proposition as his units were to him. And as he had his techniques, so had she hers. Once she had him, which was very soon, she managed always to seem slightly dissatisfied. She gave him an impression of restlessness, as though she might take flight at any moment. When she knew he was going to visit her, she made it a point to be out and to come in glowing as from some incredible experience. She complained a good deal about the difficulties of avoiding the lecherous looks and touches of men in the street who could not keep away from her. Several times she ran frightened into the house, having barely escaped a man who had followed her. When she would return in the late afternoon and find him waiting for her she would explain, "Why, I was shopping. I have to go shopping, you know." And she made it sound like a lie.

In their sexual relations she convinced him that the result was not quite satisfactory to her, that if he were a better man he could release a flood of unbelievable reaction in her. Her method was to keep him continually off balance. She saw with satisfaction his nerves begin to go, his hands take to quivering, his loss of weight, and the wild glazed look in his eyes. And when she delicately sensed the near approach of insane, punishing rage, she sat in his lap and soothed him and made him believe for a moment in her innocence. She could convince him.

Catherine wanted money, and she set about getting it as quickly and as easily as she could. When she had successfully reduced him to a pulp, and Catherine knew exactly when the time had come, she began to steal from him. She went through his pockets and took any large bills she found. He didn't dare accuse her for fear she would go away. The presents of jewelry he gave her disappeared, and although she said she had lost them he knew they had been sold. She padded the grocery bills, added to the prices of clothes. He could not bring himself to stop it. She did not sell the house but she mortgaged it for every penny she could get.

One evening his key did not fit in the lock of the front door. She answered his pounding after a long time. Yes, she had changed the locks because she had lost her key. She was afraid, living alone. Anyone could get in. She would get him another key—but she never did. He always had to ring the bell after that, and sometimes it took a long time for her to answer, and at other times his ring was not answered at all. There was no way for him to know whether she was at home or not. Mr. Edwards had her followed—and she did not know how often.

Mr. Edwards was essentially a simple man, but even a simple man has complexities which are dark and twisted. Catherine was clever, but even a clever woman misses some of the strange corridors in a man.

She made only one bad slip, and she had tried to avoid that one. As was proper, Mr. Edwards had stocked the pretty little nest with champagne. Catherine had from the first refused to touch it.

"It makes me sick," she explained. "I've tried it and I can't drink it."

"Nonsense," he said. "Just have one glass. It can't hurt you."

"No, thank you. No. I can't drink it."

Mr. Edwards thought of her reluctance as a delicate, a ladylike quality. He had never insisted until one evening when it occurred to him that he knew nothing about her. Wine might loosen her tongue. The more he thought of it, the better the idea seemed to him.

"It's not friendly of you not to have a glass with me."

"I tell you, it doesn't agree with me."

"Nonsense."

"I tell you I don't want it."

"This is silly," he said. "Do you want me to be angry with you?"

"No."

"Then drink a glass."

"I don't want it."

"Drink it." He held a glass for her, and she retreated from it.

"You don't know. It's not good for me."

"Drink it."

She took the glass and poured it down and stood still, quivering, seeming to listen. The blood flowed to her cheeks. She poured another glass for herself and another. Her eyes became set and cold. Mr. Edwards felt a fear of her. Something was happening to her which neither she nor he could control.

"I didn't want to do it. Remember that," she said calmly.

"Maybe you'd better not have any more."

She laughed and poured herself another glass. "It doesn't matter now," she said. "More won't make much difference."

"It's nice to have a glass or so," he said uneasily.

She spoke to him softly. "You fat slug," she said. "What do you know about me? Do you think I can't read every rotten thought you ever had? Want me to tell you? You wonder where a nice girl like me learned tricks. I'll tell you. I learned them in cribs—you hear?—cribs. I've worked in places you never even heard of—four years. Sailors brought me little tricks from Port Said. I know every nerve in your lousy body and I can use them."

"Catherine," he protested, "you don't know what you're saying."

"I could see it. You thought I would talk. Well, I'm talking."

She advanced slowly toward him, and Mr. Edwards overcame his impulse to edge away. He was afraid of her but he sat still. Directly in front of him she drank the last champagne in her glass, delicately struck the rim on the table, and jammed the ragged edge against his cheek.

And then he did run from the house and he could hear her laughing as he went.

3

Love to a man like Mr. Edwards is a crippling emotion. It ruined his judgment, canceled his knowledge, weakened him. He told himself that she was hysterical and tried to believe it, and it was made easier for him by Catherine. Her outbreak had terrified her, and for a time she made every effort to restore his sweet picture of her.

A man so painfully in love is capable of self-torture beyond belief. Mr. Edwards wanted with all his heart to believe in her goodness, but he was forced not to, as much by his own particular devil as by her outbreak. Almost instinctively he went about learning the truth and at the same time disbelieved it. He knew, for instance, that she would not put her money in a bank. One of his employees, using a complicated set of mirrors, found out the place in the cellar of the little brick house where she did keep it.

One day a clipping came from the agency he employed. It was an old newspaper account of a fire from a small-town weekly. Mr. Edwards studied it. His chest and stomach turned to molten metal and a redness glowed in his head behind his eyes. There was real fear mixed up in his love, and the precipitate from the mixing of these two is cruelty. He staggered dizzily to his office couch and lay face down, his forehead against the cool black leather. For a time he hung suspended, hardly breathing. Gradually his brain cleared. His mouth tasted salty, and there was a great ache of anger in his shoulders. But he was calm and his mind cut its intention through time like the sharp beam of a searchlight through a dark room. He moved slowly, checking his suitcase just as he always did when he started out to inspect his units—clean shirts and underwear, a nightgown and slippers, and the heavy quirt with the lash curving around the end of the suitcase.

He moved heavily up the little garden in front of the brick house and rang the bell.

Catherine answered it immediately. She had on her coat and hat.

"Oh!" she said. "What a shame! I must go out for a while."

Mr. Edwards put down his suitcase. "No," he said.

She studied him. Something was changed. He lumbered past her and went down into the cellar.

"Where are you going?" Her voice was shrill.

He did not reply. In a moment he came up again, carrying a small oak box. He opened his suitcase and put the box inside.

"That's mine," she said softly.

"I know."

"What are you up to?"

"I thought we'd go for a little trip."

"Where? I can't go."

"Little town in Connecticut. I have some business there. You told me once you wanted to work. You're going to work."

"I don't want to now. You can't make me. Why, I'll call the police!"

He smiled so horribly that she stepped back from him. His temples were thudding with blood. "Maybe you'd rather go to your home town," he said. "They had a big fire there several years ago. Do you remember that fire?"

Her eyes probed and searched him, seeking a soft place, but his eyes were flat and hard. "What do you want me to do?" she asked quietly.

"Just come for a little trip with me. You said you wanted to work."

She could think of only one plan. She must go along with him and wait for a chance. A man couldn't always watch. It would be dangerous to thwart him now—best go along with it and wait. That always worked. It always had. But his words had given Catherine real fear.

In the small town they got off the train at dusk, walked down its one dark street, and on out into the country. Catherine was wary and watchful. She had no access to his plan. In her purse she had a thin-bladed knife.

Mr. Edwards thought he knew what he intended to do. He meant to whip her and put her in one of the rooms at the inn, whip her and move her to another town, and so on until she was of no use any more. Then he would throw her out. The local constable would see to it that she did not run away. The knife did not bother him. He knew about that.

The first thing he did when they stopped in a private place between a stone wall and a fringe of cedars was to jerk the purse from her hand and throw it over the wall. That took care of the knife. But he didn't know about himself, because in all his life he had never been in love with a woman. He thought he only meant to punish her. After two slashes the quirt was not enough. He dropped it on the ground and used his fists. His breathing came out in squealing whines.

Catherine did her best not to fall into panic. She tried to duck his threshing fists or at least to make them ineffective, but at last fear overcame her and she tried to run. He leaped at her and brought her down, and by then his fists were not enough. His frantic hand found a stone on the ground and his cold control was burst through with a red roaring wave.

Later he looked down on her beaten face. He listened for her heartbeat and could hear nothing over the thumping of his own. Two complete and separate thoughts ran in his mind. One said, "Have to bury her, have to dig a hole and put her in it." And the other cried like a child, "I can't stand it. I couldn't bear to touch her." Then the sickness that follows rage overwhelmed him. He ran from the place, leaving his suitcase, leaving the quirt, leaving the oak box of money. He blundered away in the dusk, wondering only where he could hide his sickness for a while.

No question was ever asked of him. After a time of sickness to which his wife ministered tenderly, he went back to his business and never again let the insanity of love come near him. A man who can't learn from experience is a fool, he said. Always afterward he had a kind of fearful respect for himself. He had never known that the impulse to kill was in him.

That he had not killed Catherine was an accident. Every blow had been intended to crush her. She was a long time unconscious and a long time half-conscious. She realized her arm was broken and that she must find help if she wanted to live. Wanting to live forced her to drag herself along the dark road, looking for help. She turned in at a gate and almost made the steps of the house before she fainted. The roosters were crowing in the chickenhouse and a gray rim of dawn lay on the east.

TEN

When two men live together they usually maintain a kind of shabby neatness out of incipient rage at each other. Two men alone are constantly on the verge of fighting, and they know it. Adam Trask had not been home long before the tensions began to build up. The brothers saw too much of each other and not enough of anyone else.

For a few months they were busy getting Cyrus's money in order and out at interest. They traveled together to Washington to look at the grave, good stone and on top an iron star with seal and a hole on the top in which to insert the stick for a little flag on Decoration Day. The brothers stood by the grave a long time, then they went away and they didn't mention Cyrus.

If Cyrus had been dishonest he had done it well. No one asked questions about the money. But the subject was on Charles' mind.

Back on the farm Adam asked him, "Why don't you buy some new clothes? You're a rich man. You act like you're afraid to spend a penny."

"I am," said Charles.

"Why?"

"I might have to give it back."

"Still harping on that? If there was anything wrong, don't you think we'd have heard about it by now?"

"I don't know," said Charles. "I'd rather not talk about it."

But that night he brought up the subject again. "There's one thing bothers me," he began.

"About the money?"

"Yes, about the money. If you make that much money there's bound to be a mess."

"How do you mean?"

"Well, papers and account books and bills of sale, notes, figuring—well, we went through Father's things and there wasn't none of that."

"Maybe he burned it up."

"Maybe he did," said Charles.

The brothers lived by a routine established by Charles, and he never varied it. Charles awakened on the stroke of four-thirty as surely as though the brass pendulum of the clock had nudged him. He was awake, in fact, a split second before four-thirty. His eyes were open and had blinked once before the high gong struck. For a moment he lay still, looking up into the darkness and scratching his stomach. Then he reached to the table beside his bed and his hand fell exactly on the block of sulphur matches lying there. His fingers pulled a match free and struck it on the side of the block. The sulphur burned its little blue bead before the wood caught. Charles lighted the candle beside his bed. He threw back his blanket and got up. He wore long gray underwear that bagged over his knees and hung loose around his ankles. Yawning, he went to the door, opened it, and called, "Half-past four, Adam. Time to get up. Wake up."

Adam's voice was muffled. "Don't you ever forget?"

"It's time to get up." Charles slipped his legs into his pants and hunched them up over his hips. "You don't have to get up," he said. "You're a rich man. You can lay in bed all day."

"So are you. But we still get up before daylight."

"You don't have to get up," Charles repeated. "But if you're going to farm, you'd better farm."

Adam said ruefully, "So we're going to buy more land so we can do more work."

"Come off it," said Charles. "Go back to bed if you want to."

Adam said, "I bet you couldn't sleep if you stayed in bed. You know what I bet? I bet you get up because you want to, and then you take credit for it —like taking credit for six fingers."

Charles went into the kitchen and lighted the lamp. "You can't lay in bed and run a farm," he said, and he knocked the ashes through the grate of the stove and tore some paper over the exposed coals and blew until the flame started.

Adam was watching him through the door. "You wouldn't use a match," he said.

Charles turned angrily. "You mind your own goddam business. Stop picking at me."

"All right," said Adam. "I will. And maybe my business isn't here."

"That's up to you. Any time you want to get out, you go right ahead."

The quarrel was silly but Adam couldn't stop it. His voice went on without his willing it, making angry and irritating words. "You're damn right I'll go when I want," he said. "This is my place as much as yours."

"Then why don't you do some work on it?"

"Oh, Lord!" Adam said. "What are we fussing about? Let's not fuss."

"I don't want trouble," said Charles. He scooped lukewarm mush into two bowls and spun them on the table.

The brothers sat down. Charles buttered a slice of bread, gouged out a knifeful of jam, and spread it over the butter. He dug butter for his second slice and left a slop of jam on the butter roll.

"Goddam it, can't you wipe your knife? Look at that butter!"

Charles laid his knife and the bread on the table and placed his hands palm down on either side. "You better get off the place," he said.

Adam got up. "I'd rather live in a pigsty," he said, and he walked out of the house.

2

It was eight months before Charles saw him again. Charles came in from work and found Adam sloshing water on his hair and face from the kitchen bucket.

"Hello," said Charles. "How are you?"

"Fine," said Adam.

"Where'd you go?"

"Boston."

"No place else?"

"No. Just looked at the city."

The brothers settled back to their old life, but each took precautions against anger. In a way each protected the other and so saved himself. Charles, always the early riser, got breakfast ready before he awakened Adam. And Adam kept the house clean and started a set of books on the farm. In this guarded way they lived for two years before their irritation grew beyond control again.

On a winter evening Adam looked up from his account book. "It's nice in California," he said. "It's nice in the winter. And you can raise anything there."

"Sure you can raise it. But when you got it, what are you going to do with it?"

"How about wheat? They raise a lot of wheat in California."

"The rust will get to it," said Charles.

"What makes you so sure? Look, Charles, things grow so fast in California they say you have to plant and step back quick or you'll get knocked down."

Charles said, "Why the hell don't you go there? I'll buy you out any time you say."

Adam was quiet then, but in the morning while he combed his hair and peered in the small mirror he began it again.

"They don't have any winter in California," he said. "It's just like spring all the time."

"I like the winter," said Charles.

Adam came toward the stove. "Don't be cross," he said.

"Well, stop picking at me. How many eggs?"

"Four," said Adam.

Charles placed seven eggs on top of the warming oven and built his fire carefully of small pieces of kindling until it burned fiercely. He put the skillet down next to the flame. His sullenness left him as he fried the bacon.

"Adam," he said, "I don't know whether you notice it, but it seems like every other word you say is California. Do you really want to go?"

Adam chuckled. "That's what I'm trying to figure out," he said. "I don't know. It's like getting up in the morning. I don't want to get up but I don't want to stay in bed either."

"You sure make a fuss about it," said Charles.

Adam went on, "Every morning in the army that damned bugle would sound. And I swore to God if I ever got out I would sleep till noon every day. And here I get up a half-hour before reveille. Will you tell me, Charles, what in hell we're working for?"

"You can't lay in bed and run a farm," said Charles. He stirred the hissing bacon around with a fork.

"Take a look at it," Adam said earnestly. "Neither one of us has got a chick or a child, let alone a wife. And the way we're going it don't look like we ever will. We don't have time to look around for a wife. And here we're figuring to add the Clark place to ours if the price is right. What for?"

"It's a damn fine piece," said Charles. "The two of them together would make one of the best farms in this section. Say! You thinking of getting married?"

"No. And that's what I'm talking about. Come a few years and we'll have the finest farm in this section. Two lonely old farts working our tails off. Then one of us will die off and the fine farm will belong to one lonely old fart, and then he'll die off—"

"What the hell are you talking about?" Charles demanded. "Fellow can't get comfortable. You make me itch. Get it out—what's on your mind?"

"I'm not having any fun," said Adam. "Or anyway I'm not having enough. I'm working too hard for what I'm getting, and I don't have to work at all."

"Well, why don't you quit?" Charles shouted at him. "Why don't you get the hell out? I don't see any guards holding you. Go down to the South Seas and lay in a hammock if that's what you want."

"Don't be cross," said Adam quietly. "It's like getting up. I don't want to get up and I don't want to stay down. I don't want to stay here and I don't want to go away."

"You make me itch," said Charles.

"Think about it, Charles. You like it here?"

"Yes."

"And you want to live here all your life?"

"Yes."

"Jesus, I wish I had it that easy. What do you suppose is the matter with me?"

"I think you've got knocker fever. Come in to the inn tonight and get it cured up."

"Maybe that's it," said Adam. "But I never took much satisfaction in a whore."

"It's all the same," Charles said. "You shut your eyes and you can't tell the difference."

"Some of the boys in the regiment used to keep a squaw around. I had one for a while."

Charles turned to him with interest. "Father would turn in his grave if he knew you was squawing around. How was it?"

"Pretty nice. She'd wash my clothes and mend and do a little cooking."

"I mean the other—how was that?"

"Good. Yes, good. And kind of sweet—kind of soft and sweet. Kind of gentle and soft."

"You're lucky she didn't put a knife in you while you were asleep."

"She wouldn't. She was sweet."

"You've got a funny look in your eye. I guess you were kind of gone on that squaw."

"I guess I was," said Adam.

"What happened to her?"

"Smallpox."

"You didn't get another one?"

Adam's eyes were pained. "We piled them up like they were logs, over two hundred, arms and legs sticking out. And we piled brush on top and poured coal oil on."

"I've heard they can't stand smallpox."

"It kills them," said Adam. "You're burning that bacon."

Charles turned quickly back to the stove. "It'll just be crisp," he said, "I like it crisp." He shoveled the bacon out on a plate and broke the eggs in the hot grease and they jumped and fluttered their edges to brown lace and made clucking sounds.

"There was a schoolteacher," Charles said. "Prettiest thing you ever saw. Had little tiny feet. Bought all her clothes in New York. Yellow hair, and you never saw such little feet. Sang too, in the choir. Everybody took to going to church. Damn near stampeded getting into church. That was quite a while ago."

"'Bout the time you wrote about thinking of getting married?"

Charles grinned. "I guess so. I guess there wasn't a young buck in the county didn't get the marrying fever."

"What happened to her?"

"Well, you know how it is. The women got kind of restless with her here. They got together. First thing you knew they had her out. I heard she wore silk underwear. Too hoity toity. School board had her out halfway through the term. Feet no longer than that. Showed her ankles too, like it was an accident. Always showing her ankles."

"Did you get to know her?" Adam asked.

"No. I only went to church. Couldn't hardly get in. Girl that pretty's got no right in a little town. Just makes people uneasy. Causes trouble."

Adam said, "Remember that Samuels girl? She was real pretty. What happened to her?"

"Same thing. Just caused trouble. She went away. I heard she's living in Philadelphia. Does dressmaking. I heard she gets ten dollars just for making one dress."

"Maybe we ought to go away from here," Adam said.

Charles said, "Still thinking of California?"

"I guess so."

Charles' temper tore in two. "I want you out of here!" he shouted. "I want you to get off the place. I'll buy you or sell you or anything. Get out, you son of a bitch—" He stopped. "I guess I don't mean that last. But goddam it, you make me nervous."

"I'll go," said Adam.

3

In three months Charles got a colored picture postcard of the bay at Rio, and Adam had written on the back with a splottery pen, "It's summer here when it's winter there. Why don't you come down?"

Six months later there was another card, from Buenos Aires. "Dear Charles—my God this is a big city. They speak French and Spanish both. I'm sending you a book."

But no book came. Charles looked for it all the following winter and well into the spring. And instead of the book Adam arrived. He was brown and his clothes had a foreign look.

"How are you?" Charles asked.

"Fine. Did you get the book?"

"No."

"I wonder what happened to it? It had pictures."

"Going to stay?"

"I guess so. I'll tell you about that country."

"I don't want to hear about it," said Charles.

"Christ, you're mean," said Adam.

"I can just see it all over again. You'll stay around a year or so and then you'll get restless and you'll make me restless. We'll get mad at each other and then we'll get polite to each other—and that's worse. Then we'll blow up and you'll go away again, and then you'll come back and we'll do it all over again."

Adam asked, "Don't you want me to stay?"

"Hell, yes," said Charles. "I miss you when you're not here. But I can see how it's going to be just the same."

And it was just that way. For a while they reviewed old times, for a while they recounted the times when they were apart, and finally they relapsed into the long ugly silences, the hours of speechless work, the guarded courtesy, the flashes of anger. There were no boundaries to time so that it seemed endless passing.

On an evening Adam said, "You know, I'm going to be thirty-seven. That's half a life."

"Here it comes," said Charles. "Wasting your life. Look, Adam, could we not have a fight this time?"

"How do you mean?"

"Well, if we run true to form we'll fight for three or four weeks, getting you ready to go away. If you're getting restless, couldn't you just go away and save all the trouble?"

Adam laughed and the tension went out of the room. "I've got a pretty smart brother," he said. "Sure, when I get the itch bad enough I'll go without fighting. Yes, I like that. You're getting rich, aren't you, Charles?"

"I'm doing all right. I wouldn't say rich."

"You wouldn't say you bought four buildings and the inn in the village?"

"No, I wouldn't say it."

"But you did. Charles, you've made this about the prettiest farm anywhere about. Why don't we build a new house—bathtub and running water and a water closet? We're not poor people any more. Why, they say you're nearly the richest man in this section."

"We don't need a new house," Charles said gruffly. "You take your fancy ideas away."

"It would be nice to go to the toilet without going outside."

"You take your fancy ideas away."

Adam was amused. "Maybe I'll build a pretty little house right over by the woodlot. Say, how would that be? Then we wouldn't get on each other's nerves."

"I don't want it on the place."

"The place is half mine."

"I'll buy you out."

"But I don't have to sell."

Charles' eyes blazed. "I'll burn your goddam house down."

"I believe you would," Adam said, suddenly sobered. "I believe you really would. What are you looking like that for?"

Charles said slowly, "I've thought about it a lot. And I've wanted for you to bring it up. I guess you aren't ever going to."

"What do you mean?"

"You remember when you sent me a telegram for a hundred dollars?"

"You bet I do. Saved my life, I guess. Why?"

"You never paid it back."

"I must have."

"You didn't."

Adam looked down at the old table where Cyrus had sat, knocking on his wooden leg with a stick. And the old oil lamp was hanging over the center of the table, shedding its unstable yellow light from the round Rochester wick.

Adam said slowly, "I'll pay you in the morning."

"I gave you plenty of time to offer."

"Sure you did, Charles. I should have remembered." He paused, considering, and at last he said, "You don't know why I needed the money."

"I never asked."

"And I never told. Maybe I was ashamed. I was a prisoner, Charles. I broke jail—I escaped."

Charles' mouth was open. "What are you talking about?"

"I'm going to tell you. I was a tramp and I got taken up for vagrancy and put on a road gang—leg irons at night. Got out in six months and picked right up again. That's how they get their roads built. I served three days less than the second six months and then I escaped—got over the Georgia line, robbed a store for clothes, and sent you the telegram."

"I don't believe you," Charles said. "Yes, I do. You don't tell lies. Of course I believe you. Why didn't you tell me?"

"Maybe I was ashamed. But I'm more ashamed that I didn't pay you."

"Oh, forget it," said Charles. "I don't know why I mentioned it."

"Good God, no. I'll pay you in the morning."

"I'll be damned," said Charles. "My brother a jailbird!"

"You don't have to look so happy."

"I don't know why," said Charles, "but it makes me kind of proud. My brother a jailbird! Tell me this, Adam—why did you wait till just three days before they let you go to make your break?"

Adam smiled. "Two or three reasons," he said. "I was afraid if I served out my time, why, they'd pick me up again. And I figured if I waited till the end they wouldn't expect me to run away."

"That makes sense," said Charles. "But you said there was one more reason."

"I guess the other was the most important," Adam said, "and it's the hardest to explain. I figured I owed the state six months. That was the sentence. I didn't feel right about cheating. I only cheated three days."

Charles exploded with laughter. "You're a crazy son of a bitch," he said with affection. "But you say you robbed a store."

"I sent the money back with ten per cent interest," Adam said.

Charles leaned forward. "Tell me about the road gang, Adam."

"Sure I will, Charles. Sure I will."

ELEVEN

Charles had more respect for Adam after he knew about the prison. He felt the warmth for his brother you can feel only for one who is not perfect and therefore no target for your hatred. Adam took some advantage of it too. He tempted Charles.

"Did you ever think, Charles, that we've got enough money to do anything we want to do?"

"All right, what do we want?"

"We could go to Europe, we could walk around Paris."

"What's that?"

"What's what?"

"I thought I heard someone on the stoop."

"Probably a cat."

"I guess so. Have to kill off some of them pretty soon."

"Charles, we could go to Egypt and walk around the Sphinx."

"We could stay right here and make some good use of our money. And we could get the hell out to work and make some use of the day. Those goddam cats!" Charles jumped to the door and yanked it open and said, "Get!" Then he was silent, and Adam saw him staring at the steps. He moved beside him.

A dirty bundle of rags and mud was trying to worm its way up the steps. One skinny hand clawed slowly at the stairs. The other dragged helplessly. There was a caked face with cracked lips and eyes peering out of swollen, blackened lids. The forehead was laid open, oozing blood back into the matted hair.

Adam went down the stairs and knelt beside the figure. "Give me a hand," he said. "Come on, let's get her in. Here—look out for that arm. It looks broken."

She fainted when they carried her in.

"Put her in my bed," Adam said. "Now I think you better go for the doctor."

"Don't you think we better hitch up and take her in?"

"Move her? No. Are you crazy?"

"Maybe not as crazy as you. Think about it a minute."

"For God's sake, think about what?"

"Two men living alone and they've got this in their house."

Adam was shocked. "You don't mean it."

"I mean it all right. I think we better take her in. It'll be all over the county in two hours. How do you know what she is? How'd she get here? What happened to her? Adam, you're taking an awful chance."

Adam said coldly, "If you don't go now, I'll go and leave you here."

"I think you're making a mistake. I'll go, but I tell you we'll suffer for it."

"I'll do the suffering," said Adam. "You go."

After Charles left, Adam went to the kitchen and poured hot water from the teakettle into a basin. In his bedroom he dampened a handkerchief in the water and loosened the caked blood and dirt on the girl's face. She reeled up to consciousness and her blue eyes glinted at him. His mind went back—it was this room, this bed. His stepmother was standing over him with a damp cloth in her hand, and he could feel the little running pains as the water cut through. And she had said something over and over. He heard it but he could not remember what it was.

"You'll be all right," he said to the girl. "We're getting a doctor. He'll be here right off."

Her lips moved a little.

"Don't try to talk," he said. "Don't try to say anything." As he worked gently with his cloth a huge warmth crept over him. "You can stay here," he said. "You can stay here as long as you want. I'll take care of you." He squeezed out the cloth and sponged her matted hair and lifted it out of the gashes in her scalp.

He could hear himself talking as he worked, almost as though he were a stranger listening. "There, does that hurt? The poor eyes—I'll put some brown paper over your eyes. You'll be all right. That's a bad one on your forehead. I'm afraid you'll have a scar there. Could you tell me your name? No, don't try. There's lots of time. There's lots of time. Do you hear that? That's the doctor's rig. Wasn't that quick?" He moved to the kitchen door. "In here, Doc. She's in here," he called.

2

She was very badly hurt. If there had been X-rays in that time the doctor might have found more injuries than he did. As it was he found enough. Her left arm and three ribs were broken and her jaw was cracked. Her skull was cracked too, and the teeth on the left side were missing. Her scalp was ripped and torn and her forehead laid open to the skull. So much the doctor could see and identify. He set her arm, taped her ribs, and sewed up her scalp. With a pipette and an alcohol flame he bent a glass tube to go through the aperture where a tooth was missing so that she could drink and take liquid food without moving her cracked jaw. He gave her a large shot of morphine, left a bottle of opium pills, washed his hands, and put on his coat. His patient was asleep before he left the room.

In the kitchen he sat down at the table and drank the hot coffee Charles put in front of him.

"All right, what happened to her?" he asked.

"How do we know?" Charles said truculently. "We found her on our porch. If you want to see, go look at the marks on the road where she dragged herself."

"Know who she is?"

"God, no."

"You go upstairs at the inn—is she anybody from there?"

"I haven't been there lately. I couldn't recognize her in that condition anyway."

The doctor turned his head toward Adam. "You ever see her before?"

Adam shook his head slowly.

Charles said harshly, "Say, what you mousing around at?"

"I'll tell you, since you're interested. That girl didn't fall under a harrow even if she looks that way. Somebody did that to her, somebody who didn't like her at all. If you want the truth, somebody tried to kill her."

"Why don't you ask her?" Charles said.

"She won't be talking for quite a while. Besides, her skull is cracked, and God knows what that will do to her. What I'm getting at is, should I bring the sheriff into it?"

"No!" Adam spoke so explosively that the two looked at him. "Let her alone. Let her rest."

"Who's going to take care of her?"

"I am," said Adam.

"Now, you look here—" Charles began.

"Keep out of it!"

"It's my place as much as yours."

"Do you want me to go?"

"I didn't mean that."

"Well, I'll go if she has to go."

The doctor said, "Steady down. What makes you so interested?"

"I wouldn't put a hurt dog out."

"You wouldn't get mad about it either. Are you holding something back? Did you go out last night? Did you do it?"

"He was here all night," said Charles. "He snores like a goddam train."

Adam said, "Why can't you let her be? Let her get well."

The doctor stood up and dusted his hands. "Adam," he said, "your father was one of my oldest friends. I know you and your family. You aren't stupid. I don't know why you don't recognize ordinary facts, but you don't seem to. Have to talk to you like a baby. That girl was assaulted. I believe whoever did it tried to kill her. If I don't tell the sheriff about it, I'm breaking the law. I admit I break a few, but not that one."

"Well, tell him. But don't let him bother her until she's better."

"It's not my habit to let my patients be bothered," the doctor said. "You still want to keep her here?"

"Yes."

"Your funeral. I'll look in tomorrow. She'll sleep. Give her water and warm soup through the tube if she wants it." He stalked out.

Charles turned on his brother. "Adam, for God's sake, what is this?"

"Let me alone."

"What's got into you?"

"Let me alone—you hear? Just let me alone."

"Christ!" said Charles and spat on the floor and went restlessly and uneasily to work.

Adam was glad he was gone. He moved about the kitchen, washed the breakfast dishes, and swept the floor. When he had put the kitchen to rights he went in and drew a chair up to the bed. The girl snored thickly through the morphine. The swelling was going down on her face but the eyes were blackened and swollen. Adam sat very still, looking at her. Her set and splinted arm lay on her stomach, but her right arm lay on top of the coverlet, the fingers curled like a nest. It was a child's hand, almost a baby's hand. Adam touched her wrist with his finger, and her fingers moved a little in reflex. Her wrist was warm. Secretly then, as though he were afraid he might be caught, he straightened her hand and touched the little cushion pads on the fingertips. Her fingers were pink and soft, but the skin on the back of her hand seemed to have an underbloom like a pearl. Adam chuckled with delight. Her breathing stopped and he became electrically alert—then her throat clicked and the rhythmed snoring continued. Gently he worked her hand and arm under the cover before he tiptoed out of the room.

For several days Cathy lay in a cave of shock and opium. Her skin felt like lead, and she moved very little because of the pain. She was aware of movement around her. Gradually her head and her eyes cleared. Two young men were with her, one occasionally and the other a great deal. She knew that another man who came in was the doctor, and there was also a tall lean man, who interested her more than any of the others, and the interest grew out of fear. Perhaps in her drugged sleep she had picked something up and stored it.

Very slowly her mind assembled the last days and rearranged them. She saw the face of Mr. Edwards, saw it lose its placid self-sufficiency and dissolve into murder. She had never been so afraid before in her life, but she had learned fear now. And her mind sniffed about like a rat looking for an escape. Mr. Edwards knew about the fire. Did anyone else? And how did he know? A blind nauseating terror rose in her when she thought of that.

From things she heard she learned that the tall man was the sheriff and wanted to question her, and that the young man named Adam was protecting her from the questioning. Maybe the sheriff knew about the fire.

Raised voices gave her the cue to her method. The sheriff said, "She must have a name. Somebody must know her."

"How could she answer? Her jaw is broken." Adam's voice.

"If she's right-handed she could spell out answers. Look here, Adam, if somebody tried to kill her I'd better catch him while I can. Just give me a pencil and let me talk to her."

Adam said, "You heard the doctor say her skull was cracked. How do you know she can remember?"

"Well, you give me paper and pencil and we'll see."

"I don't want you to bother her."

"Adam, goddam it, it doesn't matter what you want. I'm telling you I want a paper and pencil."

Then the other young man's voice. "What's the matter with you? You make it sound like it was you who did it. Give him a pencil."

She had her eyes closed when the three men came quietly into her room. "She's asleep," Adam whispered.

She opened her eyes and looked at them.

The tall man came to the side of the bed. "I don't want to bother you, Miss. I'm the sheriff. I know you can't talk, but will you just write some things on this?"

She tried to nod and winced with pain. She blinked her eyes rapidly to indicate assent.

"That's the girl," said the sheriff. "You see? She wants to." He put the tablet on the bed beside her and molded her fingers around the pencil. "There we are. Now. What is your name?"

The three men watched her face. Her mouth grew thin and her eyes squinted. She closed her eyes and the pencil began to move. "I don't know," it scrawled in huge letters.

"Here, now there's a fresh sheet. What do you remember?"

"All black. Can't think," the pencil wrote before it went over the edge of the tablet.

"Don't you remember who you are, where you came from? Think!"

She seemed to go through a great struggle and then her face gave up and became tragic. "No. Mixed up. Help me."

"Poor child," the sheriff said. "I thank you for trying anyway. When you get better we'll try again. No, you don't have to write any more."

The pencil wrote, "Thank you," and fell from her fingers.

She had won the sheriff. He ranged himself with Adam. Only Charles was against her. When the brothers were in her room, and it took two of them to help her on the bedpan without hurting her, she studied Charles' dark sullenness. He had something in his face that she recognized, that made her uneasy. She saw that he touched the scar on his forehead very often, rubbed it, and drew its outline with his fingers. Once he caught her watching. He looked guiltily at his fingers. Charles said brutally, "Don't you worry. You're going to have one like it, maybe even a better one."

She smiled at him, and he looked away. When Adam came in with her warm soup Charles said, "I'm going in town and drink some beer."

3

Adam couldn't remember ever having been so happy. It didn't bother him that he did not know her name. She had said to call her Cathy, and that was enough for him. He cooked for Cathy, going through recipes used by his mother and his stepmother.

Cathy's vitality was great. She began to recover very quickly. The swelling went out of her cheeks and the prettiness of convalescence came to her face. In a short time she could be helped to a sitting position. She opened and closed her mouth very carefully, and she began to eat soft foods that required little chewing. The bandage was still on her forehead but the rest of her face was little marked except for the hollow cheek on the side where the teeth were missing.

Cathy was in trouble and her mind ranged for a way out of it. She spoke little even when it was not so difficult.

One afternoon she heard someone moving around in the kitchen. She called, "Adam, is it you?"

Charles' voice answered, "No, it's me."

"Would you come in here just for a minute, please?"

He stood in the doorway. His eyes were sullen.

"You don't come in much," she said.

"That's right."

"You don't like me."

"I guess that's right too."

"Will you tell me why?"

He struggled to find an answer. "I don't trust you."

"Why not?"

"I don't know. And I don't believe you lost your memory."

"But why should I lie?"

"I don't know. That's why I don't trust you. There's something—I almost recognize."

"You never saw me in your life."

"Maybe not. But there's something that bothers me—that I ought to know. And how do you know I never saw you?"

She was silent, and he moved to leave. "Don't go," she said. "What do you intend to do?"

"About what?"

"About me."

He regarded her with a new interest. "You want the truth?"

"Why else would I ask?"

"I don't know, but I'll tell you. I'm going to get you out of here just as soon as I can. My brother's turned fool, but I'll bring him around if I have to lick him."

"Could you do that? He's a big man."

"I could do it."

She regarded him levelly. "Where is Adam?"

"Gone in town to get some more of your goddam medicine."

"You're a mean man."

"You know what I think? I don't think I'm half as mean as you are under that nice skin. I think you're a devil."

She laughed softly. "That makes two of us," she said. "Charles, how long do I have?"

"For what?"

"How long before you put me out? Tell me truly."

"All right, I will. About a week or ten days. Soon as you can get around."

"Suppose I don't go."

He regarded her craftily, almost with pleasure at the thought of combat. "All right, I'll tell you. When you had all that dope you talked a lot, like in your sleep."

"I don't believe that."

He laughed, for he had seen the quick tightening of her mouth. "All right, don't. And if you just go about your business as soon as you can, I won't tell. But if you don't, you'll know all right, and so will the sheriff."

"I don't believe I said anything bad. What could I say?"

"I won't argue with you. And I've got work to do. You asked me and I told you."

He went outside. Back of the henhouse he leaned over and laughed and slapped his leg. "I thought she was smarter," he said to himself. And he felt more easy than he had for days.

4

Charles had frightened her badly. And if he had recognized her, so had she recognized him. He was the only person she had ever met who played it her way. Cathy followed his thinking, and it did not reassure her. She knew that her tricks would not work with him, and she needed protection and rest. Her money was gone. She had to be sheltered, and would have to be for a long time. She was tired and sick, but her mind went skipping among possibilities.

Adam came back from town with a bottle of Pain Killer. He poured a tablespoonful. "This will taste horrible," he said. "It's good stuff though."

She took it without protest, did not even make much of a face about it. "You're good to me," she said. "I wonder why? I've brought you trouble."

"You have not. You've brightened up the whole house. Never complain or anything, hurt as bad as you are."

"You're so good, so kind."

"I want to be."

"Do you have to go out? Couldn't you stay and talk to me?"

"Sure I could. There's nothing so important to do."

"Draw up a chair, Adam, and sit down."

When he was seated she stretched her right hand toward him, and he took it in both of his. "So good and kind," she repeated. "Adam, you keep promises, don't you?"

"I try to. What are you thinking about?"

"I'm alone and I'm afraid," she cried. "I'm afraid."

"Can't I help you?"

"I don't think anyone can help me."

"Tell me and let me try."

"That's the worst part. I can't even tell you."

"Why not? If it's a secret I won't tell it."

"It's not my secret, don't you see?"

"No, I don't."

Her fingers gripped his hand tightly. "Adam, I didn't ever lose my memory."

"Then why did you say—"

"That's what I'm trying to tell you. Did you love your father, Adam?"

"I guess I revered him more than loved him."

"Well, if someone you revered were in trouble, wouldn't you do anything to save him from destruction?"

"Well, sure. I guess I would."

"Well, that's how it is with me."

"But how did you get hurt?"

"That's part of it. That's why I can't tell."

"Was it your father?"

"Oh, no. But it's all tied up together."

"You mean, if you tell me who hurt you, then your father will be in trouble?"

She sighed. He would make up the story himself. "Adam, will you trust me?"

"Of course."

"It's an awful thing to ask."

"No, it isn't, not if you're protecting your father."

"You understand, it's not my secret. If it were I'd tell you in a minute."

"Of course I understand. I'd do the same thing myself."

"Oh, you understand so much." Tears welled up in her eyes. He leaned down toward her, and she kissed him on the cheek.

"Don't you worry," he said, "I'll take care of you."

She lay back against the pillow. "I don't think you can."

"What do you mean?"

"Well, your brother doesn't like me. He wants me to get out of here."

"Did he tell you that?"

"Oh, no. I can just feel it. He hasn't your understanding."

"He has a good heart."

"I know that, but he doesn't have your kindness. And when I have to go— the sheriff is going to begin asking questions and I'll be all alone."

He stared into space. "My brother can't make you go. I own half of this farm. I have my own money."

"If he wanted me to go I would have to. I can't spoil your life."

Adam stood up and strode out of the room. He went to the back door and looked out on the afternoon. Far off in the field his brother was lifting stones from a sled and piling them on the stone wall. Adam looked up at the sky. A blanket of herring clouds was rolling in from the east. He sighed deeply and his breath made a tickling, exciting feeling in his chest. His ears seemed suddenly clear, so that he heard the chickens cackling and the east wind blowing over the ground. He heard horses' hoofs plodding on the road and far-off pounding on wood where a neighbor was shingling a barn. And all these sounds related into a kind of music. His eyes were clear too. Fences and walls and sheds stood staunchly out in the yellow afternoon, and they were related too. There was change in everything. A flight of sparrows dropped into the dust and scrabbled for bits of food and then flew off like a gray scarf twisting in the light. Adam looked back at his brother. He had lost track of time and he did not know how long he had been standing in the doorway.

No time had passed. Charles was still struggling with the same large stone. And Adam had not released the full, held breath he had taken when time stopped.

Suddenly he knew joy and sorrow felted into one fabric. Courage and fear were one thing too. He found that he had started to hum a droning little tune. He turned, walked through the kitchen, and stood in the doorway, looking at Cathy. She smiled weakly at him, and he thought, What a child! What a helpless child! and a surge of love filled him.

"Will you marry me?" he asked.

Her face tightened and her hand closed convulsively.

"You don't have to tell me now," he said. "I want you to think about it. But if you would marry me I could protect you. No one could hurt you again."

Cathy recovered in an instant. "Come here, Adam. There, sit down. Here, give me your hand. That's good, that's right." She raised his hand and put the back of it against her cheek. "My dear," she said brokenly. "Oh, my dear. Look, Adam, you have trusted me. Now will you promise me something? Will you promise not to tell your brother you have asked me?"

"Asked you to marry me? Why shouldn't I?"

"It's not that. I want this night to think. I'll want maybe more than this night. Could you let me do that?" She raised her hand to her head. "You know I'm not sure I can think straight. And I want to."

"Do you think you might marry me?"

"Please, Adam. Let me alone to think. Please, my dear."

He smiled and said nervously, "Don't make it long. I'm kind of like a cat up a tree so far he can't come down."

"Just let me think. And, Adam—you're a kind man."

He went outside and walked toward where his brother was loading stones.

When he was gone Cathy got up from her bed and moved unsteadily to the bureau. She leaned forward and looked at her face. The bandage was still on her forehead. She raised the edge of it enough to see the angry red underneath. She had not only made up her mind to marry Adam but she had so decided before he had asked her. She was afraid. She needed protection and money. Adam could give her both. And she could control him—she knew that. She did not want to be married, but for the time being it was a refuge. Only one thing bothered her. Adam had a warmth toward her which she did not understand since she had none toward him, nor had ever experienced it toward anyone. And Mr. Edwards had really frightened her. That had been the only time in her life she had lost control of a situation. She determined never to let it happen again. She smiled to herself when she thought what Charles would say. She felt a kinship to Charles. She didn't mind his suspicion of her.

5

Charles straightened up when Adam approached. He put his palms against the small of his back and massaged the tired muscles. "My God, there's lots of rocks," he said.

"Fellow in the army told me there's valleys in California—miles and miles—and you can't find a stone, not even a little one."

"There'll be something else," said Charles. "I don't think there's any farm without something wrong with it. Out in the Middle West it's locusts, someplace else it's tornadoes. What's a few stones?"

"I guess you're right. I thought I would give you a hand."

"That's nice of you. I thought you'd spend the rest of your life holding hands with that in there. How long is she going to stay?"

Adam was on the point of telling him of his proposal but the tone of Charles' voice made him change his mind.

"Say," Charles said, "Alex Platt came by a little while ago. You'd never think what happened to him. He's found a fortune."

"How do you mean?"

"Well, you know the place on his property where that clump of cedars sticks out—you know, right on the county road?"

"I know. What about it?"

"Alex went in between those trees and his stone wall. He was hunting rabbits. He found a suitcase and a man's clothes, all packed nice. Soaked up with rain though. Looked like it had been there some time. And there was a wooden box with a lock, and when he broke it open there was near four thousand dollars in it. And he found a purse too. There wasn't anything in it."

"No name or anything?"

"That's the strange part—no name; no name on the clothes, no labels on the suits. It's just like the fellow didn't want to be traced."

"Is Alex going to keep it?"

"He took it in to the sheriff, and the sheriff is going to advertise it, and if nobody answers Alex can keep it."

"Somebody's sure to claim it."

"I guess so. I didn't tell Alex that. He's feeling so good about it. That's funny about no labels—not cut out, just didn't have any."

"That's a lot of money," Adam said. "Somebody's bound to claim it."

"Alex hung around for a while. You know, his wife goes around a lot." Charles was silent. "Adam," he said finally, "we got to have a talk. The whole county's doing plenty of talking."

"What about? What do you mean?"

"Goddam it, about that—that girl. Two men can't have a girl living with them. Alex says the women are pretty riled up about it. Adam, we can't have it. We live here. We've got a good name."

"You want me to throw her out before she's well?"

"I want you to get rid of her—get her out. I don't like her."

"You never have."

"I know it. I don't trust her. There's something—something—I don't know what it is, but I don't like it. When you going to get her out?"

"Tell you what," Adam said slowly. "Give her one more week and then I'll do something about her."

"You promise?"

"Sure I promise."

"Well, that's something. I'll get the word to Alex's wife. From there on she'll handle the news. Good Lord, I'll be glad to have the house to ourselves again. I don't suppose her memory's come back?"

"No," said Adam.

6

Five days later, when Charles had gone to buy some calf feed, Adam drove the buggy to the kitchen steps. He helped Cathy in, tucked a blanket around her knees, and put another around her shoulders. He drove to the county seat and was married to her by a justice of the peace.

Charles was home when they returned. He looked sourly at them when they came into the kitchen. "I thought you'd took her in to put her on the train."

"We got married," Adam said simply.

Cathy smiled at Charles.

"Why? Why did you do it?"

"Why not? Can't a man get married?"

Cathy went quickly into the bedroom and closed the door.

Charles began to rave. "She's no damn good, I tell you. She's a whore."

"Charles!"

"I tell you, she's just a two-bit whore. I wouldn't trust her with a bit piece—why, that bitch, that slut!"

"Charles, stop it! Stop it, I tell you! You keep your filthy mouth shut about my wife!"

"She's no more a wife than an alley cat."

Adam said slowly, "I think you're jealous, Charles. I think you wanted to marry her."

"Why, you goddam fool! Me jealous? I won't live in the same house with her!"

Adam said evenly, "You won't have to. I'm going away. You can buy me out if you want. You can have the farm. You always wanted it. You can stay here and rot."

Charles' voice lowered. "Won't you get rid of her? Please, Adam. Throw her out. She'll tear you to pieces. She'll destroy you, Adam, she'll destroy you!"

"How do you know so much about her?"

Charles' eyes were bleak. "I don't," he said, and his mouth snapped shut.

Adam did not even ask Cathy whether she wanted to come out for dinner. He carried two plates into the bedroom and sat beside her.

"We're going to go away," he said.

"Let me go away. Please, let me. I don't want to make you hate your brother. I wonder why he hates me?"

"I think he's jealous."

Her eyes narrowed. "Jealous?"

"That's what it looks like to me. You don't have to worry. We're getting out. We're going to California."

She said quietly, "I don't want to go to California."

"Nonsense. Why, it's nice there, sun all the time and beautiful."

"I don't want to go to California."

"You are my wife," he said softly. "I want you to go with me."

She was silent and did not speak of it again.

They heard Charles slam out the door, and Adam said, "That will be good for him. He'll get a little drunk and he'll feel better."

Cathy modestly looked at her fingers. "Adam, I can't be a wife to you until I'm well."

"I know," he said. "I understand. I'll wait."

"But I want you to stay with me. I'm afraid of Charles. He hates me so."

"I'll bring my cot in here. Then you can call me if you're frightened. You can reach out and touch me."

"You're so good," she said. "Could we have some tea?"

"Why, sure, I'd like some myself." He brought the steaming cups in and went back for the sugar bowl. He settled himself in a chair near her bed. "It's pretty strong. Is it too strong for you?"

"I like it strong."

He finished his cup. "Does it taste strange to you? It's got a funny taste."

Her hand flew to her mouth. "Oh, let me taste it." She sipped the dregs. "Adam," she cried, "you got the wrong cup—that was mine. It had my medicine in it."

He licked his lips. "I guess it can't hurt me."

"No, it can't." She laughed softly. "I hope I don't need to call you in the night."

"What do you mean?"

"Well, you drank my sleeping medicine. Maybe you wouldn't wake up easily."

Adam went down into a heavy opium sleep though he fought to stay awake. "Did the doctor tell you to take this much?" he asked thickly.

"You're just not used to it," she said.

Charles came back at eleven o'clock. Cathy heard his tipsy footsteps. He went into his room, flung off his clothes, and got into bed. He grunted and turned, trying to get comfortable, and then he opened his eyes. Cathy was standing by his bed. "What do you want?"

"What do you think? Move over a little."

"Where's Adam?"

"He drank my sleeping medicine by mistake. Move over a little."

He breathed harshly. "I already been with a whore."

"You're a pretty strong boy. Move over a little."

"How about your broken arm?"

"I'll take care of that. It's not your worry."

Suddenly Charles laughed. "The poor bastard," he said, and he threw back the blanket to receive her.

PART TWO

PART TWO

TWELVE

You can see how this book has reached a great boundary that was called 1900. Another hundred years were ground up and churned, and what had happened was all muddied by the way folks wanted it to be—more rich and meaningful the farther back it was. In the books of some memories it was the best time that ever sloshed over the world—the old time, the gay time, sweet and simple, as though time were young and fearless. Old men who didn't know whether they were going to stagger over the boundary of the century looked forward to it with distaste. For the world was changing, and sweetness was gone, and virtue too. Worry had crept on a corroding world, and what was lost—good manners, ease and beauty? Ladies were not ladies any more, and you couldn't trust a gentleman's word.

There was a time when people kept their fly buttons fastened. And man's freedom was boiling off. And even childhood was no good any more—not the way it was. No worry then but how to find a good stone, not round exactly but flattened and water-shaped, to use in a sling pouch cut from a discarded shoe. Where did all the good stones go, and all simplicity?

A man's mind vagued up a little, for how can you remember the feel of pleasure or pain or choking emotion? You can remember only that you had them. An elder man might truly recall through water the delicate doctor-testing of little girls, but such a man forgets, and wants to, the acid emotion eating at the spleen so that a boy had to put his face flat down in the young wild oats and drum his fists against the ground and sob "Christ! Christ!" Such a man might say, and did, "What's that damned kid lying out there in the grass for? He'll catch a cold."

Oh, strawberries don't taste as they used to and the thighs of women have lost their clutch!

And some men eased themselves like setting hens into the nest of death.

History was secreted in the glands of a million historians. We must get out of this banged-up century, some said, out of this cheating, murderous century of riot and secret death, of scrabbling for public lands and damn well getting them by any means at all.

Think back, recall our little nation fringing the oceans, torn with complexities, too big for its britches. Just got going when the British took us on again. We beat them, but it didn't do us much good. What we had was a burned White House and ten thousand widows on the public pension list.

Then the soldiers went to Mexico and it was a kind of painful picnic. Nobody knows why you go to a picnic to be uncomfortable when it is so easy and pleasant to eat at home. The Mexican War did two good things though. We got a lot of western land, damn near doubled our size, and besides that it was a training ground for generals, so that when the sad self-murder settled on us the leaders knew the techniques for making it properly horrible.

And then the arguments:

Can you keep a slave?

Well if you bought him in good faith, why not?

Next they'll be saying a man can't have a horse. Who is it wants to take my property?

And there we were, like a man scratching at his own face and bleeding into his own beard.

Well, that was over and we got slowly up off the bloody ground and started westward.

There came boom and bust, bankruptcy, depression.

Great public thieves came along and picked the pockets of everyone who had a pocket.

To hell with that rotten century!

Let's get it over and the door closed shut on it! Let's close it like a book and go on reading! New chapter, new life. A man will have clean hands once we get the lid slammed shut on that stinking century. It's a fair thing ahead. There's no rot on this clean new hundred years. It's not stacked, and any bastard who deals seconds from this new deck of years—why, we'll crucify him head down over a privy.

Oh, but strawberries will never taste so good again and the thighs of women have lost their clutch!

THIRTEEN

Sometimes a kind of glory lights up the mind of a man. It happens to nearly everyone. You can feel it growing or preparing like a fuse burning toward dynamite. It is a feeling in the stomach, a delight of the nerves, of the forearms. The skin tastes the air, and every deep-drawn breath is sweet. Its beginning has the pleasure of a great stretching yawn; it flashes in the brain and the whole world glows outside your eyes. A man may have lived all of his life in the gray, and the land and trees of him dark and somber. The events, even the important ones, may have trooped by faceless and pale. And then—the glory—so that a cricket song sweetens his ears, the smell of the earth rises chanting to his nose, and dappling light under a tree blesses his eyes. Then a man pours outward, a torrent of him, and yet he is not diminished. And I guess a man's importance in the world can be measured by the quality and number of his glories. It is a lonely thing but it relates us to the world. It is the mother of all creativeness, and it sets each man separate from all other men.

I don't know how it will be in the years to come. There are monstrous changes taking place in the world, forces shaping a future whose face we do not know. Some of these forces seem evil to us, perhaps not in themselves but because their tendency is to eliminate other things we hold good. It is true that two men can lift a bigger stone than one man. A group can build automobiles quicker and better than one man, and bread from a huge factory is cheaper and more uniform. When our food and clothing and housing all are born in the complication of mass production, mass method is bound to get into our thinking and to eliminate all other thinking. In our time mass or collective production has entered our economics, our politics, and even our religion, so that some nations have substituted the idea collective for the idea God. This in my time is the danger. There is great tension in the world, tension toward a breaking point, and men are unhappy and confused.

At such a time it seems natural and good to me to ask myself these questions. What do I believe in? What must I fight for and what must I fight against?

Our species is the only creative species, and it has only one creative instrument, the individual mind and spirit of a man. Nothing was ever created by two men. There are no good collaborations, whether in music, in art, in poetry, in mathematics, in philosophy. Once the miracle of creation has taken place, the group can build and extend it, but the group never invents anything. The preciousness lies in the lonely mind of a man.

And now the forces marshaled around the concept of the group have declared a war of extermination on that preciousness, the mind of man. By disparagement, by starvation, by repressions, forced direction, and the stunning hammerblows of conditioning, the free, roving mind is being pursued, roped, blunted, drugged. It is a sad suicidal course our species seems to have taken.

And this I believe: that the free, exploring mind of the individual human is the most valuable thing in the world. And this I would fight for: the freedom of the mind to take any direction it wishes, undirected. And this I must fight against: any idea, religion, or government which limits or destroys the individual. This is what I am and what I am about. I can understand why a system built on a pattern must try to destroy the free mind, for that is one thing which can by inspection destroy such a system. Surely I can understand this, and I hate it and I will fight against it to preserve the one thing that separates us from the uncreative beasts. If the glory can be killed, we are lost.

2

Adam Trask grew up in grayness, and the curtains of his life were like dusty cobwebs, and his days a slow file of half-sorrows and sick dissatisfactions, and then, through Cathy, the glory came to him.

It doesn't matter that Cathy was what I have called a monster. Perhaps we can't understand Cathy, but on the other hand we are capable of many things in all directions, of great virtues and great sins. And who in his mind has not probed the black water?

Maybe we all have in us a secret pond where evil and ugly things germinate and grow strong. But this culture is fenced, and the swimming brood climbs up only to fall back. Might it not be that in the dark pools of some men the evil grows strong enough to wriggle over the fence and swim free? Would not such a man be our monster, and are we not related to him in our hidden water? It would be absurd if we did not understand both angels and devils, since we invented them.

Whatever Cathy may have been, she set off the glory in Adam. His spirit rose flying and released him from fear and bitterness and rancid memories. The glory lights up the world and changes it the way a star shell changes a battleground. Perhaps Adam did not see Cathy at all, so lighted was she by his eyes. Burned in his mind was an image of beauty and tenderness, a sweet and holy girl, precious beyond thinking, clean and loving, and that image was Cathy to her husband, and nothing Cathy did or said could warp Adam's Cathy.

She said she did not want to go to California and he did not listen, because *his* Cathy took his arm and started first. So bright was his glory that he did not notice the sullen pain in his brother, did not see the glinting in his brother's eyes. He sold his share of the farm to Charles, for less than it was worth, and with that and his half of his father's money he was free and rich.

The brothers were strangers now. They shook hands at the station, and Charles watched the train pull out and rubbed his scar. He went to the inn, drank four quick whiskies, and climbed the stairs to the top floor. He paid the girl and then could not perform. He cried in her arms until she put him out. He raged at his farm, forced it, added to it, drilled and trimmed, and his boundaries extended. He took no rest, no recreation, and he became rich without pleasure and respected without friends.

Adam stopped in New York long enough to buy clothes for himself and Cathy before they climbed on the train which bore them across the continent. How they happened to go to the Salinas Valley is very easy to understand.

In that day the railroads—growing, fighting among themselves, striving to increase and to dominate—used every means to increase their traffic. The companies not only advertised in the newspapers, they issued booklets and broadsides describing and picturing the beauty and richness of the West. No claim was too extravagant—wealth was unlimited. The Southern Pacific Railroad, headed by the wild energy of Leland Stanford, had begun to dominate the Pacific Coast not only in transportation but in politics. Its rails extended down the valleys. New towns sprang up, new sections were opened and populated, for the company had to create customers to get custom.

The long Salinas Valley was part of the exploitation. Adam had seen and studied a fine color broadside which set forth the valley as that region which heaven unsuccessfully imitated. After reading the literature, anyone who did not want to settle in the Salinas Valley was crazy.

Adam did not rush at his purchase. He bought a rig and drove around, meeting the earlier comers, talking of soil and water, climate and crops, prices and facilities. It was not speculation with Adam. He was here to settle, to found a home, a family, perhaps a dynasty.

Adam drove exuberantly from farm to farm, picked up dirt and crumbled it in his fingers, talked and planned and dreamed. The people of the valley liked him and were glad he had come to live there, for they recognized a man of substance.

He had only one worry, and that was for Cathy. She was not well. She rode around the country with him, but she was listless. One morning she complained of feeling ill and stayed in her room in the King City hotel while Adam drove into the country. He returned at about five in the afternoon to find her nearly dead from loss of blood. Luckily Adam found Dr. Tilson at his supper and dragged him from his roast beef. The doctor made a quick examination, inserted a packing, and turned to Adam.

"Why don't you wait downstairs?" he suggested.

"Is she all right?"

"Yes. I'll call you pretty soon."

Adam patted Cathy's shoulder, and she smiled up at him.

Dr. Tilson closed the door behind him and came back to the bed. His face was red with anger. "Why did you do it?"

Cathy's mouth was a thin tight line.

"Does your husband know you are pregnant?"

Her head moved slowly from side to side.

"What did you do it with?"

She stared up at him.

He looked around the room. He stepped to the bureau and picked up a knitting needle. He shook it in her face. "The old offender—the old criminal," he said. "You're a fool. You've nearly killed yourself and you haven't lost your baby. I suppose you took things too, poisoned yourself, inserted camphor, kerosene, red pepper. My God! Some of the things you women do!"

Her eyes were as cold as glass.

He pulled a chair up beside her bed. "Why don't you want to have the baby?" he asked softly. "You've got a good husband. Don't you love him? Don't you intend to speak to me at all? Tell me, damn it! Don't turn mulish."

Her lips did not move and her eyes did not flicker.

"My dear," he said, "can't you see? You must not destroy life. That's the one thing gets me crazy. God knows I lose patients because I don't know enough. But I try—I always try. And then I see a deliberate killing." He talked rapidly on. He dreaded the sick silence between his sentences. This woman puzzled him. There was something inhuman about her. "Have you met Mrs. Laurel? She's wasting and crying for a baby. Everything she has or can get she would give to have a baby, and you—you try to stab yours with a knitting needle. All right," he cried, "you won't speak—you don't have to. But I'm going to tell you. The baby is safe. Your aim was bad. And I'm telling you this—you're going to have that baby. Do you know what the law in this state has to say about abortion? You don't have to answer, but you listen to me! If this happens again, if you lose this baby and I have any reason to suspect monkey business, I will charge you, I will testify against you, and I will see you punished. Now I hope you have sense enough to believe me, because I mean it."

Cathy moistened her lips with a little pointed tongue. The cold went out of her eyes and a weak sadness took its place. "I'm sorry," she said. "I'm sorry. But you don't understand."

"Then why don't you tell me?" His anger disappeared like mist. "Tell me, my dear."

"It's hard to tell. Adam is so good, so strong. I am—well, I'm tainted. Epilepsy."

"Not you!"

"No, but my grandfather and my father—and my brother." She covered her eyes with her hands. "I couldn't bring that to my husband."

"Poor child," he said. "My poor child. You can't be certain. It's more than probable that your baby will be fine and healthy. Will you promise me not to try any more tricks?"

"Yes."

"All right then. I won't tell your husband what you did. Now lie back and let me see if the bleeding's stopped."

In a few minutes he closed his satchel and put the knitting needle in his pocket. "I'll look in tomorrow morning," he said.

Adam swarmed on him as he came down the narrow stairs into the lobby. Dr. Tilson warded off a flurry of "How is she? Is she all right? What caused it? Can I go up?"

"Whoa, hold up—hold up." And he used his trick, his standard joke. "Your wife is sick."

"Doctor—"

"She has the only good sickness there is—"

"Doctor—"

"Your wife is going to have a baby." He brushed past Adam and left him staring. Three men sitting around the stove grinned at him. One of them observed dryly, "If it was me now—why, I'd invite a few, maybe three, friends to have a drink." His hint was wasted. Adam bolted clumsily up the narrow stairs.

Adam's attention narrowed to the Bordoni ranch a few miles south of King City, almost equidistant, in fact, between San Lucas and King City.

The Bordonis had nine hundred acres left of a grant of ten thousand acres which had come to Mrs. Bordoni's great-grandfather from the Spanish crown. The Bordonis were Swiss, but Mrs. Bordoni was the daughter and heiress of a Spanish family that had settled in the Salinas Valley in very early times. And as happened with most of the old families, the land slipped away. Some was lost in gambling, some chipped off for taxes, and some acres torn off like coupons to buy luxuries—a horse, a diamond, or a pretty woman. The nine hundred remaining acres were the core of the original Sanchez grant, and the best of it too. They straddled the river and tucked into the foothills on both sides, for at this point the valley narrows and then opens out again. The original Sanchez house was still usable. Built of adobe, it stood in a tiny opening in the foothills, a miniature valley fed by a precious ever-running spring of sweet water. That of course was why the first Sanchez had built his seat there. Huge live oaks shaded the valley, and the earth had a richness and a greenness foreign to this part of the country. The walls of the low house were four feet thick, and the round pole rafters were tied on with rawhide ropes which had been put on wet. The hide shrank and pulled joist and rafter tight together, and the leather ropes became hard as iron and nearly imperishable. There is only one drawback to this building method. Rats will gnaw at the hide if they are let.

The old house seemed to have grown out of the earth, and it was lovely. Bordoni used it for a cow barn. He was a Swiss, an immigrant, with his national passion for cleanliness. He distrusted the thick mud walls and built a frame house some distance away, and his cows put their heads out the deep recessed windows of the old Sanchez house.

The Bordonis were childless, and when the wife died in ripe years a lonely longing for his Alpine past fell on her husband. He wanted to sell the ranch and go home. Adam Trask refused to buy in a hurry, and Bordoni was asking a big price and using the selling method of pretending not to care whether he sold or not. Bordoni knew Adam was going to buy his land long before Adam knew it.

Where Adam settled he intended to stay and to have his unborn children stay. He was afraid he might buy one place and then see another he liked better, and all the time the Sanchez place was drawing him. With the ad-

vent of Cathy, his life extended long and pleasantly ahead of him. But h
went through all the motions of carefulness. He drove and rode and walke
over every foot of the land. He put a post-hole augur down through th
subsoil to test and feel and smell the under earth. He inquired about th
small wild plants of field and riverside and hill. In damp places he kne
down and examined the game tracks in the mud, mountain lion and dee
coyote and wild cat, skunk and raccoon, weasel and rabbit, all overlaid wit
the pattern of quail tracks. He threaded among willows and sycamores an
wild blackberry vines in the riverbed, patted the trunks of live oak and scru
oak, madrone, laurel, toyon.

Bordoni watched him with squinting eyes and poured tumblers of re
wine squeezed from the grapes of his small hillside vineyard. It was Bor
doni's pleasure to get a little drunk every afternoon. And Adam, who hac
never tasted wine, began to like it.

Over and over he asked Cathy's opinion of the place. Did she like it?
Would she be happy there? And he didn't listen to her noncommittal an
swers. He thought that she linked arms with his enthusiasm. In the lobby o
the King City hotel he talked to the men who gathered around the stove
and read the papers sent down from San Francisco.

"It's water I think about," he said one evening. "I wonder how deep you'd
have to go to bring in a well."

A rancher crossed his denim knees. "You ought to go see Sam Hamilton,"
he said. "He knows more about water than anybody around here. He's a
water witch and a well-digger too. He'll tell you. He's put down half the
wells in this part of the valley."

His companion chuckled. "Sam's got a real legitimate reason to be interested in water. Hasn't got a goddam drop of it on his own place."

"How do I find him?" Adam asked.

"I'll tell you what. I'm going out to have him make some angle-irons. I'll
take you with me if you want. You'll like Mr. Hamilton. He's a fine man."

"Kind of a comical genius," his companion said.

3

They went to the Hamilton ranch in Louis Lippo's buckboard—Louis and
Adam Trask. The iron straps rattled around in the box, and a leg of venison,
wrapped in wet burlap to keep it cool, jumped around on top of the iron. It
was customary in that day to take some substantial lump of food as a present
when you went calling on a man, for you had to stay to dinner unless you
wished to insult his house. But a few guests could set back the feeding plans
for the week if you did not build up what you destroyed. A quarter of pork
or a rump of beef would do. Louis had cut down the venison and Adam
provided a bottle of whisky.

"Now I'll have to tell you," Louis said. "Mr. Hamilton will like that, but

Mrs. Hamilton has got a skunner on it. If I was you I'd leave it under the seat, and when we drive around to the shop, why, then you can get it out. That's what we always do."

"Doesn't she let her husband take a drink?"

"No bigger than a bird," said Louis. "But she's got brassbound opinions. Just you leave the bottle under the seat."

They left the valley road and drove into the worn and rutted hills over a set of wheel tracks gulleyed by the winter rains. The horses strained into their collars and the buckboard rocked and swayed. The year had not been kind to the hills, and already in June they were dry and the stones showed through the short, burned feed. The wild oats had headed out barely six inches above the ground, as though with knowledge that if they didn't make seed quickly they wouldn't get to seed at all.

"It's not likely looking country," Adam said.

"Likely? Why, Mr. Trask, it's country that will break a man's heart and eat him up. Likely! Mr. Hamilton has a sizable piece and he'd of starved to death on it with all those children. The ranch don't feed them. He does all kinds of jobs, and his boys are starting to bring in something now. It's a fine family."

Adam stared at a line of dark mesquite that peeked out of a draw. "Why in the world would he settle on a place like this?"

Louis Lippo, as does every man, loved to interpret, to a stranger particularly, if no native was present to put up an argument. "I'll tell you," he said. "Take me—my father was Italian. Came here after the trouble but he brought a little money. My place isn't very big but it's nice. My father bought it. He picked it out. And take you—I don't know how you're fixed and wouldn't ask, but they say you're trying to buy the old Sanchez place and Bordoni never gave anything away. You're pretty well fixed or you wouldn't even ask about it."

"I'm comfortably off," said Adam modestly.

"I'm talking the long way around," said Louis. "When Mr. and Mrs. Hamilton came into the valley they didn't have a pot to piss in. They had to take what was left—government land that nobody else wanted. Twenty-five acres of it won't keep a cow alive even in good years, and they say the coyotes move away in bad years. There's people say they don't know how the Hamiltons lived. But of course Mr. Hamilton went right to work—that's how they lived. Worked as a hired hand till he got his threshing machine built."

"Must have made a go of it. I hear of him all over."

"He made a go of it all right. Raised nine children. I'll bet he hasn't got four bits laid away. How could he?"

One side of the buckboard leaped up, rolled over a big round stone, and dropped down again. The horses were dark with sweat and lathered under collar and britching.

"I'll be glad to talk to him," said Adam.

"Well, sir, he raised one fine crop—he had good children and he raised them fine. All doing well—maybe except Joe. Joe—he's the youngest—they're talking about sending him to college, but all the rest are doing fine. Mr. Hamilton can be proud. The house is just on the other side of the next rise. Don't forget and bring out that whisky—she'll freeze you to the ground."

The dry earth was ticking under the sun and the crickets rasped. "It's real godforsaken country," said Louis.

"Makes me feel mean," said Adam.

"How's that?"

"Well, I'm fixed so I don't have to live on a place like this."

"Me too, and I don't feel mean. I'm just goddam glad."

When the buckboard topped the rise Adam could look down on the little cluster of buildings which composed the Hamilton seat—a house with many lean-tos, a cow shed, a shop, and a wagon shed. It was a dry and sun-eaten sight—no big trees and a small hand-watered garden.

Louis turned to Adam, and there was just a hint of hostility in his tone. "I want to put you straight on one or two things, Mr. Trask. There's people that when they see Samuel Hamilton the first time might get the idea he's full of bull. He don't talk like other people. He's an Irishman. And he's all full of plans—a hundred plans a day. And he's all full of hope. My Christ, he'd have to be to live on this land! But you remember this—he's a fine worker, a good blacksmith, and some of his plans work out. And I've heard him talk about things that were going to happen and they did."

Adam was alarmed at the hint of threat. "I'm not a man to run another man down," he said, and he felt that suddenly Louis thought of him as a stranger and an enemy.

"I just wanted you to get it straight. There's some people come in from the East and they think if a man hasn't got a lot of money he's no good."

"I wouldn't think of—"

"Mr. Hamilton maybe hasn't got four bits put away, but he's our people and he's as good as we got. And he's raised the nicest family you're likely to see. I just want you to remember that."

Adam was on the point of defending himself and then he said, "I'll remember. Thanks for telling me."

Louis faced around front again. "There he is—see, out by the shop? He must of heard us."

"Has he got a beard?" Adam asked, peering.

"Yes, got a nice beard. It's turning white fast, beginning to grizzle up."

They drove past the frame house and saw Mrs. Hamilton looking out the window at them, and they drew up in front of the shop where Samuel stood waiting for them.

Adam saw a big man, bearded like a patriarch, his graying hair stirring in the air like thistledown. His cheeks above his beard were pink where the sun had burned his Irish skin. He wore a clean blue shirt, overalls, and a leather apron. His sleeves were rolled up, and his muscular arms were clean too. Only his hands were blackened from the forge. After a quick glance Adam came back to the eyes, light blue and filled with a young delight. The wrinkles around them were drawn in radial lines inward by laughter.

"Louis," he said, "I'm glad to see you. Even in the sweetness of our little heaven here, we like to see our friends." He smiled at Adam, and Louis said, "I brought Mr. Adam Trask to see you. He's a stranger from down east, come to settle."

"I'm glad," said Samuel. "We'll shake another time. I wouldn't soil your hand with these forge hooks."

"I brought some strap iron, Mr. Hamilton. Would you make some angles for me? The whole frame of my header bed is fallen to hell."

"Sure I will, Louis. Get down, get down. We'll put the horses to the shade."

"There's a piece of venison behind, and Mr. Trask brought a little something."

Samuel glanced toward the house. "Maybe we'll get out the 'little something' when we've got the rig behind the shed."

Adam could hear the singing lilt of his speech and yet could detect no word pronounced in a strange manner except perhaps in sharpened *t*'s and *l*'s held high on the tongue.

"Louis, will you out-span your team? I'll take the venison in. Liza will be glad. She likes a venison stew."

"Any of the young ones home?"

"Well, no, they aren't. George and Will came home for the weekend, and they all went last night to a dance up Wild Horse Canyon at the Peach Tree schoolhouse. They'll come trooping back by dusk. We lack a sofa because of that. I'll tell you later—Liza will have a vengeance on them—it was Tom did it. I'll tell you later." He laughed and started toward the house, carrying the wrapped deer's haunch. "If you want you can bring the 'little something' into the shop, so you don't let the sun glint on it."

They heard him calling as he came near the house. "Liza, you'll never guess. Louis Lippo has brought a piece of venison bigger than you."

Louis drove in back of the shed, and Adam helped him take the horses out, tie up the tugs, and halter them in the shade. "He meant that about the sun shining on the bottle," said Louis.

"She must be a holy terror."

"No bigger than a bird but she's brassbound."

"'Out-span,'" Adam said. "I think I've heard it said that way, or read it."

Samuel rejoined them in the shop. "Liza will be happy if you will stay to dinner," he said.

"She didn't expect us," Adam protested.

"Hush, man. She'll make some extra dumplings for the stew. It's a pleasure to have you here. Give me your straps, Louis, and let's see how you want them."

He built a chip fire in the black square of the forge and pulled a bellows breeze on it and then fed wet coke over with his fingers until it glowed. "Here, Louis," he said, "wave your wing on my fire. Slow, man, slow and even." He laid the strips of iron on the glowing coke. "No, sir, Mr. Trask, Liza's used to cooking for nine starving children. Nothing can startle her." He tonged the iron to more advantageous heat, and he laughed. "I'll take that last back as a holy lie," he said. "My wife is rumbling like round stones in the surf. And I'll caution the both of you not to mention the word 'sofa.' It's a word of anger and sorrow to Liza."

"You said something about it," Adam said.

"If you knew my boy Tom, you'd understand it better, Mr. Trask. Louis knows him."

"Sure I know him," Louis said.

Samuel went on, "My Tom is a hell-bent boy. Always takes more on his plate than he can eat. Always plants more than he can harvest. Pleasures too much, sorrows too much. Some people are like that. Liza thinks I'm like that. I don't know what will come to Tom. Maybe greatness, maybe the noose—well, Hamiltons have been hanged before. And I'll tell you about that sometime."

"The sofa," Adam suggested politely.

"You're right. I do, and Liza says I do, shepherd my words like rebellious sheep. Well, came the dance at the Peach Tree School and the boys, George, Tom, Will, and Joe, all decided to go. And of course the girls were asked. George and Will and Joe, poor simple boys, each asked one lady friend, but Tom—he took too big a helping as usual. He asked two Williams sisters, Jennie and Belle. How many screw holes do you want, Louis?"

"Five," said Louis.

"All right. Now I must tell you, Mr. Trask, that my Tom has all the egotism and self-love of a boy who thinks he's ugly. Mostly lets himself go fallow, but comes a celebration and he garlands himself like a maypole, and he glories like spring flowers. This takes him quite a piece of time. You notice the wagon house was empty? George and Will and Joe started early and not so beautiful as Tom. George took the rig, Will had the buggy, and Joe got the little two-wheeled cart." Samuel's blue eyes shone with pleasure. "Well then, Tom came out as shy and shining as a Roman emperor and the only thing left with wheels was a hay rake, and you can't take even one Williams sister on that. For good or bad, Liza was taking her nap. Tom sat on the steps and thought it out. Then I saw him go to the shed and hitch up two horses and take the doubletree off the hay rake. He wrestled the sofa out of the house and ran a fifth-chain under the legs—the fine gooseneck horsehair sofa that Liza loves better than anything. I gave it to her to rest on before George was born. The last I saw, Tom went dragging up the hill, reclining at his ease on the sofa to get the Williams girls. And, oh, Lord, it'll be worn thin as a wafer from scraping by the time he gets it back." Samuel put down his tongs and placed his hands on his hips the better to laugh. "And Liza has the smoke of brimstone coming out her nostrils. Poor Tom."

Adam said, smiling, "Would you like to take a little something?"

"That I would," said Samuel. He accepted the bottle and took a quick swallow of whisky and passed it back.

"*Uisquebaugh*—it's an Irish word—whisky, water of life—and so it is."

He took the red straps to his anvil and punched screw holes in them and bent the angles with his hammer and the forked sparks leaped out. Then he dipped the iron hissing into his half-barrel of black water. "There you are," he said and threw them on the ground.

"I thank you," said Louis. "How much will that be?"

"The pleasure of your company."

"It's always like that," Louis said helplessly.

"No, when I put your new well down you paid my price."

"That reminds me—Mr. Trask here is thinking of buying the Bordoni place—the old Sanchez grant—you remember?"

"I know it well," said Samuel. "It's a fine piece."

"He was asking about water, and I told him you knew more about that than anybody around here."

Adam passed the bottle, and Samuel took a delicate sip and wiped his mouth on his forearm above the soot.

"I haven't made up my mind," said Adam. "I'm just asking some questions."

"Oh, Lord, man, now you've put your foot in it. They say it's a dangerous thing to question an Irishman because he'll tell you. I hope you know what you're doing when you issue me a license to talk. I've heard two ways of looking at it. One says the silent man is the wise man and the other that a man without words is a man without thought. Naturally I favor the second —Liza says to a fault. What do you want to know?"

"Well, take the Bordoni place. How deep would you have to go to get water?"

"I'd have to see the spot—some places thirty feet, some places a hundred and fifty, and in some places clear to the center of the world."

"But you could develop water?"

"Nearly every place except my own."

"I've heard you have a lack here."

"Heard? Why, God in heaven must have heard! I've screamed it loud enough."

"There's a four-hundred-acre piece beside the river. Would there be water under it?"

"I'd have to look. It seems to me it's an odd valley. If you'll hold your patience close, maybe I can tell you a little bit about it, for I've looked at it and poked my stinger down into it. A hungry man gorges with his mind—he does indeed."

Louis Lippo said, "Mr. Trask is from New England. He plans to settle here. He's been west before though—in the army, fighting Indians."

"Were you now? Then it's you should talk and let me learn."

"I don't want to talk about it."

"Why not? God help my family and my neighbors if I had fought the Indians!"

"I didn't want to fight them, sir." The "sir" crept in without his knowing it.

"Yes, I can understand that. It must be a hard thing to kill a man you don't know and don't hate."

"Maybe that makes it easier," said Louis.

"You have a point, Louis. But some men are friends with the whole world in their hearts, and there are others that hate themselves and spread their hatred around like butter on hot bread."

"I'd rather you told me about this land," Adam said uneasily, for a sick picture of piled-up bodies came into his mind.

"What time is it?"

Louis stepped out and looked at the sun. "Not past ten o'clock."

"If I get started I have no self-control. My son Will says I talk to trees when I can't find a human vegetable." He sighed and sat down on a nail keg. "I said it was a strange valley, but maybe that's because I was born in a green place. Do you find it strange, Louis?"

"No, I never been out of it."

"I've dug into it plenty," Samuel said. "Something went on under it— maybe still is going on. There's an ocean bed underneath, and below that another world. But that needn't bother a farming man. Now, on top is good soil, particularly on the flats. In the upper valley it is light and sandy, but mixed in with that, the top sweetness of the hills that washed down on it in the winters. As you go north the valley widens out, and the soil gets blacker and heavier and perhaps richer. It's my belief that marshes were there once, and the roots of centuries rotted into the soil and made it black and fertilized it. And when you turn it up, a little greasy clay mixes and holds it together. That's from about Gonzales north to the river mouth. Off to the sides, around Salinas and Blanco and Castroville and Moss Landing, the marshes are still there. And when one day those marshes are drained off, that will be the richest of all land in this red world."

"He always tells what it will be like someday," Louis threw in.

"Well, a man's mind can't stay in time the way his body does."

"If I'm going to settle here I need to know about how and what will be," said Adam. "My children, when I have them, will be on it."

Samuel's eyes looked over the heads of his friends, out of the dark forge to the yellow sunlight. "You'll have to know that under a good part of the valley, some places deep and others pretty near the surface, there's a layer called hard-pan. It's a clay, hard-packed, and it feels greasy too. Some places it is only a foot thick, and more in others. And this hard-pan resists water. If it were not there the winter rains would go soaking down and dampen the earth, and in the summer it would rise up to the roots again. But when the earth above the hard-pan is soaked full, the rest runs fresheting off or stands rotting on top. And that's one of the main curses of our valley."

"Well, it's a pretty good place to live, isn't it?"

"Yes, it is, but a man can't entirely rest when he knows it could be richer. I've thought that if you could drive thousands of holes through it to let the water in, it might solve it. And then I tried something with a few sticks of dynamite. I punched a hole through the hard-pan and blasted. That broke it up and the water could get down. But, God in heaven, think of the amount of dynamite! I've read that a Swede—the same man who invented dynamite—has got a new explosive stronger and safer. Maybe that might be the answer."

Louis said half derisively and half with admiration, "He's always thinking about how to change things. He's never satisfied with the way they are."

Samuel smiled at him. "They say man lived in trees one time. Somebody had to get dissatisfied with a high limb or your feet would not be touching flat ground now." And then he laughed again. "I can see myself sitting on my dust heap making a world in my mind as surely as God created this one. But God saw his world. I'll never see mine except—this way. This will be a valley of great richness one day. It could feed the world, and maybe it will. And happy people will live here, thousands and thousands—" A cloud seemed to come over his eyes and his face set in sadness and he was silent.

"You make it sound like a good place to settle," Adam said. "Where else could I raise my children with that coming?"

Samuel went on, "There's a thing I don't understand. There's a blackness on this valley. I don't know what it is, but I can feel it. Sometimes on a white blinding day I can feel it cutting off the sun and squeezing the light out of it like a sponge." His voice rose. "There's a black violence on this valley. I don't know—I don't know. It's as though some old ghost haunted it out of the dead ocean below and troubled the air with unhappiness. It's as secret as hidden sorrow. I don't know what it is, but I see it and feel it in the people here."

Adam shivered. "I just remembered I promised to get back early. Cathy, my wife, is going to have a baby."

"But Liza's getting ready."

"She'll understand when you tell her about the baby. My wife is feeling poorly. And I thank you for telling me about the water."

"Have I depressed you with my rambling?"

"No, not at all—not at all. It's Cathy's first baby and she's miserable."

Adam struggled all night with his thoughts and the next day he drove out and shook hands with Bordoni and the Sanchez place was his.

FOURTEEN

There is so much to tell about the Western country in that day that it is hard to know where to start. One thing sets off a hundred others. The problem is to decide which one to tell first.

You remember that Samuel Hamilton said his children had gone to a dance at the Peach Tree School. The country schools were the centers of culture then. The Protestant churches in the towns were fighting for their existence in a country where they were newcomers. The Catholic church, first on the scene and deeply dug in, sat in comfortable tradition while the missions were gradually abandoned and their roofs fell in and pigeons roosted on the stripped altars. The library (in Latin and Spanish) of the San Antonio Mission was thrown into a granary, where the rats ate off the sheep-skin bindings. In the country the repository of art and science was the school, and the schoolteacher shielded and carried the torch of learning and of beauty. The schoolhouse was the meeting place for music, for debate. The polls were set in the schoolhouse for elections. Social life, whether it was the crowning of a May queen, the eulogy to a dead president, or an all-night dance, could be held nowhere else. And the teacher was not only an intellectual paragon and a social leader, but also the matrimonial catch of the countryside. A family could indeed walk proudly if a son married the schoolteacher. Her children were presumed to have intellectual advantages both inherited and conditioned.

The daughters of Samuel Hamilton were not destined to become work-destroyed farm wives. They were handsome girls and they carried with them the glow of their descent from the kings of Ireland. They had a pride that transcended their poverty. No one ever thought of them as deserving pity. Samuel raised a distinctly superior breed. They were better read and better bred than most of their contemporaries. To all of them Samuel communicated his love of learning, and he set them apart from the prideful ignorance of their time. Olive Hamilton became a teacher. That meant that she left home at fifteen and went to live in Salinas, where she could go to secondary school. At seventeen she took county board examinations, which covered all the arts and sciences, and at eighteen she was teaching school at Peach Tree.

In her school there were pupils older and bigger than she was. It required great tact to be a schoolteacher. To keep order among the big undisciplined boys without pistol and bull whip was a difficult and dangerous business. In one school in the mountains a teacher was raped by her pupils.

Olive Hamilton had not only to teach everything, but to all ages. Very few youths went past the eighth grade in those days, and what with farm duties some of them took fourteen or fifteen years to do it. Olive also had to practice a rudimentary medicine, for there were constant accidents. She sewed up knife cuts after a fight in the schoolyard. When a small barefooted boy was bitten by a rattlesnake, it was her duty to suck his toe to draw the poison out.

She taught reading to the first grade and algebra to the eighth. She led the singing, acted as a critic of literature, wrote the social notes that went weekly to the *Salinas Journal*. In addition, the whole social life of the area was in her hands, not only graduation exercises, but dances, meetings, debates, chorals, Christmas and May Day festivals, patriotic exudations on Decoration Day and the Fourth of July. She was on the election board and headed and held together all charities. It was far from an easy job, and it had duties and obligations beyond belief. The teacher had no private life. She was watched jealously for any weakness of character. She could not board with one family for more than one term, for that would cause jealousy—a family gained social ascendancy by boarding the teacher. If a marriageable son belonged to the family where she boarded a proposal was automatic; if there was more than one claimant, vicious fights occurred over her hand. The Aguita boys, three of them, nearly clawed each other to death over Olive Hamilton. Teachers rarely lasted very long in the country schools. The work was so hard and the proposals so constant that they married within a very short time.

This was a course Olive Hamilton determined she would not take. She did not share the intellectual enthusiasms of her father, but the time she had spent in Salinas determined her not to be a ranch wife. She wanted to live in a town, perhaps not so big as Salinas but at least not a crossroads. In Salinas, Olive had experienced niceties of living, the choir and vestments, Altar Guild, and bean suppers of the Episcopal church. She had partaken of the arts—road companies of plays and even operas, with their magic and promise of an aromatic world outside. She had gone to parties, played charades, competed in poetry readings, joined a chorus and orchestra. Salinas had tempted her. There she could go to a party dressed for the party and come home in the same dress, instead of rolling her clothes in a saddlebag and riding ten miles, then unrolling and pressing them.

Busy though she was with her teaching, Olive longed for the metropolitan life, and when the young man who had built the flour mill in King City sued properly for her hand, she accepted him subject to a long and secret engagement. The secrecy was required because if it were known there would be trouble among the young men in the neighborhood.

Olive had not her father's brilliance, but she did have a sense of fun, together with her mother's strong and undeviating will. What light and beauty could be forced down the throats of her reluctant pupils, she forced.

There was a wall against learning. A man wanted his children to read, to figure, and that was enough. More might make them dissatisfied and flighty. And there were plenty of examples to prove that learning made a boy leave the farm to live in the city—to consider himself better than his father. Enough arithmetic to measure land and lumber and to keep accounts, enough writing to order goods and write to relatives, enough reading for newspapers, almanacs, and farm journals, enough music for religious and patriotic display—that was enough to help a boy and not to lead him astray. Learning was for doctors, lawyers, and teachers, a class set off and not considered related to other people. There were some sports, of course, like Samuel Hamilton, and he was tolerated and liked, but if he had not been able to dig a well, shoe a horse, or run a threshing machine, God knows what would have been thought of the family.

Olive did marry her young man and did move, first to Paso Robles, then to King City, and finally to Salinas. She was as intuitive as a cat. Her acts were based on feelings rather than thoughts. She had her mother's firm chin and button nose and her father's fine eyes. She was the most definite of any of the Hamiltons except her mother. Her theology was a curious mixture of Irish fairies and an Old Testament Jehovah whom in her later life she confused with her father. Heaven was to her a nice home ranch inhabited by her dead relatives. External realities of a frustrating nature she obliterated by refusing to believe in them, and when one resisted her disbelief she raged at it. It was told of her that she cried bitterly because she could not go to two dances on one Saturday night. One was in Greenfield and the other in San Lucas—twenty miles apart. To have gone to both and then home would have entailed a sixty-mile horseback ride. This was a fact she could not blast with her disbelief, and so she cried with vexation and went to neither dance.

As she grew older she developed a scattergun method for dealing with unpleasant facts. When I, her only son, was sixteen I contracted pleural pneumonia, in that day a killing disease. I went down and down, until the wing tips of the angels brushed my eyes. Olive used her scattergun method of treating pleural pneumonia, and it worked. The Episcopalian minister prayed with and for me, the Mother Superior and nuns of the convent next to our house held me up to Heaven for relief twice a day, a distant relative who was a Christian Science reader held the thought for me. Every incantation, magic, and herbal formula known was brought out, and she got two good nurses and the town's best doctors. Her method was practical. I got well. She was loving and firm with her family, three girls and me, trained us in housework, dish washing, clothes washing, and manners. When angered she had a terrible eye which could blanch the skin off a bad child as easily as if he were a boiled almond.

When I recovered from my pneumonia it came time for me to learn to walk again. I had been nine weeks in bed, and the muscles had gone lax and the laziness of recovery had set in. When I was helped up, every nerve cried, and the wound in my side, which had been opened to drain the pus from the pleural cavity, pained horribly. I fell back in bed, crying, "I can't do it! I can't get up!"

Olive fixed me with her terrible eye. "Get up!" she said. "Your father has worked all day and sat up all night. He has gone into debt for you. Now get up!"

And I got up.

Debt was an ugly word and an ugly concept to Olive. A bill unpaid past the fifteenth of the month was a debt. The word had connotations of dirt and slovenliness and dishonor. Olive, who truly believed that her family was the best in the world, quite snobbishly would not permit it to be touched by debt. She planted that terror of debt so deeply in her children that even now, in a changed economic pattern where indebtedness is a part of living, I become restless when a bill is two days overdue. Olive never accepted the time-payment plan when it became popular. A thing bought on time was a thing you did not own and for which you were in debt. She saved for things she wanted, and this meant that the neighbors had new gadgets as much as two years before we did.

2

Olive had great courage. Perhaps it takes courage to raise children. And I must tell you what she did about the First World War. Her thinking was not international. Her first boundary was the geography of her family, second her town, Salinas, and finally there was a dotted line, not clearly defined, which was the county line. Thus she did not quite believe in the war, not even when Troop C, our militia cavalry, was called out, loaded its horses on a train, and set out for the open world.

Martin Hopps lived around the corner from us. He was wide, short, red-haired. His mouth was wide, and he had red eyes. He was almost the shyest boy in Salinas. To say good morning to him was to make him itch with self-consciousness. He belonged to Troop C because the armory had a basketball court.

If the Germans had known Olive and had been sensible they would have gone out of their way not to anger her. But they didn't know or they were stupid. When they killed Martin Hopps they lost the war because that made my mother mad and she took out after them. She had liked Martin Hopps. He had never hurt anyone. When they killed him Olive declared war on the German empire.

She cast about for a weapon. Knitting helmets and socks was not deadly enough for her. For a time she put on a Red Cross uniform and met other ladies similarly dressed in the armory, where bandages were rolled and reputations unrolled. This was all right, but it was not driving at the heart of the Kaiser. Olive wanted blood for the life of Martin Hopps. She found her weapon in Liberty bonds. She had never sold anything in her life beyond

an occasional angel cake for the Altar Guild in the basement of the Episcopal church, but she began to sell bonds by the bale. She brought ferocity to
her work. I think she made people afraid not to buy them. And when they
did buy from Olive she gave them a sense of actual combat, of putting a
bayonet in the stomach of Germany.

As her sales skyrocketed and stayed up, the Treasury Department began
to notice this new Amazon. First there came mimeographed letters of com-
mendation, then real letters signed by the Secretary of the Treasury, and
not with a rubber stamp either. We were proud but not so proud as when
prizes began to arrive, a German helmet (too small for any of us to wear), a
bayonet, a jagged piece of shrapnel set on an ebony base. Since we were not
eligible for armed conflict beyond marching with wooden guns, our mother's
war seemed to justify us. And then she outdid herself, and outdid everyone
in our part of the country. She quadrupled her already fabulous record and
she was awarded the fairest prize of all—a ride in an army airplane.

Oh, we were proud kids! Even vicariously this was an eminence we could
hardly stand. But my poor mother—I must tell you that there are certain
things in the existence of which my mother did not believe, against any
possible evidence to the contrary. One was a bad Hamilton and another was
the airplane. The fact that she had seen them didn't make her believe in
them one bit more.

In the light of what she did I have tried to imagine how she felt. Her
soul must have crawled with horror, for how can you fly in something that
does not exist? As a punishment the ride would have been cruel and unusual, but it was a prize, a gift, an honor, and an eminence. She must have
looked into our eyes and seen the shining idolatry there and understood
that she was trapped. Not to have gone would have let her family down. She
was surrounded, and there was no honorable way out save death. Once she
had decided to go up in the nonexistent thing she seemed to have had no
idea whatever that she would survive it.

Olive made her will—took lots of time with it and had it checked to be
sure it was legal. Then she opened her rosewood box wherein were the letters
her husband had written to her in courtship and since. We had not known
he wrote poetry to her, but he had. She built a fire in the grate and burned
every letter. They were hers, and she wanted no other human to see them.
She bought all new underwear. She had a horror of being found dead with
mended or, worse, unmended underclothes. I think perhaps she saw the
wide twisted mouth and embarrassed eyes of Martin Hopps on her and felt
that in some way she was reimbursing him for his stolen life. She was very
gentle with us and did not notice a badly washed dinner plate that left a
greasy stain on the dish towel.

This glory was scheduled to take place at the Salinas Race Track and Ro-
deo Grounds. We were driven to the track in an army automobile, feeling
more solemn and golden than at a good funeral. Our father was working at

the Spreckles Sugar Factory, five miles from town and could not get off, or perhaps didn't want to, for fear he could not stand the strain. But Olive had made arrangements, on pain of not going up, for the plane to try to fly as far as the sugar factory before it crashed.

I realize now that the several hundred people who had gathered simply came to see the airplane, but at that time we thought they were there to do my mother honor. Olive was not a tall woman and at that age she had begun to put on weight. We had to help her out of the car. She was probably stiff with fright but her little chin was set.

The plane stood in the field around which the race track was laid out. It was appallingly little and flimsy—an open cockpit biplane with wooden struts, tied with piano wire. The wings were covered with canvas. Olive was stunned. She went to the side as an ox to the knife. Over the clothes she was convinced were her burial clothes, two sergeants slipped on a coat, a padded coat, and a flight coat, and she grew rounder and rounder with each layer. Then a leather helmet and goggles, and with her little button of a nose and her pink cheeks you really had something. She looked like a goggled ball. The two sergeants hoisted her bodily into the cockpit and wedged her in. She filled the opening completely. As they strapped her in she suddenly came to life and began waving frantically for attention. One of the soldiers climbed up, listened to her, came over to my sister Mary, and led her to the side of the plane. Olive was tugging at the thick padded flight glove on her left hand. She got her hands free, took off her engagement ring with its tiny diamond, and handed it down to Mary. She set her gold wedding ring firmly, pulled the gloves back on, and faced the front. The pilot climbed into the front cockpit, and one of the sergeants threw his weight on the wooden propeller. The little ship taxied away and turned, and down the field it roared and staggered into the air, and Olive was looking straight ahead and probably her eyes were closed.

We followed it with our eyes as it swept up and away, leaving a lonesome silence behind it. The bond committee, the friends and relatives, the simple unhonored spectators didn't think of leaving the field. The plane became a speck in the sky toward Spreckles and disappeared. It was fifteen minutes before we saw it again, flying serenely and very high. Then to our horror it seemed to stagger and fall. It fell endlessly, caught itself, climbed, and made a loop. One of the sergeants laughed. For a moment the plane steadied and then it seemed to go crazy. It barrel-rolled, made Immelmann turns, inside and outside loops, and turned over and flew over the field upside down. We could see the black bullet which was our mother's helmet. One of the soldiers said quietly, "I think he's gone nuts. She's not a young woman."

The airplane landed steadily enough and ran up to the group. The motor died. The pilot climbed out, shaking his head in perplexity. "Goddamest woman I ever saw," he said. He reached up and shook Olive's nerveless hand and walked hurriedly away.

It took four men and quite a long time to get Olive out of the cockpit. She was so rigid they could not bend her. We took her home and put her to bed, and she didn't get up for two days.

What had happened came out slowly. The pilot talked some and Olive talked some, and both stories had to be put together before they made sense. They had flown out and circled the Spreckles Sugar Factory as ordered— circled it three times so that our father would be sure to see, and then the pilot thought of a joke. He meant no harm. He shouted something, and his face looked contorted. Olive could not hear over the noise of the engine. The pilot throttled down and shouted, "Stunt?" It was a kind of joke. Olive saw his goggled face and the slip stream caught his word and distorted it. What Olive heard was the word "stuck."

Well, she thought, here it is just as I knew it would be. Here was her death. Her mind flashed to see if she had forgotten anything—will made, let- ters burned, new underwear, plenty of food in the house for dinner. She wondered whether she had turned out the light in the back room. It was all in a second. Then she thought there might be an outside chance of survival. The young soldier was obviously frightened and fear might be the worst thing that could happen to him in handling the situation. If she gave way to the panic that lay on her heart it might frighten him more. She decided to encourage him. She smiled brightly and nodded to give him courage, and then the bottom fell out of the world. When he leveled out of his loop the pilot looked back again and shouted, "More?"

Olive was way beyond hearing anything, but her chin was set and she was determined to help the pilot so that he would not be too afraid before they hit the earth. She smiled and nodded again. At the end of each stunt he looked back, and each time she encouraged him. Afterward he said over and over, "She's the goddamest woman I ever saw. I tore up the rule book and she wanted more. Good Christ, what a pilot she would have made!"

FIFTEEN

Adam sat like a contented cat on his land. From the entrance to the little draw under a giant oak, which dipped its roots into underground water, he could look out over the acres lying away to the river and across to an alluvial flat and then up the rounded foothills on the western side. It was a fair place even in the summer when the sun laced into it. A line of river willows and sycamores banded it in the middle, and the western hills were yellow- brown with feed. For some reason the mountains to the west of the Salinas Valley have a thicker skin of earth on them than have the eastern foothills, so that the grass is richer there. Perhaps the peaks store rain and distribute it more evenly, and perhaps, being more wooded, they draw more rainfall.

Very little of the Sanchez, now Trask, place was under cultivation, but Adam in his mind could see the wheat growing tall and squares of green alfalfa near the river. Behind him he could hear the rackety hammering of the carpenters brought all the way from Salinas to rebuild the old Sanchez house. Adam had decided to live in the old house. Here was a place in which to plant his dynasty. The manure was scraped out, the old floors torn up, neck-rubbed window casings ripped away. New sweet wood was going in, pine sharp with resin and velvety redwood and a new roof of long split shakes. The old thick walls sucked in coat after coat of whitewash made with lime in salt water, which, as it dried, seemed to have a luminosity of its own.

He planned a permanent seat. A gardener had trimmed the ancient roses, planted geraniums, laid out the vegetable flat, and brought the living spring in little channels to wander back and forth through the garden. Adam foretasted comfort for himself and his descendants. In a shed, covered with tarpaulins, lay the crated heavy furniture sent from San Francisco and carted out from King City.

He would have good living too. Lee, his pigtailed Chinese cook, had made a special trip to Pajaro to buy the pots and kettles and pans, kegs, jars, copper, and glass for his kitchen. A new pigsty was building far from the house and downwind, with chicken and duck runs near and a kennel for the dogs to keep the coyotes away. It was no quick thing Adam contemplated, to be finished and ready in a hurry. His men worked deliberately and slowly. It was a long job. Adam wanted it well done. He inspected every wooden joint, stood off to study paint samples on a shingle. In the corner of his room catalogues piled up—catalogues for machinery, furnishings, seeds, fruit trees. He was glad now that his father had left him a rich man. In his mind a darkness was settling over his memory of Connecticut. Perhaps the hard flat light of the West was blotting out his birthplace. When he thought back to his father's house, to the farm, the town, to his brother's face, there was a blackness over all of it. And he shook off the memories.

Temporarily he had moved Cathy into the white-painted, clean spare house of Bordoni, there to await the home and the child. There was no doubt whatever that the child would be finished well before the house was ready. But Adam was unhurried.

"I want it built strong," he directed over and over. "I want it to last— copper nails and hard wood—nothing to rust and rot."

He was not alone in his preoccupation with the future. The whole valley, the whole West was that way. It was a time when the past had lost its sweetness and its sap. You'd go a good long road before you'd find a man, and he very old, who wished to bring back a golden past. Men were notched and comfortable in the present, hard and unfruitful as it was, but only as a doorstep into a fantastic future. Rarely did two men meet, or three stand in a bar, or a dozen gnaw tough venison in camp, that the valley's future, paralyz-ing in its grandeur, did not come up, not as conjecture but as a certainty.

"It'll be—who knows? maybe in our lifetime," they said.

And people found happiness in the future according to their present lack. Thus a man might bring his family down from a hill ranch in a drag—a big box nailed on oaken runners which pulled bumping down the broken hills. In the straw of the box, his wife would brace the children against the tooth-shattering, tongue-biting crash of the runners against stone and ground. And the father would set his heels and think, When the roads come in—then will be the time. Why, we'll sit high and happy in a surrey and get clear into King City in three hours—and what more in the world could you want than that?

Or let a man survey his grove of live-oak trees, hard as coal and hotter, the best firewood in the world. In his pocket might be a newspaper with a squib: "Oak cord wood is bringing ten dollars a cord in Los Angeles." Why, hell, when the railroad puts a branch out here, I could lay it down neat, broke up and seasoned, right beside the track, for a dollar and a half a cord. Let's go whole hog and say the Southern Pacific will charge three-fifty to carry it. There's still five dollars a cord, and there's three thousand cords in that little grove alone. That's fifteen thousand dollars right there.

There were others who prophesied, with rays shining on their foreheads, about the sometime ditches that would carry water all over the valley—who knows? maybe in our lifetime—or deep wells with steam engines to pump the water up out of the guts of the world. Can you imagine? Just think what this land would raise with plenty of water! Why, it will be a frigging garden!

Another man, but he was crazy, said that someday there'd be a way, maybe ice, maybe some other way, to get a peach like this here I got in my hand clear to Philadelphia.

In the towns they talked of sewers and inside toilets, and some already had them; and arc lights on the street corners—Salinas had those—and tele-phones. There wasn't any limit, no boundary at all, to the future. And it would be so a man wouldn't have room to store his happiness. Contentment would flood raging down the valley like the Salinas River in March of a thirty-inch year.

They looked over the flat dry dusty valley and the ugly mushroom towns and they saw a loveliness—who knows? maybe in our lifetime. That's one reason you couldn't laugh too much at Samuel Hamilton. He let his mind range more deliciously than any other, and it didn't sound so silly when you heard what they were doing in San Jose. Where Samuel went haywire was wondering whether people would be happy when all that came.

Happy? He's haywire now. Just let us get it, and we'll show you hap-piness.

And Samuel could remember hearing of a cousin of his mother's in Ire-land, a knight and rich and handsome, and anyway shot himself on a silken couch, sitting beside the most beautiful woman in the world who loved him.

"There's a capacity for appetite," Samuel said, "that a whole heaven and earth of cake can't satisfy."

Adam Trask nosed some of his happiness into futures but there was present contentment in him too. He felt his heart smack up against his throat when he saw Cathy sitting in the sun, quiet, her baby growing, and a transparency to her skin that made him think of the angels on Sunday School cards. Then a breeze would move her bright hair, or she would raise her eyes, and Adam would swell out in his stomach with a pressure of ecstasy that was close kin to grief.

If Adam rested like a sleek fed cat on his land, Cathy was catlike too. She had the inhuman attribute of abandoning what she could not get and of waiting for what she could get. These two gifts gave her great advantages. Her pregnancy had been an accident. When her attempt to abort herself failed and the doctor threatened her, she gave up that method. This does not mean that she reconciled herself to pregnancy. She sat it out as she would have weathered an illness. Her marriage to Adam had been the same. She was trapped and she took the best possible way out. She had not wanted to go to California either, but other plans were denied her for the time being. As a very young child she had learned to win by using the momentum of her opponent. It was easy to guide a man's strength where it was impossible to resist him. Very few people in the world could have known that Cathy did not want to be where she was and in the condition she was. She relaxed and waited for the change she knew must come some time. Cathy had the one quality required of a great and successful criminal: she trusted no one, confided in no one. Her self was an island. It is probable that she did not even look at Adam's new land or building house, or turn his towering plans to reality in her mind, because she did not intend to live here after her sickness was over, after her trap opened. But to his questions she gave proper answers; to do otherwise would be waste motion, and dissipated energy, and foreign to a good cat.

"See, my darling, how the house lies—windows looking down the valley?"

"It's beautiful."

"You know, it may sound foolish, but I find myself trying to think the way old Sanchez did a hundred years ago. How was the valley then? He must have planned so carefully. You know, he had pipes? He did—made out of redwood with a hole bored or burned through to carry the water down from the spring. We dug up some pieces of it."

"That's remarkable," she said. "He must have been clever."

"I'd like to know more about him. From the way the house sets, the trees he left, the shape and proportion of the house, he must have been a kind of an artist."

"He was a Spaniard, wasn't he? They're artistic people, I've heard. I remember in school about a painter—no, he was a Greek."

"I wonder where I could find out about old Sanchez."

"Well, somebody must know."

"All of his work and planning, and Bordoni kept cows in the house. You know what I wonder about most?"

"What, Adam?"

"I wonder if he had a Cathy and who she was."

She smiled and looked down and away from him. "The things you say."

"He must have had! He must have had. I never had energy or direction or —well, even a very great desire to live before I had you."

"Adam, you embarrass me. Adam, be careful. Don't joggle me, it hurts."

"I'm sorry. I'm so clumsy."

"No, you're not. You just don't think. Should I be knitting or sewing, do you suppose? I'm so comfortable just sitting."

"We'll buy everything we need. You just sit and be comfortable. I guess in a way you're working harder than anyone here. But the pay—the pay is wonderful."

"Adam, the scar on my forehead isn't going to go away, I'm afraid."

"The doctor said it would fade in time."

"Well, sometimes it seems to be getting fainter, and then it comes back. Don't you think it's darker today?"

"No, I don't."

But it was. It looked like a huge thumbprint, even to whorls of wrinkled skin. He put his finger near, and she drew her head away.

"Don't," she said. "It's tender to the touch. It turns red if you touch it."

"It will go away. Just takes a little time, that's all."

She smiled as he turned, but when he walked away her eyes were flat and directionless. She shifted her body restlessly. The baby was kicking. She relaxed and all her muscles loosened. She waited.

Lee came near where her chair was set under the biggest oak tree. "Missy likee tea?"

"No—yes, I would too."

Her eyes inspected him and her inspection could not penetrate the dark brown of his eyes. He made her uneasy. Cathy had always been able to shovel into the mind of any man and dig up his impulses and his desires. But Lee's brain gave and repelled like rubber. His face was lean and pleasant, his forehead broad, firm, and sensitive, and his lips curled in a perpetual smile. His long black glossy braided queue, tied at the bottom with a narrow piece of black silk, hung over his shoulder and moved rhythmically against his chest. When he did violent work he curled his queue on top of his head. He wore narrow cotton trousers, black heelless slippers, and a frogged Chinese smock. Whenever he could he hid his hands in his sleeves as though he were afraid for them, as most Chinese did in that day.

"I bling litta table," he said, bowed slightly, and shuffled away.

Cathy looked after him, and her eyebrows drew down in a scowl. She was not afraid of Lee, yet she was not comfortable with him either. But he was a good and respectful servant—the best. And what harm could he do her?

2

The summer progressed and the Salinas River retired underground or stood in green pools under high banks. The cattle lay drowsing all day long under the willows and only moved out at night to feed. An umber tone came to the grass. And the afternoon winds blowing inevitably down the valley started a dust that was like fog and raised it into the sky almost as high as the mountaintops. The wild oat roots stood up like nigger-heads where the winds blew the earth away. Along a polished earth, pieces of straw and twigs scampered until they were stopped by some rooted thing; and little stones rolled crookedly before the wind.

It became more apparent than ever why old Sanchez had built his house in the little draw, for the wind and the dust did not penetrate, and the spring, while it diminished, still gushed a head of cold clear water. But Adam, looking out over his dry dust-obscured land, felt the panic the Eastern man always does at first in California. In a Connecticut summer two weeks without rain is a dry spell and four a drought. If the countryside is not green it is dying. But in California it does not ordinarily rain at all between the end of May and the first of November. The Eastern man, though he has been told, feels the earth is sick in the rainless months.

Adam sent Lee with a note to the Hamilton place to ask Samuel to visit him and discuss the boring of some wells on his new place.

Samuel was sitting in the shade, watching his son Tom design and build a revolutionary coon trap, when Lee drove up in the Trask cart. Lee folded his hands in his sleeves and waited. Samuel read the note. "Tom," he said, "do you think you could keep the estate going while I run down and talk water with a dry man?"

"Why don't I go with you? You might need some help."

"At talking?—that I don't. It won't come to digging for some time if I'm any judge. With wells there's got to be a great deal of talk—five or six hundred words for every shovel of dirt."

"I'd like to go—it's Mr. Trask, isn't it? I didn't meet him when he came here."

"You'll do that when the digging starts. I'm older than you. I've got first claim on the talk. You know, Tom, a coon is going to reach his pretty little hand through here and let himself out. You know how clever they are."

"See this piece here? It screws on and turns down here. You couldn't get out of that yourself."

"I'm not so clever as a coon. I think you've worked it out, though. Tom, boy, would you saddle Doxology while I go tell your mother where I'm going?"

"I bling lig," said Lee.

"Well, I have to come home some time."

"I bling back."

"Nonsense," said Samuel. "I'll lead my horse in and ride back."

Samuel sat in the buggy beside Lee, and his clobber-footed saddle horse shuffled clumsily behind.

"What's your name?" Samuel asked pleasantly.

"Lee. Got more name. Lee papa family name. Call Lee."

"I've read quite a lot about China. You born in China?"

"No. Born here."

Samuel was silent for quite a long time while the buggy lurched down the wheel track toward the dusty valley. "Lee," he said at last, "I mean no disrespect, but I've never been able to figure why you people still talk pidgin when an illiterate baboon from the black bogs of Ireland, with a head full of Gaelic and a tongue like a potato, learns to talk a poor grade of English in ten years."

Lee grinned. "Me talkee Chinese talk," he said.

"Well, I guess you have your reasons. And it's not my affair. I hope you'll forgive me if I don't believe it, Lee."

Lee looked at him and the brown eyes under their rounded upper lids seemed to open and deepen until they weren't foreign any more, but man's eyes, warm with understanding. Lee chuckled. "It's more than a convenience," he said. "It's even more than self-protection. Mostly we have to use it to be understood at all."

Samuel showed no sign of having observed any change. "I can understand the first two," he said thoughtfully, "but the third escapes me."

Lee said, "I know it's hard to believe, but it has happened so often to me and to my friends that we take it for granted. If I should go up to a lady or a gentleman, for instance, and speak as I am doing now, I wouldn't be understood."

"Why not?"

"Pidgin they expect, and pidgin they'll listen to. But English from me they don't listen to, and so they don't understand it."

"Can that be possible? How do I understand you?"

"That's why I'm talking to you. You are one of the rare people who can separate your observation from your preconception. You see what is, where most people see what they expect."

"I hadn't thought of it. And I've not been so tested as you, but what you say has a candle of truth. You know, I'm very glad to talk to you. I've wanted to ask so many questions."

"Happy to oblige."

"So many questions. For instance, you wear the queue. I've read that it is a badge of slavery imposed by conquest by the Manchus on the Southern Chinese."

"That is true."

"Then why in the name of God do you wear it here, where the Manchus can't get at you?"

"Talkee Chinese talk. Queue Chinese fashion—you savvy?"

Samuel laughed loudly. "That does have the green touch of convenience," he said. "I wish I had a hidey-hole like that."

"I'm wondering whether I can explain," said Lee. "Where there is no likeness of experience it's very difficult. I understand you were not born in America."

"No, in Ireland."

"And in a few years you can almost disappear; while I, who was born in Grass Valley, went to school and several years to the University of California, have no chance of mixing."

"If you cut your queue, dressed and talked like other people?"

"No. I tried it. To the so-called whites I was still a Chinese, but an untrustworthy one; and at the same time my Chinese friends steered clear of me. I had to give it up."

Lee pulled up under a tree, got out and unfastened the check rein. "Time for lunch," he said. "I made a package. Would you like some?"

"Sure I would. Let me get down in the shade there. I forget to eat sometimes, and that's strange because I'm always hungry. I'm interested in what you say. It has a sweet sound of authority. Now it peeks into my mind that you should go back to China."

Lee smiled satirically at him. "In a few minutes I don't think you'll find a loose bar I've missed in a lifetime of search. I did go back to China. My father was a fairly successful man. It didn't work. They said I looked like a foreign devil; they said I spoke like a foreign devil. I made mistakes in manners, and I didn't know delicacies that had grown up since my father left. They wouldn't have me. You can believe it or not—I'm less foreign here than I was in China."

"I'll have to believe you because it's reasonable. You've given me things to think about until at least February twenty-seventh. Do you mind my questions?"

"As a matter of fact, no. The trouble with pidgin is that you get to thinking in pidgin. I write a great deal to keep my English up. Hearing and reading aren't the same as speaking and writing."

"Don't you ever make a mistake? I mean, break into English?"

"No, I don't. I think it's a matter of what is expected. You look at a man's eyes, you see that he expects pidgin and a shuffle, so you speak pidgin and shuffle."

"I guess that's right," said Samuel. "In my own way I tell jokes because people come all the way to my place to laugh. I try to be funny for them even when the sadness is on me."

"But the Irish are said to be a happy people, full of jokes."

"There's your pidgin and your queue. They're not. They're a dark people with a gift for suffering way past their deserving. It's said that without whisky to soak and soften the world, they'd kill themselves. But they tell jokes because it's expected of them."

Lee unwrapped a little bottle. "Would you like some of this? Chinee drink ng-ka-py."

"What is it?"

"Chinee blandy. Stlong dlink—as a matter of fact it's a brandy with a dosage of wormwood. Very powerful. It softens the world."

Samuel sipped from the bottle. "Tastes a little like rotten apples," he said.

"Yes, but nice rotten apples. Taste it back along your tongue toward the roots."

Samuel took a big swallow and tilted his head back. "I see what you mean. That *is* good."

"Here are some sandwiches, pickles, cheese, a can of buttermilk."

"You do well."

"Yes, I see to it."

Samuel bit into a sandwich. "I was shuffling over half a hundred questions. What you said brings the brightest one up. You don't mind?"

"Not at all. The only thing I do want to ask of you is not to talk this way when other people are listening. It would only confuse them and they wouldn't believe it anyway."

"I'll try," said Samuel. "If I slip, just remember that I'm a comical genius. It's hard to split a man down the middle and always to reach for the same half."

"I think I can guess what your next question is."

"What?"

"Why am I content to be a servant?"

"How in the world did you know?"

"It seemed to follow."

"Do you resent the question?"

"Not from you. There are no ugly questions except those clothed in condescension. I don't know where being a servant came into disrepute. It is the refuge of a philosopher, the food of the lazy, and, properly carried out, it is a position of power, even of love. I can't understand why more intelligent people don't take it as a career—learn to do it well and reap its benefits. A good servant has absolute security, not because of his master's kindness, but because of habit and indolence. It's a hard thing for a man to change spices or lay out his own socks. He'll keep a bad servant rather than change. But a good servant, and I am an excellent one, can completely control his master, tell him what to think, how to act, whom to marry, when to divorce, reduce him to terror as a discipline, or distribute happiness to him, and finally be mentioned in his will. If I had wished I could have

obbed, stripped, and beaten anyone I've worked for and come away with
hanks. Finally, in my circumstances I am unprotected. My master will de-
end me, protect me. You have to work and worry. I work less and worry less.
And I am a good servant. A bad one does no work and does no worrying, and
he still is fed, clothed, and protected. I don't know any profession where the
field is so cluttered with incompetents and where excellence is so rare."

Samuel leaned toward him, listening intently.

Lee went on, "It's going to be a relief after that to go back to pidgin."

"It's a very short distance to the Sanchez place. Why did we stop so
near?" Samuel asked.

"Allee time talkee. Me Chinee number one boy. You leddy go now?"

"What? Oh, sure. But it must be a lonely life."

"That's the only fault with it," said Lee. "I've been thinking of going to
San Francisco and starting a little business."

"Like a laundry? Or a grocery store?"

"No. Too many Chinese laundries and restaurants. I thought perhaps a
bookstore. I'd like that, and the competition wouldn't be too great. I probably won't do it though. A servant loses his initiative."

3

In the afternoon Samuel and Adam rode over the land. The wind came up
as it did every afternoon, and the yellow dust ran into the sky.

"Oh, it's a good piece," Samuel cried. "It's a rare piece of land."

"Seems to me it's blowing away bit by bit," Adam observed.

"No, it's just moving over a little. You lose some to the James ranch but
you get some from the Southeys."

"Well, I don't like the wind. Makes me nervous."

"Nobody likes wind for very long. It makes animals nervous and restless
too. I don't know whether you noticed, but a little farther up the valley
they're planting windbreaks of gum trees. Eucalyptus—comes from Australia.
They say the gums grow ten feet a year. Why don't you try a few rows and
see what happens? In time they should back up the wind a little, and they
make grand firewood."

"Good idea," Adam said. "What I really want is water. This wind would
pump all the water I could find. I thought if I could bring in a few wells
and irrigate, the topsoil wouldn't blow away. I might try some beans."

Samuel squinted into the wind. "I'll try to get you water if you want," he
said. "And I've got a little pump I made that will bring it up fast. It's my
own invention. A windmill is a pretty costly thing. Maybe I could build them
for you and save you some money."

"That's good," said Adam. "I wouldn't mind the wind if it worked for me.
And if I could get water I might plant alfalfa."

"It's never brought much of a price."

"I wasn't thinking of that. Few weeks ago I took a drive up around Green field and Gonzales. Some Swiss have moved in there. They've got nice little dairy herds, and they get four crops of alfalfa a year."

"I heard about them. They brought in Swiss cows."

Adam's face was bright with plans. "That's what I want to do. Sell butter and cheese and feed the milk to pigs."

"You're going to bring credit to the valley," Samuel said. "You're going to be a real joy to the future."

"If I can get water."

"I'll get you water if there's any to be got. I'll find it. I brought my magic wand." He patted a forked stick tied to his saddle.

Adam pointed to the left where a wide flat place was covered with a low growth of sagebrush. "Now then," he said, "thirty-six acres and almost level as a floor. I put an auger down. Topsoil averages three and a half feet, sand on top and loam within plow reach. Think you could get water there?"

"I don't know," Samuel said. "I'll see."

He dismounted, handed his reins to Adam, and untied his forked wand. He took the forks in his two hands and walked slowly, his arms out and stretched before him and the wand tip up. His steps took a zigzag course. Once he frowned and backed up a few steps, then shook his head and went on. Adam rode slowly along behind, leading the other horse.

Adam kept his eyes on the stick. He saw it quiver and then jerk a little, as though an invisible fish were tugging at a line. Samuel's face was taut with attention. He continued on until the point of the wand seemed to be pulled strongly downward against his straining arms. He made a slow circle, broke off a piece of sagebrush, and dropped it on the ground. He moved well outside his circle, held up his stick again, and moved inward toward his marker. As he came near it, the point of the stick was drawn down again. Samuel sighed and relaxed and dropped his wand on the ground. "I can get water here," he said. "And not very deep. The pull was strong, plenty of water."

"Good," said Adam. "I want to show you a couple more places."

Samuel whittled out a stout piece of sagewood and drove it into the soil. He made a split on the top and fitted a crosspiece on for a mark. Then he kicked the brittle brush down in the area so he could find his marker again.

On a second try three hundred yards away the wand seemed nearly torn downward out of his hands. "Now there's a whole world of water here," he said.

The third try was not so productive. After half an hour he had only the slightest sign.

The two men rode slowly back toward the Trask house. The afternoon was golden, for the yellow dust in the sky gilded the light. As always the wind began to drop as the day waned, but it sometimes took half the night for the dust to settle out of the air. "I knew it was a good place," Samuel said. "Anyone can see that. But I didn't know it was that good. You must have a great drain under your land from the mountains. You know how to pick land, Mr. Trask."

Adam smiled. "We had a farm in Connecticut," he said. "For six generations we dug stones out. One of the first things I remember is sledding stones over to the walls. I thought that was the way all farms were. It's strange to me and almost sinful here. If you wanted a stone, you'd have to go a long way for it."

"The ways of sin are curious," Samuel observed. "I guess if a man had to shuck off everything he had, inside and out, he'd manage to hide a few little sins somewhere for his own discomfort. They're the last things we'll give up."

"Maybe that's a good thing to keep us humble. The fear of God in us."

"I guess so," said Samuel. "And I guess humility must be a good thing, since it's a rare man who has not a piece of it, but when you look at humbleness it's hard to see where its value rests unless you grant that it is a pleasurable pain and very precious. Suffering—I wonder has it been properly looked at."

"Tell me about your stick," Adam said. "How does it work?"

Samuel stroked the fork now tied to his saddle strings. "I don't really believe in it save that it works." He smiled at Adam. "Maybe it's this way. Maybe I know where the water is, feel it in my skin. Some people have a gift in this direction or that. Suppose—well, call it humility, or a deep disbelief in myself, forced me to do a magic to bring up to the surface the thing I know anyway. Does that make any sense to you?"

"I'd have to think about it," said Adam.

The horses picked their own way, heads hung low, reins loosened against the bits.

"Can you stay the night?" Adam asked.

"I can but better not. I didn't tell Liza I'd be away the night. I'd not like to give her a worry."

"But she knows where you are."

"Sure she knows. But I'll ride home tonight. It doesn't matter the time. If you'd like to ask me to supper I'd be glad. And when do you want me to start on the wells?"

"Now—as soon as you can."

"You know it's no cheap thing, indulging yourself with water. I'd have to charge you fifty cents or more a foot, depending on what we find down there. It can run into money."

"I have the money. I want the wells. Look, Mr. Hamilton—"

" 'Samuel' would be easier."

"Look, Samuel, I mean to make a garden of my land. Remember my name is Adam. So far I've had no Eden, let alone been driven out."

"It's the best reason I ever heard for making a garden," Samuel exclaimed. He chuckled. "Where will the orchard be?"

Adam said, "I won't plant apples. That would be looking for accidents."

"What does Eve say to that? She has a say, you remember. And Eves delight in apples."

"Not this one." Adam's eyes were shining. "You don't know this Eve. She'll celebrate my choice. I don't think anyone can know her goodness."

"You have a rarity. Right now I can't recall any greater gift."

They were coming near to the entrance to the little side valley in which was the Sanchez house. They could see the rounded green tops of the great live oaks.

"Gift," Adam said softly. "You can't know. No one can know. I had a gray life, Mr. Hamilton—Samuel. Not that it was bad compared to other lives, but it was nothing. I don't know why I tell you this."

"Maybe because I like to hear."

"My mother—died—before my memory. My stepmother was a good woman but troubled and ill. My father was a stern, fine man—maybe a great man."

"You couldn't love him?"

"I had the kind of feeling you have in church, and not a little fear in it."

Samuel nodded. "I know—and some men want that." He smiled ruefully. "I've always wanted the other. Liza says it's the weak thing in me."

"My father put me in the army, in the West, against the Indians."

"You told me. But you don't think like a military man."

"I wasn't a good one. I seem to be telling you everything."

"You must want to. There's always a reason."

"A soldier must want to do the things we had to do—or at least be satisfied with them. I couldn't find good enough reasons for killing men and women, nor understand the reasons when they were explained."

They rode on in silence for a time. Adam went on, "I came out of the army like dragging myself muddy out of a swamp. I wandered for a long time before going home to a remembered place I did not love."

"Your father?"

"He died, and home was a place to sit around or work around, waiting for death the way you might wait for a dreadful picnic."

"Alone?"

"No, I have a brother."

"Where is he—waiting for the picnic?"

"Yes—yes, that's exactly what. Then Cathy came. Maybe I will tell you some time when I can tell and you want to hear."

"I'll want to hear," Samuel said. "I eat stories like grapes."

"A kind of light spread out from her. And everything changed color. And the world opened out. And a day was good to awaken to. And there were no limits to anything. And the people of the world were good and handsome. And I was not afraid any more."

"I recognize it," Samuel said. "That's an old friend of mine. It never dies but sometimes it moves away, or you do. Yes, that's my acquaintance—eyes, nose, mouth, and hair."

"All this coming out of a little hurt girl."

"And not out of you?"

"Oh, no, or it would have come before. No, Cathy brought it, and it lives around her. And now I've told you why I want the wells. I have to repay somehow for value received. I'm going to make a garden so good, so beautiful, that it will be a proper place for her to live and a fitting place for her light to shine on."

Samuel swallowed several times, and he spoke with a dry voice out of a pinched-up throat. "I can see my duty," he said. "I can see it plainly before me if I am any kind of man, any kind of friend to you."

"What do you mean?"

Samuel said satirically, "It's my duty to take this thing of yours and kick it in the face, then raise it up and spread slime on it thick enough to blot out its dangerous light." His voice grew strong with vehemence. "I should hold it up to you muck-covered and show you its dirt and danger. I should warn you to look closer until you can see how ugly it really is. I should ask you to think of inconstancy and give you examples. I should give you Othello's handkerchief. Oh, I know I should. And I should straighten out your tangled thoughts, show you that the impulse is gray as lead and rotten as a dead cow in wet weather. If I did my duty well, I could give you back your bad old life and feel good about it, and welcome you back to the musty membership in the lodge."

"Are you joking? Maybe I shouldn't have told—"

"It is the duty of a friend. I had a friend who did the duty once for me. But I'm a false friend. I'll get no credit for it among my peers. It's a lovely thing, preserve it, and glory in it. And I'll dig your wells if I have to drive my rig to the black center of the earth. I'll squeeze water out like juice from an orange."

They rode under the great oaks and toward the house. Adam said, "There she is, sitting outside." He shouted, "Cathy, he says there's water—lots of it." Aside he said excitedly, "Did you know she's going to have a baby?"

"Even at this distance she looks beautiful," Samuel said.

4

Because the day had been hot, Lee set a table outside under an oak tree, and as the sun neared the western mountains he padded back and forth from the kitchen, carrying the cold meats, pickles, potato salad, coconut cake, and peach pie which were supper. In the center of the table he placed a gigantic stoneware pitcher full of milk.

Adam and Samuel came from the wash house, their hair and faces shining with water, and Samuel's beard was fluffy after its soaping. They stood at the trestle table and waited until Cathy came out.

She walked slowly, picking her way as though she were afraid she would fall. Her full skirt and apron concealed to a certain extent her swelling abdomen. Her face was untroubled and childlike, and she clasped her hands in front of her. She had reached the table before she looked up and glanced from Samuel to Adam.

Adam held her chair for her. "You haven't met Mr. Hamilton, dear," he said.

She held out her hand. "How do you do," she said.

Samuel had been inspecting her. "It's a beautiful face," he said, "I'm glad to meet you. You are well, I hope?"

"Oh, yes. Yes, I'm well."

The men sat down. "She makes it formal whether she wants to or not. Every meal is a kind of occasion," Adam said.

"Don't talk like that," she said. "It isn't true."

"Doesn't it feel like a party to you, Samuel?" he asked.

"It does so, and I can tell you there's never been such a candidate for a party as I am. And my children—they're worse. My boy Tom wanted to come today. He's spoiling to get off the ranch."

Samuel suddenly realized that he was making his speech last to prevent silence from falling on the table. He paused, and the silence dropped. Cathy looked down at her plate while she ate a sliver of roast lamb. She looked up as she put it between her small sharp teeth. Her wide-set eyes communicated nothing. Samuel shivered.

"It isn't cold, is it?" Adam asked.

"Cold? No. A goose walked over my grave, I guess."

"Oh, yes, I know that feeling."

The silence fell again. Samuel waited for some speech to start up, knowing in advance that it would not.

"Do you like our valley, Mrs. Trask?"

"What? Oh, yes."

"If it isn't impertinent to ask, when is your baby due?"

"In about six weeks," Adam said. "My wife is one of those paragons—a woman who does not talk very much."

"Sometimes a silence tells the most," said Samuel, and he saw Cathy's eyes leap up and down again, and it seemed to him that the scar on her forehead grew darker. Something had flicked her the way you'd flick a horse with the braided string popper on a buggy whip. Samuel couldn't recall what he had said that had made her give a small inward start. He felt a tenseness coming over him that was somewhat like the feeling he had just before the water wand pulled down, an awareness of something strange and strained. He glanced at Adam and saw that he was looking raptly at his wife. Whatever was strange was not strange to Adam. His face had happiness on it.

Cathy was chewing a piece of meat, chewing with her front teeth. Samuel had never seen anyone chew that way before. And when she had swallowed, her little tongue flicked around her lips. Samuel's mind repeated, "Something—something—can't find what it is. Something wrong," and the silence hung on the table.

There was a shuffle behind him. He turned. Lee set a teapot on the table and shuffled away.

Samuel began to talk to push the silence away. He told how he had first come to the valley fresh from Ireland, but within a few words neither Cathy nor Adam was listening to him. To prove it, he used a trick he had devised to discover whether his children were listening when they begged him to read to them and would not let him stop. He threw in two sentences of nonsense. There was no response from either Adam or Cathy. He gave up.

He bolted his supper, drank his tea scalding hot, and folded his napkin. "Ma'am, if you'll excuse me, I'll ride off home. And I thank you for your hospitality."

"Good night," she said.

Adam jumped to his feet. He seemed torn out of a reverie. "Don't go now. I hoped to persuade you to stay the night."

"No, thank you, but that I can't. And it's not a long ride. I think—of course, I know—there'll be a moon."

"When will you start the wells?"

"I'll have to get my rig together, do a piece of sharpening, and put my house in order. In a few days I'll send the equipment with Tom."

The life was flowing back into Adam. "Make it soon," he said. "I want it soon. Cathy, we're going to make the most beautiful place in the world. There'll be nothing like it anywhere."

Samuel switched his gaze to Cathy's face. It did not change. The eyes were flat and the mouth with its small up-curve at the corners was carven.

"That will be nice," she said.

For just a moment Samuel had an impulse to do or say something to shock her out of her distance. He shivered again.

"Another goose?" Adam asked.

"Another goose." The dusk was falling and already the tree forms were dark against the sky. "Good night, then."

"I'll walk down with you."

"No, stay with your wife. You haven't finished your supper."

"But I—"

"Sit down, man. I can find my own horse, and if I can't I'll steal one of yours." Samuel pushed Adam gently down in his chair. "Good night. Good night. Good night, ma'am." He walked quickly toward the shed.

Old platter-foot Doxology was daintily nibbling hay from the manger with lips like two flounders. The halter chain clinked against wood. Samuel lifted down his saddle from the big nail where it hung by one wooden

stirrup and swung it over the broad back. He was lacing the latigo through
the cinch rings when there was a small stir behind him. He turned and saw
the silhouette of Lee against the last light from the open shadows.

"When you come back?" the Chinese asked softly.

"I don't know. In a few days or a week. Lee, what is it?"

"What is what?"

"By God, I got creepy! Is there something wrong here?"

"What do you mean?"

"You know damn well what I mean."

"Chinee boy jus' workee—not hear, not talkee."

"Yes. I guess you're right. Sure, you're right. Sorry I asked you. It wasn't
very good manners." He turned back, slipped the bit in Dox's mouth, and
laced the big flop ears into the headstall. He slipped the halter and dropped
it in the manger. "Good night, Lee," he said.

"Mr. Hamilton—"

"Yes?"

"Do you need a cook?"

"On my place I can't afford a cook."

"I'd work cheap."

"Liza would kill you. Why—you want to quit?"

"Just thought I'd ask," said Lee. "Good night."

<h1 style="text-align:center">5</h1>

Adam and Cathy sat in the gathering dark under the tree.

"He's a good man," Adam said. "I like him. I wish I could persuade him
to take over here and run this place—kind of superintendent."

Cathy said, "He's got his own place and his own family."

"Yes, I know. And it's the poorest land you ever saw. He could make
more at wages from me. I'll ask him. It does take a time to get used to a
new country. It's like being born again and having to learn all over. I used
to know from what quarter the rains came. It's different here. And once I
knew in my skin whether wind would blow, when it would be cold. But I'll
learn. It just takes a little time. Are you comfortable, Cathy?"

"Yes."

"One day, and not too far away, you'll see the whole valley green with
alfalfa—see it from the fine big windows of the finished house. I'll plant
rows of gum trees, and I'm going to send away for seeds and plants—put in
a kind of experimental farm. I might try lichee nuts from China. I wonder
if they would grow here. Well, I can try. Maybe Lee could tell me. And once
the baby's born you can ride over the whole place with me. You haven't
really seen it. Did I tell you? Mr. Hamilton is going to put up windmills,
and we'll be able to see them turning from here." He stretched his legs out

comfortably under the table. "Lee should bring candles," he said. "I wonder what's keeping him."

Cathy spoke very quietly. "Adam, I didn't want to come here. I am not going to stay here. As soon as I can I will go away."

"Oh, nonsense." He laughed. "You're like a child away from home for the first time. You'll love it once you get used to it and the baby is born. You know, when I first went away to the army I thought I was going to die of homesickness. But I got over it. We all get over it. So don't say silly things like that."

"It's not a silly thing."

"Don't talk about it, dear. Everything will change after the baby is born. You'll see. You'll see."

He clapped his hands behind his head and looked up at the faint stars through the tree branches.

SIXTEEN

Samuel Hamilton rode back home in a night so flooded with moonlight that the hills took on the quality of the white and dusty moon. The trees and earth were moon-dry, silent and airless and dead. The shadows were black without shading and the open places white without color. Here and there Samuel could see secret movement, for the moon-feeders were at work—the deer which browse all night when the moon is clear and sleep under thickets in the day. Rabbits and field mice and all other small hunted that feel safer in the concealing light crept and hopped and crawled and froze to resemble stones or small bushes when ear or nose suspected danger. The predators were working too—the long weasels like waves of brown light; the cobby wildcats crouching near to the ground, almost invisible except when their yellow eyes caught light and flashed for a second; the foxes, sniffling with pointed up-raised noses for a warm-blooded supper; the raccoons padding near still water, talking frogs. The coyotes nuzzled along the slopes and, torn with sorrow-joy, raised their heads and shouted their feeling, half keen, half laughter, at their goddess moon. And over all the shadowy screech owls sailed, drawing a smudge of shadowy fear below them on the ground. The wind of the afternoon was gone and only a little breeze like a sigh was stirred by the restless thermals of the warm, dry hills.

Doxology's loud off-beat hoofsteps silenced the night people until after he had passed. Samuel's beard glinted white, and his graying hair stood up high on his head. He had hung his black hat on his saddle horn. An ache was on the top of his stomach, an apprehension that was like a sick thought.

It was a *Weltschmerz*—which we used to call "Welshrats"—the world sadness that rises into the soul like a gas and spreads despair so that you probe for the offending event and can find none.

Samuel went back in his mind over the fine ranch and the indications of water—no Welshrats could come out of that unless he sheltered a submerged envy. He looked in himself for envy and could find none. He went on to Adam's dream of a garden like Eden and to Adam's adoration of Cathy. Nothing there unless—unless his secret mind brooded over his own healed loss. But that was so long ago he had forgotten the pain. The memory was mellow and warm and comfortable, now that it was all over. His loins and his thighs had forgotten hunger.

As he rode through the light and dark of tree-shade and open his mind moved on. When had the Welshrats started crawling in his chest? He found it then—and it was Cathy, pretty, tiny, delicate Cathy. But what about her? She was silent, but many women were silent. What was it? Where had it come from? He remembered that he had felt an imminence akin to the one that came to him when he held the water wand. And he remembered the shivers when the goose walked over his grave. Now he had pinned it down in time and place and person. It had come at dinner and it had come from Cathy.

He built her face in front of him and studied her wide-set eyes, delicate nostrils, mouth smaller than he liked but sweet, small firm chin, and back to her eyes. Were they cold? Was it her eyes? He was circling to the point. The eyes of Cathy had no message, no communication of any kind. There was nothing recognizable behind them. They were not human eyes. They reminded him of something—what was it?—some memory, some picture. He strove to find it and then it came of itself.

It rose out of the years complete with all its colors and its cries, its crowded feelings. He saw himself, a very little boy, so small that he had to reach high for his father's hand. He felt the cobbles of Londonderry under his feet and the crush and gaiety of the one big city he had seen. A fair, it was, with puppet shows and stalls of produce and horses and sheep penned right in the street for sale or trade or auction, and other stalls of bright-colored knickknackery, desirable, and because his father was gay, almost possessable.

And then the people turned like a strong river, and they were carried along a narrow street as though they were chips on a flood tide, pressure at chest and back and the feet keeping up. The narrow street opened out to a square, and against the gray wall of a building there was a high structure of timbers and a noosed rope hanging down.

Samuel and his father were pushed and bunted by the water of people, pushed closer and closer. He could hear in his memory ear his father saying, "It's no thing for a child. It's no thing for anybody, but less for a child." His father struggled to turn, to force his way back against the flood wave of people. "Let us out. Please let us out. I've a child here."

The wave was faceless and it pushed without passion. Samuel raised his head to look at the structure. A group of dark-clothed, dark-hatted men had climbed up on the high platform. And in their midst was a man with golden hair, dressed in dark trousers and a light blue shirt open at the throat. Samuel and his father were so close that the boy had to raise his head high to see.

The golden man seemed to have no arms. He looked out over the crowd and then looked down, looked right at Samuel. The picture was clear, lighted and perfect. The man's eyes had no depth—they were not like other eyes, not like the eyes of a man.

Suddenly there was quick movement on the platform, and Samuel's father put both his hands on the boy's head so that his palms cupped over the ears and his fingers met behind. The hands forced Samuel's head down and forced his face tight in against his father's black best coat. Struggle as he would, he could not move his head. He could see only a band of light around the edges of his eyes and only a muffled roar of sound came to his ears through his father's hands. He heard heartbeats in his ears. Then he felt his father's hands and arms grow rigid with set muscles, and against his face he could feel his father's deep-caught breathing and then deep intake and held breath, and his father's hands, trembling.

A little more there was to it, and he dug it up and set it before his eyes in the air ahead of the horse's head—a worn and battered table at a pub, loud talk and laughter. A pewter mug was in front of his father, and a cup of hot milk, sweet and aromatic with sugar and cinnamon, before himself. His father's lips were curiously blue and there were tears in his father's eyes.

"I'd never have brought you if I'd known. It's not fit for any man to see, and sure not for a small boy."

"I didn't see any," Samuel piped. "You held my head down."

"I'm glad of that."

"What was it?"

"I'll have to tell you. They were killing a bad man."

"Was it the golden man?"

"Yes, it was. And you must put no sorrow on him. He had to be killed. Not once but many times he did dreadful things—things only a fiend could think of. It's not his hanging sorrows me but that they make a holiday of it that should be done secretly, in the dark."

"I saw the golden man. He looked right down at me."

"For that even more I thank God he's gone."

"What did he do?"

"I'll never tell you nightmare things."

"He had the strangest eyes, the golden man. They put me in mind of a goat's eyes."

"Drink your sweety-milk and you shall have a stick with ribbons and a long whistle like silver."

"And the shiny box with a picture into it?"

"That also, so you drink up your sweety-milk and beg no more."

There it was, mined out of the dusty past.

Doxology was climbing the last rise before the hollow of the home ranch and the big feet stumbled over stones in the roadway.

It was the eyes, of course, Samuel thought. Only twice in my life have I seen eyes like that—not like human eyes. And he thought, It's the night and the moon. Now what connection under heaven can there be between the golden man hanged so long ago and the sweet little bearing mother? Liza's right. My imagination will get me a passport to hell one day. Let me dig this nonsense out, else I'll be searching that poor child for evil. This is how we can get trapped. Now think hard and then lose it. Some accident of eye shape and eye color, it is. But no, that's not it. It's a look and has no reference to shape or color. Well, why is a look evil then? Maybe such a look may have been sometime on a holy face. Now, stop this romancing and never let it trouble again—ever. He shivered. I'll have to set up a goose fence around my grave, he thought.

And Samuel Hamilton resolved to help greatly with the Salinas Valley Eden, to make a secret guilt-payment for his ugly thoughts.

2

Liza Hamilton, her apple cheeks flaming red, moved like a caged leopard in front of the stove when Samuel came into the kitchen in the morning. The oakwood fire roared up past an open damper to heat the oven for the bread, which lay white and rising in the pans. Liza had been up before dawn. She always was. It was just as sinful to her to lie abed after light as it was to be abroad after dark. There was no possible virtue in either. Only one person in the world could with impunity and without crime lie between her crisp ironed sheets after dawn, after sunup, even to the far reaches of mid-morning, and that was her youngest and last born, Joe.

Only Tom and Joe lived on the ranch now. And Tom, big and red, already cultivating a fine flowing mustache, sat at the kitchen table with his sleeves rolled down as he had been mannered. Liza poured thick batter from a pitcher onto a soapstone griddle. The hot cakes rose like little hassocks, and small volcanos formed and erupted on them until they were ready to be turned. A cheerful brown, they were, with tracings of darker brown. And the kitchen was full of the good sweet smell of them.

Samuel came in from the yard where he had been washing himself. His face and beard gleamed with water, and he turned down the sleeves of his blue shirt as he entered the kitchen. Rolled-up sleeves at the table were not acceptable to Mrs. Hamilton. They indicated either an ignorance or a flouting of the niceties.

"I'm late, Mother," Samuel said.

She did not look around at him. Her spatula moved like a striking snake and the hot cakes settled their white sides hissing on the soapstone. "What time was it you came home?" she asked.

"Oh, it was late—late. Must have been near eleven. I didn't look, fearing to waken you."

"I did not waken," Liza said grimly. "And maybe you can find it healthy to rove all night, but the Lord God will do what He sees fit about that." It was well known that Liza Hamilton and the Lord God held similar convictions on nearly every subject. She turned and reached and a plate of crisp hot cakes lay between Tom's hands. "How does the Sanchez place look?" she asked.

Samuel went to his wife, leaned down from his height, and kissed her round red cheek. "Good morning, Mother. Give me your blessing."

"Bless you," said Liza automatically.

Samuel sat down at the table and said, "Bless you, Tom. Well, Mr. Trask is making great changes. He's fitting up the old house to live in."

Liza turned sharply from the stove. "The one where the cows and pigs have slept the years?"

"Oh, he's ripped out the floors and window casings. All new and new painted."

"He'll never get the smell of pigs out," Liza said firmly. "There's a pungency left by a pig that nothing can wash out or cover up."

"Well, I went inside and looked around, Mother, and I could smell nothing except paint."

"When the paint dries you'll smell pig," she said.

"He's got a garden laid out with spring water running through it, and he's set a place apart for flowers, roses and the like, and some of the bushes are coming clear from Boston."

"I don't see how the Lord God puts up with such waste," she said grimly. "Not that I don't like a rose myself."

"He said he'd try to root some cuttings for me," Samuel said.

Tom finished his hot cakes and stirred his coffee. "What kind of a man is he, Father?"

"Well, I think he's a fine man—has a good tongue and a fair mind. He's given to dreaming—"

"Hear now the pot blackguarding the kettle," Liza interrupted.

"I know, Mother, I know. But have you ever thought that my dreaming takes the place of something I haven't? Mr. Trask has practical dreams and the sweet dollars to make them solid. He wants to make a garden of his land, and he will do it too."

"What's his wife like?" Liza asked.

"Well, she's very young and very pretty. She's quiet, hardly speaks, but then she's having her first baby soon."

"I know that," Liza said. "What was her name before?"

"I don't know."

"Well, where did she come from?"

"I don't know."

She put his plate of hot cakes in front of him and poured coffee in his cup and refilled Tom's cup. "What did you learn then? How does she dress?"

"Why, very nice, pretty—a blue dress and a little coat, pink but tight about the waist."

"You've an eye for that. Would you say they were made clothes or store bought?"

"Oh, I think store bought."

"You would not know," Liza said firmly. "You thought the traveling suit Dessie made to go to San Jose was store bought."

"Dessie's the clever love," said Samuel. "A needle sings in her hands."

Tom said, "Dessie's thinking of opening a dressmaking shop in Salinas."

"She told me," Samuel said. "She'd make a great success of it."

"Salinas?" Liza put her hands on her hips. "Dessie didn't tell me."

"I'm afraid we've done bad service to our dearie," Samuel said. "Here she wanted to save it for a real tin-plate surprise to her mother and we've leaked it like wheat from a mouse-hole sack."

"She might have *told* me," said Liza. "I don't like surprises. Well, go on— what was she doing?"

"Who?"

"Why, Mrs. Trask of course."

"Doing? Why, sitting, sitting in a chair under an oak tree. Her time's not far."

"Her hands, Samuel, her hands—what was she doing with her hands?"

Samuel searched his memory. "Nothing I guess. I remember—she had little hands and she held them clasped in her lap."

Liza sniffed. "Not sewing, not mending, not knitting?"

"No, Mother."

"I don't know that it's a good idea for you to go over there. Riches and idleness, devil's tools, and you've not a very sturdy resistance."

Samuel raised his head and laughed with pleasure. Sometimes his wife delighted him but he could never tell her how. "It's only the riches I'll be going there for, Liza. I meant to tell you after breakfast so you could sit down to hear. He wants me to bore four or five wells for him, and maybe put windmills and storage tanks."

"Is it all talk? Is it a windmill turned by water? Will he pay you or will you come back excusing as usual. 'He'll pay when his crop comes in,'" she mimicked, "'He'll pay when his rich uncle dies.' It's my experience,

Samuel, and should be yours, that if they don't pay presently they never pay at all. We could buy a valley farm with your promises."

"Adam Trask will pay," said Samuel. "He's well fixed. His father left him a fortune. It's a whole winter of work, Mother. We'll lay something by and we'll have a Christmas to scrape the stars. He'll pay fifty cents a foot, and the windmills, Mother. I can make everything but the casings right here. I'll need the boys to help. I want to take Tom and Joe."

"Joe can't go," she said. "You know he's delicate."

"I thought I might scrape off some of his delicacy. He can starve on delicacy."

"Joe can't go," she said finally. "And who is to run the ranch while you and Tom are gone?"

"I thought I'd ask George to come back. He doesn't like a clerk's job even if it is in King City."

"Like it he may not, but he can take a measure of discomfort for eight dollars a week."

"Mother," Samuel cried, "here's our chance to scratch our name in the First National Bank! Don't throw the weight of your tongue in the path of fortune. Please, Mother!"

She grumbled to herself all morning over her work while Tom and Samuel went over the boring equipment, sharpened bits, drew sketches of windmills new in design, and measured for timbers and redwood water tanks. In the midmorning Joe came out to join them, and he became so fascinated that he asked Samuel to let him go.

Samuel said, "Offhand I'd say I'm against it, Joe. Your mother needs you here."

"But I want to go, Father. And don't forget, next year I'll be going to college in Palo Alto. And that's going away, isn't it? Please let me go. I'll work hard."

"I'm sure you would if you could come. But I'm against it. And when you talk to your mother about it, I'll thank you to let it slip that I'm against it. You might even throw in that I refused you."

Joe grinned, and Tom laughed aloud.

"Will you let her persuade you?" Tom asked.

Samuel scowled at his sons. "I'm a hard-opinioned man," he said. "Once I've set my mind, oxen can't stir me. I've looked at it from all angles and my word is—Joe can't go. You wouldn't want to make a liar of my word, would you?"

"I'll go in and talk to her now," said Joe.

"Now, son, take it easy," Samuel called after him. "Use your head. Let her do most of it. Meanwhile I'll set my stubborn up."

Two days later the big wagon pulled away, loaded with timbers and tackle. Tom drove four horses, and beside him Samuel and Joe sat swinging their feet.

SEVENTEEN

When I said Cathy was a monster it seemed to me that it was so. Now I have bent close with a glass over the small print of her and reread the footnotes, and I wonder if it was true. The trouble is that since we cannot know what she wanted, we will never know whether or not she got it. If rather than running toward something, she ran away from something, we can't know whether she escaped. Who knows but that she tried to tell someone or everyone what she was like and could not, for lack of a common language. Her life may have been her language, formal, developed, indecipherable. It is easy to say she was bad, but there is little meaning unless we know why.

I've built the image in my mind of Cathy, sitting quietly waiting for her pregnancy to be over, living on a farm she did not like, with a man she did not love.

She sat in her chair under the oak tree, her hands clasped each to each in love and shelter. She grew very big—abnormally big, even at a time when women gloried in big babies and counted extra pounds with pride. She was misshapen; her belly, tight and heavy and distended, made it impossible for her to stand without supporting herself with her hands. But the great lump was local. Shoulders, neck, arms, hands, face, were unaffected, slender and girlish. Her breasts did not grow and her nipples did not darken. There was no quickening of milk glands, no physical planning to feed the newborn. When she sat behind a table you could not see that she was pregnant at all.

In that day there was no measuring of pelvic arch, no testing of blood, no building with calcium. A woman gave a tooth for a child. It was the law. And a woman was likely to have strange tastes, some said for filth, and it was set down to the Eve nature still under sentence for original sin.

Cathy's odd appetite was simple compared to some. The carpenters, repairing the old house, complained that they could not keep the lumps of chalk with which they coated their chalk lines. Again and again the scored hunks disappeared. Cathy stole them and broke them in little pieces. She carried the chips in her apron pocket, and when no one was about she crushed the soft lime between her teeth. She spoke very little. Her eyes were remote. It was as though she had gone away, leaving a breathing doll to conceal her absence.

Activity surged around her. Adam went happily about building and planning his Eden. Samuel and his boys brought in a well at forty feet and put down the newfangled expensive metal casing, for Adam wanted the best.

The Hamiltons moved their rig and started another hole. They slept in a tent beside the work and cooked over a campfire. But there was always one or another of them riding home for a tool or with a message.

Adam fluttered like a bewildered bee confused by too many flowers. He sat by Cathy and chatted about the pieplant roots just come in. He sketched for her the new fan blade Samuel had invented for the windmill. It had a variable pitch and was an unheard-of thing. He rode out to the well rig and slowed the work with his interest. And naturally, as he discussed wells with Cathy, his talk was all of birth and child care at the well head. It was a good time for Adam, the best time. He was the king of his wide and spacious life. And summer passed into a hot and fragrant autumn.

2

The Hamiltons at the well rig had finished their lunch of Liza's bread and rat cheese and venomous coffee cooked in a can over the fire. Joe's eyes were heavy and he was considering how he could get away into the brush to sleep for a while.

Samuel knelt in the sandy soil, looking at the torn and broken edges of his bit. Just before they had stopped for lunch the drill had found something thirty feet down that had mangled the steel as though it were lead. Samuel scraped the edge of the blade with his pocketknife and inspected the scrapings in the palm of his hand. His eyes shone with a childlike excitement. He held out his hand and poured the scrapings into Tom's hand.

"Take a look at it, son. What do you think it is?"

Joe wandered over from his place in front of the tent. Tom studied the fragments in his hand. "Whatever it is, it's hard," he said. "Couldn't be a diamond that big. Looks like metal. Do you think we've bored into a buried locomotive?"

His father laughed. "Thirty feet down," he said admiringly.

"It looks like tool steel," said Tom. "We haven't got anything that can touch it." Then he saw the faraway joyous look on his father's face and a shiver of shared delight came to him. The Hamilton children loved it when their father's mind went free. Then the world was peopled with wonders.

Samuel said, "Metal, you say. You think, steel. Tom, I'm going to make a guess and then I'm going to get an assay. Now hear my guess—and remember it. I think we'll find nickel in it, and silver maybe, and carbon and manganese. How I would like to dig it up! It's in sea sand. That's what we've been getting."

Tom said, "Say, what do you think it is with—nickel and silver—"

"It must have been long thousand centuries ago," Samuel said, and his sons knew he was seeing it. "Maybe it was all water here—an inland sea with the seabirds circling and crying. And it would have been a pretty thing if it happened at night. There would come a line of light and then a pencil of white light and then a tree of blinding light drawn in a long arc from heaven. Then there'd be a great water spout and a big mushroom of steam. And your ears would be staggered by the sound because the soaring cry of its coming would be on you at the same time the water exploded. And then it would be black night again, because of the blinding light. And gradually you'd see the killed fish coming up, showing silver in the starlight, and the crying birds would come to eat them. It's a lonely, lovely thing to think about, isn't it?"

He made them see it as he always did.

Tom said softly, "You think it's a meteorite, don't you?"

"That I do, and we can prove it by assay."

Joe said eagerly, "Let's dig it up."

"You dig it, Joe, while we bore for water."

Tom said seriously, "If the assay showed enough nickel and silver, wouldn't it pay to mine it?"

"You're my own son," said Samuel. "We don't know whether it's big as a house or little as a hat."

"But we could probe down and see."

"That we could if we did it secretly and hid our thinking under a pot."

"Why, what do you mean?"

"Now, Tom, have you no kindness toward your mother? We give her enough trouble, son. She's told me plain that if I spend any more money patenting things, she'll give us trouble to remember. Have pity on her! Can't you see her shame when they ask her what we're doing? She's a truthful woman, your mother. She'd have to say, 'They're at digging up a star.'" He laughed happily. "She'd never live it down. And she'd make us smart. No pies for three months."

Tom said, "We can't get through it. We'll have to move to another place."

"I'll put some blasting powder down," said his father, "and if that doesn't crack it aside we'll start a new hole." He stood up. "I'll have to go home for powder and to sharpen the drill. Why don't you boys ride along with me and we'll give Mother a surprise so that she'll cook the whole night and complain. That way she'll dissemble her pleasure."

Joe said, "Somebody's coming, coming fast." And indeed they could see a horseman riding toward them at full gallop, but a curious horseman who flopped about on his mount like a tied chicken. When he came a little closer they saw that it was Lee, his elbows waving like wings, his queue lashing about like a snake. It was surprising that he stayed on at all and still drove the horse at full tilt. He pulled up, breathing heavily. "Missy Adam say come! Missy Cathy bad—come quick. Missy yell, scream."

Samuel said, "Hold on, Lee. When did it start?"

"Mebbe bleakfus time."

"All right. Calm yourself. How is Adam?"

"Missy Adam clazy. Cly—laugh—make vomit."

"Sure," said Samuel. "These new fathers. I was one once. Tom, throw a saddle on for me, will you?"

Joe said, "What is it?"

"Why, Mrs. Trask is about to have her baby. I told Adam I'd stand by."

"You?" Joe asked.

Samuel leveled his eyes on his youngest son. "I brought both of you into the world," he said. "And you've given no evidence you think I did a bad service to the world. Tom, you get all the tools gathered up. And go back to the ranch and sharpen the metal. Bring back the box of powder that's on the shelf in the tool shed, and go easy with it as you love your arms and legs. Joe, I want you to stay here and look after things."

Joe said plaintively, "But what will I do here alone?"

Samuel was silent for a moment. Then he said, "Joe, do you love me?"

"Why, sure."

"If you heard I'd committed some great crime would you turn me over to the police?"

"What are you talking about?"

"Would you?"

"No."

"All right then. In my basket, under my clothes, you'll find two books— new, so be gentle with them. It's two volumes by a man the world is going to hear from. You can start reading if you want and it will raise up your lid a little. It's called *The Principles of Psychology* and it's by an Eastern man named William James. No relative to the train robber. And, Joe, if you ever let on about the books I'll run you off the ranch. If your mother ever found out I spent the money on them she'd run me off the ranch."

Tom led a saddled horse to him. "Can I read it next?"

"Yes," said Samuel, and he slipped his leg lightly over the saddle. "Come on, Lee."

The Chinese wanted to break into a gallop but Samuel restrained him. "Take it easy, Lee. Birthing takes longer than you think, mostly."

For a time they rode in silence, and then Lee said, "I'm sorry you bought those books. I have the condensed form, in one volume, the textbook. You could have borrowed it."

"Have you now? Do you have many books?"

"Not many here—thirty or forty. But you're welcome to any of them you haven't read."

"Thank you, Lee. And you may be sure I'll look the first moment I can. You know, you could talk to my boys. Joe's a little flighty but Tom's all right and it would do him good."

"It's a hard bridge to cross, Mr. Hamilton. Makes me timid to talk to a new person, but I'll try if you say so."

They walked the horses rapidly toward the little draw of the Trask place. Samuel said, "Tell me, how is it with the mother?"

"I'd rather you saw for yourself and thought for yourself," Lee said. "You know when a man lives alone as much as I do, his mind can go off on an irrational tangent just because his social world is out of kilter."

"Yes, I know. But I'm not lonely and I'm on a tangent too. But maybe not the same one."

"You don't think I imagine it then?"

"I don't know what it is, but I'll tell you for your reassurance that I've a sense of strangeness."

"I guess that's all it is with me too," said Lee. He smiled. "I'll tell you how far it got with me though. Since I've come here I find myself thinking of Chinese fairy tales my father told me. We Chinese have a well-developed demonology."

"You think she is a demon?"

"Of course not," said Lee. "I hope I'm a little beyond such silliness. I don't know what it is. You know, Mr. Hamilton, a servant develops an ability to taste the wind and judge the climate of the house he works in. And there's a strangeness here. Maybe that's what makes me remember my father's demons."

"Did your father believe in them?"

"Oh, no. He thought I should know the background. You Occidentals perpetuate a good many myths too."

Samuel said, "Tell me what happened to set you off. This morning, I mean."

"If you weren't coming I would try," said Lee. "But I would rather not. You can see for yourself. I may be crazy. Of course Mr. Adam is strung so tight he may snap like a banjo string."

"Give me a little hint. It might save time. What did she do?"

"Nothing. That's just it. Mr. Hamilton, I've been at births before, a good many of them, but this is something new to me."

"How?"

"It's—well—I'll tell you the one thing I can think of. This is much more like a bitter, deadly combat than a birth."

As they rode into the draw and under the oak trees Samuel said, "I hope you haven't got me in a state, Lee. It's a strange day, and I don't know why."

"No wind," said Lee. "It's the first day in a month when there hasn't been wind in the afternoon."

"That's so. You know I've been so close to the details I've paid no attention to the clothing of the day. First we find a buried star and now we go to dig up a mint-new human." He looked up through the oak branches at the yellow-lit hills. "What a beautiful day to be born in!" he said. "If signs have their fingers on a life, it's a sweet life coming. And, Lee, if Adam plays true, he'll be in the way. Stay close, will you? In case I need something. Look, the men, the carpenters, are sitting under that tree."

"Mr. Adam stopped the work. He thought the hammering might disturb his wife."

Samuel said, "You stay close. That sounds like Adam playing true. He doesn't know his wife probably couldn't hear God Himself beating a tattoo on the sky."

The workmen sitting under the tree waved to him. "How do, Mr. Hamilton. How's your family?"

"Fine, fine. Say, isn't that Rabbit Holman? Where've you been, Rabbit?"

"Went prospecting, Mr. Hamilton."

"Find anything, Rabbit?"

"Hell, Mr. Hamilton, I couldn't even find the mule I went out with."

They rode on toward the house. Lee said quickly, "If you ever get a minute, I'd like to show you something."

"What is it, Lee?"

"Well, I've been trying to translate some old Chinese poetry into English. I'm not sure it can be done. Will you take a look?"

"I'd like to, Lee. Why, that would be a treat for me."

3

Bordoni's white frame house was very quiet, almost broodingly quiet, and the shades were pulled down. Samuel dismounted at the stoop, untied his bulging saddlebags, and gave his horse to Lee. He knocked and got no answer and went in. It was dusky in the living room after the outside light. He looked in the kitchen, scrubbed to the wood grain by Lee. A gray stoneware pilon coffeepot grunted on the back of the stove. Samuel tapped lightly on the bedroom door and went in.

It was almost pitch-black inside, for not only were the shades down but blankets were tacked over the windows. Cathy was lying in the big four-poster bed, and Adam sat beside her, his face buried in the coverlet. He raised his head and looked blindly out.

Samuel said pleasantly, "Why are you sitting in the dark?"

Adam's voice was hoarse. "She doesn't want the light. It hurts her eyes."

Samuel walked into the room and authority grew in him with each step. "There will have to be light," he said. "She can close her eyes. I'll tie a black cloth over them if she wants." He moved to the window and grasped the blanket to pull it down, but Adam was upon him before he could yank.

"Leave it. The light hurts her," he said fiercely.

Samuel turned on him. "Now, Adam, I know what you feel. I promised you I'd take care of things, and I will. I only hope one of those things isn't you." He pulled the blanket down and rolled up the shade to let the golden afternoon light in.

Cathy made a little mewing sound from the bed, and Adam went to her. "Close your eyes, dear. I'll put a cloth over your eyes."

Samuel dropped his saddlebags in a chair and stood beside the bed. "Adam," he said firmly, "I'm going to ask you to go out of the room and to stay out."

"No, I can't. Why?"

"Because I don't want you in the way. It's considered a sweet practice fo: you to get drunk."

"I couldn't."

Samuel said, "Anger's a slow thing in me and disgust is slower, but I can taste the beginnings of both of them. You'll get out of the room and give me no trouble or I'll go away and you'll have a basket of trouble."

Adam went finally, and from the doorway Samuel called, "And I don't want you bursting in if you hear anything. You wait for me to come out." He closed the door, noticed there was a key in the lock, and turned it. "He's an upset, vehement man," he said. "He loves you."

He had not looked at her closely until now. And he saw true hatred in her eyes, unforgiving, murderous hatred.

"It'll be over before long, dearie. Now tell me, has the water broke?"

Her hostile eyes glared at him and her lips raised snarling from her little teeth. She did not answer him.

He stared at her. "I did not come by choice except as a friend," he said. "It's not a pleasure to me, young woman. I don't know your trouble and minute by minute I don't care. Maybe I can save you some pain—who knows? I'm going to ask you one more question. If you don't answer, if you put that snarling look on me, I'm going out and leave you to welter."

The words struck into her understanding like lead shot dropped in water. She made a great effort. And it gave him a shivering to see her face change, the steel leave her eyes, the lips thicken from line to bow, and the corners turn up. He noticed a movement of her hands, the fists unclench and the fingers turn pinkly upward. Her face became young and innocent and bravely hurt. It was like one magic-lantern slide taking the place of another.

She said softly, "The water broke at dawn."

"That's better. Have you had hard labor?"

"Yes."

"How far apart?"

"I don't know."

"Well, I've been in this room fifteen minutes."

"I've had two little ones—no big ones since you came."

"Fine. Now where's your linen?"

"In that hamper over there."

"You'll be all right, dearie," he said gently.

He opened his saddlebags and took out a thick rope covered with blue velvet and looped at either end. On the velvet hundreds of little pink flowers were embroidered. "Liza sent you her pulling rope to use," he said. "She made it when our first-born was preparing. What with our children and friends', this rope has pulled a great number of people into the world." He slipped one of the loops over each of the footposts of the bed.

Suddenly her eyes glazed and her back arched like a spring and the blood started to her cheeks. He waited for her cry or scream and looked apprehensively at the closed door. But there was no scream—only a series of grunting squeals. After a few seconds her body relaxed and the hatefulness was back in her face.

The labor struck again. "There's a dear," he said soothingly. "Was it one or two? I don't know. The more you see, the more you learn no two are alike. I'd better get my hands washed."

Her head threshed from side to side. "Good, good, my darling," he said. "I think it won't be long till your baby's here." He put his hand on her forehead where her scar showed dark and angry. "How did you get the hurt on your head?" he asked.

Her head jerked up and her sharp teeth fastened on his hand across the back and up into the palm near the little finger. He cried out in pain and tried to pull his hand away, but her jaw was set and her head twisted and turned, mangling his hand the way a terrier worries a sack. A shrill snarling came from her set teeth. He slapped her on the cheek and it had no effect. Automatically he did what he would have done to stop a dog fight. His left hand went to her throat and he cut off her wind. She struggled and tore at his hand before her jaws unclenched and he pulled his hand free. The flesh was torn and bleeding. He stepped back from the bed and looked at the damage her teeth had done. He looked at her with fear. And when he looked, her face was calm again and young and innocent.

"I'm sorry," she said quickly. "Oh, I'm sorry."

Samuel shuddered.

"It was the pain," she said.

Samuel laughed shortly. "I'll have to muzzle you, I guess," he said. "A collie bitch did the same to me once." He saw the hatred look out of her eyes for a second and then retreat.

Samuel said, "Have you got anything to put on it? Humans are more poisonous than snakes."

"I don't know."

"Well, have you got any whisky? I'll pour some whisky on it."

"In the second drawer."

He splashed whisky on his bleeding hand and kneaded the flesh against the alcohol sting. A strong quaking was in his stomach and a sickness rose up against his eyes. He took a swallow of whisky to steady himself. He dreaded to look back at the bed. "My hand won't be much good for a while," he said.

Samuel told Adam afterward, "She must be made of whalebone. The birth happened before I was ready. Popped like a seed. I'd not the water ready to wash him. Why, she didn't even touch the pulling rope to bear down. Pure whalebone, she is." He tore at the door, called Lee and demanded warm water. Adam came charging into the room. "A boy!" Samuel cried. "You've got a boy! Easy," he said, for Adam had seen the mess in the bed and a green was rising in his face.

Samuel said, "Send Lee in here. And you, Adam, if you still have the authority to tell your hands and feet what to do, get to the kitchen and make me some coffee. And see the lamps are filled and the chimneys clean."

Adam turned like a zombie and left the room. In a moment Lee looked in. Samuel pointed to the bundle in a laundry basket. "Sponge him off in warm water, Lee. Don't let a draft get on him. Lord! I wish Liza were here. I can't do everything at once."

He turned back to the bed. "Now, dearie, I'll get you cleaned up."

Cathy was bowed again, snarling in her pain. "It'll be over in a little," he said. "Takes a little time for the residue. And you're so quick. Why, you didn't even have to pull on Liza's rope." He saw something, stared, and went quickly to work. "Lord God in Heaven, it's another one!"

He worked fast, and as with the first the birth was incredibly quick. And again Samuel tied the cord. Lee took the second baby, washed it, wrapped it, and put it in the basket.

Samuel cleaned the mother and shifted her gently while he changed the linen on the bed. He found in himself a reluctance to look in her face. He worked as quickly as he could, for his bitten hand was stiffening. He drew a clean white sheet up to her chin and raised her to slip a fresh pillow under her head. At last he had to look at her.

Her golden hair was wet with perspiration but her face had changed. It was stony, expressionless. At her throat the pulse fluttered visibly.

"You have two sons," Samuel said. "Two fine sons. They aren't alike. Each one born separate in his own sack."

She inspected him coldly and without interest.

Samuel said, "I'll show your boys to you."

"No," she said without emphasis.

"Now, dearie, don't you want to see your sons?"

"No. I don't want them."

"Oh, you'll change. You're tired now, but you'll change. And I'll tell you now—this birth was quicker and easier than I've seen ever in my life."

The eyes moved from his face. "I don't want them. I want you to cover the windows and take the light away."

"It's weariness. In a few days you'll feel so different you won't remember."

"I'll remember. Go away. Take them out of the room. Send Adam in."

Samuel was caught by her tone. There was no sickness, no weariness, no softness. His words came out without his will. "I don't like you," he said and wished he could gather the words back into his throat and into his mind. But his words had no effect on Cathy.

"Send Adam in," she said.

In the little living room Adam looked vaguely at his sons and went quickly nto the bedroom and shut the door. In a moment came the sound of apping. Adam was nailing the blankets over the windows again.

Lee brought coffee to Samuel. "That's a bad-looking hand you have there," he said.

"I know. I'm afraid it's going to give me trouble."

"Why did she do it?"

"I don't know. She's a strange thing."

Lee said, "Mr. Hamilton, let me take care of that. You could lose an arm."

The life went out of Samuel. "Do what you want, Lee. A frightened sorrow has closed down over my heart. I wish I were a child so I could cry. I'm too old to be afraid like this. And I've not felt such despair since a bird died in my hand by a flowing water long ago."

Lee left the room and shortly returned, carrying a small ebony box carved with twisting dragons. He sat by Samuel and from his box took a wedge-shaped Chinese razor. "It will hurt," he said softly.

"I'll try to bear it, Lee."

The Chinese bit his lips, feeling the inflicted pain in himself while he cut deeply into the hand, opened the flesh around the toothmarks front and back, and trimmed the ragged flesh away until good red blood flowed from every wound. He shook a bottle of yellow emulsion labeled Hall's Cream Salve and poured it into the deep cuts. He saturated a handkerchief with the salve and wrapped the hand. Samuel winced and gripped the chair arm with his good hand.

"It's mostly carbolic acid," Lee said. "You can smell it."

"Thank you, Lee. I'm being a baby to knot up like this."

"I don't think I could have been so quiet," said Lee. "I'll get you another cup of coffee."

He came back with two cups and sat down by Samuel. "I think I'll go away," he said. "I never went willingly to a slaughter house."

Samuel stiffened. "What do you mean?"

"I don't know. The words came out."

Samuel shivered. "Lee, men are fools. I guess I hadn't thought about it, but Chinese men are fools too."

"What made you doubt it?"

"Oh, maybe because we think of strangers as stronger and better than we are."

"What do you want to say?"

Samuel said, "Maybe the foolishness is necessary, the dragon fighting, the boasting, the pitiful courage to be constantly knocking a chip off God's shoulder, and the childish cowardice that makes a ghost of a dead tree beside a darkening road. Maybe that's good and necessary, but—"

"What do you want to say?" Lee repeated patiently.

"I thought some wind had blown up the embers in my foolish mind,"

Samuel said. "And now I hear in your voice that you have it too. I feel wing
over this house. I feel a dreadfulness coming."

"I feel it too."

"I know you do, and that makes me take less than my usual comfort in m
foolishness. This birth was too quick, too easy—like a cat having kittens. An
I fear for these kittens. I have dreadful thoughts gnawing to get into m
brain."

"What do you want to say?" Lee asked a third time.

"I want my wife," Samuel cried. "No dreams, no ghosts, no foolishness.
want her here. They say miners take canaries into the pits to test the ai
Liza has no truck with foolishness. And, Lee, if Liza sees a ghost, it's a ghos
and not a fragment of a dream. If Liza feels trouble we'll bar the doors."

Lee got up and went to the laundry basket and looked down at the babies
He had to peer close, for the light was going fast. "They're sleeping," he
said.

"They'll be squalling soon enough. Lee, will you hitch up the rig and
drive to my place for Liza? Tell her I need her here. If Tom's still there, tel
him to mind the place. If not, I'll send him in the morning. And if Liza
doesn't want to come, tell her we need a woman's hand here and a woman's
clear eyes. She'll know what you mean."

"I'll do it," said Lee. "Maybe we're scaring each other, like two children
in the dark."

"I've thought of that," Samuel said. "And, Lee, tell her I hurt my hand
at the well head. Do not, for God's sake, tell her how it happened."

"I'll get some lamps lit and then I'll go," said Lee. "It will be a great relief
to have her here."

"That it will, Lee. That it will. She'll let some light into this cellar hole."

After Lee drove away in the dark Samuel picked up a lamp in his left
hand. He had to set it on the floor to turn the knob of the bedroom door.
The room was in pitch-blackness, and the yellow lamplight streamed upward and did not light the bed.

Cathy's voice came strong and edged from the bed. "Shut the door. I do
not want the light. Adam, go out! I want to be in the dark—alone."

Adam said hoarsely, "I want to stay with you."

"I do not want you."

"I will stay."

"Then stay. But don't talk any more. Please close the door and take the
lamp away."

Samuel went back to the living room. He put the lamp on the table by the
laundry basket and looked in on the small sleeping faces of the babies. Their
eyes were pinched shut and they sniffled a little in discomfort at the light.
Samuel put his forefinger down and stroked the hot foreheads. One of the
twins opened his mouth and yawned prodigiously and settled back to sleep.
Samuel moved the lamp and then went to the front door and opened it

and stepped outside. The evening star was so bright that it seemed to flare and crumple as it sank toward the western mountains. The air was still, and Samuel could smell the day-heated sage. The night was very dark. Samuel started when he heard a voice speaking out of the blackness.

"How is she?"

"Who is it?" Samuel demanded.

"It's me, Rabbit." The man emerged and took form in the light from the doorway.

"The mother, Rabbit? Oh, she's fine."

"Lee said twins."

"That's right—twin sons. You couldn't want better. I guess Mr. Trask will tear the river up by the roots now. He'll bring in a crop of candy canes."

Samuel didn't know why he changed the subject. "Rabbit, do you know what we bored into today? A meteorite."

"What's that, Mr. Hamilton?"

"A shooting star that fell a million years ago."

"You did? Well, think of that! How did you hurt your hand?"

"I almost said on a shooting star." Samuel laughed. "But it wasn't that interesting. I pinched it in the tackle."

"Bad?"

"No, not bad."

"Two boys," said Rabbit. "My old lady will be jealous."

"Will you come inside and sit, Rabbit?"

"No, no, thank you. I'll get out to sleep. Morning seems to come earlier every year I live."

"That it does, Rabbit. Good night then."

Liza Hamilton arrived about four in the morning. Samuel was asleep in his chair, dreaming that he had gripped a red-hot bar of iron and could not let go. Liza awakened him and looked at his hand before she even glanced at the babies. While she did well the things he had done in a lumbering, masculine way, she gave him his orders and packed him off. He was to get up this instant, saddle Doxology, and ride straight to King City. No matter what time it was, he must wake up that good-for-nothing doctor and get his hand treated. If it seemed all right he could go home and wait. And it was a criminal thing to leave your last-born, and he little more than a baby himself, sitting there by a hole in the ground with no one to care for him. It was a matter which might even engage the attention of the Lord God himself.

If Samuel craved realism and activity, he got it. She had him off the place by dawn. His hand was bandaged by eleven, and he was in his own chair at his own table by five in the afternoon, sizzling with fever, and Tom was boiling a hen to make chicken soup for him.

For three days Samuel lay in bed, fighting the fever phantoms and putting names to them too, before his great strength broke down the infection and drove it caterwauling away.

Samuel looked up at Tom with clear eyes and said, "I'll have to get up," tried it and sat weakly back, chuckling—the sound he made when any force in the world defeated him. He had an idea that even when beaten he could steal a little victory by laughing at defeat. And Tom brought him chicken soup until he wanted to kill him. The lore has not died out of the world, and you will still find people who believe that soup will cure any hurt or illness and is no bad thing to have for the funeral either.

4

Liza stayed away a week. She cleaned the Trask house from the top clear down into the grain of the wooden floors. She washed everything she could bend enough to get into a tub and sponged the rest. She put the babies on a working basis and noted with satisfaction that they howled most of the time and began to gain weight. Lee she used like a slave since she didn't quite believe in him. Adam she ignored since she couldn't use him for anything. She did make him wash the windows and then did it again after he had finished.

Liza sat with Cathy just enough to come to the conclusion that she was a sensible girl who didn't talk very much or try to teach her grandmother to suck eggs. She also checked her over and found that she was perfectly healthy, not injured and not sick, and that she would never nurse the twins. "And just as well too," she said. "Those great lummoxes would chew a little thing like you to the bone." She forgot that she was smaller than Cathy and had nursed every one of her own children.

On Saturday afternoon Liza checked her work, left a list of instructions as long as her arm to cover every possibility from colic to an inroad of grease ants, packed her traveling basket, and had Lee drive her home.

She found her house a stable of filth and abomination and she set to cleaning it with the violence and disgust of a Hercules at labor. Samuel asked questions of her in flight.

How were the babies?

They were fine, growing.

How was Adam?

Well, he moved around as if he was alive but he left no evidence. The Lord in his wisdom gave money to very curious people, perhaps because they'd starve without.

How was Mrs. Trask?

Quiet, lackadaisical, like most rich Eastern women (Liza had never known a rich Eastern woman), but on the other hand docile and respectful. "And it's a strange thing," Liza said. "I can find no real fault with her save perhaps a touch of laziness, and yet I don't like her very much. Maybe it's that scar. How did she get it?"

"I don't know," said Samuel.

Liza leveled her forefinger like a pistol between his eyes. "I'll tell you something. Unbeknownst to herself, she's put a spell on her husband. He moons around her like a sick duck. I don't think he's given the twins a thorough good look yet."

Samuel waited until she went by again. He said, "Well, if she's lazy and he's moony, who's going to take care of the sweet babies? Twin boys take a piece of looking after."

Liza stopped in mid-swoop, drew a chair close to him, and sat, resting her hands on her knees. "Remember I've never held the truth lightly if you don't believe me," she said.

"I don't think you could lie, dearie," he said, and she smiled, thinking it a compliment.

"Well, what I'm to tell you might weigh a little heavy on your belief if you did not know that."

"Tell me."

"Samuel, you know that Chinese with his slanty eyes and his outlandish talk and that braid?"

"Lee? Sure I know him."

"Well, wouldn't you say offhand he was a heathen?"

"I don't know."

"Come now, Samuel, anybody would. But he's not." She straightened up.

"What is he?"

She tapped his arm with an iron finger. "A Presbyterian, and well up—well up, I say, when you dig it out of that crazy talk. Now what do you think of that?"

Samuel's voice was unsteady with trying to clamp his laughter in. "No!" he said.

"And I say yes. Well now, who do you think is looking after the twins? I wouldn't trust a heathen from here to omega—but a Presbyterian—he learned everything I told him."

"No wonder they're taking on weight," said Samuel.

"It's a matter for praise and it's a matter for prayer."

"We'll do it too," said Samuel. "Both."

5

For a week Cathy rested and gathered her strength. On Saturday of the second week of October she stayed in her bedroom all morning. Adam tried the door and found it locked.

"I'm busy," she called, and he went away.

Putting her bureau in order, he thought, for he could hear her opening drawers and closing them.

In the late afternoon Lee came to Adam where he sat on the stoop. "Missy say I go King City buy nursey bottle," he said uneasily.

"Well, do it then," said Adam. "She's your mistress."

"Missy say not come back mebbe Monday. Take—"

Cathy spoke calmly from the doorway. "He hasn't had a day off for a long time. A rest would do him good."

"Of course," said Adam. "I just didn't think of it. Have a good time. If I need anything I'll get one of the carpenters."

"Men go home, Sunday."

"I'll get the Indian. Lopez will help."

Lee felt Cathy's eyes on him. "Lopez dlunk. Find bottle whisky."

Adam said petulantly, "I'm not helpless, Lee. Stop arguing."

Lee looked at Cathy standing in the doorway. He lowered his eyelids. "Mebbe I come back late," he said, and he thought he saw two dark lines appear between her eyes and then disappear. He turned away. "Goo-by," he said.

Cathy went back to her room as the evening came down. At seven-thirty Adam knocked. "I've got you some supper, dear. It's not much." The door opened as though she had been standing waiting. She was dressed in her neat traveling dress, the jacket edged in black braid, black velvet lapels, and large jet buttons. On her head was a wide straw hat with a tiny crown; long jet-beaded hatpins held it on. Adam's mouth dropped open.

She gave him no chance to speak. "I'm going away now."

"Cathy, what do you mean?"

"I told you before."

"You didn't."

"You didn't listen. It doesn't matter."

"I don't believe you."

Her voice was dead and metallic. "I don't give a damn what you believe. I'm going."

"The babies—"

"Throw them in one of your wells."

He cried in panic, "Cathy, you're sick. You can't go—not from me—not from me."

"I can do anything to you. Any woman can do anything to you. You're a fool."

The word got through his haze. Without warning, his hands reached for her shoulders and he thrust her backward. As she staggered he took the key from the inside of the door, slammed the door shut, and locked it.

He stood panting, his ear close to the panel, and a hysterical sickness poisoned him. He could hear her moving quietly about. A drawer was opened, and the thought leaped in him—she's going to stay. And then there was a little click he could not place. His ear was almost touching the door.

Her voice came from so near that he jerked his head back. He heard richness in her voice. "Dear," she said softly, "I didn't know you would take it so. I'm sorry, Adam."

His breath burst hoarsely out of his throat. His hand trembled, trying to turn the key, and it fell out on the floor after he had turned it. He pushed the door open. She stood three feet away. In her right hand she held his .44 Colt, and the black hole in the barrel pointed at him. He took a step toward her, saw that the hammer was back.

She shot him. The heavy slug struck him in the shoulder and flattened and tore out a piece of his shoulderblade. The flash and roar smothered him, and he staggered back and fell to the floor. She moved slowly toward him, cautiously, as she might toward a wounded animal. He stared up into her eyes, which inspected him impersonally. She tossed the pistol on the floor beside him and walked out of the house.

He heard her steps on the porch, on the crisp dry oak leaves on the path, and then he could hear her no more. And the monotonous sound that had been there all along was the cry of the twins, wanting their dinner. He had forgotten to feed them.

EIGHTEEN

Horace Quinn was the new deputy sheriff appointed to look after things around the King City district. He complained that his new job took him away from his ranch too much. His wife complained even more, but the truth of the matter was that nothing much had happened in a criminal way since Horace had been deputy. He had seen himself making a name for himself and running for sheriff. The sheriff was an important officer. His job was less flighty than that of district attorney, almost as permanent and dignified as superior court judge. Horace didn't want to stay on the ranch all his life, and his wife had an urge to live in Salinas where she had relatives.

When the rumors, repeated by the Indian and the carpenters, that Adam Trask had been shot reached Horace, he saddled up right away and left his wife to finish butchering the pig he had killed that morning.

Just north of the big sycamore tree where the Hester road turns off to the left, Horace met Julius Euskadi. Julius was trying to decide whether to go quail hunting or to King City and catch the train to Salinas to shake some of the dust out of his britches. The Euskadis were well-to-do, handsome people of Basque extraction.

Julius said, "If you'd come along with me, I'd go into Salinas. They tell me that right next door to Jenny's, two doors from the Long Green, there's a new place called Faye's. I heard it was pretty nice, run like San Francisco. They've got a piano player."

Horace rested his elbow on his saddle horn and stirred a fly from his horse's shoulder with his rawhide quirt. "Some other time," he said. "I've got to look into something."

"You wouldn't be going to Trasks, would you?"

"That's right. Did you hear anything about it?"

"Not to make any sense. I heard Mr. Trask shot himself in the shoulder with a forty-four and then fired everybody on the ranch. How do you go about shooting yourself in the shoulder with a forty-four, Horace?"

"I don't know. Them Easterners are pretty clever. I thought I'd go up and find out. Didn't his wife just have a baby?"

"Twins, I heard," said Julius. "Maybe they shot him."

"One hold the gun and the other pull the trigger? Hear anything else?"

"All mixed up, Horace. Want some company?"

"I'm not going to deputize you, Julius. Sheriff says the supervisors are raising hell about the payroll. Hornby out in the Alisal deputized his great aunt and kept her in posse three weeks just before Easter."

"You're fooling!"

"No, I'm not. And you get no star."

"Hell, I don't want to be a deputy. Just thought I'd ride along with you for company. I'm curious."

"Me too. Glad to have you, Julius. I can always fling the oath around your neck if there's any trouble. What do you say the new place is called?"

"Faye's. Sacramento woman."

"They do things pretty nice in Sacramento," and Horace told how they did things in Sacramento as they rode along.

It was a nice day to be riding. As they turned into the Sanchez draw they were cursing the bad hunting in recent years. Three things are never any good—farming, fishing, and hunting—compared to other years, that is. Julius was saying, "Christ, I wish they hadn't killed off all the grizzly bears. In eighteen-eighty my grandfather killed one up by Pleyto weighed eighteen hundred pounds."

A silence came on them as they rode in under the oaks, a silence they took from the place itself. There was no sound, no movement.

"I wonder if he finished fixing up the old house," Horace said.

"Hell, no. Rabbit Holman was working on it, and he told me Trask called them all in and fired them. Told them not to come back."

"They say Trask has got a pot of money."

"I guess he's well fixed, all right," said Julius. "Sam Hamilton is sinking four wells—if he didn't get fired too."

"How is Mr. Hamilton? I ought to go up to see him."

"He's fine. Full of hell as ever."

"I'll have to go up and pay him a visit," said Horace.

Lee came out on the stoop to meet them.

Horace said, "Hello, Ching Chong. Bossy man here?"

"He sick," said Lee.

"I'd like to see him."

"No see. He sick."

"That's enough of that," said Horace. "Tell him Deputy Sheriff Quinn wants to see him."

Lee disappeared, and in a moment he was back. "You come," he said. "I take horsy."

Adam lay in the four-poster bed where the twins had been born. He was propped high with pillows, and a mound of home-devised bandages covered his left breast and shoulder. The room reeked of Hall's Cream Salve.

Horace said later to his wife, "And if you ever saw death still breathing, there it was."

Adam's cheeks hugged the bone and pulled the skin of his nose tight and slimy. His eyes seemed to bulge out of his head and to take up the whole upper part of his face, and they were shiny with sickness, intense and myopic. His bony right hand kneaded a fist full of coverlet.

Horace said, "Howdy, Mr. Trask. Heard you got hurt." He paused, waiting for an answer. He went on, "Just thought I'd drop around and see how you were doing. How'd it happen?"

A look of transparent eagerness came over Adam's face. He shifted slightly in the bed.

"If it hurts to talk you can whisper," Horace added helpfully.

"Only when I breathe deep," Adam said softly. "I was cleaning my gun and it went off."

Horace glanced at Julius and then back. Adam saw the look and a little color of embarrassment rose in his cheeks.

"Happens all the time," said Horace. "Got the gun around?"

"I think Lee put it away."

Horace stepped to the door. "Hey there, Ching Chong, bring the pistol."

In a moment Lee poked the gun butt-first through the door. Horace looked at it, swung the cylinder out, poked the cartridges out, and smelled the empty brass cylinder of the one empty shell. "There's better shooting cleaning the damn things than pointing them. I'll have to make a report to the county, Mr. Trask. I won't take up much of your time. You were cleaning the barrel, maybe with a rod, and the gun went off and hit you in the shoulder?"

"That's right, sir," Adam said quickly.

"And cleaning it, you hadn't swung out the cylinder?"

"That's right."

"And you were poking the rod in and out with the barrel pointed toward you with the hammer cocked?"

Adam's breath rasped in a quick intake.

Horace went on, "And it must have blowed the rod right through you and took off your left hand too." Horace's pale sun-washed eyes never left

Adam's face. He said kindly, "What happened, Mr. Trask? Tell me what happened."

"I tell you truly it was an accident, sir."

"Now you wouldn't have me write a report like I just said. The sheriff would think I was crazy. What happened?"

"Well, I'm not very used to guns. Maybe it wasn't just like that, but I was cleaning it and it went off."

There was a whistle in Horace's nose. He had to breathe through his mouth to stop it. He moved slowly up from the foot of the bed, nearer to Adam's head and staring eyes. "You came from the East not very long ago, didn't you, Mr. Trask?"

"That's right. Connecticut."

"I guess people don't use guns very much there any more."

"Not much."

"Little hunting?"

"Some."

"So you'd be more used to a shotgun?"

"That's right. But I never hunted much."

"I guess you didn't hardly use a pistol at all, so you didn't know how to handle it."

"That's right," Adam said eagerly. "Hardly anybody there has a pistol."

"So when you came here you bought that forty-four because everybody out here has a pistol and you were going to learn how to use it."

"Well, I thought it might be a good thing to learn."

Julius Euskadi stood tensely, his face and body receptive, listening but uncommunicative.

Horace sighed and looked away from Adam. His eyes brushed over and past Julius and came back to his hands. He laid the gun on the bureau and carefully lined the brass and lead cartridges beside it. "You know," he said, "I've only been a deputy a little while. I thought I was going to have some fun with it and maybe in a few years run for sheriff. I haven't got the guts for it. It isn't any fun to me."

Adam watched him nervously.

"I don't think anybody's ever been afraid of me before—mad at me, yes —but not afraid. It's a mean thing, makes me feel mean."

Julius said irritably, "Get to it. You can't resign right this minute."

"The hell I can't—if I want to. All right! Mr. Trask, you served in the United States Cavalry. The weapons of the cavalry are carbines and pistols. You—" He stopped and swallowed. "What happened, Mr. Trask?"

Adam's eyes seemed to grow larger, and they were moist and edged with red. "It was an accident," he whispered.

"Anybody see it? Was your wife with you when it happened?"

Adam did not reply, and Horace saw that his eyes were closed. "Mr. Trask," he said, "I know you're a sick man. I'm trying to make it as easy on you as I can. Why don't you rest now while I have a talk with your wife?" He waited a moment and then turned to the doorway, where Lee still stood. "Ching Chong, tell Missy I would admire to talk to her a few minutes."

Lee did not reply.

Adam spoke without opening his eyes. "My wife is away on a visit."

"She wasn't here when it happened?" Horace glanced at Julius and saw a curious expression on Julius's lips. The corners of his mouth were turned slightly up in a sardonic smile. Horace thought quickly, He's ahead of me. He'd make a good sheriff. "Say," he said, "that's kind of interesting. Your wife had a baby—two babies—two weeks ago, and now she's gone on a visit. Did she take the babies with her? I thought I heard them a little while ago." Horace leaned over the bed and touched the back of Adam's clenched right hand. "I hate this, but I can't stop now. Trask!" he said loudly, "I want you to tell me what happened. This isn't nosiness. This is the law. Now, damn it, you open your eyes and tell me or, by Christ, I'll take you in to the sheriff even if you are hurt."

Adam opened his eyes, and they were blank like a sleepwalker's eyes. And his voice came out without rise or fall, without emphasis, and without any emotion. It was as though he pronounced perfectly words in a language he did not understand.

"My wife went away," he said.

"Where did she go?"

"I don't know."

"What do you mean?"

"I don't know where she went."

Julius broke in, speaking for the first time. "Why did she go?"

"I don't know."

Horace said angrily, "You watch it, Trask. You're playing pretty close to the edge and I don't like what I'm thinking. You must know why she went away."

"I don't know why she went."

"Was she sick? Did she act strange?"

"No."

Horace turned. "Ching Chong, do you know anything about this?"

"I go King City Satdy. Come back mebbe twelve night. Find Missy Tlask on floor."

"So you weren't here when it happened?"

"No, ma'am."

"All right, Trask, I'll have to get back to you. Open up that shade a little, Ching Chong, so I can see. There, that's better. Now I'm going to do it your way first until I can't any more. Your wife went away. Did she shoot you?"

"It was an accident."

"All right, an accident, but was the gun in her hand?"

"It was an accident."

"You don't make it very easy. But let's say she went away and we have to find her—see?—like a kid's game. You're making it that way. How long have you been married?"

"Nearly a year."

"What was her name before you married her?"

There was a long pause, and then Adam said softly, "I won't tell. I promised."

"Now you watch it. Where did she come from?"

"I don't know."

"Mr. Trask, you're talking yourself right into the county jail. Let's have a description. How tall was she?"

Adam's eyes gleamed. "Not tall—little and delicate."

"That's just fine. What color hair? Eyes?"

"She was beautiful."

"Was?"

"Is."

"Any scars?"

"Oh, God, no. Yes—a scar on her forehead."

"You don't know her name, where she came from, where she went, and you can't describe her. And you think I'm a fool."

Adam said, "She had a secret. I promised I wouldn't ask her. She was afraid for someone." And without warning Adam began to cry. His whole body shook, and his breath made little high sounds. It was hopeless crying.

Horace felt misery rising in him. "Come on in the other room, Julius," he said and led the way into the living room. "All right, Julius, tell me what you think. Is he crazy?"

"I don't know."

"Did he kill her?"

"That's what jumped into my mind."

"Mine too," said Horace. "My God!" He hurried into the bedroom and came back with the pistol and the shells. "I forgot them," he apologized. "I won't last long in this job."

Julius asked, "What are you going to do?"

"Well, I think it's beyond me. I told you I wouldn't put you on the payroll, but hold up your right hand."

"I don't want to get sworn in, Horace. I want to go to Salinas."

"You don't have any choice, Julius. I'll have to arrest you if you don't get your goddam hand up."

Julius reluctantly put up his hand and disgustedly repeated the oath. "And that's what I get for keeping you company," he said. "My father will skin me alive. All right, what do we do now?"

Horace said, "I'm going to run to papa. I need the sheriff. I'd take Trask in but I don't want to move him. You've got to stay, Julius. I'm sorry. Have you got a gun?"

"Hell, no."

"Well, take this one, and take my star." He unpinned it from his shirt and held it out.

"How long do you think you'll be gone?"

"Not any longer than I can help. Did you ever see Mrs. Trask, Julius?"

"No, I didn't."

"Neither did I. And I've got to tell the sheriff that Trask doesn't know her name or anything. And she's not very big and she is beautiful. That's one hell of a description! I think I'll resign before I tell the sheriff, because he's sure as hell going to fire me afterward. Do you think he killed her?"

"How the hell do I know?"

"Don't get mad."

Julius picked up the gun and put the cartridges back in the cylinder and balanced it in his hand. "You want an idea, Horace?"

"Don't it look like I need one?"

"Well, Sam Hamilton knew her—he took the babies, Rabbit says. And Mrs. Hamilton took care of her. Why don't you ride out there on your way and find out what she really looked like."

"I think maybe you better keep that star," said Horace. "That's good. I'll get going."

"You want me to look around?"

"I want you just to see that he doesn't get away—or hurt himself. Understand? Take care of yourself."

2

About midnight Horace got on a freight train in King City. He sat up in the cab with the engineer, and he was in Salinas the first thing in the morning. Salinas was the county seat, and it was a fast-growing town. Its population was due to cross the two thousand mark any time. It was the biggest town between San Jose and San Luis Obispo, and everyone felt that a brilliant future was in store for it.

Horace walked up from the Southern Pacific Depot and stopped in the Chop House for breakfast. He didn't want to get the sheriff out so early and rouse ill will when it wasn't necessary. In the Chop House he ran into young Will Hamilton, looking pretty prosperous in a salt-and-pepper business suit.

Horace sat down at the table with him. "How are you, Will?"

"Oh, pretty good."

"Up here on business?"

"Well, yes, I do have a little deal on."

"You might let me in on something sometime." Horace felt strange talking like this to such a young man, but Will Hamilton had an aura of success about him. Everybody knew he was going to be a very influential man in the county. Some people exude their futures, good or bad.

"I'll do that, Horace. I thought the ranch took all your time."

"I could be persuaded to rent it if anything turned up."

Will leaned over the table. "You know, Horace, our part of the county has been pretty much left out. Did you ever think of running for office?"

"What do you mean?"

"Well, you're a deputy—did you ever think of running for sheriff?"

"Why, no, I didn't."

"Well, you think about it. Just keep it under your hat. I'll look you up in a couple of weeks and we'll talk about it. But keep it under your hat."

"I'll certainly do that, Will. But we've got an awful good sheriff."

"I know. That's got nothing to do with it. King City hasn't got a single county officer—you see?"

"I see. I'll think about it. Oh, by the way, I stopped by and saw your father and mother yesterday."

Will's face lighted up. "You did? How were they?"

"Just fine. You know, your father is a real comical genius."

Will chuckled. "He made us laugh all the time we were growing up."

"But he's a smart man too, Will. He showed me a new kind of windmill he's invented—goddamnedest thing you ever saw."

"Oh, Lord," said Will, "here come the patent attorneys again!"

"But this is good," said Horace.

"They're all good. And the only people who make any money are the patent lawyers. Drives my mother crazy."

"I guess you've got a point there."

Will said, "The only way to make any money is to sell something somebody else makes."

"You've got a point there, Will, but this is the goddamnedest windmill you ever saw."

"He took you in, did he, Horace?"

"I guess he did. But you wouldn't want him to change, would you?"

"Oh, Lord, no!" said Will. "You think about what I said."

"All right."

"And keep it under your hat," said Will.

The sheriff's job was not an easy one, and that county which, out of the grab bag of popular elections, pulled a good sheriff was lucky. It was a complicated position. The obvious duties of the sheriff—enforcing the law and keeping the peace—were far from the most important ones. It was true that the sheriff represented armed force in the county, but in a community seething with individuals a harsh or stupid sheriff did not last long. There were water rights, boundary disputes, astray arguments, domestic relations,

paternity matters—all to be settled without force of arms. Only when everything else failed did a good sheriff make an arrest. The best sheriff was not
the best fighter but the best diplomat. And Monterey County had a good
one. He had a brilliant gift for minding his own business.

Horace went into the sheriff's office in the old county jail about ten
minutes after nine. The sheriff shook hands and discussed the weather and
the crops until Horace was ready to get down to business.

"Well, sir," Horace said finally, "I had to come up to get your advice."
And he told his story in great detail—what everybody had said and how they
looked and what time it was—everything.

After a few moments the sheriff closed his eyes and laced his fingers
together. He punctuated the account occasionally by opening his eyes, but
he made no comment.

"Well, there I was on a limb," Horace said. "I couldn't find out what
happened. I couldn't even find out what the woman looked like. It was
Julius Euskadi got the idea I should go to see Sam Hamilton."

The sheriff stirred, crossed his legs, and inspected the job. "You think he
killed her."

"Well, I did. But Mr. Hamilton kind of talked me out of it. He says
Trask hasn't got it in him to kill anybody."

"Everybody's got it in him," the sheriff said. "You just find his trigger
and anybody will go off."

"Mr. Hamilton told me some funny things about her. You know, when he
was taking her babies she bit him on the hand. You ought to see that hand,
like a wolf got him."

"Did Sam give you a description?"

"He did, and his wife did." Horace took a piece of paper from his pocket
and read a detailed description of Cathy. Between the two of them the
Hamiltons knew pretty much everything physical there was to know about
Cathy.

When Horace finished the sheriff sighed. "They both agreed about the
scar?"

"Yes, they did. And both of them remarked about how sometimes it was
darker than other times."

The sheriff closed his eyes again and leaned back in his chair. Suddenly
he straightened up, opened a drawer of his rolltop desk, and took out a
pint of whisky. "Have a drink," he said.

"Don't mind if I do. Here's looking at you." Horace wiped his mouth
and handed back the pint. "Got any ideas?" he asked.

The sheriff took three big swallows of whisky, corked the pint, and put it
back in the drawer before he replied. "We've got a pretty well-run county,"
he said. "I get along with the constables, give them a hand when they need
it, and they help me out when I need it. You take a town growing like
Salinas, and strangers in and out all the time—we could have trouble if we

didn't watch it pretty close. My office gets along fine with the local people."
He looked Horace in the eye. "Don't get restless. I'm not making a speech.
I just want to tell you how it is. We don't drive people. We've got to live
with them."

"Did I do something wrong?"

"No, you didn't, Horace. You did just right. If you hadn't come to town
or if you had brought Mr. Trask in, we'd of been in one hell of a mess. Now
hold on. I'm going to tell you—"

"I'm listening," said Horace.

"Over across the tracks down by Chinatown there's a row of whorehouses."

"I know that."

"Everybody knows it. If we closed them up they'd just move. The people
want those houses. We keep an eye on them so not much bad happens.
And the people that run those houses keep in touch with us. I've picked up
some wanted men from tips I got down there."

Horace said, "Julius told me—"

"Now wait a minute. Let me get all this said so we won't have to go back
over it. About three months ago a fine-looking woman came in to see me.
She wanted to open a house here and wanted to do it right. Came from
Sacramento. Ran a place there. She had letters from some pretty important
people—straight record—never had any trouble. A pretty damn good citizen."

"Julius told me. Name of Faye."

"That's right. Well, she opened a nice place, quiet, well run. It was about
time old Jenny and the Nigger had some competition. They were mad as
hell about it, but I told them just what I told you. It's about time they had
some competition."

"There's a piano player."

"Yes, there is. Good one too—blind fella. Say, are you going to let me
tell this?"

"I'm sorry," said Horace.

"That's all right. I know I'm slow but I'm thorough. Anyways, Faye turned
out to be just what she looks like, a good solid citizen. Now there's one
thing a good quiet whorehouse is more scared of than anything else. Take
a flighty randy girl runs off from home and goes in a house. Her old man
finds her and he begins to shovel up hell. Then the churches get into it,
and the women, and pretty soon that whorehouse has got a bad name and
we've got to close it up. You understand?"

"Yeah!" Horace said softly.

"Now don't get ahead of me. I hate to tell something you already thought
out. Faye sent me a note Sunday night. She's got a girl and she can't make
much out of her. What puzzles Faye is that this kid looks like a runaway girl
except she's a goddam good whore. She knows all the answers and all the
tricks. I went down and looked her over. She told me the usual bull, but I

can't find a thing wrong with her. She's of age and nobody's made a complaint." He spread his hands. "Well, there it is. What do we do about it?"

"You're pretty sure it's Mrs. Trask?"

The sheriff said, "Wide-set eyes, yellow hair, and a scar on her forehead, and she came in Sunday afternoon."

Adam's weeping face was in Horace's mind. "God all mighty! Sheriff, you got to get somebody else to tell him. I'll quit before I do."

The sheriff gazed into space. "You say he didn't even know her name, where she came from. She really bull-shitted him, didn't she?"

"The poor bastard," Horace said. "The poor bastard is in love with her. No, by God, somebody else has got to tell him. I won't."

The sheriff stood up. "Let's go down to the Chop House and get a cup of coffee."

They walked along the street in silence for a while. "Horace," the sheriff said, "if I told some of the things I know, this whole goddam county would go up in smoke."

"I guess that's right."

"You said she had twins?"

"Yeah, twin boys."

"You listen to me, Horace. There's only three people in the world that knows—her and you and me. I'm going to warn her that if she ever tells I'll brush her ass out of this county so fast it'll burn. And, Horace—if you should ever get an itchy tongue, before you tell anybody, even your wife, why, you think about those little boys finding out their mother is a whore."

3

Adam sat in his chair under the big oak tree. His left arm was expertly bandaged against his side so that he could not move his shoulder. Lee came out carrying the laundry basket. He set it on the ground beside Adam and went back inside.

The twins were awake, and they both looked blindly and earnestly up at the wind-moved leaves of the oak tree. A dry oak leaf came whirling down and landed in the basket. Adam leaned over and picked it out.

He didn't hear Samuel's horse until it was almost upon him, but Lee had seen him coming. He brought a chair out and led Doxology away toward the shed.

Samuel sat down quietly, and he didn't trouble Adam by looking at him too much, and he didn't trouble him by not looking at him. The wind freshened in the treetops and a fringe of it ruffled Samuel's hair. "I thought I'd better get back to the wells," Samuel said softly.

Adam's voice had gone rusty from lack of use. "No," he said, "I don't want any wells. I'll pay for the work you did."

Samuel leaned over the basket and put his finger against the small palm

of one of the twins and the fingers closed and held on. "I guess the last
bad habit a man will give up is advising."

"I don't want advice."

"Nobody does. It's a giver's present. Go through the motions, Adam."

"What motions?"

"Act out being alive, like a play. And after a while, a long while, it will
be true."

"Why should I?" Adam asked.

Samuel was looking at the twins. "You're going to pass something down
no matter what you do or if you do nothing. Even if you let yourself go
fallow, the weeds will grow and the brambles. Something will grow."

Adam did not answer, and Samuel stood up. "I'll be back," he said. "I'll
be back again and again. Go through the motions, Adam."

In the back of the shed Lee held Doxology while Sam mounted. "There
goes your bookstore, Lee," he said.

"Oh, well," said the Chinese, "maybe I didn't want it much anyway."

NINETEEN

A new country seems to follow a pattern. First come the openers, strong
and brave and rather childlike. They can take care of themselves in a
wilderness, but they are naïve and helpless against men, and perhaps that is
why they went out in the first place. When the rough edges are worn off the
new land, businessmen and lawyers come in to help with the development
—to solve problems of ownership, usually by removing the temptations to
themselves. And finally comes culture, which is entertainment, relaxation,
transport out of the pain of living. And culture can be on any level, and is.

The church and the whorehouse arrived in the Far West simultaneously.
And each would have been horrified to think it was a different facet of the
same thing. But surely they were both intended to accomplish the same
thing: the singing, the devotion, the poetry of the churches took a man out
of his bleakness for a time, and so did the brothels. The sectarian churches
came in swinging, cocky and loud and confident. Ignoring the laws of debt
and repayment, they built churches which couldn't be paid for in a hundred
years. The sects fought evil, true enough, but they also fought each other
with a fine lustiness. They fought at the turn of a doctrine. Each happily
believed all the others were bound for hell in a basket. And each for all its
bumptiousness brought with it the same thing: the Scripture on which our
ethics, our art and poetry, and our relationships are built. It took a smart
man to know where the difference lay between the sects, but anyone could
see what they had in common. And they brought music—maybe not the

best, but the form and sense of it. And they brought conscience, or, rather, nudged the dozing conscience. They were not pure, but they had a potential of purity, like a soiled white shirt. And any man could make something pretty fine of it within himself. True enough, the Reverend Billing, when they caught up with him, turned out to be a thief, an adulterer, a libertine, and a zoophilist, but that didn't change the fact that he had communicated some good things to a great number of receptive people. Billing went to jail, but no one ever arrested the good things he had released. And it doesn't matter much that his motive was impure. He used good material and some of it stuck. I use Billing only as an outrageous example. The honest preachers had energy and go. They fought the devil, no holds barred, boots and eye-gouging permitted. You might get the idea that they howled truth and beauty the way a seal bites out the National Anthem on a row of circus horns. But some of the truth and beauty remained, and the anthem was recognizable. The sects did more than this, though. They built the structure of social life in the Salinas Valley. The church supper is the grandfather of the country club, just as the Thursday poetry reading in the basement under the vestry sired the little theater.

While the churches, bringing the sweet smell of piety for the soul, came in prancing and farting like brewery horses in bock-beer time, the sister evangelism, with release and joy for the body, crept in silently and grayly, with its head bowed and its face covered.

You may have seen the spangled palaces of sin and fancy dancing in the false West of the movies, and maybe some of them existed—but not in the Salinas Valley. The brothels were quiet, orderly, and circumspect. Indeed, if after hearing the ecstatic shrieks of climactic conversion against the thumping beat of the melodeon you had stood under the window of a whorehouse and listened to the low decorous voices, you would have been likely to confuse the identities of the two ministries. The brothel was accepted while it was not admitted.

I will tell you about the solemn courts of love in Salinas. They were about the same in other towns, but the Salinas Row has a pertinence to this telling.

You walked west on Main Street until it bent. That's where Castroville Street crossed Main. Castroville Street is now called Market Street, God knows why. Streets used to be named for the place they aimed at. Thus Castroville Street, if you followed it nine miles, brought you to Castroville, Alisal Street to Alisal, and so forth.

Anyway, when you came to Castroville Street you turned right. Two blocks down, the Southern Pacific tracks cut diagonally across the street on their way south, and a street crossed Castroville Street from east to west. And for the life of me I cannot remember the name of that street. If you turned left on that street and crossed the tracks you were in Chinatown. If you turned right you were on the Row.

It was a black 'dobe street, deep shining mud in winter and hard as rutted iron in summer. In the spring the tall grass grew along its sides—wild oats and mallow weeds and yellow mustard mixed in. In the early morning the sparrows shrieked over the horse manure in the street.

Do you remember hearing that, old men? And do you remember how an easterly breeze brought odors in from Chinatown, roasting pork and punk and black tobacco and yen shi? And do you remember the deep blatting stroke of the great gong in the Joss House, and how its tone hung in the air so long?

Remember, too, the little houses, unpainted, unrepaired? They seemed very small, and they tried to efface themselves in outside neglect, and the wild overgrown front yards tried to hide them from the street. Remember how the shades were always drawn with little lines of yellow light around their edges? You could hear only a murmur from within. Then the front door would open to admit a country boy, and you'd hear laughter and perhaps the soft sentimental tone of an open-face piano with a piece of toilet chain across the strings, and then the door would close it off again.

Then you might hear horses' hoofs on the dirt street, and Pet Bulene would drive his hack up in front, and maybe four or five portly men would get out—great men, rich or official, bankers maybe, or the courthouse gang. And Pet would drive around the corner and settle down in his hack to wait for them. Big cats would ripple across the street to disappear in the tall grass.

And then—remember?—the train whistle and the boring light and a freight from King City would go stomping across Castroville Street and into Salinas and you could hear it sighing at the station. Remember?

Every town has its celebrated madams, eternal women to be sentimentalized down the years. There is something very attractive to men about a madam. She combines the brains of a businessman, the toughness of a prize fighter, the warmth of a companion, the humor of a tragedian. Myths collect around her, and, oddly enough, not voluptuous myths. The stories remembered and repeated about a madam cover every field but the bedroom. Remembering, her old customers picture her as philanthropist, medical authority, bouncer, and poetess of the bodily emotions without being involved with them.

For a number of years Salinas had sheltered two of these treasures: Jenny, sometimes called Fartin' Jenny, and the Nigger, who owned and operated the Long Green. Jenny was a good companion, a keeper of secrets, a giver of secret loans. There is a whole literature of stories about Jenny in Salinas.

The Nigger was a handsome, austere woman with snow-white hair and a dark and awful dignity. Her brown eyes, brooding deep in her skull, looked out on an ugly world with philosophic sorrow. She conducted her house like a cathedral dedicated to a sad but erect Priapus. If you wanted a good laugh and a poke in the ribs, you went to Jenny's and got your money's worth; but if the sweet world-sadness close to tears crept out of your immutable loneliness, the Long Green was your place. When you came out of there you felt that something pretty stern and important had happened. It was no jump in the hay. The dark beautiful eyes of the Nigger stayed with you for days.

When Faye came down from Sacramento and opened her house there was a flurry of animosity from the two incumbents. They got together to drive Faye out, but they discovered she was not in competition.

Faye was the motherly type, big-breasted, big-hipped, and warm. She was a bosom to cry on, a soother and a stroker. The iron sex of the Nigger and the tavern bacchanalianism of Jenny had their devotees, and they were not lost to Faye. Her house became the refuge of young men puling in puberty, mourning over lost virtue, and aching to lose some more. Faye was the reassurer of misbegotten husbands. Her house took up the slack for frigid wives. It was the cinnamon-scented kitchen of one's grandmother. If any sexual thing happened to you at Faye's you felt it was an accident but forgivable. Her house led the youths of Salinas into the thorny path of sex in the pinkest, smoothest way. Faye was a nice woman, not very bright, highly moral, and easily shocked. People trusted her and she trusted everyone. No one could want to hurt Faye once he knew her. She was no competition to the others. She was a third phase.

Just as in a store or on a ranch the employees are images of the boss, so in a whorehouse the girls are very like the madam, partly because she hires that kind and partly because a good madam imprints her personality on the business. You could stay a very long time at Faye's before you would hear an ugly or suggestive word spoken. The wanderings to the bedrooms, the payments, were so soft and casual they seemed incidental. All in all, she ran a hell of a fine house, as the constable and the sheriff knew. Faye contributed heavily to every charity. Having a revulsion against disease, she paid for regular inspection of her girls. You had less chance of contracting a difficulty at Faye's than with your Sunday School teacher. Faye soon became a solid and desirable citizen of the growing town of Salinas.

2

The girl Kate puzzled Faye—she was so young and pretty, so ladylike, so well educated. Faye took her into her own inviolate bedroom and questioned her far more than she would if Kate had been another kind of girl. There were always women knocking on the door of a whorehouse, and Faye recognized most of them instantly. She could tick them off—lazy, vengeful, lustful, unsatisfied, greedy, ambitious. Kate didn't fall into any of these classes.

"I hope you don't mind my asking you all these questions," she said. "It just seems so strange that you should come here. Why, you could get a husband and a surrey and a corner house in town with no trouble at all, no trouble at all." And Faye rolled her wedding band around and around on her fat little finger.

Kate smiled shyly. "It's so hard to explain. I hope you won't insist on knowing. The happiness of someone very near and dear to me is involved. Please don't ask me."

Faye nodded solemnly. "I've known things like that. I had one girl who was supporting her baby, and no one knew for a long, long time. That girl has a fine house and a husband in—there, I nearly told you where. I'd cut out my tongue before I'd tell. Do you have a baby, dear?"

Kate looked down to try to conceal the shine of tears in her eyes. When she could control her throat she whispered, "I'm sorry, I can't talk about it."

"That's all right. That's all right. You just take your time."

Faye was not bright, but she was far from stupid. She went to the sheriff and got herself cleared. There was no sense in taking chances. She knew something was wrong about Kate, but if it didn't harm the house it really wasn't Faye's business.

Kate might have been a chiseler, but she wasn't. She went to work right away. And when customers come back again and again and ask for a girl by name, you know you've got something. A pretty face won't do that. It was quite apparent to Faye that Kate was not learning a new trade.

There are two things it is good to know about a new girl: first, will she work? and second, will she get along with the other girls? There's nothing will upset a house like an ill-tempered girl.

Faye didn't have long to wonder about the second question. Kate put herself out to be pleasant. She helped the other girls keep their rooms clean. She served them when they were sick, listened to their troubles, answered them in matters of love, and as soon as she had some, loaned them money. You couldn't want a better girl. She became best friend to everyone in the house.

There was no trouble Kate would not take, no drudgery she was afraid of, and, in addition, she brought business. She soon had her own group of regular customers. Kate was thoughtful too. She remembered birthdays and always had a present and a cake with candles. Faye realized she had a treasure.

People who don't know think it is easy to be a madam—just sit in a big chair and drink beer and take half the money the girls make, they think. But it's not like that at all. You have to feed the girls—that's groceries and a cook. Your laundry problem is quite a bit more complicated than that of a hotel. You have to keep the girls well and as happy as possible, and some of them can get pretty ornery. You have to keep suicide at an absolute minimum, and whores, particularly the ones getting along in years, are flighty with a razor; and that gets your house a bad name.

It isn't so easy, and if you have waste too you can lose money. When Kate offered to help with the marketing and planning of meals Faye was pleased, although she didn't know when the girl found time. Well, not only did the food improve, but the grocery bills came down one-third the first month Kate took over. And the laundry—Faye didn't know what Kate said to the man but that bill suddenly dropped twenty-five per cent. Faye didn't see how she ever got along without Kate.

In the late afternoon before business they sat together in Faye's room and drank tea. It was much nicer since Kate had painted the woodwork and put up lace curtains. The girls began to realize that there were two bosses, not one, and they were glad because Kate was very easy to get along with. She made them turn more tricks but she wasn't mean about it. They'd as likely as not have a big laugh over it.

By the time a year had passed Faye and Kate were like mother and daughter. And the girls said, "You watch—she'll own this house some day."

Kate's hands were always busy, mostly at drawn work on the sheerest of lawn handkerchiefs. She could make beautiful initials. Nearly all the girls carried and treasured her handkerchiefs.

Gradually a perfectly natural thing happened. Faye, the essence of motherness, began to think of Kate as her daughter. She felt this in her breast and in her emotions, and her natural morality took hold. She did not want her daughter to be a whore. It was a perfectly reasonable sequence.

Faye thought hard how she was going to bring up the subject. It was a problem. It was Faye's nature to approach any subject sideways. She could not say, "I want you to give up whoring."

She said, "If it is a secret, don't answer, but I've always meant to ask you. What did the sheriff say to you—good Lord, is it a year ago? How the time goes! Quicker as you get older, I think. He was nearly an hour with you. He didn't—but of course not. He's a family man. He goes to Jenny's. But I don't want to pry into your affairs."

"There's no secret at all about that," said Kate. "I would have told you. He told me I should go home. He was very nice about it. When I explained that I couldn't, he was very nice and understanding."

"Did you tell him why?" Faye asked jealously.

"Of course not. Do you think I would tell him when I won't tell you? Don't be silly, darling. You're such a funny little girl."

Faye smiled and snuggled contentedly down in her chair.

Kate's face was in repose, but she was remembering every word of that interview. As a matter of fact, she rather liked the sheriff. He was direct.

3

He had closed the door of her room, glanced around with the quick record-ing eye of a good policeman—no photographs, none of the personal articles which identify, nothing but clothes and shoes.

He sat down on her little cane rocking chair and his buttocks hung over on each side. His fingers got together in conference, talking to one another like ants. He spoke in an unemotional tone, almost as though he weren't much interested in what he was saying. Maybe that was what impressed her.

At first she put on her slightly stupid demure look, but after a few of his words she gave that up and bored into him with her eyes, trying to read his thoughts. He neither looked in her eyes nor avoided them. But she was aware that he was inspecting her as she inspected him. She felt his glance go over the scar on her forehead almost as though he had touched it.

"I don't want to make a record," he said quietly. "I've held office a long time. About one more term will be enough. You know, young woman, if this were fifteen years back I'd do some checking, and I guess I'd find some-thing pretty nasty." He waited for some reaction from her but she did not protest. He nodded his head slowly. "I don't want to know," he said. "I want peace in this county, and I mean all kinds of peace, and that means people getting to sleep at night. Now I haven't met your husband," he said, and she knew he noticed the slight movement of her tightening muscles. "I hear he's a very nice man. I hear also that he's pretty hard hit." He looked into her eyes for a moment. "Don't you want to know how bad you shot him?"

"Yes," she said.

"Well, he's going to get well—smashed his shoulder, but he's going to get well. That Chink is taking pretty good care of him. Course I don't think he'll lift anything with his left arm for quite a spell. A forty-four tears hell out of a man. If the Chink hadn't come back he'd of bled to death, and you'd be staying with me in the jail."

Kate was holding her breath, listening for any hint of what was coming and not hearing any hints.

"I'm sorry," she said quietly.

The sheriff's eyes became alert. "Now that's the first time you've made a mistake," he said. "You're not sorry. I knew somebody like you once—hung him twelve years ago in front of the county jail. We used to do that here."

The little room with its dark mahogany bed, its marble-top wash stand with bowl and pitcher and a door for the pot, its wallpaper endlessly repeating little roses—little roses—the little room was silent, the sound sucked out of it.

The sheriff was staring at a picture of three cherubim—just heads, curlyaired, limpid-eyed, with wings about the size of pigeons' wings growing out of where their necks would be. He frowned. "That's a funny picture for a whorehouse," he said.

"It was here," said Kate. Apparently the preliminaries were over now.

The sheriff straightened up, undid his fingers, and held the arms of his chair. Even his buttocks pulled in a little. "You left a couple of babies," he said. "Little boys. Now you calm down. I'm not going to try to get you to go back. I guess I'd do quite a bit to keep you from going back. I think I know you. I could just run you over the county line and have the next sheriff run you, and that could keep up till you landed splash in the Atlantic Ocean. But I don't want to do that. I don't care how you live as long as you don't give me any trouble. A whore is a whore."

Kate asked evenly, "What is it you do want?"

"That's more like it," the sheriff said. "Here's what I want. I notice you changed your name. I want you to keep your new name. I guess you made up someplace you came from—well, that's where you came from. And your reason—that's when you're maybe drunk—you keep your reason about two thousand miles away from King City."

She was smiling a little, and not a forced smile. She was beginning to trust this man and to like him.

"One thing I thought of," he said. "Did you know many people around King City?"

"No."

"I heard about the knitting needle," he said casually. "Well, it could happen that somebody you knew might come in here. That your real hair color?"

"Yes."

"Dye it black for a while. Lots of people look like somebody else."

"How about this?" She touched her scar with a slender finger.

"Well, that's just a—what is that word? What is that goddam word? I had it this morning."

"Coincidence?"

"That's it—coincidence." He seemed to be finished. He got out tobacco and papers and rolled a clumsy, lumpy cigarette. He broke out a sulphur match and struck it on the block and held it away until its acrid blue flame turned yellow. His cigarette burned crookedly up the side.

Kate said, "Isn't there a threat? I mean, what you'll do if I—"

"No, there isn't. I guess I could think up something pretty ornery, though, if it came to that. No, I don't want you—what you are, what you do, or what you say—to hurt Mr. Trask or his boys. You figure you died and now you're somebody else and we'll get along fine."

He stood up and went to the door, then turned. "I've got a boy—he'll be twenty this year; big, nice-looking fellow with a broken nose. Everybody likes him. I don't want him in here. I'll tell Faye too. Let him go to Jenny's.

If he comes in, you tell him to go to Jenny's." He closed the door behind
him.

Kate smiled down at her fingers.

4

Faye twisted around in her chair to reach a piece of brown panocha studded
with walnuts. When she spoke it was around a mouth full of candy. Kate
wondered uneasily whether she could read minds, for Faye said, "I still don'
like it as well. I said it then and I say it again. I liked your hair blond better
I don't know what got into you to change it. You've got a fair complexion."

Kate caught a single thread of hair with fingernails of thumb and forefinger and gently drew it out. She was very clever. She told the best lie of
all—the truth. "I didn't want to tell you," she said. "I was afraid I might be
recognized and that would hurt someone."

Faye got up out of her chair and went to Kate and kissed her. "What a
good child it is," she said. "What a thoughtful dear."

Kate said, "Let's have some tea. I'll bring it in." She went out of the
room, and in the hall on the way to the kitchen she rubbed the kiss from
her cheek with her fingertips.

Back in her chair, Faye picked out a piece of panocha with a whole walnut
showing through. She put it in her mouth and bit into a piece of walnut
shell. The sharp, pointed fragment hit a hollow tooth and whanged into the
nerve. Blue lights of pain flashed through her. Her forehead became wet.
When Kate came back with teapot and cups on a tray Faye was clawing at
her mouth with a crooked finger and whimpering in agony.

"What is it?" Kate cried.

"Tooth—nutshell."

"Here, let me see. Open and point." Kate looked into the open mouth,
then went to the nut bowl on the fringed table for a nut pick. In a fraction
of a second she had dug out the shell and held it in the palm of her hand.
"There it is."

The nerve stopped shrieking and the pain dropped to an ache. "Only
that big? It felt like a house. Look, dear," said Faye, "open that second
drawer where my medicine is. Bring the paregoric and a piece of cotton.
Will you help me pack this tooth?"

Kate brought the bottle and pushed a little ball of saturated cotton into
the tooth with the point of the nut pick. "You ought to have it out."

"I know. I will."

"I have three teeth missing on this side."

"Well, you'd never know it. That made me feel all shaky. Bring me the
Pinkham, will you?" She poured herself a slug of the vegetable compound
and sighed with relief. "That's a wonderful medicine," she said. "The
woman who invented it was a saint."

TWENTY

It was a pleasant afternoon. Frémont's Peak was lighted pinkly by the setting sun, and Faye could see it from her window. From over on Castroville Street came the sweet sound of jingling horse bells from an eight-horse grain team down from the ridge. The cook was fighting pots in the kitchen. There was a rubbing sound on the wall and then a gentle tap on the door.

"Come in, Cotton Eye," Faye called.

The door opened and the crooked little cotton-eyed piano player stood in the entrance, waiting for a sound to tell him where she was.

"What is it you want?" Faye asked.

He turned to her. "I don't feel good, Miss Faye. I want to crawl into my bed and not do no playing tonight."

"You were sick two nights last week, Cotton Eye. Don't you like your job?"

"I don't feel good."

"Well, all right. But I wish you'd take better care of yourself."

Kate said softly, "Let the gong alone for a couple of weeks, Cotton Eye."

"Oh, Miss Kate. I didn't know you was here. I ain't been smoking."

"You've been smoking," Kate said.

"Yes, Miss Kate, I sure will let it alone. I don't feel good." He closed the door, and they could hear his hand rubbing along the wall to guide him.

Faye said, "He told me he'd stopped."

"He hasn't stopped."

"The poor thing," said Faye, "he doesn't have much to live for."

Kate stood in front of her. "You're so sweet," she said. "You believe in everybody. Someday if you don't watch, or I don't watch for you, someone will steal the roof."

"Who'd want to steal from me?" asked Faye.

Kate put her hand on Faye's plump shoulders. "Not everyone is as nice as you are."

Faye's eyes glistened with tears. She picked up a handkerchief from the chair beside her and wiped her eyes and patted delicately at her nostrils. "You're like my own daughter, Kate," she said.

"I'm beginning to believe I am. I never knew my mother. She died when I was small."

Faye drew a deep breath and plunged into the subject.

"Kate, I don't like you working here."

"Why not?"

Faye shook her head, trying to find words. "I'm not ashamed. I run a nice house. If I didn't somebody else might run a bad house. I don't do anybody any harm. I'm not ashamed."

"Why should you be?" asked Kate.

"But I don't like you working. I just don't like it. You're sort of my daughter. I don't like my daughter working."

"Don't be a silly, darling," said Kate. "I have to—here or somewhere else. I told you. I have to have the money."

"No, you don't."

"Of course I do. Where else could I get it?"

"You could be my daughter. You could manage the house. You could take care of things for me and not go upstairs. I'm not always well, you know."

"I know you're not, poor darling. But I have to have money."

"There's plenty for both of us, Kate. I could give you as much as you make and more, and you'd be worth it."

Kate shook her head sadly. "I do love you," she said. "And I wish I could do what you want. But you need your little reserve, and I—well, suppose something should happen to you? No, I must go on working. Do you know, dear, I have five regulars tonight?"

A jar of shock struck Faye. "I don't want you to work."

"I have to, Mother."

The word did it. Faye burst into tears, and Kate sat on the arm of her chair and stroked her cheek and wiped her streaming eyes. The outburst sniffled to a close.

The dusk was settling deeply on the valley. Kate's face was a glow of lightness under her dark hair. "Now you're all right. I'll go and look in on the kitchen and then dress."

"Kate, can't you tell your regulars you're sick?"

"Of course not, Mother."

"Kate, it's Wednesday. Probably won't be anybody in after one o'clock."

"The Woodmen of the World are having a do."

"Oh, yes. But on Wednesday—the Woodmen won't be here after two."

"What are you getting at?"

"Kate, when you close, you tap on my door. I'll have a little surprise for you."

"What kind of a surprise?"

"Oh, a secret surprise! Will you ask the cook to come in as you go by the kitchen?"

"Sounds like a cake surprise."

"Now don't ask questions, darling. It's a surprise."

Kate kissed her. "What a dear you are, Mother."

When she had closed the door behind her Kate stood for a moment in the hall. Her fingers caressed her little pointed chin. Her eyes were calm. Then she stretched her arms over her head and strained her body in a luxurious yawn. She ran her hands slowly down her sides from right under her breasts to her hips. Her mouth corners turned up a little, and she moved toward the kitchen.

2

The few regulars drifted in and out and two drummers walked down the Line to look them over, but not a single Woodman of the World showed up. The girls sat yawning in the parlor until two o'clock, waiting.

What kept the Woodmen away was a sad accident. Clarence Monteith had a heart attack right in the middle of the closing ritual and before supper. They laid him out on the carpet and dampened his forehead until the doctor came. Nobody felt like sitting down to the doughnut supper. After Dr. Wilde had arrived and looked Clarence over, the Woodmen made a stretcher by putting flagpoles through the sleeves of two overcoats. On the way home Clarence died, and they had to go for Dr. Wilde again. And by the time they had made plans for the funeral and written the piece for the *Salinas Journal*, nobody had any heart for a whorehouse.

The next day, when they found out what had happened, the girls all remembered what Ethel had said at ten minutes to two.

"My god!" Ethel had said, "I never heard it so quiet. No music, cat's got Kate's tongue. It's like setting up with a corpse."

Later Ethel was impressed with having said it—almost as if she knew.

Grace had said, "I wonder what cat's got Kate's tongue. Don't you feel good? Kate—I said, don't you feel good?"

Kate started. "Oh! I guess I was thinking of something."

"Well, I'm not," said Grace. "I'm sleepy. Why don't we close up? Let's ask Faye if we can't lock up. There won't even be a Chink in tonight. I'm going to ask Faye."

Kate's voice cut in on her. "Let Faye alone. She's not well. We'll close up at two."

"That clock's way wrong," said Ethel. "What's the matter with Faye?"

Kate said, "Maybe that's what I was thinking about. Faye's not well. I'm worried to death about her. She won't show it if she can help it."

"I thought she was all right," Grace said.

Ethel hit the jackpot again. "Well, she don't look good to me. She's got a kind of flush. I noticed it."

Kate spoke very softly. "Don't you girls ever let her know I told you. She wouldn't want you to worry. What a dear she is!"

"Best goddam house I ever hustled," said Grace.

Alice said, "You better not let her hear you talk words like that."

"Balls!" said Grace. "She knows all the words."

"She don't like to hear them—not from us."

Kate said patiently, "I want to tell you what happened. I was having tea with her late this afternoon and she fainted dead away. I do wish she'd see a doctor."

"I noticed she had a kind of bright flush," Ethel repeated. "That clock's way wrong but I forget which way."

Kate said, "You girls go on to bed. I'll lock up."

When they were gone Kate went to her room and put on her pretty new print dress that made her look like a little girl. She brushed and braided her hair and let it hang behind in one thick pigtail tied with a little white bow. She patted her cheeks with Florida water. For a moment she hesitated, and then from the top bureau drawer she took a little gold watch that hung from a fleur-de-lis pin. She wrapped it in one of her fine lawn handkerchiefs and went out of the room.

The hall was very dark, but a rim of light showed under Faye's door. Kate tapped softly.

Faye called, "Who is it?"

"It's Kate."

"Don't you come in yet. You wait outside. I'll tell you when." Kate heard a rustling and a scratching in the room. Then Faye called, "All right. Come in."

The room was decorated. Japanese lanterns with candles in them hung on bamboo sticks at the corners, and red crepe paper twisted in scallops from the center to the corners to give the effect of a tent. On the table, with candlesticks around it, was a big white cake and a box of chocolates, and beside these a basket with a magnum of champagne peeking out of crushed ice. Faye wore her best lace dress and her eyes were shiny with emotion.

"What in the world?" Kate cried. She closed the door. "Why, it looks like a party!"

"It is a party. It's a party for my dear daughter."

"It's not my birthday."

Faye said, "In a way maybe it is."

"I don't know what you mean. But I brought you a present." She laid the folded handkerchief in Faye's lap. "Open it carefully," she said.

Faye held the watch up. "Oh, my dear, my dear! You crazy child! No, I can't take it." She opened the face and then picked open the back with her fingernail. It was engraved—"To C. with all my heart from A."

"It was my mother's watch," Kate said softly. "I would like my new mother to have it."

"My darling child! My darling child!"

"Mother would be glad."

"But it's my party. I have a present for my dear daughter—but I'll have to do it in my own way. Now, Kate, you open the bottle of wine and pour two glasses. I want it to be fancy."

When everything was ready Faye took her seat behind the table. She raised her glass. "To my new daughter—may you have long life and happiness." And when they had drunk Kate proposed, "To my mother."

Faye said, "You'll make me cry—don't make me cry. Over on the bureau, dear. Bring the little mahogany box. There, that's the one. Now put it on the table here and open it."

In the polished box lay a rolled white paper tied with a red ribbon. "What in the world is it?" Kate asked.

"It's my gift to you. Open it."

Kate very carefully untied the red ribbon and unrolled the tube. It was written elegantly with shaded letters, and it was well and carefully drawn and witnessed by the cook.

"All my worldly goods without exception to Kate Albey because I regard her as my daughter."

It was simple, direct, and legally irreproachable. Kate read it three times, looked back at the date, studied the cook's signature. Faye watched her, and her lips were parted in expectation. When Kate's lips moved, reading, Faye's lips moved.

Kate rolled the paper and tied the ribbon around it and put it in the box and closed the lid. She sat in her chair.

Faye said at last, "Are you pleased?"

Kate's eyes seemed to peer into and beyond Faye's eyes—to penetrate the brain behind the eyes. Kate said quietly, "I'm trying to hold on, Mother. I didn't know anyone could be so good. I'm afraid if I say anything too quickly or come too close to you, I'll break to pieces."

It was more dramatic than Faye had anticipated, quiet and electric. Faye said, "It's a funny present, isn't it?"

"Funny? No, it isn't funny."

"I mean, a will is a strange present. But it means more than that. Now you are my real daughter I can tell you. I—no, we—have cash and securities in excess of sixty thousand dollars. In my desk are notations of accounts and safe-deposit boxes. I sold the place in Sacramento for a very good price. Why are you so silent, child? Is something bothering you?"

"A will sounds like death. That's thrown a pall."

"But everyone should make a will."

"I know, Mother." Kate smiled ruefully. "A thought crossed my mind. I thought of all your kin coming in angrily to break such a will as this. You can't do this."

"My poor little girl, is that what's bothering you? I have no folks. As far as I know I have no kin. And if I did have some—who would know? Do you think you are the only one with secrets? Do you think I use the name I was born with?"

Kate looked long and levelly at Faye.

"Kate," she cried, "Kate, it's a party. Don't be sad! Don't be frozen!"

Kate got up, gently pulled the table aside, and sat down on the floor. She put her cheek on Faye's knee. Her slender fingers traced a gold thread on the skirt through its intricate leaf pattern. And Faye stroked Kate's cheek and hair and touched her strange ears. Shyly Faye's fingers explored to the borders of the scar.

"I think I've never been so happy before," said Kate.

"My darling. You make me happy too. Happier than I have ever been. Now I don't feel alone. Now I feel safe."

Kate picked delicately at the gold thread with her fingernails.

They sat in the warmth for a long time before Faye stirred. "Kate," she said, "we're forgetting. It's a party. We've forgotten the wine. Pour it, child. We'll have a little celebration."

Kate said uneasily, "Do we need it, Mother?"

"It's good. Why not? I like to take on a little load. It lets the poison out. Don't you like champagne, Kate?"

"Well, I never have drunk much. It's not good for me."

"Nonsense. Pour it, darling."

Kate got up from the floor and filled the glasses.

Faye said, "Now drink it down. I'm watching you. You're not going to let an old woman get silly by herself."

"You're not an old woman, Mother."

"Don't talk—drink it. I won't touch mine until yours is empty." She held her glass until Kate had emptied hers, then gulped it. "Good, that's good," she said. "Fill them up. Now, come on dear—down the rat hole. After two or three the bad things go away."

Kate's chemistry screamed against the wine. She remembered, and she was afraid.

Faye said, "Now let me see the bottom, child—there. You see how good it is? Fill up again."

The transition came to Kate almost immediately after the second glass. Her fear evaporated, her fear of anything disappeared. This was what she had been afraid of, and now it was too late. The wine had forced a passage through all the carefully built barriers and defenses and deceptions, and she didn't care. The thing she had learned to cover and control was lost. Her voice became chill and her mouth was thin. Her wide-set eyes slitted and grew watchful and sardonic.

"Now you drink—Mother—while I watch," she said. "There's a—dear. I'll bet you can't drink two without stopping."

"Don't bet me, Kate. You'd lose. I can drink six without stopping."

"Let me see you."

"If I do, will you?"

"Of course."

The contest started, and a puddle of wine spread out over the table-top and the wine went down in the magnum.

Faye giggled. "When I was a girl—I could tell you stories maybe you wouldn't believe."

Kate said, "I could tell stories nobody would believe."

"You? Don't be silly. You're a child."

Kate laughed. "You never saw such a child. This is a child—yes—a child!" She laughed with a thin penetrating shriek.

The sound got through the wine that was muffling Faye. She centered her eyes on Kate. "You look so strange," she said. "I guess it's the lamplight. You look different."

"I am different."

"Call me 'Mother,' dear."

"*Mother—dear.*"

"Kate, we're going to have such a good life."

"You bet we are. You don't even know. You don't know."

"I've always wanted to go to Europe. We could get on a ship and have nice clothes—dresses from Paris."

"Maybe we'll do that—but not now."

"Why not, Kate? I have plenty of money."

"We'll have plenty more."

Faye spoke pleadingly, "Why don't we go now? We could sell the house. With the business we've got, we could get maybe ten thousand dollars for it."

"No."

"What do you mean, no? It's my house. I can sell it."

"Did you forget I'm your daughter?"

"I don't like your tone, Kate. What's the matter with you? Is there any more wine?"

"Sure, there's a little. Look at it through the bottle. Here, drink it out of the bottle. That's right—Mother—spill it down your neck. Get it in under your corset, Mother, against your fat stomach."

Faye wailed, "Kate, don't be mean! We were feeling so nice. What do you want to go and spoil it for?"

Kate wrenched the bottle from her hand. "Here, give me that." She tipped it up and drained it and dropped it on the floor. Her face was sharp and her eyes glinted. The lips of her little mouth were parted to show her small sharp teeth, and the canines were longer and more pointed than the others. She laughed softly. "Mother—dear Mother—I'm going to show you how to run a whorehouse. We'll fix the gray slugs that come in here and dump their nasty little loads—for a dollar. We'll give them pleasure, Mother dear."

Faye said sharply, "Kate, you're drunk. I don't know what you're talking about."

"You don't, Mother dear? Do you want me to tell you?"

"I want you to be sweet. I want you to be like you were."

"Well, it's too late. I didn't want to drink the wine. But you, you nasty fat worm, you made me. I'm your dear, sweet daughter—don't you remember? Well, I remember how surprised you were that I had regulars. Do you think I'll give them up? Do you think they give me a mean little dollar in quarters? No, they give me ten dollars, and the price is going up all the time. They can't go to anybody else. Nobody else is any good for them."

Faye wept like a child. "Kate," she said, "don't talk like that. You're not like that. You're not like that."

"Dear Mother, sweet fat Mother, take down the pants of one of my regulars. Look at the heelmarks on the groin—very pretty. And the little cuts that bleed for a long time. Oh, Mother dear, I've got the sweetest set of razors all in a case—and so sharp, so sharp."

Faye struggled to get out of her chair. Kate pushed her back. "And do you know, Mother dear, that's the way this whole house is going to be. The price will be twenty dollars, and we'll make the bastards take a bath. We'll catch the blood on white silk handkerchiefs—Mother dear—blood from the little knotted whips."

In her chair Faye began to scream hoarsely. Kate was on her instantly with a hard hand cupped over her mouth. "Don't make a noise. There's a good darling. Get snot all over your daughter's hand—but no noise." Tentatively she took her hand away and wiped it on Faye's skirt.

Faye whispered, "I want you out of the house. I want you out. I run a good house without nastiness. I want you out."

"I can't go, Mother. I can't leave you alone, poor dear." Her voice chilled. "Now I'm sick of you. Sick of you." She took a wineglass from the table, went to the bureau, and poured paregoric until the glass was half full. "Here, Mother, drink it. It will be good for you."

"I don't want to."

"There's a good dear. Drink it." She coaxed the fluid into Faye. "Now one more swallow—just one more."

Faye mumbled thickly for a while and then she relaxed in her chair and slept, snoring thickly.

3

Dread began to gather in the corners of Kate's mind, and out of dread came panic. She remembered the other time and a nausea swept through her. She gripped her hands together, and the panic grew. She lighted a candle from the lamp and went unsteadily down the dark hall to the kitchen. She poured dry mustard in a glass, stirred water into it until it was partly fluid, and drank it. She held on to the edge of the sink while the paste went burning down. She retched and strained again and again. At the end of it, her heart was pounding and she was weak—but the wine was overcome and her mind was clear.

She went over the evening in her mind, moving from scene to scene like a sniffing animal. She bathed her face and washed out the sink and put the mustard back on the shelf. Then she went back to Faye's room.

The dawn was coming, lighting up the back of Frémont's Peak so that it stood black against the sky. Faye was still snoring in her chair. Kate watched her for a few moments and then she fixed Faye's bed. Kate dragged and strained and lifted the dead weight of the sleeping woman. On the bed Kate undressed Faye and washed her face and put her clothes away.

The day was coming fast. Kate sat beside the bed and watched the relaxed face, the mouth open, lips blowing in and out.

Faye made a restless movement and her dry lips slobbered a few thick words and sighed off to a snore again.

Kate's eyes became alert. She opened the top bureau drawer and examined the bottles which constituted the medicine chest of the house—paregoric, Pain Killer, Lydia Pinkham, iron wine tonic, Hall's Cream Salve, Epsom salts, castor oil, ammonia. She carried the ammonia bottle to the bed, saturated a handkerchief, and, standing well away, held the cloth over Faye's nose and mouth.

The strangling, shocking fumes went in, and Faye came snorting and fighting out of her black web. Her eyes were wide and terrified.

Kate said, "It's all right, Mother. It's all right. You had a nightmare. You had a bad dream."

"Yes, a dream," and then sleep overcame her again and she fell back and began to snore, but the shock of the ammonia had lifted her up nearer consciousness and she was more restless. Kate put the bottle back in its drawer. She straightened the table, mopped up the spilled wine, and carried the glasses to the kitchen.

The house was dusky with dawnlight creeping in around the edges of the blinds. The cook stirred in his lean-to behind the kitchen, groping for his clothes and putting on his clodhopper shoes.

Kate moved quietly. She drank two glasses of water and filled the glass again and carried it back to Faye's room and closed the door. She lifted Faye's right eyelid, and the eye looked rakishly up at her but it was not rolled back in her head. Kate acted slowly and precisely. She picked up the handkerchief and smelled it. Some of the ammonia had evaporated but the smell was still sharp. She laid the cloth lightly over Faye's face, and when Faye twisted and turned and came near to waking, Kate took the handkerchief away and let Faye sink back. This she did three times. She put the handkerchief away and picked up an ivory crochet hook from the marble top of the bureau. She turned down the cover and pressed the blunt end of the ivory against Faye's flabby breast with a steady, increasing pressure until the sleeping woman whined and writhed. Then Kate explored the sensitive places of the body with the hook—under the arm, the groin, the ear, the clitoris, and always she removed the pressure just before Faye awakened fully.

Faye was very near the surface now. She whined and sniffled and tossed. Kate stroked her forehead and ran smooth fingers over her inner arm and spoke softly to her.

"Dear—dear. You're having such a bad dream. Come out of the bad dream, Mother."

Faye's breathing grew more regular. She heaved a great sigh and turned on her side and settled down with little grunts of comfort.

Kate stood up from the bed and a wave of dizziness rose in her head. She steadied herself, then went to the door and listened, slipped out, and moved cautiously to her own room. She undressed quickly and put on her nightgown and a robe and slippers. She brushed her hair and put it up and covered it with a sleeping cap, and she sponged her face with Florida water. She went quietly back to Faye's room.

Faye was still sleeping peacefully on her side. Kate opened the door to the hall. She carried the glass of water to the bed and poured cold water in Faye's ear.

Faye screamed, and screamed again. Ethel's frightened face looked out of her room in time to see Kate in robe and slippers at Faye's door. The cook was right behind Kate, and he put out his hand to stop her.

"Now don't go in there, Miss Kate. You don't know what's in there."

"Nonsense, Faye's in trouble." Kate burst in and ran to the bed.

Faye's eyes were wild and she was crying and moaning.

"What is it? What is it, dear?"

The cook was in the middle of the room, and three sleep-haggard girls stood in the doorway.

"Tell me, what is it?" Kate cried.

"Oh, darling—the dreams, the dreams! I can't stand them!"

Kate turned to the door. "She's had a nightmare—she'll be all right. You go back to bed. I'll stay with her a while. Alex, bring a pot of tea."

Kate was tireless. The other girls remarked on it. She put cold towels on Faye's aching head and held her shoulders and the cup of tea for her. She petted and babied her, but the look of horror would not go out of Faye's eyes. At ten o'clock Alex brought in a can of beer and without a word put it on the bureau top. Kate held a glass of it to Faye's lips.

"It will help, darling. Drink it down."

"I never want another drink."

"Nonsense! Drink it down like medicine. That's a good girl. Now just lie back and go to sleep."

"I'm afraid to sleep."

"Were the dreams so bad?"

"Horrible, horrible!"

"Tell me about them, Mother. Maybe that will help."

Faye shrank back. "I wouldn't tell anyone. How I could have dreamed hem! They weren't like my dreams."

"Poor little Mother! I love you," Kate said. "You go to sleep. I'll keep he dreams away."

Gradually Faye did slip off to sleep. Kate sat beside the bed, studying er.

TWENTY-ONE

In human affairs of danger and delicacy successful conclusion is sharply imited by hurry. So often men trip by being in a rush. If one were properly to perform a difficult and subtle act, he should first inspect the end to be achieved and then, once he had accepted the end as desirable, he should forget it completely and concentrate solely on the means. By this method he would not be moved to false action by anxiety or hurry or fear. Very few people learn this.

What made Kate so effective was the fact that she had either learned it or had been born with the knowledge. Kate never hurried. If a barrier arose, she waited until it had disappeared before continuing. She was capable of complete relaxation between the times for action. Also, she was mistress of a technique which is the basis of good wrestling—that of letting your opponent do the heavy work toward his own defeat, or of guiding his strength toward his weaknesses.

Kate was in no hurry. She thought to the end very quickly and then put it out of her mind. She set herself to work on method. She built a structure and attacked it, and if it showed the slightest shakiness she tore it down and started fresh. This she did only late at night or otherwise when she was completely alone, so that no change or preoccupation was noticeable in her manner. Her building was constructed of personalities, materials, knowledge, and time. She had access to the first and last, and she set about getting knowledge and materials, but while she did that she set in motion a series of imperceptible springs and pendulums and left them to pick up their own momenta.

First the cook told about the will. It must have been the cook. He thought he did anyway. Kate heard about it from Ethel, and she confronted him in the kitchen where he was kneading bread, his hairy big arms floured to the elbows and his hands yeast bleached.

"Do you think it was a good thing to tell about being a witness?" she said mildly. "What do you think Miss Faye is going to think?"

He looked confused. "But I didn't—"

"You didn't what—tell about it or think it would hurt?"

"I don't think I—"

"You don't think you told? Only three people knew. Do you think I told? Or do you think Miss Faye did?" She saw the puzzled look come into his eyes and knew that by now he was far from sure that he had not told. In a moment he would be sure that he had.

Three of the girls questioned Kate about the will, coming to her together for mutual strength.

Kate said, "I don't think Faye would like me to discuss it. Alex should have kept his mouth shut." Their wills wavered, and she said, "Why don't you ask Faye?"

"Oh, we wouldn't do that!"

"But you dare to talk behind her back! Come on now, let's go in to her and you can ask her the questions."

"No, Kate, no."

"Well, I'll have to tell her you asked. Wouldn't you rather be there? Don't you think she would feel better if she knew you weren't talking behind her back?"

"Well—"

"I know I would. I always like a person who comes right out." Quietly she surrounded and nudged and pushed until they stood in Faye's room.

Kate said, "They asked me about a certain you-know-what. Alex admits he let it out."

Faye was slightly puzzled. "Well, dear, I can't see that it's such a secret."

Kate said, "Oh, I'm glad you feel that way. But you can see that I couldn't mention it until you did."

"You think it's bad to tell, Kate?"

"Oh, not at all. I'm glad, but it seemed to me that it wouldn't be loyal of me to mention it before you did."

"You're sweet, Kate. I don't see any harm. You see, girls, I'm alone in the world and I have taken Kate as my daughter. She takes such care of me. Get the box, Kate."

And each girl took the will in her own hands and inspected it. It was so simple they could repeat it word for word to the other girls.

They watched Kate to see how she would change, perhaps become a tyrant, but, if anything, she was nicer to them.

A week later when Kate became ill, she went right on with her supervision of the house, and no one would have known if she hadn't been found standing rigid in the hall with agony printed on her face. She begged the girls not to tell Faye, but they were outraged, and it was Faye who forced her to bed and called Dr. Wilde.

He was a nice man and a pretty good doctor. He looked at her tongue, felt her pulse, asked her a few intimate questions, and then tapped his lower lip.

"Right here?" he asked and exerted a little pressure on the small of her back. "No? Here? Does this hurt? So. Well, I think you just need a kidney flushing." He left yellow, green, and red pills to be taken in sequence. The pills did good work.

She did have one little flare up. She told Faye, "I'll go to the doctor's office."

"I'll ask him to come here."

"To bring me some more pills? Nonsense. I'll go in the morning."

2

Dr. Wilde was a good man and an honest man. He was accustomed to say of his profession that all he was sure of was that sulphur would cure the itch. He was not casual about his practice. Like so many country doctors, he was a combination doctor, priest, psychiatrist to his town. He knew most of the secrets, weaknesses, and the braveries of Salinas. He never learned to take death easily. Indeed the death of a patient always gave him a sense of failure and hopeless ignorance. He was not a bold man, and he used surgery only as a last and fearful resort. The drugstore was coming in to help the doctors, but Dr. Wilde was one of the few to maintain his own dispensary and to compound his own prescriptions. Many years of overwork and interrupted sleep had made him a little vague and preoccupied.

At eight-thirty on a Wednesday morning Kate walked up Main Street, climbed the stairs of the Monterey County Bank Building, and walked along the corridor until she found the door which said, "Dr. Wilde—Office Hours 11–2."

At nine-thirty Dr. Wilde put his buggy in the livery stable and wearily lifted out his black bag. He had been out in the Alisal presiding at the disintegration of old, old lady German. She had not been able to terminate her life neatly. There were codicils. Even now Dr. Wilde wondered whether the tough, dry, stringy life was completely gone out of her. She was ninety-seven and a death certificate meant nothing to her. Why, she had corrected the priest who prepared her. The mystery of death was on him. It often was. Yesterday, Allen Day, thirty-seven, six feet one inch, strong as a bull and valuable to four hundred acres and a large family, had meekly surrendered his life to pneumonia after a little exposure and three days of fever. Dr. Wilde knew it was a mystery. His eyelids felt grainy. He thought he would take a sponge bath and have a drink before his first office patients arrived with their stomach aches.

He climbed the stairs and put his worn key in the lock of his office door. The key would not turn. He set his bag on the floor and exerted pressure. The key refused to budge. He grabbed the doorknob and pulled outward and rattled the key. The door was opened from within. Kate stood in front of him.

"Oh, good morning. Lock was stuck. How did you get in?"

"It wasn't locked. I was early and came in to wait."

"Wasn't locked?" He turned the key the other way and saw that, sure enough, the little bar slipped out easily.

"I'm getting old, I guess," he said. "I'm forgetful." He sighed. "I don't know why I lock it anyway. You could get in with a piece of bailing wire. And who'd want to get in anyway?" He seemed to see her for the first time. "I don't have office hours until eleven."

Kate said, "I needed some more of those pills and I couldn't come later."

"Pills? Oh, yes. You're the girl from down at Faye's."

"That's right."

"Feeling better?"

"Yes, the pills help."

"Well, they can't hurt," he said. "Did I leave the door to the dispensary open too?"

"What's a dispensary?"

"Over there—that door."

"I guess you must have."

"Getting old. How is Faye?"

"Well, I'm worried about her. She was real sick a while ago. Had cramps and went a little out of her head."

"She's had a stomach disorder before," Dr. Wilde said. "You can't live like that and eat at all hours and be very well. I can't anyway. We just call it stomach trouble. Comes from eating too much and staying up all night. Now—the pills. Do you remember what color?"

"There were three kinds, yellow, red, and green."

"Oh, yes. Yes, I remember."

While he poured pills into a round cardboard box she stood in the door. "What a lot of medicines!"

Dr. Wilde said, "Yes—and the older I get, the fewer I use. I got some of those when I started to practice. Never used them. That's a beginner's stock. I was going to experiment—alchemy."

"What?"

"Nothing. Here you are. Tell Faye to get some sleep and eat some vegetables. I've been up all night. Let yourself out, will you?" He went wavering back into the surgery.

Kate glanced after him and then her eyes flicked over the lines of bottles and containers. She closed the dispensary door and looked around the outer office. One book in the case was out of line. She pushed it back until it was shoulder to shoulder with its brothers.

She picked up her big handbag from the leather sofa and left.

In her own room Kate took five small bottles and a strip of scribbled paper from her handbag. She put the whole works in the toe of a stocking, pushed the wad into a rubber overshoe, and stood it with its fellow in the back of her closet.

3

During the following months a gradual change came over Faye's house. The girls were sloppy and touchy. If they had been told to clean themselves and their rooms a deep resentment would have set in and the house would have reeked of ill temper. But it didn't work that way.

Kate said at table one evening that she had just happened to look in Ethel's room and it was so neat and pretty she couldn't help buying her a present. When Ethel unwrapped the package right at the table it was a big bottle of Hoyt's German, enough to keep her smelling sweet for a long time. Ethel was pleased, and she hoped Kate hadn't seen the dirty clothes under the bed. After supper she not only got the clothes out but brushed the floors and swept the cobwebs out of the corners.

Then Grace looked so pretty one afternoon that Kate couldn't help giving her the rhinestone butterfly pin she was wearing. And Grace had to rush up and put on a clean shirtwaist to set it off.

Alex in the kitchen, who, if he had believed what was usually said of him would have considered himself a murderer, found that he had a magic hand with biscuits. He discovered that cooking was something you couldn't learn. You had to feel it.

Cotton Eye learned that nobody hated him. His tub-thumping piano playing changed imperceptibly.

He told Kate, "It's funny what you remember when you think back."

"Like what?" she asked.

"Well, like this," and he played for her.

"That's lovely," she said. "What is it?"

"Well, I don't know. I think it's Chopin. If I could just see the music!"

He told her how he had lost his sight, and he had never told anyone else. It was a bad story. That Saturday night he took the chain off the piano strings and played something he had been remembering and practicing in the morning, something called "Moonlight," a piece by Beethoven, Cotton Eye thought.

Ethel said it sounded like moonlight and did he know the words.

"It don't have words," said Cotton Eye.

Oscar Trip, up from Gonzales for Saturday night, said, "Well, it ought to have. It's pretty."

One night there were presents for everyone because Faye's was the best house, the cleanest, and nicest in the whole county—and who was responsible for that? Why, the girls—who else? And did they ever taste seasoning like in that stew?

Alex retired into the kitchen and shyly wiped his eyes with the back of his wrist. He bet he could make a plum pudding would knock their eyes out.

Georgia was getting up at ten every morning and taking piano lessons from Cotton Eye and her nails were clean.

Coming back from eleven o'clock mass on a Sunday morning, Grace said to Trixie, "And I was about ready to get married and give up whoring. Can you imagine?"

"It's sure nice," said Trixie. "Jenny's girls came over for Faye's birthday cake and they couldn't believe their eyes. They don't talk about nothing else but how it is at Faye's. Jenny's sore."

"Did you see the score on the blackboard this morning?"

"Sure I did—eighty-seven tricks in one week. Let Jenny or the Nigger match that when there ain't no holidays!"

"No holidays, hell. Have you forgot it's Lent? They ain't turning a trick at Jenny's."

After her illness and her evil dreams Faye was quiet and depressed. Kate knew she was being watched, but there was no help for that. And she had made sure the rolled paper was still in the box and all the girls had seen it or heard about it.

One afternoon Faye looked up from her solitaire game as Kate knocked and entered the room.

"How do you feel, Mother?"

"Fine, just fine." Her eyes were secretive. Faye wasn't very clever. "You know, Kate, I'd like to go to Europe."

"Well, how wonderful! And you deserve it and you can afford it."

"I don't want to go alone. I want you to go with me."

Kate looked at her in astonishment. "Me? You want to take me?"

"Sure, why not?"

"Oh, you sweet dear! When can we go?"

"You want to?"

"I've always dreamed of it. When can we go? Let's go soon."

Faye's eyes lost their suspicion and her face relaxed. "Maybe next summer," she said. "We can plan it for next summer. Kate!"

"Yes, Mother."

"You—you don't turn any tricks any more, do you?"

"Why should I? You take such good care of me."

Faye slowly gathered up the cards, and tapped them square, and dropped them in the table drawer.

Kate pulled up a chair. "I want to ask your advice about something."

"What is it?"

"Well, you know I'm trying to help you."

"You're doing everything, darling."

"You know our biggest expense is food, and it gets bigger in the winter."

"Yes."

"Well, right now you can buy fruit and all kinds of vegetables for two bits a lug. And in the winter you know what we pay for canned peaches and canned string beans."

"You aren't planning to start preserving?"

"Well, why shouldn't we?"

"What will Alex say to that?"

"Mother, you can believe it or not, or you can ask him. Alex suggested it."

"No!"

"Well, he did. Cross my heart."

"Well, I'll be damned—Oh, I'm sorry, sweet. It slipped out."

The kitchen turned into a cannery and all the girls helped. Alex truly believed it was his idea. At the end of the season he had a silver watch with his name engraved on the back to prove it.

Ordinarily both Faye and Kate had their supper at the long table in the dining room, but on Sunday nights when Alex was off and the girls dined on thick sandwiches, Kate served supper for two in Faye's room. It was a pleasant and a ladylike time. There was always some little delicacy, very special and good—foie gras or a tossed salad, pastry bought at Lang's Bakery just across Main Street. And instead of the white oilcloth and paper napkins of the dining room, Faye's table was covered with a white damask cloth and the napkins were linen. It had a party feeling too, candles and—something rare in Salinas—a bowl of flowers. Kate could make pretty floral arrangements using only the blossoms from weeds she picked in the fields.

"What a clever girl she is," Faye would say. "She can do anything and she can make do with anything. We're going to Europe. And did you know Kate speaks French? Well, she can. When you get her alone ask her to say something in French. She's teaching me. Know how you say bread in French?" Faye was having a wonderful time. Kate gave her excitement and perpetual planning.

4

On Saturday the fourteenth of October the first wild ducks went over Salinas. Faye saw them from her window, a great wedge flying south. When Kate came in before supper, as she always did, Faye told her about it. "I guess the winter's nearly here," she said. "We'll have to get Alex to set up the stoves."

"Ready for your tonic, Mother dear?"

"Yes, I am. You're making me lazy, waiting on me."

"I like to wait on you," said Kate. She took the bottle of Lydia Pinkham's

Vegetable Compound from the drawer and held it up to the light. "Not much left," she said. "We'll have to get some more."

"Oh, I think I have three bottles left of the dozen in my closet."

Kate picked up the glass. "There's a fly in the glass," she said. "I'll just go and wash it out."

In the kitchen she rinsed the glass. From her pocket she took the eye-dropper. The end was closed with a little piece of potato, the way you plug the spout of a kerosene can. She carefully squeezed a few drops of clear liquid into the glass, a tincture of nux vomica.

Back in Faye's room she poured the three tablespoons of vegetable compound in the glass and stirred it.

Faye drank her tonic and licked her lips. "It tastes bitter," she said.

"Does it, dear? Let me taste." Kate took a spoonful from the bottle and made a face. "So it does," she said. "I guess it's been standing around too long. I'm going to throw it out. Say, that *is* bitter. Let me get you a glass of water."

At supper Faye's face was flushed. She stopped eating and seemed to be listening.

"What's the matter?" Kate asked. "Mother, what's the matter?"

Faye seemed to tear her attention away. "Why, I don't know. I guess a little heart flutter. Just all of a sudden I felt afraid and my heart got to pounding."

"Don't you want me to help you to your room?"

"No, dear, I feel all right now."

Grace put down her fork. "Well, you got a real high flush, Faye."

Kate said, "I don't like it. I wish you'd see Dr. Wilde."

"No, it's all right now."

"You frightened me," said Kate. "Have you ever had it before?"

"Well, I'm a little short of breath sometimes. I guess I'm getting too stout."

Faye didn't feel very good that Saturday night and about ten o'clock Kate persuaded her to go to bed. Kate looked in several times until she was sure Faye was asleep.

The next day Faye felt all right. "I guess I'm just short-winded," she said.

"Well, we're going to have invalid food for my darling," said Kate. "I've made some chicken soup for you, and we'll have a string-bean salad—the way you like it, just oil and vinegar, and a cup of tea."

"Honest to God, Kate, I feel pretty good."

"It wouldn't hurt either of us to eat a little light. You frightened me last night. I had an aunt who died of heart trouble. And that leaves a memory, you know."

"I never had any trouble with my heart. Just a little short-winded when I climb the stairs."

In the kitchen Kate set the supper on two trays. She measured out the French dressing in a cup and poured it on the string-bean salad. On Faye's tray she put her favorite cup and set the soup forward on the stove to heat. Finally she took the eye-dropper from her pocket and squeezed two drops of croton oil on the string beans and stirred it in. She went to her room and swallowed the contents of a small bottle of Cascara Sagrada and hurried back to the kitchen. She poured the hot soup in the cups, filled the teapot with boiling water, and carried the trays to Faye's room.

"I didn't think I was hungry," Faye said. "But that soup smells good."

"I made a special salad dressing for you," said Kate. "It's an old recipe, rosemary and thyme. See if you like it."

"Why, it's delicious," said Faye. "Is there anything you can't do, darling?"

Kate was stricken first. Her forehead beaded with perspiration and she doubled over, crying with pain. Her eyes were staring and the saliva ran from her mouth. Faye ran to the hallway, screaming for help. The girls and a few Sunday customers crowded into the room. Kate was writhing on the floor. Two of the regulars lifted her onto Faye's bed and tried to straighten her out, but she screamed and doubled up again. The sweat poured from her body and wet her clothes.

Faye was wiping Kate's forehead with a towel when the pain struck her.

It was an hour before Dr. Wilde could be found playing euchre with a friend. He was dragged down to the Line by two hysterical whores. Faye and Kate were weak from vomiting and diarrhea and the spasms continued at intervals.

Dr. Wilde said, "What did you eat?" And then he noticed the trays. "Are these string beans home canned?" he demanded.

"Sure," said Grace. "We did them right here."

"Did any of you have them?"

"Well, no. You see—"

"Go out and break every jar," Dr. Wilde said. "Goddam the string beans!" And he unpacked his stomach pump.

On Tuesday he sat with the two pale weak women. Kate's bed had been moved into Faye's room. "I can tell you now," he said. "I didn't think you had a chance. You're pretty lucky. And let home-made string beans alone. Buy canned ones."

"What is it?" Kate asked.

"Botulism. We don't know much about it, but damn few ever get over it. I guess it's because you're young and she's tough." He asked Faye, "Are you still bleeding from the bowels?"

"Yes, a little."

"Well, here are some morphine pills. They'll bind you up. You've probably ruptured something. But they say you can't kill a whore. Now take it easy, both of you."

That was October 17.

Faye was never really well again. She would make a little gain and then go to pieces. She had a bad time on December 3, and it took even longer for her to gain her strength. February 12 the bleeding became violent and the strain seemed to have weakened Faye's heart. Dr. Wilde listened a long time through his stethoscope.

Kate was haggard and her slender body had shrunk to bones. The girls tried to spell her with Faye, but Kate would not leave.

Grace said, "God knows when's the last sleep she had. If Faye was to die I think it would kill that girl."

"She's just as like to blow her brains out," said Ethel.

Dr. Wilde took Kate into the day-darkened parlor and put his black bag on the chair. "I might as well tell you," he said. "Her heart just can't take the strain, I'm afraid. She's all torn up inside. That goddam botulism. Worse than a rattlesnake." He looked away from Kate's haggard face. "I thought it would be better to tell you so you can prepare yourself," he said lamely and put his hand on her bony shoulder. "Not many people have such loyalty. Give her a little warm milk if she can take it."

Kate carried a basin of warm water to the table beside the bed. When Trixie looked in, Kate was bathing Faye and using the fine linen napkins to do it. Then she brushed the lank blond hair and braided it.

Faye's skin had shrunk, clinging to jaw and skull, and her eyes were huge and vacant.

She tried to speak, and Kate said, "Shush! Save your strength. Save your strength."

She went to the kitchen for a glass of warm milk and put it on the bedside table. She took two little bottles from her pocket and sucked a little from each one into the eye-dropper. "Open up, Mother. This is a new kind of medicine. Now be brave, dear. This will taste bad." She squeezed the fluid far back on Faye's tongue and held up her head so she could drink a little milk to take away the taste. "Now you rest and I'll be back in a little while."

Kate slipped quietly out of the room. The kitchen was dark. She opened the outer door and crept out and moved back among the weeds. The ground was damp from the spring rains. At the back of the lot she dug a small hole with a pointed stick. She dropped in a number of small thin bottles and an eye-dropper. With the stick she crushed the glass to bits and scraped dirt over them. Rain was beginning to fall as Kate went back to the house.

At first they had to tie Kate down to keep her from hurting herself. From violence she went into a gloomy stupor. It was a long time before she regained her health. And she forgot completely about the will. It was Trixie who finally remembered.

TWENTY-TWO

On the Trask place Adam drew into himself. The unfinished Sanchez house lay open to wind and rain, and the new floorboards buckled and warped with moisture. The laid-out vegetable gardens rioted with weeds.

Adam seemed clothed in a viscosity that slowed his movements and held his thoughts down. He saw the world through gray water. Now and then his mind fought its way upward, and when the light broke in it brought him only a sickness of the mind, and he retired into the grayness again. He was aware of the twins because he heard them cry and laugh, but he felt only a thin distaste for them. To Adam they were symbols of his loss. His neighbors drove up into his little valley, and every one of them would have understood anger or sorrow—and so helped him. But they could do nothing with the cloud that hung over him. Adam did not resist them. He simply did not see them, and before long the neighbors stopped driving up the road under the oaks.

For a time Lee tried to stimulate Adam to awareness, but Lee was a busy man. He cooked and washed, he bathed the twins and fed them. Through his hard and constant work he grew fond of the two little boys. He talked to them in Cantonese, and Chinese words were the first they recognized and tried to repeat.

Samuel Hamilton went back twice to try to wedge Adam up and out of his shock. Then Liza stepped in.

"I want you to stay away from there," she said. "You come back a changed man. Samuel, you don't change him. He changes you. I can see the look of him in your face."

"Have you thought of the two little boys, Liza?" he asked.

"I've thought of your own family," she said snappishly. "You lay a crepe on us for days after."

"All right, Mother," he said, but it saddened him because Samuel could not mind his own business when there was pain in any man. It was no easy thing for him to abandon Adam to his desolation.

Adam had paid him for his work, had even paid him for the windmill parts and did not want the windmills. Samuel sold the equipment and sent Adam the money. He had no answer.

He became aware of an anger at Adam Trask. It seemed to Samuel that Adam might be pleasuring himself with sadness. But there was little leisure to brood. Joe was off to college—to that school Leland Stanford had built on his farm near Palo Alto. Tom worried his father, for Tom grew deeper and deeper into books. He did his work well enough, but Samuel felt that Tom had not joy enough.

Will and George were doing well in business, and Joe was writing letters home in rhymed verse and making as smart an attack on all the accepted verities as was healthful.

Samuel wrote to Joe, saying, "I would be disappointed if you had not become an atheist, and I read pleasantly that you have, in your age and wisdom, accepted agnosticism the way you'd take a cookie on a full stomach. But I would ask you with all my understanding heart not to try to convert your mother. Your last letter only made her think you are not well. Your mother does not believe there are many ills uncurable by good strong soup. She puts your brave attack on the structure of our civilization down to a stomach ache. It worries her. Her faith is a mountain, and you, my son, haven't even got a shovel yet."

Liza was getting old. Samuel saw it in her face, and he could not feel old himself, white beard or no. But Liza was living backwards, and that's the proof.

There was a time when she looked on his plans and prophecies as the crazy shoutings of a child. Now she felt that they were unseemly in a grown man. They three, Liza and Tom and Samuel, were alone on the ranch. Una was married to a stranger and gone away. Dessie had her dressmaking business in Salinas. Olive had married her young man, and Mollie was married and living, believe it or not, in an apartment in San Francisco. There was perfume, and a white bearskin rug in the bedroom in front of the fireplace, and Mollie smoked a gold-tipped cigarette—Violet Milo—with her coffee after dinner.

One day Samuel strained his back lifting a bale of hay, and it hurt his feelings more than his back, for he could not imagine a life in which Sam Hamilton was not privileged to lift a bale of hay. He felt insulted by his back, almost as he would have been if one of his children had been dishonest.

In King City, Dr. Tilson felt him over. The doctor grew more testy with his overworked years.

"You sprained your back."

"That I did," said Samuel.

"And you drove all the way in to have me tell you that you sprained your back and charge you two dollars?"

"Here's your two dollars."

"And you want to know what to do about it?"

"Sure I do."

"Don't sprain it any more. Now take your money back. You're not a fool, Samuel, unless you're getting childish."

"But it hurts."

"Of course it hurts. How would you know it was strained if it didn't?"

Samuel laughed. "You're good for me," he said. "You're more than two dollars good for me. Keep the money."

The doctor looked closely at him. "I think you're telling the truth, Samuel. I'll keep the money."

Samuel went in to see Will in his fine new store. He hardly knew his son, for Will was getting fat and prosperous and he wore a coat and vest and a gold ring on his little finger.

"I've got a package made up for Mother," Will said. "Some little cans of things from France. Mushrooms and liver paste and sardines so little you can hardly see them."

"She'll just send them to Joe," said Samuel.

"Can't you make her eat them?"

"No," said his father. "But she'll enjoy sending them to Joe."

Lee came into the store and his eyes lighted up. "How do, Missy," he said.

"Hello, Lee. How are the boys?"

"Boys fine."

Samuel said, "I'm going to have a glass of beer next door, Lee. Be glad to have you join me."

Lee and Samuel sat at the little round table in the barroom and Samuel drew figures on the scrubbed wood with the moisture of his beer glass. "I've wanted to go to see you and Adam but I didn't think I could do any good."

"Well, you can't do any harm. I thought he'd get over it. But he still walks around like a ghost."

"It's over a year, isn't it?" Samuel asked.

"Three months over."

"Well, what do you think I can do?"

"I don't know," said Lee. "Maybe you could shock him out of it. Nothing else has worked."

"I'm not good at shocking. I'd probably end up by shocking myself. By the way, what did he name the twins?"

"They don't have any names."

"You're making a joke, Lee."

"I am not making jokes."

"What does he call them?"

"He calls them 'they.'"

"I mean when he speaks to them."

"When he speaks to them he calls them 'you,' one or both."

"This is nonsense," Samuel said angrily. "What kind of a fool is the man?"

"I've meant to come and tell you. He's a dead man unless you can wake him up."

Samuel said, "I'll come. I'll bring a horse whip. No names! You're damn right I'll come, Lee."

"When?"

"Tomorrow."

"I'll kill a chicken," said Lee. "You'll like the twins, Mr. Hamilton. They'r
fine-looking boys. I won't tell Mr. Trask you're coming."

2

Shyly Samuel told his wife he wanted to visit the Trask place. He though
she would pile up strong walls of objection, and for one of the few time
in his life he would disobey her wish no matter how strong her objection. I
gave him a sad feeling in the stomach to think of disobeying his wife. H
explained his purpose almost as though he were confessing. Liza put he
hands on her hips during the telling and his heart sank. When he was fin
ished she continued to look at him, he thought, coldly.

Finally she said, "Samuel, do you think you can move this rock of a man?"

"Why, I don't know, Mother." He had not expected this. "I don't know."

"Do you think it is such an important matter that those babies have
names right now?"

"Well, it seemed so to me," he said lamely.

"Samuel, do you think why you want to go? Is it your natural incurable
nosiness? Is it your black inability to mind your own business?"

"Now, Liza, I know my failings pretty well. I thought it might be more
than that."

"It had better be more than that," she said. "This man has not admitted
that his sons live. He has cut them off mid-air."

"That's the way it seems to me, Liza."

"If he tells you to mind your own business—what then?"

"Well, I don't know."

Her jaw snapped shut and her teeth clicked. "If you do not get those boys
named, there'll be no warm place in this house for you. Don't you dare come
whining back, saying he wouldn't do it or he wouldn't listen. If you do I'll
have to go myself."

"I'll give him the back of my hand," Samuel said.

"No, that you won't do. You fall short in savagery, Samuel. I know you.
You'll give him sweet-sounding words and you'll come dragging back and try
to make me forget you ever went."

"I'll beat his brains out," Samuel shouted.

He slammed into the bedroom, and Liza smiled at the panels.

He came out soon in his black suit and his hard shiny shirt and collar.
He stooped down to her while she tied his black string tie. His white beard
was brushed to shining.

"You'd best take a swab at your shoes with a blacking brush," she said.

In the midst of painting the blacking on his worn shoes he looked sideways up at her. "Could I take the Bible along?" he asked. "There's no place
for getting a good name like the Bible."

"I don't much like it out of the house," she said uneasily. "And if you're late coming home, what'll I have for my reading? And the children's names are in it." She saw his face fall. She went into the bedroom and came back with a small Bible, worn and scuffed, its cover held on by brown paper and glue. "Take this one," she said.

"But that's your mother's."

"She wouldn't mind. And all the names but one in here have two dates."

"I'll wrap it so it won't get hurt," said Samuel.

Liza spoke sharply, "What my mother would mind is what I mind, and I'll tell you what I mind. You're never satisfied to let the Testament alone. You're forever picking at it and questioning it. You turn it over the way a 'coon turns over a wet rock, and it angers me."

"I'm just trying to understand it, Mother."

"What is there to understand? Just read it. There it is in black and white. Who wants you to understand it? If the Lord God wanted you to understand it He'd have given you to understand or He'd have set it down different."

"But, Mother—"

"Samuel," she said, "you're the most contentious man this world has ever seen."

"Yes, Mother."

"Don't agree with me all the time. It hints of insincerity. Speak up for yourself."

She looked after his dark figure in the buggy as he drove away. "He's a sweet husband," she said aloud, "but contentious."

And Samuel was thinking with wonder, Just when I think I know her she does a thing like that.

3

On the last half-mile, turning out of the Salinas Valley and driving up the unscraped road under the great oak trees, Samuel tried to plait a rage to take care of his embarrassment. He said heroic words to himself.

Adam was more gaunt than Samuel remembered. His eyes were dull, as though he did not use them much for seeing. It took a little time for Adam to become aware that Samuel was standing before him. A grimace of displeasure drew down his mouth.

Samuel said, "I feel small now—coming uninvited as I have."

Adam said, "What do you want? Didn't I pay you?"

"Pay?" Samuel asked. "Yes, you did. Yes, by God, you did. And I'll tell you that pay has been more than I've merited by the nature of it."

"What? What are you trying to say?"

Samuel's anger grew and put out leaves. "A man, his whole life, matches himself against pay. And how, if it's my whole life's work to find my worth, can you, sad man, write me down instant in a ledger?"

Adam exclaimed, "I'll pay. I tell you I'll pay. How much? I'll pay."

"You have, but not to me."

"Why did you come then? Go away!"

"You once invited me."

"I don't invite you now."

Samuel put his hands on his hips and leaned forward. "I'll tell you now, quiet. In a bitter night, a mustard night that was last night, a good thought came and the dark was sweetened when the day sat down. And this thought went from evening star to the late dipper on the edge of the first light— that our betters spoke of. So I invite myself."

"You are not welcome."

Samuel said, "I'm told that out of some singular glory your loins got twins."

"What business is that of yours?"

A kind of joy lighted Samuel's eyes at the rudeness. He saw Lee lurking inside the house and peeking out at him. "Don't, for the love of God, put violence on me. I'm a man hopes there'll be a picture of peace on my hatchments."

"I don't understand you."

"How could you? Adam Trask, a dog wolf with a pair of cubs, a scrubby rooster with sweet paternity for a fertilized egg! A dirty clod!"

A darkness covered Adam's cheeks and for the first time his eyes seemed to see. Samuel joyously felt hot rage in his stomach. He cried, "Oh, my friend, retreat from me! Please, I beg of you!" The saliva dampened the corners of his mouth. "Please!" he cried. "For the love of any holy thing you can remember, step back from me. I feel murder nudging my gizzard."

Adam said, "Get off my place. Go on—get off. You're acting crazy. Get off. This is my place. I bought it."

"You bought your eyes and nose," Samuel jeered. "You bought your uprightness. You bought your thumb on sideways. Listen to me, because I'm like to kill you after. You bought! You bought out of some sweet inheritance. Think now—do you deserve your children, man?"

"Deserve them? They're here—I guess. I don't understand you."

Samuel wailed, "God save me, Liza! It's not the way you think, Adam! Listen to me before my thumb finds the bad place at your throat. The precious twins—untried, unnoticed, undirected—and I say it quiet with my hands down—undiscovered."

"Get off," said Adam hoarsely. "Lee, bring a gun! This man is crazy. Lee!"

Then Samuel's hands were on Adam's throat, pressing the throbbing up to his temples, swelling his eyes with blood. And Samuel was snarling at him. "Tear away with your jelly fingers. You have not bought these boys, nor stolen them, nor passed any bit for them. You have them by some strange and lovely dispensation." Suddenly he plucked his hard thumbs out of his neighbor's throat.

Adam stood panting. He felt his throat where the blacksmith hands had
been. "What is it you want of me?"

"You have no love."

"I had—enough to kill me."

"No one ever had enough. The stone orchard celebrates too little, not too
much."

"Stay away from me. I can fight back. Don't think I can't defend myself."

"You have two weapons, and they not named."

"I'll fight you, old man. You are an old man."

Samuel said, "I can't think in my mind of a dull man picking up a rock,
who before evening would not put a name to it—like Peter. And you—for a
year you've lived with your heart's draining and you've not even laid a number to the boys."

Adam said, "What I do is my own business."

Samuel struck him with a work-heavy fist, and Adam sprawled out in the
dust. Samuel asked him to rise, and when Adam accepted struck him again,
and this time Adam did not get up. He looked stonily at the menacing old
man.

The fire went out of Samuel's eyes and he said quietly, "Your sons have no
names."

Adam replied, "Their mother left them motherless."

"And you have left them fatherless. Can't you feel the cold at night of a
lone child? What warm is there, what bird song, what possible morning can
be good? Don't you remember, Adam, how it was, even a little?"

"I didn't do it," Adam said.

"Have you undone it? Your boys have no names." He stooped down and
put his arms around Adam's shoulders and helped him to his feet. "We'll
give them names," he said. "We'll think long and find good names to clothe
them." He whipped the dust from Adam's shirt with his hands.

Adam wore a faraway yet intent look, as though he were listening to some
wind-carried music, but his eyes were not dead as they had been. He said,
"It's hard to imagine I'd thank a man for insults and for shaking me out like
a rug. But I'm grateful. It's a hurty thanks, but it's thanks."

Samuel smiled, crinkle-eyed. "Did it seem natural? Did I do it right?"
he asked.

"What do you mean?"

"Well, in a way I promised my wife I'd do it. She didn't believe I would.
I'm not a fighting man, you see. The last time I clobbered a human soul it
was over a red-nosed girl and a schoolbook in County Derry."

Adam stared at Samuel, but in his mind he saw and felt his brother
Charles, black and murderous, and that sight switched to Cathy and the
quality of her eyes over the gun barrel. "There wasn't any fear in it," Adam
said. "It was more like a weariness."

"I guess I was not angry enough."

"Samuel, I'll ask just once and then no more. Have you heard anything? Has there been any news of her—any news at all?"

"I've heard nothing."

"It's almost a relief," said Adam.

"Do you have hatred?"

"No. No—only a kind of sinking in the heart. Maybe later I'll sort it out to hatred. There was no interval from loveliness to horror, you see. I'm confused, confused."

Samuel said, "One day we'll sit and you'll lay it out on the table, neat like a solitaire deck, but now—why, you can't find all the cards."

From behind the shed there came the indignant shrieking of an outraged chicken and then a dull thump.

"There's something at the hens," said Adam.

A second shrieking started. "It's Lee at the hens," said Samuel. "You know, if chickens had government and church and history, they would take a distant and distasteful view of human joy. Let any gay and hopeful thing happen to a man, and some chicken goes howling to the block."

Now the two men were silent, breaking it only with small false courtesies —meaningless inquiries about health and weather, with answers unlistened to. And this might have continued until they were angry at each other again if Lee had not interfered.

Lee brought out a table and two chairs and set the chairs facing each other. He made another trip for a pint of whisky and two glasses and set a glass on the table in front of each chair. Then he carried out the twins, one under each arm, and put them on the ground beside the table and gave each boy a stick for his hand to shake and make shadows with.

The boys sat solemnly and looked about, stared at Samuel's beard and searched for Lee. The strange thing about them was their clothing, for the boys were dressed in the straight trousers and the frogged and braided jackets of the Chinese. One was in turquoise blue and the other in a faded rose pink, and the frogs and braid were black. On their heads sat round black silken hats, each with a bright red button on its flat top.

Samuel asked, "Where in the world did you get those clothes, Lee?"

"I didn't get them," Lee said testily. "I had them. The only other clothes they have I made myself, out of sail cloth. A boy should be well dressed on his naming day."

"You've dropped the pidgin, Lee."

"I hope for good. Of course I use it in King City." He addressed a few short sung syllables to the boys on the ground, and they both smiled up at him and waved their sticks in the air. Lee said, "I'll pour you a drink. It's some that was here."

"It's some you bought yesterday in King City," said Samuel.

Now that Samuel and Adam were seated together and the barriers were down, a curtain of shyness fell on Samuel. What he had beaten in with his fists he could not supplement easily. He thought of the virtues of courage and forbearance, which become flabby when there is nothing to use them on. His mind grinned inward at itself.

The two sat looking at the twin boys in their strange bright-colored clothes. Samuel thought, Sometimes your opponent can help you more than your friend. He lifted his eyes to Adam.

"It's hard to start," he said. "And it's like a put-off letter that gathers difficulties to itself out of the minutes. Could you give me a hand?"

Adam looked up for a moment and then back at the boys on the ground. "There's a crashing in my head," he said. "Like sounds you hear under water. I'm having to dig myself out of a year."

"Maybe you'll tell me how it was and that will get us started."

Adam tossed down his drink and poured another and rolled the glass at an angle in his hand. The amber whisky moved high on the side and the pungent fruit odor of its warming filled the air. "It's hard to remember," he said. "It was not agony but a dullness. But no—there were needles in it. You said I had not all the cards in the deck—and I was thinking of that. Maybe I'll never have all the cards."

"Is it herself trying to come out? When a man says he does not want to speak of something he usually means he can think of nothing else."

"Maybe it's that. She's all mixed up with the dullness, and I can't remember much except the last picture drawn in fire."

"She did shoot you, didn't she, Adam?"

His lips grew thin and his eyes black.

Samuel said, "There's no need to answer."

"There's no reason not to," Adam replied. "Yes, she did."

"Did she mean to kill you?"

"I've thought of that more than anything else. No, I don't think she meant to kill me. She didn't allow me that dignity. There was no hatred in her, no passion at all. I learned about that in the army. If you want to kill a man, you shoot at head or heart or stomach. No, she hit me where she intended. I can see the gun barrel moving over. I guess I wouldn't have minded so much if she had wanted my death. That would have been a kind of love. But I was an annoyance, not an enemy."

"You've given it a lot of thought," said Samuel.

"I've had lots of time for it. I want to ask you something. I can't remember behind the last ugly thing. Was she very beautiful, Samuel?"

"To you she was because you built her. I don't think you ever saw her—only your own creation."

Adam mused aloud, "I wonder who she was—what she was. I was content not to know."

"And now you want to?"

Adam dropped his eyes. "It's not curiosity. But I would like to know what kind of blood is in my boys. When they grow up—won't I be looking for something in them?"

"Yes, you will. And I will warn you now that not their blood but your suspicion might build evil in them. They will be what you expect of them."

"But their blood—"

"I don't very much believe in blood," said Samuel. "I think when a man finds good or bad in his children he is seeing only what he planted in them after they cleared the womb."

"You can't make a race horse of a pig."

"No," said Samuel, "but you can make a very fast pig."

"No one hereabouts would agree with you. I think even Mrs. Hamilton would not."

"That's exactly right. She most of all would disagree, and so I would not say it to her and let loose the thunder of her disagreement. She wins all arguments by the use of vehemence and the conviction that a difference of opinion is a personal affront. She's a fine woman, but you have to learn to feel your way with her. Let's speak of the boys."

"Will you have another drink?"

"That I will, thank you. Names are a great mystery. I've never known whether the name is molded by the child or the child changed to fit the name. But you can be sure of this—whenever a human has a nickname it is a proof that the name given him was wrong. How do you favor the standard names—John or James or Charles?"

Adam was looking at the twins and suddenly with the mention of the name he saw his brother peering out of the eyes of one of the boys. He leaned forward.

"What is it?" Samuel asked.

"Why," Adam cried, "these boys are not alike! They don't look alike."

"Of course they don't. They're not identical twins."

"That one—that one looks like my brother. I just saw it. I wonder if the other looks like me."

"Both of them do. A face has everything in it right back to the beginning."

"It's not so much now," said Adam. "But for a moment I thought I was seeing a ghost."

"Maybe that's what ghosts are," Samuel observed.

Lee brought dishes out and put them on the table.

"Do you have Chinese ghosts?" Samuel asked.

"Millions," said Lee. "We have more ghosts than anything else. I guess nothing in China ever dies. It's very crowded. Anyway, that's the feeling I got when I was there."

Samuel said, "Sit down, Lee. We're trying to think of names."

"I've got chicken frying. It will be ready pretty soon."

Adam looked up from the twins and his eyes were warmed and softened. "Will you have a drink, Lee?"

"I'm nipping at the ng-ka-py in the kitchen," said Lee and went back to the house.

Samuel leaned down and gathered up one of the boys and held him on his lap. "Take that one up," he said to Adam. "We ought to see whether there's something that draws names to them."

Adam held the other child awkwardly on his knee. "They look some alike," he said, "but not when you look close. This one has rounder eyes than that one."

"Yes, and a rounder head and bigger ears," Samuel added. "But this one is more like—like a bullet. This one might go farther but not so high. And this one is going to be darker in the hair and skin. This one will be shrewd, I think, and shrewdness is a limitation on the mind. Shrewdness tells you what you must not do because it would not be shrewd. See how this one supports himself! He's farther along than that one—better developed. Isn't it strange how different they are when you look close?"

Adam's face was changing as though he had opened and come out on his surface. He held up his finger, and the child made a lunge for it and missed and nearly fell off his lap. "Whoa!" said Adam. "Take it easy. Do you want to fall?"

"It would be a mistake to name them for qualities we think they have," Samuel said. "We might be wrong—so wrong. Maybe it would be good to give them a high mark to shoot at—a name to live up to. The man I'm named for had his name called clear by the Lord God, and I've been listening all my life. And once or twice I've thought I heard my name called—but not clear, not clear."

Adam, holding the child by his upper arm, leaned over and poured whisky in both glasses. "I thank you for coming, Samuel," he said. "I even thank you for hitting me. That's a strange thing to say."

"It was a strange thing for me to do. Liza will never believe it, and so I'll never tell her. An unbelieved truth can hurt a man much more than a lie. It takes great courage to back truth unacceptable to our times. There's a punishment for it, and it's usually crucifixion. I haven't the courage for that."

Adam said, "I've wondered why a man of your knowledge would work a desert hill place."

"It's because I haven't courage," said Samuel. "I could never quite take the responsibility. When the Lord God did not call my name, I might have called His name—but I did not. There you have the difference between greatness and mediocrity. It's not an uncommon disease. But it's nice for a mediocre man to know that greatness must be the loneliest state in the world."

"I'd think there are degrees of greatness," Adam said.

"I don't think so," said Samuel. "That would be like saying there is a little bigness. No. I believe when you come to that responsibility the hugeness and you are alone to make your choice. On one side you have warmth and companionship and sweet understanding, and on the other—cold, lonely greatness. There you make your choice. I'm glad I chose mediocrity, but how am I to say what reward might have come with the other? None of my children will be great either, except perhaps Tom. He's suffering over the choosing right now. It's a painful thing to watch. And somewhere in me I want him to say yes. Isn't that strange? A father to want his son condemned to greatness! What selfishness that must be."

Adam chuckled. "This naming is no simple business, I see."

"Did you think it would be?"

"I didn't know it could be so pleasant," said Adam.

Lee came out with a platter of fried chicken, a bowl of smoking boiled potatoes, and a deep dish of pickled beets, all carried on a pastry board. "I don't know how good it will be," he said. "The hens are a little old. We don't have any pullets. The weasels got the baby chicks this year."

"Pull up," said Samuel.

"Wait until I get my ng-ka-py," said Lee.

While he was gone Adam said, "It's strange to me—he used to speak differently."

"He trusts you now," Samuel said. "He has a gift of resigned loyalty without hope of reward. He's maybe a much better man than either of us could dream of being."

Lee came back and took his seat at the end of the table. "Just put the boys on the ground," he said.

The twins protested when they were set down. Lee spoke to them sharply in Cantonese and they were silent.

The men ate quietly as nearly all country people do. Suddenly Lee got up and hurried into the house. He came back with a jug of red wine. "I forgot it," he said. "I found it in the house."

Adam laughed. "I remember drinking wine here before I bought the place. Maybe I bought the place because of the wine. The chicken's good, Lee. I don't think I've been aware of the taste of food for a long time."

"You're getting well," Samuel said. "Some people think it's an insult to the glory of their sickness to get well. But the time poultice is no respecter of glories. Everyone gets well if he waits around."

4

Lee cleared the table and gave each of the boys a clean drumstick. They sat solemnly holding their greasy batons and alternately inspecting and sucking them. The wine and the glasses stayed on the table.

"We'd best get on with the naming," Samuel said. "I can feel a little tightening on my halter from Liza."

"I can't think what to name them," Adam said.

"You have no family name you want—no inviting trap for a rich relative, no proud name to re-create?"

"No, I'd like them to start fresh, insofar as that is possible."

Samuel knocked his forehead with his knuckles. "What a shame," he said. "What a shame it is that the proper names for them they cannot have."

"What do you mean?" Adam asked.

"Freshness, you said. I thought last night—" He paused. "Have you thought of your own name?"

"Mine?"

"Of course. Your first-born—Cain and Abel."

Adam said, "Oh, no. No, we can't do that."

"I know we can't. That would be tempting whatever fate there is. But isn't it odd that Cain is maybe the best-known name in the whole world and as far as I know only one man has ever borne it?"

Lee said, "Maybe that's why the name has never changed its emphasis."

Adam looked into the ink-red wine in his glass. "I got a shiver when you mentioned it," he said.

"Two stories have haunted us and followed us from our beginning," Samuel said. "We carry them along with us like invisible tails—the story of original sin and the story of Cain and Abel. And I don't understand either of them. I don't understand them at all but I feel them. Liza gets angry with me. She says I should not try to understand them. She says why should we try to explain a verity. Maybe she's right—maybe she's right. Lee, Liza says you're a Presbyterian—do you understand the Garden of Eden and Cain and Abel?"

"She thought I should be something, and I went to Sunday School long ago in San Francisco. People like you to be something, preferably what they are."

Adam said, "He asked you if you understood."

"I think I understand the Fall. I could perhaps feel that in myself. But the brother murder—no. Well, maybe I don't remember the details very well."

Samuel said, "Most people don't read the details. It's the details that astonish me. And Abel had no children." He looked up at the sky. "Lord, how the day passes! It's like a life—so quickly when we don't watch it and so slowly when we do. No," he said, "I'm having enjoyment. And I made a promise to myself that I would not consider enjoyment a sin. I take a pleasure in inquiring into things. I've never been content to pass a stone without looking under it. And it is a black disappointment to me that I can never see the far side of the moon."

"I don't have a Bible," Adam said. "I left the family one in Connecticut."

"I have," said Lee. "I'll get it."

"No need," said Samuel. "Liza let me take her mother's. It's here in my pocket." He took out the package and unwrapped the battered book. "This one has been scraped and gnawed at," he said. "I wonder what agonies have settled here. Give me a used Bible and I will, I think, be able to tell you about a man by the places that are edged with the dirt of seeking fingers. Liza wears a Bible down evenly. Here we are—this oldest story. If it troubles us it must be that we find the trouble in ourselves."

"I haven't heard it since I was a child," said Adam.

"You think it's long then, and it's very short," said Samuel. "I'll read it through and then we'll go back. Give me a little wine, my throat's dried out with wine. Here it is—such a little story to have made so deep a wound." He looked down at the ground. "See!" he said. "The boys have gone to their sleep, there in the dust."

Lee got up. "I'll cover them," he said.

"The dust is warm," said Samuel. "Now it goes this way. 'And Adam knew Eve his wife; and she conceived, and bare Cain, and said, "I have gotten a man from the Lord." '"

Adam started to speak and Samuel looked up at him and he was silent and covered his eyes with his hand. Samuel read, "'And she again bare his brother Abel. And Abel was a keeper of sheep, but Cain was a tiller of the ground. And in the process of time it came to pass that Cain brought of the fruit of the ground an offering unto the Lord. And Abel, he also brought of the firstlings of his flock and of the fat thereof. And the Lord had respect unto Abel and to his offering. But unto Cain and to his offering he had not respect.'"

Lee said, "Now there—no, go on, go on. We'll come back."

Samuel read, "'And Cain was very wroth, and his countenance fell. And the Lord said unto Cain, "Why art thou wroth? And why is thy countenance fallen? If thou doest well, shalt thou not be accepted? And if thou doest not well, sin lieth at the door. And unto thee shall be his desire, and thou shalt rule over him."

"'And Cain talked with Abel his brother: and it came to pass, when they were in the field, that Cain rose up against Abel his brother and slew him. And the Lord said unto Cain, "Where is Abel thy brother?" And he said, "I know not. Am I my brother's keeper?" And he said, "What hast thou done? The voice of thy brother's blood crieth unto me from the ground. And now art thou cursed from the earth, which hath opened her mouth to receive thy brother's blood from thy hand. When thou tillest the ground it shall not henceforth yield unto thee her strength; a fugitive and a vagabond shalt thou be in the earth." And Cain said unto the Lord, "My punishment is greater than I can bear. Behold, thou hast driven me out this day from the face of the earth, and from thy face shall I be hid. And I shall be a fugitive and a vagabond in the earth; and it shall come to pass that everyone that findeth me shall slay me." And the Lord said unto him, "Therefore whosoever slayeth Cain, vengeance shall be taken on him sevenfold." And the Lord set a mark upon Cain, lest any finding him should kill him. And Cain went out from the presence of the Lord and dwelt in the land of Nod on the east of Eden.' "

Samuel closed the loose cover of the book almost with weariness. "There t is," he said. "Sixteen verses, no more. And oh, Lord! I had forgotten how dreadful it is—no single tone of encouragement. Maybe Liza's right. There's nothing to understand."

Adam sighed deeply. "It's not a comforting story, is it?"

Lee poured a tumbler full of dark liquor from his round stone bottle and sipped it and opened his mouth to get the double taste on the back of his tongue. "No story has power, nor will it last, unless we feel in ourselves that it is true and true of us. What a great burden of guilt men have!"

Samuel said to Adam, "And you have tried to take it all."

Lee said, "So do I, so does everyone. We gather our arms full of guilt as though it were precious stuff. It must be that we want it that way."

Adam broke in, "It makes me feel better, not worse."

"How do you mean?" Samuel asked.

"Well, every little boy thinks he invented sin. Virtue we think we learn, because we are told about it. But sin is our own designing."

"Yes, I see. But how does this story make it better?"

"Because," Adam said excitedly, "we are descended from this. This is our father. Some of our guilt is absorbed in our ancestry. What chance did we have? We are the children of our father. It means we aren't the first. It's an excuse, and there aren't enough excuses in the world."

"Not convincing ones anyway," said Lee. "Else we would long ago have wiped out guilt, and the world would not be filled with sad, punished people."

Samuel said, "But do you think of another frame to this picture? Excuse or not, we are snapped back to our ancestry. We have guilt."

Adam said, "I remember being a little outraged at God. Both Cain and Abel gave what they had, and God accepted Abel and rejected Cain. I never thought that was a just thing. I never understood it. Do you?"

"Maybe we think out of a different background," said Lee. "I remember that this story was written by and for a shepherd people. They were not farmers. Wouldn't the god of shepherds find a fat lamb more valuable than a sheaf of barley? A sacrifice must be the best and most valuable."

"Yes, I can see that," said Samuel. "And Lee, let me caution you about bringing your Oriental reasoning to Liza's attention."

Adam was excited. "Yes, but why did God condemn Cain? That's an injustice."

Samuel said, "There's an advantage to listening to the words. God did not condemn Cain at all. Even God can have a preference, can't he? Let's suppose God liked lamb better than vegetables. I think I do myself. Cain brought him a bunch of carrots maybe. And God said, 'I don't like this. Try again. Bring me something I like and I'll set you up alongside your brother.'

But Cain got mad. His feelings were hurt. And when a man's feelings are hurt he wants to strike at something, and Abel was in the way of his anger."

Lee said, "St. Paul says to the Hebrews that Abel had faith."

"There's no reference to it in Genesis," Samuel said. "No faith or lack of faith. Only a hint of Cain's temper."

Lee asked, "How does Mrs. Hamilton feel about the paradoxes of the Bible?"

"Why, she does not feel anything because she does not admit they are there."

"But—"

"Hush, man. Ask her. And you'll come out of it older but not less confused."

Adam said, "You two have studied this. I only got it through my skin and not much of it stuck. Then Cain was driven out for murder?"

"That's right—for murder."

"And God branded him?"

"Did you listen? Cain bore the mark not to destroy him but to save him. And there's a curse called down on any man who shall kill him. It was a preserving mark."

Adam said, "I can't get over a feeling that Cain got the dirty end of the stick."

"Maybe he did," said Samuel. "But Cain lived and had children, and Abel lives only in the story. We are Cain's children. And isn't it strange that three grown men, here in a century so many thousands of years away, discuss this crime as though it happened in King City yesterday and hadn't come up for trial?"

One of the twins awakened and yawned and looked at Lee and went to sleep again.

Lee said, "Remember, Mr. Hamilton, I told you I was trying to translate some old Chinese poetry into English? No, don't worry. I won't read it. Doing it, I found some of the old things as fresh and clear as this morning. And I wondered why. And, of course, people are interested only in themselves. If a story is not about the hearer he will not listen. And I here make a rule—a great and lasting story is about everyone or it will not last. The strange and foreign is not interesting—only the deeply personal and familiar."

Samuel said, "Apply that to the Cain-Abel story."

And Adam said, "I didn't kill my brother—" Suddenly he stopped and his mind went reeling back in time.

"I think I can," Lee answered Samuel. "I think this is the best-known story in the world because it is everybody's story. I think it is the symbol story of the human soul. I'm feeling my way now—don't jump on me if I'm not clear. The greatest terror a child can have is that he is not loved, and rejection is the hell he fears. I think everyone in the world to a large or small extent has felt rejection. And with rejection comes anger, and with anger some kind of crime in revenge for the rejection, and with the crime guilt—and there is the story of mankind. I think that if rejection could be amputated, the human would not be what he is. Maybe there would be fewer crazy people. I am sure in myself there would not be many jails. It is all there—the start, the beginning. One child, refused the love he craves, kicks the cat and hides his secret guilt; and another steals so that money will make him loved; and a third conquers the world—and always the guilt and revenge and more guilt. The human is the only guilty animal. Now wait! Therefore I think this old and terrible story is important because it is a chart of the soul—the secret, rejected, guilty soul. Mr. Trask, you said you did not kill your brother and then you remembered something. I don't want to know what it was, but was it very far apart from Cain and Abel? And what do you think of my Oriental patter, Mr. Hamilton? You know I am no more Oriental than you are."

Samuel had leaned his elbows on the table and his hands covered his eyes and his forehead. "I want to think," he said. "Damn you, I want to think. I'll want to take this off alone where I can pick it apart and see. Maybe you've tumbled a world for me. And I don't know what I can build in my world's place."

Lee said softly, "Couldn't a world be built around accepted truth? Couldn't some pains and insanities be rooted out if the causes were known?"

"I don't know, damn you. You've disturbed my pretty universe. You've taken a contentious game and made an answer of it. Let me alone—let me think! Your damned bitch is having pups in my brain already. Oh, I wonder what my Tom will think of this! He'll cradle it in the palm of his mind. He'll turn it slow in his brain like a roast of pork before the fire. Adam, come out now. You've been long enough in whatever memory it was."

Adam started. He sighed deeply. "Isn't it too simple?" he asked. "I'm always afraid of simple things."

"It isn't simple at all," said Lee. "It's desperately complicated. But at the end there's light."

"There's not going to be light long," Samuel said. "We've sat and let the evening come. I drove over to help name the twins and they're not named. We've swung ourselves on a pole. Lee, you better keep your complications out of the machinery of the set-up churches or there might be a Chinese with nails in his hands and feet. They like complications but they like their own. I'll have to be driving home."

Adam said desperately, "Name me some names."

"From the Bible?"

"From anyplace."

"Well, let's see. Of all the people who started out of Egypt only two came to the Promised Land. Would you like them for a symbol?"

"Who?"

"Caleb and Joshua."

"Joshua was a soldier—a general. I don't like soldiering."

"Well, Caleb was a captain."

"But not a general. I kind of like Caleb—Caleb Trask."

One of the twins woke up and without interval began to wail.

"You called his name," said Samuel. "You don't like Joshua, and Caleb's named. He's the smart one—the dark one. See, the other one is awake too. Well, Aaron I've always liked, but he didn't make it to the Promised Land."

The second boy almost joyfully began to cry.

"That's good enough," said Adam.

Suddenly Samuel laughed. "In two minutes," he said, "and after a waterfall of words. Caleb and Aaron—now you are people and you have joined the fraternity and you have the right to be damned."

Lee took the boys up under his arms. "Have you got them straight?" he asked.

"Of course," said Adam. "That one is Caleb and you are Aaron."

Lee lugged the yelling twins toward the house in the dusk.

"Yesterday I couldn't tell them apart," said Adam. "Aaron and Caleb."

"Thank the good Lord we had produce from our patient thought," Samuel said. "Liza would have preferred Joshua. She loves the crashing walls of Jericho. But she likes Aaron too, so I guess it's all right. I'll go and hitch up my rig."

Adam walked to the shed with him. "I'm glad you came," he said. "There's a weight off me."

Samuel slipped the bit in Doxology's reluctant mouth, set the brow band, and buckled the throatlatch. "Maybe you'll now be thinking of the garden in the flat land," he said. "I can see it there the way you planned it."

Adam was long in answering. At last he said, "I think that kind of energy is gone out of me. I can't feel the pull of it. I have money enough to live. I never wanted it for myself. I have no one to show a garden to."

Samuel wheeled on him and his eyes were filled with tears. "Don't think it will ever die," he cried. "Don't expect it. Are you better than other men? I tell you it won't ever die until you do." He stood panting for a moment and then he climbed into the rig and whipped Doxology and he drove away, his shoulders hunched, without saying good-by.

PART THREE

PART THREE

TWENTY-THREE

The Hamiltons were strange, high-strung people, and some of them were tuned too high and they snapped. This happens often in the world.

Of all his daughters Una was Samuel's greatest joy. Even as a little girl she hungered for learning as a child does for cookies in the late afternoon. Una and her father had a conspiracy about learning—secret books were borrowed and read and their secrets communicated privately.

Of all the children Una had the least humor. She met and married an intense dark man—a man whose fingers were stained with chemicals, mostly silver nitrate. He was one of those men who live in poverty so that their lines of questioning may continue. His question was about photography. He believed that the exterior world could be transferred to paper—not in the ghost shadings of black and white but in the colors the human eye perceives.

His name was Anderson and he had little gift for communication. Like most technicians, he had a terror and a contempt for speculation. The inductive leap was not for him. He dug a step and pulled himself up one single step, the way a man climbs the last shoulder of a mountain. He had great contempt, born of fear, for the Hamiltons, for they all half believed they had wings—and they got some bad falls that way.

Anderson never fell, never slipped back, never flew. His steps moved slowly, slowly upward, and in the end, it is said, he found what he wanted—color film. He married Una, perhaps, because she had little humor, and this reassured him. And because her family frightened and embarrassed him, he took her away to the north, and it was black and lost where he went—somewhere on the borders of Oregon. He must have lived a very primitive life with his bottles and papers.

Una wrote bleak letters without joy but also without self-pity. She was well and she hoped her family was well. Her husband was near to his discovery.

And then she died and her body was shipped home.

I never knew Una. She was dead before I remember, but George Hamilton told me about it many years later and his eyes filled with tears and his voice croaked in the telling.

"Una was not a beautiful girl like Mollie," he said. "But she had the loveliest hands and feet. Her ankles were as slender as grass and she moved like grass. Her fingers were long and the nails narrow and shaped like almonds. And Una had lovely skin too, translucent, even glowing.

"She didn't laugh and play like the rest of us. There was something set apart about her. She seemed always to be listening. When she was reading, her face would be like the face of one listening to music. And when we asked her any question, why, she gave the answer, if she knew it—not pointed up and full of color and 'maybes' and 'it-might-bes' the way the rest of us would. We were always full of bull. There was some pure simple thing in Una," George said.

"And then they brought her home. Her nails were broken to the quick and her fingers cracked and all worn out. And her poor, dear feet—" George could not go on for a while, and then he said with the fierceness of a man trying to control himself, "Her feet were broken and gravel-cut and briar-cut. Her dear feet had not worn shoes for a long time. And her skin was rough as rawhide.

"We think it was an accident," he said. "So many chemicals around. We think it was."

But Samuel thought and mourned in the thought that the accident was pain and despair.

Una's death struck Samuel like a silent earthquake. He said no brave and reassuring words, he simply sat alone and rocked himself. He felt that it was his neglect had done it.

And now his tissue, which had fought joyously against time, gave up a little. His young skin turned old, his clear eyes dulled, and a little stoop came to his great shoulders. Liza with her acceptance could take care of tragedy; she had no real hope this side of Heaven. But Samuel had put up a laughing wall against natural laws, and Una's death breached his battlements. He became an old man.

His other children were doing well. George was in the insurance business. Will was getting rich. Joe had gone east and was helping to invent a new profession called advertising. Joe's very faults were virtues in this field. He found that he could communicate his material daydreaming—and, properly applied, that is all advertising is. Joe was a big man in a new field.

The girls were married, all except Dessie, and she had a successful dressmaking business in Salinas. Only Tom had never got started.

Samuel told Adam Trask that Tom was arguing with greatness. And the father watched his son and could feel the drive and the fear, the advance and the retreat, because he could feel it in himself.

Tom did not have his father's lyric softness or his gay good looks. But you could feel Tom when you came near to him—you could feel strength and warmth and an iron integrity. And under all of this was a shrinking—a shy shrinking. He could be as gay as his father, and suddenly in the middle it would be cut the way you would cut a violin string, and you could watch Tom go whirling into darkness.

He was a dark-faced man; his skin, perhaps from sun, was a black red, as though some Norse or perhaps Vandal blood was perpetuated in him. His hair and beard and mustache were dark red too, and his eyes gleamed startlingly blue against his coloring. He was powerful, heavy of shoulders and arm, but his hips were slim. He could lift and run and hike and ride with anyone, but he had no sense of competition whatever. Will and George were gamblers and often tried to entice their brother into the joys and sorrows of venture.

Tom said, "I've tried and it just seems tiresome. I've thought why this must be. I get no great triumph when I win and no tragedy when I lose. Without these it is meaningless. It is not a way to make money, that we know, and unless it can simulate birth and death, joy and sorrow, it seems, at least to me—it feels—it doesn't feel at all. I would do it if I felt anything—good or bad."

Will did not understand this. His whole life was competitive and he lived by one kind of gambling or another. He loved Tom and he tried to give him the things he himself found pleasant. He took him into business and tried to inoculate him with the joys of buying and selling, of outwitting other men, of judging them for a bluff, of living by maneuver.

Always Tom came back to the ranch, puzzled, not critical, but feeling that somewhere he had lost track. He felt that he should take joy in the man-pleasures of contest, but he could not pretend to himself that he did.

Samuel had said that Tom always took too much on his plate, whether it was beans or women. And Samuel was wise, but I think he knew only one side of Tom. Maybe Tom opened up a little more for children. What I set down about him will be the result of memory plus what I know to be true plus conjecture built on the combination. Who knows whether it will be correct?

We lived in Salinas and we knew when Tom had arrived—I think he always arrived at night—because under our pillows, Mary's and mine, there would be packages of gum. And gum was valuable in those days just as a nickel was valuable. There were months when he did not come, but every morning as soon as we awakened we put our hands under our pillows to see. And I still do it, and it has been many years since there has been gum there.

My sister Mary did not want to be a girl. It was a misfortune she could not get used to. She was an athlete, a marble player, a pitcher of one-o'-cat, and the trappings of a girl inhibited her. Of course this was long before the compensations for being a girl were apparent to her.

Just as we knew that somewhere on our bodies, probably under the arm, there was a button which if pressed just right would permit us to fly, so Mary had worked out a magic for herself to change her over into the tough little boy she wanted to be. If she went to sleep in a magical position, knees crooked just right, head at a magical angle, fingers all crossed one over the other, in the morning she would be a boy. Every night she tried to find

exactly the right combination, but she never could. I used to help her cros
her fingers like shiplap.

She was despairing of ever getting it right when one morning there wa
gum under the pillow. We each peeled a stick and solemnly chewed it; i
was Beeman's peppermint, and nothing so delicious has been made since

Mary was pulling on her long black ribbed stockings when she said with
great relief, "Of course."

"Of course what?" I asked.

"Uncle Tom," she said and chewed her gum with great snapping sounds.

"Uncle Tom what?" I demanded.

"He'll know how to get to be a boy."

There it was—just as simple as that. I wondered why I hadn't thought of it
myself.

Mother was in the kitchen overseeing a new little Danish girl who worked
for us. We had a series of girls. New-come Danish farm families put their
daughters out to service with American families, and they learned not only
English but American cooking and table setting and manners and all the
little niceties of high life in Salinas. At the end of a couple of years of this,
at twelve dollars a month, the girls were highly desirable wives for American
boys. Not only did they have American manners but they could still work
like horses in the fields. Some of the most elegant families in Salinas today
are descended from these girls.

It would be flaxen-haired Mathilde in the kitchen, with Mother clucking
over her like a hen.

We charged in. "Is he up?"

"Sh!" said Mother. "He got in late. You let him sleep."

But the water was running in the basin of the back bedroom so we knew
he was up. We crouched like cats at his door, waiting for him to emerge.

There was always a little diffidence between us at first. I think Uncle Tom
was as shy as we were. I think he wanted to come running out and toss us
in the air, but instead we were all formal.

"Thank you for the gum, Uncle Tom."

"I'm glad you liked it."

"Do you think we'll have an oyster loaf late at night while you're here?"

"We'll certainly try, if your mother will let you."

We drifted into the sitting room and sat down. Mother's voice called
from the kitchen, "Children, you let him alone."

"They're all right, Ollie," he called back.

We sat in a triangle in the living room. Tom's face was so dark and his
eyes so blue. He wore good clothes but he never seemed well dressed. In
this he was very different from his father. His red mustache was never neat
and his hair would not lie down and his hands were hard from work.

Mary said, "Uncle Tom, how do you get to be a boy?"

"How? Why, Mary, you're just born a boy."

"No, that's not what I mean. How do *I* get to be a boy?"

Tom studied her gravely. "You?" he asked.

Her words poured out. "I don't want to be a girl, Uncle Tom. I want to be a boy. A girl's all kissing and dolls. I don't want to be a girl. I don't want to." Tears of anger welled up in Mary's eyes.

Tom looked down at his hands and picked at a loose piece of callus with a broken nail. He wanted to say something beautiful, I think. He wished for words like his father's words, sweet winged words, cooing and lovely. "I wouldn't like you to be a boy," he said.

"Why not?"

"I like you as a girl."

An idol was crashing in Mary's temple. "You mean you like girls?"

"Yes, Mary, I like girls very much."

A look of distaste crossed Mary's face. If it were true, Tom was a fool. She put on her don't-give-me-any-of-that-crap tone. "All right," she said, "but how do *I* go about being a boy?"

Tom had a good ear. He knew he was reeling down in Mary's estimation and he wanted her to love him and to admire him. At the same time there was a fine steel wire of truthfulness in him that cut off the heads of fast-traveling lies. He looked at Mary's hair, so light that it was almost white, and braided tight to be out of the way, and dirty at the end of the braid, for Mary wiped her hands on her braid before she made a difficult marble shot. Tom studied her cold and hostile eyes.

"I don't think you really want to change."

"I do."

Tom was wrong—she really did.

"Well," he said, "you can't. And someday you'll be glad."

"I won't be glad," said Mary, and she turned to me and said with frigid contempt, "He doesn't know!"

Tom winced and I shivered at the immensity of her criminal charge. Mary was braver and more ruthless than most. That's why she won every marble in Salinas.

Tom said uneasily, "If your mother says it's all right, I'll order the oyster loaf this morning and pick it up tonight."

"I don't like oyster loaves," said Mary and stalked to our bedroom and slammed the door.

Tom looked ruefully after her. "She's a girl all right," he said.

Now we were alone together and I felt that I had to heal the wound Mary had made. "I love oyster loaves," I said.

"Sure you do. So does Mary."

"Uncle Tom, don't you think there's some way for her to be a boy?"

"No, I don't," he said sadly. "I would have told her if I had known."

"She's the best pitcher in the West End."

Tom sighed and looked down at his hands again, and I could see his failure on him and I was sorry for him, aching sorry. I brought out my hollowed cork with pins stuck down to make bars. "Would you like to have my fly cage, Uncle Tom?"

Oh, he was a great gentleman. "Do you want me to have it?"

"Yes. You see, you pull up a pin to get the fly in and then he sits in there and buzzes."

"I'd like to have it very much. Thank you, John."

He worked all day with a sharp tiny pocketknife on a small block of wood, and when we came home from school he had carved a little face. The eyes and ears and lips were movable, and little perches connected them with the inside of the hollow head. At the bottom of the neck there was a hole closed by a cork. And this was very wonderful. You caught a fly and eased him through the hole and set the cork. And suddenly the head became alive. The eyes moved and the lips talked and the ears wiggled as the frantic fly crawled over the little perches. Even Mary forgave him a little, but she never really trusted him until after she was glad she was a girl, and then it was too late. He gave the head not to me but to us. We still have it put away somewhere, and it still works.

Sometimes Tom took me fishing. We started before the sun came up and drove in the rig straight toward Frémont's Peak, and as we neared the mountains the stars would pale out and the light would rise to blacken the mountains. I can remember riding and pressing my ear and cheek against Tom's coat. And I can remember that his arm would rest lightly over my shoulders and his hand pat my arm occasionally. Finally we would pull up under an oak tree and take the horse out of the shafts, water him at the stream side, and halter him to the back of the rig.

I don't remember that Tom talked. Now that I think of it, I can't remember the sound of his voice or the kind of words he used. I can remember both about my grandfather, but when I think of Tom it is a memory of a kind of warm silence. Maybe he didn't talk at all. Tom had beautiful tackle and made his own flies. But he didn't seem to care whether we caught trout or not. He needed not to triumph over animals.

I remember the five-fingered ferns growing under little waterfalls, bobbing their green fingers as the droplets struck them. And I remember the smells of the hills, wild azalea and a very distant skunk and the sweet cloy of lupin and horse sweat on harness. I remember the sweeping lovely dance of high buzzards against the sky and Tom looking long up at them, but I can't remember that he ever said anything about them. I remember holding the bite of a line while Tom drove pegs and braided a splice. I remember the smell of crushed ferns in the creel and the delicate sweet odor of fresh damp rainbow trout lying so prettily on the green bed. And finally I can remember coming back to the rig and pouring rolled barley into the leather feedbag and buckling it over the horse's head behind the ears. And I have no sound of his voice or words in my ear; he is dark and silent and hugely warm in my memory.

Tom felt his darkness. His father was beautiful and clever, his mother was short and mathematically sure. Each of his brothers and sisters had looks or gifts or fortune. Tom loved all of them passionately, but he felt heavy and earth-bound. He climbed ecstatic mountains and floundered in the rocky darkness between the peaks. He had spurts of bravery but they were bracketed in battens of cowardice.

Samuel said that Tom was quavering over greatness, trying to decide whether he could take the cold responsibility. Samuel knew his son's quality and felt the potential of violence, and it frightened him, for Samuel had no violence—even when he hit Adam Trask with his fist he had no violence. And the books that came into the house, some of them secretly—well, Samuel rode lightly on top of a book and he balanced happily among ideas the way a man rides white rapids in a canoe. But Tom got into a book, crawled and groveled between the covers, tunneled like a mole among the thoughts, and came up with the book all over his face and hands.

Violence and shyness—Tom's loins needed women and at the same time he did not think himself worthy of a woman. For long periods he would welter in a howling celibacy, and then he would take a train to San Francisco and roll and wallow in women, and then he would come silently back to the ranch, feeling weak and unfulfilled and unworthy, and he would punish himself with work, would plow and plant unprofitable land, would cut tough oakwood until his back was breaking and his arms were weary rags.

It is probable that his father stood between Tom and the sun, and Samuel's shadow fell on him. Tom wrote secret poetry, and in those days it was only sensible to keep it secret. The poets were pale emasculates, and Western men held them in contempt. Poetry was a symptom of weakness, of degeneracy and decay. To read it was to court catcalls. To write it was to be suspected and ostracized. Poetry was a secret vice, and properly so. No one knows whether Tom's poetry was any good or not, for he showed it to only one person, and before he died he burned every word. From the ashes in the stove there must have been a great deal of it.

Of all his family Tom loved Dessie best. She was gay. Laughter lived on her doorstep.

Her shop was a unique institution in Salinas. It was a woman's world. Here all the rules, and the fears that created the iron rules, went down. The door was closed to men. It was a sanctuary where women could be themselves—smelly, wanton, mystic, conceited, truthful, and interested. The whalebone corsets came off at Dessie's, the sacred corsets that molded and warped woman-flesh into goddess-flesh. At Dessie's they were women who went to the toilet and overate and scratched and farted. And from this freedom came laughter, roars of laughter.

Men could hear the laughter through the closed door and were properl
frightened at what was going on, feeling, perhaps, that they were the but
of the laughter—which to a large extent was true.

I can see Dessie now, her gold pince-nez wabbling on a nose not properl
bridged for pince-nez, her eyes streaming with hilarious tears, and her whol
front constricted with muscular spasms of laughter. Her hair would com
down and drift between her glasses and her eyes, and the glasses woul
fall off her wet nose and spin and swing at the end of their black ribbon

You had to order a dress from Dessie months in advance, and you mad
twenty visits to her shop before you chose material and pattern. Nothing s
healthy as Dessie had ever happened to Salinas. The men had their lodges
their clubs, their whorehouses; the women nothing but the Altar Guild an
the mincing coquetry of the minister until Dessie came along.

And then Dessie fell in love. I do not know any details of her love affair—
who the man was or what the circumstances, whether it was religion or a
living wife, a disease or a selfishness. I guess my mother knew, but it was
one of those things put away in the family closet and never brought out.
And if other people in Salinas knew, they must have kept it a loyal town
secret. All I do know is that it was a hopeless thing, gray and terrible. After
a year of it the joy was all drained out of Dessie and the laughter had ceased.

Tom raged crazily through the hills like a lion in horrible pain. In the
middle of a night he saddled and rode away, not waiting for the morning
train, to Salinas. Samuel followed him and sent a telegram from King City
to Salinas.

And when in the morning Tom, his face black, spurred his spent horse up
John Street in Salinas, the sheriff was waiting for him. He disarmed Tom
and put him in a cell and fed him black coffee and brandy until Samuel
came for him.

Samuel did not lecture Tom. He took him home and never mentioned the
incident. And a stillness fell on the Hamilton place.

2

On Thanksgiving of 1911 the family gathered at the ranch—all the children
except Joe, who was in New York, and Lizzie, who had left the family and
joined another, and Una, who was dead. They arrived with presents and
more food than even this clan could eat. They were all married save Dessie
and Tom. Their children filled the Hamilton place with riot. The home
place flared up—noisier than it had ever been. The children cried and
screamed and fought. The men made many trips to the forge and came
back self-consciously wiping their mustaches.

Liza's little round face grew redder and redder. She organized and ordered. The kitchen stove never went out. The beds were full, and com-
forters laid on pillows on the floor were for children.

Samuel dug up his old gaiety. His sardonic mind glowed and his speech took on its old singing rhythm. He hung on with the talk and the singing and the memories, and then suddenly, and it not midnight, he tired. Weariness came down on him, and he went to his bed where Liza had been for two hours. He was puzzled at himself, not that he had to go to bed but that he wanted to.

When the mother and father were gone, Will brought the whisky in from the forge and the clan had a meeting in the kitchen with whisky passed around in round-bottomed jelly glasses. The mothers crept to the bedrooms to see that the children were covered and then came back. They all spoke softly, not to disturb the children and the old people. There were Tom and Dessie, George and his pretty Mamie, who had been a Dempsey, Mollie and William J. Martin, Olive and Ernest Steinbeck, Will and his Deila.

They all wanted to say the same thing—all ten of them. Samuel was an old man. It was as startling a discovery as the sudden seeing of a ghost. Somehow they had not believed it could happen. They drank their whisky and talked softly of the new thought.

His shoulders—did you see how they slump? And there's no spring in his step.

His toes drag a little, but it's not that—it's in his eyes. His eyes are old.

He never would go to bed until last.

Did you notice he forgot what he was saying right in the middle of a story?

It's his skin told me. It's gone wrinkled, and the backs of his hands have turned transparent.

He favors his right leg.

Yes, but that's the one the horse broke.

I know, but he never favored it before.

They said these things in outrage. This can't happen, they were saying. Father can't be an old man. Samuel is young as the dawn—the perpetual dawn.

He might get old as midday maybe, but sweet God! the evening cannot come, and the night—? Sweet God, no!

It was natural that their minds leaped on and recoiled, and they would not speak of that, but their minds said, There can't be any world without Samuel.

How could we think about anything without knowing what he thought about it?

What would the spring be like, or Christmas, or rain? There couldn't be a Christmas.

Their minds shrank away from such thinking and they looked for a victim —someone to hurt because they were hurt. They turned on Tom.

You were here. You've been here all along!

How did this happen? When did it happen?

Who did this to him?

Have you by any chance done this with your craziness?

And Tom could stand it because he had been with it. "It was Una," he said hoarsely. "He couldn't get over Una. He told me how a man, a real man, had no right to let sorrow destroy him. He told me again and again how I must believe that time would take care of it. He said it so often that I knew he was losing."

"Why didn't you tell us? Maybe we could have done something."

Tom leaped up, violent and cringing. "Goddam it! What was there to tell? That he was dying of sorrow? That the marrow had melted out of his bones? What was there to tell? You weren't here. I had to look at it and see his eyes die down—goddam it." Tom went out of the room and they heard his clodhopper feet knocking on the flinty ground outside.

They were ashamed. Will Martin said, "I'll go out and bring him back."

"Don't do it," George said quickly, and the blood kin nodded. "Don't do it. Let him alone. We know him from the insides of ourselves."

In a little while Tom came back. "I want to apologize," he said. "I'm very sorry. Maybe I'm a little drunk. Father calls it 'jolly' when I do it. One night I rode home"—it was a confession—"and I came staggering across the yard and I fell into the rosebush and crawled up the stairs on my hands and knees and I was sick on the floor beside my bed. In the morning I tried to tell him I was sorry, and do you know what he said? 'Why, Tom, you were just jolly.' 'Jolly,' if I did it. A drunken man didn't crawl home. Just jolly."

George stopped the crazy flow of talk. "We want to apologize to you, Tom," he said. "Why, we sounded as though we were blaming you and we didn't mean to. Or maybe we did mean to. And we're sorry."

Will Martin said realistically, "It's too hard a life here. Why don't we get him to sell out and move to town? He could have a long and happy life. Mollie and I would like them to come and live with us."

"I don't think he'd do it," said Will. "He's stubborn as a mule and proud as a horse. He's got a pride like brass."

Olive's husband, Ernest, said, "Well, there'd be no harm in asking him. We would like to have him—or both of them—with us."

Then they were silent again, for the idea of not having the ranch, the dry, stony desert of heartbreaking hillside and unprofitable hollow, was shocking to them.

Will Hamilton from instinct and training in business had become a fine reader of the less profound impulses of men and women. He said, "If we ask him to close up shop it will be like asking him to close his life, and he won't do it."

"You're right, Will," George agreed. "He would think it was like quitting. He'd feel it was a cowardice. No, he will never sell out, and if he did I don't think he would live a week."

Will said, "There's another way. Maybe he could come for a visit. Tom can run the ranch. It's time Father and Mother saw something of the world. All kinds of things are happening. It would freshen him, and then he could come back and go to work again. And after a while maybe he wouldn't have to. He says himself that thing about time doing the job dynamite can't touch."

Dessie brushed the hair out of her eyes. "I wonder if you really think he's that stupid," she said.

And Will said out of his experience, "Sometimes a man wants to be stupid if it lets him do a thing his cleverness forbids. We can try it anyway. What do you all think?"

There was a nodding of heads in the kitchen, and only Tom sat rocklike and brooding.

"Tom, wouldn't you be willing to take over the ranch?" George asked.

"Oh, that's nothing," said Tom. "It's no trouble to run the ranch because the ranch doesn't run—never has."

"Then why don't you agree?"

"I'd find a reluctance to insult my father," Tom said. "He'd know."

"But where's the harm in suggesting it?"

Tom rubbed his ears until he forced the blood out of them and for a moment they were white. "I don't forbid you," he said. "But I can't do it."

George said, "We could write it in a letter—a kind of invitation, full of jokes. And when he got tired of one of us, why, he could go to another. There's years of visiting among the lot of us." And that was how they left it.

3

Tom brought Olive's letter from King City, and because he knew what it contained he waited until he caught Samuel alone before he gave it to him. Samuel was working in the forge and his hands were black. He took the envelope by a tiny corner and put it on the anvil, and then he scrubbed his hands in the half-barrel of black water into which he plunged hot iron. He slit the letter open with the point of a horseshoe nail and went into the sunlight to read it. Tom had the wheels off the buckboard and was buttering the axles with yellow axle grease. He watched his father from the corners of his eyes.

Samuel finished the letter and folded it and put it back in its envelope. He sat down on the bench in front of the shop and stared into space. Then he opened the letter and read it again and folded it again and put it in his blue shirt pocket. Then Tom saw him stand up and walk slowly up the eastern hill, kicking at the flints on the ground.

There had been a little rain and a fuzz of miserly grass had started up.

Halfway up the hill Samuel squatted down and took up a handful of the
harsh gravelly earth in his palm and spread it with his forefinger, flint and
sandstone and bits of shining mica and a frail rootlet and a veined stone.
He let it slip from his hand and brushed his palms. He picked a spear of
grass and set it between his teeth and stared up the hill to the sky. A gray
nervous cloud was scurrying eastward, searching for trees on which to rain.

Samuel stood up and sauntered down the hill. He looked into the tool
shed and patted the four-by-four supports. He paused near Tom and spun
one of the free-running wheels of the buckboard, and he inspected Tom as
though he saw him for the first time. "Why, you're a grown-up man," he
said.

"Didn't you know?"

"I guess I did—I guess I did," said Samuel and sauntered on. There was
the sardonic look on his face his family knew so well—the joke on himself
that made him laugh inwardly. He walked by the sad little garden and all
around the house—not a new house any more. Even the last added lean-to
bedrooms were old and weathered and the putty around the windowpanes
had shrunk away from the glass. At the porch he turned and surveyed the
whole home cup of the ranch before he went inside.

Liza was rolling out pie crust on the floury board. She was so expert with
the rolling pin that the dough seemed alive. It flattened out and then pulled
back a little from tension in itself. Liza lifted the pale sheet of it and laid
it over one of the pie tins and trimmed the edges with a knife. The prepared
berries lay deep in red juice in a bowl.

Samuel sat down in a kitchen chair and crossed his legs and looked at
her. His eyes were smiling.

"Can't you find something to do this time of day?" she asked.

"Oh, I guess I could, Mother, if I wanted to."

"Well, don't sit there and make me nervous. The paper's in the other
room if you're feeling day-lazy."

"I've read it," said Samuel.

"All of it?"

"All I want to."

"Samuel, what's the matter with you? You're up to something. I can see
it in your face. Now tell it, and let me get on with my pies."

He swung his leg and smiled at her. "Such a little bit of a wife," he said.
"Three of her is hardly a bite."

"Samuel, now you stop this. I don't mind a joke in the evening sometimes,
but it's not eleven o'clock. Now you go along."

Samuel said, "Liza, do you know the meaning of the English word 'vacation'?"

"Now don't you make jokes in the morning."

"Do you, Liza?"

"Of course I do. Don't play me for a fool."

"What does it mean?"

"Going away for a rest to the sea and the beach. Now, Samuel, get out with your fooling."

"I wonder how you know the word."

"Will you tell me what you're after? Why shouldn't I know?"

"Did you ever have one, Liza?"

"Why, I—" She stopped.

"In fifty years, did you ever have a vacation, you little, silly, half-pint, smidgin of a wife?"

"Samuel, please go out of my kitchen," she said apprehensively.

He took the letter from his pocket and unfolded it. "It's from Ollie," he said. "She wants us to come and visit in Salinas. They've fixed over the upstairs rooms. She wants us to get to know the children. She's got us tickets for the Chautauqua season. Billy Sunday's going to wrestle with the Devil and Bryan is going to make his Cross of Gold speech. I'd like to hear that. It's an old fool of a speech but they say he gives it in a way to break your heart."

Liza rubbed her nose and floured it with her finger. "Is it very costly?" she asked anxiously.

"Costly? Ollie has bought the tickets. They're a present."

"We can't go," said Liza. "Who'd run the ranch?"

"Tom would—what running there is to do in the winter."

"He'd be lonely."

"George would maybe come out and stay a while to go quail hunting. See what's in the letter, Liza."

"What are those?"

"Two tickets to Salinas on the train. Ollie says she doesn't want to give us a single escape."

"You can just turn them in and send her back the money."

"No, I can't. Why, Liza—Mother—now don't. Here—here's a handkerchief."

"That's a dish towel," said Liza.

"Sit here, Mother. There! I guess the shock of taking a rest kind of threw you. Here! I know it's a dish towel. They say that Billy Sunday drives the Devil all over the stage."

"That's a blasphemy," said Liza.

"But I'd like to see it, wouldn't you? What did you say? Hold up your head. I didn't hear you. What did you say?"

"I said yes," said Liza.

Tom was making a drawing when Samuel came in to him. Tom looked at his father with veiled eyes, trying to read the effect of Olive's letter.

Samuel looked at the drawing. "What is it?"

"I'm trying to work out a gate-opener so a man won't have to get out of his rig. Here's the pull-rod to open the latch."

"What's going to open it?"

"I figured a strong spring."

Samuel studied the drawing. "Then what's going to close it?"

"This bar here. It would slip to this spring with the tension the other way."

"I see," said Samuel. "It might work too, if the gate was truly hung. And it would only take twice as much time to make and keep up as twenty years of getting out of the rig and opening the gate."

Tom protested, "Sometimes with a skittish horse—"

"I know," said his father. "But the main reason is that it's fun."

Tom grinned. "Caught me," he said.

"Tom, do you think you could look after the ranch if your mother and I took a little trip?"

"Why, sure," said Tom. "Where do you plan to go?"

"Ollie wants us to stay with her for a while in Salinas."

"Why, that would be fine," said Tom. "Is Mother agreeable?"

"She is, always forgetting the expense."

"That's fine," said Tom. "How long do you plan to be gone?"

Samuel's jeweled, sardonic eyes dwelt on Tom's face until Tom said, "What's the matter, Father?"

"It's the little tone, son—so little that I could barely hear it. But it was there. Tom, my son, if you have a secret with your brothers and sisters, I don't mind. I think that's good."

"I don't know what you mean," said Tom.

"You may thank God you didn't want to be an actor, Tom, because you would have been a very bad one. You worked it out at Thanksgiving, I guess, when you were all together. And it's working smooth as butter. I see Will's hand in this. Don't tell me if you don't want to."

"I wasn't in favor of it," said Tom.

"It doesn't sound like you," his father said. "You'd be for scattering the truth out in the sun for me to see. Don't tell the others I know." He turned away and then came back and put his hand on Tom's shoulder. "Thank you for wanting to honor me with the truth, my son. It's not clever but it's more permanent."

"I'm glad you're going."

Samuel stood in the doorway of the forge and looked at the land. "They say a mother loves best an ugly child," he said, and he shook his head sharply. "Tom, I'll trade you honor for honor. You will please hold this in your dark secret place, nor tell any of your brothers and sisters—I know why I'm going—and, Tom, I know where I'm going, and I am content."

TWENTY-FOUR

I have wondered why it is that some people are less affected and torn by the verities of life and death than others. Una's death cut the earth from under Samuel's feet and opened his defended keep and let in old age. On the other hand Liza, who surely loved her family as deeply as did her husband, was not destroyed or warped. Her life continued evenly. She felt sorrow but she survived it.

I think perhaps Liza accepted the world as she accepted the Bible, with all of its paradoxes and its reverses. She did not like death but she knew it existed, and when it came it did not surprise her.

Samuel may have thought and played and philosophized about death, but he did not really believe in it. His world did not have death as a member. He, and all around him, was immortal. When real death came it was an outrage, a denial of the immortality he deeply felt, and the one crack in his wall caused the whole structure to crash. I think he had always thought he could argue himself out of death. It was a personal opponent and one he could lick.

To Liza it was simply death—the thing promised and expected. She could go on and in her sorrow put a pot of beans in the oven, bake six pies, and plan to exactness how much food would be necessary properly to feed the funeral guests. And she could in her sorrow see that Samuel had a clean white shirt and that his black broadcloth was brushed and free of spots and his shoes blacked. Perhaps it takes these two kinds to make a good marriage, riveted with several kinds of strengths.

Once Samuel accepted, he could probably go farther than Liza, but the process of accepting tore him to pieces. Liza watched him closely after the decision to go to Salinas. She didn't quite know what he was up to but, like a good and cautious mother, she knew he was up to something. She was a complete realist. Everything else being equal, she was glad to be going to visit her children. She was curious about them and their children. She had no love of places. A place was only a resting stage on the way to Heaven. She did not like work for itself, but she did it because it was there to be done. And she was tired. Increasingly it was more difficult to fight the aches and stiffnesses which tried to keep her in bed in the morning—not that they ever succeeded.

And she looked forward to Heaven as a place where clothes did not get dirty and where food did not have to be cooked and dishes washed. Privately there were some things in Heaven of which she did not quite approve. There was too much singing, and she didn't see how even the Elect could survive for very long the celestial laziness which was promised. She would find something to do in Heaven. There must be something to take up one's time—some clouds to darn, some weary wings to rub with liniment. Maybe the collars of the robes needed turning now and then, and when you come right down to it, she couldn't believe that even in Heaven there would not be cobwebs in some corner to be knocked down with a cloth-covered broom.

She was gay and frightened about the visit to Salinas. She liked the idea so well that she felt there must be something bordering on sin involved in it. And the Chautauqua? Well, she didn't have to go and probably wouldn't. Samuel would run wild—she would have to watch him. She never lost her feeling that he was young and helpless. It was a good thing that she did not know what went on in his mind, and, through his mind, what happened to his body.

Places were very important to Samuel. The ranch was a relative, and when he left it he plunged a knife into a darling. But having made up his mind, Samuel set about doing it well. He made formal calls on all of his neighbors, the old-timers who remembered how it used to be and how it was. And when he drove away from his old friends they knew they would not see him again, although he did not say it. He took to gazing at the mountains and the trees, even at faces, as though to memorize them for eternity.

He saved his visit to the Trask place for last. He had not been there for months. Adam was not a young man any more. The boys were eleven years old, and Lee—well, Lee did not change much. Lee walked to the shed with Samuel.

"I've wanted to talk to you for a long time," said Lee. "But there's so much to do. And I try to get to San Francisco at least once a month."

"You know how it is," Samuel said. "When you know a friend is there you do not go to see him. Then he's gone and you blast your conscience to shreds that you did not see him."

"I heard about your daughter. I'm sorry."

"I got your letter, Lee. I have it. You said good things."

"Chinese things," said Lee. "I seem to get more Chinese as I get older."

"There's something changed about you, Lee. What is it?"

"It's my queue, Mr. Hamilton. I've cut off my queue."

"That's it."

"We all did. Haven't you heard? The Dowager Empress is gone. China is free. The Manchus are not overlords and we do not wear queues. It was a proclamation of the new government. There's not a queue left anywhere."

"Does it make a difference, Lee?"

"Not much. It's easier. But there's a kind of looseness on the scalp that makes me uneasy. It's hard to get used to the convenience of it."

"How is Adam?"

"He's all right. But he hasn't changed much. I wonder what he was like before."

"Yes, I've wondered about that. It was a short flowering. The boys must be big."

"They are big. I'm glad I stayed here. I learned a great deal from seeing the boys grow and helping a little."

"Did you teach them Chinese?"

"No. Mr. Trask didn't want me to. And I guess he was right. It would have been a needless complication. But I'm their friend—yes, I'm their friend. They admire their father, but I think they love me. And they're very different. You can't imagine how different."

"In what way, Lee?"

"You'll see when they come home from school. They're like two sides of a medal. Cal is sharp and dark and watchful, and his brother—well, he's a boy you like before he speaks and like more afterwards."

"And you don't like Cal?"

"I find myself defending him—to myself. He's fighting for his life and his brother doesn't have to fight."

"I have the same thing in my brood," said Samuel. "I don't understand it. You'd think with the same training and the same blood they'd be alike, but they're not—not at all."

Later Samuel and Adam walked down the oak-shadowed road to the entrance to the draw where they could look out at the Salinas Valley.

"Will you stay to dinner?" Adam asked.

"I will not be responsible for the murder of more chickens," said Samuel.

"Lee's got a pot roast."

"Well, in that case—"

Adam still carried one shoulder lower than the other from the old hurt. His face was hard and curtained, and his eyes looked at generalities and did not inspect details. The two men stopped in the road and looked out at the valley, green tinged from the early rains.

Samuel said softly, "I wonder you do not feel a shame at leaving that land fallow."

"I had no reason to plant it," Adam said. "We had that out before. You thought I would change. I have not changed."

"Do you take pride in your hurt?" Samuel asked. "Does it make you seem large and tragic?"

"I don't know."

"Well, think about it. Maybe you're playing a part on a great stage with only yourself as audience."

A slight anger came into Adam's voice. "Why do you come to lecture me? I'm glad you've come, but why do you dig into me?"

"To see whether I can raise a little anger in you. I'm a nosy man. But there's all that fallow land, and here beside me is all that fallow man. It seems a waste. And I have a bad feeling about waste because I could never afford it. Is it a good feeling to let your life lie fallow?"

"What else could I do?"

"You could try again."

Adam faced him. "I'm afraid to, Samuel," he said. "I'd rather just go about it this way. Maybe I haven't the energy or the courage."

"How about your boys—do you love them?"

"Yes—yes."

"Do you love one more than the other?"

"Why do you say that?"

"I don't know. Something about your tone."

"Let's go back to the house," said Adam. They strolled back under the trees. Suddenly Adam said, "Did you ever hear that Cathy was in Salinas? Did you ever hear such a rumor?"

"Did you?"

"Yes—but I don't believe it. I can't believe it."

Samuel walked silently in the sandy wheel rut of the road. His mind turned sluggishly in the pattern of Adam and almost wearily took up a thought he had hoped was finished. He said at last, "You have never let her go."

"I guess not. But I've let the shooting go. I don't think about it any more."

"I can't tell you how to live your life," Samuel said, "although I do be telling you how to live it. I know that it might be better for you to come out from under your might-have-beens, into the winds of the world. And while I tell you, I am myself sifting my memories, the way men pan the dirt under a barroom floor for the bits of gold dust that fall between the cracks. It's small mining—small mining. You're too young a man to be panning memories, Adam. You should be getting yourself some new ones, so that the mining will be richer when you come to age."

Adam's face was bent down, and his jawbone jutted below his temples from clenching.

Samuel glanced at him. "That's right," he said. "Set your teeth in it. How we do defend a wrongness! Shall I tell you what you do, so you will not think you invented it? When you go to bed and blow out the lamp—then she stands in the doorway with a little light behind her, and you can see her nightgown stir. And she comes sweetly to your bed, and you, hardly breathing, turn back the covers to receive her and move your head over on the pillow to make room for her head beside yours. You can smell the sweetness of her skin, and it smells like no other skin in the world—"

"Stop it," Adam shouted at him. "Goddam you, stop it! Stop nosing over my life! You're like a coyote sniffing around a dead cow."

"The way I know," Samuel said softly, "is that one came to me that selfsame way—night after month after year, right to the very now. And I think I should have double-bolted my mind and sealed off my heart against her, but I did not. All of these years I've cheated Liza. I've given her an untruth, a counterfeit, and I've saved the best for those dark sweet hours. And now I could wish that she may have had some secret caller too. But I'll never know that. I think she would maybe have bolted her heart shut and thrown the key to hell."

Adam's hands were clenched and the blood was driven out of his white knuckles. "You make me doubt myself," he said fiercely. "You always have. I'm afraid of you. What should I do, Samuel? Tell me! I don't know how you saw the thing so clear. What should I do?"

"I know the 'shoulds,' although I never do them, Adam. I always know the 'shoulds.' You should try to find a new Cathy. You should let the new Cathy kill the dream Cathy—let the two of them fight it out. And you, sitting by, should marry your mind to the winner. That's the second-best should. The best would be to search out and find some fresh new loveliness to cancel out the old."

"I'm afraid to try," said Adam.

"That's what you've said. And now I'm going to put a selfishness on you. I'm going away, Adam. I came to say good-by."

"What do you mean?"

"My daughter Olive has asked Liza and me to visit with her in Salinas, and we're going—day after tomorrow."

"Well, you'll be back."

Samuel went on, "After we've visited with Olive for maybe a month or two, there will come a letter from George. And his feelings will be hurt if we don't visit him in Paso Robles. And after that Mollie will want us in San Francisco, and then Will, and maybe even Joe in the East, if we should live so long."

"Well, won't you like that? You've earned it. You've worked hard enough on that dust heap of yours."

"I love that dust heap," Samuel said. "I love it the way a bitch loves her runty pup. I love every flint, the plow-breaking outcroppings, the thin and barren topsoil, the waterless heart of her. Somewhere in my dust heap there's a richness."

"You deserve a rest."

"There, you've said it again," said Samuel. "That's what I had to accept, and I have accepted. When you say I deserve a rest, you are saying that my life is over."

"Do you believe that?"

"That's what I have accepted."

Adam said excitedly, "You can't do that. Why, if you accept that you won't live!"

"I know," said Samuel.

"But you can't do that."

"Why not?"

"I don't want you to."

"I'm a nosy old man, Adam. And the sad thing to me is that I'm losing my nosiness. That's maybe how I know it's time to visit my children. I'm having to pretend to be nosy a good deal of the time."

"I'd rather you worked your guts out on your dust heap."

Samuel smiled at him. "What a nice thing to hear! And I thank you. It's a good thing to be loved, even late."

Suddenly Adam turned in front of him so that Samuel had to stop. "I know what you've done for me," Adam said. "I can't return anything. But I can ask you for one more thing. If I asked you, would you do me one more kindness, and maybe save my life?"

"I would if I could."

Adam swung out his hand and made an arc over the west. "That land out there—would you help me to make the garden we talked of, the windmills and the wells and the flats of alfalfa? We could raise flowerseeds. There's money in that. Think what it would be like, acres of sweet peas and gold squares of calendulas. Maybe ten acres of roses for the gardens of the West. Think how they would smell on the west wind!"

"You're going to make me cry," Samuel said, "and that would be an unseemly thing in an old man." And indeed his eyes were wet. "I thank you, Adam," he said. "The sweetness of your offer is a good smell on the west wind."

"Then you'll do it?"

"No, I will not do it. But I'll see it in my mind when I'm in Salinas, listening to William Jennings Bryan. And maybe I'll get to believe it happened."

"But I want to do it."

"Go and see my Tom. He'll help you. He'd plant the world with roses, poor man, if he could."

"You know what you're doing, Samuel?"

"Yes, I know what I'm doing, know so well that it's half done."

"What a stubborn man you are!"

"Contentious," said Samuel. "Liza says I am contentious, but now I'm caught in a web of my children—and I think I like it."

2

The dinner table was set in the house. Lee said, "I'd have liked to serve it under the tree like the other times, but the air is chilly."

"So it is, Lee," said Samuel.

The twins came in silently and stood shyly staring at their guest.

"It's a long time since I've seen you, boys. But we named you well. You're Caleb, aren't you?"

"I'm Cal."

"Well, Cal then." And he turned to the other. "Have you found a way to rip the backbone out of your name?"

"Sir?"

"Are you called Aaron?"

"Yes, sir."

Lee chuckled. "He spells it with one *a*. The two *a*'s seem a little fancy to his friends."

"I've got thirty-five Belgian hares, sir," Aron said. "Would you like to see them, sir? The hutch is up by the spring. I've got eight newborns—just born yesterday."

"I'd like to see them, Aron." His mouth twitched. "Cal, don't tell me you're a gardener?"

Lee's head snapped around and he inspected Samuel. "Don't do that," Lee said nervously.

Cal said, "Next year my father is going to let me have an acre in the flat."

Aron said, "I've got a buck rabbit weighs fifteen pounds. I'm going to give it to my father for his birthday."

They heard Adam's bedroom door opening. "Don't tell him," Aron said quickly. "It's a secret."

Lee sawed at the pot roast. "Always you bring trouble for my mind, Mr. Hamilton," he said. "Sit down, boys."

Adam came in, turning down his sleeves, and took his seat at the head of the table. "Good evening, boys," he said, and they replied in unison, "Good evening, Father."

And, "Don't you tell," said Aron.

"I won't," Samuel assured him.

"Don't tell what?" Adam asked.

Samuel said, "Can't there be a privacy? I have a secret with your son."

Cal broke in, "I'll tell you a secret too, right after dinner."

"I'll like to hear it," said Samuel. "And I do hope I don't know already what it is."

Lee looked up from his carving and glared at Samuel. He began piling meat on the plates.

The boys ate quickly and quietly, wolfed their food. Aron said, "Will you excuse us, Father?"

Adam nodded, and the two boys went quickly out. Samuel looked after them. "They seem older than eleven," he said. "I seem to remember that at eleven my brood were howlers and screamers and runners in circles. These seem like grown men."

"Do they?" Adam asked.

Lee said, "I think I see why that is. There is no woman in the house to put a value on babies. I don't think men care much for babies, and so it was never an advantage to these boys to be babies. There was nothing to gain by it. I don't know whether that is good or bad."

Samuel wiped up the remains of gravy in his plate with a slice of bread. "Adam, I wonder whether you know what you have in Lee. A philosopher who can cook, or a cook who can think? He has taught me a great deal. You must have learned from him, Adam."

Adam said, "I'm afraid I didn't listen enough—or maybe he didn't talk."

"Why didn't you want the boys to learn Chinese, Adam?"

Adam thought for a moment. "It seems a time for honesty," he said at last. "I guess it was plain jealousy. I gave it another name, but maybe I didn't want them to be able so easily to go away from me in a direction I couldn't follow."

"That's reasonable enough and almost too human," said Samuel. "But knowing it—that's a great jump. I wonder whether I have ever gone so far."

Lee brought the gray enameled coffeepot to the table and filled the cups and sat down. He warmed the palm of his hand against the rounded side of his cup. And then Lee laughed. "You've given me great trouble, Mr. Hamilton, and you've disturbed the tranquillity of China."

"How do you mean, Lee?"

"It almost seems that I have told you this," said Lee. "Maybe I only composed it in my mind, meaning to tell you. It's an amusing story anyway."

"I want to hear," said Samuel, and he looked at Adam. "Don't you want to hear, Adam? Or are you slipping into your cloud bath?"

"I was thinking of that," said Adam. "It's funny—a kind of excitement is coming over me."

"That's good," said Samuel. "Maybe that's the best of all good things that can happen to a human. Let's hear your story, Lee."

The Chinese reached to the side of his neck and he smiled. "I wonder whether I'll ever get used to the lack of a queue," he said. "I guess I used it more than I knew. Yes, the story. I told you, Mr. Hamilton, that I was growing more Chinese. Do you ever grow more Irish?"

"It comes and goes," said Samuel.

"Do you remember when you read us the sixteen verses of the fourth chapter of Genesis and we argued about them?"

"I do indeed. And that's a long time ago."

"Ten years nearly," said Lee. "Well, the story bit deeply into me and I went into it word for word. The more I thought about the story, the more profound it became to me. Then I compared the translations we have—and they were fairly close. There was only one place that bothered me. The King James version says this—it is when Jehovah has asked Cain why he is angry. Jehovah says, 'If thou doest well, shalt thou not be accepted? and if thou doest not well, sin lieth at the door. And unto thee shall be his desire, and *thou shalt* rule over him.' It was the 'thou shalt' that struck me, because it was a promise that Cain would conquer sin."

Samuel nodded. "And his children didn't do it entirely," he said.

Lee sipped his coffee. "Then I got a copy of the American Standard Bible. It was very new then. And it was different in this passage. It says, 'Do thou rule over him.' Now this is very different. This is not a promise, it is an order. And I began to stew about it. I wondered what the original word of the original writer had been that these very different translations could be made."

Samuel put his palms down on the table and leaned forward and the old young light came into his eyes. "Lee," he said, "don't tell me you studied Hebrew!"

Lee said, "I'm going to tell you. And it's a fairly long story. Will you have a touch of ng-ka-py?"

"You mean the drink that tastes of good rotten apples?"

"Yes. I can talk better with it."

"Maybe I can listen better," said Samuel.

While Lee went to the kitchen Samuel asked, "Adam, did you know about this?"

"No," said Adam. "He didn't tell me. Maybe I wasn't listening."

Lee came back with his stone bottle and three little porcelain cups so thin and delicate that the light shone through them. "Dlinkee Chinee fashion," he said and poured the almost black liquor. "There's a lot of wormwood in this. It's quite a drink," he said. "Has about the same effect as absinthe if you drink enough of it."

Samuel sipped the drink. "I want to know why you were so interested," he said.

"Well, it seemed to me that the man who could conceive this great story would know exactly what he wanted to say and there would be no confusion in his statement."

"You say 'the man.' Do you then not think this is a divine book written by the inky finger of God?"

"I think the mind that could think this story was a curiously divine mind. We have had a few such minds in China too."

"I just wanted to know," said Samuel. "You're not a Presbyterian after all."

"I told you I was getting more Chinese. Well, to go on, I went to San Francisco to the headquarters of our family association. Do you know about them? Our great families have centers where any member can get help or give it. The Lee family is very large. It takes care of its own."

"I have heard of them," said Samuel.

"You mean Chinee hatchet man fightee Tong war over slave girl?"

"I guess so."

"It's a little different from that, really," said Lee. "I went there because in our family there are a number of ancient reverend gentlemen who are great scholars. They are thinkers in exactness. A man may spend many years pondering a sentence of the scholar you call Confucius. I thought there might be experts in meaning who could advise me.

"They are fine old men. They smoke their two pipes of opium in the afternoon and it rests and sharpens them, and they sit through the night and their minds are wonderful. I guess no other people have been able to use opium well."

Lee dampened his tongue in the black brew. "I respectfully submitted my problem to one of these sages, read him the story, and told him what I understood from it. The next night four of them met and called me in. We discussed the story all night long."

Lee laughed. "I guess it's funny," he said. "I know I wouldn't dare tell it to many people. Can you imagine four old gentlemen, the youngest is over ninety now, taking on the study of Hebrew? They engaged a learned rabbi. They took to the study as though they were children. Exercise books, grammar, vocabulary, simple sentences. You should see Hebrew written in Chinese ink with a brush! The right to left didn't bother them as much as it would you, since we write up to down. Oh, they were perfectionists! They went to the root of the matter."

"And you?" said Samuel.

"I went along with them, marveling at the beauty of their proud clean brains. I began to love my race, and for the first time I wanted to be Chinese. Every two weeks I went to a meeting with them, and in my room here I covered pages with writing. I bought every known Hebrew dictionary. But the old gentlemen were always ahead of me. It wasn't long before they were ahead of our rabbi; he brought a colleague in. Mr. Hamilton, you should have sat through some of those nights of argument and discussion. The questions, the inspection, oh, the lovely thinking—the beautiful thinking.

"After two years we felt that we could approach your sixteen verses of the fourth chapter of Genesis. My old gentlemen felt that these words were very important too—'Thou shalt' and 'Do thou.' And this was the gold from our mining: '*Thou mayest.*' 'Thou mayest rule over sin.' The old gentlemen smiled and nodded and felt the years were well spent. It brought them out of their Chinese shells too, and right now they are studying Greek."

Samuel said, "It's a fantastic story. And I've tried to follow and maybe I've missed somewhere. Why is this word so important?"

Lee's hand shook as he filled the delicate cups. He drank his down in one gulp. "Don't you see?" he cried. "The American Standard translation *orders* men to triumph over sin, and you can call sin ignorance. The King James translation makes a promise in 'Thou shalt,' meaning that men will surely triumph over sin. But the Hebrew word, the word *timshel*—'Thou mayest'— that gives a choice. It might be the most important word in the world. That says the way is open. That throws it right back on a man. For if 'Thou mayest'—it is also true that 'Thou mayest not.' Don't you see?"

"Yes, I see. I do see. But you do not believe this is divine law. Why do you feel its importance?"

"Ah!" said Lee. "I've wanted to tell you this for a long time. I even anticipated your questions and I am well prepared. Any writing which has influenced the thinking and the lives of innumerable people is important. Now, there are many millions in their sects and churches who feel the order, 'Do thou,' and throw their weight into obedience. And there are millions more who feel predestination in 'Thou shalt.' Nothing they may do can interfere with what will be. But 'Thou mayest'! Why, that makes a man great, that gives him stature with the gods, for in his weakness and his filth and his murder of his brother he has still the great choice. He can choose his course and fight it through and win." Lee's voice was a chant of triumph.

Adam said, "Do you believe that, Lee?"

"Yes, I do. Yes, I do. It is easy out of laziness, out of weakness, to throw oneself into the lap of deity, saying, 'I couldn't help it; the way was set.' But think of the glory of the choice! That makes a man a man. A cat has no choice, a bee must make honey. There's no godliness there. And do you know, those old gentlemen who were sliding gently down to death are too interested to die now?"

Adam said, "Do you mean these Chinese men believe the Old Testament?"

Lee said, "These old men believe a true story, and they know a true story when they hear it. They are critics of truth. They know that these sixteen verses are a history of humankind in any age or culture or race. They do not believe a man writes fifteen and three-quarter verses of truth and tells a lie with one verb. Confucius tells men how they should live to have good and successful lives. But this—this is a ladder to climb to the stars." Lee's eyes shone. "You can never lose that. It cuts the feet from under weakness and cowardliness and laziness."

Adam said, "I don't see how you could cook and raise the boys and take care of me and still do all this."

"Neither do I," said Lee. "But I take my two pipes in the afternoon, no more and no less, like the elders. And I feel that I am a man. And I feel that a man is a very important thing—maybe more important than a star. This is not theology. I have no bent toward gods. But I have a new love for that glittering instrument, the human soul. It is a lovely and unique thing in the universe. It is always attacked and never destroyed—because 'Thou mayest.'"

3

Lee and Adam walked out to the shed with Samuel to see him off. Lee carried a tin lantern to light the way, for it was one of those clear early winter nights when the sky riots with stars and the earth seems doubly dark because of them. A silence lay on the hills. No animal moved about, neither grass-eater nor predator, and the air was so still that the dark limbs and leaves of the live oaks stood unmoving against the Milky Way. The three men were silent. The bail of the tin lantern squeaked a little as the light swung in Lee's hand.

Adam asked, "When do you think you'll be back from your trip?"

Samuel did not answer.

Doxology stood patiently in the stall, head down, his milky eyes staring at the straw under his feet.

"You've had that horse forever," Adam said.

"He's thirty-three," said Samuel. "His teeth are worn off. I have to feed him warm mash with my fingers. And he has bad dreams. He shivers and cries sometimes in his sleep."

"He's about as ugly a crow bait as I ever saw," Adam said.

"I know it. I think that's why I picked him when he was a colt. Do you know I paid two dollars for him thirty-three years ago? Everything was wrong with him, hoofs like flapjacks, a hock so thick and short and straight there seems no joint at all. He's hammerheaded and swaybacked. He has a pinched chest and a big behind. He has an iron mouth and he still fights the crupper. With a saddle he feels as though you were riding a sled over a gravel pit. He can't trot and he stumbles over his feet when he walks. I have never in thirty-three years found one good thing about him. He even has an ugly disposition. He is selfish and quarrelsome and mean and disobedient. To this day I don't dare walk behind him because he will surely take a kick at me. When I feed him mash he tries to bite my hand. And I love him."

Lee said, "And you named him 'Doxology.'"

"Surely," said Samuel, "so ill endowed a creature deserved, I thought, one grand possession. He hasn't very long now."

Adam said, "Maybe you should put him out of his misery."

"What misery?" Samuel demanded. "He's one of the few happy and consistent beings I've ever met."

"He must have aches and pains."

"Well, he doesn't think so. Doxology still thinks he's one hell of a horse. Would you shoot him, Adam?"

"Yes, I think I would. Yes, I would."

"You'd take the responsibility?"

"Yes, I think I would. He's thirty-three. His lifespan is long over."

Lee had set his lantern on the ground. Samuel squatted beside it and instinctively stretched his hands for warmth to the butterfly of yellow light.

"I've been bothered by something, Adam," he said.

"What is that?"

"You would really shoot my horse because death might be more comfortable?"

"Well, I meant—"

Samuel said quickly, "Do you like your life, Adam?"

"Of course not."

"If I had a medicine that might cure you and also might kill you, should I give it to you? Inspect yourself, man."

"What medicine?"

"No," said Samuel. "If I tell you, believe me when I say it may kill you."

Lee said, "Be careful, Mr. Hamilton. Be careful."

"What is this?" Adam demanded. "Tell me what you're thinking of."

Samuel said softly, "I think for once I will not be careful. Lee, if I am wrong—listen—if I am mistaken, I accept the responsibility and I will take what blame there is to take."

"Are you sure you're right?" Lee asked anxiously.

"Of course I'm not sure. Adam, do you want the medicine?"

"Yes. I don't know what it is but give it to me."

"Adam, Cathy is in Salinas. She owns a whorehouse, the most vicious and depraved in this whole end of the country. The evil and ugly, the distorted and slimy, the worst things humans can think up are for sale there. The crippled and crooked come there for satisfaction. But it is worse than that. Cathy, and she is now called Kate, takes the fresh and young and beautiful and so maims them that they can never be whole again. Now, there's your medicine. Let's see what it does to you."

"You're a liar!" Adam said.

"No, Adam. Many things I am, but a liar I am not."

Adam whirled on Lee. "Is this true?"

"I'm no antidote," said Lee. "Yes. It's true."

Adam stood swaying in the lantern light and then he turned and ran. They could hear his heavy steps running and tripping. They heard him falling over the brush and scrambling and clawing his way upward on the slope. The sound of him stopped only when he had gone over the brow of the hill.

Lee said, "Your medicine acts like poison."

"I take responsibility," said Samuel. "Long ago I learned this: When a dog has eaten strychnine and is going to die, you must get an ax and carry him to a chopping block. Then you must wait for his next convulsion, and in that moment—chop off his tail. Then, if the poison has not gone too far, your dog may recover. The shock of pain can counteract the poison. Without the shock he will surely die."

"But how do you know this is the same?" Lee asked.

"I don't. But without it he would surely die."

"You're a brave man," Lee said.

"No, I'm an old man. And if I should have anything on my conscience it won't be for long."

Lee asked, "What do you suppose he'll do?"

"I don't know," said Samuel, "but at least he won't sit around and mope. Here, hold the lantern for me, will you?"

In the yellow light Samuel slipped the bit in Doxology's mouth, a bit worn so thin that it was a flake of steel. The check rein had been abandoned long ago. The old hammerhead was free to drag his nose if he wished, or to pause and crop grass beside the road. Samuel didn't care. Tenderly he buckled the crupper, and the horse edged around to try to kick him.

When Dox was between the shafts of the cart Lee asked, "Would you mind if I rode along with you a little? I'll walk back."

"Come along," said Samuel, and he tried not to notice that Lee helped him up into the cart.

The night was very dark, and Dox showed his disgust for night-traveling by stumbling every few steps.

Samuel said, "Get on with it, Lee. What is it you want to say?"

Lee did not appear surprised. "Maybe I'm nosy the way you say you are. I get to thinking. I know probabilities, but tonight you fooled me completely. I would have taken any bet that you of all men would not have told Adam."

"Did you know about her?"

"Of course," said Lee.

"Do the boys know?"

"I don't think so, but that's only a matter of time. You know how cruel children are. Someday in the schoolyard it will be shouted at them."

"Maybe he ought to take them away from here," said Samuel. "Think about that, Lee."

"My question isn't answered, Mr. Hamilton. How were you able to do what you did?"

"Do you think I was that wrong?"

"No, I don't mean that at all. But I've never thought of you as taking any strong unchanging stand on anything. This has been my judgment. Are you interested?"

"Show me the man who isn't interested in discussing himself," said Samuel. "Go on."

"You're a kind man, Mr. Hamilton. And I've always thought it was the kindness that comes from not wanting any trouble. And your mind is as facile as a young lamb leaping in a daisy field. You have never to my knowledge taken a bulldog grip on anything. And then tonight you did a thing that tears down my whole picture of you."

Samuel wrapped the lines around a stick stuck in the whip socket, and Doxology stumbled on down the rutty road. The old man stroked his beard, and it shone very white in the starlight. He took off his black hat and laid it in his lap. "I guess it surprised me as much as it did you," he said. "But if you want to know why—look into yourself."

"I don't understand you."

"If you had only told me about your studies earlier it might have made a great difference, Lee."

"I still don't understand you."

"Careful, Lee, you'll get me talking. I told you my Irish came and went. It's coming now."

Lee said, "Mr. Hamilton, you're going away and you're not coming back. You do not intend to live very much longer."

"That's true, Lee. How did you know?"

"There's death all around you. It shines from you."

"I didn't know anyone could see it," Samuel said. "You know, Lee, I think of my life as a kind of music, not always good music but still having form and melody. And my life has not been a full orchestra for a long time now. A single note only—and that note unchanging sorrow. I'm not alone in my attitude, Lee. It seems to me that too many of us conceive of a life as ending in defeat."

Lee said, "Maybe everyone is too rich. I have noticed that there is no dissatisfaction like that of the rich. Feed a man, clothe him, put him in a good house, and he will die of despair."

"It was your two-word retranslation, Lee—'Thou mayest.' It took me by the throat and shook me. And when the dizziness was over, a path was open, new and bright. And my life which is ending seems to be going on to an ending wonderful. And my music has a new last melody like a bird song in the night."

Lee was peering at him through the darkness. "That's what it did to those old men of my family."

" 'Thou mayest rule over sin,' Lee. That's it. I do not believe all men are destroyed. I can name you a dozen who were not, and they are the ones the world lives by. It is true of the spirit as it is true of battles—only the winners are remembered. Surely most men are destroyed, but there are others who like pillars of fire guide frightened men through the darkness. 'Thou mayest, Thou mayest!' What glory! It is true that we are weak and sick and quarrelsome, but if that is all we ever were, we would, millenniums ago, have disappeared from the face of the earth. A few remnants of fossilized jawbone, some broken teeth in strata of limestone, would be the only mark man would have left of his existence in the world. But the choice, Lee, the choice of winning! I had never understood it or accepted it before. Do you see now why I told Adam tonight? I exercised the choice. Maybe I was wrong, but by telling him I also forced him to live or get off the pot. What is that word, Lee?"

"Timshel," said Lee. "Will you stop the cart?"

"You'll have a long walk back."

Lee climbed down. "Samuel!" he said.

"Here am I." The old man chuckled. "Liza hates for me to say that."

"Samuel, you've gone beyond me."

"It's time, Lee."

"Good-by, Samuel," Lee said, and he walked hurriedly back along the road. He heard the iron tires of the cart grinding on the road. He turned and looked after it, and on the slope he saw old Samuel against the sky, his white hair shining with starlight.

TWENTY-FIVE

It was a deluge of a winter in the Salinas Valley, wet and wonderful. The rains fell gently and soaked in and did not freshet. The feed was deep in January, and in February the hills were fat with grass and the coats of the cattle looked tight and sleek. In March the soft rains continued, and each storm waited courteously until its predecessor sank beneath the ground. Then warmth flooded the valley and the earth burst into bloom—yellow and blue and gold.

Tom was alone on the ranch, and even that dust heap was rich and lovely and the flints were hidden in grass and the Hamilton cows were fat and the Hamilton sheep sprouted grass from their damp backs.

At noon on March 15 Tom sat on the bench outside the forge. The sunny morning was over, and gray water-bearing clouds sailed in over the mountains from the ocean, and their shadows slid under them on the bright earth.

Tom heard a horse's clattering hoofs and he saw a small boy, elbows flapping, urging a tired horse toward the house. He stood up and walked toward the road. The boy galloped up to the house, yanked off his hat, flung a yellow envelope on the ground, spun his horse around, and kicked up a gallop again.

Tom started to call after him, and then he leaned wearily down and picked up the telegram. He sat in the sun on the bench outside the forge, holding the telegram in his hand. And he looked at the hills and at the old house, as though to save something, before he tore open the envelope and read the inevitable four words, the person, the event, and the time.

Tom slowly folded the telegram and folded it again and again until it was a square no larger than his thumb. He walked to the house, through the kitchen, through the little living room, and into his bedroom. He took his dark suit out of the clothespress and laid it over the back of a chair, and he put a white shirt and a black tie on the seat of the chair. And then he lay down on the bed and turned his face to the wall.

2

The surreys and the buggies had driven out of the Salinas cemetery. The family and friends went back to Olive's house on Central Avenue to eat nd to drink coffee, to see how each one was taking it, and to do and say the decent things.

George offered Adam Trask a lift in his rented surrey, but Adam refused. He wandered around the cemetery and sat down on the cement curb of the Williams family plot. The traditional dark cypresses wept around the edge of the cemetery, and white violets ran wild in the pathways. Someone had brought them in and they had become weeds.

The cold wind blew over the tombstones and cried in the cypresses. There were many cast-iron stars, marking the graves of Grand Army men, and on each star a small wind-bitten flag from a year ago Decoration Day.

Adam sat looking at the mountains to the east of Salinas, with the noble point of Frémont's Peak dominating. The air was crystalline as it sometimes is when rain is coming. And then the light rain began to blow on the wind although the sky was not properly covered with cloud.

Adam had come up on the morning train. He had not intended to come at all, but something drew him beyond his power to resist. For one thing, he could not believe that Samuel was dead. He could hear the rich, lyric voice in his ears, the tones rising and falling in their foreignness, and the curious music of oddly chosen words tripping out so that you were never sure what the next word would be. In the speech of most men you are ab- solutely sure what the next word will be.

Adam had looked at Samuel in his casket and knew that he didn't want him to be dead. And since the face in the casket did not look like Samuel's face, Adam walked away to be by himself and to preserve the man alive.

He had to go to the cemetery. Custom would have been outraged else. But he stood well back where he could not hear the words, and when the sons filled in the grave he had walked away and strolled in the paths where the white violets grew.

The cemetery was deserted and the dark crooning of the wind bowed the heavy cypress trees. The rain droplets grew larger and drove stinging along.

Adam stood up, shivered, and walked slowly over the white violets and past the new grave. The flowers had been laid evenly to cover the mound of new-turned damp earth, and already the wind had frayed the blossoms and flung the smaller bouquets out into the path. Adam picked them up and laid them back on the mound.

He walked out of the cemetery. The wind and the rain were at his back, and he ignored the wetness that soaked through his black coat. Romie Lane was muddy with pools of water standing in the new wheel ruts, and the tall wild oats and mustard grew beside the road, with wild turnip forcing its boisterous way up and stickery beads of purple thistles rising above the green riot of the wet spring.

The black 'dobe mud covered Adam's shoes and splashed the bottoms of his dark trousers. It was nearly a mile to the Monterey road. Adam was dirty and soaking when he reached it and turned east into the town of

Salinas. The water was standing in the curved brim of his derby hat and his collar was wet and sagging.

At John Street the road angled and became Main Street. Adam stamped the mud off his shoes when he reached the pavement. The buildings cut the wind from him and almost instantly he began to shake with a chill. He increased his speed. Near the other end of Main Street he turned into the Abbot House bar. He ordered brandy and drank it quickly and his shivering increased.

Mr. Lapierre behind the bar saw the chill. "You'd better have another one," he said. "You'll get a bad cold. Would you like a hot rum? That will knock it out of you."

"Yes, I would," said Adam.

"Well, here. You sip another cognac while I get some hot water."

Adam took his glass to a table and sat uncomfortably in his wet clothes. Mr. Lapierre brought a steaming kettle from the kitchen. He put the squat glass on a tray and brought it to the table. "Drink it as hot as you can stand it," he said. "That will shake the chill out of an aspen." He drew a chair up, sat down, then stood up. "You've made me cold," he said. "I'm going to have one myself." He brought his glass back to the table and sat across from Adam. "It's working," he said. "You were so pale you scared me when you came in. You're a stranger?"

"I'm from near King City," Adam said.

"Come up for the funeral?"

"Yes—he was an old friend."

"Big funeral?"

"Oh, yes."

"I'm not surprised. He had lots of friends. Too bad it couldn't have been a nice day. You ought to have one more and then go to bed."

"I will," said Adam. "It makes me comfortable and peaceful."

"That's worth something. Might have saved you from pneumonia too."

After he had served another toddy he brought a damp cloth from behind the bar. "You can wipe off some of that mud," he said. "A funeral isn't very gay, but when it gets rained on—that's really mournful."

"It didn't rain till after," said Adam. "It was walking back I got wet."

"Why don't you get a nice room right here? You get into bed and I'll send a toddy up to you, and in the morning you'll be fine."

"I think I'll do that," said Adam. He could feel the blood stinging his cheeks and running hotly in his arms, as though it were some foreign warm fluid taking over his body. Then the warmth melted through into the cold concealed box where he stored forbidden thoughts, and the thoughts came timidly up to the surface like children who do not know whether they will be received. Adam picked up the damp cloth and leaned down to sponge off the bottoms of his trousers. The blood pounded behind his eyes. "I might have one more toddy," he said.

Mr. Lapierre said, "If it's for cold, you've had enough. But if you just want a drink I've got some old Jamaica rum. I'd rather you'd have that straight. It's fifty years old. The water would kill the flavor."

"I just want a drink," said Adam.

"I'll have one with you. I haven't opened that jug in months. Not much call for it. This is a whisky-drinking town."

Adam wiped off his shoes and dropped the cloth on the floor. He took a drink of the dark rum and coughed. The heavy-muscled drink wrapped its sweet aroma around his head and struck at the base of his nose like a blow. The room seemed to tip sideways and then right itself.

"Good, isn't it?" Mr. Lapierre asked. "But it can knock you over. I wouldn't have more than one—unless of course you want to get knocked over. Some do."

Adam leaned his elbows on the table. He felt a garrulousness coming on him and he was frightened at the impulse. His voice did not sound like his voice, and his words amazed him.

"I don't get up here much," he said. "Do you know a place called Kate's?"

"Jesus! That rum is better than I thought," Mr. Lapierre said, and he went on sternly, "You live on a ranch?"

"Yes. Got a place near King City. My name's Trask."

"Glad to meet you. Married?"

"No. Not now."

"Widower?"

"Yes."

"You go to Jenny's. Let Kate alone. That's not good for you. Jenny's is right next door. You go there and you'll get everything you need."

"Right next door?"

"Sure, you go east a block and a half and turn right. Anybody'll tell you where the Line is."

Adam's tongue was getting thick. "What's the matter with Kate's?"

"You go to Jenny's," said Mr. Lapierre.

3

It was a dirty gusty evening. Castroville Street was deep in sticky mud, and Chinatown was so flooded that its inhabitants had laid planks across the narrow street that separated their hutches. The clouds against the evening sky were the gray of rats, and the air was not damp but dank. I guess the difference is that dampness comes down but dankness rises up out of rot and fermentation. The afternoon wind had dropped away and left the air raw and wounded. It was cold enough to shake out the curtains of rum in Adam's head without restoring his timidity. He walked quickly down the unpaved sidewalks, his eyes on the ground to avoid stepping in puddles. The row was dimly lit by the warning lantern where the railroad crossed the street and by one small carbon-filamented globe that burned on the porch of Jenny's.

Adam had his instructions. He counted two houses and nearly missed the third, so high and unbridled were the dark bushes in front of it. He looked in through the gateway at the dark porch, slowly opened the gate, and went up the overgrown path. In the half-darkness he could see the sagging dilapidated porch and the shaky steps.

The paint had long disappeared from the clapboard walls and no work had ever been done on the garden. If it had not been for the vein of light around the edges of the drawn shades he would have passed on, thinking the house deserted. The stair treads seemed to crumple under his weight and the porch planks squealed as he crossed them.

The front door opened, and he could see a dim figure holding the knob.

A soft voice said, "Won't you come in?"

The reception room was dimly lighted by small globes set under rose-colored shades. Adam could feel a thick carpet under his feet. He could see the shine of polished furniture and the gleam of gold picture frames. He got a quick impression of richness and order.

The soft voice said, "You should have worn a raincoat. Do we know you?"

"No, you don't," said Adam.

"Who sent you?"

"A man at the hotel." Adam peered at the girl before him. She was dressed in black and wore no ornaments. Her face was sharp—pretty and sharp. He tried to think of what animal, what night prowler, she reminded him. It was some secret and predatory animal.

The girl said, "I'll move nearer to a lamp if you like."

"No."

She laughed. "Sit down—over here. You did come here for something, didn't you? If you'll tell me what you want I'll call the proper girl." The low voice had a precise and husky power. And she picked her words as one picks flowers in a mixed garden and took her time choosing.

She made Adam seem clumsy to himself. He blurted out, "I want to see Kate."

"Miss Kate is busy now. Does she expect you?"

"No."

"I can take care of you, you know."

"I want to see Kate."

"Can you tell me what you want to see her about?"

"No."

The girl's voice took on the edge of a blade sharpened on a stone. "You can't see her. She's busy. If you don't want a girl or something else, you'd better go away."

"Well, will you tell her I'm here?"

"Does she know you?"

"I don't know." He felt his courage going. This was a remembered cold. "I don't know. But will you tell her that Adam Trask would like to see her? She'll know then whether I know her or not."

"I see. Well, I'll tell her." She moved silently to a door on the right and opened it. Adam heard a few muffled words and a man looked through the door. The girl left the door open so that Adam would know he was not alone. On one side of the room heavy dark portieres hung over a doorway. The girl parted the deep folds and disappeared. Adam sat back in his chair. Out of the side of his eyes he saw the man's head thrust in and then withdrawn.

Kate's private room was comfort and efficiency. It did not look at all like the room where Faye had lived. The walls were clad in saffron silk and the drapes were apple green. It was a silken room—deep chairs with silk-upholstered cushions, lamps with silken shades, a broad bed at the far end of the room with a gleaming white satin cover on which were piled gigantic pillows. There was no picture on the wall, no photograph or personal thing of any kind. A dressing table near the bed had no bottle or vial on its ebony top, and its sheen was reflected in triple mirrors. The rug was old and deep and Chinese, an apple-green dragon on saffron. One end of the room was bedroom, the center was social, and the other end was office—filing cabinets of golden oak, a large safe, black with gold lettering, and a rolltop desk with a green-hooded double lamp over it, a swivel chair behind it and a straight chair beside it.

Kate sat in the swivel chair behind the desk. She was still pretty. Her hair was blond again. Her mouth was little and firm and turned up at the corners as always. But her outlines were not sharp anywhere. Her shoulders had become plump while her hands grew lean and wrinkled. Her cheeks were chubby and the skin under her chin was crepe. Her breasts were still tiny, but a padding of fat protruded her stomach a little. Her hips were slender, but her legs and feet had thickened so that a bulge hung over her low shoes. And through her stockings, faintly, could be seen the wrappings of elastic bandage to support the veins.

Still, she was pretty and neat. Only her hands had really aged, the palms and fingerpads shining and tight, the backs wrinkled and splotched with brown. She was dressed severely in a dark dress with long sleeves, and the only contrast was billowing white lace at her wrists and throat.

The work of the years had been subtle. If one had been near by it is probable that no change at all would have been noticed. Kate's cheeks were unlined, her eyes sharp and shallow, her nose delicate, and her lips thin and firm. The scar on her forehead was barely visible. It was covered with a powder tinted to match Kate's skin.

Kate inspected a sheaf of photographs on her rolltop desk, all the same size, all taken by the same camera and bright with flash powder. And although the characters were different in each picture, there was a dreary simi-

larity about their postures. The faces of the women were never toward th
camera.

Kate arranged the pictures in four piles and slipped each pile into a heav
manila envelope. When the knock came on her door she put the envelope
in a pigeonhole of her desk. "Come in. Oh, come in, Eva. Is he here?"

The girl came to the desk before she replied. In the increased light he
face showed tight and her eyes were shiny. "It's a new one, a stranger. H
says he wants to see you."

"Well, he can't, Eva. You know who's coming."

"I told him you couldn't see him. He said he thought he knew you."

"Well, who is he, Eva?"

"He's a big gangly man, a little bit drunk. He says his name is Adan
Trask."

Although Kate made no movement or sound Eva knew something hac
struck home. The fingers of Kate's right hand slowly curled around the palm
while the left hand crept like a lean cat toward the edge of the desk. Kate sat
still as though she held her breath. Eva was jittery. Her mind went to the
box in her dresser drawer where her hypodermic needle lay.

Kate said at last, "Sit over there in that big chair, Eva. Just sit still a minute." When the girl did not move Kate whipped one word at her. "Sit!" Eva
cringed and went to the big chair.

"Don't pick your nails," said Kate.

Eva's hands separated, and each one clung to an arm of the chair.

Kate stared straight ahead at the green glass shades of her desk lamp.
Then she moved so suddenly that Eva jumped and her lips quivered. Kate
opened the desk drawer and took out a folded paper. "Here! Go to your room
and fix yourself up. Don't take it all—no, I won't trust you." Kate tapped the
paper and tore it in two; a little white powder spilled before she folded the
ends and passed one to Eva. "Now hurry up! When you come downstairs, tell
Ralph I want him in the hall close enough to hear the bell but not the
voices. Watch him to see he doesn't creep up. If he hears the bell—no, tell
him—no, let him do it his own way. After that bring Mr. Adam Trask
to me."

"Will you be all right, Miss Kate?"

Kate looked at her until she turned away. Kate called after her, "You can
have the other half as soon as he goes. Now hurry up."

After the door had closed Kate opened the right-hand drawer of her desk
and took out a revolver with a short barrel. She swung the cylinder sideways and looked at the cartridges, snapped it shut and put it on her desk,
and laid a sheet of paper over it. She turned off one of the lights and settled
back in her chair. She clasped her hands on the desk in front of her.

When the knock came on the door she called, "Come in," hardly moving
her lips.

Eva's eyes were wet, and she was relaxed. "Here he is," she said and closed the door behind Adam.

He glanced quickly about before he saw Kate sitting so quietly behind the desk. He stared at her, and then he moved slowly toward her.

Her hands unclasped and her right hand moved toward the paper. Her eyes, cold and expressionless, remained on his eyes.

Adam saw her hair, her scar, her lips, her creping throat, her arms and shoulders and flat breasts. He sighed deeply.

Kate's hand shook a little. She said, "What do you want?"

Adam sat down in the straight chair beside the desk. He wanted to shout with relief, but he said, "Nothing now. I just wanted to see you. Sam Hamilton told me you were here."

The moment he sat down the shake went out of her hand. "Hadn't you heard before?"

"No," he said. "I hadn't heard. It made me a little crazy at first, but now I'm all right."

Kate relaxed and her mouth smiled and her little teeth showed, the long canines sharp and white. She said, "You frightened me."

"Why?"

"Well, I didn't know what you'd do."

"Neither did I," said Adam, and he continued to stare at her as though she were not alive.

"I expected you for a long time, and when you didn't come I guess I forgot you."

"I didn't forget you," he said. "But now I can."

"What do you mean?"

He laughed pleasantly. "Now I see you, I mean. You know, I guess it was Samuel said I'd never seen you, and it's true. I remember your face but I had never seen it. Now I can forget it."

Her lips closed and straightened and her wide-set eyes narrowed with cruelty. "You think you can?"

"I know I can."

She changed her manner. "Maybe you won't have to," she said. "If you feel all right about everything, maybe we could get together."

"I don't think so," said Adam.

"You were such a fool," she said. "Like a child. You didn't know what things to do with yourself. I can teach you now. You seem to be a man."

"You have taught me," he said. "It was a pretty sharp lesson."

"Would you like a drink?"

"Yes," he said.

"I can smell your breath—you've been drinking rum." She got up and went to a cabinet for a bottle and two glasses, and when she turned back she noticed that he was looking at her fattened ankles. Her quick rage did not change the little smile on her lips.

She carried the bottle to the round table in the middle of the room and filled the two small glasses with rum. "Come, sit over here," she said. "It's more comfortable." As he moved to a big chair she saw that his eyes were on her protruding stomach. She handed him a glass, sat down, and folded her hands across her middle.

He sat holding his glass, and she said, "Drink it. It's very good rum." He smiled at her, a smile she had never seen. She said, "When Eva told me you were here I thought at first I would have you thrown out."

"I would have come back," he said. "I had to see you—not that I mistrusted Samuel, but just to prove it to myself."

"Drink your rum," she said.

He glanced at her glass.

"You don't think I'd poison you—" She stopped and was angry that she had said it.

Smiling, he still gazed at her glass. Her anger came through to her face. She picked up her glass and touched her lips to it. "Liquor makes me sick," she said. "I never drink it. It poisons me." She shut her mouth tight and her sharp teeth bit down on her lower lip.

Adam continued to smile at her.

Her rage was rising beyond her control. She tossed the rum down her throat and coughed, and her eyes watered and she wiped her tears away with the back of her hand. "You don't trust me very much," she said.

"No, I don't." He raised his glass and drank his rum, then got up and filled both glasses.

"I will not drink any more," she said in panic.

"You don't have to," Adam said. "I'll just finish this and go along."

The biting alcohol burned in her throat and she felt the stirring in her that frightened her. "I'm not afraid of you or anyone else," she said, and she drank off her second glass.

"You haven't any reason to be afraid of me," said Adam. "You can forget me now. But you said you had already." He felt gloriously warm and safe, better than he had for many years. "I came up to Sam Hamilton's funeral," he said. "That was a fine man. I'll miss him. Do you remember, Cathy, he helped you with the twins?"

In Kate the liquor raged. She fought and the strain of the fight showed on her face.

"What's the matter?" Adam asked.

"I told you it poisoned me. I told you it made me sick."

"I couldn't take the chance," he calmly said. "You shot me once. I don't know what else you've done."

"What do you mean?"

"I've heard some scandal," he said. "Just dirty scandal."

For the moment she had forgotten her will-fight against the cruising alcohol, and now she had lost the battle. The redness was up in her brain

.nd her fear was gone and in its place was cruelty without caution. She
:natched the bottle and filled her glass.

Adam had to get up to pour his own. A feeling completely foreign to him
:.ad arisen. He was enjoying what he saw in her. He liked to see her strug-
;ling. He felt good about punishing her, but he was also watchful. "Now I
nust be careful," he told himself. "Don't talk, don't talk."

He said aloud, "Sam Hamilton has been a good friend to me all the years.
['ll miss him."

She had spilled some rum, and it moistened the corners of her mouth.
'I hated him," she said. "I would have killed him if I could."

"Why? He was kind to us."

"He looked—he looked into me."

"Why not? He looked into me too, and he helped me."

"I hate him," she said. "I'm glad he's dead."

"Might have been good if I had looked into you," Adam said.

Her lip curled. "You are a fool," she said. "I don't hate you. You're just a
weak fool."

As her tension built up, a warm calm settled on Adam.

"Sit there and grin," she cried. "You think you're free, don't you? A few
drinks and you think you're a man! I could crook my little finger and you'd
come back slobbering, crawling on your knees." Her sense of power was loose
and her vixen carefulness abandoned. "I know you," she said. "I know your
cowardly heart."

Adam went on smiling. He tasted his drink, and that reminded her to
pour another for herself. The bottle neck chattered against her glass.

"When I was hurt I needed you," she said. "But you were slop. And when
I didn't need you any more you tried to stop me. Take that ugly smirk off
your face."

"I wonder what it is you hate so much."

"You wonder, do you?" Her caution was almost entirely gone. "It isn't
hatred, it's contempt. When I was a little girl I knew what stupid lying fools
they were—my own mother and father pretending goodness. And they
weren't good. I knew them. I could make them do whatever I wanted. I
could always make people do what I wanted. When I was half-grown I made
a man kill himself. He pretended to be good too, and all he wanted was to
go to bed with me—a little girl."

"But you say he killed himself. He must have been very sorry about
something."

"He was a fool," said Kate. "I heard him come to the door and beg. I
laughed all night."

Adam said, "I wouldn't like to think I'd driven anybody out of the world."

"You're a fool too. I remember how they talked. 'Isn't she a pretty little
thing, so sweet, so dainty?' And no one knew me. I made them jump through
hoops, and they never knew it."

Adam drained his glass. He felt remote and inspective. He thought he could see her impulses crawling like ants and could read them. The sense of deep understanding that alcohol sometimes gives was on him. He said, "It doesn't matter whether you liked Sam Hamilton. I found him wise. I remember he said one time that a woman who knows all about men usually knows one part very well and can't conceive the other parts, but that doesn't mean they aren't there."

"He was a liar and a hypocrite too." Kate spat out her words. "That's what I hate, the liars, and they're all liars. That's what it is. I love to show them up. I love to rub their noses in their own nastiness."

Adam's brows went up. "Do you mean that in the whole world there's only evil and folly?"

"That's exactly what I mean."

"I don't believe it," Adam said quietly.

"You don't believe it! You don't believe it!" She mimicked him. "Would you like me to prove it?"

"You can't," he said.

She jumped up, ran to her desk, and brought the brown envelopes to the table. "Take a look at those," she said.

"I don't want to."

"I'll show you anyway." She took out a photograph. "Look there. That's a state senator. He thinks he's going to run for Congress. Look at his fat stomach. He's got bubs like a woman. He likes whips. That streak there— that's a whip mark. Look at the expression on his face! He's got a wife and four kids and he's going to run for Congress. You don't believe! Look at this! This piece of white blubber is a councilman; this big red Swede has a ranch out near Blanco. Look here! This is a professor at Berkeley. Comes all the way down here to have the toilet splashed in his face—professor of philosophy. And look at this! This is a minister of the Gospel, a little brother of Jesus. He used to burn a house down to get what he wanted. We give it to him now another way. See that lighted match under his skinny flank?"

"I don't want to see these," said Adam.

"Well, you have seen them. And you don't believe it! I'll have you begging to get in here. I'll have you screaming at the moon." She tried to force her will on him, and she saw that he was detached and free. Her rage congealed to poison. "No one has ever escaped," she said softly. Her eyes were flat and cold but her fingernails were tearing at the upholstery of the chair, ripping and fraying the silk.

Adam sighed. "If I had those pictures and those men knew it, I wouldn't think my life was very safe," he said. "I guess one of those pictures could destroy a man's whole life. Aren't you in danger?"

"Do you think I'm a child?" she asked.

"Not any more," said Adam. "I'm beginning to think you're a twisted human—or no human at all."

She smiled. "Maybe you've struck it," she said. "Do you think I want to be human? Look at those pictures! I'd rather be a dog than a human. But I'm not a dog. I'm smarter than humans. Nobody can hurt me. Don't worry about danger." She waved at the filing cabinets. "I have a hundred beautiful pictures in there, and those men know that if anything should happen to me—anything—one hundred letters, each one with a picture, would be dropped in the mail, and each letter will go where it will do the most harm. No, they won't hurt me."

Adam asked, "But suppose you had an accident, or maybe a disease?"

"That wouldn't make any difference," she said. She leaned closer to him. "I'm going to tell you a secret none of those men knows. In a few years I'll be going away. And when I do—those envelopes will be dropped in the mail anyway." She leaned back in her chair, laughing.

Adam shivered. He looked closely at her. Her face and her laughter were childlike and innocent. He got up and poured himself another drink, a short drink. The bottle was nearly empty. "I know what you hate. You hate something in them you can't understand. You don't hate their evil. You hate the good in them you can't get at. I wonder what you want, what final thing."

"I'll have all the money I need," she said. "I'll go to New York and I won't be old. I'm not old. I'll buy a house, a nice house in a nice neighborhood, and I'll have nice servants. And first I will find a man, if he's still alive, and very slowly and with the greatest attention to pain I will take his life away. If I do it well and carefully, he will go crazy before he dies."

Adam stamped on the floor impatiently. "Nonsense," he said. "This isn't true. This is crazy. None of this is true. I don't believe any of it."

She said, "Do you remember when you first saw me?"

His face darkened. "Oh, Lord, yes!"

"You remember my broken jaw and my split lips and my missing teeth?"

"I remember. I don't want to remember."

"My pleasure will be to find the man who did that," she said. "And after that—there will be other pleasures."

"I have to go," Adam said.

She said, "Don't go, dear. Don't go now, my love. My sheets are silk. I want you to feel those sheets against your skin."

"You don't mean that?"

"Oh, I do, my love. I do. You aren't clever at love, but I can teach you. I will teach you." She stood up unsteadily and laid her hand on his arm. Her face seemed fresh and young. Adam looked down at her hand and saw it wrinkled as a pale monkey's paw. He moved away in revulsion.

She saw his gesture and understood it and her mouth hardened.

"I don't understand," he said. "I know, but I can't believe. I know I won't believe it in the morning. It will be a nightmare dream. But no, it—it can't be a dream—no. Because I remember you are the mother of my boys. You haven't asked about them. You are the mother of my sons."

Kate put her elbows on her knees and cupped her hands under her chin so that her fingers covered her pointed ears. Her eyes were bright with triumph. Her voice was mockingly soft. "A fool always leaves an opening," she said. "I discovered that when I was a child. I am the mother of your sons. Your sons? I am the mother, yes—but how do you know you are the father?"

Adam's mouth dropped open. "Cathy, what do you mean?"

"My name is Kate," she said. "Listen, my darling, and remember. How many times did I let you come near enough to me to have children?"

"You were hurt," he said. "You were terribly hurt."

"Once," said Kate, "just once."

"The pregnancy made you ill," he protested. "It was hard on you."

She smiled at him sweetly. "I wasn't too hurt for your brother."

"My brother?"

"Have you forgotten Charles?"

Adam laughed. "You are a devil," he said. "But do you think I could believe that of my brother?"

"I don't care what you believe," she said.

Adam said, "I don't believe it."

"You will. At first you will wonder, and then you'll be unsure. You'll think back about Charles—all about him. I could have loved Charles. He was like me in a way."

"He was not."

"You'll remember," she said. "Maybe one day you will remember some tea that tasted bitter. You took my medicine by mistake—remember? Slept as you had never slept before and awakened late—thick-headed?"

"You were too hurt to plan a thing like that."

"I can do anything," she said. "And now, my love, take off your clothes. And I will show you what else I can do."

Adam closed his eyes and his head reeled with the rum. He opened his eyes and shook his head violently. "It wouldn't matter—even if it were true," he said. "It wouldn't matter at all." And suddenly he laughed because he knew that this was so. He stood too quickly and had to grab the back of his chair to steady himself against dizziness.

Kate leaped up and put both of her hands on his elbow. "Let me help you take off your coat."

Adam twisted her hands from his arm as though they were wire. He moved unsteadily toward the door.

Uncontrolled hatred shone in Kate's eyes. She screamed, a long and shrill animal screech. Adam stopped and turned toward her. The door banged open. The house pimp took three steps, poised, pivoted with his whole weight, and his fist struck Adam under the ear. Adam crashed to the floor.

Kate screamed, "The boots! Give him the boots!"

Ralph moved closer to the fallen man and measured the distance. He noticed Adam's open eyes staring up at him. He turned nervously to Kate.

Her voice was cold. "I said give him the boots. Break his face!"

Ralph said, "He ain't fighting back. The fight's all out of him."

Kate sat down. She breathed through her mouth. Her hands writhed in er lap. "Adam," she said, "I hate you. I hate you now for the first time. hate you! Adam, are you listening? I hate you!"

Adam tried to sit up, fell back, and tried again. Sitting on the floor, he ooked up at Kate. "It doesn't matter," he said. "It doesn't matter at all."

He got to his knees and rested with his knuckles against the floor. He aid, "Do you know, I loved you better than anything in the world? I did. t was so strong that it took quite a killing."

"You'll come crawling back," she said. "You'll drag your belly on the loor—begging, begging!"

"You want the boots now, Miss Kate?" Ralph asked.

She did not answer.

Adam moved very slowly toward the door, balancing his steps carefully. His hand fumbled at the doorjamb.

Kate called, "Adam!"

He turned slowly. He smiled at her as a man might smile at a memory. Then he went out and closed the door gently behind him.

Kate sat staring at the door. Her eyes were desolate.

TWENTY-SIX

On the train back to King City from his trip to Salinas, Adam Trask was in a cloud of vague forms and sounds and colors. He was not conscious of any thought at all.

I believe there are techniques of the human mind whereby, in its dark deep, problems are examined, rejected or accepted. Such activities sometimes concern facets a man does not know he has. How often one goes to sleep troubled and full of pain, not knowing what causes the travail, and in the morning a whole new direction and a clearness is there, maybe the result of the black reasoning. And again there are mornings when ecstasy bubbles in the blood, and the stomach and chest are tight and electric with joy, and nothing in the thoughts to justify it or cause it.

Samuel's funeral and the talk with Kate should have made Adam sad and bitter, but they did not. Out of the gray throbbing an ecstasy arose. He felt young and free and filled with a hungry gaiety. He got off the train in King City, and, instead of going directly to the livery stable to claim his horse and buggy, he walked to Will Hamilton's new garage.

Will was sitting in his glass-walled office from which he could watch the

activity of his mechanics without hearing the clamor of their work. Will'
stomach was beginning to fill out richly.

He was studying an advertisement for cigars shipped direct and often
from Cuba. He thought he was mourning for his dead father, but he wa.
not. He did have some little worry about Tom, who had gone directly from
the funeral to San Francisco. He felt that it was more dignified to lose one
self in business, as he intended to do, than in alcohol, as Tom was probably
doing.

He looked up when Adam came into the office and waved his hand to
one of the big leather chairs he had installed to lull his customers past the
size of the bills they were going to have to pay.

Adam sat down. "I don't know whether I offered my condolences," he
said.

"It's a sad time," said Will. "You were at the funeral?"

"Yes," said Adam. "I don't know whether you know how I felt about your
father. He gave me things I will never forget."

"He was respected," said Will. "There were over two hundred people at
the cemetery—over two hundred."

"Such a man doesn't really die," Adam said, and he was discovering it
himself. "I can't think of him dead. He seems maybe more alive to me than
before."

"That's true," said Will, and it was not true to him. To Will, Samuel was
dead.

"I think of things he said," Adam went on. "When he said them I didn't
listen very closely, but now they come back, and I can see his face when he
said them."

"That's true," said Will. "I was just thinking the same thing. Are you
going back to your place?"

"Yes, I am. But I thought I would come in and talk to you about buying
an automobile."

A subtle change came over Will, a kind of silent alertness. "I would have
said you'd be the last man in the valley to get a car," he observed and
watched through half-closed eyes for Adam's reaction.

Adam laughed. "I guess I deserved that," he said. "Maybe your father
is responsible for a change in me."

"How do you mean?"

"I don't know as I could explain it. Anyway, let's talk about a car."

"I'll give you the straight dope on it," said Will. "The truth of the matter
is I'm having one hell of a time getting enough cars to fill my orders. Why,
I've got a list of people who want them."

"Is that so? Well, maybe I'll just have to put my name on the list."

"I'd be glad to do that, Mr. Trask, and—" He paused. "You've been so
close to the family that—well, if there should be a cancellation I'd be glad
to move you up on the list."

"That's kind of you," said Adam.

"How would you like to arrange it?"

"How do you mean?"

"Well, I can arrange it so you pay only so much a month."

"Isn't it more expensive that way?"

"Well, there's interest and carrying charge. Some people find it convenient."

"I think I'll pay cash," said Adam. "There'd be no point in putting it off."

Will chuckled. "Not very many people feel that way," he said. "And there's going to come a time when I won't be able to sell for cash without losing money."

"I'd never thought of that," said Adam. "You will put me on the list though?"

Will leaned toward him. "Mr. Trask, I'm going to put you on the top of the list. The first car that comes in, you're going to have."

"Thank you."

"I'll be glad to do it for you," said Will.

Adam asked, "How is your mother holding up?"

Will leaned back in his chair and an affectionate smile came on his face. "She's a remarkable woman," he said. "She's like a rock. I think back on all the hard times we had, and we had plenty of them. My father wasn't very practical. He was always off in the clouds or buried in a book. I think my mother held us together and kept the Hamiltons out of the poorhouse."

"She's a fine woman," Adam said.

"Not only fine. She's strong. She stands on her two feet. She's a tower of strength. Did you come back to Olive's house after the funeral?"

"No, I didn't."

"Well over a hundred people did. And my mother fried all that chicken and saw that everybody had enough."

"She didn't!"

"Yes, she did. And when you think—it was her own husband."

"A remarkable woman," Adam repeated Will's phrase.

"She's practical. She knew they had to be fed and she fed them."

"I guess she'll be all right, but it must be a great loss to her."

"She'll be all right," Will said. "And she'll outlive us all, little tiny thing that she is."

On his drive back to the ranch Adam found that he was noticing things he had not seen for years. He saw the wildflowers in the heavy grass, and he saw the red cows against the hillsides, moving up the easy ascending paths and eating as they went. When he came to his own land Adam felt a quick pleasure so sharp that he began to examine it. And suddenly he found himself saying aloud in rhythm with his horse's trotting feet, "I'm free, I'm free. I don't have to worry any more. I'm free. She's gone. She's out of me. Oh, Christ Almighty, I'm free!"

He reached out and stripped the fur from the silver-gray sage beside the road, and when his fingers were sticky with the sap he smelled the sharp penetrating odor on his fingers, breathed it deep into his lungs. He was glad to be going home. He wanted to see how the twins had grown in the two days he had been gone—he wanted to see the twins.

"I'm free, she's gone," he chanted aloud.

2

Lee came out of the house to meet Adam, and he stood at the horse's head while Adam climbed down from the buggy.

"How are the boys?" Adam asked.

"They're fine. I made them some bows and arrows and they went hunting rabbits in the river bottom. I'm not keeping the pan hot though."

"Everything all right here?"

Lee looked at him sharply, was about to exclaim, changed his mind. "How was the funeral?"

"Lots of people," Adam said. "He had lots of friends. I can't get it through my head that he's gone."

"My people bury them with drums and scatter papers to confuse the devils and put roast pigs instead of flowers on the grave. We're a practical people and always a little hungry. But our devils aren't very bright. We can outthink them. That's some progress."

"I think Samuel would have liked that kind of funeral," said Adam. "It would have interested him." He noticed that Lee was staring at him. "Put the horse away, Lee, and then come in and make some tea. I want to talk to you."

Adam went into the house and took off his black clothes. He could smell the sweet and now sickish odor of rum about himself. He removed all of his clothes and sponged his skin with yellow soap until the odor was gone from his pores. He put on a clean blue shirt and overalls washed until they were soft and pale blue and lighter blue at the knees where the wear came. He shaved slowly and combed his hair while the rattle of Lee at the stove sounded from the kitchen. Then he went to the living room. Lee had set out one cup and a bowl of sugar on the table beside his big chair. Adam looked around at the flowered curtains washed so long that the blossoms were pale. He saw the worn rugs on the floor and the brown path on the linoleum in the hall. And it was all new to him.

When Lee came in with the teapot Adam said, "Bring yourself a cup, Lee. And if you've got any of that drink of yours, I could use a little. I got drunk last night."

Lee said, "You drunk? I can hardly believe it."

"Well, I was. And I want to talk about it. I saw you looking at me."

"Did you?" asked Lee, and he went to the kitchen to bring his cup and glasses and his stone bottle of ng-ka-py.

He said when he came back, "The only times I've tasted it for years have been with you and Mr. Hamilton."

"Is that the same one we named the twins with?"

"Yes, it is." Lee poured the scalding green tea. He grimaced when Adam put two spoonfuls of sugar in his cup.

Adam stirred his tea and watched the sugar crystals whirl and disappear into liquid. He said, "I went down to see her."

"I thought you might," said Lee. "As a matter of fact I don't see how a human man could have waited so long."

"Maybe I wasn't a human man."

"I thought of that too. How was she?"

Adam said slowly, "I can't understand it. I can't believe there is such a creature in the world."

"The trouble with you Occidentals is that you don't have devils to explain things with. Did you get drunk afterward?"

"No, before and during. I needed it for courage, I guess."

"You look all right now."

"I am all right," said Adam. "That's what I want to talk to you about." He paused and said ruefully, "This time last year I would have run to Sam Hamilton to talk."

"Maybe both of us have got a piece of him," said Lee. "Maybe that's what immortality is."

"I seemed to come out of a sleep," said Adam. "In some strange way my eyes have cleared. A weight is off me."

"You even use words that sound like Mr. Hamilton," said Lee. "I'll build a theory for my immortal relatives."

Adam drank his cup of black liquor and licked his lips. "I'm free," he said. "I have to tell it to someone. I can live with my boys. I might even see a woman. Do you know what I'm saying?"

"Yes, I know. And I can see it in your eyes and in the way your body stands. A man can't lie about a thing like that. You'll like the boys, I think."

"Well, at least I'm going to give myself a chance. Will you give me another drink and some more tea?"

Lee poured the tea and picked up his cup.

"I don't know why you don't scald your mouth, drinking it that hot."

Lee was smiling inwardly. Adam, looking at him, realized that Lee was not a young man any more. The skin on his cheeks was stretched tight, and its surface shone as though it were glazed. And there was a red irritated rim around his eyes.

Lee studied the shell-thin cup in his hand and his was a memory smile. "Maybe if you're free, you can free me."

"What do you mean, Lee?"

"Could you let me go?"

"Why, of course you can go. Aren't you happy here?"

"I don't think I've ever known what you people call happiness. We think of contentment as the desirable thing, and maybe that's negative."

Adam said, "Call it that then. Aren't you contented here?"

Lee said, "I don't think any man is contented when there are things undone he wishes to do."

"What do you want to do?"

"Well, one thing it's too late for. I wanted to have a wife and sons of my own. Maybe I wanted to hand down the nonsense that passes for wisdom in a parent, to force it on my own helpless children."

"You're not too old."

"Oh, I guess I'm physically able to father a child. That's not what I'm thinking. I'm too closely married to a quiet reading lamp. You know, Mr. Trask, once I had a wife. I made her up just as you did, only mine had no life outside my mind. She was good company in my little room. I would talk and she would listen, and then she would talk, would tell me all the happenings of a woman's afternoon. She was very pretty and she made coquettish little jokes. But now I don't know whether I would listen to her. And I wouldn't want to make her sad or lonely. So there's my first plan gone."

"What was the other?"

"I talked to Mr. Hamilton about that. I want to open a bookstore in Chinatown in San Francisco. I would live in the back, and my days would be full of discussions and arguments. I would like to have in stock some of those dragon-carved blocks of ink from the dynasty of Sung. The boxes are worm-bored, and that ink is made from fir smoke and a glue that comes only from wild asses' skin. When you paint with that ink it may physically be black but it suggests to your eye and persuades your seeing that it is all the colors in the world. Maybe a painter would come by and we could argue about method and haggle about price."

Adam said, "Are you making this up?"

"No. If you are well and if you are free, I would like to have my little bookshop at last. I would like to die there."

Adam sat silently for a while, stirring sugar into his lukewarm tea. Then he said, "Funny. I found myself wishing you were a slave so I could refuse you. Of course you can go if you want to. I'll even lend you money for your bookstore."

"Oh, I have the money. I've had it a long time."

"I never thought of your going," Adam said. "I took you for granted." He straightened his shoulders. "Could you wait a little while?"

"What for?"

"I want you to help me get acquainted with my boys. I want to put this place in shape, or maybe sell it or rent it. I'll want to know how much money I have left and what I can do with it."

"You wouldn't lay a trap for me?" Lee asked. "My wish isn't as strong as it once was. I'm afraid I could be talked out of it or, what would be worse, I could be held back just by being needed. Please try not to need me. That's the worst bait of all to a lonely man."

Adam said, "A lonely man. I must have been far down in myself not to have thought of that."

"Mr. Hamilton knew," said Lee. He raised his head and his fat lids let only two sparks from his eyes show through. "We're controlled, we Chinese," he said. "We show no emotion. I loved Mr. Hamilton. I would like to go to Salinas tomorrow if you will permit it."

"Do anything you want," said Adam. "God knows you've done enough for me."

"I want to scatter devil papers," Lee said. "I want to put a little roast pig on the grave of my father."

Adam got up quickly and knocked over his cup and went outside and left Lee sitting there.

TWENTY-SEVEN

That year the rains had come so gently that the Salinas River did not overflow. A slender stream twisted back and forth in its broad bed of gray sand, and the water was not milky with silt but clear and pleasant. The willows that grow in the river bed were well leafed, and the wild blackberry vines were thrusting their spiky new shoots along the ground.

It was very warm for March, and the kite wind blew steadily from the south and turned up the silver undersides of the leaves.

Against the perfect cover of vine and bramble and tangled drift sticks, a little gray brush rabbit sat quietly in the sun, drying his breast fur, wet by the grass dew of his early feeding. The rabbit's nose crinkled, and his ears slewed around now and then, investigating small sounds that might possibly be charged with danger to a brush rabbit. There had been a rhythmic vibration in the ground audible through the paws, so that ears swung and nose wrinkled, but that had stopped. Then there had been a movement of willow branches twenty-five yards away and downwind, so that no odor of fear came to the rabbit.

For the last two minutes there had been sounds of interest but not of danger—a snap and then a whistle like that of the wings of a wild dove. The rabbit stretched out one hind leg lazily in the warm sun. There was a snap and a whistle and a grunting thud on fur. The rabbit sat perfectly

still and his eyes grew large. A bamboo arrow was through his chest, and
its iron tip deep in the ground on the other side. The rabbit slumped over
on his side and his feet ran and scampered in the air for a moment before
he was still.

From the willow two crouching boys crept. They carried four-foot bows,
and tufts of arrows stuck their feathers up from the quivers behind their
left shoulders. They were dressed in overalls and faded blue shirts, but
each boy wore one perfect turkey tailfeather tied with tape against his
temple.

The boys moved cautiously, bending low, self-consciously toeing-in like
Indians. The rabbit's flutter of death was finished when they bent over to
examine their victim.

"Right through the heart," said Cal as though it could not be any other
way. Aron looked down and said nothing. "I'm going to say you did it,"
Cal went on. "I won't take credit. And I'll say it was a hard shot."

"Well, it was," said Aron.

"Well, I'm telling you. I'll give you credit to Lee and to Father."

"I don't know as I want credit—not all of it," said Aron. "Tell you what.
If we get another one we'll say we each hit one, and if we don't get any
more, why don't we say we both shot together and we don't know who hit?"

"Don't you want credit?" Cal asked subtly.

"Well, not full credit. We could divide it up."

"After all, it was my arrow," said Cal.

"No, it wasn't."

"You look at the feathers. See that nick? That's mine."

"How did it get in my quiver? I don't remember any nick."

"Maybe you don't remember. But I'm going to give you credit anyway."

Aron said gratefully, "No, Cal. I don't want that. We'll say we both shot
at once."

"Well, if that's what you want. But suppose Lee sees it was my arrow?"

"We'll just say it was in my quiver."

"You think he'll believe that? He'll think you're lying."

Aron said helplessly, "If he thinks you shot it, why, we'll just let him
think that."

"I just wanted you to know," said Cal. "Just in case he'd think that."
He drew the arrow through the rabbit so that the white feathers were dark
red with heart blood. He put the arrow in his quiver. "You can carry him,"
he said magnanimously.

"We ought to start back," said Aron. "Maybe Father is back by now."

Cal said, "We could cook that old rabbit and have him for our supper
and stay out all night."

"It's too cold at night, Cal. Don't you remember how you shivered this
morning?"

"It's not too cold for me," said Cal. "I never feel cold."

"You did this morning."

"No, I didn't. I was just making fun of you, shivering and chattering like a milk baby. Do you want to call me a liar?"

"No," said Aron. "I don't want to fight."

"Afraid to fight?"

"No. I just don't want to."

"If I was to say you was scared, would you want to call me a liar?"

"No."

"Then you're scared, aren't you?"

"I guess so."

Aron wandered slowly away, leaving the rabbit on the ground. His eyes were very wide and he had a beautiful soft mouth. The width between his blue eyes gave him an expression of angelic innocence. His hair was fine and golden. The sun seemed to light up the top of his head.

He was puzzled—but he was often puzzled. He knew his brother was getting at something, but he didn't know what. Cal was an enigma to him. He could not follow the reasoning of his brother, and he was always surprised at the tangents it took.

Cal looked more like Adam. His hair was dark brown. He was bigger than his brother, bigger of bone, heavier in the shoulder, and his jaw had the square sternness of Adam's jaw. Cal's eyes were brown and watchful, and sometimes they sparkled as though they were black. But Cal's hands were very small for the size of the rest of him. The fingers were short and slender, the nails delicate. Cal protected his hands. There were few things that could make him cry, but a cut finger was one of them. He never ventured with his hands, never touched an insect or carried a snake about. And in a fight he picked up a rock or a stick to fight with.

As Cal watched his brother walking away from him there was a small sure smile on his lips. He called, "Aron, wait for me!"

When he caught up with his brother he held out the rabbit. "You can carry it," he said kindly, putting his arm around his brother's shoulders. "Don't be mad with me."

"You always want to fight," said Aron.

"No, I don't. I was only making a joke."

"Were you?"

"Sure. Look—you can carry the rabbit. And we'll start back now if you want."

Aron smiled at last. He was always relieved when his brother let the tension go. The two boys trudged up out of the river bottom and up the crumbling cliff to the level land. Aron's right trouser leg was well bloodied from the rabbit.

Cal said, "They'll be surprised we got a rabbit. If Father's home, let's give it to him. He likes a rabbit for his supper."

"All right," Aron said happily. "Tell you what. We'll both give it to him and we won't say which one hit it."

"All right, if you want to," said Cal.

They walked along in silence for a time and then Cal said, "All this is our land—way to hell over the river."

"It's Father's."

"Yes, but when he dies it's going to be ours."

This was a new thought to Aron. "What do you mean, when he dies?"

"Everybody dies," said Cal. "Like Mr. Hamilton. He died."

"Oh, yes," Aron said. "Yes, he died." He couldn't connect the two—the dead Mr. Hamilton and the live father.

"They put them in a box and then they dig a hole and put the box in," said Cal.

"I know that." Aron wanted to change the subject, to think of something else.

Cal said, "I know a secret."

"What is it?"

"You'd tell."

"No, I wouldn't, if you said not."

"I don't know if I ought."

"Tell me," Aron begged.

"You won't tell?"

"No, I won't."

Cal said, "Where do you think our mother is?"

"She's dead."

"No, she isn't."

"She is too."

"She ran away," said Cal. "I heard some men talking."

"They were liars."

"She ran away," said Cal. "You won't tell I told you?"

"I don't believe it," said Aron. "Father said she was in Heaven."

Cal said quietly, "Pretty soon I'm going to run away and find her. I'll bring her back."

"Where did the men say she is?"

"I don't know, but I'll find her."

"She's in Heaven," said Aron. "Why would Father tell a lie?" He looked at his brother, begging him silently to agree. Cal didn't answer him. "Don't you think she's in Heaven with the angels?" Aron insisted. And when Cal still did not answer, "Who were the men who said it?"

"Just some men. In the post office at King City. They didn't think I could hear. But I got good ears. Lee says I can hear the grass grow."

Aron said, "What would she want to run away for?"

"How do I know? Maybe she didn't like us."

Aron inspected this heresy. "No," he said. "The men were liars. Father said she's in Heaven. And you know how he don't like to talk about her."

"Maybe that's because she ran away."

"No. I asked Lee. Know what Lee said? Lee said, 'Your mother loved you and she still does.' And Lee gave me a star to look at. He said maybe that was our mother and she would love us as long as that light was there. Do you think Lee is a liar?" Through his gathering tears Aron could see his brother's eyes, hard and reasonable. There were no tears in Cal's eyes.

Cal felt pleasantly excited. He had found another implement, another secret tool, to use for any purpose he needed. He studied Aron, saw his quivering lips, but he noticed in time the flaring nostrils. Aron would cry, but sometimes, pushed to tears, Aron would fight too. And when Aron cried and fought at the same time he was dangerous. Nothing could hurt him and nothing could stop him. Once Lee had held him in his lap, clasping his still flailing fists to his sides, until after a long time he relaxed. And his nostrils had flared then.

Cal put his new tool away. He could bring it out anytime, and he knew it was the sharpest weapon he had found. He would inspect it at his ease and judge just when and how much to use it.

He made his decision almost too late. Aron leaped at him and the limp body of the rabbit slashed against his face. Cal jumped back and cried, "I was just joking. Honest, Aron, it was only a joke."

Aron stopped. Pain and puzzlement were on his face. "I don't like that joke," he said, and he sniffled and wiped his nose on his sleeve.

Cal came close to him and hugged him and kissed him on the cheek. "I won't do it any more," he said.

The boys trudged along silently for a while. The light of day began to withdraw. Cal looked over his shoulder at a thunderhead sailing blackly over the mountains on the nervous March wind. "Going to storm," he said. "Going to be a bastard."

Aron said, "Did you really hear those men?"

"Maybe I only thought I did," Cal said quickly. "Jesus, look at that cloud!"

Aron turned around to look at the black monster. It ballooned in great dark rolls above, and beneath it drew a long trailing skirt of rain, and as they looked the cloud rumbled and flashed fire. Borne on the wind, the cloudburst drummed hollowly on the fat wet hills across the valley and moved out over the flat lands. The boys turned and ran for home, and the cloud boomed at their backs and the lightning shattered the air into quaking pieces. The cloud caught up with them, and the first stout drops plopped on the ground out of the riven sky. They could smell the sweet odor of ozone. Running, they sniffed the thunder smell.

As they raced across the county road and onto the wheel tracks that led to their own home draw the water struck them. The rain fell in sheets and in columns. Instantly they were soaked through, and their hair plastered down on their foreheads and streamed into their eyes, and the turkey feathers at their temples bent over with the weight of water.

Now that they were as wet as they could get the boys stopped running. There was no reason to run for cover. They looked at each other and laughed for joy. Aron wrung out the rabbit and tossed it in the air and caught it and threw it to Cal. And Cal, feeling silly, put it around his neck with the head and hind feet under his chin. Both boys leaned over and laughed hysterically. The rain roared on the oak trees in the home draw and the wind disturbed their high dignity.

2

The twins came in sight of the ranch buildings in time to see Lee, his head through the center hole of a yellow oilskin poncho, leading a strange horse and a flimsy rubber-tired buggy toward the shed. "Somebody's here," said Cal. "Will you look at that rig?"

They began to run again, for there was a certain deliciousness about visitors. Near the steps they slowed down, moved cautiously around the house, for there was a certain fearsomeness about visitors too. They went in the back way and stood dripping in the kitchen. They heard voices in the living room—their father's voice and another, a man's voice. And then a third voice stiffened their stomachs and rippled a little chill up their spines. It was a woman's voice. These boys had had very little experience with women. They tiptoed into their own room and stood looking at each other.

"Who do you 'spose it is?" Cal asked.

An emotion like a light had burst in Aron. He wanted to shout, "Maybe it's our mother. Maybe she's come back." And then he remembered that she was in Heaven and people do not come back from there. He said, "I don't know. I'm going to put on dry clothes."

The boys put on dry clean clothes, which were exact replicas of the sopping clothes they were taking off. They took off the wet turkey feathers and combed their hair back with their fingers. And all the while they could hear the voices, mostly low pitched, and then the high woman's voice, and once they froze, listening, for they heard a child's voice—a girl's voice—and this was such an excitement that they did not even speak of hearing it.

Silently they edged into the hall and crept toward the door to the living room. Cal turned the doorknob very, very slowly and lifted it up so that no creak would betray them.

Only the smallest crack was open when Lee came in the back door, shuffled along the hall, getting out of his poncho, and caught them there. "Lilly boy peek?" he said in pidgin, and when Cal closed the door and the latch clicked Lee said quickly, "Your father's home. You'd better go in."

Aron whispered hoarsely, "Who else is there?"

"Just some people going by. The rain drove them in." Lee put his hand over Cal's on the doorknob and turned it and opened the door.

"Boys come long home," he said and left them there, exposed in the opening.

Adam cried, "Come in, boys! Come on in!"

The two carried their heads low and darted glances at the strangers and shuffled their feet. There was a man in city clothes and a woman in the fanciest clothes ever. Her duster and hat and veil lay on a chair beside her, and she seemed to the boys to be clad entirely in black silk and lace. Black lace even climbed up little sticks and hugged her throat. That was enough for one day, but it wasn't all. Beside the woman sat a girl, a little younger maybe than the twins, but not much. She wore a blue-checked sunbonnet with lace around the front. Her dress was flowery, and a little apron with pockets was tied around her middle. Her skirt was turned back, showing a petticoat of red knitted yarn with tatting around the edge. The boys could not see her face because of the sunbonnet, but her hands were folded in her lap, and it was easy to see the little gold seal ring she wore on her third finger.

Neither boy had drawn a breath and the red rings were beginning to flare in back of their eyes from holding their breath.

"These are my boys," their father said. "They're twins. That's Aron and this is Caleb. Boys, shake hands with our guests."

The boys moved forward, heads down, hands up, in a gesture very like surrender and despair. Their limp fins were pumped by the gentleman and then by the lacy lady. Aron was first, and he turned away from the little girl, but the lady said, "Aren't you going to say how do to my daughter?"

Aron shuddered and surrendered his hand in the direction of the girl with the hidden face. Nothing happened. His lifeless sausages were not gripped, or wrung, or squeezed, or racheted. His hand simply hung in the air in front of her. Aron peeked up through his eyelashes to see what was going on.

Her head was down too, and she had the advantage of the sunbonnet. Her small right hand with the signet ring on the middle finger was stuck out too, but it made no move toward Aron's hand.

He stole a glance at the lady. She was smiling, her lips parted. The room seemed crushed with silence. And then Aron heard a ripping snicker from Cal.

Aron reached out and grabbed her hand and pumped it up and down three times. It was as soft as a handful of petals. He felt a pleasure that burned him. He dropped her hand and concealed his in his overall pocket. As he backed hastily away he saw Cal step up and shake hands formally and say, "How do." Aron had forgotten to say it, so he said it now, after his brother, and it sounded strange. Adam and his guests laughed.

Adam said, "Mr. and Mrs. Bacon nearly got caught in the rain."

"We were lucky to be lost here," Mr. Bacon said. "I was looking for th
Long ranch."

"That's farther. You should have taken the next left turn off the count
road to the south." Adam continued to the boys, "Mr. Bacon is a count
supervisor."

"I don't know why, but I take the job very seriously," said Mr. Bacon
and he too addressed the boys. "My daughter's name is Abra, boys. Isn'
that a funny name?" He used the tone adults employ with children. H
turned to Adam and said in poetic singsong, " 'Abra was ready ere I calle
her name; And though I called another, Abra came.' Matthew Prior. I won'
say I hadn't wanted a son—but Abra's such a comfort. Look up, dear."

Abra did not move. Her hands were again clasped in her lap. Her fathe
repeated with relish, " 'And though I called another, Abra came.' "

Aron saw his brother looking at the little sunbonnet without an ounce o
fear. And Aron said hoarsely, "I don't think Abra's a funny name."

"He didn't mean funny that way," Mrs. Bacon explained. "He only mean
curious." And she explained to Adam, "My husband gets the strangest thing
out of books. Dear, shouldn't we be going?"

Adam said eagerly, "Oh, don't go yet, ma'am. Lee is making some tea
It will warm you up."

"Well, how pleasant!" Mrs. Bacon said, and she continued, "Children,
it isn't raining any more. Go outside and play." Her voice had such authority
that they filed out—Aron first and Cal second and Abra following.

3

In the living room Mr. Bacon crossed his legs. "You have a fine prospect
here," he said. "Is it a sizable piece?"

Adam said, "I have a good strip. I cross the river to the other side. It's
a good piece."

"That's all yours across the county road then?"

"Yes, it is. I'm kind of ashamed to admit it. I've let it go badly. I haven't
farmed it at all. Maybe I got too much farming as a child."

Both Mr. and Mrs. Bacon were looking at Adam now, and he knew he
had to make some explanation for letting his good land run free. He said,
"I guess I'm a lazy man. And my father didn't help me when he left me
enough to get along on without working." He dropped his eyes but he
could feel the relief on the part of the Bacons. It was not laziness if he was a
rich man. Only the poor were lazy. Just as only the poor were ignorant. A
rich man who didn't know anything was spoiled or independent.

"Who takes care of the boys?" Mrs. Bacon asked.

Adam laughed. "What taking care of they get, and it isn't much, is Lee's
work."

"Lee?"

Adam became a little irritated with the questioning. "I only have one man," he said shortly.

"You mean the Chinese we saw?" Mrs. Bacon was shocked.

Adam smiled at her. She had frightened him at first, but now he was more comfortable. "Lee raised the boys, and he has taken care of me," he said.

"But didn't they ever have a woman's care?"

"No, they didn't."

"The poor lambs," she said.

"They're wild but I guess they're healthy," Adam said. "I guess we've all gone wild like the land. But now Lee is going away. I don't know what we'll do."

Mr. Bacon carefully cleared the phlegm from his throat so it wouldn't be run over by his pronouncement. "Have you thought about the education of your sons?"

"No—I guess I haven't thought about it much."

Mrs. Bacon said, "My husband is a believer in education."

"Education is the key to the future," Mr. Bacon said.

"What kind of education?" asked Adam.

Mr. Bacon went on, "All things come to men who know. Yes, I'm a believer in the torch of learning." He leaned close and his voice became confidential. "So long as you aren't going to farm your land, why don't you rent it and move to the county seat—near our good public schools?"

For just a second Adam thought of saying, "Why don't you mind your own goddam business?" but instead he asked, "You think that would be a good idea?"

"I think I could get you a good reliable tenant," Mr. Bacon said. "No reason why you shouldn't have something coming in from your land if you don't live on it."

Lee made a great stir coming in with the tea. He had heard enough of the tones through the door to be sure Adam was finding them tiresome. Lee was pretty certain they didn't like tea, and if they did, they weren't likely to favor the kind he had brewed. And when they drank it with compliments he knew that the Bacons had their teeth in something. Lee tried to catch Adam's eye but could not. Adam was studying the rug between his feet.

Mrs. Bacon was saying, "My husband has served on his school board for many years—" but Adam didn't hear the discussion that followed.

He was thinking of a big globe of the world, suspended and swaying from a limb of one of his oak trees. And for no reason at all that he could make out, his mind leaped to his father, stumping about on his wooden leg, rapping on his leg for attention with a walking stick. Adam could see the stern and military face of his father as he forced his sons through drill and made them carry heavy packs to develop their shoulders. Through his memory Mrs. Bacon's voice droned on. Adam felt the pack loaded with rocks. He saw Charles' face grinning sardonically—Charles—the mean, fierce eyes, the hot temper. Suddenly Adam wanted to see Charles. He would take a trip—take the boys. He slapped his leg with excitement.

Mr. Bacon paused in his talk. "I beg your pardon?"

"Oh, I'm sorry," Adam said. "I just remembered something I've neglected to do." Both Bacons were patiently, politely waiting for his explanation. Adam thought, Why not? I'm not running for supervisor. I'm not on the school board. Why not? He said to his guests, "I just remembered that I have forgotten to write to my brother for over ten years." They shuddered under his statement and exchanged glances.

Lee had been refilling the teacups. Adam saw his cheeks puff out and heard his happy snort as he passed to the safety of the hallway. The Bacons didn't want to comment on the incident. They wanted to be alone to discuss it.

Lee anticipated that it would be this way. He hurried out to harness up and bring the rubber-tired buggy to the front door.

4

When Abra and Cal and Aron went out, they stood side by side on the small covered porch, looking at the rain splashing and dripping down from the wide-spreading oak trees. The cloudburst had passed into a distant echoing thunder roll, but it had left a rain determined to go on for a long time.

Aron said, "That lady told us the rain was stopped."

Abra answered him wisely, "She didn't look. When she's talking she never looks."

Cal demanded, "How old are you?"

"Ten, going on eleven," said Abra.

"Ho!" said Cal. "We're eleven, going on twelve."

Abra pushed her sunbonnet back. It framed her head like a halo. She was pretty, with dark hair in two braids. Her little forehead was round and domed, and her brows were level. One day her nose would be sweet and turned up where now it still was button-form. But two features would be with her always. Her chin was firm and her mouth was as sweet as a flower and very wide and pink. Her hazel eyes were sharp and intelligent and completely fearless. She looked straight into the faces of the boys, straight into their eyes, one after the other, and there was no hint of the shyness she had pretended inside the house.

"I don't believe you're twins," she said. "You don't look alike."

"We are too," said Cal.

"We are too," said Aron.

"Some twins don't look alike," Cal insisted.

"Lots of them don't," Aron said. "Lee told us how it is. If the lady has one egg, the twins look alike. If she has two eggs, they don't."

"We're two eggs," said Cal.

Abra smiled with amusement at the myths of these country boys. "Eggs," she said. "Ho! Eggs." She didn't say it loudly or harshly, but Lee's theory tottered and swayed and then she brought it crashing down. "Which one of you is fried?" she asked. "And which one is poached?"

The boys exchanged uneasy glances. It was their first experience with the inexorable logic of women, which is overwhelming even, or perhaps especially, when it is wrong. This was new to them, exciting and frightening.

Cal said, "Lee is a Chinaman."

"Oh, well," said Abra kindly, "why don't you say so? Maybe you're china eggs then, like they put in a nest." She paused to let her shaft sink in. She saw opposition, struggle, disappear. Abra had taken control. She was the boss.

Aron suggested, "Let's go to the old house and play there. It leaks a little but it's nice."

They ran under the dripping oaks to the old Sanchez house and plunged in through its open door, which squeaked restlessly on rusty hinges.

The 'dobe house had entered its second decay. The great sala all along the front was half plastered, the line of white halfway around and then stopping, just as the workmen had left it over ten years before. And the deep windows with their rebuilt sashes remained glassless. The new floor was streaked with water stain, and a clutter of old papers and darkened nail bags with their nails rusted to prickly balls filled the corner of the room.

As the children stood in the entrance a bat flew from the rear of the house. The gray shape swooped from side to side and disappeared through the doorway.

The boys conducted Abra through the house—opened closets to show wash basins and toilets and chandeliers, still crated and waiting to be installed. A smell of mildew and of wet paper was in the air. The three children walked on tiptoe, and they did not speak for fear of the echoes from the walls of the empty house.

Back in the big sala the twins faced their guest. "Do you like it?" Aron asked softly because of the echo.

"Yee-es," she admitted hesitantly.

"Sometimes we play here," Cal said boldly. "You can come here and play with us if you like."

"I live in Salinas," Abra said in such a tone that they knew they were dealing with a superior being who hadn't time for bumpkin pleasures.

Abra saw that she had crushed their highest treasure, and while she knew the weaknesses of men she still liked them, and, besides, she was a lady. "Sometimes, when we are driving by, I'll come and play with you—a little," she said kindly, and both boys felt grateful to her.

"I'll give you my rabbit," said Cal suddenly. "I was going to give it to m
father, but you can have it."

"What rabbit?"

"The one we shot today—right through the heart with an arrow. He hardl
even kicked."

Aron looked at him in outrage. "It was my—"

Cal interrupted, "We will let you have it to take home. It's a pretty bi;
one."

Abra said, "What would I want with a dirty old rabbit all covered witl
blood?"

Aron said, "I'll wash him off and put him in a box and tie him witl
string, and if you don't want to eat him, you can have a funeral when you
get time—in Salinas."

"I go to real funerals," said Abra. "Went to one yesterday. There wa:
flowers high as this roof."

"Don't you want our rabbit?" Aron asked.

Abra looked at his sunny hair, tight-curled now, and at his eyes that
seemed near to tears, and she felt the longing and the itching burn in her
chest that is the beginning of love. Also, she wanted to touch Aron, and
she did. She put her hand on his arm and felt him shiver under her fingers.
"If you put it in a box," she said.

Now that she had got herself in charge, Abra looked around and inspected
her conquests. She was well above vanity now that no male principle
threatened her. She felt kindly toward these boys. She noticed their thin
washed-out clothes patched here and there by Lee. She drew on her fairy
tales. "You poor children," she said, "does your father beat you?"

They shook their heads. They were interested but bewildered.

"Are you very poor?"

"How do you mean?" Cal asked.

"Do you sit in the ashes and have to fetch water and faggots?"

"What's faggots?" Aron asked.

She avoided that by continuing. "Poor darlings," she began, and she
seemed to herself to have a little wand in her hand tipped by a twinkling
star. "Does your wicked stepmother hate you and want to kill you?"

"We don't have a stepmother," said Cal.

"We don't have any kind," said Aron. "Our mother's dead."

His words destroyed the story she was writing but almost immediately
supplied her with another. The wand was gone but she wore a big hat
with an ostrich plume and she carried an enormous basket from which a
turkey's feet protruded.

"Little motherless orphans," she said sweetly. "I'll be your mother. I'll
hold you and rock you and tell you stories."

"We're too big," said Cal. "We'd overset you."

Abra looked away from his brutality. Aron, she saw, was caught up in her story. His eyes were smiling and he seemed almost to be rocking in her arms, and she felt again the tug of love for him. She said pleasantly, "Tell me, did your mother have a nice funeral?"

"We don't remember," said Aron. "We were too little."

"Well, where is she buried? You could put flowers on her grave. We always do that for Grandma and Uncle Albert."

"We don't know," said Aron.

Cal's eyes had a new interest, a gleaming interest that was close to triumph. He said naïvely, "I'll ask our father where it is so we can take flowers."

"I'll go with you," said Abra. "I can make a wreath. I'll show you how." She noticed that Aron had not spoken. "Don't you want to make a wreath?"

"Yes," he said.

She had to touch him again. She patted his shoulder and then touched his cheek. "Your mama will like that," she said. "Even in Heaven they look down and notice. My father says they do. He knows a poem about it."

Aron said, "I'll go wrap up the rabbit. I've got the box my pants came in." He ran out of the old house. Cal watched him go. He was smiling.

"What are you laughing at?" Abra asked.

"Oh, nothing," he said. Cal's eyes stayed on her.

She tried to stare him down. She was an expert at staring down, but Cal did not look away. At very first he had felt a shyness, but that was gone now, and the sense of triumph at destroying Abra's control made him laugh. He knew she preferred his brother, but that was nothing new to him. Nearly everyone preferred Aron with his golden hair and the openness that allowed his affection to plunge like a puppy. Cal's emotions hid deep in him and peered out, ready to retreat or attack. He was starting to punish Abra for liking his brother, and this was nothing new either. He had done it since he first discovered he could. And secret punishment had grown to be almost a creative thing with him.

Maybe the difference between the two boys can best be described in this way. If Aron should come upon an anthill in a little clearing in the brush, he would lie on his stomach and watch the complications of ant life—he would see some of them bringing food in the ant roads and others carrying the white eggs. He would see how two members of the hill on meeting put their antennas together and talked. For hours he would lie absorbed in the economy of the ground.

If, on the other hand, Cal came upon the same anthill, he would kick it to pieces and watch while the frantic ants took care of their disaster. Aron was content to be a part of his world, but Cal must change it.

Cal did not question the fact that people liked his brother better, but he had developed a means for making it all right with himself. He planned and waited until one time that admiring person exposed himself, and then something happened and the victim never knew how or why. Out of revenge

Cal extracted a fluid of power, and out of power, joy. It was the strongest, purest emotion he knew. Far from disliking Aron, he loved him because he was usually the cause for Cal's feelings of triumph. He had forgotten —if he had ever known—that he punished because he wished he could be loved as Aron was loved. It had gone so far that he preferred what he had to what Aron had.

Abra had started a process in Cal by touching Aron and by the softness of her voice toward him. Cal's reaction was automatic. His brain probed for a weakness in Abra, and so clever was he that he found one almost at once in her words. Some children want to be babies and some want to be adults. Few are content with their age. Abra wanted to be an adult. She used adult words and simulated, insofar as she was able, adult attitudes and emotions. She had left babyhood far behind, and she was not capable yet of being one of the grownups she admired. Cal sensed this, and it gave him the instrument to knock down her anthill.

He knew about how long it would take his brother to find the box. He could see in his mind what would happen. Aron would try to wash the blood off the rabbit, and this would take time. Finding string would take more time, and the careful tying of the bow knots still more time. And meanwhile Cal knew he was beginning to win. He felt Abra's certainty wavering and he knew that he could prod it further.

Abra looked away from him at last and said, "What do you stare at a person for?"

Cal looked at her feet and slowly raised his eyes, going over her as coldly as if she were a chair. This, he knew, could make even an adult nervous.

Abra couldn't stand it. She said, "See anything green?"

Cal asked, "Do you go to school?"

"Of course I do."

"What grade?"

"High fifth."

"How old are you?"

"Going on eleven."

Cal laughed.

"What's wrong with that?" she demanded. He didn't answer her. "Come on, tell me! What's wrong with that?" Still no answer. "You think you're mighty smart," she said, and when he continued to laugh at her she said uneasily, "I wonder what's taking your brother so long. Look, the rain's stopped."

Cal said, "I guess he's looking around for it."

"You mean, for the rabbit?"

"Oh, no. He's got that all right—it's dead. But maybe he can't catch the other. It gets away."

"Catch what? What gets away?"

"He wouldn't want me to tell," said Cal. "He wants it to be a surprise. He caught it last Friday. It bit him too."

"Whatever are you talking about?"

"You'll see," said Cal, "when you open the box. I bet he tells you not to open it right off." This was not a guess. Cal knew his brother.

Abra knew she was losing not only the battle but the whole war. She began to hate this boy. In her mind she went over the deadly retorts she knew and gave them all up in helplessness, feeling they would have no effect. She retired into silence. She walked out of the door and looked toward the house where her parents were.

"I think I'll go back," she said.

"Wait," said Cal.

She turned as he came up with her. "What do you want?" she asked coldly.

"Don't be mad with me," he said. "You don't know what goes on here. You should see my brother's back."

His change of pace bewildered her. He never let her get set in an attitude, and he had properly read her interest in romantic situations. His voice was low and secret. She lowered her voice to match his.

"What do you mean? What's wrong with his back?"

"All scars," said Cal. "It's the Chinaman."

She shivered and tensed with interest. "What does he do? Does he beat him?"

"Worse than that," said Cal.

"Why don't you tell your father?"

"We don't dare. Do you know what would happen if we told?"

"No. What?"

He shook his head. "No"—he seemed to think carefully—"I don't even dare tell you."

At that moment Lee came from the shed leading the Bacons' horse hitched to the high spindly rig with rubber tires. Mr. and Mrs. Bacon came out of the house and automatically they all looked up at the sky.

Cal said, "I can't tell you now. The Chinaman would know if I told."

Mrs. Bacon called, "Abra! Hurry! We're going."

Lee held the restive horse while Mrs. Bacon was helped up into the rig.

Aron came dashing around the house, carrying a cardboard box intricately tied with string in fancy bow knots. He thrust it at Abra. "Here," he said. "Don't untie it until you get home."

Cal saw revulsion on Abra's face. Her hands shrank away from the box.

"Take it, dear," her father said. "Hurry, we're very late." He thrust the box into her hands.

Cal stepped close to her. "I want to whisper," he said. He put his mouth to her ear. "You've wet your pants," he said. She blushed and pulled the

sunbonnet up over her head. Mr. Bacon picked her up under the arms and
passed her into the buggy.

Lee and Adam and the twins watched the horse pick up a fine trot.

Before the first turn Abra's hand came up and the box went sailing backward into the road. Cal watched his brother's face and saw misery come
into Aron's eyes. When Adam had gone back into the house and Lee was
moving out with a pan of grain to feed the chickens, Cal put his arm
around his brother's shoulders and hugged him reassuringly.

"I wanted to marry her," Aron said. "I put a letter in the box, asking her."

"Don't be sad," said Cal. "I'm going to let you use my rifle."

Aron's head jerked around. "You haven't got a rifle."

"Haven't I?" Cal said. "Haven't I though?"

TWENTY-EIGHT

It was at the supper table that the boys discovered the change in their
father. They knew him as a presence—as ears that heard but did not listen,
eyes that looked and did not notice. He was a cloud of a father. The boys
had never learned to tell him of their interests and discoveries, or of their
needs. Lee had been their contact with the adult world, and Lee had
managed not only to raise, feed, clothe, and discipline the boys, but he had
also given them a respect for their father. He was mystery to the boys,
and his word, his law, was carried down by Lee, who naturally made it up
himself and ascribed it to Adam.

This night, the first after Adam's return from Salinas, Cal and Aron were
first astonished and then a little embarrassed to find that Adam listened to
them and asked questions, looked at them and saw them. The change made
them timid.

Adam said, "I hear you were hunting today."

The boys became cautious as humans always are, faced with a new situation. After a pause Aron admitted, "Yes, sir."

"Did you get anything?"

This time a longer pause, and then, "Yes, sir."

"What did you get?"

"A rabbit."

"With bows and arrows? Who got him?"

Aron said, "We both shot. We don't know which one hit."

Adam said, "Don't you know your own arrows? We used to mark our
arrows when I was a boy."

This time Aron refused to answer and get into trouble. And Cal, after waiting, said, "Well, it was my arrow, all right, but we think it might have got in Aron's quiver."

"What makes you think that?"

"I don't know," Cal said. "But I think it was Aron hit the rabbit."

Adam swung his eyes. "And what do you think?"

"I think maybe I hit it—but I'm not sure."

"Well, you both seem to handle the situation very well."

The alarm went out of the faces of the boys. It did not seem to be a trap.

"Where is the rabbit?" Adam asked.

Cal said, "Aron gave it to Abra as a present."

"She threw it out," said Aron.

"Why?"

"I don't know. I wanted to marry her too."

"You did?"

"Yes, sir."

"How about you, Cal?"

"I guess I'll let Aron have her," said Cal.

Adam laughed, and the boys could not recall ever having heard him laugh. "Is she a nice little girl?" he asked.

"Oh, yes," said Aron. "She's nice, all right. She's good and nice."

"Well, I'm glad of that if she's going to be my daughter-in-law."

Lee cleared the table and after a quick rattling in the kitchen he came back. "Ready to go to bed?" he asked the boys.

They glared in protest. Adam said, "Sit down and let them stay a while."

"I've got the accounts together. We can go over them later," said Lee.

"What accounts, Lee?"

"The house and ranch accounts. You said you wanted to know where you stood."

"Not the accounts for over ten years, Lee!"

"You never wanted to be bothered before."

"I guess that's right. But sit a while. Aron wants to marry the little girl who was here today."

"Are they engaged?" Lee asked.

"I don't think she's accepted him yet," said Adam. "That may give us some time."

Cal had quickly lost his awe of the changed feeling in the house and had been examining this anthill with calculating eyes, trying to determine just how to kick it over. He made his decision.

"She's a real nice girl," he said. "I like her. Know why? Well, she said to ask you where our mother's grave is, so we can take some flowers."

"Could we, Father?" Aron asked. "She said she would teach us how to make wreaths."

Adam's mind raced. He was not good at lying to begin with, and he hadn't practiced. The solution frightened him, it came so quickly to his mind and so glibly to his tongue. Adam said, "I wish we could do that boys. But I'll have to tell you. Your mother's grave is clear across the country where she came from."

"Why?" Aron asked.

"Well, some people want to be buried in the place they came from."

"How did she get there?" Cal asked.

"We put her on a train and sent her home—didn't we, Lee?"

Lee nodded. "It's the same with us," he said. "Nearly all Chinese get sent home to China after they die."

"I know that," said Aron. "You told us that before."

"Did I?" Lee asked.

"Sure you did," said Cal. He was vaguely disappointed.

Adam quickly changed the subject. "Mr. Bacon made a suggestion this afternoon," he began. "I'd like you boys to think about it. He said it might be better for you if we moved to Salinas—better schools and lots of other children to play with."

The thought stunned the twins. Cal asked, "How about here?"

"Well, we'd keep the ranch in case we want to come back."

Aron said, "Abra lives in Salinas." And that was enough for Aron. Already he had forgotten the sailing box. All he could think of was a small apron and a sunbonnet and soft little fingers.

Adam said, "Well, you think about it. Maybe you should go to bed now. Why didn't you go to school today?"

"The teacher's sick," said Aron.

Lee verified it. "Miss Culp has been sick for three days," he said. "They don't have to go back until Monday. Come on, boys."

They followed him obediently from the room.

2

Adam sat smiling vaguely at the lamp and tapping his knee with a forefinger until Lee came back. Adam said, "Do they know anything?"

"I don't know," said Lee.

"Well, maybe it was just the little girl."

Lee went to the kitchen and brought back a big cardboard box. "Here are the accounts. Every year has a rubber band around it. I've been over it. It's complete."

"You mean all accounts?"

Lee said, "You'll find a book for each year and receipted bills for everything. You wanted to know how you stood. Here it is—all of it. Do you really think you'll move?"

"Well, I'm thinking of it."

"I wish there were some way you could tell the boys the truth."

"That would rob them of the good thoughts about their mother, Lee."

"Have you thought of the other danger?"

"What do you mean?"

"Well, suppose they find out the truth. Plenty of people know."

"Well, maybe when they're older it will be easier for them."

"I don't believe that," said Lee. "But that's not the worst danger."

"I guess I don't follow you, Lee."

"It's the lie I'm thinking of. It might infect everything. If they ever found out you'd lied to them about this, the true things would suffer. They wouldn't believe anything then."

"Yes, I see. But what can I tell them? I couldn't tell them the whole truth."

"Maybe you can tell them a part truth, enough so that you won't suffer if they find out."

"I'll have to think about that, Lee."

"If you go to live in Salinas it will be more dangerous."

"I'll have to think about it."

Lee went on insistently, "My father told me about my mother when I was very little, and he didn't spare me. He told me a number of times as I was growing. Of course it wasn't the same, but it was pretty dreadful. I'm glad he told me though. I wouldn't like not to know."

"Do you want to tell me?"

"No, I don't want to. But it might persuade you to make some change for your own boys. Maybe if you just said she went away and you don't know where."

"But I do know."

"Yes, there's the trouble. It's bound to be all truth or part lie. Well, I can't force you."

"I'll think about it," said Adam. "What's the story about your mother?"

"You really want to hear?"

"Only if you want to tell me."

"I'll make it very short," said Lee. "My first memory is of living in a little dark shack alone with my father in the middle of a potato field, and with it the memory of my father telling me the story of my mother. His language was Cantonese, but whenever he told the story he spoke in high and beautiful Mandarin. All right then. I'll tell you—" And Lee looked back in time.

"I'll have to tell you first that when you built the railroads in the West the terrible work of grading and laying ties and spiking the rails was done by many thousands of Chinese. They were cheap, they worked hard, and if they died no one had to worry. They were recruited largely from Canton, for the Cantonese are short and strong and durable, and also they are not quarrelsome. They were brought in by contract, and perhaps the history of my father was a fairly typical one.

"You must know that a Chinese must pay all of his debts on or before our New Year's day. He starts every year clean. If he does not, he loses face; but not only that—his family loses face. There are no excuses."

"That's not a bad idea," said Adam.

"Well, good or bad, that's the way it was. My father had some bad luck. He could not pay a debt. The family met and discussed the situation. Ours is an honorable family. The bad luck was nobody's fault, but the unpaid debt belonged to the whole family. They paid my father's debt and then he had to repay them, and that was almost impossible.

"One thing the recruiting agents for the railroad companies did—they paid down a lump of money on the signing of the contract. In this way they caught a great many men who had fallen into debt. All of this was reasonable and honorable. There was only one black sorrow.

"My father was a young man recently married, and his tie to his wife was very strong and deep and warm, and hers to him must have been—overwhelming. Nevertheless, with good manners they said good-by in the presence of the heads of the family. I have often thought that perhaps formal good manners may be a cushion against heartbreak.

"The herds of men went like animals into the black hold of a ship, there to stay until they reached San Francisco six weeks later. And you can imagine what those holes were like. The merchandise had to be delivered in some kind of working condition so it was not mistreated. And my people have learned through the ages to live close together, to keep clean and fed under intolerable conditions.

"They were a week at sea before my father discovered my mother. She was dressed like a man and she had braided her hair in a man's queue. By sitting very still and not talking, she had not been discovered, and of course there were no examinations or vaccinations then. She moved her mat close to my father. They could not talk except mouth to ear in the dark. My father was angry at her disobedience, but he was glad too.

"Well, there it was. They were condemned to hard labor for five years. It did not occur to them to run away once they were in America, for they were honorable people and they had signed the contract."

Lee paused. "I thought I could tell it in a few sentences," he said. "But you don't know the background. I'm going to get a cup of water—do you want some?"

"Yes," said Adam. "But there's one thing I don't understand. How could a woman do that kind of work?"

"I'll be back in a moment," said Lee, and he went to the kitchen. He brought back tin cups of water and put them on the table. He asked, "Now what did you want to know?"

"How could your mother do a man's work?"

Lee smiled. "My father said she was a strong woman, and I believe a strong woman may be stronger than a man, particularly if she happens to have love in her heart. I guess a loving woman is almost indestructible."

Adam made a wry grimace.

Lee said, "You'll see one day, you'll see."

"I didn't mean to think badly," said Adam. "How could I know out of one experience? Go on."

"One thing my mother did not whisper in my father's ear during that long miserable crossing. And because a great many were deadly seasick, no remark was made of her illness."

Adam cried, "She wasn't pregnant!"

"She was pregnant," said Lee. "And she didn't want to burden my father with more worries."

"Did she know about it when she started?"

"No, she did not. I set my presence in the world at the most inconvenient time. It's a longer story than I thought."

"Well, you can't stop now," said Adam.

"No, I suppose not. In San Francisco the flood of muscle and bone flowed into cattle cars and the engines puffed up the mountains. They were going to dig hills aside in the Sierras and burrow tunnels under the peaks. My mother got herded into another car, and my father didn't see her until they got to their camp on a high mountain meadow. It was very beautiful, with green grass and flowers and the snow mountains all around. And only then did she tell my father about me.

"They went to work. A woman's muscles harden just as a man's do, and my mother had a muscular spirit too. She did the pick and shovel work expected of her, and it must have been dreadful. But a panic worry settled on them about how she was going to have the baby."

Adam said, "Were they ignorant? Why couldn't she have gone to the boss and told him she was a woman and pregnant? Surely they would have taken care of her."

"You see?" said Lee. "I haven't told you enough. And that's why this is so long. They were not ignorant. These human cattle were imported for one thing only—to work. When the work was done, those who were not dead were to be shipped back. Only males were brought—no females. The country did not want them breeding. A man and a woman and a baby have a way of digging in, of pulling the earth where they are about them and scratching out a home. And then it takes all hell to root them out. But a crowd of men, nervous, lusting, restless, half sick with loneliness for women—why, they'll go anywhere, and particularly will they go home. And my mother was the only woman in this pack of half-crazy, half-savage men. The longer the men worked and ate, the more restless they became. To the bosses they were not people but animals which could be dangerous if not controlled. You can see why my mother did not ask for help. Why, they'd have rushed her out of the camp and—who knows?—perhaps shot and buried her like a diseased cow. Fifteen men were shot for being a little mutinous.

"No—they kept order the only way our poor species has ever learned to keep order. We think there must be better ways but we never learn them —always the whip, the rope, and the rifle. I wish I hadn't started to tell you this—"

"Why should you not tell me?" Adam asked.

"I can see my father's face when he told me. An old misery comes back, raw and full of pain. Telling it, my father had to stop and gain possession of himself, and when he continued he spoke sternly and he used hard sharp words almost as though he wanted to cut himself with them.

"These two managed to stay close together by claiming she was my father's nephew. The months went by and fortunately for them there was very little abdominal swelling, and she worked in pain and out of it. My father could only help her a little, apologizing, 'My nephew is young and his bones are brittle.' They had no plan. They did not know what to do.

"And then my father figured out a plan. They would run into the high mountains to one of the higher meadows, and there beside a lake they would make a burrow for the birthing, and when my mother was safe and the baby born, my father would come back and take his punishment. And he would sign for an extra five years to pay for his delinquent nephew. Pitiful as their escape was, it was all they had, and it seemed a brightness. The plan had two requirements—the timing had to be right and a supply of food was necessary."

Lee said, "My parents"—and he stopped, smiling over his use of the word, and it felt so good that he warmed it up—"my dear parents began to make their preparations. They saved a part of their daily rice and hid it under their sleeping mats. My father found a length of string and filed out a hook from a piece of wire, for there were trout to be caught in the mountain lakes. He stopped smoking to save the matches issued. And my mother collected every tattered scrap of cloth she could find and unraveled edges to make thread and sewed this ragbag together with a splinter to make swaddling clothes for me. I wish I had known her."

"So do I," said Adam. "Did you ever tell this to Sam Hamilton?"

"No. I didn't. I wish I had. He loved a celebration of the human soul. Such things were like a personal triumph to him."

"I hope they got there," said Adam.

"I know. And when my father would tell me I would say to him, 'Get to that lake—get my mother there—don't let it happen again, not this time. Just once let's tell it: how you got to the lake and built a house of fir boughs.' And my father became very Chinese then. He said, 'There's more beauty in the truth even if it is dreadful beauty. The storytellers at the city gate twist life so that it looks sweet to the lazy and the stupid and the weak, and this only strengthens their infirmities and teaches nothing, cures nothing, nor does it let the heart soar.'"

"Get on with it," Adam said irritably.

Lee got up and went to the window, and he finished the story, looking out at the stars that winked and blew in the March wind.

"A little boulder jumped down a hill and broke my father's leg. They set the leg and gave him cripples' work, straightening used nails with a hammer on a rock. And whether with worry or work—it doesn't matter—my mother went into early labor. And then the half-mad men knew and they went all mad. One hunger sharpened another hunger, and one crime blotted out the one before it, and the little crimes committed against those starving men flared into one gigantic maniac crime.

"My father heard the shout 'Woman' and he knew. He tried to run and his leg rebroke under him and he crawled up the ragged slope to the roadbed where it was happening.

"When he got there a kind of sorrow had come over the sky, and the Canton men were creeping away to hide and to forget that men can be like this. My father came to her on the pile of shale. She had not even eyes to see out of, but her mouth still moved and she gave him his instructions. My father clawed me out of the tattered meat of my mother with his fingernails. She died on the shale in the afternoon."

Adam was breathing hard. Lee continued in a singsong cadence, "Before you hate those men you must know this. My father always told it at the last: No child ever had such care as I. The whole camp became my mother. It is a beauty—a dreadful kind of beauty. And now good night. I can't talk any more."

3

Adam restlessly opened drawers and looked up at the shelves and raised the lids of boxes in his house and at last he was forced to call Lee back and ask, "Where's the ink and the pen?"

"You don't have any," said Lee. "You haven't written a word in years. I'll lend you mine if you want." He went to his room and brought back a squat bottle of ink and a stub pen and a pad of paper and an envelope and laid them on the table.

Adam asked, "How do you know I want to write a letter?"

"You're going to try to write to your brother, aren't you?"

"That's right."

"It will be a hard thing to do after so long," said Lee.

And it was hard. Adam nibbled and munched on the pen and his mouth made strained grimaces. Sentences were written and the page thrown away and another started. Adam scratched his head with the penholder. "Lee, if I wanted to take a trip east, would you stay with the twins until I get back?"

"It's easier to go than to write," said Lee. "Sure I'll stay."

"No. I'm going to write."

"Why don't you ask your brother to come out here?"

"Say, that's a good idea, Lee. I didn't think of it."

"It also gives you a reason for writing, and that's a good thing."

The letter came fairly easily then, was corrected and copied fair. Adam read it slowly to himself before he put it in the envelope.

"Dear brother Charles," it said. "You will be surprised to hear from me after so long. I have thought of writing many times, but you know how a man puts it off.

"I wonder how this letter finds you. I trust in good health. For all I know you may have five or even ten children by now. Ha! Ha! I have two sons and they are twins. Their mother is not here. Country life did not agree with her. She lives in a town nearby and I see her now and then.

"I have got a fine ranch, but I am ashamed to say I do not keep it up very well. Maybe I will do better from now on. I always did make good resolutions. But for a number of years I felt poorly. I am well now.

"How are you and how do you prosper? I would like to see you. Why don't you come to visit here? It is a great country and you might even find a place where you would like to settle. No cold winters here. That makes a difference to 'old men' like us. Ha! Ha!

"Well, Charles, I hope you will think about it and let me know. The trip would do you good. I want to see you. I have much to tell you that I can't write down.

"Well, Charles, write me a letter and tell me all the news of the old home. I suppose many things have happened. As you get older you hear mostly about people you knew that died. I guess that is the way of the world. Write quick and tell me if you will come to visit. Your brother Adam."

He sat holding the letter in his hand and looking over it at his brother's dark face with its scarred forehead. Adam could see the glinting heat in the brown eyes, and as he looked he saw the lips writhe back from the teeth and the blind destructive animal take charge. He shook his head to rid his memory of the vision, and he tried to rebuild the face smiling. He tried to remember the forehead before the scar, but he could not bring either into focus. He seized the pen and wrote below his signature, "P.S. Charles, I never hated you no matter what. I always loved you because you were my brother."

Adam folded the letter and forced the creases sharp with his fingernails. He sealed the envelope flap with his fist. "Lee!" he called, "Oh, Lee!"

The Chinese looked in through the door.

"Lee, how long does it take a letter to go east—clear east?"

"I don't know," said Lee. "Two weeks maybe."

TWENTY-NINE

After his first letter to his brother in over ten years was mailed Adam became impatient for an answer. He forgot how much time had elapsed. Before the letter got as far as San Francisco he was asking aloud in Lee's hearing, "I wonder why he doesn't answer. Maybe he's mad at me for not writing. But he didn't write either. No—he didn't know where to write. Maybe he's moved away."

Lee answered, "It's only been gone a few days. Give it time."

"I wonder whether he would really come out here?" Adam asked himself, and he wondered whether he wanted Charles. Now that the letter was gone, Adam was afraid Charles might accept. He was like a restless child whose fingers stray to every loose article. He interfered with the twins, asked them innumerable questions about school.

"Well, what did you learn today?"

"Nothing!"

"Oh, come! You must have learned something. Did you read?"

"Yes, sir."

"What did you read?"

"That old one about the grasshopper and the ant."

"Well, that's interesting."

"There's one about an eagle carries a baby away."

"Yes, I remember that one. I forget what happens."

"We aren't to it yet. We saw the pictures."

The boys were disgusted. During one of Adam's moments of fatherly bungling Cal borrowed his pocketknife, hoping he would forget to ask for it back. But the sap was beginning to run freely in the willows. The bark would slip easily from a twig. Adam got his knife back to teach the boys to make willow whistles, a thing Lee had taught them three years before. To make it worse, Adam had forgotten how to make the cut. He couldn't get a peep out of his whistles.

At noon one day Will Hamilton came roaring and bumping up the road in a new Ford. The engine raced in its low gear, and the high top swayed like a storm-driven ship. The brass radiator and the Prestolite tank on the running board were blinding with brass polish.

Will pulled up the brake lever, turned the switch straight down, and sat back in the leather seat. The car backfired several times without ignition because it was overheated.

"Here she is!" Will called with a false enthusiasm. He hated Fords with a deadly hatred, but they were daily building his fortune.

Adam and Lee hung over the exposed insides of the car while Will

Hamilton, puffing under the burden of his new fat, explained the workings of a mechanism he did not understand himself.

It is hard now to imagine the difficulty of learning to start, drive, and maintain an automobile. Not only was the whole process complicated, but one had to start from scratch. Today's children breathe in the theory, habits, and idiosyncrasies of the internal combustion engine in their cradles, but then you started with the blank belief that it would not run at all, and sometimes you were right. Also, to start the engine of a modern car you do just two things, turn a key and touch the starter. Everything else is automatic. The process used to be more complicated. It required not only a good memory, a strong arm, an angelic temper, and a blind hope, but also a certain amount of practice of magic, so that a man about to turn the crank of a Model T might be seen to spit on the ground and whisper a spell.

Will Hamilton explained the car and went back and explained it again. His customers were wide-eyed, interested as terriers, cooperative, and did not interrupt, but as he began for the third time Will saw that he was getting no place.

"Tell you what!" he said brightly. "You see, this isn't my line. I wanted you to see her and listen to her before I made delivery. Now, I'll go back to town and tomorrow I'll send out this car with an expert, and he'll tell you more in a few minutes than I could in a week. But I just wanted you to see her."

Will had forgotten some of his own instructions. He cranked for a while and then borrowed a buggy and a horse from Adam and drove to town, but he promised to have a mechanic out the next day.

2

There was no question of sending the twins to school the next day. They wouldn't have gone. The Ford stood tall and aloof and dour under the oak tree where Will had stopped it. Its new owners circled it and touched it now and then, the way you touch a dangerous horse to soothe him.

Lee said, "I wonder whether I'll ever get used to it."

"Of course you will," Adam said without conviction. "Why, you'll be driving all over the county first thing you know."

"I will try to understand it," Lee said. "But drive it I will not."

The boys made little dives in and out, to touch something and leap away. "What's this do-hickey, Father?"

"Get your hands off that."

"But what's it for?"

"I don't know, but don't touch it. You don't know what might happen."

"Didn't the man tell you?"

"I don't remember what he said. Now you boys get away from it or I'll have to send you to school. Do you hear me, Cal? Don't open that."

They had got up and were ready very early in the morning. By eleven o'clock hysterical nervousness had set in. The mechanic drove up in the buggy in time for the midday meal. He wore box-toed shoes and Duchess trousers and his wide square coat came almost to his knees. Beside him in the buggy was a satchel in which were his working clothes and tools. He was nineteen and chewed tobacco, and from his three months in automobile school he had gained a great though weary contempt for human beings. He spat and threw the lines at Lee.

"Put this hayburner away," he said. "How do you tell which end is the front?" And he climbed down from the rig as an ambassador comes out of a state train. He sneered at the twins and turned coldly to Adam. "I hope I'm in time for dinner," he said.

Lee and Adam stared at each other. They had forgotten about the noonday meal.

In the house the godling grudgingly accepted cheese and bread and cold meat and pie and coffee and a piece of chocolate cake.

"I'm used to a hot dinner," he said. "You better keep those kids away if you want any car left." After a leisurely meal and a short rest on the porch the mechanic took his satchel into Adam's bedroom. In a few minutes he emerged, dressed in striped overalls and a white cap which had "Ford" printed on the front of its crown.

"Well," he said. "Done any studying?"

"Studying?" Adam asked.

"Ain't you even read the litature in the book under the seat?"

"I didn't know it was there," said Adam.

"Oh, Lord," said the young man disgustedly. With a courageous gathering of his moral forces he moved with decision toward the car. "Might as well get started," he said. "God knows how long it's going to take if you ain't studied."

Adam said, "Mr. Hamilton couldn't start it last night."

"He always tries to start it on the magneto," said the sage. "All right! All right, come along. Know the principles of a internal combustion engine?"

"No," said Adam.

"Oh, Jesus Christ!" He lifted the tin flaps. "This-here is a internal combustion engine," he said.

Lee said quietly, "So young to be so erudite."

The boy swung around toward him, scowling. "What did you say?" he demanded, and he asked Adam, "What did the Chink say?"

Lee spread his hands and smiled blandly. "Say velly smaht fella," he observed quietly. "Mebbe go college. Velly wise."

"Just call me Joe!" the boy said for no reason at all, and he added, "College! What do them fellas know? Can they set a timer, huh? Can they file a point? College!" And he spat a brown disparaging comment on the ground. The twins regarded him with admiration, and Cal collected spit on the back of his tongue to practice.

Adam said, "Lee was admiring your grasp of the subject."

The truculence went out of the boy and a magnanimity took its place. "Just call me Joe," he said. "I *ought* to know it. Went to automobile school in Chicago. That's a real school—not like no college." And he said, "My old man says you take a good Chink, I mean a good one—why, he's about as good as anybody. They're honest."

"But not the bad ones," said Lee.

"Hell no! Not no highbinders nor nothing like that. But good Chinks."

"I hope I may be included in that group?"

"You look like a good Chink to me. Just call me Joe."

Adam was puzzled at the conversation, but the twins weren't. Cal said experimentally to Aron, "Jus' call me Joe," and Aron moved his lips, trying out, "Jus' call me Joe."

The mechanic became professional again but his tone was kinder. An amused friendliness took the place of his former contempt. "This-here," he said, "is a internal combustion engine." They looked down at the ugly lump of iron with a certain awe.

Now the boy went on so rapidly that the words ran together into a great song of the new era. "Operates through the explosion of gases in a enclosed space. Power of explosion is exerted on piston and through connecting rod and crankshaft through transmission thence to rear wheels. Got that?" They nodded blankly, afraid to stop the flow. "They's two kinds, two cycle and four cycle. This-here is four cycle. Got that?"

Again they nodded. The twins, looking up into his face with adoration, nodded.

"That's interesting," said Adam.

Joe went on hurriedly, "Main difference of a Ford automobile from other kinds is its planetary transmission which operates on a rev-rev-a-lu-shun-ary principle." He pulled up for a moment, his face showing strain. And when his four listeners nodded again he cautioned them, "Don't get the idea you know it all. The planetary system is, don't forget, rev-a-lu-shun-ary. You better study up on it in the book. Now, if you got all that we'll go on to Operation of the Automobile." He said this in boldface type, capital letters. He was obviously glad to be done with the first part of his lecture, but he was no gladder than his listeners. The strain of concentration was beginning to tell on them, and it was not made any better by the fact that they had not understood one single word.

"Come around here," said the boy. "Now you see that-there? That's the ignition key. When you turn that-there you're ready to go ahead. Now, you push this do-hickey to the left. That puts her on battery—see, where it says Bat. That means battery." They craned their necks into the car. The twins were standing on the running board.

"No—wait. I got ahead of myself. First you got to retard the spark and advance the gas, else she'll kick your goddam arm off. This-here—see it?—this-here's the spark. You push it up—get it?—*up*. Clear up. And this-here's the gas—you push her down. Now I'm going to explain it and then I'm going to do it. I want you to pay attention. You kids get off the car. You're in my light. Get down, goddam it." The boys reluctantly climbed down from the running board; only their eyes looked over the door.

He took a deep breath. "Now you ready? Spark retarded, gas advanced. Spark up, gas down. Now switch to battery—left, remember—left." A buzzing like that of a gigantic bee sounded. "Hear that? That's the contact in one of the coil boxes. If you don't get that, you got to adjust the points or maybe file them." He noticed a look of consternation on Adam's face. "You can study up on that in the book," he said kindly.

He moved to the front of the car. "Now this-here is the crank and—see this little wire sticking out of the radiator?—that's the choke. Now watch careful while I show you. You grab the crank like this and push till she catches. See how my thumb is turned down? If I grabbed her the other way with my thumb around her, and she was to kick, why, she'd knock my thumb off. Got it?"

He didn't look up but he knew they were nodding.

"Now," he said, "look careful. I push in and bring her up until I got compression, and then, why, I pull out this wire and I bring her around careful to suck gas in. Hear that sucking sound? That's choke. But don't pull her too much or you'll flood her. Now, I let go the wire and I give her a hell of a spin, and as soon as she catches I run around and advance the spark and retard the gas and I reach over and throw the switch quick over to magneto—see where it says Mag?—and there you are."

His listeners were limp. After all this they had just got the engine started.

The boy kept at them. "I want you to say after me now so you learn it. Spark up—gas down."

They repeated in chorus, "Spark up—gas down."

"Switch to Bat."

"Switch to Bat."

"Crank to compression, thumb down."

"Crank to compression, thumb down."

"Easy over—choke out."

"Easy over—choke out."

"Spin her."

"Spin her."

"Spark down—gas up."

"Spark down—gas up."

"Switch to Mag."

"Switch to Mag."

"Now, we'll go over her again. Just call me Joe."

"Just call you Joe."

"Not that. Spark up—gas down."

A kind of weariness settled on Adam as they went over the litany for the fourth time. The process seemed silly to him. He was relieved when a short time later Will Hamilton drove up in his low sporty red car. The boy looked at the approaching vehicle. "That-there's got sixteen valves," he said in a reverent tone. "Special job."

Will leaned out of his car. "How's it going?" he asked.

"Just fine," said the mechanic. "They catch on quick."

"Look, Roy, I've got to take you in. The new hearse knocked out a bearing. You'll have to work late to get it ready for Mrs. Hawks at eleven tomorrow."

Roy snapped to efficient attention. "I'll get my clos'," he said and ran for the house. As he tore back with his satchel Cal stood in his way.

"Hey," Cal said, "I thought your name was Joe."

"How do you mean, Joe?"

"You told us to call you Joe. Mr. Hamilton says you're Roy."

Roy laughed and jumped into the roadster. "Know why I say call me Joe?"

"No. Why?"

"Because my name is Roy." In the midst of his laughter he stopped and said sternly to Adam, "You get that book under the seat and you study up. Hear me?"

"I will," said Adam.

THIRTY

Even as in Biblical times, there were miracles on the earth in those days. One week after the lesson a Ford bumped up the main street of King City and pulled to a shuddering stop in front of the post office. Adam sat at the wheel with Lee beside him and the two boys straight and grand in the back seat.

Adam looked down at the floorboards, and all four chanted in unison, "Brake on—advance gas—switch off." The little engine roared and then stopped. Adam sat back for a moment, limp but proud, before he got out.

The postmaster looked out between the bars of his golden grill. "I see you've got one of the damn things," he said.

"Have to keep up with the times," said Adam.

"I predict there'll come a time when you can't find a horse, Mr. Trask."

"Maybe so."

"They'll change the face of the countryside. They get their clatter into everything," the postmaster went on. "We even feel it here. Man used to come for his mail once a week. Now he comes every day, sometimes twice a day. He just can't wait for his damn catalogue. Running around. Always running around." He was so violent in his dislike that Adam knew he hadn't bought a Ford yet. It was a kind of jealousy coming out. "I wouldn't have one around," the postmaster said, and this meant that his wife was at him to buy one. It was the women who put the pressure on. Social status was involved.

The postmaster angrily shuffled through the letters from the T box and tossed out a long envelope. "Well, I'll see you in the hospital," he said viciously.

Adam smiled at him and took his letter and walked out.

A man who gets few letters does not open one lightly. He hefts it for weight, reads the name of the sender on the envelope and the address, looks at the handwriting, and studies the postmark and the date. Adam was out of the post office and across the sidewalk to his Ford before he had done all of these things. The left-hand corner of the envelope had printed on it, Bellows and Harvey, Attorneys at Law, and their address was the town in Connecticut from which Adam had come.

He said in a pleasant tone, "Why, I know Bellows and Harvey, know them well. I wonder what they want?" He looked closely at the envelope. "I wonder how they got my address?" He turned the envelope over and looked at the back. Lee watched him, smiling. "Maybe the questions are answered in the letter."

"I guess so," Adam said. Once having decided to open the letter, he took out his pocketknife, opened the big blade, and inspected the envelope for a point of ingress, found none, held the letter up to the sun to make sure not to cut the message, tapped the letter to one end of the envelope, and cut off the other end. He blew in the end and extracted the letter with two fingers. He read the letter very slowly.

"Mr. Adam Trask, King City, California, Dear Sir," it began testily, "For the last six months we have exhausted every means of locating you. We have advertised in newspapers all over the country without success. It was only when your letter to your brother was turned over to us by the local postmaster that we were able to ascertain your whereabouts." Adam could feel their impatience with him. The next paragraph began a complete change of mood. "It is our sad duty to inform you that your brother Charles Trask is deceased. He died of a lung ailment October 12 after an illness of two weeks, and his body rests in the Odd Fellows cemetery. No stone marks his grave. We presume you will want to undertake this sorrowful duty yourself."

Adam drew a deep full breath and held it while he read the paragraph again. He breathed out slowly to keep the release from being a sigh. "My brother Charles is dead," he said.

"I'm sorry," said Lee.

Cal said, "Is he our uncle?"

"He was your Uncle Charles," said Adam.

"Mine too?" Aron asked.

"Yours too."

"I didn't know we had him," Aron said. "Maybe we can put some flowe:
on his grave. Abra would help us. She likes to."

"It's a long way off—clear across the country."

Aron said excitedly, "I know! When we take flowers to our mother we'
take some to our Uncle Charles." And he said a little sadly, "I wish't I knev
I had him before he was dead." He felt that he was growing rich in dea
relatives. "Was he nice?" Aron asked.

"Very nice," said Adam. "He was my only brother, just like Cal is you
only brother."

"Were you twins too?"

"No—not twins."

Cal asked, "Was he rich?"

"Of course not," said Adam. "Where'd you get that idea?"

"Well, if he was rich we'd get it, wouldn't we?"

Adam said sternly, "At a time of death it isn't a nice thing to talk abou
money. We're sad because he died."

"How can I be sad?" said Cal. "I never even saw him."

Lee covered his mouth with his hand to conceal his smile. Adam looked
back at the letter, and again it changed mood with its paragraph.

"As attorneys for the deceased it is our pleasant duty to inform you that
your brother through industry and judgment amassed a considerable fortune,
which in land, securities, and cash is well in excess of one hundred thousand
dollars. His will, which was drawn and signed in this office, is in our hands
and will be sent to you on your request. By its terms it leaves all money,
property, and securities to be divided equally between you and your wife.
In the event that your wife is deceased, the total goes to you. The will also
stipulates that if you are deceased, all property goes to your wife. We judge
from your letter that you are still in the land of the living and we wish to
offer our congratulations. Your obedient servants, Bellows and Harvey, by
George B. Harvey." And at the bottom of the page was scrawled, "Dear
Adam: Forget not thy servants in the days of thy prosperity. Charles never
spent a dime. He pinched a dollar until the eagle screamed. I hope you and
your wife will get some pleasure from the money. Is there an opening out
there for a good lawyer? I mean myself. Your old friend, Geo. Harvey."

Adam looked over the edge of the letter at the boys and at Lee. All three
were waiting for him to continue. Adam's mouth shut to a line. He folded
the letter, put it in its envelope, and placed the envelope carefully in his
inside pocket.

"Any complications?" Lee asked.

"No."

"I just thought you looked concerned."

"I'm not. I'm sad about my brother." Adam was trying to arrange the letter's information in his mind, and it was as restless as a setting hen scrounging into the nest. He felt that he would have to be alone to absorb it. He climbed into the car and looked blankly at the mechanism. He couldn't remember a single procedure.

Lee asked, "Want some help?"

"Funny!" said Adam. "I can't remember where to start."

Lee and the boys began softly, "Spark up—gas down, switch over to Bat."

"Oh, yes. Of course, of course." And while the loud bee hummed in the coil box Adam cranked the Ford and ran to advance the spark and throw the switch to Mag.

They were driving slowly up the lumpy road of the home draw under the oak trees when Lee said, "We forgot to get meat."

"Did we? I guess we did. Well, can't we have something else?"

"How about bacon and eggs?"

"That's fine. That's good."

"You'll want to mail your answer tomorrow," said Lee. "You can buy meat then."

"I guess so," said Adam.

While dinner was preparing Adam sat staring into space. He knew he would have to have help from Lee, if only the help of a listener to clear his own thinking.

Cal had led his brother outside and conducted him to the wagon shed where the tall Ford rested. Cal opened the door and sat behind the wheel. "Come on, get in!" he said.

Aron protested, "Father told us to stay out of it."

"He won't ever know. Get in!"

Aron climbed in timidly and eased back in the seat. Cal turned the wheel from side to side. "Honk, honk," he said, and then, "Know what I think? I think Uncle Charles was rich."

"He was not."

"I bet you anything he was."

"You think our father'd tell a lie."

"I won't say that. I just bet he was rich." They were silent for a while. Cal steered wildly around imaginary curves. He said, "I bet you I can find out."

"How do you mean?"

"What you got to bet?"

"Nothing," said Aron.

"How about your deer's-leg whistle? I bet you this-here taw against that deer's-leg whistle that we get sent to bed right after supper. Is it a bet?"

"I guess so," Aron said vaguely. "I don't see why."

Cal said, "Father will want to talk to Lee. And I'm going to listen."

"You won't dare."

"You think I won't."

"'Spose I was to tell."

Cal's eyes turned cold and his face darkened. He leaned so close that his voice dropped to a whisper. "You won't tell. Because if you do—I'll tell who stole his knife."

"Nobody stole his knife. He's got his knife. He opened the letter with it."

Cal smiled bleakly. "I mean tomorrow," he said. And Aron saw what he meant and knew he couldn't tell. He couldn't do anything about it. Cal was perfectly safe.

Cal saw the confusion and helplessness on Aron's face and felt his power, and it made him glad. He could outthink and outplan his brother. He was beginning to think he could do the same thing to his father. With Lee, Cal's tricks did not work, for Lee's bland mind moved effortlessly ahead of him and was always there waiting, understanding, and at the last moment cautioning quietly, "Don't do it." Cal had respect for Lee and a little fear of him. But Aron here, looking helplessly at him, was a lump of soft mud in his hands. Cal suddenly felt a deep love for his brother and an impulse to protect him in his weakness. He put his arm around Aron.

Aron did not flinch or respond. He drew back a little to see Cal's face.

Cal said, "See any green grass growing out of my head?"

Aron said, "I don't know why you go for to do it."

"How do you mean? Do what?"

"All the tricky, sneaky things," said Aron.

"What do you mean, sneaky?"

"Well, about the rabbit, and sneaking here in the car. And you did something to Abra. I don't know what, but it was you made her throw the box away."

"Ho," said Cal. "Wouldn't you like to know!" But he was uneasy.

Aron said slowly, "I wouldn't want to know that. I'd like to know *why* you do it. You're always at something. I just wonder why you do it. I wonder what's it good for."

A pain pierced Cal's heart. His planning suddenly seemed mean and dirty to him. He knew that his brother had found him out. And he felt a longing for Aron to love him. He felt lost and hungry and he didn't know what to do.

Aron opened the door of the Ford and climbed down and walked out of the wagon shed. For a few moments Cal twisted the steering wheel and tried to imagine he was racing down the road. But it wasn't any good, and soon he followed Aron back toward the house.

2

When supper was finished and Lee had washed the dishes Adam said, "I think you boys had better go to bed. It's been a big day."

Aron looked quickly at Cal and slowly took his deer's-leg whistle out of his pocket.

Cal said, "I don't want it."

Aron said, "It's yours now."

"Well, I don't want it. I won't have it."

Aron laid the bone whistle on the table. "It'll be here for you," he said.

Adam broke in, "Say, what is this argument? I said you boys should go to bed."

Cal put on his "little boy" face. "Why?" he asked. "It's too early to go to bed."

Adam said, "That wasn't quite the truth I told you. I want to talk privately to Lee. And it's getting dark so you can't go outside, so I want you boys to go to bed—at least to your room. Do you understand?"

Both boys said, "Yes, sir," and they followed Lee down the hall to their bedroom at the back of the house. In their nightgowns they returned to say good night to their father.

Lee came back to the living room and closed the door to the hall. He picked up the deer's-leg whistle and inspected it and laid it down. "I wonder what went on there," he said.

"How do you mean, Lee?"

"Well, some bet was made before supper, and just after supper Aron lost the bet and paid off. What were we talking about?"

"All I can remember is telling them to go to bed."

"Well, maybe it will come out later," said Lee.

"Seems to me you put too much stock in the affairs of children. It probably didn't mean anything."

"Yes, it meant something." Then he said, "Mr. Trask, do you think the thoughts of people suddenly become important at a given age? Do you have sharper feelings or clearer thoughts now than when you were ten? Do you see as well, hear as well, taste as vitally?"

"Maybe you're right," said Adam.

"It's one of the great fallacies, it seems to me," said Lee, "that time gives much of anything but years and sadness to a man."

"And memory."

"Yes, memory. Without that, time would be unarmed against us. What did you want to talk to me about?"

Adam took the letter from his pocket and put it on the table. "I want you to read this, to read it carefully, and then—I want to talk about it." Lee took out his half-glasses and put them on. He opened the letter under th lamp and read it.

Adam asked, "Well?"

"*Is* there an opening here for a lawyer?"

"How do you mean? Oh, I see. Are you making a joke?"

"No," said Lee, "I was not making a joke. In my obscure but courteou Oriental manner I was indicating to you that I would prefer to know you opinion before I offered mine."

"Are you speaking sharply to me?"

"Yes, I am," said Lee. "I'll lay aside my Oriental manner. I'm getting ol and cantankerous. I am growing impatient. Haven't you heard of all Chines servants that when they get old they remain loyal but they turn mean?'

"I don't want to hurt your feelings."

"They aren't hurt. You want to talk about this letter. Then talk, and will know from your talk whether I can offer an honest opinion or whethe it is better to reassure you in your own."

"I don't understand it," said Adam helplessly.

"Well, you knew your brother. If you don't understand it, how can I who never saw him?"

Adam got up and opened the hall door and did not see the shadow that slipped behind it. He went to his room and returned and put a faded brown daguerreotype on the table in front of Lee. "That is my brother Charles," he said, and he went back to the hall door and closed it.

Lee studied the shiny metal under the lamp, shifting the picture this way and that to overcome the highlights. "It's a long time ago," Adam said. "Before I went into the army."

Lee leaned close to the picture. "It's hard to make out. But from his expression I wouldn't say your brother had much humor."

"He hadn't any," said Adam. "He never laughed."

"Well, that wasn't exactly what I meant. When I read the terms of your brother's will it struck me that he might have been a man with a particularly brutal sense of play. Did he like you?"

"I don't know," said Adam. "Sometimes I thought he loved me. He tried to kill me once."

Lee said, "Yes, that's in his face—both the love and the murder. And the two made a miser of him, and a miser is a frightened man hiding in a fortress of money. Did he know your wife?"

"Yes."

"Did he love her?"

"He hated her."

Lee sighed. "It doesn't really matter. That's not your problem, is it?"

"No. It isn't."

"Would you like to bring the problem out and look at it?"

"That's what I want."

"Go ahead then."

"I can't seem to get my mind to work clearly."

"Would you like me to lay out the cards for you? The uninvolved can sometimes do that."

"That's what I want."

"Very well then." Suddenly Lee grunted and a look of astonishment came over his face. He held his round chin in his thin small hand. "Holy horns!" he said. "I didn't think of that."

Adam stirred uneasily. "I wish you'd get off the tack you're sitting on," he said irritably. "You make me feel like a column of figures on a blackboard."

Lee took a pipe from his pocket, a long slender ebony stem with a little cuplike brass bowl. He filled the thimble bowl with tobacco so fine-cut it looked like hair, then lighted the pipe, took four long puffs, and let the pipe go out.

"Is that opium?" Adam demanded.

"No," said Lee. "It's a cheap brand of Chinese tobacco, and it has an unpleasant taste."

"Why do you smoke it then?"

"I don't know," said Lee. "I guess it reminds me of something—something I associate with clarity. Not very complicated." Lee's eyelids half closed. "All right then—I'm going to try to pull out your thoughts like egg noodles and let them dry in the sun. The woman is still your wife and she is still alive. Under the letter of the will she inherits something over fifty thousand dollars. That is a great deal of money. A sizable chunk of good or of evil could be done with it. Would your brother, if he knew where she is and what she is doing, want her to have the money? Courts always try to follow the wishes of the testator."

"My brother would not want that," said Adam. And then he remembered the girls upstairs in the tavern and Charles' periodic visits.

"Maybe you'll have to think for your brother," said Lee. "What your wife is doing is neither good nor bad. Saints can spring from any soil. Maybe with this money she would do some fine thing. There's no springboard to philanthropy like a bad conscience."

Adam shivered. "She told me what she would do if she had money. It was closer to murder than to charity."

"You don't think she should have the money then?"

"She said she would destroy many reputable men in Salinas. She can do it too."

"I see," said Lee. "I'm glad I can take a detached view of this. The pants of their reputations must have some thin places. Morally, then, you would be against giving her the money?"

"Yes."

"Well, consider this. She has no name, no background. A whore springs full blown from the earth. She couldn't very well claim the money, if she knew about it, without your help."

"I guess that's so. Yes, I can see that she might not be able to claim it without my help."

Lee took up the pipe and picked out the ash with a little brass pin and filled the bowl again. While he drew in the four slow puffs his heavy lids raised and he watched Adam.

"It's a very delicate moral problem," he said. "With your permission I shall offer it for the consideration of my honorable relatives—using no names of course. They will go over it as a boy goes over a dog for ticks. I'm sure they will get some interesting results." He laid his pipe on the table. "But you don't have any choice, do you?"

"What do you mean by that?" Adam demanded.

"Well, do you? Do you know yourself so much less than I do?"

"I don't know what to do," said Adam. "I'll have to give it a lot of thought."

Lee said angrily, "I guess I've been wasting my time. Are you lying to yourself or only to me?"

"Don't speak to me like that!" Adam said.

"Why not? I have always disliked deception. Your course is drawn. What you will do is written—written in every breath you've ever taken. I'll speak any way I want to. I'm crochety. I feel sand under my skin. I'm looking forward to the ugly smell of old books and the sweet smell of good thinking. Faced with two sets of morals, you'll follow your training. What you call thinking won't change it. The fact that your wife is a whore in Salinas won't change a thing."

Adam got to his feet. His face was angry. "You are insolent now that you've decided to go away," he cried. "I tell you I haven't made up my mind what to do about the money."

Lee sighed deeply. He pushed his small body erect with his hands against his knees. He walked wearily to the front door and opened it. He turned back and smiled at Adam. "Bull shit!" he said amiably, and he went out and closed the door behind him.

3

Cal crept quietly down the dark hall and edged into the room where he and his brother slept. He saw the outline of his brother's head against the pillow in the double bed, but he could not see whether Aron slept. Very gently he eased himself in on his side and turned slowly and laced his fingers behind his head and stared at the myriads of tiny colored dots that make up darkness. The window shade bellied slowly in and then the night wind fell and the worn shade flapped quietly against the window.

A gray, quilted melancholy descended on him. He wished with all his heart that Aron had not walked away from him out of the wagon shed. He wished with all his heart that he had not crouched listening at the hall door. He moved his lips in the darkness and made the words silently in his head and yet he could hear them.

"Dear Lord," he said, "let me be like Aron. Don't make me mean. I don't want to be. If you will let everybody like me, why, I'll give you anything in the world, and if I haven't got it, why, I'll go for to get it. I don't want to be mean. I don't want to be lonely. For Jesus' sake, Amen." Slow warm tears were running down his cheeks. His muscles were tight and he fought against making any crying sound or sniffle.

Aron whispered from his pillow in the dark, "You're cold. You've got a chill." He stretched out his hand to Cal's arm and felt the goose bumps there. He asked softly, "Did Uncle Charles have any money?"

"No," said Cal.

"Well, you were out there long enough. What did Father want to talk about?"

Cal lay still, trying to control his breathing.

"Don't you want to tell me?" Aron asked. "I don't care if you don't tell me."

"I'll tell," Cal whispered. He turned on his side so that his back was toward his brother. "Father is going to send a wreath to our mother. A great big goddam wreath of carnations."

Aron half sat up in bed and asked excitedly, "He is? How's he going to get it clear there?"

"On the train. Don't talk so loud."

Aron dropped back to a whisper. "But how's it going to keep fresh?"

"With ice," said Cal. "They're going to pack ice all around it."

Aron asked, "Won't it take a lot of ice?"

"A whole hell of a lot of ice," said Cal. "Go to sleep now."

Aron was silent, and then he said, "I hope it gets there fresh and nice."

"It will," said Cal. And in his mind he cried, "Don't let me be mean."

THIRTY-ONE

Adam brooded around the house all morning, and at noon he went to find Lee, who was spading the dark composted earth of his vegetable garden and planting his spring vegetables, carrots and beets, turnips, peas, and string beans, rutabaga and kale. The rows were straight planted under a tight-stretched string, and the pegs at the row ends carried the seed package to identify the row. On the edge of the garden in a cold frame the tomato and bell pepper and cabbage sets were nearly ready for transplanting, waiting only for the passing of the frost danger.

Adam said, "I guess I was stupid."

Lee leaned on his spading fork and regarded him quietly.

"When are you going?" he asked.

"I thought I would catch the two-forty. Then I can get the eight o'clock back."

"You could put it in a letter, you know," said Lee.

"I've thought of that. Would you write a letter?"

"No. You're right. I'm the stupid one there. No letters."

"I have to go," said Adam. "I thought in all directions and always a leash snapped me back."

Lee said, "You can be unhonest in many ways, but not in that way. Well, good luck. I'll be interested to hear what she says and does."

"I'll take the rig," said Adam. "I'll leave it at the stable in King City. I'm nervous about driving the Ford alone."

It was four-fifteen when Adam climbed the rickety steps and knocked on the weather-beaten door of Kate's place. A new man opened the door, a square-faced Finn, dressed in shirt and trousers; red silk armbands held up his full sleeves. He left Adam standing on the porch and in a moment came back and led him to the dining room.

It was a large undecorated room, the walls and woodwork painted white. A long square table filled the center of the room, and on the white oilcloth cover the places were set—plates, cups and saucers, and the cups upside down in the saucers.

Kate sat at the head of the table with an account book open before her. Her dress was severe. She wore a green eyeshade, and she rolled a yellow pencil restlessly in her fingers. She looked coldly at Adam as he stood in the doorway.

"What do you want now?" she asked.

The Finn stood behind Adam.

Adam did not reply. He walked to the table and laid the letter in front of her on top of the account book.

"What's this?" she asked, and without waiting for a reply she read the letter quickly. "Go out and close the door," she told the Finn.

Adam sat at the table beside her. He pushed the dishes aside to make a place for his hat.

When the door was closed Kate said, "Is this a joke? No, you haven't got a joke in you." She considered. "Your brother might be joking. You sure he's dead?"

"All I have is the letter," said Adam.

"What do you want me to do about it?"

Adam shrugged his shoulders.

Kate said, "If you want me to sign anything, you're wasting your time. What do you want?"

Adam drew his finger slowly around his black ribbon hatband. "Why don't you write down the name of the firm and get in touch with them yourself?"

"What have you told them about me?"

"Nothing," said Adam. "I wrote to Charles and said you were living in another town, nothing more. He was dead when the letter got there. The letter went to the lawyers. It tells about it."

"The one who wrote the postscript seems to be a friend of yours. What have you written him?"

"I haven't answered the letter yet."

"What do you intend to say when you answer it?"

"The same thing—that you live in another town."

"You can't say we've been divorced. We haven't been."

"I don't intend to."

"Do you want to know how much it will take to buy me off? I'll take forty-five thousand in cash."

"No."

"What do you mean—no? You can't bargain."

"I'm not bargaining. You have the letter, you know as much as I do. Do what you want."

"What makes you so cocky?"

"I feel safe."

She peered at him from under the green transparent eyeshade. Little curls of her hair lay on the bill like vines on a green roof. "Adam, you're a fool. If you had kept your mouth shut nobody would ever have known I was alive."

"I know that."

"You know it? Did you think I might be afraid to claim the money? You're a damn fool if you thought that."

Adam said patiently, "I don't care what you do."

She smiled cynically at him. "You don't, huh? Suppose I should tell you that there's a permanent order in the sheriff's office, left there by the old sheriff, that if I ever use your name or admit I'm your wife I'll get a floater out of the county and out of the state. Does that tempt you?"

"Tempt me to do what?"

"To get me floated and take all the money."

"I brought you the letter," Adam said patiently.

"I want to know why."

Adam said, "I'm not interested in what you think or in what you think of me. Charles left you the money in his will. He didn't put any strings on it. I haven't seen the will, but he wanted you to have the money."

"You're playing a close game with fifty thousand dollars," she said, "and you're not going to get away with it. I don't know what the trick is, but I'm going to find out." And then she said, "What am I thinking about? You're not smart. Who's advising you?"

"No one."

"How about that Chinaman? He's smart."

"He gave me no advice." Adam was interested in his own complete lack of emotion. He didn't really feel that he was here at all. When he glanced at her he surprised an emotion on her face he had never seen before. Kate was afraid—she was afraid of him. But why?

She controlled her face and whipped the fear from it. "You're just doing it because you're honest, is that it? You're just too sugar sweet to live."

"I hadn't thought of it," Adam said. "It's your money and I'm not a thief. It doesn't matter to me what you think about it."

Kate pushed the eyeshade back on her head. "You want me to think you're just dropping this money in my lap. Well, I'll find out what you're up to. Don't think I won't take care of myself. Did you think I'd take such a stupid bait?"

"Where do you get your mail?" he asked patiently.

"What's that to you?"

"I'll write the lawyers where to get in touch with you."

"Don't you do it!" she said. She put the letter in the account book and closed the cover. "I'll keep this. I'll get legal advice. Don't think I won't. You can drop the innocence now."

"You do that," Adam said. "I want you to have what is yours. Charles willed you the money. It isn't mine."

"I'll find the trick. I'll find it."

Adam said, "I guess you can't understand it. I don't much care. There are so many things I don't understand. I don't understand how you could shoot me and desert your sons. I don't understand how you or anyone could live like this." He waved his hand to indicate the house.

"Who asked you to understand?"

Adam stood up and took his hat from the table. "I guess that's all," he said. "Good-by." He walked toward the door.

She called after him, "You're changed, Mr. Mouse. Have you got a woman at last?"

Adam stopped and slowly turned and his eyes were thoughtful. "I hadn't considered before," he said, and he moved toward her until he towered over her and she had to tilt back her head to look into his face. "I said I didn't understand about you," he said slowly. "Just now it came to me what you don't understand."

"What don't I understand, Mr. Mouse?"

"You know about the ugliness in people. You showed me the pictures. You use all the sad, weak parts of a man, and God knows he has them."

"Everybody—"

Adam went on, astonished at his own thoughts, "But you—yes, that's ight—you don't know about the rest. You don't believe I brought you the etter because I don't want your money. You don't believe I loved you. And the men who come to you here with their ugliness, the men in the pictures—you don't believe those men could have goodness and beauty in hem. You see only one side, and you think—more than that, you're sure —that's all there is."

She cackled at him derisively. "In sticks and stones. What a sweet dreamer is Mr. Mouse! Give me a sermon, Mr. Mouse."

"No. I won't because I seem to know that there's a part of you missing. Some men can't see the color green, but they may never know they can't. I think you are only a part of a human. I can't do anything about that. But I wonder whether you ever feel that something invisible is all around you. It would be horrible if you knew it was there and couldn't see it or feel it. That would be horrible."

Kate pushed back her chair and stood up. Her fists were clenched at her sides and hiding in the folds of her skirt. She tried to prevent the shrillness that crept into her voice.

"Our Mouse is a philosopher," she said. "But our Mouse is no better at that than he is at other things. Did you ever hear of hallucinations? If there are things I can't see, don't you think it's possible that they are dreams manufactured in your own sick mind?"

"No, I don't," said Adam. "No, I don't. And I don't think you do either." He turned and went out and closed the door behind him.

Kate sat down and stared at the closed door. She was not aware that her fists beat softly on the white oilcloth. But she did know that the square white door was distorted by tears and that her body shook with something that felt like rage and also felt like sorrow.

2

When Adam left Kate's place he had over two hours to wait for the train back to King City. On an impulse he turned off Main Street and walked up Central Avenue to number 130, the high white house of Ernest Steinbeck. It was an immaculate and friendly house, grand enough but not pretentious, and it sat inside its white fence, surrounded by its clipped lawn, and roses and catoneasters lapped against its white walls.

Adam walked up the wide veranda steps and rang the bell. Olive came to the door and opened it a little, while Mary and John peeked around the edges of her.

Adam took off his hat. "You don't know me. I'm Adam Trask. Your father was a friend of mine. I thought I'd like to pay my respects to Mrs. Hamilton. She helped me with the twins."

"Why, of course," Olive said and swung the wide doors open. "We've heard about you. Just a moment. You see, we've made a kind of retreat for Mother."

She knocked on a door off the wide front hall and called, "Mother! There's a friend to see you."

She opened the door and showed Adam into the pleasant room where Liza lived. "You'll have to excuse me," she said to Adam. "Catrina's frying chicken and I have to watch her. John! Mary! Come along. Come along."

Liza seemed smaller than ever. She sat in a wicker rocking chair and she was old and old. Her dress was a full wide-skirted black alpaca, and at her throat she wore a pin which spelled "Mother" in golden script.

The pleasant little bed-sitting room was crowded with photographs, bottles of toilet water, lace pincushions, brushes and combs, and the china and silver bureau-knacks of many birthdays and Christmases.

On the wall hung a huge tinted photograph of Samuel, which had captured a cold and aloof dignity, a scrubbed and dressed remoteness, which did not belong to him living. There was no twinkle in the picture of him, nor any of his inspective joyousness. The picture hung in a heavy gold frame, and to the consternation of all children its eyes followed a child about the room.

On a wicker table beside Liza was the cage of Polly parrot. Tom had bought the parrot from a sailor. He was an old bird, reputed to be fifty years old, and he had lived a ribald life and acquired the vigorous speech of a ship's fo'c'sle. Try as she would, Liza could not make him substitute psalms for the picturesque vocabulary of his youth.

Polly cocked his head sideways, inspecting Adam, and scratched the feathers at the base of his beak with a careful foreclaw. "Come off it, you bastard," said Polly unemotionally.

Liza frowned at him. "Polly," she said sternly, "that's not polite."

"Bloody bastard!" Polly observed.

Liza ignored the vulgarity. She held out her tiny hand. "Mr. Trask," she said, "I'm glad to see you. Sit down, won't you?"

"I was passing by, and I wanted to offer my condolences."

"We got your flowers." And she remembered, too, every bouquet after all this time. Adam had sent a fine pillow of everlastings.

"It must be hard to rearrange your life."

Liza's eyes brimmed over and she snapped her little mouth shut on her weakness.

Adam said, "Maybe I shouldn't bring up your hurt, but I miss him."

Liza turned her head away. "How is everything down your way?" she asked.

"Good this year. Lots of rainfall. The feed's deep already."

"Tom wrote me," she said.

"Button up," said the parrot, and Liza scowled at him as she had at her growing children when they were mutinous.

"What brings you up to Salinas, Mr. Trask?" she asked.

"Why, some business." He sat down in a wicker chair and it cricked under his weight. "I'm thinking of moving up here. Thought it might be better for my boys. They get lonely on the ranch."

"We never got lonely on the ranch," she said harshly.

"I thought maybe the schools would be better here. My twins could have the advantages."

"My daughter Olive taught at Peachtree and Pleyto and the Big Sur." Her tone made it clear that there were no better schools than those. Adam began to feel a warm admiration for her iron gallantry.

"Well, I was just thinking about it," he said.

"Children raised in the country do better." It was the law, and she could prove it by her own boys. Then she centered closely on him. "Are you looking for a house in Salinas?"

"Well, yes, I guess I am."

"Go see my daughter Dessie," she said. "Dessie wants to move back to the ranch with Tom. She's got a nice little house up the street next to Reynaud's Bakery."

"I'll certainly do that," said Adam. "I'll go now. I'm glad to see you doing so well."

"Thank you," she said. "I'm comfortable." Adam was moving toward the door when she said, "Mr. Trask, do you ever see my son Tom?"

"Well, no, I don't. You see, I haven't been off the ranch."

"I wish you would go and see him," she said quickly. "I think he's lonely." She stopped as though horrified at this breaking over.

"I will. I surely will. Good-by, ma'am."

As he closed the door he heard the parrot say, "Button up, you bloody bastard!" And Liza, "Polly, if you don't watch your language, I'll thrash you."

Adam let himself out of the house and walked up the evening street toward Main. Next to Reynaud's French Bakery he saw Dessie's house set back in its little garden. The yard was so massed with tall privets that he couldn't see much of the house. A neatly painted sign was screwed to the front gate. It read: Dessie Hamilton, Dressmaker.

The San Francisco Chop House was on the corner of Main and Central and its windows were on both streets. Adam went in to get some dinner. Will Hamilton sat at the corner table, devouring a rib steak. "Come and sit with me," he called to Adam. "Up on business?"

"Yes," said Adam. "I went to pay a call on your mother."

Will laid down his fork. "I'm just up here for an hour. I didn't go to see her because it gets her excited. And my sister Olive would tear the house down getting a special dinner for me. I just didn't want to disturb them. Besides, I have to go right back. Order a rib steak. They've got good ones. How is Mother?"

"She's got great courage," said Adam. "I find I admire her more all the time."

"That she has. How she kept her good sense with all of us and with my father, I don't know."

"Rib steak, medium," said Adam to the waiter.

"Potatoes?"

"No—yes, french fried. Your mother is worried about Tom. Is he all right?"

Will cut off the edging of fat from his steak and pushed it to the side of his plate. "She's got reason to worry," he said. "Something's the matter with Tom. He's moping around like a monument."

"I guess he depended on Samuel."

"Too much," said Will. "Far too much. He can't seem to come out of it. In some ways Tom is a great big baby."

"I'll go and see him. Your mother says Dessie is going to move back to the ranch."

Will laid his knife and fork down on the tablecloth and stared at Adam. "She can't do it," he said. "I won't let her do it."

"Why not?"

Will covered up. "Well," he said, "she's got a nice business here. Makes a good living. It would be a shame to throw it away." He picked up his knife and fork, cut off a piece of the fat, and put it in his mouth.

"I'm catching the eight o'clock home," Adam said.

"So am I," said Will. He didn't want to talk any more.

THIRTY-TWO

Dessie was the beloved of the family. Mollie the pretty kitten, Olive the strong-headed, Una with clouds on her head, all were loved, but Dessie was the warm-beloved. Hers was the twinkle and the laughter infectious as chickenpox, and hers the gaiety that colored a day and spread to people so that they carried it away with them.

I can put it this way. Mrs. Clarence Morrison of 122 Church Street, Salinas, had three children and a husband who ran a dry goods store. On certain mornings, at breakfast, Agnes Morrison would say, "I'm going to Dessie Hamilton's for a fitting after dinner."

The children would be glad and would kick their copper toes against the table legs until cautioned. And Mr. Morrison would rub his palms together and go to his store, hoping some drummer would come by that day. And any drummer who did come by was likely to get a good order. Maybe the children and Mr. Morrison would forget why it was a good day with a promise on its tail.

Mrs. Morrison would go to the house next to Reynaud's Bakery at two o'clock and she would stay until four. When she came out her eyes would be wet with tears and her nose red and streaming. Walking home, she would dab her nose and wipe her eyes and laugh all over again. Maybe all Dessie had done was to put several black pins in a cushion to make it look like the Baptist minister, and then had the pincushion deliver a short dry sermon. Maybe she had recounted a meeting with Old Man Taylor, who bought old houses and moved them to a big vacant lot he owned until he had so many it looked like a dry-land Sargasso Sea. Maybe she had read a poem from *Chatterbox* with gestures. It didn't matter. It was warm-funny, it was catching funny.

The Morrison children, coming home from school, would find no aches, no carping, no headache. Their noise was not a scandal nor their dirty faces a care. And when the giggles overcame them, why, their mother was giggling too.

Mr. Morrison, coming home, would tell of the day and get listened to, and he would try to retell the drummer's stories—some of them at least. The supper would be delicious—omelets never fell and cakes rose to balloons of lightness, biscuits fluffed up, and no one could season a stew like Agnes Morrison. After supper, when the children had laughed themselves to sleep, like as not Mr. Morrison would touch Agnes on the shoulder in their old, old signal and they would go to bed and make love and be very happy.

The visit to Dessie might carry its charge into two days more before it petered out and the little headaches came back and business was not so good as last year. That's how Dessie was and that's what she could do. She carried excitement in her arms just as Samuel had. She was the darling, she was the beloved of the family.

Dessie was not beautiful. Perhaps she wasn't even pretty, but she had the glow that makes men follow a woman in the hope of reflecting a little of it. You would have thought that in time she would have got over her first love affair and found another love, but she did not. Come to think of it, none of the Hamiltons, with all their versatility, had any versatility in love. None of them seemed capable of light or changeable love.

Dessie did not simply throw up her hands and give up. It was much worse than that. She went right on doing and being what she was—without the glow. The people who loved her ached for her, seeing her try, and they got to trying for her.

Dessie's friends were good and loyal but they were human, and humans love to feel good and they hate to feel bad. In time the Mrs. Morrisons found unassailable reasons for not going to the little house by the bakery. They weren't disloyal. They didn't want to be sad as much as they wanted to be happy. It is easy to find a logical and virtuous reason for not doing what you don't want to do.

Dessie's business began to fall off. And the women who had thought they wanted dresses never realized that what they had wanted was happiness. Times were changing and the ready-made dress was becoming popular. It was no longer a disgrace to wear one. If Mr. Morrison was stocking ready-mades, it was only reasonable that Agnes Morrison should be seen in them.

The family was worried about Dessie, but what could you do when she would not admit there was anything wrong with her? She did admit to pains in her side, quite fierce, but they lasted only a little while and came only at intervals.

Then Samuel died and the world shattered like a dish. His sons and daughters and friends groped about among the pieces, trying to put some kind of world together again.

Dessie decided to sell her business and go back to the ranch to live with Tom. She hadn't much of any business to sell out. Liza knew about it, and Olive, and Dessie had written to Tom. But Will, sitting scowling at the table in the San Francisco Chop House, had not been told. Will frothed inwardly and finally he balled up his napkin and got up. "I forgot something," he said to Adam. "I'll see you on the train."

He walked the half-block to Dessie's house and went through the high grown garden and rang Dessie's bell.

She was having her dinner alone, and she came to the door with her napkin in her hand. "Why, hello, Will," she said and put up her pink cheek for him to kiss. "When did you get in town?"

"Business," he said. "Just here between trains. I want to talk to you."

She led him back to her kitchen and dining-room combined, a warm little room papered with flowers. Automatically she poured a cup of coffee and placed it for him and put the sugar bowl and the cream pitcher in front of it.

"Have you seen Mother?" she asked.

"I'm just here over trains," he said gruffly. "Dessie, is it true you want to go back to the ranch?"

"I was thinking of it."

"I don't want you to go."

She smiled uncertainly. "Why not? What's wrong with that? Tom's lonely down there."

"You've got a nice business here," he said.

"I haven't any business here," she replied. "I thought you knew that."

"I don't want you to go," he repeated sullenly.

Her smile was wistful and she tried her best to put a little mockery in her manner. "My big brother is masterful. Tell Dessie why not."

"It's too lonely down there."

"It won't be as lonely with the two of us."

Will pulled at his lips angrily. He blurted, "Tom's not himself. You shouldn't be alone with him."

"Isn't he well? Does he need help?"

Will said, "I didn't want to tell you—I don't think Tom's ever got over—the death. He's strange."

She smiled affectionately. "Will, you've always thought he was strange. You thought he was strange when he didn't like business."

"That was different. But now he's broody. He doesn't talk. He goes walking alone in the hills at night. I went out to see him and—he's been writing poetry—pages of it all over the table."

"Didn't you ever write poetry, Will?"

"I did not."

"I have," said Dessie. "Pages and pages of it all over the table."

"I don't want you to go."

"Let me decide," she said softly. "I've lost something. I want to try to find it again."

"You're talking foolish."

She came around the table and put her arms around his neck. "Dear brother," she said, "please let me decide."

He went angrily out of the house and barely caught his train.

2

Tom met Dessie at the King City station. She saw him out of the train window, scanning every coach for her. He was burnished, his face shaved so close that its darkness had a shine like polished wood. His red mustache was clipped. He wore a new Stetson hat with a flat crown, a tan Norfolk jacket with a belt buckle of mother-of-pearl. His shoes glinted in the noonday light so that it was sure he had gone over them with his handkerchief just before the train arrived. His hard collar stood up against his strong red neck, and he wore a pale blue knitted tie with a horseshoe tie pin. He tried to conceal his excitement by clasping his rough brown hands in front of him.

Dessie waved wildly out the window, crying, "Here I am, Tom, here I am!" though she knew he couldn't hear her over the grinding wheels of the train as the coach slid past him. She climbed down the steps and saw him looking frantically about in the wrong direction. She smiled and walked up behind him.

"I beg your pardon, stranger," she said quietly. "Is there a Mister Tom Hamilton here?"

He spun around and he squealed with pleasure and picked her up in a bear hug and danced her around. He held her off the ground with one arm and spanked her bottom with his free hand. He nuzzled her cheek with his harsh mustache. Then he held her back by the shoulders and looked at her. Both of them threw back their heads and howled with laughter.

The station agent leaned out his window and rested his elbows, protected with black false sleeves, on the sill. He said over his shoulder to the telegrapher, "Those Hamiltons! Just look at them!"

Tom and Dessie, fingertips touching, were doing a courtly heel-and-toe while he sang Doodle-doodle-doo and Dessie sang Deedle-deedle-dee, and then they embraced again.

Tom looked down at her. "Aren't you Dessie Hamilton? I seem to remember you. But you've changed. Where are your pigtails?"

It took him quite a fumbling time to get her luggage checks, to lose them in his pockets, to find them and pick up the wrong pieces. At last he had her baskets piled in the back of the buckboard. The two bay horses pawed the hard ground and threw up their heads so that the shined pole jumped and the doubletrees squeaked. The harness was polished and the horse brasses glittered like gold. There was a red bow tied halfway up the buggy whip and red ribbons were braided into the horses' manes and tails.

Tom helped Dessie into the seat and pretended to peek coyly at her ankle. Then he snapped up the check reins and unfastened the leather tie reins from the bits. He unwrapped the lines from the whip stock, and the horses turned so sharply that the wheel screamed against the guard.

Tom said, "Would you care to make a tour of King City? It's a lovely town."

"No," she said. "I think I remember it." He turned left and headed south and lifted the horses to a fine swinging trot.

Dessie said, "Where's Will?"

"I don't know," he answered gruffly.

"Did he talk to you?"

"Yes. He said you shouldn't come."

"He told me the same thing," said Dessie. "He got George to write to me too."

"Why shouldn't you come if you want to?" Tom raged. "What's Will got to do with it?"

She touched his arm. "He thinks you're crazy. Says you're writing poetry."

Tom's face darkened. "He must have gone in the house when I wasn't there. What's he want anyway? He had no right to look at my papers."

"Gently, gently," said Dessie. "Will's your brother. Don't forget that."

"How would he like me to go through his papers?" Tom demanded.

"He wouldn't let you," Dessie said dryly. "They'd be locked in the safe. Now let's not spoil the day with anger."

"All right," he said. "God knows all right! But he makes me mad. If I don't want to live his kind of life I'm crazy—just crazy."

Dessie changed the subject, forced the change. "You know, I had quite a time at the last," she said. "Mother wanted to come. Have you ever seen Mother cry, Tom?"

"No, not that I can remember. No, she's not a crier."

"Well, she cried. Not much, but a lot for her—a choke and two sniffles and a wiped nose and polished her glasses and snapped shut like a watch."

Tom said, "Oh, Lord, Dessie, it's good to have you back! It's good. Makes me feel I'm well from a sickness."

The horses spanked along the county road. Tom said, "Adam Trask has bought a Ford. Or maybe I should say Will sold him a Ford."

"I didn't know about the Ford," said Dessie. "He's buying my house. Giving me a very good price for it." She laughed. "I put a very high price on the house. I was going to come down during negotiations. Mr. Trask accepted the first price. It put me in a fix."

"What did you do, Dessie?"

"Well, I had to tell him about the high price and that I had planned to be argued down. He didn't seem to care either way."

Tom said, "Let me beg you never to tell that story to Will. He'd have you locked up."

"But the house wasn't worth what I asked!"

"I repeat what I said about Will. What's Adam want with your house?"

"He's going to move there. Wants the twins to go to school in Salinas."

"What'll he do with his ranch?"

"I don't know. He didn't say."

Tom said, "I wonder what would have happened if Father'd got hold of a ranch like that instead of Old Dry and Dusty."

"It isn't such a bad place."

"Fine for everything except making a living."

Dessie said earnestly, "Have you ever known any family that had more fun?"

"No, I don't. But that was the family, not the land."

"Tom, remember when you took Jenny and Belle Williams to the Peachtree dance on the sofa?"

"Mother never let me forget it. Say, wouldn't it be good to ask Jenny and Belle down for a visit?"

"They'd come too," Dessie said. "Let's do it."

When they turned off the county road she said, "Somehow I remember it differently."

"Drier?"

"I guess that's it. Tom, there's so much grass."

"I'm getting twenty head of stock to eat it."

"You must be rich."

"No, and the good year will break the price of beef. I wonder what Will would do. He's a scarcity man. He told me. He said, 'Always deal in scarcities.' Will's smart."

The rutty road had not changed except that the ruts were deeper and the round stones stuck up higher.

Dessie said, "What's the card on that mesquite bush?" She picked it off as they drove by, and it said, "Welcome Home."

"Tom, you did it!"

"I did not. Someone's been here."

Every fifty yards there was another card sticking on a bush, or hanging from the branches of a madrone, or tacked to the trunk of a buckeye, and all of them said, "Welcome Home." Dessie squealed with delight over each one.

They topped the rise above the little valley of the old Hamilton place and Tom pulled up to let her enjoy the view. On the hill across the valley, spelled out in whitewashed stones, were the huge words, "Welcome Home, Dessie." She put her head against his lapel and laughed and cried at the same time.

Tom looked sternly ahead of him. "Now who could have done that?" he said. "A man can't leave the place any more."

In the dawn Dessie was awakened by the chill of pain that came to her at intervals. It was a rustle and a threat of pain; it scampered up from her side and across her abdomen, a nibbling pinch and then a little grab and then a hard catch and finally a fierce grip as though a huge hand had wrenched her. When that relaxed she felt a soreness like a bruise. It didn't last very long, but while it went on the outside world was blotted out, and she seemed to be listening to the struggle in her body.

When only the soreness remained she saw how the dawn had come silver to the windows. She smelled the good morning wind rippling the curtains, bringing in the odor of grass and roots and damp earth. After that sounds joined the parade of perception—sparrows haggling among themselves, a bawling cow monotonously berating a punching hungry calf, a blue jay's squawk of false excitement, the sharp warning of a cock quail on guard and the answering whisper of the hen quail somewhere near in the tall grass. The chickenyard boiled with excitement over an egg, and a big lady Rhode Island Red, who weighed four pounds, hypocritically protested the horror of being lustfully pinned to the ground by a scrawny wreck of a rooster she could have blasted with one blow of her wing.

The cooing of pigeons brought memory into the procession. Dessie remembered how her father had said, sitting at the head of the table, "I told Rabbit I was going to raise some pigeons and—do you know?—he said, 'No white pigeons.' 'Why not white?' I asked him, and he said, 'They're the rare worst of bad luck. You take a flight of white pigeons and they'll bring sadness and death. Get gray ones.' 'I like white ones.' 'Get gray ones,' he told me. And as the sky covers me, I'll get white ones."

And Liza said patiently, "Why do you be forever testing, Samuel? Gray ones taste just as good and they're bigger."

"I'll let no flimsy fairy tale push me," Samuel said.

And Liza said with her dreadful simplicity, "You're already pushed by your own contentiousness. You're a mule of contention, a very mule!"

"Someone's got to do these things," he said sullenly. "Else Fate would not ever get nose-thumbed and mankind would still be clinging to the top branches of a tree."

And of course he got white pigeons and waited truculently for sadness and death until he'd proved his point. And here were the great-great-grand squabs cooing in the morning and rising to fly like a whirling white scarf around the wagon shed.

As Dessie remembered, she heard the words and the house around her grew peopled. Sadness and death, she thought, and death and sadness, and it wrenched in her stomach against the soreness. You just have to wait around long enough and it will come.

She heard the air whooshing into the big bellows in the forge and the practice tap for range of hammer on anvil. She heard Liza open the oven door and the thump of a kneaded loaf on the floury board. Then Joe wandered about, looking in unlikely places for his shoes, and at last found them where he had left them under the bed.

She heard Mollie's sweet high voice in the kitchen, reading a morning text from the Bible, and Una's full cold throaty correction.

And Tom had cut Mollie's tongue with his pocketknife and died in his heart when he realized his courage.

"Oh, dear Tom," she said, and her lips moved.

Tom's cowardice was as huge as his courage, as it must be in great men. His violence balanced his tenderness, and himself was a pitted battlefield of his own forces. He was confused now, but Dessie could hold his bit and point him, the way a handler points a thoroughbred at the barrier to show his breeding and his form.

Dessie lay part in pain and a part of her dangled still in sleep while the morning brightened against the window. She remembered that Mollie was going to lead the Grand March at the Fourth of July picnic with no less than Harry Forbes, State Senator. And Dessie had not finished putting the braid on Mollie's dress. She struggled to get up. There was so much braid, and here she lay drowsing.

She cried, "I'll get it done, Mollie. It will be ready."

She got up from her bed and threw her robe around her and walked barefooted through the house crowded with Hamiltons. In the hall they were gone to the bedrooms. In the bedrooms, with the beds neat-made, they were all in the kitchen, and in the kitchen—they dispersed and were gone. Sadness and death. The wave receded and left her in dry awakeness.

The house was clean, scrubbed and immaculate, curtains washed, windows polished, but all as a man does it—the ironed curtains did not hang quite straight and there were streaks on the windows and a square showed on the table when a book was moved.

The stove was warming, with orange light showing around the lids and the soft thunder of drafty flame leaping past the open damper. The kitchen clock flashed its pendulum behind its glass skirt, and it ticked like a little wooden hammer striking on an empty wooden box.

From outside came a whistle as wild and raucous as a reed and pitched high and strange. The whistling scattered a savage melody. Then Tom's steps sounded on the porch, and he came in with an armload of oakwood so high he could not see over it. He cascaded the wood into the woodbox.

"You're up," he said. "That was to wake you if you were still sleeping." His face was lighted with joy. "This is a morning light as down and no time to be slugging."

"You sound like your father," Dessie said, and she laughed with him.

His joy hardened to fierceness. "Yes," he said loudly. "And we'll have that time again, right here. I've been dragging myself in misery like a spine-broken snake. No wonder Will thought I was cracked. But now you're back, and I'll show you. I'll breathe life into life again. Do you hear? This house is going to be alive."

"I'm glad I came," she said, and she thought in desolation how brittle he was now and how easy to shatter, and how she would have to protect him.

"You must have worked day and night to get the house so clean," she said.

"Nothing," said Tom. "A little twist with the fingers."

"I know that twist, but it was with bucket and mop and on your knees—unless you've invented some way to do it by chicken power or the harnessed wind."

"Invented—now that's why I have no time. I've invented a little slot that lets a necktie slip around freely in a stiff collar."

"You don't wear stiff collars."

"I did yesterday. That's when I invented it. And chickens—I'm going to raise millions of them—little houses all over the ranch and a ring on the roof to dip them in a whitewash tank. And the eggs will come through on a little conveyor belt—here! I'll draw it."

"I want to draw some breakfast," Dessie said. "What's the shape of a fried egg? How would you color the fat and lean of a strip of bacon?"

"You'll have it," he cried, and he opened the stove lid and assaulted the fire with the stove lifter until the hairs on his hand curled and charred. He pitched wood in and started his high whistling.

Dessie said, "You sound like some goat-foot with a wheat flute on a hill in Greece."

"What do you think I am?" he shouted.

Dessie thought miserably, If his is real, why can't my heart be light? Why can't I climb out of my gray ragbag? I will, she screeched inside herself. If he can—I will.

She said, "Tom!"

"Yes."

"I want a purple egg."

THIRTY-THREE

The green lasted on the hills far into June before the grass turned yellow. The heads of the wild oats were so heavy with seed that they hung over on their stalks. The little springs trickled on late in the summer. The range cattle staggered under their fat and their hides shone with health. It was a year when the people of the Salinas Valley forgot the dry years. Farmers bought more land than they could afford and figured their profits on the covers of their checkbooks.

Tom Hamilton labored like a giant, not only with his strong arms and rough hands but also with his heart and spirit. The anvil rang in the forge again. He painted the old house white and whitewashed the sheds. He went to King City and studied a flush toilet and then built one of craftily bent tin and carved wood. Because the water came so slowly from the spring, he put a redwood tank beside the house and pumped the water up to it with a handmade windmill so cleverly made that it turned in the slightest wind. And he made metal and wood models of two ideas to be sent to the patent office in the fall.

That was not all—he labored with humor and good spirits. Dessie had to rise very early to get in her hand at the housework before Tom had it all done. She watched his great red happiness, and it was not light as Samuel's happiness was light. It did not rise out of his roots and come floating up. He was manufacturing happiness as cleverly as he knew how, molding it and shaping it.

Dessie, who had more friends than anyone in the whole valley, had no confidants. When her trouble had come upon her she had not talked about it. And the pains were a secret in herself.

When Tom found her rigid and tight from the grabbing pain and cried in alarm, "Dessie, what's the matter?" she controlled her face and said, "A little crick, that's all. Just a little crick. I'm all right now." And in a moment they were laughing.

They laughed a great deal, as though to reassure themselves. Only when Dessie went to her bed did her loss fall on her, bleak and unendurable. And Tom lay in the dark of his room, puzzled as a child. He could hear his heart beating and rasping a little in its beat. His mind fell away from thought and clung for safety to little plans, designs, machines.

Sometimes in the summer evenings they walked up the hill to watch the afterglow clinging to the tops of the western mountains and to feel the breeze drawn into the valley by the rising day-heated air. Usually they stood silently for a while and breathed in peacefulness. Since both were shy they never talked about themselves. Neither knew about the other at all.

It was startling to both of them when Dessie said one evening on the hil "Tom, why don't you get married?"

He looked quickly at her and away. He said, "Who'd have me?"

"Is that a joke or do you really mean it?"

"Who'd have me?" he said again. "Who'd want a thing like me?"

"It sounds to me as though you really mean it." Then she violated thei unstated code. "Have you been in love with someone?"

"No," he said shortly.

"I wish I knew," she said as though he had not answered.

Tom did not speak again as they walked down the hill. But on the porcl he said suddenly, "You're lonely here. You don't want to stay." He waited fo a moment. "Answer me. Isn't that true?"

"I want to stay here more than I want to stay anyplace else." She asked "Do you ever go to women?"

"Yes," he said.

"Is it any good to you?"

"Not much."

"What are you going to do?"

"I don't know."

In silence they went back to the house. Tom lighted the lamp in the old living room. The horsehair sofa he had rebuilt raised its gooseneck against the wall, and the green carpet had tracks worn light between the doors.

Tom sat down by the round center table. Dessie sat on the sofa, and she could see that he was still embarrassed from his last admission. She thought, How pure he is, how unfit for a world that even she knew more about than he did. A dragon killer, he was, a rescuer of damsels, and his small sins seemed so great to him that he felt unfit and unseemly. She wished her father were here. Her father had felt greatness in Tom. Perhaps he would know now how to release it out of its darkness and let it fly free.

She took another tack to see whether she could raise some spark in him. "As long as we're talking about ourselves, have you ever thought that our whole world is the valley and a few trips to San Francisco, and have you ever been farther south than San Luis Obispo? I never have."

"Neither have I," said Tom.

"Well, isn't that silly?"

"Lots of people haven't," he said.

"But it's not a law. We could go to Paris and to Rome or to Jerusalem. I would dearly love to see the Colosseum."

He watched her suspiciously, expecting some kind of joke. "How could we?" he asked. "That takes a lot of money."

"I don't think it does," she said. "We wouldn't have to stay in fancy places. We could take the cheapest boats and the lowest class. That's how our father came here from Ireland. And we could go to Ireland."

Still he watched her, but a burning was beginning in his eyes.

Dessie went on, "We could take a year for work, save every penny. I can get some sewing to do in King City. Will would help us. And next summer you could sell all the stock and we could go. There's no law forbids it."

Tom got up and went outside. He looked up at the summer stars, at blue Venus and red Mars. His hands flexed at his sides, closed to fists and opened. Then he turned and went back into the house. Dessie had not moved.

"Do you want to go, Dessie?"

"More than anything in the world."

"Then we will go!"

"Do you want to go?"

"More than anything in the world," he said, and then, "Egypt—have you given a thought to Egypt?"

"Athens," she said.

"Constantinople!"

"Bethlehem!"

"Yes, Bethlehem," and he said suddenly, "Go to bed. We've got a year of work—a year. Get some rest. I'm going to borrow money from Will to buy a hundred shoats."

"What will you feed them?"

"Acorns," said Tom. "I'll make a machine to gather acorns."

After he had gone to his room she could hear him knocking around and talking softly to himself. Dessie looked out her window at the starlit night and she was glad. But she wondered whether she really wanted to go, or whether Tom did. And as she wondered the whisper of pain grew up from her side.

When Dessie got up in the morning Tom was already at his drawing board, beating his forehead with his fist and growling to himself. Dessie looked over his shoulder. "Is it the acorn machine?"

"It should be easy," he said. "But how to get out the sticks and rocks?"

"I know you're the inventor, but I invented the greatest acorn picker in the world and it's ready to go."

"What do you mean?"

"Children," she said. "Those restless little hands."

"They wouldn't do it, not even for pay."

"They would for prizes. A prize for everyone and a big prize for the winner—maybe a hundred-dollar prize. They'd sweep the valley clean. Will you let me try?"

He scratched his head. "Why not?" he said. "But how would you collect the acorns?"

"The children will bring them in," said Dessie. "Just let me take care of it. I hope you have plenty of storage space."

"It would be exploiting the young, wouldn't it?"

"Certainly it would," Dessie agreed. "When I had my shop I exploited the girls who wanted to learn to sew—and they exploited me. I think I will call this The Great Monterey County Acorn Contest. And I won't let everyone in. Maybe bicycles for prizes—wouldn't you pick up acorns in hope of a bicycle, Tom?"

"Sure I would," he said. "But couldn't we pay them too?"

"Not with money," Dessie said. "That would reduce it to labor, and they will not labor if they can help it. Nor will I."

Tom leaned back from his board and laughed. "Nor will I," he said. "All right, you are in charge of acorns and I am in charge of pigs."

Dessie said, "Tom, wouldn't it be ridiculous if we made money, we of all people?"

"But you made money in Salinas," he said.

"Some—not much. But oh, I was rich in promises. If the bills had ever been paid we wouldn't need pigs. We could go to Paris tomorrow."

"I'm going to drive in and talk to Will," said Tom. He pushed his chair back from the drawing board. "Want to come with me?"

"No, I'll stay and make my plans. Tomorrow I start The Great Acorn Contest."

2

On the ride back to the ranch in the late afternoon Tom was depressed and sad. As always, Will had managed to chew up and spit out his enthusiasm. Will had pulled his lip, rubbed his eyebrows, scratched his nose, cleaned his glasses, and made a major operation of cutting and lighting a cigar. The pig proposition was full of holes, and Will was able to put his finger in the holes.

The Acorn Contest wouldn't work although he was not explicit about why it wouldn't. The whole thing was shaky, particularly in these times. The very best Will was able to do was to agree to think about it.

At one time during the talk Tom had thought to tell Will about Europe, but a quick instinct stopped him. The idea of traipsing around Europe, unless, of course, you were retired and had your capital out in good securities, would be to Will a craziness that would make the pig plan a marvel of business acumen. Tom did not tell him, and he left Will to "think it over," knowing that the verdict would be against the pigs and the acorns.

Poor Tom did not know and could not learn that dissembling successfully is one of the creative joys of a businessman. To indicate enthusiasm was to be idiotic. And Will really did mean to think it over. Parts of the plan fascinated him. Tom had stumbled on a very interesting thing. If you could buy shoats on credit, fatten them on food that cost next to nothing, sell them, pay off your loan, and take your profit, you would really have done something. Will would not rob his brother. He would cut him in on the profits, but Tom was a dreamer and could not be trusted with a good sound plan. Tom, for instance, didn't even know the price of pork and its probable trend. If it worked out, Will could be depended on to give Tom a very substantial present—maybe even a Ford. And how about a Ford as first and only prize for acorns? Everybody in the whole valley would pick acorns.

Driving up the Hamilton road, Tom wondered how to break it to Dessie that their plan was no good. The best way would be to have another plan to substitute for it. How could they make enough money in one year to go to Europe? And suddenly he realized that he didn't know how much they'd need. He didn't know the price of a steamship ticket. They might spend the evening figuring.

He half expected Dessie to run out of the house when he drove up. He would put on his best face and tell a joke. But Dessie didn't run out. Maybe taking a nap, he thought. He watered the horses and stabled them and pitched hay into the manger.

Dessie was lying on the gooseneck sofa when Tom came in. "Taking a nap?" he asked, and then he saw the color of her face. "Dessie," he cried, "what's the matter?"

She rallied herself against pain. "Just a stomach ache," she said. "A pretty severe one."

"Oh," said Tom. "You scared me. I can fix up a stomach ache." He went to the kitchen and brought back a glass of pearly liquid. He handed it to her.

"What is it, Tom?"

"Good old-fashioned salts. It may gripe you a little but it'll do the job."

She drank it obediently and made a face. "I remember that taste," she said. "Mother's remedy in green apple season."

"Now you lie still," Tom said. "I'll rustle up some dinner."

She could hear him knocking about in the kitchen. The pain roared through her body. And on top of the pain there was fear. She could feel the medicine burn down to her stomach. After a while she dragged herself to the new homemade flush toilet and tried to vomit the salts. The perspiration ran from her forehead and blinded her. When she tried to straighten up the muscles over her stomach were set, and she could not break free.

Later Tom brought her some scrambled eggs. She shook her head slowly. "I can't," she said, smiling. "I think I'll just go to bed."

"The salts should work pretty soon," Tom assured her. "Then you'll be all right." He helped her to bed. "What do you suppose you ate to cause it?"

Dessie lay in her bedroom and her will battled the pain. About ten o'clock in the evening her will began to lose its fight. She called, "Tom! Tom!" He opened the door. He had the *World Almanac* in his hand. "Tom," she said, "I'm sorry. But I'm awfully sick, Tom. I'm terribly sick."

He sat down on the edge of her bed in the half-darkness. "Are the gripes bad?"

"Yes, awful."

"Can you go to the toilet now?"

"No, not now."

"I'll bring a lamp and sit with you," he said. "Maybe you can get some sleep. It'll be gone in the morning. The salts will do the job."

Her will took hold again and she lay still while Tom read bits out of the *Almanac* to soothe her. He stopped reading when he thought she was sleeping, and he dozed in his chair beside the lamp.

A thin scream awakened him. He stepped beside the struggling bedclothes. Dessie's eyes were milky and crazy, like those of a maddened horse. Her mouth corners erupted thick bubbles and her face was on fire. Tom put his hand under the cover and felt muscles knotted like iron. And then her struggle stopped and her head fell back and the light glinted on her half-closed eyes.

Tom put only a bridle on the horse and flung himself on bareback. He groped and ripped out his belt to beat the frightened horse to an awkward run over the stony, rutted wheel track.

The Duncans, asleep upstairs in their two-story house on the county road, didn't hear the banging on their door, but they heard the bang and ripping sound as their front door came off, carrying lock and hinges with it. By the time Red Duncan got downstairs with a shotgun Tom was screaming into the wall telephone at the King City central. "Dr. Tilson! Get him! I don't care. Get him! Get him, goddam it." Red Duncan sleepily had the gun on him.

Dr. Tilson said, "Yes! Yes—yes, I hear. You're Tom Hamilton. What's the matter with her? Is her stomach hard? What did you do? Salts! You goddam fool!"

Then the doctor controlled his anger. "Tom," he said, "Tom, boy. Pull yourself together. Go back and lay cold cloths—cold as you can get them. I don't suppose you have any ice. Well, keep changing the cloths. I'll be out as fast as I can. Do you hear me? Tom, do you hear me?"

He hung the receiver up and dressed. In angry weariness he opened the wall cabinet and collected scalpels and clamps, sponges and tubes of sutures, to put in his bag. He shook his gasoline pressure lantern to make sure it was full and arranged ether can and mask beside it on his bureau. His wife in boudoir cap and nightgown looked in. Dr. Tilson said, "I'm walking over to the garage. Call Will Hamilton. Tell him I want him to drive me to his father's place. If he argues tell him his sister is—dying."

3

Tom came riding back to the ranch a week after Dessie's funeral, riding high and prim, his shoulders straight and chin in, like a guardsman on parade. Tom had done everything slowly, perfectly. His horse was curried and brushed, and his Stetson hat was square on his head. Not even Samuel could have held himself in more dignity than Tom as he rode back to the

d house. A hawk driving down on a chicken with doubled fists did not
make him turn his head.

At the barn he dismounted, watered his horse, held him a moment at the
door, haltered him, and put rolled barley in the box beside the manger. He
took off the saddle and turned the blanket inside out to dry. Then the barley
was finished and he led the bay horse out and turned him free to graze on
every unfenced inch of the world.

In the house the furniture, chairs, and stove seemed to shrink back and
way from him in distaste. A stool avoided him as he went to the living
room. His matches were soft and damp, and with a feeling of apology he
went to the kitchen for more. The lamp in the living room was fair and
lonely. Tom's first match flame ran quickly around the Rochester wick and
then stood up a full inch of yellow flame.

Tom sat down in the evening and looked around. His eyes avoided the
horsehair sofa. A slight noise of mice in the kitchen made him turn, and he
saw his shadow on the wall and his hat was on. He removed it and laid it on
the table beside him.

He thought dawdling, protective thoughts, sitting under the lamp, but he
knew that pretty soon his name would be called and he would have to go up
before the bench with himself as judge and his own crimes as jurors.

And his name *was* called, shrilly in his ears. His mind walked in to face
the accusers: Vanity, which charged him with being ill dressed and dirty
and vulgar; and Lust, slipping him the money for his whoring; Dishonesty,
to make him pretend to talent and thought he did not have; Laziness and
Gluttony arm in arm. Tom felt comforted by these because they screened the
great Gray One in the back seat, waiting—the gray and dreadful crime. He
dredged up lesser things, used small sins almost like virtues to save himself.
There were Covetousness of Will's money, Treason toward his mother's
God, Theft of time and hope, sick Rejection of love.

Samuel spoke softly but his voice filled the room. "Be good, be pure, be
great, be Tom Hamilton."

Tom ignored his father. He said, "I'm busy greeting my friends," and he
nodded to Discourtesy and Ugliness and Unfilial Conduct and Unkempt
Fingernails. Then he started with Vanity again. The Gray One shouldered
up in front. It was too late to stall with baby sins. This Gray One was
Murder.

Tom's hand felt the chill of the glass and saw the pearly liquid with the
dissolving crystals still turning over and lucent bubbles rising, and he repeated aloud in the empty, empty room, "This will do the job. Just wait till
morning. You'll feel fine then." That's how it had sounded, exactly how,
and the walls and chairs and the lamp had all heard it and they could prove
it. There was no place in the whole world for Tom Hamilton to live. But it
wasn't for lack of trying. He shuffled possibilities like cards. London? No!
Egypt—pyramids in Egypt and the Sphinx. No! Paris? No! Now wait—they

do all your sins lots better there. No! Well, stand aside and maybe we'
come back to you. Bethlehem? Dear God, no! It would be lonely there for
stranger.

And here interpolated—it's so hard to remember how you die or wher
An eyebrow raised or a whisper—they may be it; or a night mottled wit
splashed light until powder-driven lead finds your secret and lets out th
fluid in you.

Now this is true, Tom Hamilton was dead and he had only to do a fe
decent things to make it final.

The sofa cricked in criticism, and Tom looked at it and at the smokin
lamp to which the sofa referred. "Thank you," Tom said to the sofa. "
hadn't noticed it," and he turned down the wick until the smoking stopped

His mind dozed. Murder slapped him aware again. Now Red Tom, Gun
Tom, was too tired to kill himself. That takes some doing, with maybe pair
and maybe hell.

He remembered that his mother had a strong distaste for suicide, feeling
that it combined three things of which she strongly disapproved—bad manners, cowardice, and sin. It was almost as bad as adultery or stealing—maybe
just as bad. There must be a way to avoid Liza's disapproval. She could make
one suffer if she disapproved.

Samuel wouldn't make it hard, but on the other hand you couldn't avoid
Samuel because he was in the air every place. Tom had to tell Samuel. He
said, "My father, I'm sorry. I can't help it. You overestimated me. You
were wrong. I wish I could justify the love and the pride you squandered on
me. Maybe you could figure a way out, but I can't. I cannot live. I've killed
Dessie and I want to sleep."

And his mind spoke for his father absent, saying, "Why, I can understand how that would be. There are so many patterns to choose from in the
arc from birth back to birth again. But let's think how we can make it all
right with Mother. Why are you so impatient, dear?"

"I can't wait, that's why," Tom said. "I can't wait any more."

"Why, sure you can, my son, my darling. You're grown great as I knew
you would. Open the table drawer and then make use of that turnip you call
your head."

Tom opened the drawer and saw a tablet of Crane's Linen Lawn and a
package of envelopes to match and two gnawed and crippled pencils and
in the dust corner at the back a few stamps. He laid out the tablet and
sharpened the pencils with his pocketknife.

He wrote, "Dear Mother, I hope you keep yourself well. I am going to
plan to spend more time with you. Olive asked me for Thanksgiving and you
know I'll be there. Our little Olive can cook a turkey nearly to match yours,
but I know you will never believe that. I've had a stroke of good luck. Bought
a horse for fifteen dollars—a gelding, and he looks like a blood-horse to me.
I got him cheap because he has taken a dislike to mankind. His former owner

pent more time on his own back than on the gelding's. I must say he's a pretty cute article. He's thrown me twice but I'll get him yet, and if I can break him I'll have one of the best horses in the whole county. And you can be sure I'll break him if it takes all winter. I don't know why I go on about him, only the man I bought him from said a funny thing. He said, 'That horse is so mean he'd eat a man right off his back.' Well, remember what Father used to say when we went rabbit hunting? 'Come back with your shield or on it.' I'll see you Thanksgiving. Your son Tom."

He wondered whether it was good enough, but he was too tired to do it again. He added, "P.S. I notice that Polly has not reformed one bit. That parrot makes me blush."

On another sheet he wrote, "Dear Will, No matter what you yourself may think—please help me now. For Mother's sake—please. I was killed by a horse—thrown and kicked in the head—please! Your brother Tom."

He stamped the letters and put them in his pocket and he asked Samuel, "Is that all right?"

In his bedroom he broke open a new box of shells and put one of them in the cylinder of his well-oiled Smith and Wesson .38 and he set the loaded chamber one space to the left of the firing pin.

His horse standing sleepily near the fence came to his whistle and stood drowsing while he saddled up.

It was three o'clock in the morning when he dropped the letters in the post office at King City and mounted and turned his horse south toward the unproductive hills of the old Hamilton place.

He was a gallant gentleman.

PART FOUR

PART FOUR

THIRTY-FOUR

A child may ask, "What is the world's story about?" And a grown man or woman may wonder, "What way will the world go? How does it end and, while we're at it, what's the story about?"

I believe that there is one story in the world, and only one, that has frightened and inspired us, so that we live in a Pearl White serial of continuing thought and wonder. Humans are caught—in their lives, in their thoughts, in their hungers and ambitions, in their avarice and cruelty, and in their kindness and generosity too—in a net of good and evil. I think this is the only story we have and that it occurs on all levels of feeling and intelligence. Virtue and vice were warp and woof of our first consciousness, and they will be the fabric of our last, and this despite any changes we may impose on field and river and mountain, on economy and manners. There is no other story. A man, after he has brushed off the dust and chips of his life, will have left only the hard, clean questions: Was it good or was it evil? Have I done well—or ill?

Herodotus, in the Persian War, tells a story of how Croesus, the richest and most-favored king of his time, asked Solon the Athenian a leading question. He would not have asked it if he had not been worried about the answer. "Who," he asked, "is the luckiest person in the world?" He must have been eaten with doubt and hungry for reassurance. Solon told him of three lucky people in old times. And Croesus more than likely did not listen, so anxious was he about himself. And when Solon did not mention him, Croesus was forced to say, "Do you not consider me lucky?"

Solon did not hesitate in his answer. "How can I tell?" he said. "You aren't dead yet."

And this answer must have haunted Croesus dismally as his luck disappeared, and his wealth and his kingdom. And as he was being burned on a tall fire, he may have thought of it and perhaps wished he had not asked or not been answered.

And in our time, when a man dies—if he has had wealth and influence and power and all the vestments that arouse envy, and after the living take stock of the dead man's property and his eminence and works and monuments—the question is still there: Was his life good or was it evil?—which is another way of putting Croesus's question. Envies are gone, and the measuring stick is: "Was he loved or was he hated? Is his death felt as a loss or does a kind of joy come of it?"

I remember clearly the deaths of three men. One was the richest man of the century, who, having clawed his way to wealth through the souls and bodies of men, spent many years trying to buy back the love he had forfeited and by that process performed great service to the world and, perhaps, had much more than balanced the evils of his rise. I was on a ship when he died. The news was posted on the bulletin board, and nearly everyone received the news with pleasure. Several said, "Thank God that son of a bitch is dead."

Then there was a man, smart as Satan, who, lacking some perception of human dignity and knowing all too well every aspect of human weakness and wickedness, used his special knowledge to warp men, to buy men, to bribe and threaten and seduce until he found himself in a position of great power. He clothed his motives in the names of virtue, and I have wondered whether he ever knew that no gift will ever buy back a man's love when you have removed his self-love. A bribed man can only hate his briber. When this man died the nation rang with praise and, just beneath, with gladness that he was dead.

There was a third man, who perhaps made many errors in performance but whose effective life was devoted to making men brave and dignified and good in a time when they were poor and frightened and when ugly forces were loose in the world to utilize their fears. This man was hated by the few. When he died the people burst into tears in the streets and their minds wailed, "What can we do now? How can we go on without him?"

In uncertainty I am certain that underneath their topmost layers of frailty men want to be good and want to be loved. Indeed, most of their vices are attempted short cuts to love. When a man comes to die, no matter what his talents and influence and genius, if he dies unloved his life must be a failure to him and his dying a cold horror. It seems to me that if you or I must choose between two courses of thought or action, we should remember our dying and try so to live that our death brings no pleasure to the world.

We have only one story. All novels, all poetry, are built on the never-ending contest in ourselves of good and evil. And it occurs to me that evil must constantly respawn, while good, while virtue, is immortal. Vice has always a new fresh young face, while virtue is venerable as nothing else in the world is.

THIRTY-FIVE

Lee helped Adam and the two boys move to Salinas, which is to say he did it all, packed the things to be taken, saw them on the train, loaded the back seat of the Ford, and, arriving in Salinas, unpacked and saw the family settled in Dessie's little house. When he had done everything he could think of to make them comfortable, and a number of things unnecessary, and more things for the sake of delay, he waited on Adam formally one evening after the twins had gone to bed. Perhaps Adam caught his intention from Lee's coldness and formality.

Adam said, "All right. I've been expecting it. Tell me."

That broke up Lee's memorized speech, which he had intended to begin, "For a number of years I have served you to the best of my ability and now I feel—"

"I've put it off as long as I could," said Lee. "I have a speech all ready. Do you want to hear it?"

"Do you want to say it?"

"No," said Lee. "I don't. And it's a pretty good speech too."

"When do you want to go?" Adam asked.

"As soon as possible. I'm afraid I might lose my intention if I don't go soon. Do you want me to wait until you get someone else?"

"Better not," said Adam. "You know how slow I am. It might be some time. I might never get around to it."

"I'll go tomorrow then."

"It will tear the boys to pieces," Adam said. "I don't know what they'll do. Maybe you'd better sneak off and let me tell them afterward."

"It's my observation that children always surprise us," said Lee.

And so it was. At breakfast the next morning Adam said, "Boys, Lee is going away."

"Is he?" said Cal. "There's a basketball game tonight, costs ten cents. Can we go?"

"Yes. But did you hear what I said?"

"Sure," Aron said. "You said Lee's going away."

"But he's not coming back."

Cal asked, "Where's he going?"

"To San Francisco to live."

"Oh!" said Aron. "There's a man on Main Street, right on the street, and he's got a little stove and he cooks sausages and puts them in buns. They cost a nickel. And you can take all the mustard you want."

Lee stood in the kitchen door, smiling at Adam.

When the twins got their books together Lee said, "Good-by, boys."

They shouted, "Good-by!" and tumbled out of the house.

Adam stared into his coffee cup and said in apology, "What little brutes I guess that's your reward for over ten years of service."

"I like it better that way," Lee said. "If they pretended sorrow they'd b liars. It doesn't mean anything to them. Maybe they'll think of me some times—privately. I don't want them to be sad. I hope I'm not so small souled as to take satisfaction in being missed." He laid fifty cents on the table in front of Adam. "When they start for the basketball game tonight give them this from me and tell them to buy the sausage buns. My farewel gift may be ptomaine, for all I know."

Adam looked at the telescope basket Lee brought into the dining room "Is that all your stuff, Lee?"

"Everything but my books. They're in boxes in the cellar. If you don't mind I'll send for them or come for them after I get settled."

"Why, sure. I'm going to miss you, Lee, whether you want me to or not. Are you really going to get your bookstore?"

"That is my intention."

"You'll let us hear from you?"

"I don't know. I'll have to think about it. They say a clean cut heals soonest. There's nothing sadder to me than associations held together by nothing but the glue of postage stamps. If you can't see or hear or touch a man, it's best to let him go."

Adam stood up from the table. "I'll walk to the depot with you."

"No!" Lee said sharply. "No. I don't want that. Good-by, Mr. Trask. Good-by, Adam." He went out of the house so fast that Adam's "Good-by" reached him at the bottom of the front steps and Adam's "Don't forget to write" sounded over the click of the front gate.

2

That night after the basketball game Cal and Aron each had five sausages on buns, and it was just as well, for Adam had forgotten to provide any supper. Walking home, the twins discussed Lee for the first time.

"I wonder why he went away?" Cal asked.

"He's talked about going before."

"What do you suppose he'll do without us?"

"I don't know. I bet he comes back," Aron said.

"How do you mean? Father said he was going to start a bookstore. That's funny. A Chinese bookstore."

"He'll come back," said Aron. "He'll get lonesome for us. You'll see."

"Bet you ten cents he don't."

"Before when?"

"Before forever."

"That's a bet," said Aron.

Aron was not able to collect his winnings for nearly a month, but he won six days later.

Lee came in on the ten-forty and let himself in with his own key. There was a light in the dining room but Lee found Adam in the kitchen, scraping at a thick black crust in the frying pan with the point of a can opener.

Lee put down his basket. "If you soak it overnight it will come right out."

"Will it? I've burned everything I've cooked. There's a saucepan of beets out in the yard. Smelled so bad I couldn't have them in the house. Burned beets are awful—Lee!" he cried, and then, "Is anything the matter?"

Lee took the black iron pan from him and put it in the sink and ran water in it. "If we had a new gas stove we could make a cup of coffee in a few minutes," he said. "I might as well build up the fire."

"Stove won't burn," said Adam.

Lee lifted a lid. "Have you ever taken the ashes out?"

"Ashes?"

"Oh, go in the other room," said Lee. "I'll make some coffee."

Adam waited impatiently in the dining room but he obeyed his orders. At last Lee brought in two cups of coffee and set them on the table. "Made it in a skillet," he said. "Much faster." He leaned over his telescope basket and untied the rope that held it shut. He brought out the stone bottle. "Chinese absinthe," he said. "Ng-ka-py maybe last ten more years. I forgot to ask whether you had replaced me."

"You're beating around the bush," said Adam.

"I know it. And I also know the best way would be just to tell it and get it over with."

"You lost your money in a fan-tan game."

"No. I wish that was it. No, I have my money. This damn cork's broken— I'll have to shove it in the bottle." He poured the black liquor into his coffee. "I never drank it this way," he said. "Say, it's good."

"Tastes like rotten apples," said Adam.

"Yes, but remember Sam Hamilton said like good rotten apples."

Adam said, "When do you think you'll get around to telling me what happened to you?"

"Nothing happened to me," said Lee. "I got lonesome. That's all. Isn't that enough?"

"How about your bookstore?"

"I don't want a bookstore. I think I knew it before I got on the train, but I took all this time to make sure."

"Then there's your last dream gone."

"Good riddance." Lee seemed on the verge of hysteria. "Missy Tlask, Chinee boy sink gung get dlunk."

Adam was alarmed. "What's the matter with you anyway?"

Lee lifted the bottle to his lips and took a deep hot drink and panted the fumes out of his burning throat. "Adam," he said, "I am incomparably, incredibly, overwhelmingly glad to be home. I've never been so goddam lonesome in my life."

THIRTY-SIX

Salinas had two grammar schools, big yellow structures with tall windows, and the windows were baleful and the doors did not smile. These schools were called the East End and the West End. Since the East End School was way to hell and gone across town and the children who lived east of Main Street attended there, I will not bother with it.

The West End, a huge building of two stories, fronted with gnarled poplars, divided the play yards called girlside and boyside. Behind the school a high board fence separated girlside from boyside, and the back of the play yard was bounded by a slough of standing water in which tall tules and even cattails grew. The West End had grades from third to eighth. The first- and second-graders went to Baby School some distance away.

In the West End there was a room for each grade—third, fourth, and fifth on the ground floor, sixth, seventh, and eighth on the second floor. Each room had the usual desks of battered oak, a platform and square teacher's desk, one Seth Thomas clock and one picture. The pictures identified the rooms, and the pre-Raphaelite influence was overwhelming. Galahad standing in full armor pointed the way for third-graders; Atalanta's race urged on the fourth, the Pot of Basil confused the fifth grade, and so on until the denunciation of Cataline sent the eighth-graders on to high school with a sense of high civic virtue.

Cal and Aron were assigned to the seventh grade because of their age, and they learned every shadow of its picture—Laocoön completely wrapped in snakes.

The boys were stunned by the size and grandeur of the West End after their background in a one-room country school. The opulence of having a teacher for each grade made a deep impression on them. It seemed wasteful. But as is true of all humans, they were stunned for one day, admiring on the second, and on the third day could not remember very clearly ever having gone to any other school.

The teacher was dark and pretty, and by a judicious raising or withholding of hands the twins had no worries. Cal worked it out quickly and explained it to Aron. "You take most kids," he said, "if they know the answer, why, they hold up their hands, and if they don't know they just crawl under the desk. Know what we're going to do?"

"No. What?"

"Well, you notice the teacher don't always call on somebody with his hand up. She lets drive at the others and, sure enough, they don't know."

"That's right," said Aron.

"Now, first week we're going to work like bedamned but we won't stick up our hands. So she'll call on us and we'll know. That'll throw her. So the second week we won't work and we'll stick up our hands and she won't call on us. Third week we'll just sit quiet, and she won't ever know whether we got the answer or not. Pretty soon she'll let us alone. She isn't going to waste her time calling on somebody that knows."

Cal's method worked. In a short time the twins were not only let alone but got themselves a certain reputation for smartness. As a matter of fact, Cal's method was a waste of time. Both boys learned easily enough.

Cal was able to develop his marble game and set about gathering in all the chalkies and immies, glassies and agates, in the schoolyard. He traded them for tops just as marble season ended. At one time he had and used as legal tender at least forty-five tops of various sizes and colors, from the thick clumsy baby tops to the lean and dangerous splitters with their needle points.

Everyone who saw the twins remarked on their difference one from the other and seemed puzzled that this should be so. Cal was growing up dark-skinned, dark-haired. He was quick and sure and secret. Even though he may have tried, he could not conceal his cleverness. Adults were impressed with what seemed to them a precocious maturity, and they were a little frightened at it too. No one liked Cal very much and yet everyone was touched with fear of him and through fear with respect. Although he had no friends he was welcomed by his obsequious classmates and took up a natural and cold position of leadership in the schoolyard.

If he concealed his ingenuity, he concealed his hurts too. He was regarded as thick-skinned and insensitive—even cruel.

Aron drew love from every side. He seemed shy and delicate. His pink-and-white skin, golden hair, and wide-set blue eyes caught attention. In the schoolyard his very prettiness caused some difficulty until it was discovered by his testers that Aron was a dogged, steady, and completely fearless fighter, particularly when he was crying. Word got around, and the natural punishers of new boys learned to let him alone. Aron did not attempt to hide his disposition. It was concealed by being the opposite of his appearance. He was unchanging once a course was set. He had few facets and very little versatility. His body was as insensitive to pain as was his mind to subtleties.

Cal knew his brother and could handle him by keeping him off balance, but this only worked up to a certain point. Cal had learned when to sidestep, when to run away. Change of direction confused Aron, but that was the only thing that confused him. He set his path and followed it and he did not see nor was he interested in anything beside his path. His emotions were few and heavy. All of him was hidden by his angelic face, and for this he had no more concern or responsibility than has a fawn for the dappling spots on its young hide.

2

On Aron's first day in school he waited eagerly for the recess. He went over to the girlside to talk to Abra. A mob of squealing girls could not drive him out. It took a full-grown teacher to force him back to the boyside.

At noon he missed her, for her father came by in his high-wheeled buggy and drove her home for her lunch. He waited outside the schoolyard gate for her after school.

She came out surrounded by girls. Her face was composed and gave no sign that she expected him. She was far the prettiest girl in the school, but it is doubtful whether Aron had noticed that.

The cloud of girls hung on and hung on. Aron marched along three paces behind them, patient and unembarrassed even when the girls tossed their squealing barbs of insult over their shoulders at him. Gradually some drifted away to their own homes, and only three girls were with Abra when she came to the white gate of her yard and turned in. Her friends stared at him a moment, giggled, and went on their way.

Aron sat down on the edge of the sidewalk. After a moment the latch lifted, the white gate opened, and Abra emerged. She walked across the walk and stood over him. "What do you want?"

Aron's wide eyes looked up at her. "You aren't engaged to anybody?"

"Silly," she said.

He struggled up to his feet. "I guess it will be a long time before we can get married," he said.

"Who wants to get married?"

Aron didn't answer. Perhaps he didn't hear. He walked along beside her.

Abra moved with firm and deliberate steps and she faced straight ahead. There was wisdom and sweetness in her expression. She seemed deep in thought. And Aron, walking beside her, never took his eyes from her face. His attention seemed tied to her face by a taut string.

They walked silently past the Baby School, and there the pavement ended. Abra turned right and led the way through the stubble of the summer's hayfield. The black 'dobe clods crushed under their feet.

On the edge of the field stood a little pump house, and a willow tree flourished beside it, fed by the overspill of water. The long skirts of the willow hung down nearly to the ground.

Abra parted the switches like a curtain and went into the house of leaves made against the willow trunk by the sweeping branches. You could see out through the leaves, but inside it was sweetly protected and warm and safe. The afternoon sunlight came yellow through the aging leaves.

Abra sat down on the ground, or rather she seemed to drift down, and her full skirts settled in a billow around her. She folded her hands in her lap almost as though she were praying.

Aron sat down beside her. "I guess it will be a long time before we can get married," he said again.

"Not so long," Abra said.

"I wish it was now."

"It won't be so long," said Abra.

Aron asked, "Do you think your father will let you?"

It was a new thought to her, and she turned and looked at him. "Maybe I won't ask him."

"But your mother?"

"Let's not disturb them," she said. "They'd think it was funny or bad. Can't you keep a secret?"

"Oh, yes. I can keep secrets better than anybody. And I've got some too."

Abra said, "Well, you just put this one with the others."

Aron picked up a twig and drew a line on the dark earth. "Abra, do you know how you get babies?"

"Yes," she said. "Who told you?"

"Lee told me. He explained the whole thing. I guess we can't have any babies for a long time."

Abra's mouth turned up at the corners with a condescending wisdom. "Not so long," she said.

"We'll have a house together some time," Aron said, bemused. "We'll go in and close the door and it will be nice. But that will be a long time."

Abra put out her hand and touched him on the arm. "Don't you worry about long times," she said. "This is a kind of a house. We can play like we live here while we're waiting. And you will be my husband and you can call me wife."

He tried it over under his breath and then aloud. "Wife," he said.

"It'll be like practicing," said Abra.

Aron's arm shook under her hand, and she put it, palm up, in her lap.

Aron said suddenly, "While we're practicing, maybe we could do something else."

"What?"

"Maybe you wouldn't like it."

"What is it?"

"Maybe we could pretend like you're my mother."

"That's easy," she said.

"Would you mind?"

"No, I'd like it. Do you want to start now?"

"Sure," Aron said. "How do you want to go about it?"

"Oh, I can tell you that," said Abra. She put a cooing tone in her voice and said, "Come, my baby, put your head in Mother's lap. Come, my little son. Mother will hold you." She drew his head down, and without warning Aron began to cry and could not stop. He wept quietly, and Abra stroked his cheek and wiped the flowing tears away with the edge of her skirt.

The sun crept down toward its setting place behind the Salinas River, and a bird began to sing wonderfully from the golden stubble of the field. It was as beautiful under the branches of the willow tree as anything in the world can be.

Very slowly Aron's weeping stopped, and he felt good and he felt warm.

"My good little baby," Abra said. "Here, let Mother brush your hair back."

Aron sat up and said almost angrily, "I don't hardly ever cry unless I'm mad. I don't know why I cried."

Abra asked, "Do you remember your mother?"

"No. She died when I was a little bit of a baby."

"Don't you know what she looked like?"

"No."

"Maybe you saw a picture."

"No, I tell you. We don't have any pictures. I asked Lee and he said no pictures—no, I guess it was Cal asked Lee."

"When did she die?"

"Right after Cal and I were born."

"What was her name?"

"Lee says it was Cathy. Say, what you asking so much for?"

Abra went on calmly, "How was she complected?"

"What?"

"Light or dark hair?"

"I don't know."

"Didn't your father tell you?"

"We never asked him."

Abra was silent, and after a while Aron asked, "What's the matter—cat got your tongue?"

Abra inspected the setting sun.

Aron asked uneasily, "You mad with me"—and he added tentatively—"wife?"

"No, I'm not mad. I'm just wondering."

"What about?"

"About something." Abra's firm face was tight against a seething inner argument. She asked, "What's it like not to have any mother?"

"I don't know. It's like anything else."

"I guess you wouldn't even know the difference."

"I would too. I wish you would talk out. You're like riddles in the *Bulletin*."

Abra continued in her concentrated imperturbability, "Do you want to have a mother?"

"That's crazy," said Aron. " 'Course I do. Everybody does. You aren't trying to hurt my feelings, are you? Cal tries that sometimes and then he laughs."

Abra looked away from the setting sun. She had difficulty seeing past the purple spots the light had left on her eyes. "You said a little while ago you could keep secrets."

"I can."

"Well, do you have a double-poison-and-cut-my-throat secret?"

"Sure I have."

Abra said softly, "Tell me what it is, Aron." She put a caress in his name.

"Tell you what?"

"Tell me the deepest down hell-and-goddam secret you know."

Aron reared back from her in alarm. "Why, I will not," he said. "What right you got to ask me? I wouldn't tell anybody."

"Come on, my baby—tell Mother," she crooned.

There were tears crowding up in his eyes again, but this time they were tears of anger. "I don't know as I want to marry you," he said. "I think I'm going home now."

Abra put her hand on his wrist and hung on. Her voice lost its coquetry. "I wanted to see. I guess you can keep secrets all right."

"Why did you go for to do it? I'm mad now. I feel sick."

"I think I'm going to tell you a secret," she said.

"Ho!" he jeered at her. "Who can't keep a secret now?"

"I was trying to decide," she said. "I think I'm going to tell you this secret because it might be good for you. It might make you glad."

"Who told you not to tell?"

"Nobody," she said. "I only told myself."

"Well, I guess that's a little different. What's your old secret?"

The red sun leaned its rim on the rooftree of Tollot's house on the Blanco Road, and Tollot's chimney stuck up like a black thumb against it.

Abra said softly, "Listen, you remember when we came to your place that time?"

"Sure!"

"Well, in the buggy I went to sleep, and when I woke up my father and mother didn't know I was awake. They said your mother wasn't dead. They said she went away. They said something bad must have happened to her, and she went away."

Aron said hoarsely, "She's dead."

"Wouldn't it be nice if she wasn't?"

"My father says she's dead. He's not a liar."

"Maybe he thinks she's dead."

He said, "I think he'd know." But there was uncertainty in his tone.

Abra said, "Wouldn't it be nice if we could find her? 'Spose she lost her memory or something. I've read about that. And we could find her and that would make her remember." The glory of the romance caught her like a rip tide and carried her away.

Aron said, "I'll ask my father."

"Aron," she said sternly, "what I told you is a secret."

"Who says?"

"I say. Now you just say after me—'I'll take double poison and cut my throat if I tell.'"

For a moment he hesitated and then he repeated, "I'll take double poison and cut my throat if I tell."

She said, "Now spit in your palm—like this—that's right. Now you give me your hand—see?—squidge the spit all together. Now rub it dry on your hair." The two followed the formula, and then Abra said solemnly, "Now, I'd just like to see you tell that one. I knew one girl that told a secret after that oath and she burned up in a barn fire."

The sun was gone behind Tollot's house and the gold light with it. The evening star shimmered over Mount Toro.

Abra said, "They'll skin me alive. Come on. Hurry! I bet my father's got the dog whistle out for me. I'll get whipped."

Aron looked at her in disbelief. "Whipped! They don't whip you?"

"That's what you think!"

Aron said passionately, "You just let them try. If they go for to whip you, you tell them I'll kill them." His wide-set blue eyes were slitted and glinting. "Nobody's going to whip my wife," he said.

Abra put her arms around his neck in the dusk under the willow tree. She kissed him on his open mouth. "I love you, husband," she said, and then she turned and bolted, holding up her skirts above her knees, her lace-edged white drawers flashing as she ran toward home.

3

Aron went back to the trunk of the willow tree and sat on the ground and leaned back against the bark. His mind was a grayness and there were churnings of pain in his stomach. He tried to sort out the feeling into thoughts and pictures so the pain would go away. It was hard. His slow deliberate mind could not accept so many thoughts and emotions at once. The door was shut against everything except physical pain. After a while the door opened a little and let in one thing to be scrutinized and then another and another, until all had been absorbed, one at a time. Outside his closed mind a huge thing was clamoring to get in. Aron held it back until last.

First he let Abra in and went over her dress, her face, the feel of her hand on his cheek, the odor that came from her, like milk a little and like cut grass a little. He saw and felt and heard and smelled her all over again. He thought how clean she was, her hands and fingernails, and how straightforward and unlike the gigglers in the schoolyard.

Then, in order, he thought of her holding his head and his baby crying, crying with longing, wanting something and in a way feeling that he was getting it. Perhaps the getting it was what had made him cry.

Next he thought of her trick—her testing of him. He wondered what she would have done if he had told her a secret. What secret could he have told her if he had wished? Right now he didn't recall any secret except the one that was beating on the door to get into his mind.

The sharpest question she had asked, "How does it feel not to have a mother?" slipped into his mind. And how did it feel? It didn't feel like anything. Ah, but in the schoolroom, at Christmas and graduation, when the mothers of other children came to the parties—then was the silent cry and the wordless longing. That's what it was like.

Salinas was surrounded and penetrated with swamps, with tule-filled ponds, and every pond spawned thousands of frogs. With the evening the air was so full of their song that it was a kind of roaring silence. It was a veil, a background, and its sudden disappearance, as after a clap of thunder, was a shocking thing. It is possible that if in the night the frog sound should have stopped, everyone in Salinas would have awakened, feeling that there was a great noise. In their millions the frog songs seemed to have a beat and a cadence, and perhaps it is the ears' function to do this just as it is the eyes' business to make stars twinkle.

It was quite dark under the willow tree now. Aron wondered whether he was ready for the big thing, and while he wondered it slipped through and was in.

His mother was alive. Often he had pictured her lying underground, still and cool and unrotted. But this was not so. Somewhere she moved about and spoke, and her hands moved and her eyes were open. And in the midst of his flood of pleasure a sorrow came down on him and a sense of loss, of dreadful loss. Aron was puzzled. He inspected the cloud of sadness. If his mother was alive, his father was a liar. If one was alive, the other was dead. Aron said aloud under the tree, "My mother is dead. She's buried some place in the East."

In the darkness he saw Lee's face and heard Lee's soft speech. Lee had built very well. Having a respect that amounted to reverence for the truth, he had also its natural opposite, a loathing of a lie. He had made it very clear to the boys exactly what he meant. If something was untrue and you didn't know it, that was error. But if you knew a true thing and changed it to a false thing, both you and it were loathsome.

Lee's voice said, "I know that sometimes a lie is used in kindness. I don't believe it ever works kindly. The quick pain of truth can pass away, but the slow, eating agony of a lie is never lost. That's a running sore." And Lee had worked patiently and slowly and he had succeeded in building Adam as the center, the foundation, the essence of truth.

Aron shook his head in the dark, shook it hard in disbelief. "If my father is a liar, Lee is a liar too." He was lost. He had no one to ask. Cal was a liar, but Lee's conviction had made Cal a clever liar. Aron felt that something had to die—his mother or his world.

His solution lay suddenly before him. Abra had not lied. She had told him only what she had heard, and her parents had only heard it too. He got to his feet and pushed his mother back into death and closed his mind against her.

He was late for supper. "I was with Abra," he explained. After supper, when Adam sat in his new comfortable chair, reading the *Salinas Index*, he felt a stroking touch on his shoulder and looked up. "What is it, Aron?" he asked.

"Good night, Father," Aron said.

THIRTY-SEVEN

February in Salinas is likely to be damp and cold and full of miseries. The heaviest rains fall then, and if the river is going to rise, it rises then. February of 1915 was a year heavy with water.

The Trasks were well established in Salinas. Lee, once he had given up his brackish bookish dream, made a new kind of place for himself in the house beside Reynaud's Bakery. On the ranch his possessions had never really been unpacked, for Lee had lived poised to go someplace else. Here, for the first time in his life, he built a home for himself, feathered with comfort and permanence.

The large bedroom nearest the street door fell to him. Lee dipped into his savings. He had never before spent a needless penny, since all money had been earmarked for his bookstore. But now he bought a little hard bed and a desk. He built bookshelves and unpacked his books, invested in a soft rug and tacked prints on the walls. He placed a deep and comfortable Morris chair under the best reading lamp he could find. And last he bought a typewriter and set about learning to use it.

Having broken out of his own Spartanism, he remade the Trask household, and Adam gave him no opposition. A gas stove came into the house and electric wires and a telephone. He spent Adam's money remorselessly—new furniture, new carpets, a gas water-heater, and a large icebox. In a short time there was hardly a house in Salinas so well equipped. Lee defended himself to Adam, saying, "You have plenty of money. It would be a shame not to enjoy it."

"I'm not complaining," Adam protested. "Only I'd like to buy something too. What shall I buy?"

"Why don't you go to Logan's music store and listen to one of the new phonographs?"

"I think I'll do that," said Adam. And he bought a Victor victrola, a tall Gothic instrument, and he went regularly to see what new records had come in.

The growing century was shucking Adam out of his shell. He subscribed to the *Atlantic Monthly* and the *National Geographic*. He joined the Masons and seriously considered the Elks. The new icebox fascinated him. He bought a textbook on refrigeration and began to study it.

The truth was that Adam needed work. He came out of his long sleep needing to do something.

"I think I'll go into business," he said to Lee.

"You don't need to. You have enough to live on."

"But I'd like to be doing something."

"That's different," said Lee. "Know what you want to do? I don't think you'd be very good at business."

"Why not?"

"Just a thought," said Lee.

"Say, Lee, I want you to read an article. It says they've dug up a mastodon in Siberia. Been in the ice thousands of years. And the meat's still good."

Lee smiled at him. "You've got a bug in your bonnet somewhere," he said. "What have you got in all of those little cups in the icebox?"

"Different things."

"Is that the business? Some of the cups smell bad."

"It's an idea," Adam said. "I can't seem to stay away from it. I just can't seem to get over the idea that you can keep things if you get them cold enough."

"Let's not have any mastodon meat in our icebox," said Lee.

If Adam had conceived thousands of ideas, the way Sam Hamilton had, they might all have drifted away, but he had only the one. The frozen mastodon stayed in his mind. His little cups of fruit, of pudding, of bits of meat, both cooked and raw, continued in the icebox. He bought every available book on bacteria and began sending for magazines that printed articles of a mildly scientific nature. And as is usually true of a man of one idea, he became obsessed.

Salinas had a small ice company, not large but enough to supply the few houses with iceboxes and to service the ice-cream parlors. The horse-drawn ice wagon went its route every day.

Adam began to visit the ice plant, and pretty soon he was taking his little cups to the freezing chambers. He wished with all his heart that Sam Hamilton were alive to discuss cold with him. Sam would have covered the field very quickly, he thought.

Adam was walking back from the ice plant one rainy afternoon, thinking about Sam Hamilton, when he saw Will Hamilton go into the Abbot House

Bar. He followed him and leaned against the bar beside him. "Why don
you come up and have some supper with us?"

"I'd like to," Will said. "I'll tell you what—I've got a deal I'm trying
put through. If I get finished in time I'll walk by. Is there something in
portant?"

"Well, I don't know. I've been doing some thinking and I'd like to as
your advice."

Nearly every business proposition in the county came sooner or later t
Will Hamilton's attention. He might have excused himself if he had nc
remembered that Adam was a rich man. An idea was one thing, but backe
up with cash it was quite another. "You wouldn't entertain a reasonabl
offer for your ranch, would you?" he asked.

"Well, the boys, particularly Cal, they like the place. I think I'll hang o:
to it."

"I think I can turn it over for you."

"No, it's rented, paying its own taxes. I'll hold on to it."

"If I can't get in for supper I might be able to come in afterward," saic
Will.

Will Hamilton was a very substantial businessman. No one knew exactl
how many pies his thumb had explored, but it was known that he was a
clever and comparatively rich man. His business deal had been non-existent
It was a part of his policy always to be busy and occupied.

He had supper alone in the Abbot House. After a considered time he
walked around the corner on Central Avenue and rang the bell of Adam
Trask's house.

The boys had gone to bed. Lee sat with a darning basket, mending the
long black stockings the twins wore to school. Adam had been reading the
Scientific American. He let Will in and placed a chair for him. Lee brought
a pot of coffee and went back to his mending.

Will settled himself into a chair, took out a fat black cigar, and lighted
up. He waited for Adam to open the game.

"Nice weather for a change. And how's your mother?" Adam said.

"Just fine. Seems younger every day. The boys must be growing up."

"Oh, they are. Cal's going to be in his school play. He's quite an actor.
Aron's a real good student. Cal wants to go to farming."

"Nothing wrong with that if you go about it right. Country could use
some forward-looking farmers." Will waited uneasily. He wondered if it
could be that Adam's money was exaggerated. Could Adam be getting ready
to borrow money? Will quickly worked out how much he would lend on the
Trask ranch and how much he could borrow on it. The figures were not the
same, nor was the interest rate. And still Adam did not come up with his
proposition. Will grew restless. "I can't stay very long," he said. "Told a fellow I'd meet him later tonight."

"Have another cup of coffee," Adam suggested.

"No, thanks. Keeps me awake. Did you have something you wanted to see me about?"

Adam said, "I was thinking about your father and I thought I'd like to talk to a Hamilton."

Will relaxed a little in his chair. "He was a great old talker."

"Somehow he made a man better than he was," said Adam.

Lee looked up from his darning egg. "Perhaps the best conversationalist in the world is the man who helps others to talk."

Will said, "You know, it sounds funny to hear you use all those two-bit words. I'd swear to God you used to talk pidgin."

"I used to," said Lee. "It was vanity, I guess." He smiled at Adam and said to Will, "Did you hear that somewhere up in Siberia they dug a mastodon out of the ice? It had been there a hundred thousand years and the meat was still fresh."

"Mastodon?"

"Yes, a kind of elephant that hasn't lived on the earth for a long time."

"Meat was still fresh?"

"Sweet as a pork chop," said Lee. He shoved the wooden egg into the shattered knee of a black stocking.

"That's very interesting," said Will.

Adam laughed. "Lee hasn't wiped my nose yet, but that will come," he said. "I guess I'm pretty roundabout. The whole thing comes up because I'm tired of just sitting around. I want to get something to take up my time."

"Why don't you farm your place?"

"No. That doesn't interest me. You see, Will, I'm not like a man looking for a job. I'm looking for work. I don't need a job."

Will came out of his cautiousness. "Well, what can I do for you?"

"I thought I'd tell you an idea I had, and you might give me an opinion. You're a businessman."

"Of course," said Will. "Anything I can do."

"I've been looking into refrigeration," said Adam. "I got an idea and I can't get rid of it. I go to sleep and it comes right back at me. Never had anything give me so much trouble. It's a kind of a big idea. Maybe it's full of holes."

Will uncrossed his legs and pulled at his pants where they were binding him. "Go ahead—shoot," he said. "Like a cigar?"

Adam didn't hear the offer, nor did he know the implication. "The whole country's changing," Adam said. "People aren't going to live the way they used to. Do you know where the biggest market for oranges in the winter is?"

"No. Where?"

"New York City. I read that. Now in the cold parts of the country, don't you think people get to wanting perishable things in the winter—like peas and lettuce and cauliflower? In a big part of the country they don't have those things for months and months. And right here in the Salinas Valley we can raise them all the year round."

"Right here isn't right there," said Will. "What's your idea?"

"Well, Lee made me get a big icebox, and I got kind of interested. I put different kinds of vegetables in there. And I got to arranging them different ways. You know, Will, if you chop ice fine and lay a head of lettuce in it and wrap it in waxed paper, it will keep three weeks and come out fresh and good."

"Go on," said Will cautiously.

"Well, you know the railroads built those fruit cars. I went down and had a look at them. They're pretty good. Do you know we could ship lettuce right to the east coast in the middle of winter?"

Will asked, "Where do you come in?"

"I was thinking of buying the ice plant here in Salinas and trying to ship some things."

"That would cost a lot of money."

"I have quite a lot of money," said Adam.

Will Hamilton pulled his lip angrily. "I don't know why I got into this," he said. "I know better."

"How do you mean?"

"Look here," said Will. "When a man comes to me for advice about an idea, I know he doesn't want advice. He wants me to agree with him. And if I want to keep his friendship I tell him his idea is fine and go ahead. But I like you and you're a friend of my family, so I'm going to stick my neck out."

Lee put down his darning, moved his sewing basket to the floor, and changed his glasses.

Adam remonstrated, "What are you getting upset about?"

"I come from a whole goddam family of inventors," said Will. "We had ideas for breakfast. We had ideas instead of breakfast. We had so many ideas we forgot to make the money for groceries. When we got a little ahead my father, or Tom, patented something. I'm the only one in the family, except my mother, who didn't have ideas, and I'm the only one who ever made a dime. Tom had ideas about helping people, and some of it was pretty darn near socialism. And if you tell me you don't care about making a profit, I'm going to throw that coffee pot right at your head."

"Well, I don't care much."

"You stop right there, Adam. I've got my neck out. If you want to drop forty or fifty thousand dollars quick, you just go on with your idea. But I'm telling you—let your damned idea die. Kick dust over it."

"What's wrong with it?"

"Everything's wrong with it. People in the East aren't used to vegetables in the winter. They wouldn't buy them. You get your cars stuck on a siding

d you'll lose the shipment. The market is controlled. Oh, Jesus Christ! It
akes me mad when babies try to ride into business on an idea."

Adam sighed. "You make Sam Hamilton sound like a criminal," he said.

"Well, he was my father and I loved him, but I wish to God he had let
deas alone." Will looked at Adam and saw amazement in his eyes, and
iddenly Will was ashamed. He shook his head slowly from side to side. "I
idn't mean to run down my people," he said. "I think they were good
eople. But my advice to you stands. Let refrigeration alone."

Adam turned slowly to Lee. "Have we got any more of that lemon pie
ve had for supper?" he asked.

"I don't think so," said Lee. "I thought I heard mice in the kitchen.
'm afraid there will be white of egg on the boys' pillows. You've got half a
uart of whisky."

"Have I? Why don't we have that?"

"I got excited," said Will, and he tried to laugh at himself. "A drink
vould do me good." His face was fiery red and his voice was strained in his
hroat. "I'm getting too fat," he said.

But he had two drinks and relaxed. Sitting comfortably, he instructed
Adam. "Some things don't ever change their value," he said. "If you want
:o put money into something, you look around at the world. This war in Europe is going to go on a long time. And when there's war there's going to be
hungry people. I won't say it is so, but it wouldn't surprise me if we got into
it. I don't trust this Wilson—he's all theory and big words. And if we do get
into it, there's going to be fortunes made in imperishable foods. You take
rice and corn and wheat and beans, they don't need ice. They keep, and people can stay alive on them. I'd say if you were to plant your whole damned
bottom land to beans and just put them away, why, your boys wouldn't
have to worry about the future. Beans are up to three cents now. If we get
into the war I wouldn't be surprised if they went to ten cents. And you keep
beans dry and they'll be right there, waiting for a market. If you want to turn
a profit, you plant beans."

He went away feeling good. The shame that had come over him was gone
and he knew he had given sound advice.

After Will had gone Lee brought out one-third of a lemon pie and cut it
in two. "He's getting too fat," Lee said.

Adam was thinking. "I only said I wanted something to do," he observed.

"How about the ice plant?"

"I think I'll buy it."

"You might plant some beans too," said Lee.

2

Late in the year Adam made his great try, and it was a sensation in a year
of sensations, both local and international. As he got ready, businessmen

spoke of him as farseeing, forward-looking, progress-minded. The departur
of six carloads of lettuce packed in ice was given a civic overtone. The Cham
ber of Commerce attended the departure. The cars were decorated with bi
posters which said, "Salinas Valley Lettuce." But no one wanted to inves
in the project.

Adam untapped energy he did not suspect he had. It was a big job t
gather, trim, box, ice, and load the lettuce. There was no equipment fo
such work. Everything had to be improvised, a great many hands hired anc
taught to do the work. Everyone gave advice but no one helped. It was esti
mated that Adam had spent a fortune on his idea, but how big a fortune nc
one knew. Adam did not know. Only Lee knew.

The idea looked good. The lettuce was consigned to commission mer
chants in New York at a fine price. Then the train was gone and everyone
went home to wait. If it was a success any number of men were willing to
dig down to put money in. Even Will Hamilton wondered whether he had
not been wrong with his advice.

If the series of events had been planned by an omnipotent and unfor
giving enemy it could not have been more effective. As the train came to
Sacramento a snow slide closed the Sierras for two days and the six cars
stood on a siding, dripping their ice away. On the third day the freight
crossed the mountains, and that was the time for unseasonable warm weather
throughout the Middle West. In Chicago there developed a confusion of
orders—no one's fault—just one of those things that happen, and Adam's six
cars of lettuce stood in the yard for five more days. That was enough, and
there is no reason to go into it in detail. What arrived in New York was six
carloads of horrible slop with a sizable charge just to get rid of it.

Adam read the telegram from the commission house and he settled back
in his chair and a strange enduring smile came on his face and did not go
away.

Lee kept away from him to let him get a grip on himself. The boys heard
the reaction in Salinas. Adam was a fool. These know-it-all dreamers always
got into trouble. Businessmen congratulated themselves on their foresight in
keeping out of it. It took experience to be a businessman. People who in
herited their money always got into trouble. And if you wanted any proof—
just look at how Adam had run his ranch. A fool and his money were soon
parted. Maybe that would teach him a lesson. And he had doubled the out
put of the ice company.

Will Hamilton recalled that he had not only argued against it but had
foretold in detail what would happen. He did not feel pleasure, but what
could you do when a man wouldn't take advice from a sound businessman?
And, God knows, Will had plenty of experience with fly-by-night ideas. In a
roundabout way it was recalled that Sam Hamilton had been a fool too.
And as for Tom Hamilton—he had been just crazy.

When Lee felt that enough time had passed he did not beat around the bush. He sat directly in front of Adam to get and to keep his attention.

"How do you feel?" he asked.

"All right."

"You aren't going to crawl back in your hole, are you?"

"What makes you think that?" Adam asked.

"Well, you have the look on your face you used to wear. And you've got that sleepwalker light in your eyes. Does this hurt your feelings?"

"No," said Adam. "The only thing I was wondering about was whether I'm wiped out."

"Not quite," said Lee. "You have about nine thousand dollars left and the ranch."

"There's a two-thousand-dollar bill for garbage disposal," said Adam.

"That's before the nine thousand."

"I owe quite a bit for the new ice machinery."

"That's paid."

"I have nine thousand?"

"And the ranch," said Lee. "Maybe you can sell the ice plant."

Adam's face tightened up and lost the dazed smile. "I still believe it will work," he said. "It was a whole lot of accidents. I'm going to keep the ice plant. Cold does preserve things. Besides, the plant makes some money. Maybe I can figure something out."

"Try not to figure something that costs money," said Lee. "I would hate to leave my gas stove."

3

The twins felt Adam's failure very deeply. They were fifteen years old and they had known so long that they were sons of a wealthy man that the feeling was hard to lose. If only the affair had not been a kind of carnival it would not have been so bad. They remembered the big placards on the freight cars with horror. If the businessmen made fun of Adam, the high-school group was much more cruel. Overnight it became the thing to refer to the boys as "Aron and Cal Lettuce," or simply as "Lettuce-head."

Aron discussed his problem with Abra. "It's going to make a big difference," he told her.

Abra had grown to be a beautiful girl. Her breasts were rising with the leaven of her years, and her face had the calm and warmth of beauty. She had gone beyond prettiness. She was strong and sure and feminine.

She looked at his worried face and asked, "Why is it going to make a difference?"

"Well, one thing, I think we're poor."

"You would have worked anyway."

"You know I want to go to college."

"You still can. I'll help you. Did your father lose all his money?"

"I don't know. That's what they say."

"Who is 'they'?" Abra asked.

"Why, everybody. And maybe your father and mother won't want you to marry me."

"Then I won't tell them about it," said Abra.

"You're pretty sure of yourself."

"Yes," she said, "I'm pretty sure of myself. Will you kiss me?"

"Right here? Right in the street?"

"Why not?"

"Everybody'd see."

"I want them to," said Abra.

Aron said, "No. I don't like to make things public like that."

She stepped around in front of him and stopped him. "You look here, mister. You kiss me now."

"Why?"

She said slowly, "So everybody will know that I'm Mrs. Lettuce-head."

He gave her a quick embarrassed peck and then forced her beside him again. "Maybe I ought to call it off myself," he said.

"What do you mean?"

"Well, I'm not good enough for you now. I'm just another poor kid. You think I haven't seen the difference in your father?"

"You're just crazy," Abra said. And she frowned a little because she had seen the difference in her father too.

They went into Bell's candy store and sat at a table. The rage was celery tonic that year. The year before it had been root-beer ice-cream sodas.

Abra stirred bubbles delicately with her straw and thought how her father had changed since the lettuce failure. He had said to her, "Don't you think it would be wise to see someone else for a change?"

"But I'm engaged to Aron."

"Engaged!" he snorted at her. "Since when do children get engaged? You'd better look around a little. There are other fish in the sea."

And she remembered that recently there had been references to suitability of families and once a hint that some people couldn't keep a scandal hidden forever. This had happened only when Adam was reputed to have lost all of his money.

She leaned across the table. "You know what we could really do is so simple it will make you laugh."

"What?"

"We could run your father's ranch. My father says it's beautiful land."

"No," Aron said quickly.

"Why not?"

"I'm not going to be a farmer and you're not going to be a farmer's wife."

"I'm going to be Aron's wife, no matter what he is."

"I'm not going to give up college," he said.

"I'll help you," Abra said again.

"Where would you get the money?"

"Steal it," she said.

"I want to get out of this town," he said. "Everybody's sneering at me. I can't stand it here."

"They'll forget it pretty soon."

"No, they won't either. I don't want to stay two years more to finish high school."

"Do you want to go away from me, Aron?"

"No. Oh, damn it, why did he have to mess with things he doesn't know about?"

Abra reproved him. "Don't you blame your father. If it had worked everybody'd been bowing to him."

"Well, it didn't work. He sure fixed me. I can't hold up my head. By God! I hate him."

Abra said sternly, "Aron! You stop talking like that!"

"How do I know he didn't lie about my mother?"

Abra's face reddened with anger. "You ought to be spanked," she said. "If it wasn't in front of everybody I'd spank you myself." She looked at his beautiful face, twisted now with rage and frustration, and suddenly she changed her tactics. "Why don't you ask about your mother? Just come right out and ask him."

"I can't, I promised you."

"You only promised not to say what I told you."

"Well, if I asked him he'd want to know where I heard."

"All right," she cried, "you're a spoiled baby! I let you out of your promise. Go ahead and ask him."

"I don't know if I will or not."

"Sometimes I want to kill you," she said. "But, Aron—I do love you so. I do love you so." There was giggling from the stools in front of the soda fountain. Their voices had risen and they were overheard by their peers. Aron blushed and tears of anger started in his eyes. He ran out of the store and plunged away up the street.

Abra calmly picked up her purse and straightened her skirt and brushed it with her hand. She walked calmly over to Mr. Bell and paid for the celery tonics. On her way to the door she stopped by the giggling group. "You let him alone," she said coldly. She walked on, and a falsetto followed her—"Oh, Aron, I do love you so."

In the street she broke into a run to try to catch up with Aron, but she couldn't find him. She called on the telephone. Lee said that Aron had not come home. But Aron was in his bedroom, lapped in resentments—Lee had seen him creep in and close his door behind him.

Abra walked up and down the streets of Salinas, hoping to catch sight of him. She was angry at him, but she was also bewilderingly lonely. Aron hadn't ever run away from her before. Abra had lost her gift for being alone.

Cal had to learn loneliness. For a very short time he tried to join Abra and Aron, but they didn't want him. He was jealous and tried to attract the girl to himself and failed.

His studies he found easy and not greatly interesting. Aron had to work harder to learn, wherefore Aron had a greater sense of accomplishment when he did learn, and he developed a respect for learning out of all proportion to the quality of the learning. Cal drifted through. He didn't care much for the sports at school or for the activities. His growing restlessness drove him out at night. He grew tall and rangy, and always there was the darkness about him.

THIRTY-EIGHT

From his first memory Cal had craved warmth and affection, just as everyone does. If he had been an only child or if Aron had been a different kind of boy, Cal might have achieved his relationship normally and easily. But from the very first people were won instantly to Aron by his beauty and his simplicity. Cal very naturally competed for attention and affection in the only way he knew—by trying to imitate Aron. And what was charming in the blond ingenuousness of Aron became suspicious and unpleasant in the dark-faced, slit-eyed Cal. And since he was pretending, his performance was not convincing. Where Aron was received, Cal was rebuffed for doing or saying exactly the same thing.

And as a few strokes on the nose will make a puppy head shy, so a few rebuffs will make a boy shy all over. But whereas a puppy will cringe away or roll on its back, groveling, a little boy may cover his shyness with nonchalance, with bravado, or with secrecy. And once a boy has suffered rejection, he will find rejection even where it does not exist—or, worse, will draw it forth from people simply by expecting it.

In Cal the process had been so long and so slow that he felt no strangeness. He had built a wall of self-sufficiency around himself, strong enough to defend him against the world. If his wall had any weak places they may have been on the sides nearest Aron and Lee, and particularly nearest Adam. Perhaps in his father's very unawareness Cal had felt safety. Not being noticed at all was better than being noticed adversely.

When he was quite small Cal had discovered a secret. If he moved very quietly to where his father was sitting and if he leaned very lightly against his father's knee, Adam's hand would rise automatically and his fingers would caress Cal's shoulder. It is probable that Adam did not even know he did it, but the caress brought such a raging flood of emotion to the boy that he saved this special joy and used it only when he needed it. It was a magic to be depended upon. It was the ceremonial symbol of a dogged adoration.

Things do not change with a change of scene. In Salinas, Cal had no more friends than he had in King City. Associates he had, and authority and some admiration, but friends he did not have. He lived alone and walked alone.

2

If Lee knew that Cal left the house at night and returned very late, he gave no sign, since he couldn't do anything about it. The night constables sometimes saw him walking alone. Chief Heiserman made it a point to speak to the truant officer, who assured him that Cal not only had no record for playing hooky but actually was a very good student. The chief knew Adam of course, and since Cal broke no windows and caused no disturbance he told the constables to keep their eyes open but to let the boy alone unless he got into trouble.

Old Tom Watson caught up with Cal one night and asked, "Why do you walk around so much at night?"

"I'm not bothering anybody," said Cal defensively.

"I know you're not. But you ought to be home in bed."

"I'm not sleepy," said Cal, and this didn't make any sense at all to Old Tom, who couldn't remember any time in his whole life when he wasn't sleepy. The boy looked in on the fan-tan games in Chinatown, but he didn't play. It was a mystery, but then fairly simple things were mysteries to Tom Watson and he preferred to leave them that way.

On his walks Cal often recalled the conversation between Lee and Adam he had heard on the ranch. He wanted to dig out the truth. And his knowledge accumulated slowly, a reference heard in the street, the gibing talk in the pool hall. If Aron had heard the fragments he would not have noticed, but Cal collected them. He knew that his mother was not dead. He knew also, both from the first conversation and from the talk he heard, that Aron was not likely to be pleased at discovering her.

One night Cal ran into Rabbit Holman, who was up from San Ardo on his semi-annual drunk. Rabbit greeted Cal effusively, as a country man always greets an acquaintance in a strange place. Rabbit, drinking from a pint flask in the alley behind the Abbot House, told Cal all the news he could think of. He had sold a piece of his land at a fine price and he was in Salinas to celebrate, and celebration meant the whole shebang. He was going down the Line and show the whores what a real man could do.

Cal sat quietly beside him, listening. When the whisky got low in Rabbit's pint Cal slipped away and got Louis Schneider to buy him another one. And Rabbit put down his empty pint and reached for it again and came up with a full pint.

"Funny," he said, "thought I only had one. Well, it's a good mistake."

Halfway down the second pint Rabbit had not only forgotten who Cal was but how old he was. He remembered, however, that his companion was his very dear old friend.

"Tell you what, George," he said. "You let me get a little more of this here lead in my pencil and you and me will go down the Line. Now don't say you can't afford it. The whole shebang's on me. Did I tell you I sold forty acres? Wasn't no good neither."

And he said, "Harry, tell you what let's do. Let's keep away from them two-bit whores. We'll go to Kate's place. Costs high, ten bucks, but what the hell! They got a circus down there. Ever seen a circus, Harry? Well, it's a lulu. Kate sure knows her stuff. You remember who Kate is, don't you, George? She's Adam Trask's wife, mother of them damn twins. Jesus! I never forget the time she shot him and ran away. Plugged him in the shoulder and just run off. Well, she wasn't no good as a wife but she's sure as hell a good whore. Funny too—you know how they say a whore makes a good wife? Ain't nothing new for them to experiment with. Help me up a little, will you, Harry? What was I saying?"

"Circus," said Cal softly.

"Oh, yeah. Well, this circus of Kate's will pop your eyes out. Know what they do?"

Cal walked a little behind so that Rabbit would not notice him. Rabbit told what they did. And what they did wasn't what made Cal sick. That just seemed to him silly. It was the men who watched. Seeing Rabbit's face under the streetlights, Cal knew what the watchers at the circus would look like.

They went through the overgrown yard and up on the unpainted porch. Although Cal was tall for his age he walked high on his toes. The guardian of the door didn't look at him very closely. The dim room with its low secret lamps and the nervous waiting men concealed his presence.

3

Always before, Cal had wanted to build a dark accumulation of things seen and things heard—a kind of a warehouse of materials that, like obscure tools, might come in handy, but after the visit to Kate's he felt a desperate need for help.

One night Lee, tapping away at his typewriter, heard a quiet knock on his door and let Cal in. The boy sat down on the edge of the bed, and Lee let his thin body down in the Morris chair. He was amused that a chair could give him so much pleasure. Lee folded his hands over his stomach as though he wore Chinese sleeves and waited patiently. Cal was looking at a spot in the air right over Lee's head.

Cal spoke softly and rapidly. "I know where my mother is and what she's doing. I saw her."

Lee's mind said a convulsive prayer for guidance. "What do you want to know?" he asked softly.

"I haven't thought yet. I'm trying to think. Would you tell me the truth?"

"Of course."

The questions whirling in Cal's head were so bewildering he had trouble picking one out. "Does my father know?"

"Yes."

"Why did he say she was dead?"

"To save you from pain."

Cal considered. "What did my father do to make her leave?"

"He loved her with his whole mind and body. He gave her everything he could imagine."

"Did she shoot him?"

"Yes."

"Why?"

"Because he didn't want her to go away."

"Did he ever hurt her?"

"Not that I know of. It wasn't in him to hurt her."

"Lee, why did she do it?"

"I don't know."

"Don't know or won't say?"

"Don't know."

Cal was silent for so long that Lee's fingers began to creep a little, holding to his wrists. He was relieved when Cal spoke again. The boy's tone was different. There was a pleading in it.

"Lee, you knew her. What was she like?"

Lee sighed and his hands relaxed. "I can only say what I think. I may be wrong."

"Well, what did you think?"

"Cal," he said, "I've thought about it for a great many hours and I still don't know. She is a mystery. It seems to me that she is not like other people. There is something she lacks. Kindness maybe, or conscience. You can only understand people if you feel them in yourself. And I can't feel her. The moment I think about her my feeling goes into darkness. I don't know what she wanted or what she was after. She was full of hatred, but why or toward what I don't know. It's a mystery. And her hatred wasn't healthy. It wasn't angry. It was heartless. I don't know that it is good to talk to you like this."

"I need to know."

"Why? Didn't you feel better before you knew?"

"Yes. But I can't stop now."

"You're right," said Lee. "When the first innocence goes, you can't stop—unless you're a hypocrite or a fool. But I can't tell you any more because I don't know any more."

Cal said, "Tell me about my father then."

"That I can do," said Lee. He paused. "I wonder if anyone can hear us talking? Speak softly."

"Tell me about him," said Cal.

"I think your father has in him, magnified, the things his wife lacks. I think in him kindness and conscience are so large that they are almost faults. They trip him up and hinder him."

"What did he do when she left?"

"He died," said Lee. "He walked around but he was dead. And only recently has he come half to life again." Lee saw a strange new expression on Cal's face. The eyes were open wider, and the mouth, ordinarily tight and muscular, was relaxed. In his face, now for the first time, Lee could see Aron's face in spite of the different coloring. Cal's shoulders were shaking a little, like a muscle too long held under a strain.

"What is it, Cal?" Lee asked.

"I love him," Cal said.

"I love him too," said Lee. "I guess I couldn't have stayed around so long if I hadn't. He is not smart in a worldly sense but he's a good man. Maybe the best man I have ever known."

Cal stood up suddenly. "Good night, Lee," he said.

"Now you wait just a moment. Have you told anyone?"

"No."

"Not Aron—no, of course you wouldn't."

"Suppose he finds out?"

"Then you'd have to stand by to help him. Don't go yet. When you leave this room we may not be able to talk again. You may dislike me for knowing you know the truth. Tell me this—do you hate your mother?"

"Yes," said Cal.

"I wondered," said Lee. "I don't think your father ever hated her. He had only sorrow."

Cal drifted toward the door, slowly, softly. He shoved his fists deep in his pockets. "It's like you said about knowing people. I hate her because I know why she went away. I know—because I've got her in me." His head was down and his voice was heartbroken.

Lee jumped up. "You stop that!" he said sharply. "You hear me? Don't let me catch you doing that. Of course you may have that in you. Everybody has. But you've got the other too. Here—look up! Look at me!"

Cal raised his head and said wearily, "What do you want?"

"You've got the other too. Listen to me! You wouldn't even be wondering if you didn't have it. Don't you dare take the lazy way. It's too easy to excuse yourself because of your ancestry. Don't let me catch you doing it! Now—look close at me so you will remember. Whatever you do, it will be you who do it—not your mother."

"Do you believe that, Lee?"

"Yes, I believe it, and you'd better believe it or I'll break every bone in your body."

After Cal had gone Lee went back to his chair. He thought ruefully, I wonder what happened to my Oriental repose?

4

Cal's discovery of his mother was more a verification than a new thing to him. For a long time he had known without details that the cloud was there. And his reaction was twofold. He had an almost pleasant sense of power in knowing, and he could evaluate actions and expressions, could interpret vague references, could even dip up and reorganize the past. But these did not compensate for the pain in his knowledge.

His body was rearranging itself toward manhood, and he was shaken by the veering winds of adolescence. One moment he was dedicated and pure and devoted; the next he wallowed in filth; and the next he groveled in shame and emerged rededicated.

His discovery sharpened all of his emotions. It seemed to him that he was unique, having such a heritage. He could not quite believe Lee's words or conceive that other boys were going through the same thing.

The circus at Kate's remained with him. At one moment the memory inflamed his mind and body with pubescent fire, and the next moment nauseated him with revulsion and loathing.

He looked at his father more closely and saw perhaps more sadness and frustration in Adam than may have been there. And in Cal there grew up a passionate love for his father and a wish to protect him and to make it up to him for the things he had suffered. In Cal's own sensitized mind that suffering was unbearable. He blundered into the bathroom while Adam was bathing and saw the ugly bullet scar and heard himself ask against his will, "Father, what's that scar?"

Adam's fingers went up as though to conceal the scar. He said, "It's an old wound, Cal. I was in the Indian campaigns. I'll tell you about it some time."

Cal, watching Adam's face, had seen his mind leap into the past for a lie. Cal didn't hate the lie but the necessity for telling it. Cal lied for reasons of profit of one kind or another. To be driven to a lie seemed shameful to him. He wanted to shout, "I know how you got it and it's all right." But, of course, he did not. "I'd like to hear about it," he said.

Aron was caught in the roil of change too, but his impulses were more sluggish than Cal's. His body did not scream at him so shrilly. His passions took a religious direction. He decided on the ministry for his future. He attended all services in the Episcopal church, helped with the flowers and leaves at feast times, and spent many hours with the young and curly-haired clergyman, Mr. Rolf. Aron's training in worldliness was gained from a young man of no experience, which gave him the ability for generalization only the inexperienced can have.

Aron was confirmed in the Episcopal church and took his place in the choir on Sundays. Abra followed him. Her feminine mind knew that such things were necessary but unimportant.

It was natural that the convert Aron should work on Cal. First Aron prayed silently for Cal, but finally he approached him. He denounced Cal's godlessness, demanded his reformation.

Cal might have tried to go along if his brother had been more clever. But Aron had reached a point of passionate purity that made everyone else foul. After a few lectures Cal found him unbearably smug and told him so. It was a relief to both of them when Aron abandoned his brother to eternal damnation.

Aron's religion inevitably took a sexual turn. He spoke to Abra of the necessity for abstinence and decided that he would live a life of celibacy. Abra in her wisdom agreed with him, feeling and hoping that this phase would pass. Celibacy was the only state she had known. She wanted to marry Aron and bear any number of his children, but for the time being she did not speak of it. She had never been jealous before, but now she began to find in herself an instinctive and perhaps justified hatred of the Reverend Mr. Rolf.

Cal watched his brother triumph over sins he had never committed. He thought sardonically of telling him about his mother, to see how he would handle it, but he withdrew the thought quickly. He didn't think Aron could handle it at all.

THIRTY-NINE

At intervals Salinas suffered from a mild eructation of morality. The process never varied much. One burst was like another. Sometimes it started in the pulpit and sometimes with a new ambitious president of the Women's Civic Club. Gambling was invariably the sin to be eradicated. There were certain advantages in attacking gambling. One could discuss it, which was not true of prostitution. It was an obvious evil and most of the games were operated by Chinese. There was little chance of treading on the toes of a relative.

From church and club the town's two newspapers caught fire. Editorials demanded a clean-up. The police agreed but pleaded short-handedness and tried for increased budget and sometimes succeeded.

When it got to the editorial stage everyone knew the cards were down. What followed was as carefully produced as a ballet. The police got ready, the gambling houses got ready, and the papers set up congratulatory editorials in advance. Then came the raid, deliberate and sure. Twenty or more Chinese, imported from Pajaro, a few bums, six or eight drummers, who, being strangers, were not warned, fell into the police net, were booked, jailed, and in the morning fined and released. The town relaxed in its new spotlessness and the houses lost only one night of business plus the fines. It is one of the triumphs of the human that he can know a thing and still not believe it.

In the fall of 1916 Cal was watching the fan-tan game at Shorty Lim's one night when the raid scooped him up. In the dark no one noticed him, and the chief was embarrassed to find him in the tank in the morning. The chief telephoned Adam, got him up from his breakfast. Adam walked the two blocks to the City Hall, picked up Cal, crossed the street to the post office for his mail, and then the two walked home.

Lee had kept Adam's eggs warm and had fried two for Cal.

Aron walked through the dining room on his way to school. "Want me to wait for you?" he asked Cal.

"No," said Cal. He kept his eyes down and ate his eggs.

Adam had not spoken except to say, "Come along!" at the City Hall after he had thanked the chief.

Cal gulped down a breakfast he did not want, darting glances up through his eyelashes at his father's face. He could make nothing of Adam's expression. It seemed at once puzzled and angry and thoughtful and sad.

Adam stared down into his coffee cup. The silence grew until it had the weight of age so hard to lift aside.

Lee looked in. "Coffee?" he asked.

Adam shook his head slowly. Lee withdrew and this time closed the kitchen door.

In the clock-ticking silence Cal began to be afraid. He felt a strength flowing out of his father he had never known was there. Itching prickles of agony ran up his legs, and he was afraid to move to restore the circulation. He knocked his fork against his plate to make a noise and the clatter was swallowed up. The clock struck nine deliberate strokes and they were swallowed up.

As the fear began to chill, resentment took its place. So might a trapped fox feel anger at the paw which held him to the trap.

Suddenly Cal jumped up. He hadn't known he was going to move. He shouted and he hadn't known he was going to speak. He cried, "Do what you're going to do to me! Go ahead! Get it over!"

And his shout was sucked into the silence.

Adam slowly raised his head. It is true that Cal had never looked into his father's eyes before, and it is true that many people never look into their father's eyes. Adam's irises were light blue with dark radial lines leading into the vortices of his pupils. And deep down in each pupil Cal saw his own face reflected, as though two Cals looked out at him.

Adam said slowly, "I've failed you, haven't I?"

It was worst than an attack. Cal faltered, "What do you mean?"

"You were picked up in a gambling house. I don't know how you go there, what you were doing there, why you went there."

Cal sat limply down and looked at his plate.

"Do you gamble, son?"

"No, sir. I was just watching."

"Had you been there before?"

"Yes, sir. Many times."

"Why do you go?"

"I don't know. I get restless at night—like an alley cat, I guess." He thought of Kate and his weak joke seemed horrible to him. "When I can't sleep I walk around," he said, "to try to blot it out."

Adam considered his words, inspected each one, "Does your brother walk around too?"

"Oh, no, sir. He wouldn't think of it. He's—he's not restless."

"You see, I don't know," said Adam. "I don't know anything about you."

Cal wanted to throw his arms about his father, to hug him and to be hugged by him. He wanted some wild demonstration of sympathy and love. He picked up his wooden napkin ring and thrust his forefinger through it. "I'd tell you if you asked," he said softly.

"I didn't ask. I didn't ask! I'm as bad a father as my father was."

Cal had never heard this tone in Adam's voice. It was hoarse and breaking with warmth and he fumbled among his words, feeling for them in the dark.

"My father made a mold and forced me into it," Adam said. "I was a bad casting but I couldn't be remelted. Nobody can be remelted. And so I remained a bad casting."

Cal said, "Sir, don't be sorry. You've had too much of that."

"Have I? Maybe—but maybe the wrong kind. I don't know my sons. I wonder whether I could learn."

"I'll tell you anything you want to know. Just ask me."

"Where would I start? Right at the beginning?"

"Are you sad or mad because I was in jail?"

To Cal's surprise Adam laughed. "You were just there, weren't you? You didn't do anything wrong."

"Maybe being there was wrong." Cal wanted a blame for himself.

"One time I was just there," said Adam. "I was a prisoner for nearly a year for just being there."

Cal tried to absorb this heresy. "I don't believe it," he said.

"Sometimes I don't either, but I know that when I escaped I robbed a store and stole some clothes."

"I don't believe it," Cal said weakly, but the warmth, the closeness, was so delicious that he clung to it. He breathed shallowly so that the warmth might not be disturbed.

Adam said, "Do you remember Samuel Hamilton?—sure you do. When you were a baby he told me I was a bad father. He hit me, knocked me down, to impress it on me."

"That old man?"

"He was a tough old man. And now I know what he meant. I'm the same as my father was. He didn't allow me to be a person, and I haven't seen my sons as people. That's what Samuel meant." He looked right into Cal's eyes and smiled, and Cal ached with affection for him.

Cal said, "We don't think you're a bad father."

"Poor things," said Adam. "How would you know? You've never had any other kind."

"I'm glad I was in jail," said Cal.

"So am I. So am I." He laughed. "We've both been in jail—we can talk together." A gaiety grew in him. "Maybe you can tell me what kind of a boy you are—can you?"

"Yes, sir."

"Will you?"

"Yes, sir."

"Well, tell me. You see, there's a responsibility in being a person. It's more than just taking up space where air would be. What are you like?"

"No joke?" Cal asked shyly.

"No joke—oh, surely, no joke. Tell me about yourself—that is, if you want to."

Cal began, "Well—I'm—" He stopped. "It's not so easy when you try," he said.

"I guess it would be—maybe impossible. Tell me about your brother."

"What do you want to know about him?"

"What you think of him, I guess. That's all you could tell me."

Cal said, "He's good. He doesn't do bad things. He doesn't think bad things."

"Now you're telling about yourself."

"Sir?"

"You're saying you do and think bad things."

Cal's cheeks reddened. "Well, I do."

"Very bad things?"

"Yes, sir. Do you want me to tell?"

"No, Cal. You've told. Your voice tells and your eyes tell you're at war with yourself. But you shouldn't be ashamed. It's awful to be ashamed. Is Aron ever ashamed?"

"He doesn't do anything to be ashamed of."

Adam leaned forward. "Are you sure?"

"Pretty sure."

"Tell me, Cal—do you protect him?"

"How do you mean, sir?"

"I mean like this—if you heard something bad or cruel or ugly, would you keep it from him?"

"I—I think so."

"You think he's too weak to bear things you can bear?"

"It's not that, sir. He's good. He's really good. He never does anyone harm. He never says bad things about anyone. He's not mean and he never complains and he's brave. He doesn't like to fight but he will."

"You love your brother, don't you?"

"Yes, sir. And I do bad things to him. I cheat him and I fool him. Sometimes I hurt him for no reason at all."

"And then you're miserable?"

"Yes, sir."

"Is Aron ever miserable?"

"I don't know. When I didn't want to join the Church he felt bad. And once when Abra got angry and said she hated him he felt awful bad. He was sick. He had a fever. Don't you remember? Lee sent for the doctor."

Adam said with wonder, "I could live with you and not know any of these things! Why was Abra mad?"

Cal said, "I don't know if I ought to tell."

"I don't want you to then."

"It's nothing bad. I guess it's all right. You see, sir, Aron wants to be a minister. Mr. Rolf—well, he likes high church, and Aron liked that, and he thought maybe he would never get married and maybe go to a retreat."

"Like a monk, you mean?"

"Yes, sir."

"And Abra didn't like that?"

"Like it? She got spitting mad. She can get mad sometimes. She took Aron's fountain pen and threw it on the sidewalk and tramped on it. She said she'd wasted half her life on Aron."

Adam laughed. "How old is Abra?"

"Nearly fifteen. But she's—well, more than that some ways."

"I should say she is. What did Aron do?"

"He just got quiet but he felt awful bad."

Adam said, "I guess you could have taken her away from him then."

"Abra is Aron's girl," said Cal.

Adam looked deeply into Cal's eyes. Then he called, "Lee!" There was no answer. "Lee!" he called again. He said, "I didn't hear him go out. I want some fresh coffee."

Cal jumped up. "I'll make it."

"Say," said Adam, "you should be in school."

"I don't want to go."

"You ought to go. Aron went."

"I'm happy," Cal said. "I want to be with you."

Adam looked down at his hands. "Make the coffee," he said softly and his voice was shy.

When Cal was in the kitchen Adam looked inward at himself with wonder. His nerves and muscles throbbed with an excited hunger. His fingers yearned to grasp, his legs to run. His eyes avidly brought the room into focus. He saw the chairs, the pictures, the red roses on the carpet, and new sharp things—almost people things but friendly things. And in his brain was born sharp appetite for the future—a pleased warm anticipation, as though the coming minutes and weeks must bring delight. He felt a dawn emotion, with a lovely day to slip golden and quiet over him. He laced his fingers behind his head and stretched his legs out stiff.

In the kitchen Cal urged on the water heating in the coffeepot, and yet he was pleased to be waiting. A miracle once it is familiar is no longer a miracle; Cal had lost his wonder at the golden relationship with his father but the pleasure remained. The poison of loneliness and the gnawing envy of the unlonely had gone out of him, and his person was clean and sweet, and he knew it was. He dredged up an old hatred to test himself, and he found the hatred gone. He wanted to serve his father, to give him some great gift, to perform some huge good task in honor of his father.

The coffee boiled over and Cal spent minutes cleaning up the stove. He said to himself, "I wouldn't have done this yesterday."

Adam smiled at him when he carried in the steaming pot. Adam sniffed and said, "That's a smell could raise me out of a concrete grave."

"It boiled over," said Cal.

"It has to boil over to taste good," Adam said. "I wonder where Lee went."

"Maybe in his room. Shall I look?"

"No. He'd have answered."

"Sir, when I finish school, will you let me run the ranch?"

"You're planning early. How about Aron?"

"He wants to go to college. Don't tell him I told you. Let him tell you, and you be surprised."

"Why, that's fine," said Adam. "But don't you want to go to college too?"

"I bet I could make money on the ranch—enough to pay Aron's way through college."

Adam sipped his coffee. "That's a generous thing," he said. "I don't know whether I ought to tell you this but—well, when I asked you earlier what kind of boy Aron was, you defended him so badly I thought you might dislike him or even hate him."

"I have hated him," Cal said vehemently. "And I've hurt him too. But, sir, can I tell you something? I don't hate him now. I won't ever hate him again. I don't think I will hate anyone, not even my mother—" He stopped, astonished at his slip, and his mind froze up tight and helpless.

Adam looked straight ahead. He rubbed his forehead with the palm of

his hand. Finally he said quietly, "You know about your mother." It was no
a question.

"Yes—yes, sir."

"All about her?"

"Yes, sir."

Adam leaned back in his chair. "Does Aron know?"

"Oh, no! No—no, sir. He doesn't know."

"Why do you say it that way?"

"I wouldn't dare to tell him."

"Why not?"

Cal said brokenly, "I don't think he could stand it. He hasn't enough
badness in him to stand it." He wanted to continue, "—any more than you
could, sir," but he left the last unsaid.

Adam's face looked weary. He moved his head from side to side. "Cal,
listen to me. Do you think there's any chance of keeping Aron from knowing? Think carefully."

Cal said, "He doesn't go near places like that. He's not like me."

"Suppose someone told him?"

"I don't think he would believe it, sir. I think he would lick whoever told
him and think it was a lie."

"You've been there?"

"Yes, sir. I had to know." And Cal went on excitedly, "If he went away to
college and never lived in this town again—"

Adam nodded. "Yes. That might be. But he has two more years here."

"Maybe I could make him hurry it up and finish in one year. He's smart."

"But you're smarter?"

"A different kind of smart," said Cal.

Adam seemed to grow until he filled one side of the room. His face was
stern and his blue eyes sharp and penetrating. "Cal!" he said harshly.

"Sir?"

"I trust you, son," said Adam.

2

Adam's recognition brought a ferment of happiness to Cal. He walked on
the balls of his feet. He smiled more often than he frowned, and the secret
darkness was seldom on him.

Lee, noticing the change in him, asked quietly, "You haven't found a
girl, have you?"

"Girl? No. Who wants a girl?"

"Everybody," said Lee.

And Lee asked Adam, "Do you know what's got into Cal?"

Adam said, "He knows about her."

"Does he?" Lee stayed out of trouble. "Well, you remember I thought you should have told them."

"I didn't tell him. He knew."

"What do you think of that!" said Lee. "But that's not information to make a boy hum when he studies and play catch with his cap when he walks. How about Aron?"

"I'm afraid of that," said Adam. "I don't think I want him to know."

"It might be too late."

"I might have a talk with Aron. Kind of feel around."

Lee considered. "Something's happened to you too."

"Has it? I guess it has," said Adam.

But humming and sailing his cap, driving quickly through his schoolwork, were only the smallest of Cal's activities. In his new joy he appointed himself guardian of his father's content. It was true what he had said about not feeling hatred for his mother. But that did not change the fact that she had been the instrument of Adam's hurt and shame. Cal reasoned that what she could do before, she could do again. He set himself to learn all he could about her. A known enemy is less dangerous, less able to surprise.

At night he was drawn to the house across the tracks. Sometimes in the afternoon he lay hidden in the tall weeds across the street, watching the place. He saw the girls come out, dressed somberly, even severely. They left the house always in pairs, and Cal followed them with his eyes to the corner of Castroville Street, where they turned left toward Main Street. He discovered that if you didn't know where they had come from you couldn't tell what they were. But he was not waiting for the girls to come out. He wanted to see his mother in the light of day. He found that Kate emerged every Monday at one-thirty.

Cal made arrangements in school, by doing extra and excellent work, to make up for his absences on Monday afternoons. To Aron's questions he replied that he was working on a surprise and was duty bound to tell no one. Aron was not much interested anyway. In his self-immersion Aron soon forgot the whole thing.

Cal, after he had followed Kate several times, knew her route. She always went to the same places—first to the Monterey County Bank where she was admitted behind the shining bars that defended the safe-deposit vault. She spent fifteen or twenty minutes there. Then she moved slowly along Main Street, looking in the store windows. She stepped into Porter and Irvine's and looked at dresses and sometimes made a purchase—elastic, safety pins, a veil, a pair of gloves. About two-fifteen she entered Minnie Franken's beauty parlor, stayed an hour, and came out with her hair pinned up in tight curls and a silk scarf around her head and tied under her chin.

At three-thirty she climbed the stairs to the offices over the Farmers' Mercantile and went into the consulting room of Dr. Rosen. When she came down from the doctor's office she stopped for a moment at Bell's candy store and bought a two-pound box of mixed chocolates. She never varied the route. From Bell's she went directly back to Castroville Street and thence to her house.

There was nothing strange about her clothing. She dressed exactly like any well-to-do Salinas woman out shopping on a Monday afternoon—except that she always wore gloves, which was unusual for Salinas.

The gloves made her hands seem puffed and pudgy. She moved as though she were surrounded by a glass shell. She spoke to no one and seemed to see no one. Occasionally a man turned and looked after her and then nervously went about his business. But for the most part she slipped past like an invisible woman.

For a number of weeks Cal followed Kate. He tried not to attract her attention. And since Kate walked always looking straight ahead, he was convinced that she did not notice him.

When Kate entered her own yard Cal strolled casually by and went home by another route. He could not have said exactly why he followed her, except that he wanted to know all about her.

The eighth week he took the route she completed her journey and went into her overgrown yard as usual.

Cal waited a moment, then strolled past the rickety gate.

Kate was standing behind a tall ragged privet. She said to him coldly, "What do you want?"

Cal froze in his steps. He was suspended in time, barely breathing. Then he began a practice he had learned when he was very young. He observed and catalogued details outside his main object. He noticed how the wind from the south bent over the new little leaves of the tall privet bush. He saw the muddy path beaten to black mush by many feet, and Kate's feet standing far to the side out of the mud. He heard a switch engine in the Southern Pacific yards discharging steam in shrill dry spurts. He felt the chill air on the growing fuzz on his cheeks. And all the time he was staring at Kate and she was staring back at him. And he saw in the set and color of her eyes and hair, even in the way she held her shoulders—high in a kind of semi-shrug—that Aron looked very like her. He did not know his own face well enough to recognize her mouth and little teeth and wide cheekbones as his own. They stood thus for the moment, between two gusts of the southern wind.

Kate said, "This isn't the first time you've followed me. What do you want?"

He dipped his head. "Nothing," he said.

"Who told you to do it?" she demanded.

"Nobody—ma'am."

"You won't tell me, will you?"

Cal heard his own next speech with amazement. It was out before he could

top it. "You're my mother and I wanted to see what you're like." It was the
xact truth and it had leaped out like the stroke of a snake.

"What? What is this? Who are you?"

"I'm Cal Trask," he said. He felt the delicate change of balance as when
, seesaw moves. His was the upper seat now. Although her expression had
10t changed Cal knew she was on the defensive.

She looked at him closely, observed every feature. A dim remembered
)icture of Charles leaped into her mind. Suddenly she said, "Come with
ne!" She turned and walked up the path, keeping well to the side, out of
the mud.

Cal hesitated only for a moment before following her up the steps. He
remembered the big dim room, but the rest was strange to him. Kate pre-
:eded him down a hall and into her room. As she went past the kitchen
entrance she called, "Tea. Two cups!"

In her room she seemed to have forgotten him. She removed her coat,
tugging at the sleeves with reluctant fat gloved fingers. Then she went to a
new door cut in the wall in the end of the room where her bed stood. She
opened the door and went into a new little lean-to. "Come in here!" she
said. "Bring that chair with you."

He followed her into a box of a room. It had no windows, no decorations
of any kind. Its walls were painted a dark gray. A solid gray carpet covered
the floor. The only furniture in the room was a huge chair puffed with gray
silk cushions, a tilted reading table, and a floor lamp deeply hooded. Kate
pulled the light chain with her gloved hand, holding it deep in the crotch
between her thumb and forefinger as though her hand were artificial.

"Close the door!" Kate said.

The light threw a circle on the reading table and only diffused dimly
through the gray room. Indeed the gray walls seemed to suck up the light
and destroy it.

Kate settled herself gingerly among the thick down cushions and slowly
removed her gloves. The fingers of both hands were bandaged.

Kate said angrily, "Don't stare. It's arthritis. Oh—so you want to see, do
you?" She unwrapped the oily-looking bandage from her right forefinger
and stuck the crooked finger under the light. "There—look at it," she said.
"It's arthritis." She whined in pain as she tenderly wrapped the bandage
loosely. "God, those gloves hurt!" she said. "Sit down."

Cal crouched on the edge of his chair.

"You'll probably get it," Kate said. "My great-aunt had it and my mother
was just beginning to get it—" She stopped. The room was very silent.

There was a soft knock on the door. Kate called, "Is that you, Joe? Set the
tray down out there. Joe, are you there?"

A mutter came through the door.

Kate said tonelessly, "There's a litter in the parlor. Clean it up. Anne
hasn't cleaned her room. Give her one more warning. Tell her it's the last.

Eva got smart last night. I'll take care of her. And, Joe, tell the cook if h‑
serves carrots again this week he can pack up. Hear me?"

The mutter came through the door.

"That's all," said Kate. "The dirty pigs!" she muttered. "They'd rot if
didn't watch them. Go out and bring in the tea tray."

The bedroom was empty when Cal opened the door. He carried the tra
into the lean-to and set it gingerly on the tilted reading table. It was a large
silver tray, and on it were a pewter teapot, two paper-thin white teacups
sugar, cream, and an open box of chocolates.

"Pour the tea," said Kate. "It hurts my hands." She put a chocolate in he:
mouth. "I saw you looking at this room," she went on when she had swal
lowed her candy. "The light hurts my eyes. I come in here to rest." She saw
Cal's quick glance at her eyes and said with finality, "The light hurts my
eyes." She said harshly, "What's the matter? Don't you want tea?"

"No, ma'am," said Cal, "I don't like tea."

She held the thin cup with her bandaged fingers. "All right. What *do* you
want?"

"Nothing, ma'am."

"Just wanted to look at me?"

"Yes, ma'am."

"Are you satisfied?"

"Yes, ma'am."

"How do I look?" She smiled crookedly at him and showed her sharp white
little teeth.

"All right."

"I might have known you'd cover up. Where's your brother?"

"In school, I guess, or home."

"What's he like?"

"He looks more like you."

"Oh, he does? Well, *is* he like me?"

"He wants to be a minister," said Cal.

"I guess that's the way it should be—looks like me and wants to go into
the church. A man can do a lot of damage in the church. When someone
comes here, he's got his guard up. But in church a man's wide open."

"He means it," said Cal.

She leaned toward him, and her face was alive with interest. "Fill my
cup. Is your brother dull?"

"He's nice," said Cal.

"I asked you if he's dull."

"No, ma'am," said Cal.

She settled back and lifted her cup. "How's your father?"

"I don't want to talk about him," Cal said.

"Oh, no! You like him then?"

"I love him," said Cal.

Kate peered closely at him, and a curious spasm shook her—an aching
:wist rose in her chest. And then she closed up and her control came back.

"Don't you want some candy?" she asked.

"Yes, ma'am. Why did you do it?"

"Why did I do what?"

"Why did you shoot my father and run away from us?"

"Did he tell you that?"

"No. He didn't tell us."

She touched one hand with the other and her hands leaped apart as
though the contact burned them. She asked, "Does your father ever have
any—girls or young women come to your house?"

"No," said Cal. "Why did you shoot him and go away?"

Her cheeks tightened and her mouth straightened, as though a net of
muscles took control. She raised her head, and her eyes were cold and
shallow.

"You talk older than your age," she said. "But you don't talk old enough.
Maybe you'd better run along and play—and wipe your nose."

"Sometimes I work my brother over," he said. "I make him squirm, I've
made him cry. He doesn't know how I do it. I'm smarter than he is. I don't
want to do it. It makes me sick."

Kate picked it up as though it were her own conversation. "They thought
they were so smart," she said. "They looked at me and thought they knew
about me. And I fooled them. I fooled every one of them. And when they
thought they could tell me what to do—oh! that's when I fooled them best.
Charles, I really fooled them then."

"My name is Caleb," Cal said. "Caleb got to the Promised Land. That's
what Lee says, and it's in the Bible."

"That's the Chinaman," Kate said, and she went on eagerly, "Adam
thought he had me. When I was hurt, all broken up, he took me in and he
waited on me, cooked for me. He tried to tie me down that way. Most
people get tied down that way. They're grateful, they're in debt, and that's
the worst kind of handcuffs. But nobody can hold me. I waited and waited
until I was strong, and then I broke out. Nobody can trap me," she said. "I
knew what he was doing. I waited."

The gray room was silent except for her excited wheezing breath.

Cal said, "Why did you shoot him?"

"Because he tried to stop me. I could have killed him but I didn't. I just
wanted him to let me go."

"Did you ever wish you'd stayed?"

"Christ, no! Even when I was a little girl I could do anything I wanted.
They never knew how I did it. Never. They were always so sure they were
right. And they never knew—no one ever knew." A kind of realization came
to her. "Sure, you're my kind. Maybe you're the same. Why wouldn't you
be?"

Cal stood up and clasped his hands behind his back. He said, "When you were little, did you"—he paused to get the thought straight—"did you ever have the feeling like you were missing something? Like as if the others knew something you didn't—like a secret they wouldn't tell you? Did you ever feel that way?"

While he spoke her face began to close against him, and by the time he paused she was cut off and the open way between them was blocked.

She said, "What am I doing, talking to kids!"

Cal unclasped his hands from behind him and shoved them in his pockets.

"Talking to snot-nosed kids," she said. "I must be crazy."

Cal's face was alight with excitement, and his eyes were wide with vision. Kate said, "What's the matter with you?"

He stood still, his forehead glistening with sweat, his hands clenched into fists.

Kate, as she had always, drove in the smart but senseless knife of her cruelty. She laughed softly. "I may have given you some interesting things, like this—" She held up her crooked hands. "But if it's epilepsy—fits—you didn't get it from me." She glanced brightly up at him, anticipating the shock and beginning worry in him.

Cal spoke happily. "I'm going," he said. "I'm going now. It's all right. What Lee said was true."

"What did Lee say?"

Cal said, "I was afraid I had you in me."

"You have," said Kate.

"No, I haven't. I'm my own. I don't have to be you."

"How do you know that?" she demanded.

"I just know. It just came to me whole. If I'm mean, it's my own mean."

"This Chinaman has really fed you some pap. What are you looking at me like that for?"

Cal said, "I don't think the light hurts your eyes. I think you're afraid."

"Get out!" she cried. "Go on, get out!"

"I'm going." He had his hand on the doorknob. "I don't hate you," he said. "But I'm glad you're afraid."

She tried to shout "Joe!" but her voice thickened to a croak.

Cal wrenched open the door and slammed it behind him.

Joe was talking to one of the girls in the parlor. They heard the stutter of light quick footsteps. But by the time they looked up a streaking figure had reached the door, opened it, slipped through, and the heavy front door banged. There was only one step on the porch and then a crunch as jumping feet struck earth.

"What in hell was that?" the girl asked.

"God knows," said Joe. "Sometimes I think I'm seeing things."

"Me too," said the girl. "Did I tell you Clara's got bugs under her skin?"

"I guess she seen the shadow of the needle," said Joe. "Well, the way I
gure, the less you know, the better off you are."

"That's the truth you said there," the girl agreed.

FORTY

ate sat back in her chair against the deep down cushions. Waves of nerves
ruised over her body, raising the little hairs and making ridges of icy burn
s they went.

She spoke softly to herself. "Steady now," she said. "Quiet down. Don't
et it hit you. Don't think for a while. The goddam snot-nose!"

She thought suddenly of the only person who had ever made her feel this
anic hatred. It was Samuel Hamilton, with his white beard and his pink
heeks and the laughing eyes that lifted her skin and looked underneath.

With her bandaged forefinger she dug out a slender chain which hung
round her neck and pulled the chain's burden up from her bodice. On the
hain were strung two safe-deposit keys, a gold watch with a fleur-de-lis pin,
nd a little steel tube with a ring on its top. Very carefully she unscrewed
he top from the tube and, spreading her knees, shook out a gelatine capsule.
She held the capsule under the light and saw the white crystals inside—six
grains of morphine, a good, sure margin. Very gently she eased the capsule
nto its tube, screwed on the cap, and dropped the chain inside her dress.

Cal's last words had been repeating themselves over and over in her head.
'I'm glad you're afraid." She said the words aloud to herself to kill the
sound. The rhythm stopped, but a strong picture formed in her mind and she
let it form so that she could inspect it again.

2

It was before the lean-to was built. Kate had collected the money Charles
had left. The check was converted to large bills, and the bills in their bales
were in the safe-deposit box at the Monterey County Bank.

It was about the time the first pains began to twist her hands. There was
enough money now to go away. It was just a matter of getting the most she
could out of the house. But also it was better to wait until she felt quite
well again.

She never felt quite well again. New York seemed cold and very far away.

A letter came to her signed "Ethel." Who in hell was Ethel? Whoever
she was, she must be crazy to ask for money. Ethel—there were hundreds of
Ethels. Ethels grew on every bush. And this one scrawled illegibly on a
lined pad.

Not very long afterward Ethel came to see Kate, and Kate hardly re=
ognized her.

Kate sat at her desk, watchful, suspicious, and confident. "It's been a lon=
time," she said.

Ethel responded like a soldier who comes in his cushion age upon th=
sergeant who trained him. "I've been poorly," she said. Her flesh had thick=
ened and grown heavy all over her. Her clothes had the strained cleanlines=
that means poverty.

"Where are you—staying now?" Kate asked, and she wondered how soo=
the old bag would be able to come to her point.

"Southern Pacific Hotel. I got a room."

"Oh, then you don't work in a house now?"

"I couldn't never get started again," said Ethel. "You shouldn't of run m=
off." She wiped big tears from the corners of her eyes with the tip of a cotto=
glove. "Things are bad," she said. "First I had trouble when we got that ne=
judge. Ninety days, and I didn't have no record—not here anyways. I com=
out of that and I got the old Joe. I didn't know I had it. Give it to a regula=
—nice fella, worked on the section gang. He got sore an' busted me up, hur=
my nose, lost four teeth, an' that new judge he give me a hundred an=
eighty. Hell, Kate, you lose all your contacts in a hundred and eighty days=
They forget you're alive. I just never could get started."

Kate nodded her head in cold and shallow sympathy. She knew that
Ethel was working up to the bite. Just before it came Kate made a move.
She opened her desk drawer and took out some money and held it out to
Ethel. "I never let a friend down," she said. "Why don't you go to a new
town, start fresh? It might change your luck."

Ethel tried to keep her fingers from grabbing at the money. She fanned
the bills like a poker hand—four tens. Her mouth began to work with emotion.

Ethel said, "I kind of hoped you'd see your way to let me take more than
forty bucks."

"What do you mean?"

"Didn't you get my letter?"

"What letter?"

"Oh!" said Ethel. "Well, maybe it got lost in the mail. They don't take
no care of things. Anyways, I thought you might look after me. I don't feel
good hardly ever. Got a kind of weight dragging my guts down." She sighed
and then she spoke so rapidly that Kate knew it had been rehearsed.

"Well, maybe you remember how I've got like second sight," Ethel began. "Always predicting things that come true. Always dreaming stuff and
it come out. Fella says I should go in the business. Says I'm a natural
medium. You remember that?"

"No," said Kate, "I don't."

"Don't? Well, maybe you never noticed. All the others did. I told 'em lots of things and they come true."

"What are you trying to say?"

"I had this-here dream. I remember when it was because it was the same night Faye died." Her eyes flicked up at Kate's cold face. She continued doggedly, "It rained that night, and it was raining in my dream—anyways, it was wet. Well, in my dream I seen you come out the kitchen door. It wasn't pitch-dark—moon was coming through a little. And the dream thing was you. You went out to the back of the lot and stooped over. I couldn't see what you done. Then you come creeping back.

"Next thing I knew—why, Faye was dead." She paused and waited for some comment from Kate, but Kate's face was expressionless.

Ethel waited until she was sure Kate would not speak. "Well, like I said, I always believed in my dreams. It's funny, there wasn't nothing out there except some smashed medicine bottles and a little rubber tit from an eye-dropper."

Kate said lazily, "So you took them to a doctor. What did he say had been in the bottles?"

"Oh, I didn't do nothing like that."

"You should have," said Kate.

"I don't want to see nobody get in trouble. I've had enough trouble myself. I put that broke glass in an envelope and stuck it away."

Kate said softly, "And so you are coming to me for advice?"

"Yes, ma'am."

"I'll tell you what I think," said Kate. "I think you're a worn-out old whore and you've been beaten over the head too many times."

"Don't you start saying I'm nuts—" Ethel began.

"No, maybe you're not, but you're tired and you're sick. I told you I never let a friend down. You can come back here. You can't work but you can help around, clean and give the cook a hand. You'll have a bed and you'll get your meals. How would that be? And a little spending money."

Ethel stirred uneasily. "No, ma'am," she said. "I don't think I want to—sleep here. I don't carry that envelope around. I left it with a friend."

"What did you have in mind?" Kate asked.

"Well, I thought if you could see your way to let me have a hundred dollars a month, why, I could make out and maybe get my health back."

"You said you lived at the Southern Pacific Hotel?"

"Yes, ma'am—and my room is right up the hall from the desk. The night clerk's a friend of mine. He don't never sleep when he's on duty. Nice fella."

Kate said, "Don't wet your pants, Ethel. All you've got to worry about is how much does the 'nice fella' cost. Now wait a minute." She counted six more ten-dollar bills from the drawer in front of her and held them out. "Will it come the first of the month or do I have to come here for it?"

"I'll send it to you," said Kate. "And, Ethel," she continued quietly, "I still think you ought to have those bottles analyzed."

Ethel clutched the money tightly in her hand. She was bubbling over with triumph and good feeling. It was one of the few things that had ever worked out for her. "I wouldn't think of doing that," she said. "Not unless I had to."

After she had gone Kate strolled out to the back of the lot behind the house. And even after years she could see from the unevenness of the earth that it must have been pretty thoroughly dug over.

The next morning the judge heard the usual chronicle of small violence and nocturnal greed. He only half listened to the fourth case and at the end of the terse testimony of the complaining witness he asked, "How much did you lose?"

The dark-haired man said, "Pretty close to a hundred dollars."

The judge turned to the arresting officer. "How much did she have?"

"Ninety-six dollars. She got whisky and cigarettes and some magazines from the night clerk at six o'clock this morning."

Ethel cried, "I never seen this guy in my life."

The judge looked up from his papers. "Twice for prostitution and now robbery. You're costing too much. I want you out of town by noon." He turned to the officer. "Tell the sheriff to run her over the county line." And he said to Ethel, "If you come back, I'll give you to the county for the limit, and that's San Quentin. Do you understand?"

Ethel said, "Judge, I want to see you alone."

"Why?"

"I got to see you," said Ethel. "This is a frame."

"Everything's a frame," said the judge. "Next."

While a deputy sheriff drove Ethel to the county line on the bridge over the Pajaro River, the complaining witness strolled down Castroville Street toward Kate's, changed his mind and went back to Kenoe's barbershop to get a hair cut.

3

Ethel's visit did not disturb Kate very much when it happened. She knew about what attention would be paid to a whore with a grievance, and that an analysis of the broken bottles would not show anything recognizable as poison. She had nearly forgotten Faye. The forcible recalling was simply an unpleasant memory.

Gradually, however, she found herself thinking about it. One night when she was checking the items on a grocery bill a thought shot into her mind, shining and winking like a meteor. The thought flashed and went out so quickly that she had to stop what she was doing to try to find it. How was the dark face of Charles involved in the thought? And Sam Hamilton's puzzled and merry eyes? And why did she get a shiver of fear from the thought, What about Charles, had then it come to her.

She gave it up and went back to her work, but the face of Charles was behind her, looking over her shoulder. Her fingers began to hurt her. She put the accounts away and made a tour through the house. It was a slow, listless night—a Tuesday night. There weren't even enough customers to put on the circus.

Kate knew how the girls felt about her. They were desperately afraid of her. She kept them that way. It was probable that they hated her, and that didn't matter either. But they trusted her, and that did matter. If they followed the rules she laid down, followed them exactly, Kate would take care of them and protect them. There was no love involved and no respect. She never rewarded them and she punished an offender only twice before she removed her. The girls did have the security of knowing that they would not be punished without cause.

As Kate walked about, the girls became elaborately casual. Kate knew about that too and expected it. But on this night she felt that she was not alone. Charles seemed to walk to the side and behind her.

She went through the dining room and into the kitchen, opened the icebox and looked in. She lifted the cover of the garbage can and inspected it for waste. She did this every night, but this night she carried some extra charge.

When she had left the parlor the girls looked at each other and raised their shoulders in bewilderment. Eloise, who was talking to the dark-haired Joe, said, "Anything the matter?"

"Not that I know of. Why?"

"I don't know. She seems nervous."

"Well, there was some kind of rat race."

"What was it?"

"Wait a minute!" said Joe. "I don't know and you don't know."

"I get it. Mind my own business."

"You're goddam right," said Joe. "Let's keep it that way, shall we?"

"I don't want to know," said Eloise.

"Now you're talking," Joe said.

Kate ranged back from her tour. "I'm going to bed," she said to Joe. "Don't call me unless you have to."

"Anything I can do?"

"Yes, make me a pot of tea. Did you press that dress, Eloise?"

"Yes, ma'am."

"You didn't do it very well."

"Yes, ma'am."

Kate was restless. She put all her papers neatly in the pigeonholes of her desk, and when Joe brought the tea tray she had him put it beside her bed.

Lying back among her pillows and sipping the tea, she probed for her thought. What about Charles? And then it came to her.

Charles was clever. In his crazy way Sam Hamilton was clever. That was the fear-driven thought—there were clever people. Both Sam and Charles were dead, but maybe there were others. She worked it out very slowly.

Suppose I had been the one to dig up the bottles? What would I think and what would I do? A rim of panic rose in her breast. Why were the bottles broken and buried? So it wasn't a poison! Then why bury them? What had made her do that? She should have dropped them in the gutter on Main Street or tossed them in the garbage can. Dr. Wilde was dead. But what kind of records did he keep? She didn't know. Suppose she had found the glass and learned what had been in them. Wouldn't she have asked someone who knew—"Suppose you gave croton oil to a person. What would happen?"

"Well, suppose you gave little doses and kept it up a long time?" She would know. Maybe somebody else would know.

"Suppose you heard about a rich madam who willed everything to a new girl and then died." Kate knew perfectly well what her first thought would be. What insanity had made her get Ethel floated? Now she couldn't be found. Ethel should have been paid and tricked into turning over the glass. Where was the glass now? In an envelope—but where? How could Ethel be found?

Ethel would know why and how she had been floated. Ethel wasn't bright, but she might tell somebody who was bright. That chattering voice might tell the story, how Faye was sick, and what she looked like, and about the will.

Kate was breathing quickly and little prickles of fear were beginning to course over her body. She should go to New York or someplace—not bother to sell the house. She didn't need the money. She had plenty. Nobody could find her. Yes, but if she ran out and the clever person heard Ethel tell the story, wouldn't that cinch it?

Kate got up from her bed and took a heavy dose of bromide.

From that time on the crouching fear had always been at her side. She was almost glad when she learned that the pain in her hands was developing arthritis. An evil voice had whispered that it might be a punishment.

She had never gone out in the town very much, but now she developed a reluctance to go out at all. She knew that men stared secretly after her, knowing who she was. Suppose one of those men should have Charles' face or Samuel's eyes. She had to drive herself to go out once a week.

Then she built the lean-to and had it painted gray. She said it was because the light troubled her eyes, and gradually she began to believe the light did trouble her eyes. Her eyes burned after a trip to the town. She spent more and more time in her little room.

It is possible to some people, and it was possible for Kate, to hold two opposing thoughts at the same time. She believed that the light pained her eyes, and also that the gray room was a cave to hide in, a dark burrow in the earth, a place where no eyes could stare at her. Once, sitting in her pillowed chair, she considered having a secret door built so that she would have an avenue of escape. And then a feeling rather than a thought threw out the plan. She would not be protected then. If she could get out, some-thing could get in—that something which had begun to crouch outside the house, to crawl close to the walls at night, and to rise silently, trying to look through the windows. It required more and more will power for Kate to leave the house on Monday afternoons.

When Cal began to follow her she had a terrible leap of fear. And when she waited for him behind the privet she was very near to panic.

But now her head dug deep in her soft pillows and her eyes felt the gentle weight of the bromide.

FORTY-ONE

The nation slid imperceptibly toward war, frightened and at the same time attracted. People had not felt the shaking emotion of war in nearly sixty years. The Spanish affair was more nearly an expedition than a war. Mr. Wilson was re-elected President in November on his platform promise to keep us out of war, and at the same time he was instructed to take a firm hand, which inevitably meant war. Business picked up and prices began to rise. British purchasing agents roved about the country, buying food and cloth and metals and chemicals. A charge of excitement ran through the country. People didn't really believe in war even while they planned it. The Salinas Valley lived about as it always had.

2

Cal walked to school with Aron.

"You look tired," Aron said.

"Do I?"

"I heard you come in last night. Four o'clock. What do you do so late?"

"I was walking around—thinking. How would you like to quit school and go back to the ranch?"

"What for?"

"We could make some money for Father."

"I'm going to college. I wish I could go now. Everybody is laughing at us. I want to get out of town."

"You act mad."

"I'm not mad. But I didn't lose the money. I didn't have a crazy lettuce idea. But people laugh at me just the same. And I don't know if there's enough money for college."

"He didn't mean to lose the money."

"But he lost it."

Cal said, "You've got this year to finish and next before you can go to college."

"Do you think I don't know it?"

"If you worked hard, maybe you could take entrance examinations next summer and go in the fall."

Aron swung around. "I couldn't do it."

"I think you could. Why don't you talk to the principal? And I bet the Reverend Rolf would help you."

Aron said, "I want to get out of this town. I don't ever want to come back. They still call us Lettuce-heads. They laugh at us."

"How about Abra?"

"Abra will do what's best."

Cal asked, "Would she want you to go away?"

"Abra's going to do what I want her to do."

Cal thought for a moment. "I'll tell you what. I'm going to try to make some money. If you knuckle down and pass examinations a year early, why, I'll help you through college."

"You will?"

"Sure I will."

"Why, I'll go and see the principal right away." He quickened his steps.

Cal called, "Aron, wait! Listen! If he says he thinks you can do it, don't tell Father."

"Why not?"

"I was just thinking how nice it would be if you went to him and told him you'd done it."

"I don't see what difference it makes."

"You don't?"

"No, I don't," said Aron. "It sounds silly to me."

Cal had a violent urge to shout, "I know who our mother is! I can show her to you." That would cut through and get inside of Aron.

Cal met Abra in the hall before the schoolbell rang.

"What's the matter with Aron?" he demanded.

"I don't know."

"Yes, you do," he said.

"He's just in a cloud. I think it's that minister."

"Does he walk home with you?"

"Sure he does. But I can see right through him. He's wearing wings."

"He's still ashamed about the lettuce."

"I know he is," said Abra. "I try to talk him out of it. Maybe he's enjoying it."

"What do you mean?"

"Nothing," said Abra.

After supper that night Cal said, "Father, would you mind if I went down to the ranch Friday afternoon?"

Adam turned in his chair. "What for?"

"Just want to see. Just want to look around."

"Does Aron want to go?"

"No. I want to go alone."

"I don't see why you shouldn't. Lee, do you see any reason why he shouldn't go?"

"No," said Lee. He studied Cal. "Thinking seriously of going to farming?"

"I might. If you'd let me take it over, I'd farm it, Father."

"The lease has more than a year to run," Adam said.

"After that can I farm it?"

"How about school?"

"I'll be through school."

"Well, we'll see," said Adam. "You might want to go to college."

When Cal started for the front door Lee followed and walked out with him.

"Can you tell me what it's about?" Lee asked.

"I just want to look around."

"All right, I guess I'm left out." Lee turned to go back into the house. Then he called, "Cal!" The boy stopped. "You worried, Cal?"

"No."

"I've got five thousand dollars if you ever need it."

"Why would I need it?"

"I don't know," said Lee.

3

Will Hamilton liked his glass cage of an office in the garage. His business interests were much wider than the automobile agency, but he did not get another office. He loved the movement that went on outside his square glass cage. And he had put in double glass to kill the noise of the garage.

He sat in his big red leather swivel chair, and most of the time he enjoyed his life. When people spoke of his brother Joe making so much money in advertising in the East, Will always said he himself was a big frog in a little puddle.

"I'd be afraid to go to a big city," he said. "I'm just a country boy." And he liked the laugh that always followed. It proved to him that his friends knew he was well off.

Cal came in to see him one Saturday morning. Seeing Will's puzzled look, he said, "I'm Cal Trask."

"Oh, sure. Lord, you're getting to be a big boy. Is your father down?"

"No. I came alone."

"Well, sit down. I don't suppose you smoke."

"Sometimes. Cigarettes."

Will slid a package of Murads across the desk. Cal opened the box and then closed it. "I don't think I will right now."

Will looked at the dark-faced boy and he liked him. He thought, This boy is sharp. He's nobody's fool. "I guess you'll be going into business pretty soon," he said.

"Yes, sir. I thought I might run the ranch when I get out of high school."

"There's no money in that," said Will. "Farmers don't make any money. It's the man who buys from him and sells. You'll never make any money farming." Will knew that Cal was feeling him, testing him, observing him, and he approved of that.

And Cal had made up his mind, but first he asked, "Mr. Hamilton, you haven't any children, have you?"

"Well, no. And I'm sorry about that. I guess I'm sorriest about that." And then, "What makes you ask?"

Cal ignored the question. "Would you give me some advice?"

Will felt a glow of pleasure. "If I can, I'll be glad to. What is it you want to know?"

And then Cal did something Will Hamilton approved even more. He used candor as a weapon. He said, "I want to make a lot of money. I want you to tell me how."

Will overcame his impulse to laugh. Naïve as the statement was, he didn't think Cal was naïve. "Everybody wants that," he said. "What do you mean by a lot of money?"

"Twenty or thirty thousand dollars."

"Good God!" said Will, and he screeched his chair forward. And now he did laugh, but not in derision. Cal smiled along with Will's laughter.

Will said, "Can you tell me why you want to make so much?"

"Yes, sir," said Cal, "I can." And Cal opened the box of Murads and took out one of the oval cork-tipped cigarettes and lighted it. "I'll tell you why," he said.

Will leaned his chair back in enjoyment.

"My father lost a lot of money."

"I know," said Will. "I warned him not to try to ship lettuce across the country."

"You did? Why did you?"

"There were no guarantees," said Will. "A businessman has to protect himself. If anything happened, he was finished. And it happened. Go on."

"I want to make enough money to give him back what he lost."

Will gaped at him. "Why?" he asked.

"I want to."

Will said, "Are you fond of him?"

"Yes."

Will's fleshy face contorted and a memory swept over him like a chilling wind. He did not move slowly over the past, it was all there in one flash, all of the years, a picture, a feeling and a despair, all stopped the way a fast camera stops the world. There was the flashing Samuel, beautiful as dawn with a fancy like a swallow's flight, and the brilliant, brooding Tom who was dark fire, Una who rode the storms, and lovely Mollie, Dessie of laughter, George handsome and with a sweetness that filled a room like the perfume of flowers, and there was Joe, the youngest, the beloved. Each one without effort brought some gift into the family.

Nearly everyone has his box of secret pain, shared with no one. Will had concealed his well, laughed loud, exploited perverse virtues, and never let his jealousy go wandering. He thought of himself as slow, doltish, conservative, uninspired. No great dream lifted him high and no despair forced self-destruction. He was always on the edge, trying to hold on to the rim of the family with what gifts he had—care, and reason, application. He kept the books, hired the attorneys, called the undertaker, and eventually paid the bills. The others didn't even know they needed him. He had the ability to get money and to keep it. He thought the Hamiltons despised him for his one ability. He had loved them doggedly, had always been at hand with his money to pull them out of their errors. He thought they were ashamed of him, and he fought bitterly for their recognition. All of this was in the frozen wind that blew through him.

His slightly bulging eyes were damp as he stared past Cal, and the boy asked, "What's the matter, Mr. Hamilton? Don't you feel well?"

Will had sensed his family but he had not understood them. And they had accepted him without knowing there was anything to understand. And now this boy came along. Will understood him, felt him, sensed him, recognized him. This was the son he should have had, or the brother, or the father. And the cold wind of memory changed to a warmth toward Cal which gripped him in the stomach and pushed up against his lungs.

He forced his attention to the glass office. Cal was sitting back in his chair, waiting.

Will did not know how long his silence had lasted. "I was thinking," he said lamely. He made his voice stern. "You asked me something. I'm a businessman. I don't give things away. I sell them."

"Yes, sir." Cal was watchful but he felt that Will Hamilton liked him.

Will said, "I want to know something and I want the truth. Will you tell me the truth?"

"I don't know," said Cal.

"I like that. How do you know until you know the question? I like that.

That's smart—and honest. Listen—you have a brother. Does your father like him better than you?"

"Everybody does," said Cal calmly. "Everybody loves Aron."

"Do you?"

"Yes, sir. At least—yes, I do."

"What's the 'at least'?"

"Sometimes I think he's stupid but I like him."

"Now, how about your father?"

"I love him," said Cal.

"And he loves your brother better."

"I don't know."

"Now, you say you want to give back the money your father lost. Why?"

Ordinarily Cal's eyes were squinted and cautious, but now they were so wide that they seemed to look around and through Will. Cal was as close to his own soul as it is possible to get.

"My father is good," he said. "I want to make it up to him because I am not good."

"If you do that, wouldn't you be good?"

"No," said Cal. "I think bad."

Will had never met anyone who spoke so nakedly. He was near to embarrassment because of the nakedness, and he knew how safe Cal was in his stripped honesty. "Only one more," he said, "and I won't mind if you don't answer it. I don't think I would answer it. Here it is. Suppose you should get this money and give it to your father—would it cross your mind that you were trying to buy his love?"

"Yes, sir. It would. And it would be true."

"That's all I want to ask. That's all." Will leaned forward and put his hands against his sweating, pulsing forehead. He could not remember when he had been so shaken. And in Cal there was a cautious leap of triumph. He knew he had won and he closed his face against showing it.

Will raised his head and took off his glasses and wiped the moisture from them. "Let's go outside," he said. "Let's go for a drive."

Will drove a big Winton now, with a hood as long as a coffin and a powerful, panting mutter in its bowels. He drove south from King City over the county road, through the gathering forces of spring, and the meadowlarks flew ahead, bubbling melody from the fence wires. Pico Blanco stood up against the West with a full head of snow, and in the valley the lines of eucalyptus, which stretched across the valley to break the winds, were gleaming silver with new leaves.

When he came to the side road that led into the home draw of the Trask place Will pulled up on the side of the road. He had not spoken since the Winton rolled out of King City. The big motor idled with a deep whisper.

Will, looking straight ahead, said, "Cal—do you want to be partners with me?"

"Yes, sir."

"I don't like to take a partner without money. I could lend you the money, but there's only trouble in that."

"I can get money," said Cal.

"How much?"

"Five thousand dollars."

"You—I don't believe it."

Cal didn't answer.

"I believe it," said Will. "Borrowed?"

"Yes, sir."

"What interest?"

"None."

"That's a good trick. Where will you get it?"

"I won't tell you, sir."

Will shook his head and laughed. He was filled with pleasure. "Maybe I'm being a fool, but I believe you—and I'm not a fool." He gunned his motor and then let it idle again. "I want you to listen. Do you read the papers?"

"Yes, sir."

"We're going to be in this war any minute now."

"That's what it looks like."

"Well, a lot of people think so. Now, do you know the present price of beans? I mean, what can you sell a hundred sacks for in Salinas?"

"I'm not sure. I think about three to three and a half cents a pound."

"What do you mean you're not sure? How do you know that?"

"Well, I was thinking about asking my father to let me run the ranch."

"I see. But you don't want to farm. You're too smart. Your father's tenant is named Rantani. He's a Swiss Italian, a good farmer. He's put nearly five hundred acres under cultivation. If we can guarantee him five cents a pound and give him a seed loan, he'll plant beans. So will every other farmer around here. We could contract five thousand acres of beans."

Cal said, "What are we going to do with five-cent beans in a three-cent market? Oh, yes! But how can we be sure?"

Will said, "Are we partners?"

"Yes, sir."

"Yes, Will!"

"Yes, Will."

"How soon can you get five thousand dollars?"

"By next Wednesday."

"Shake!" Solemnly the stout man and the lean dark boy shook hands.

Will, still holding Cal's hand, said, "Now we're partners. I have a contact with the British Purchasing Agency. And I have a friend in the Quartermaster Corps. I bet we can sell all the dried beans we can find at ten cents a pound or more."

"When can you sell?"

"I'll sell before we sign anything. Now, would you like to go up to the ol place and talk to Rantani?"

"Yes, sir," said Cal.

Will double-clutched the Winton and the big green car lumbered int the side road.

FORTY-TWO

A war comes always to someone else. In Salinas we were aware that the United States was the greatest and most powerful nation in the world. Every American was a rifleman by birth, and one American was worth ten or twenty foreigners in a fight.

Pershing's expedition into Mexico after Villa had exploded one of our myths for a little while. We had truly believed that Mexicans can't shoot straight and besides were lazy and stupid. When our own Troop C came wearily back from the border they said that none of this was true. Mexicans could shoot straight, goddam it! And Villa's horsemen had outridden and outlasted our town boys. The two evenings a month of training had not toughened them very much. And last, the Mexicans seemed to have out-thought and outambushed Black Jack Pershing. When the Mexicans were joined by their ally, dysentery, it was godawful. Some of our boys didn't really feel good again for years.

Somehow we didn't connect Germans with Mexicans. We went right back to our myths. One American was as good as twenty Germans. This being true, we had only to act in a stern manner to bring the Kaiser to heel. He wouldn't dare interfere with our trade—but he did. He wouldn't stick out his neck and sink our ships—and he did. It was stupid, but he did, and so there was nothing for it but to fight him.

The war, at first anyway, was for other people. We, I, my family and friends, had kind of bleacher seats, and it was pretty exciting. And just as war is always for somebody else, so it is also true that someone else always gets killed. And Mother of God! that wasn't true either. The dreadful tele-grams began to sneak sorrowfully in, and it was everybody's brother. Here we were, over six thousand miles from the anger and the noise, and that didn't save us.

It wasn't much fun then. The Liberty Belles could parade in white caps and uniforms of white sharkskin. Our uncle could rewrite his Fourth of July speech and use it to sell bonds. We in high school could wear olive drab and campaign hats and learn the manual of arms from the physics teacher, but, Jesus Christ! Marty Hopps dead, the Berges boy, from across the street, the handsome one our little sister was in love with from the time she was three, blown to bits!

And the gangling, shuffling loose-jointed boys carrying suitcases were marching awkwardly down Main Street to the Southern Pacific Depot. They were sheepish, and the Salinas Band marched ahead of them, playing the "Stars and Stripes Forever," and the families walking along beside them were crying, and the music sounded like a dirge. The draftees wouldn't look at their mothers. They didn't dare. We'd never thought the war could happen to us.

There were some in Salinas who began to talk softly in the poolrooms and the bars. These had private information from a soldier—we weren't getting the truth. Our men were being sent in without guns. Troopships were sunk and the government wouldn't tell us. The German army was so far superior to ours that we didn't have a chance. That Kaiser was a smart fellow. He was getting ready to invade America. But would Wilson tell us this? He would not. And usually these carrion talkers were the same ones who had said one American was worth twenty Germans in a scrap—the same ones.

Little groups of British in their outlandish uniforms (but they did look smart) moved about the country, buying everything that wasn't nailed down and paying for it and paying big. A good many of the British purchasing men were crippled, but they wore their uniforms just the same. Among other things they bought beans, because beans are easy to transport and they don't spoil and a man can damn well live on them. Beans were twelve and a half cents a pound and hard to find. And farmers wished they hadn't contracted their beans for a lousy two cents a pound above the going price six months ago.

The nation and the Salinas Valley changed its songs. At first we sang of how we would knock the hell out of Helgoland and hang the Kaiser and march over there and clean up the mess them damn foreigners had made. And then suddenly we sang, "In the war's red curse stands the Red Cross nurse. She's the rose of No Man's Land," and we sang, "Hello, central, give me Heaven, 'cause my Daddy's there," and we sang, "Just a baby's prayer at twilight, when lights are low. She climbs upstairs and says her prayers—Oh, God! please tell my daddy thaddy must take care—" I guess we were like a tough but inexperienced little boy who gets punched in the nose in the first flurry and it hurts and we wished it was over.

FORTY-THREE

Late in the summer Lee came in off the street, carrying his big market basket. Lee had become American conservative in his clothes since he had lived in Salinas. He regularly wore black broadcloth when he went out of the house. His shirts were white, his collars high and stiff, and he affected narrow black string ties, like those which once were the badge for Southern senators. His hats were black, round of crown and straight of brim, and un-crushed as though he still left room for a coiled queue. He was immaculate.

Once Adam had remarked on the quiet splendor of Lee's clothes, and Lee had grinned at him. "I have to do it," he said. "One must be very rich to dress as badly as you do. The poor are forced to dress well."

"Poor!" Adam exploded. "You'll be lending us money before we're through."

"That might be," said Lee.

This afternoon he set his heavy basket on the floor. "I'm going to try to make a winter melon soup," he said. "Chinese cooking. I have a cousin in Chinatown, and he told me how. My cousin is in the firecracker and fan-tan business."

"I thought you didn't have any relatives," said Adam.

"All Chinese are related, and the ones named Lee are closest," said Lee. "My cousin is a Suey Dong. Recently he went into hiding for his health and he learned to cook. You stand the melon in a pot, cut off the top care-fully, put in a whole chicken, mushrooms, water chestnuts, leeks, and just a touch of ginger. Then you put the top back on the melon and cook it as slowly as possible for two days. Ought to be good."

Adam was lying back in his chair, his palms clasped behind his head, and he was smiling at the ceiling. "Good, Lee, good," he said.

"You didn't even listen," said Lee.

Adam drew himself upright. He said, "You think you know your own chil-dren and then you find you don't at all."

Lee smiled. "Has some detail of their lives escaped you?" he asked.

Adam chuckled. "I only found out by accident," he said. "I knew that Aron wasn't around very much this summer, but I thought he was just out playing."

"Playing!" said Lee. "He hasn't played for years."

"Well, whatever he does." Adam continued, "Today I met Mr. Kilkenny —you know, from the high school? He thought I knew all about it. Do you know what that boy is doing?"

"No," said Lee.

"He's covered all next year's work. He's going to take examinations for college and save a year. And Kilkenny is confident that he will pass. Now, what do you think of that?"

"Remarkable," said Lee. "Why is he doing it?"

"Why, to save a year!"

"What does he want to save it for?"

"Goddam it, Lee, he's ambitious. Can't you understand that?"

"No," said Lee. "I never could."

Adam said, "He never spoke of it. I wonder if his brother knows."

"I guess Aron wants it to be a surprise. We shouldn't mention it until he does."

"I guess you're right. Do you know, Lee?—I'm proud of him. Terribly proud. This makes me feel good. I wish Cal had some ambition."

"Maybe he has," said Lee. "Maybe he has some kind of a secret too."

"Maybe. God knows we haven't seen much of him lately either. Do you think it's good for him to be away so much?"

"Cal's trying to find himself," said Lee. "I guess this personal hide-and-seek is not unusual. And some people are 'it' all their lives—hopelessly 'it.' "

"Just think," said Adam. "A whole year's work ahead. When he tells us we ought to have a present for him."

"A gold watch," said Lee.

"That's right," said Adam. "I'm going to get one and have it engraved and ready. What should it say?"

"The jeweler will tell you," said Lee. "You take the chicken out after two days and cut it off the bone and put the meat back."

"What chicken?"

"Winter melon soup," said Lee.

"Have we got money enough to send him to college, Lee?"

"If we're careful and he doesn't develop expensive tastes."

"He wouldn't," Adam said.

"I didn't think I would—but I have." Lee inspected the sleeve of his coat with admiration.

2

The rectory of St. Paul's Episcopal Church was large and rambling. It had been built for ministers with large families. Mr. Rolf, unmarried and simple in his tastes, closed up most of the house, but when Aron needed a place to study he gave him a large room and helped him with his studies.

Mr. Rolf was fond of Aron. He liked the angelic beauty of his face and his smooth cheeks, his narrow hips, and long straight legs. He liked to sit in the room and watch Aron's face straining with effort to learn. He understood why Aron could not work at home in an atmosphere not conducive to hard clean thought. Mr. Rolf felt that Aron was his product, his spiritual son, his contribution to the church. He saw him through his travail of celibacy and felt that he was guiding him into calm waters.

Their discussions were long and close and personal. "I know I am criticized," Mr. Rolf said. "I happen to believe in a higher church than some people. No one can tell me that confession is not just as important a sacrament as communion. And you mind my word—I am going to bring it back, but cautiously, gradually."

"When I have a church I'll do it too."

"It requires great tact," said Mr. Rolf.

Aron said, "I wish we had in our church, well—well, I might as well say it
I wish we had something like the Augustines or the Franciscans. Someplace
to withdraw. Sometimes I feel dirty. I want to get away from the dirt and be
clean."

"I know how you feel," Mr. Rolf said earnestly. "But there I cannot go
along with you. I can't think that our Lord Jesus would want his priest-
hood withdrawn from service to the world. Think how he insisted that we
preach the Gospel, help the sick and poor, even lower ourselves into filth to
raise sinners from the slime. We must keep the exactness of His example
always before us."

His eyes began to glow and his voice took on the throatiness he used in
sermons. "Perhaps I shouldn't tell you this. And I hope you won't find any
pride in me in telling it. But there is a kind of glory in it. For the last five
weeks a woman has been coming to evening service. I don't think you can
see her from the choir. She sits always in the last row on the left-hand side
—yes, you can see her too. She is off at an angle. Yes, you can see her. She
wears a veil and she always leaves before I can get back after recessional."

"Who is she?" Aron asked.

"Well, you'll have to learn these things. I made very discreet inquiries
and you would never guess. She is the—well—the owner of a house of ill
fame."

"Here in Salinas?"

"Here in Salinas." Mr. Rolf leaned forward. "Aron, I can see your revulsion. You must get over that. Don't forget our Lord and Mary Magdalene.
Without pride I say I would be glad to raise her up."

"What does she want here?" Aron demanded.

"Perhaps what we have to offer—salvation. It will require great tact. I can
see how it will be. And mark my words—these people are timid. One day
there will come a tap on my door and she will beg to come in. Then, Aron,
I pray that I may be wise and patient. You must believe me—when that
happens, when a lost soul seeks the light, it is the highest and most beautiful
experience a priest can have. That's what we are for, Aron. That's what we
are for."

Mr. Rolf controlled his breathing with difficulty. "I pray God I may not
fail," he said.

3

Adam Trask thought of the war in terms of his own now dimly remembered
campaign against the Indians. No one knew anything about huge and general
war. Lee read European history, trying to discern from the filaments of the
past some pattern of the future.

Liza Hamilton died with a pinched little smile on her mouth, and her cheekbones were shockingly high when the red was gone from them.

And Adam waited impatiently for Aron to bring news of his examinations. The massive gold watch lay under his handkerchiefs in the top drawer of his bureau, and he kept it wound and set and checked its accuracy against his own watch.

Lee had his instructions. On the evening of the day of the announcement he was to cook a turkey and bake a cake.

"We'll want to make a party of it," Adam said. "What would you think of champagne?"

"Very nice," said Lee. "Did you ever read von Clausewitz?"

"Who is he?"

"Not very reassuring reading," said Lee. "One bottle of champagne?"

"That's enough. It's just for toasts, you know. Makes a party of it." It didn't occur to Adam that Aron might fail.

One afternoon Aron came in and asked Lee, "Where's father?"

"He's shaving."

"I won't be in for dinner," said Aron.

In the bathroom he stood behind his father and spoke to the soap-faced image in the mirror. "Mr. Rolf asked me to have dinner at the rectory."

Adam wiped his razor on a folded piece of toilet paper. "That's nice," he said.

"Can I get a bath?"

"I'll be out of here in just a minute," said Adam.

When Aron walked through the living room and said good night and went out, Cal and Adam looked after him. "He got into my cologne," said Cal. "I can still smell him."

"It must be quite a party," Adam said.

"I don't blame him for wanting to celebrate. That was a hard job."

"Celebrate?"

"The exams. Didn't he tell you? He passed them."

"Oh, yes—the exams," said Adam. "Yes, he told me. A fine job. I'm proud of him. I think I'll get him a gold watch."

Cal said sharply, "He didn't tell you!"

"Oh, yes—yes, he did. He told me this morning."

"He didn't know this morning," said Cal, and he got up and went out.

He walked very fast in the gathering darkness, out Central Avenue, past the park and past Stonewall Jackson Smart's house clear to the place beyond the streetlights where the street became a county road and angled to avoid Tollot's farm house.

At ten o'clock Lee, going out to mail a letter, found Cal sitting on the lowest step of the front porch. "What happened to you?" he asked.

"I went for a walk."

"What's the matter with Aron?"

"I don't know."

"He seems to have some kind of grudge. Want to walk to the post office with me?"

"No."

"What are you sitting out here for?"

"I'm going to beat the hell out of him."

"Don't do it," said Lee.

"Why not?"

"Because I don't think you can. He'd slaughter you."

"I guess you're right," said Cal. "The son of a bitch!"

"Watch your language."

Cal laughed. "I guess I'll walk along with you."

"Did you ever read von Clausewitz?"

"I never even heard of him."

When Aron came home it was Lee who was waiting for him on the lowest step of the front porch. "I saved you from a licking," Lee said. "Sit down."

"I'm going to bed."

"Sit down! I want to talk to you. Why didn't you tell your father you passed the tests?"

"He wouldn't understand."

"You've got a bug up your ass."

"I don't like that kind of language."

"Why do you think I used it? I am not profane by accident. Aron, your father has been living for this."

"How did he know about it?"

"You should have told him yourself."

"This is none of your business."

"I want you to go in and wake him up if he's asleep, but I don't think he'll be asleep. I want you to tell him."

"I won't do it."

Lee said softly, "Aron, did you ever have to fight a little man, a man half your size?"

"What do you mean?"

"It's one of the most embarrassing things in the world. He won't stop and pretty soon you have to hit him and that's worse. Then you're really in trouble all around."

"What are you talking about?"

"If you don't do as I tell you, Aron, I'm going to fight you. Isn't that ridiculous?"

Aron tried to pass. Lee stood up in front of him, his tiny fists doubled ineffectually, his stance and position so silly that he began to laugh. "I don't know how to do it, but I'm going to try," he said.

Aron nervously backed away from him. And when finally he sat down on the steps Lee sighed deeply. "Thank heaven that's over," he said. "It would

ave been awful. Look, Aron, can't you tell me what's the matter with
ou? You always used to tell me."

Suddenly Aron broke down. "I want to go away. It's a dirty town."

"No, it isn't. It's just the same as other places."

"I don't belong here. I wish we hadn't ever come here. I don't know what's
he matter with me. I want to go away." His voice rose to a wail.

Lee put his arm around the broad shoulders to comfort him. "You're
rowing up. Maybe that's it," he said softly. "Sometimes I think the world
ests us most sharply then, and we turn inward and watch ourselves with
orror. But that's not the worst. We think everybody is seeing into us. Then
irt is very dirty and purity is shining white. Aron, it will be over. Wait only
 little while and it will be over. That's not much relief to you because you
on't believe it, but it's the best I can do for you. Try to believe that things
re neither so good nor so bad as they seem to you now. Yes, I can help you.
Go to bed now, and in the morning get up early and tell your father about
he tests. Make it exciting. He's lonelier than you are because he has no
ovely future to dream about. Go through the motions. Sam Hamilton said
that. Pretend it's true and maybe it will be. Go through the motions. Do
that. And go to bed. I've got to bake a cake—for breakfast. And, Aron—your
father left a present on your pillow."

FORTY-FOUR

It was only after Aron went away to college that Abra really got to know his
family. Aron and Abra had fenced themselves in with themselves. With
Aron gone, she attached herself to the other Trasks. She found that she
trusted Adam more, and loved Lee more, than her own father.

About Cal she couldn't decide. He disturbed her sometimes with anger,
sometimes with pain, and sometimes with curiosity. He seemed to be in a
perpetual contest with her. She didn't know whether he liked her or not, and
so she didn't like him. She was relieved when, calling at the Trask house,
Cal was not there, to look secretly at her, judge, appraise, consider, and look
away when she caught him at it.

Abra was a straight, strong, fine-breasted woman, developed and ready
and waiting to take her sacrament—but waiting. She took to going to the
Trask house after school, sitting with Lee, reading him parts of Aron's daily
letter.

Aron was lonely at Stanford. His letters were drenched with lonesome
longing for his girl. Together they were matter of fact, but from the university, ninety miles away, he made passionate love to her, shut himself off

from the life around him. He studied, ate, slept, and wrote to Abra, and this was his whole life.

In the afternoons she sat in the kitchen with Lee and helped him to string beans or slip peas from their pods. Sometimes she made fudge and very often she stayed to dinner rather than go home to her parents. There was no subject she could not discuss with Lee. And the few things she could talk about to her father and mother were thin and pale and tired and mostly not even true. There Lee was different also. Abra wanted to tell Lee only true things even when she wasn't quite sure what was true.

Lee would sit smiling a little, and his quick fragile hands flew about their work as though they had independent lives. Abra wasn't aware that she spoke exclusively of herself. And sometimes while she talked Lee's mind wandered out and came back and went out again like a ranging dog, and Lee would nod at intervals and make a quiet humming sound.

He liked Abra and he felt strength and goodness in her, and warmth too. Her features had the bold muscular strength which could result finally either in ugliness or in great beauty. Lee, musing through her talk, thought of the round smooth faces of the Cantonese, his own breed. Even thin they were moon-faced. Lee should have liked that kind best since beauty must be somewhat like ourselves, but he didn't. When he thought of Chinese beauty the iron predatory faces of the Manchus came to his mind, arrogant and unyielding faces of a people who had authority by unquestioned inheritance.

She said, "Maybe it was there all along. I don't know. He never talked much about his father. It was after Mr. Trask had the—you know—the lettuce. Aron was angry then."

"Why?" Lee asked.

"People were laughing at him."

Lee's whole mind popped back. "Laughing at Aron? Why at him? He didn't have anything to do with it."

"Well, that's the way he felt. Do you want to know what I think?"

"Of course," said Lee.

"I figured this out and I'm not quite finished figuring. I thought he always felt—well, kind of crippled—maybe unfinished, because he didn't have a mother."

Lee's eyes opened wide and then drooped again. He nodded. "I see. Do you figure Cal is that way too?"

"No."

"Then why Aron?"

"Well, I haven't got that yet. Maybe some people need things more than others, or hate things more. My father hates turnips. He always did. Never came from anything. Turnips make him mad, real mad. Well, one time my mother was—well, huffy, and she made a casserole of mashed turnips with lots of pepper and cheese on top and got it all brown on top. My father ate half a dish of it before he asked what it was. My mother said turnips, and he threw the dish on the floor and got up and went out. I don't think he ever forgave her."

Lee chuckled. "He can forgive her because she said turnips. But, Abra, suppose he'd asked and she had said something else and he liked it and had another dish. And then afterward he found out. Why, he might have murdered her."

"I guess so. Well, anyway, I figure Aron needed a mother more than Cal did. And I think he always blamed his father."

"Why?"

"I don't know. That's what I think."

"You do get around, don't you?"

"Shouldn't I?"

"Of course you should."

"Shall I make some fudge?"

"Not today. We still have some."

"What can I do?"

"You can pound flour into the top round. Will you eat with us?"

"No. I'm going to a birthday party, thank you. Do you think he'll be a minister?"

"How do I know?" said Lee. "Maybe it's just an idea."

"I hope he doesn't," said Abra, and she clapped her mouth shut in astonishment at having said it.

Lee got up and pulled out the pastry board and laid out the red meat and a flour sifter beside it. "Use the back side of the knife," he said.

"I know." She hoped he hadn't heard her.

But Lee asked, "Why don't you want him to be a minister?"

"I shouldn't say it."

"You should say anything you want to. You don't have to explain." He went back to his chair, and Abra sifted flour over the steak and pounded the meat with a big knife. Tap-tap—"I shouldn't talk like this"—tap-tap.

Lee turned his head away to let her take her own pace.

"He goes all one way," she said over the pounding. "If it's church it's got to be high church. He was talking about how priests shouldn't be married."

"That's not the way his last letter sounded," Lee observed.

"I know. That was before." Her knife stopped its pounding. Her face was young perplexed pain. "Lee, I'm not good enough for him."

"Now, what do you mean by that?"

"I'm not being funny. He doesn't think about me. He's made someone up, and it's like he put my skin on her. I'm not like that—not like the made-up one."

"What's she like?"

"Pure!" said Abra. "Just absolutely pure. Nothing but pure—never a bad thing. I'm not like that."

"Nobody is," said Lee.

"He doesn't know me. He doesn't even want to know me. He wants that —white—ghost."

Lee rubbled a piece of cracker. "Don't you like him? You're pretty young, but I don't think that makes any difference."

" 'Course I like him. I'm going to be his wife. But I want him to like me too. And how can he, if he doesn't know anything about me? I used to think he knew me. Now I'm not sure he ever did."

"Maybe he's going through a hard time that isn't permanent. You're a smart girl—very smart. Is it pretty hard trying to live up to the one—in your skin?"

"I'm always afraid he'll see something in me that isn't in the one he made up. I'll get mad or I'll smell bad—or something else. He'll find out."

"Maybe not," said Lee. "But it must be hard living the Lily Maid, the Goddess-Virgin, and the other all at once. Humans just do smell bad sometimes."

She moved toward the table. "Lee, I wish—"

"Don't spill flour on my floor," he said. "What do you wish?"

"It's from my figuring out. I think Aron, when he didn't have a mother —why, he made her everything good he could think of."

"That might be. And then you think he dumped it all on you." She stared at him and her fingers wandered delicately up and down the blade of the knife. "And you wish you could find some way to dump it all back."

"Yes."

"Suppose he wouldn't like you then?"

"I'd rather take a chance on that," she said. "I'd rather be myself."

Lee said, "I never saw anybody get mixed up in other people's business the way I do. And I'm a man who doesn't have a final answer about anything. Are you going to pound that meat or shall I do it?"

She went back to work. "Do you think it's funny to be so serious when I'm not even out of high school?" she asked.

"I don't see how it could be any other way," said Lee. "Laughter comes later, like wisdom teeth, and laughter at yourself comes last of all in a mad race with death, and sometimes it isn't in time."

Her tapping speeded up and its beat became erratic and nervous. Lee moved five dried lima beans in patterns on the table—a line, an angle, a circle.

The beating stopped. "Is Mrs. Trask alive?"

Lee's forefinger hung over a bean for a moment and then slowly fell and pushed it to make the O into a Q. He knew she was looking at him. He could even see in his mind how her expression would be one of panic at her question. His thought raced like a rat new caught in a wire trap. He

.;hed and gave it up. He turned slowly and looked at her, and his picture ..d been accurate.

Lee said tonelessly, "We've talked a lot and I don't remember that we .ve ever discussed me—ever." He smiled shyly. "Abra, let me tell you .)out myself. I'm a servant. I'm old. I'm Chinese. These three you know. .m tired and I'm cowardly."

"You're not—" she began.

"Be silent," he said. "I am so cowardly. I will not put my finger in any .uman pie."

"What do you mean?"

"Abra, is your father mad at anything except turnips?"

Her face went stubborn. "I asked you a question."

"I did not hear a question," he said softly and his voice became con- .dent. "You did not ask a question, Abra."

"I guess you think I'm too young—" Abra began.

Lee broke in, "Once I worked for a woman of thirty-five who had .uccessfully resisted experience, learning, and beauty. If she had been six .he would have been the despair of her parents. And at thirty-five she was .ermitted to control money and the lives of people around her. No, Abra, .ge has nothing to do with it. If I had anything at all to say—I would say .t to you."

The girl smiled at him. "I'm clever," she said. "Shall I be clever?"

"God help me—no," Lee protested.

"Then you don't want me to try to figure it out?"

"I don't care what you do as long as I don't have anything to do with it. I guess no matter how weak and negative a good man is, he has as many .ins on him as he can bear. I have enough sins to trouble me. Maybe they aren't very fine sins compared to some, but, the way I feel, they're all I .an take care of. Please forgive me."

Abra reached across the table and touched the back of his hand with .loury fingers. The yellow skin on his hand was tight and glazed. He looked down at the white powdery smudges her fingers left.

Abra said, "My father wanted a boy. I guess he hates turnips and girls. He tells everyone how he gave me my crazy name. 'And though I called another, Abra came.'"

Lee smiled at her. "You're such a nice girl," he said. "I'll buy some turnips tomorrow if you'll come to dinner."

Abra asked softly, "Is she alive?"

"Yes," said Lee.

The front door slammed, and Cal came into the kitchen. "Hello, Abra. Lee, is father home?"

"No, not yet. What are you grinning all over for?"

Cal handed him a check. "There. That's for you."

Lee looked at it. "I didn't want interest," he said.

"It's better. I might want to borrow it back."

"You won't tell me where you got it?"

"No. Not yet. I've got a good idea—" His eyes flicked to Abra.

"I have to go home now," she said.

Cal said, "She might as well be in on it. I decided to do it Thanksgiving and Abra'll probably be around and Aron will be home."

"Do what?" she asked.

"I've got a present for my father."

"What is it?" Abra asked.

"I won't tell. You'll find out then."

"Does Lee know?"

"Yes, but he won't tell."

"I don't think I ever saw you so—gay," Abra said. "I don't think I ever saw you gay at all." She discovered in herself a warmth for him.

After Abra had gone Cal sat down. "I don't know whether to give it to him before Thanksgiving dinner or after," he said.

"After," said Lee. "Have you really got the money?"

"Fifteen thousand dollars."

"Honestly?"

"You mean, did I steal it?"

"Yes."

"Honestly," said Cal. "Remember how we had champagne for Aron? We'll get champagne. And—well, we'll maybe decorate the dining room. Maybe Abra'll help."

"Do you really think your father wants money?"

"Why wouldn't he?"

"I hope you're right," said Lee. "How have you been doing in school?"

"Not very well. I'll pick up after Thanksgiving," said Cal.

2

After school the next day Abra hurried and caught up with Cal.

"Hello, Abra," he said. "You make good fudge."

"That last was dry. It should be creamy."

"Lee is just crazy about you. What have you done to him?"

"I like Lee," she said and then, "I want to ask you something, Cal."

"Yes?"

"What's the matter with Aron?"

"What do you mean?"

"He just seems to think only about himself."

"I don't think that's very new. Have you had a fight with him?"

"No. When he had all that about going into the church and not getting married, I tried to fight with him, but he wouldn't."

"Not get married to you? I can't imagine that."

"Cal, he writes me love letters now—only they aren't to me."

"Then who are they to?"

"It's like they were to—himself."

Cal said, "I know about the willow tree."

She didn't seem surprised. "Do you?" she asked.

"Are you mad at Aron?"

"No, not mad. I just can't find him. I don't know him."

"Wait around," said Cal. "Maybe he's going through something."

"I wonder if I'll be all right. Do you think I could have been wrong all the time?"

"How do I know?"

"Cal," she said, "is it true that you go out late at night and even go—to—bad houses?"

"Yes," he said. "That's true. Did Aron tell you?"

"No, not Aron. Well, why do you go there?"

He walked beside her and did not answer.

"Tell me," she said.

"What's it to you?"

"Is it because you're bad?"

"What's it sound like to you?"

"I'm not good either," she said.

"You're crazy," said Cal. "Aron will knock that out of you."

"Do you think he will?"

"Why, sure," said Cal. "He's got to."

FORTY-FIVE

Joe Valery got along by watching and listening and, as he said himself, not sticking his neck out. He had built his hatreds little by little—beginning with a mother who neglected him, a father who alternately whipped and slobbered over him. It had been easy to transfer his developing hatred to the teacher who disciplined him and the policeman who chased him and the priest who lectured him. Even before the first magistrate looked down on him, Joe had developed a fine stable of hates toward the whole world he knew.

Hate cannot live alone. It must have love as a trigger, a goad, or a stimulant. Joe early developed a gentle protective love for Joe. He comforted and flattered and cherished Joe. He set up walls to save Joe from a hostile world. And gradually Joe became proof against wrong. If Joe got into trouble, it was because the world was in angry conspiracy against him. And if Joe attacked the world, it was revenge and they damn well deserved it—the sons

of bitches. Joe lavished every care on his love, and he perfected a lonely se
of rules which might have gone like this:

1. Don't believe nobody. The bastards are after you.
2. Keep your mouth shut. Don't stick your neck out.
3. Keep your ears open. When they make a slip, grab on to it and wait.
4. Everybody's a son of a bitch and whatever you do they got it coming
5. Go at everything roundabout.
6. Don't never trust no dame about nothing.
7. Put your faith in dough. Everybody wants it. Everybody will sell ou
for it.

There were other rules, but they were refinements. His system worked
and since he knew no other, Joe had no basis of comparison with other
systems. He knew it was necessary to be smart and he considered himsel
smart. If he pulled something off, that was smart; if he failed, that was bad
luck. Joe was not very successful but he got by and with a minimum of
effort. Kate kept him because she knew he would do anything in the world
if he were paid to do it or was afraid not to do it. She had no illusions about
him. In her business Joes were necessary.

When he first got the job with Kate, Joe looked for the weaknesses on
which he lived—vanity, voluptuousness, anxiety or conscience, greed,
hysteria. He knew they were there because she was a woman. It was a matter
of considerable shock to him to learn that, if they were there, he couldn't
find them. This dame thought and acted like a man—only tougher, quicker,
and more clever. Joe made a few mistakes and Kate rubbed his nose in
them. He developed an admiration for her based on fear.

When he found that he couldn't get away with some things, he began
to believe he couldn't get away with anything. Kate made a slave of him
just as he had always made slaves of women. She fed him, clothed him, gave
him orders, punished him.

Once Joe recognized her as more clever than himself, it was a short step
to the belief that she was more clever than anybody. He thought that she
possessed the two great gifts: she was smart and she got the breaks—and you
couldn't want no better than that. He was glad to do her hatchet work—and
afraid not to. Kate don't make no mistakes, Joe said. And if you played
along with her, Kate took care of you. This went beyond thought and became a habit pattern. When he got Ethel floated over the county line, it
was all in the day's work. It was Kate's business and she was smart.

2

Kate did not sleep well when the arthritic pains were bad. She could almost
feel her joints thicken and knot. Sometimes she tried to think of other
things, even unpleasant ones, to drive the pain and the distorted fingers
from her mind. Sometimes she tried to remember every detail in a room she

had not seen for a long time. Sometimes she looked at the ceiling and projected columns of figures and added them. Sometimes she used memories. She built Mr. Edwards' face and his clothes and the word that was stamped on the metal clasp of his suspenders. She had never noticed it, but she knew the word was "Excelsior."

Often in the night she thought of Faye, remembered her eyes and hair and the tone of her voice and how her hands fluttered and the little lump of flesh beside her left thumbnail, a scar from an ancient cut. Kate went into her feeling about Faye. Did she hate or love her? Did she pity her? Was she sorry she had killed her? Kate inched over her own thoughts like a measuring worm. She found she had no feeling about Faye. She neither liked nor disliked her or her memory. There had been a time during her dying when the noise and the smell of her had made anger rise in Kate so that she considered killing her quickly to get it over.

Kate remembered how Faye had looked the last time she saw her, lying in her purple casket, dressed in white, with the undertaker's smile on her lips and enough powder and rouge to cover her sallow skin.

A voice behind Kate had said, "She looks better than she has in years." And another voice had answered, "Maybe the same thing would do me some good," and there was a double snicker. The first voice would be Ethel, and the second Trixie. Kate remembered her own half-humorous reaction. Why, she had thought, a dead whore looks like anybody else.

Yes, the first voice must have been Ethel. Ethel always got into the night thinking, and Ethel always brought a shrinking fear with her, the stupid, clumsy, nosy bitch—the lousy old bag. And it happened very often that Kate's mind would tell her, "Now wait a moment. Why is she a lousy old bag? Isn't it because you made a mistake? Why did you float her? If you'd used your head and kept her here—"

Kate wondered where Ethel was. How about one of those agencies to find Ethel—at least to find where she went? Yes, and then Ethel would tell about that night and show the glass. Then there'd be two noses sniffing instead of one. Yes, but what difference would that make? Every time Ethel got a beer in her she would be telling somebody. Oh, sure, but they would think she was just a buzzed old hustler. Now an agency man—no—no agencies.

Kate spent many hours with Ethel. Did the judge have any idea it was a frame—too simple? It shouldn't have been an even hundred dollars. That was obvious. And how about the sheriff? Joe said they dropped her over the line into Santa Cruz County. What did Ethel tell the deputy who drove her out? Ethel was a lazy old bat. Maybe she had stayed in Watsonville. There was Pajaro, and that was a railroad section, and then the Pajaro River and the bridge into Watsonville. Lots of section hands went back and forth, Mexicans, some Hindus. That puddlehead Ethel might have thought she could turn enough tricks with the track workers. Wouldn't it be funny if she had never left Watsonville, thirty miles away? She could even slip in over the line and see her friends if she wanted to. Maybe she came to Salinas some-times. She might be in Salinas right now. The cops weren't likely to keep too much on the look for her. Maybe it would be a good idea to send Joe over to Watsonville to see if Ethel was there. She might have gone on to Santa Cruz. Joe could look there too. It wouldn't take him long. Joe could find any hooker in any town in a few hours. If he found her they could get her back somehow. Ethel was a fool. But maybe when he found her it would be better if Kate went to her. Lock the door. Leave a "Do not disturb" sign. She could get to Watsonville, do her business, and get back. No taxis. Take a bus. Nobody saw anybody on the night buses. People sleeping with their shoes off and coats rolled up behind their heads. Suddenly she knew she would be afraid to go to Watsonville. Well, she could make herself go. It would stop all this wondering. Strange she hadn't thought of sending Joe before. That was perfect. Joe was good at some things, and the dumb bastard thought he was clever. That was the kind easiest to handle. Ethel was stupid. That made her hard to handle.

As her hands and her mind grew more crooked, Kate began to rely more and more on Joe Valery as her assistant in chief, as her go-between, and as her executioner. She had a basic fear of the girls in the house—not that they were more untrustworthy than Joe but that the hysteria which lay very close to the surface might at any time crack through their caution and shatter their sense of self-preservation and tear down not only themselves but their sur-roundings. Kate had always been able to handle this ever-present danger, but now the slow-depositing calcium and the slow growth of apprehension caused her to need help and to look for it from Joe. Men, she knew, had a little stronger wall against self-destruction than the kind of women she knew.

She felt that she could trust Joe, because she had in her files a notation relating to one Joseph Venuta who had walked away from a San Quentin road gang in the fourth year of a five-year sentence for robbery. Kate had never mentioned this to Joe Valery, but she thought it might have a sooth-ing influence on him if he got out of hand.

Joe brought the breakfast tray every morning—green China tea and cream and toast. When he had set it on her bedside table he made his report and got his orders for the day. He knew that she was depending on him more and more. And Joe was very slowly and quietly exploring the possibility of taking over entirely. If she got sick enough there might be a chance. But very profoundly Joe was afraid of her.

"Morning," he said.

"I'm not going to sit up for it, Joe. Just give me the tea. You'll have to hold it."

"Hands bad?"

"Yes. They get better after a flare up."

"Looks like you had a bad night."

"No," said Kate. "I had a good night. I've got some new medicine."

Joe held the cup to her lips, and she drank the tea in little sips, breathing in over it to cool it. "That's enough," she said when the cup was only half empty. "How was the night?"

"I almost came to tell you last night," said Joe. "Hick came in from King City. Just sold his crop. Bought out the house. Dropped seven hundred not counting what he give the girls."

"What was his name?"

"I don't know. But I hope he comes in again."

"You should get the name, Joe. I've told you that."

"He was cagey."

"All the more reason to get his name. Didn't any of the girls frisk him?"

"I don't know."

"Well, find out."

Joe sensed a mild geniality in her and it made him feel good. "I'll find out," he assured her. "I got enough to go on."

Her eyes went over him, testing and searching, and he knew something was coming. "You like it here?" she asked softly.

"Sure. I got it good here."

"You could have it better—or worse," she said.

"I like it good here," he said uneasily, and his mind cast about for a fault in himself. "I got it real nice here."

She moistened her lips with her arrow-shaped tongue. "You and I can work together," she said.

"Any way you want it," he said ingratiatingly, and a surge of pleasant expectation grew in him. He waited patiently. She took a good long time to begin.

At last she said, "Joe, I don't like to have anything stolen."

"I didn't take nothing."

"I didn't say you did."

"Who?"

"I'll get to it, Joe. Do you remember that old buzzard we had to move?"

"You mean Ethel what's-her-name?"

"Yes. That's the one. She got away with something. I didn't know it then."

"What?"

A coldness crept into her voice. "Not your business, Joe. Listen to me! You're a smart fellow. Where would you go to look for her?"

Joe's mind worked quickly, not with reason but with experience and instinct. "She was pretty beat up. She wouldn't go far. An old hustler don't go far."

"You're smart. You think she might be in Watsonville?"

"There or maybe Santa Cruz. Anyways, I'll give odds she ain't farther away than San Jose."

She caressed her fingers tenderly. "Would you like to make five hundred, Joe?"

"You want I should find her?"

"Yes. Just find her. When you do, don't let her know. Just bring me the address. Got that? Just tell me where she is."

"Okay," said Joe. "She must of rolled you good."

"That's not your business, Joe."

"Yes, ma'am," he said. "You want I should start right off?"

"Yes. Make it quick, Joe."

"Might be a little tough," he said. "It's been a long time."

"That's up to you."

"I'll go to Watsonville this afternoon."

"That's good, Joe."

She was thoughtful. He knew she was not finished and that she was wondering whether she should go on. She decided.

"Joe, did—did she do anything—well, peculiar—that day in court?"

"Hell, no. Said she was framed like they always do."

And then something came back to him that he hadn't noticed at the time. Out of his memory Ethel's voice came, saying, "Judge, I got to see you alone. I got to tell you something." He tried to bury his memory deep so that his face would not speak.

Kate said, "Well, what was it?"

He had been too late. His mind leaped for safety. "There's something," he said to gain time. "I'm trying to think."

"Well, think!" Her voice was edged and anxious.

"Well—" He had it. "Well, I heard her tell the cops—let's see—she said why couldn't they let her go south. She said she had relatives in San Luis Obispo."

Kate leaned quickly toward him. "Yes?"

"And the cops said it was too damn far."

"You're smart, Joe. Where will you go first?"

"Watsonville," he said. "I got a friend in San Luis. He'll look around for me. I'll give him a ring."

"Joe," she said sharply, "I want this quiet."

"For five hundred you'll get it quiet and quick," said Joe. He felt fine even though her eyes were slitted and inspective again. Her next words jarred his stomach loose from his backbone.

"Joe, not to change the subject—does the name Venuta mean anything to you?"

He tried to answer before his throat tightened. "Not a thing," he said.

"Come back as soon as you can," Kate said. "Tell Helen to come in. She'll take over for you."

3

Joe packed his suitcase, went to the depot, and bought a ticket for Watson-ville. At Castroville, the first station north, he got off and waited four hours for the Del Monte express from San Francisco to Monterey, which is at the end of a spur line. In Monterey he climbed the stairs of the Central Hotel, registered as John Vicker. He went downstairs and ate a steak at Pop Ernst's, bought a bottle of whisky, and retired to his room.

He took off his shoes and his coat and vest, removed his collar and tie, and lay down on the bed. The whisky and a glass were on the table beside the brass bed. The overhead light shining in his face didn't bother him. He didn't notice it. Methodically he primed his brain with half a tumbler of whisky and then he crossed his hands behind his head and crossed his ankles and he brought out thoughts and impressions and perceptions and instincts and began matching them.

It had been a good job and he had thought he had her fooled. Well, he'd underrated her. But how in hell had she got onto it he was wanted? He thought he might go to Reno or maybe to Seattle. Seaport towns—always good. And then—now wait a minute. Think about it.

Ethel didn't steal nothing. She had something. Kate was scared of Ethel. Five hundred was a lot of dough to dig out a beat-up whore. What Ethel wanted to tell the judge was, number one, true; and, number two, Kate was scared of it. Might be able to use that. Hell!—not with her holding that jail-break over him. Joe wasn't going to serve out the limit with penalties.

But no harm in thinking about it. Suppose he was to gamble four years against—well, let's say ten grand. Was that a bad bet? No need to decide. She knew it before and didn't turn him in. Suppose she thought he was a good dog.

Maybe Ethel might be a hole-card.

Now—wait—just think about it. Maybe it was the breaks. Maybe he ought to draw his hand and see. But she was so goddam smart. Joe wondered if he could play against her. But how, if he just played along?

Joe sat up and filled his glass full. He turned off his light and raised his shade. And as he drank his whisky he watched a skinny little woman in a bathrobe washing her stockings in a basin in a room on the other side of the air shaft. And the whisky muttered in his ears.

It might be the breaks. God knows, Joe had waited long enough. God knows, he hated the bitch with her sharp little teeth. No need to decide right now.

He raised his window quietly and threw the writing pen from the table against the window across the air shaft. He enjoyed the scene of fear and apprehension before the skinny dame yanked her shade down.

With the third glass of whisky the pint was empty. Joe felt a wish to go

out in the street and look the town over. But then his discipline took over
He had made a rule, and kept to it, never to leave his room when he wa
drinking. That way a man never got in trouble. Trouble meant cops, an
cops meant a check-up, and that would surely mean a trip across the bay to
San Quentin and no road gang for good behavior this time. He put the
street out of his mind.

Joe had another pleasure he saved for times when he was alone, and he
was not aware it was a pleasure. He indulged it now. He lay on the brass bed
and went back in time over his sullen and miserable childhood and his fretful and vicious growing up. No luck—he never got the breaks. The big shots
got the breaks. A few snatch jobs he got away with, but the tray of pocketknives? Cops came right in his house and got him. Then he was on the
books and they never let him alone. Guy in Daly City couldn't shag a crate
of strawberries off a truck without they'd pick up Joe. In school he didn't
have no luck neither. Teachers against him, principal against him. Guy
couldn't take that crap. Had to get out.

Out of his memory of bad luck a warm sadness grew, and he pushed it
with more memories until the tears came to his eyes and his lips quivered
with pity for the lonely lost boy he had been. And here he was now—look at
him—a rap against him, working in a whorehouse when other men had
homes and cars. They were safe and happy and at night their blinds were
pulled down against Joe. He wept quietly until he fell asleep.

Joe got up at ten in the morning and ate a monster breakfast at Pop
Ernst's. In the early afternoon he took a bus to Watsonville and played
three games of snooker with a friend who came to meet him in answer to a
phone call. Joe won the last game and racked his cue. He handed his friend
two ten-dollar bills.

"Hell," said his friend, "I don't want your money."

"Take it," said Joe.

"It ain't like I give you anything."

"You give me plenty. You say she ain't here and you're the baby that
would know."

"Can't tell me what you want her for?"

"Wilson, I tol' you right first an' I tell you now, I don't know. I'm jus'
doing a job of work."

"Well, that's all I can do. Seems like there was this convention—what was
it?—dentists, or maybe Owls. I don't know whether she said she was going or
I just figured it myself. I got it stuck in my mind. Give Santa Cruz a whirl.
Know anybody?"

"I got a few acquaintances," said Joe.

"Look up H. V. Mahler. Hal Mahler. He runs Hal's poolroom. Got a
game in back."

"Thanks," said Joe.

"No—look, Joe. I don't want your money."

"It ain't my money—buy a cigar," said Joe.

The bus dropped him two doors from Hal's place. It was suppertime but the stud game was still going. It was an hour before Hal got up to go to the can and Joe could follow and make a connection. Hal peered at Joe with large pale eyes made huge by thick glasses. He buttoned his fly slowly and adjusted his black alpaca sleeve guards and squared his green eyeshade. "Stick around till the game breaks," he said. "Care to sit in?"

"How many playing for you, Hal?"

"Only one."

"I'll play for you."

"Five bucks an hour," said Hal.

"An' ten per cent if I win?"

"Well, okay. Sandy-haired fella Williams is the house."

At one o'clock in the morning Hal and Joe went to Barlow's Grill. "Two rib steaks and french fries. You want soup?" Hal asked Joe.

"No. And no french fries. They bind me up."

"Me too," said Hal. "But I eat them just the same. I don't get enough exercise."

Hal was a silent man until he was eating. He rarely spoke unless his mouth was full. "What's your pitch?" he asked around steak.

"Just a job. I make a hundred bucks and you get twenty-five—okay?"

"Got to have like proof—like papers?"

"No. Be good but I'll get by without them."

"Well, she come in and wants me to steer for her. She wasn't no good. I didn't take twenty a week off her. I probably wouldn't of knew what become of her only Bill Primus seen her in my place and when they found her he come in an' ast me about her. Nice fella, Bill. We got a nice force here."

Ethel was not a bad woman—lazy, sloppy, but good-hearted. She wanted dignity and importance. She was just not very bright and not very pretty and, because of these two lacks, not very lucky. It would have bothered Ethel if she had known that when they pulled her out of the sand where waves had left her half buried her skirts were pulled around her ass. She would have liked more dignity.

Hal said, "We got some crazy bohunk bastards in the sardine fleet. Get loaded with ink an' they go nuts. Way I figure, one of them sardine crews took her out an' then jus' pushed her overboard. I don't see how else she'd get in the water."

"Maybe she jumped off the pier?"

"Her?" said Hal through potatoes. "Hell, no! She was too blamed lazy to kill herself. You want to check?"

"If you say it's her, it's her," said Joe, and he pushed a twenty and a five across the table.

Hal rolled the bills like a cigarette and put them in his vest pocket. He cut out the triangle of meat from the rib steak and put it in his mouth. "It was her," he said. "Want a piece of pie?"

Joe meant to sleep until noon but he awakened at seven and lay in bed for quite a long time. He planned not to get back to Salinas until after midnight. He needed more time to think.

When he got up he looked in the mirror and inspected the expression he planned to wear. He wanted to look disappointed but not too disappointed. Kate was so goddam clever. Let her lead. Just follow suit. She was about as wide open as a fist. Joe had to admit that he was scared to death of her.

His caution said to him, "Just go in and tell her and get your five hundred."

And he answered his caution savagely, "Breaks. How many breaks did I ever get? Part of the breaks is knowing a break when you get it. Do I want to be a lousy pimp all my life? Just play it close. Let her do the talking. No harm in that. I can always tell her later like I just found out if it don't go good."

"She could have you in a cell block in six hours flat."

"Not if I play 'em close. What I got to lose? What breaks did I ever get?"

4

Kate was feeling better. The new medicine seemed to be doing her some good. The pain in her hands was abated, and it seemed to her that her fingers were straighter, the knuckles not so swollen. She had had a good night's sleep, the first in a long time, and she felt good, even a little excited. She planned to have a boiled egg for breakfast. She got up and put on a dressing gown and brought a hand mirror back to the bed. Lying high against the pillows, she studied her face.

The rest had done wonders. Pain makes you set your jaw, and your eyes grow falsely bright with anxiety, and the muscles over the temples and along the cheeks, even the weak muscles near to the nose, stand out a little, and that is the look of sickness and of resistance to suffering.

The difference in her rested face was amazing. She looked ten years younger. She opened her lips and looked at her teeth. Time to go for a cleaning. She took care of her teeth. The gold bridge where the molars were gone was the only repair in her mouth. It was remarkable how young she looked, Kate thought. Just one night's sleep and she snapped back. That was another thing that fooled them. They thought she would be weak and delicate. She smiled to herself—delicate like a steel trap. But then she always took care of herself—no liquor, no drugs, and recently she had stopped drinking coffee. And it paid off. She had an angelic face. She put the mirror a little higher so that the crepe at her throat did not reflect.

Her thought jumped to that other angelic face so like hers—what was his name?—what the hell was his name—Alec? She could see him, moving slowly past, his white surplice edged with lace, his sweet chin down and his hair glowing under the candlelight. He held the oaken staff and its brass cross angled ahead of him. There was something frigidly beautiful about him, something untouched and untouchable. Well, had anything or anybody ever really touched Kate—really got through and soiled her? Certainly not. Only the hard outside had been brushed by contacts. Inside she was intact—as clean and bright as this boy Alec—was that his name?

She chuckled—mother of two sons—and she looked like a child. And if anyone had seen her with the blond one—could they have any doubt? She thought how it would be to stand beside him in a crowd and let people find out for themselves. What would—Aron, that was the name—what would he do if he knew? His brother knew. That smart little son of a bitch—wrong word—must not call him that. Might be too true. Some people believed it. And not smart bastard either—born in holy wedlock. Kate laughed aloud. She felt good. She was having a good time.

The smart one—the dark one—bothered her. He was like Charles. She had respected Charles—and Charles would probably have killed her if he could.

Wonderful medicine—it not only stopped the arthritic pain, it gave her back her courage. Pretty soon she could sell out and go to New York as she had always planned. Kate thought of her fear of Ethel. How sick she must have been—the poor dumb old bag! How would it be to murder her with kindness? When Joe found her, how about—well, how about taking her on to New York? Keep her close.

A funny notion came to Kate. That would be a comical murder, and a murder no one under any circumstances could solve or even suspect. Chocolates—boxes of chocolate, bowls of fondant, bacon, crisp bacon—fat, port wine, and then butter, everything soaked in butter and whipped cream; no vegetables, no fruit—and no amusement either. Stay in the house, dear. I trust you. Look after things. You're tired. Go to bed. Let me fill your glass. I got these new sweets for you. Would you like to take the box to bed? Well, if you don't feel good why don't you take a physic? These cashews are nice, don't you think? The old bitch would blow up and burst in six months. Or how about a tapeworm? Did anyone ever use tapeworms? Who was the man who couldn't get water to his mouth in a sieve—Tantalus?

Kate's lips were smiling sweetly and a gaiety was coming over her. Before she went it might be good to give a party for her sons. Just a simple little party with a circus afterward for her darlings—her jewels. And then she thought of Aron's beautiful face so like her own and a strange pain—a little collapsing pain—arose in her chest. He wasn't smart. He couldn't protect himself. The dark brother might be dangerous. She had felt his quality. Cal had beaten her. Before she went away she would teach him a lesson. Maybe —why, sure—maybe a dose of the clap might set that young man back on his heels.

Suddenly she knew that she did not want Aron to know about her. Maybe he could come to her in New York. He would think she had always lived in an elegant little house on the East Side. She would take him to the theater to the opera, and people would see them together and wonder at their loveliness, and recognize that they were either brother and sister or mother and son. No one could fail to know. They could go together to Ethel's funeral. She would need an oversized coffin and six wrestlers to carry it. Kate was so filled with amusement at her thoughts that she did not hear Joe's knocking on the door. He opened it a crack and looked in and he saw her gay and smiling face.

"Breakfast," he said and nudged the door open with the edge of the linen-covered tray. He pushed the door closed with his knee. "Want it there?" he asked and gestured toward the gray room with his chin.

"No. I'll have it right here. And I want a boiled egg and a piece of cinnamon toast. Four and a half minutes on the egg. Make sure. I don't want it gooey."

"You must feel better, ma'am."

"I do," she said. "That new medicine is wonderful. You look dragged by dogs, Joe. Don't you feel well?"

"I'm all right," he said and set the tray on the table in front of the big deep chair. "Four and a half minutes?"

"That's right. And if there's a good apple—a crisp apple—bring that too."

"You ain't et like this since I knew you," he said.

In the kitchen, waiting for the cook to boil the egg, he was apprehensive. Maybe she knew. He'd have to be careful. But hell! she couldn't hate him for something he didn't know. No crime in that.

Back in her room he said, "Didn't have no apples. He said this was a good pear."

"I'd like that even better," said Kate.

He watched her chip off the egg and dip a spoon into the shell. "How is it?"

"Perfect!" said Kate. "Just perfect."

"You look good," he said.

"I feel good. You look like hell. What's the matter?"

Joe went into it warily. "Ma'am, there ain't nobody needs five hundred like I do."

She said playfully, "There isn't *anyone* who needs—"

"What?"

"Forget it. What are you trying to say? You couldn't find her—is that it? Well, if you did a good job looking, you'll get your five hundred. Tell me about it." She picked up the salt shaker and scattered a few grains into the open eggshell.

Joe put an artificial joy on his face. "Thanks," he said. "I'm in a spot. I need it. Well, I looked in Pajaro and Watsonville. Got a line on her in Watsonville but she'd went to Santa Cruz. Got a smell of her there but she was gone."

Kate tasted the egg and added more salt. "That all?"

"No," said Joe. "I went it blind there. Dropped down to San Luis an' she had been there too but gone."

"No trace? No idea where she went?"

Joe fiddled with his fingers. His whole pitch, maybe his whole life, depended on his next words, and he was reluctant to say them.

"Come on," she said at last. "You got something—what is it?"

"Well, it ain't much. I don't know what to think of it."

"Don't think. Just tell. I'll think," she said sharply.

"Might not even be true."

"For Christ's sake!" she said angrily.

"Well, I talked to the last guy that seen her. Guy named Joe, like me—"

"Did you get his grandmother's name?" she asked sarcastically.

"This guy Joe says she loaded up on beer one night an' she said how she's going to come back to Salinas an' lay low. Then she dropped out of sight. This guy Joe didn't know nothing more."

Kate was startled out of control. Joe read her quick start, the apprehension, and then the almost hopeless fear and weariness. Whatever it was, Joe had something. He had got the breaks at last.

She looked up from her lap and her twisted fingers. "We'll forget the old fart," she said. "You'll get your five hundred, Joe."

Joe breathed shallowly, afraid that any sound might drag her out of her self-absorption. She had believed him. More than that, she was believing things he had not told her. He wanted to get out of the room as quickly as possible. He said, "Thank you, ma'am," but very softly, and he moved silently toward the door.

His hand was on the knob when she spoke with elaborate casualness. "Joe, by the way—"

"Ma'am?"

"If you should hear anything about—her, let me know, will you?"

"I sure will. Want me to dig into it?"

"No. Don't bother. It isn't that important."

In his room, with the door latched, Joe sat down and folded his arms. He smiled to himself. And instantly he began to work out the future course. He decided to let her brood on it till, say, next week. Let her relax, and then bring up Ethel again. He did not know what his weapon was or how he was going to use it. But he did know that it was very sharp and he itched to use it. He would have laughed out loud if he had known that Kate had gone to the gray room and locked its door, and that she sat still in the big chair and her eyes were closed.

FORTY-SIX

Sometimes, but not often, a rain comes to the Salinas Valley in November. It is so rare that the *Journal* or the *Index* or both carry editorials about it. The hills turn to a soft green overnight and the air smells good. Rain at this time is not particularly good in an agricultural sense unless it is going to continue, and this is extremely unusual. More commonly, the dryness comes back and the fuzz of grass withers or a little frost curls it and there's that amount of seed wasted.

The war years were wet years, and there were many people who blamed the strange intransigent weather on the firing of the great guns in France. This was seriously considered in articles and in arguments.

We didn't have many troops in France that first winter, but we had millions in training, getting ready to go.

Painful as the war was, it was exciting too. The Germans were not stopped. In fact, they had taken the initiative again, driving methodically toward Paris, and God knew when they could be stopped—if they could be stopped at all. General Pershing would save us if we could be saved. His trim, beautifully uniformed soldierly figure made its appearance in every paper every day. His chin was granite and there was no wrinkle on his tunic. He was the epitome of a perfect soldier. No one knew what he really thought.

We knew we couldn't lose and yet we seemed to be going about losing. You couldn't buy flour, white flour, any more without taking four times the quantity of brown flour. Those who could afford it ate bread and biscuits made with white flour and made mash for the chickens with the brown.

In the old Troop C armory the Home Guard drilled, men over fifty and not the best soldier material, but they took setting-up exercises twice a week, wore Home Guard buttons and overseas caps, snapped orders at one another, and wrangled eternally about who should be officers. William C. Burt died right on the armory floor in the middle of a push-up. His heart couldn't take it.

There were Minute Men too, so called because they made one-minute speeches in favor of America in moving-picture theaters and in churches. They had buttons too.

The women rolled bandages and wore Red Cross uniforms and thought of themselves as Angels of Mercy. And everybody knitted something for someone. There were wristlets, short tubes of wool to keep the wind from whistling up soldiers' sleeves, and there were knitted helmets with only a hole in front to look out of. These were designed to keep the new tin helmets from freezing to the head.

Every bit of really first-grade leather was taken for officers' boots and for Sam Browne belts. These belts were handsome and only officers could wear them. They consisted of a wide belt and a strap that crossed the chest and passed under the left epaulet. We copied them from the British, and even the British had forgotten their original purpose, which was possibly to support a heavy sword. Swords were not carried except on parade, but an officer would not be caught dead without a Sam Browne belt. A good one cost as much as twenty-five dollars.

We learned a lot from the British—and if they had not been good fighting men we wouldn't have taken it. Men began to wear their handkerchiefs in their sleeves and some foppish lieutenants carried swagger sticks. One thing we resisted for a long time, though. Wristwatches were just too silly. It didn't seem likely that we would ever copy the Limeys in that.

We had our internal enemies too, and we exercised vigilance. San Jose had a spy scare, and Salinas was not likely to be left behind—not the way Salinas was growing.

For about twenty years Mr. Fenchel had done hand tailoring in Salinas. He was short and round and he had an accent that made you laugh. All day he sat cross-legged on his table in the little shop on Alisal Street, and in the evening he walked home to his small white house far out on Central Avenue. He was forever painting his house and the white picket fence in front of it. Nobody had given his accent a thought until the war came along, but suddenly we knew. It was German. We had our own personal German. It didn't do him any good to bankrupt himself buying war bonds. That was too easy a way to cover up.

The Home Guard wouldn't take him in. They didn't want a spy knowing their secret plans for defending Salinas. And who wanted to wear a suit made by an enemy? Mr. Fenchel sat all day on his table and he didn't have anything to do, so he basted and ripped and sewed and ripped on the same piece of cloth over and over.

We used every cruelty we could think of on Mr. Fenchel. He was our German. He passed our house every day, and there had been a time when he spoke to every man and woman and child and dog, and everyone had answered. Now no one spoke to him, and I can see now in my mind his tubby loneliness and his face full of hurt pride.

My little sister and I did our part with Mr. Fenchel, and it is one of those memories of shame that still makes me break into a sweat and tighten up around the throat. We were standing in our front yard on the lawn one evening and we saw him coming with little fat steps. His black homburg was brushed and squarely set on his head. I don't remember that we discussed our plan but we must have, to have carried it out so well.

As he came near, my sister and I moved slowly across the street side by side. Mr. Fenchel looked up and saw us moving toward him. We stopped in the gutter as he came by.

He broke into a smile and said, "Gut efning, Chon. Gut efning, Mary."

We stood stiffly side by side and we said in unison, "Hoch der Kaiser!"

I can see his face now, his startled innocent blue eyes. He tried to say something and then he began to cry. Didn't even try to pretend he wasn't. He just stood there sobbing. And do you know?—Mary and I turned around and walked stiffly across the street and into our front yard. We felt horrible. I still do when I think of it.

We were too young to do a good job on Mr. Fenchel. That took strong men—about thirty of them. One Saturday night they collected in a bar and marched in a column of fours out Central Avenue, saying, "Hup! Hup!" in unison. They tore down Mr. Fenchel's white picket fence and burned the front out of his house. No Kaiser-loving son of a bitch was going to get away with it with us. And then Salinas could hold up its head with San Jose.

Of course that made Watsonville get busy. They tarred and feathered a Pole they thought was a German. He had an accent.

We of Salinas did all of the things that are inevitably done in a war, and we thought the inevitable thoughts. We screamed over good rumors and died of panic at bad news. Everybody had a secret that he had to spread obliquely to keep its identity as a secret. Our pattern of life changed in the usual manner. Wages and prices went up. A whisper of shortage caused us to buy and store food. Nice quiet ladies clawed one another over a can of tomatoes.

It wasn't all bad or cheap or hysterical. There was heroism too. Some men who could have avoided the army enlisted, and others objected to the war on moral or religious grounds and took the walk up Golgotha which normally comes with that. There were people who gave everything they had to the war because it was the last war and by winning it we would remove war like a thorn from the flesh of the world and there wouldn't be any more such horrible nonsense.

There is no dignity in death in battle. Mostly that is a splashing about of human meat and fluid, and the result is filthy, but there is a great and almost sweet dignity in the sorrow, the helpless, the hopeless sorrow, that comes down over a family with the telegram. Nothing to say, nothing to do, and only one hope—I hope he didn't suffer—and what a forlorn and last-choice hope that is. And it is true that there were some people who, when their sorrow was beginning to lose its savor, gently edged it toward pride and felt increasingly important because of their loss. Some of these even made a good thing of it after the war was over. That is only natural, just as it is natural for a man whose life function is the making of money to make money out of a war. No one blamed a man for that, but it was expected that he should invest a part of his loot in war bonds. We thought we invented all of it in Salinas, even the sorrow.

FORTY-SEVEN

In the Trask house next to Reynaud's Bakery, Lee and Adam put up a map of the western front with lines of colored pins snaking down, and this gave them a feeling of participation. Then Mr. Kelly died and Adam Trask was appointed to take his place on the draft board. He was the logical man for the job. The ice plant did not take up much of his time, and he had a clear service record and an honorable discharge himself.

Adam Trask had seen a war—a little war of maneuver and butchery, but at least he had experienced the reversal of the rules where a man is permitted to kill all the humans he can. Adam didn't remember his war very well. Certain sharp pictures stood out in his memory, a man's face, the piled and burning bodies, the clang of saber scabbards at fast trot, the uneven, tearing sound of firing carbines, the thin cold voice of a bugle in the night. But Adam's pictures were frozen. There was no motion or emotion in them—illustrations in the pages of a book, and not very well drawn.

Adam worked hard and honestly and sadly. He could not get over the feeling that the young men he passed to the army were under sentence of death. And because he knew he was weak, he grew more and more stern and painstaking and much less likely to accept an excuse or a borderline disability. He took the lists home with him, called on parents, in fact, did much more work than was expected of him. He felt like a hanging judge who hates the gallows.

Henry Stanton watched Adam grow more gaunt and more silent, and Henry was a man who liked fun—needed it. A sour-pussed associate could make him sick.

"Relax," he told Adam. "You're trying to carry the weight of the war. Now, look—it's not your responsibility. You got put in here with a set of rules. Just follow the rules and relax. You aren't running the war."

Adam moved the slats of the blind so that the late afternoon sun would not shine in his eyes, and he gazed down at the harsh parallel lines the sun threw on his desk. "I know," he said wearily. "Oh, I know that! But, Henry, it's when there's a choice, and it's my own judgment of the merits, that's when it gets me. I passed Judge Kendal's boy and he was killed in training."

"It's not your business, Adam. Why don't you take a few drinks at night? Go to a movie—sleep on it." Henry put his thumbs in the armholes of his vest and leaned back in his chair. "While we're talking about it, Adam, it seems to me it don't do a candidate a damn bit of good for you to worry. You pass boys I could be talked into letting off."

"I know," said Adam. "I wonder how long it will last?"

Henry inspected him shrewdly and took a pencil from his stuffed vest pocket and rubbed the eraser against his big white front teeth. "I see what you mean," he said softly.

Adam looked at him, startled. "What do I mean?" he demanded.

"Now don't get huffy. I never thought I was lucky before, just having girls."

Adam traced one of the slat shadows on his desk with his forefinger. "Yes," he said in a voice as soft as a sigh.

"It's a long time before your boys will be called up."

"Yes." Adam's finger entered a line of light and slid slowly back.

Henry said, "I'd hate to—"

"Hate to what?"

"I was just wondering how I'd feel if I had to pass on my own sons."

"I'd resign," said Adam.

"Yes. I can see that. A man would be tempted to reject them—I mean, his own."

"No," said Adam. "I'd resign because I couldn't reject them. A man couldn't let his own go free."

Henry laced his fingers and made one big fist of his two hands and laid the fist on the desk in front of him. His face was querulous. "No," he said, "you're right. A man couldn't." Henry liked fun and avoided when he could any solemn or serious matter, for he confused these with sorrow. "How's Aron doing at Stanford?"

"Fine. He writes that it's hard but he thinks he'll make out all right. He'll be home for Thanksgiving."

"I'd like to see him. I saw Cal on the street last night. There's a smart boy."

"Cal didn't take college tests a year ahead," said Adam.

"Well, maybe that's not what he's cut out for. I didn't go to college. Did you?"

"No," said Adam. "I went into the army."

"Well, it's a good experience. I'll bet you wouldn't take a good bit for the experience."

Adam stood up slowly and picked his hat from the deer horns on the wall. "Good night, Henry," he said.

2

Walking home, Adam pondered his responsibility. As he passed Reynaud's Bakery Lee came out, carrying a golden loaf of French bread.

"I have a hunger for some garlic bread," Lee said.

"I like it with steak," said Adam.

"We're having steak. Was there any mail?"

"I forgot to look in the box."

They entered the house and Lee went to the kitchen. In a moment Adam

)llowed him and sat at the kitchen table. "Lee," he said, "suppose we send
boy to the army and he is killed, are we responsible?"

"Go on," said Lee. "I would rather have the whole thing at once."

"Well, suppose there's a slight doubt that the boy should be in the army
nd we send him and he gets killed."

"I see. Is it responsibility or blame that bothers you?"

"I don't want blame."

"Sometimes responsibility is worse. It doesn't carry any pleasant egotism."

"I was thinking about that time when Sam Hamilton and you and I had
long discussion about a word," said Adam. "What was that word?"

"Now I see. The word was *timshel*."

"*Timshel*—and you said—"

"I said that word carried a man's greatness if he wanted to take advantage
f it."

"I remember Sam Hamilton felt good about it."

"It set him free," said Lee. "It gave him the right to be a man, separate
:rom every other man."

"That's lonely."

"All great and precious things are lonely."

"What is the word again?"

"*Timshel*—thou mayest."

3

Adam looked forward to Thanksgiving when Aron would come home from
college. Even though Aron had been away such a short time Adam had forgotten him and changed him the way any man changes someone he loves.
With Aron gone, the silences were the result of his going, and every little
painful event was somehow tied to his absence. Adam found himself talking
and boasting about his son, telling people who weren't very interested how
smart Aron was and how he had jumped a year in school. He thought it
would be a good thing to have a real celebration at Thanksgiving to let the
boy know his effort was appreciated.

Aron lived in a furnished room in Palo Alto, and he walked the mile to
and from the campus every day. He was miserable. What he had expected
to find at the university had been vague and beautiful. His picture—never
really inspected—had been of clean-eyed young men and immaculate girls,
all in academic robes and converging on a white temple on the crown of a
wooded hill in the evening. Their faces were shining and dedicated and their
voices rose in chorus and it was never any time but evening. He had no idea
where he had got his picture of academic life—perhaps from the Doré illustrations of Dante's *Inferno* with its massed and radiant angels. Leland
Stanford University was not like that. A formal square of brown sandstone
blocks set down in a hayfield; a church with an Italian mosaic front; class-

rooms of varnished pine; and the great world of struggle and anger re
enacted in the rise and fall of fraternities. And those bright angels wer
youths in dirty corduroy trousers, some study-raddled and some learning the
small vices of their fathers.

Aron, who had not known he had a home, was nauseatingly homesick
He did not try to learn the life around him or to enter it. He found the
natural noise and fuss and horseplay of undergraduates horrifying, after his
dream. He left the college dormitory for a dreary furnished room where
he could decorate another dream which had only now come into being. In
the new and neutral hiding place he cut the university out, went to his
classes and left as soon as he could, to live in his new-found memories. The
house next to Reynaud's Bakery became warm and dear, Lee the epitome
of friend and counselor, his father the cool, dependable figure of godhead,
his brother clever and delightful, and Abra—well, of Abra he made his
immaculate dream and, having created her, fell in love with her. At night
when his studying was over he went to his nightly letter to her as one goes
to a scented bath. And as Abra became more radiant, more pure and beautiful, Aron took an increasing joy in a concept of his own wickedness. In a
frenzy he poured joyous abjectness on paper to send to her, and he went to
bed purified, as a man is after sexual love. He set down every evil thought
he had and renounced it. The results were love letters that dripped with
longing and by their high tone made Abra very uneasy. She could not know
that Aron's sexuality had taken a not unusual channel.

He had made a mistake. He could admit the mistake but as yet he could
not reverse himself. He made a compact with himself. At Thanksgiving he
would go home, and then he would be sure. He might never come back. He
remembered that Abra had once suggested that they go to live on the ranch,
and that became his dream. He remembered the great oaks and the clear
living air, the clean sage-laced wind from the hills and the brown oak leaves
scudding. He could see Abra there, standing under a tree, waiting for him to
come in from his work. And it was evening. There, after work of course, he
could live in purity and peace with the world, cut off by the little draw. He
could hide from ugliness—in the evening.

FORTY-EIGHT

Late in November the Nigger died and was buried in black austerity, as
her will demanded. She lay for a day in Muller's Funeral Chapel in an
ebony and silver casket, her lean and severe profile made even more ascetic
by the four large candles set at the four corners of the casket.

Her little black husband crouched like a cat by her right shoulder, and for many hours he seemed as still as she. There were no flowers, as ordered, no ceremony, no sermon, and no grief. But a strange and catholic selection of citizens tiptoed to the chapel door and peered in and went away—lawyers and laborers and clerks and bank tellers, most of them past middle age. Her girls came in one at a time and looked at her for decency and for luck and went away.

An institution was gone from Salinas, dark and fatal sex, as hopeless and deeply hurtful as human sacrifice. Jenny's place would still jangle with honky-tonk and rock with belching laughter. Kate's would rip the nerves to a sinful ecstasy and leave a man shaken and weak and frightened at himself. But the somber mystery of connection that was like a voodoo offering was gone forever.

The funeral was also by order of the will, the hearse and one automobile with the small black man crouched back in a corner. It was a gray day, and when Muller's service had lowered the casket with oiled and silent winches the hearse drove away and the husband filled the grave himself with a new shovel. The caretaker, cutting dry weeds a hundred yards away, heard a whining carried on the wind.

Joe Valery had been drinking a beer with Butch Beavers at the Owl, and he went with Butch to have a look at the Nigger. Butch was in a hurry because he had to go out to Natividad to auction a small herd of white-face Herefords for the Tavernettis.

Coming out of the mortuary, Joe found himself in step with Alf Nichelson—crazy Alf Nichelson, who was a survival from an era that was past. Alf was a jack-of-all-trades, carpenter, tinsmith, blacksmith, electrician, plasterer, scissors grinder, and cobbler. Alf could do anything, and as a result he was a financial failure although he worked all the time. He knew everything about everybody back to the beginning of time.

In the past, in the period of his success, two kinds of people had access to all homes and all gossip—the seamstress and the handy man. Alf could tell you about everybody on both sides of Main Street. He was a vicious male gossip, insatiably curious and vindictive without malice.

He looked at Joe and tried to place him. "I know you," he said. "Don't tell me."

Joe edged away. He was wary of people who knew him.

"Wait a minute. I got it. Kate's. You work at Kate's."

Joe sighed with relief. He had thought Alf might have known him earlier. "That's right," he said shortly.

"Never forget a face," said Alf. "Seen you when I built that crazy lean-to for Kate. Now why in hell did she want that for? No window."

"Wanted it dark," said Joe. "Eyes bother her."

Alf sniffed. He hardly ever believed anything simple or good about anybody. You could say good morning to Alf and he'd work it around to a password. He was convinced that everyone lived secretly and that only he could see through them.

He jerked his head back at Muller's. "Well, it's a milestone," he said. "Nearly all the old-timers gone. When Fartin' Jenny goes that'll be the end. And Jenny's getting along."

Joe was restless. He wanted to get away—and Alf knew he did. Alf was an expert in people who wanted to get away from him. Come to think of it, maybe that is why he carried his bag of stories. No one really went away when he could hear some juicy stuff about someone. Everybody is a gossip at heart. Alf was not liked for his gift but he was listened to. And he knew that Joe was on the point of making an excuse and getting out. It occurred to him that he didn't know much about Kate's place lately. Joe might trade him some new stuff for some old stuff. "The old days was pretty good," he said. "'Course you're just a kid."

"I got to meet a fella," said Joe.

Alf pretended not to hear him. "You take Faye," he said. "She was a case," and, parenthetically, "You know Faye run Kate's place. Nobody really knows how Kate come to own it. It was pretty mysterious, and there was some that had their suspicions." He saw with satisfaction that the fella Joe was going to meet would wait a long time.

"What was they suspicious about?" Joe asked.

"Hell, you know how people talk. Probably nothing in it. But I got to admit it looked kind of funny."

"Like to have a beer?" Joe asked.

"Now you got something there," said Alf. "They say a fella jumps from a funeral to the bedroom. I ain't as young as I was. Funeral makes me thirsty. The Nigger was quite a citizen. I could tell you stuff about her. I've knew her for thirty-five—no, thirty-seven years."

"Who was Faye?" Joe asked.

They went into Mr. Griffin's saloon. Mr. Griffin didn't like anything about liquor, and he hated drunks with a deadly scorn. He owned and operated Griffin's Saloon on Main Street, and on a Saturday night he might refuse to serve twenty men he thought had had enough. The result was that he got the best trade in his cool, orderly, quiet place. It was a saloon in which to make deals and to talk quietly without interruption.

Joe and Alf sat at the round table at the back and had three beers apiece. Joe learned everything true and untrue, founded and unfounded, every ugly conjecture. Out of it he got complete confusion but a few ideas. Something might have been not exactly on the level about the death of Faye. Kate might be the wife of Adam Trask. He hid that quickly—Trask might want to pay off. The Faye thing might be too hot to touch. Joe had to think about that—alone.

At the end of a couple of hours Alf was restive. Joe had not played ball. He had traded nothing, not one single piece of information or guess. Alf found himself thinking, Fella that close-mouthed must have something to hide. Wonder who would have a line on him?

Alf said finally, "Understand, I like Kate. She gives me a job now and then and she's generous and quick to pay. Probably nothing to all the palaver bout her. Still, when you think of it, she's a pretty cold piece of woman. She's got a real bad eye. You think?"

"I get along fine," said Joe.

Alf was angry at Joe's perfidy, so he put in a needle. "I had a funny idea," he said. "It was when I built that lean-to without no window. She laid that old eye on me one day and the idea come to me. If she knew all the things I heard, and she was to offer me a drink or even a cupcake—why, I'd say, 'No thank you, ma'am.' "

"Me and her get along just fine," said Joe. "I got to meet a guy."

Joe went to his room to think. He was uneasy. He jumped up and looked in his suitcase and opened all the bureau drawers. He thought somebody had been going through his things. Just came to him. There was nothing to find. It made him nervous. He tried to arrange the things he had heard.

There was a tap on the door and Thelma came in, her eyes swollen and her nose red. "What's got into Kate?"

"She's been sick."

"I don't mean that. I was in the kitchen shaking up a milkshake in a fruit jar and she came in and worked me over."

"Was you maybe shaking up a little bourbon in it?"

"Hell, no. Just vanilla extract. She can't talk like that to me."

"She did, didn't she?"

"Well, I won't take it."

"Oh, yes, you will," said Joe. "Get out, Thelma!"

Thelma looked at him out of her dark, handsome, brooding eyes, and she regained the island of safety a woman depends on. "Joe," she asked, "are you really just pure son of a bitch or do you just pretend to be?"

"What do you care?" Joe asked.

"I don't," said Thelma. "You son of a bitch."

2

Joe planned to move slowly, cautiously, and only after long consideration. "I got the breaks, I got to use 'em right," he told himself.

He went in to get his evening orders and took them from the back of Kate's head. She was at her desk, green eyeshade low, and she did not look around at him. She finished her terse orders and then went on, "Joe, I wonder if you've been attending to business. I've been sick. But I'm well again or very nearly well."

"Something wrong?"

"Just a symptom. I'd rather Thelma drank whisky than vanilla extract, an
I don't want her to drink whisky. I think you've been slipping."

His mind scurried for a hiding place. "Well, I been busy," he said.

"Busy?"

"Sure. Doing that stuff for you."

"What stuff?"

"You know—about Ethel."

"Forget Ethel!"

"Okay," said Joe. And then it came without his expecting it. "I met a fell:
yesterday said he seen her."

If Joe had not known her he would not have given the little pause, the
rigid ten seconds of silence, its due.

At the end of it Kate asked softly, "Where?"

"Here."

She turned her swivel chair slowly around to face him. "I shouldn't have
let you work in the dark, Joe. It's hard to confess a fault but I owe it to you.
I don't have to remind you I got Ethel floated out of the county. I thought
she'd done something to me." A melancholy came into her voice. "I was
wrong. I found out later. It's been working on me ever since. She didn't
do anything to me. I want to find her and make it up to her. I guess you
think it's strange for me to feel that way."

"No, ma'am."

"Find her for me, Joe. I'll feel better when I've made it up to her—the
poor old girl."

"I'll try, ma'am."

"And, Joe—if you need any money, let me know. And if you find her,
just tell her what I said. If she doesn't want to come here, find out where
I can telephone her. Need any money?"

"Not right now, ma'am. But I'll have to go out of the house more than
I ought."

"You go ahead. That's all, Joe."

He wanted to hug himself. In the hall he gripped his elbows and let his
joy run through him. And he began to believe he had planned the whole
thing. He went through the darkened parlor with its low early evening
spatter of conversation. He stepped outside and looked up at the stars swimming in schools through the wind-driven clouds.

Joe thought of his bumbling father—because he remembered something
the old man had told him. "Look out for a soup carrier," Joe's father had
said. "Take one of them dames that's always carrying soup to somebody
—she wants something, and don't you forget it."

Joe said under his breath, "A soup carrier. I thought she was smarter than
that." He went over her tone and words to make sure he hadn't missed

something. No—a soup carrier. And he thought of Alf saying, "If she was to offer a drink or even a cupcake—"

3

Kate sat at her desk. She could hear the wind in the tall privet in the yard, and the wind and the darkness were full of Ethel—fat, sloppy Ethel oozing near like a jellyfish. A dull weariness came over her.

She went into the lean-to, the gray room, and closed the door and sat in the darkness, listening to the pain creep back into her fingers. Her temples beat with pounding blood. She felt for the capsule hanging in its tube on the chain around her neck, she rubbed the metal tube, warm from her breast, against her cheek, and her courage came back. She washed her face and put on make-up, combed and puffed her hair in a loose pompadour. She moved into the hall and at the door of the parlor she paused, as always, listening.

To the right of the door two girls and a man were talking. As soon as Kate stepped inside the talk stopped instantly. Kate said, "Helen, I want to see you if you aren't busy right now."

The girl followed her down the hall and into her room. She was a pale blonde with a skin like clean and polished bone. "Is something the matter, Miss Kate?" she asked fearfully.

"Sit down. No. Nothing's the matter. You went to the Nigger's funeral."

"Didn't you want me to?"

"I don't care about that. You went."

"Yes, ma'am."

"Tell me about it."

"What about it?"

"Tell me what you remember—how it was."

Helen said nervously, "Well, it was kind of awful and—kind of beautiful."

"How do you mean?"

"I don't know. No flowers, no nothing, but there was—there was a—well, a kind of—dignity. The Nigger was just laying there in a black wood coffin with the biggest goddam silver handles. Made you feel—I can't say it. I don't know how to say it."

"Maybe you said it. What did she wear?"

"Wear, ma'am?"

"Yes—wear. They didn't bury her naked, did they?"

A struggle of effort crossed Helen's face. "I don't know," she said at last. "I don't remember."

"Did you go to the cemetery?"

"No, ma'am. Nobody did—except him."

"Who?"

"Her man."

Kate said quickly—almost too quickly, "Have you got any regulars to night?"

"No, ma'am. Day before Thanksgiving. Bound to be slow."

"I'd forgotten," said Kate. "Get back out." She watched the girl out of the room and moved restlessly back to her desk. And as she looked at an item-ized bill for plumbing her left hand strayed to her neck and touched the chain. It was comfort and reassurance.

FORTY-NINE

Both Lee and Cal tried to argue Adam out of going to meet the train, the Lark night train from San Francisco to Los Angeles.

Cal said, "Why don't we let Abra go alone? He'll want to see her first."

"I think he won't know anybody else is there," said Lee. "So it doesn't matter whether we go or not."

"I want to see him get off the train," said Adam. "He'll be changed. I want to see what change there is."

Lee said, "He's only been gone a couple of months. He can't be very changed, nor much older."

"He'll be changed. Experience will do that."

"If you go we'll all have to go," said Cal.

"Don't you want to see your brother?" Adam asked sternly.

"Sure, but he won't want to see me—not right at first."

"He will too," said Adam. "Don't you underrate Aron."

Lee threw up his hands. "I guess we all go," he said.

"Can you imagine?" said Adam. "He'll know so many new things. I won-der if he'll talk different. You know, Lee, in the East a boy takes on the speech of his school. You can tell a Harvard man from a Princeton man. At least that's what they say."

"I'll listen," said Lee. "I wonder what dialect they speak at Stanford." He smiled at Cal.

Adam didn't think it was funny. "Did you put some fruit in his room?" he asked. "He loves fruit."

"Pears and apples and muscat grapes," said Lee.

"Yes, he loves muscats. I remember he loves muscats."

Under Adam's urging they got to the Southern Pacific Depot half an hour before the train was due. Abra was already there.

"I can't come to dinner tomorrow, Lee," she said. "My father wants me home. I'll come as soon after as I can."

"You're a little breathless," said Lee.

"Aren't you?"

"I guess I am," said Lee. "Look up the track and see if the block's turned green."

Train schedules are a matter of pride and of apprehension to nearly everyone. When, far up the track, the block signal snapped from red to green and the long, stabbing probe of the headlight sheered the bend and blared on the station, men looked at their watches and said, "On time."

There was pride in it, and relief too. The split second has been growing more and more important to us. And as human activities become more and more intermeshed and integrated, the split tenth of a second will emerge, and then a new name must be made for the split hundredth, until one day, although I don't believe it, we'll say, "Oh, the hell with it. What's wrong with an hour?" But it isn't silly, this preoccupation with small time units. One thing late or early can disrupt everything around it, and the disturbance runs outward in bands like the waves from a dropped stone in a quiet pool.

The Lark came rushing in as though it had no intention of stopping. And only when the engine and baggage cars were well past did the air brakes give their screaming hiss and the straining iron protest to a halt.

The train delivered quite a crowd for Salinas, returning relatives home for Thanksgiving, their hands entangled in cartons and gift-wrapped paper boxes. It was a moment or two before his family could locate Aron. And then they saw him, and he seemed bigger than he had been.

He was wearing a flat-topped, narrow-brimmed hat, very stylish, and when he saw them he broke into a run and yanked off his hat, and they could see that his bright hair was clipped to a short brush of a pompadour that stood straight up. And his eyes shone so that they laughed with pleasure to see him.

Aron dropped his suitcase and lifted Abra from the ground in a great hug. He set her down and gave Adam and Cal his two hands. He put his arms around Lee's shoulders and nearly crushed him.

On the way home they all talked at once. "Well, how are you?" "You look fine." "Abra, you're so pretty."

"I am not. Why did you cut your hair?"

"Oh, everybody wears it that way."

"But you have such nice hair."

They hurried up to Main Street and one short block and around the corner on Central past Reynaud's with stacked French bread in the window and black-haired Mrs. Reynaud waved her flour-pale hand at them and they were home.

Adam said, "Coffee, Lee?"

"I made it before we left. It's on the simmer." He had the cups laid out too. Suddenly they were together—Aron and Abra on the couch, Adam in his chair under the light, Lee passing coffee, and Cal braced in the doorway to the hall. And they were silent, for it was too late to say hello and too early to begin other things.

Adam did say, "I'll want to hear all about it. Will you get good marks?"

"Finals aren't until next month, Father."

"Oh, I see. Well, you'll get good marks, all right. I'm sure you will."

In spite of himself a grimace of impatience crossed Aron's face.

"I'll bet you're tired," said Adam. "Well, we can talk tomorrow."

Lee said, "I'll bet he's not. I'll bet he'd like to be alone."

Adam looked at Lee and said, "Why, of course—of course. Do you think we should all go to bed?"

Abra solved it for them. "I can't stay out long," she said. "Aron, why don't you walk me home? We'll be together tomorrow."

On the way Aron clung to her arm. He shivered. "There's going to be a frost," he said.

"You're glad to be back."

"Yes, I am. I have a lot to talk about."

"Good things?"

"Maybe. I hope you think so."

"You sound serious."

"It is serious."

"When do you have to go back?"

"Not until Sunday night."

"We'll have lots of time. I want to tell you some things too. We have tomorrow and Friday and Saturday and all day Sunday. Would you mind not coming in tonight?"

"Why not?"

"I'll tell you later."

"I want to know now."

"Well, my father's got one of his streaks."

"Against me?"

"Yes. I can't go to dinner with you tomorrow, but I won't eat much at home, so you can tell Lee to save a plate for me."

He was turning shy. She could feel it in the relaxing grip on her arm and in his silence, and she could see it in his raised face. "I shouldn't have told you that tonight."

"Yes, you should," he said slowly. "Tell me the truth. Do you still—want to be with me?"

"Yes, I do."

"Then all right. I'll go away now. We'll talk tomorrow."

He left her on her porch with the feeling of a light-brushed kiss on her lips. She felt hurt that he had agreed so easily, and she laughed sourly at herself that she could ask a thing and be hurt when she got it. She watched his tall quick step through the radiance of the corner streetlight. She thought, I must be crazy. I've been imagining things.

2

In his bedroom after he had said his good night, Aron sat on the edge of his bed and peered down at his hands cupped between his knees. He felt let down and helpless, packed like a bird's egg in the cotton of his father's ambition for him. He had not known its strength until tonight, and he wondered whether he would have the strength to break free of its soft, persistent force. His thoughts would not coagulate. The house seemed cold with a dampness that made him shiver. He got up and softly opened his door. There was a light under Cal's door. He tapped and went in without waiting for a reply.

Cal sat at a new desk. He was working with tissue paper and a bolt of red ribbon, and as Aron came in he hastily covered something on his desk with a large blotter.

Aron smiled. "Presents?"

"Yes," said Cal and left it at that.

"Can I talk to you?"

"Sure! Come on in. Talk low or Father will come in. He hates to miss a moment."

Aron sat down on the bed. He was silent so long that Cal asked, "What's the matter—you got trouble?"

"No, not trouble. I just wanted to talk to you. Cal, I don't want to go on at college."

Cal's head jerked around. "You don't? Why not?"

"I just don't like it."

"You haven't told Father, have you? He'll be disappointed. It's bad enough that I don't want to go. What do you want to do?"

"I thought I'd like to take over the ranch."

"How about Abra?"

"She told me a long time ago that's what she'd like."

Cal studied him. "The ranch has got a lease to run."

"Well, I was just thinking about it."

Cal said, "There's no money in farming."

"I don't want much money. Just to get along."

"That's not good enough for me," said Cal. "I want a lot of money and I'm going to get it too."

"How?"

Cal felt older and surer than his brother. He felt protective toward him. "If you'll go on at college, why, I'll get started and lay in a foundation. Then when you finish we can be partners. I'll have one kind of thing and you'll have another. That might be pretty good."

"I don't want to go back. Why do I have to go back?"

"Because Father wants you to."

"That won't make me go."

Cal stared fiercely at his brother, at the pale hair and the wide-set eyes, and suddenly he knew why his father loved Aron, knew it beyond doubt. "Sleep on it," he said quickly. "It would be better if you finish out the term at least. Don't do anything now."

Aron got up and moved toward the door. "Who's the present for?" he asked.

"It's for Father. You'll see it tomorrow—after dinner."

"It's not Christmas."

"No," said Cal, "it's better than Christmas."

When Aron had gone back to his room Cal uncovered his present. He counted the fifteen new bills once more, and they were so crisp they made a sharp, cracking sound. The Monterey County Bank had to send to San Francisco to get them, and only did so when the reason for them was told. It was a matter of shock and disbelief to the bank that a seventeen-year-old boy should, first, own them, and, second, carry them about. Bankers do not like money to be lightly handled even if the handling is sentimental. It had taken Will Hamilton's word to make the bank believe that the money belonged to Cal, that it was honestly come by, and that he could do what he wanted to with it.

Cal wrapped the bills in tissue and tied it with red ribbon finished in a blob that was faintly recognizable as a bow. The package might have been a handkerchief. He concealed it under the shirts in his bureau and went to bed. But he could not sleep. He was excited and at the same time shy. He wished the day was over and the gift given. He went over what he planned to say.

"This is for you."

"What is it?"

"A present."

From then on he didn't know what would happen. He tossed and rolled in bed, and at dawn he got up and dressed and crept out of the house.

On Main Street he saw Old Martin sweeping the street with a stable broom. The city council was discussing the purchase of a mechanical sweeper. Old Martin hoped he would get to drive it, but he was cynical about it. Young men got the cream of everything. Bacigalupi's garbage wagon went by, and Martin looked after it spitefully. *There* was a good business. Those wops were getting rich.

Main Street was empty except for a few dogs sniffing at closed entrances and the sleepy activity around the San Francisco Chop House. Pet Bulene's new taxi was parked in front, for Pet had been alerted the night before to take the Williams girls to the morning train for San Francisco.

Old Martin called to Cal, "Got a cigarette, young fella?"

Cal stopped and took out his cardboard box of Murads.

"Oh, fancy ones!" Martin said. "I ain't got a match either."

Cal lighted the cigarette for him, careful not to set fire to the grizzle round Martin's mouth.

Martin leaned on the handle of his brush and puffed disconsolately. "Young fellas gets the cream," he said. "They won't let me drive it."

"What?" Cal asked.

"Why, the new sweeper. Ain't you heard? Where you been, boy?" It was incredible to him that any reasonably informed human did not know about the sweeper. He forgot Cal. Maybe the Bacigalupis would give him a job. They were coining money. Three wagons and a new truck.

Cal turned down Alisal Street, went into the post office, and looked in the glass window of box 632. It was empty. He wandered back home and found Lee up and stuffing a very large turkey.

"Up all night?" Lee asked.

"No. I just went for a walk."

"Nervous?"

"Yes."

"I don't blame you. I would be too. It's hard to give people things—I guess it's harder to be given things, though. Seems silly, doesn't it? Want some coffee?"

"I don't mind."

Lee wiped his hands and poured coffee for himself and for Cal. "How do you think Aron looks?"

"All right, I guess."

"Did you get to talk to him?"

"No," said Cal. It was easier that way. Lee would want to know what he said. It wasn't Aron's day. It was Cal's day. He had carved this day out for himself and he wanted it. He meant to have it.

Aron came in, his eyes still misty with sleep. "What time do you plan to have dinner, Lee?"

"Oh, I don't know—three-thirty or four."

"Could you make it about five?"

"I guess so, if Adam says it's all right. Why?"

"Well, Abra can't get here before then. I've got a plan I want to put to my father and I want her to be here."

"I guess that will be all right," said Lee.

Cal got up quickly and went to his room. He sat at his desk with the student light turned on and he churned with uneasiness and resentment. Without effort, Aron was taking his day away from him. It would turn out to be Aron's day. Then, suddenly, he was bitterly ashamed. He covered his eyes with his hands and he said, "It's just jealousy. I'm jealous. That's what I am. I'm jealous. I don't want to be jealous." And he repeated over and over, "Jealous—jealous—jealous," as though bringing it into the open might destroy it. And having gone this far, he proceeded with his self-punishment. "Why am I giving the money to my father? Is it for his good? No. It's for my

good. Will Hamilton said it—I'm trying to buy him. There's not one decen
thing about it. There's not one decent thing about me. I sit here wallowin,
in jealousy of my brother. Why not call things by their names?"

He whispered hoarsely to himself. "Why not be honest? I know why m
father loves Aron. It's because he looks like her. My father never got ove
her. He may not know it, but it's true. I wonder if he does know it. Tha
makes me jealous of her too. Why don't I take my money and go away.
They wouldn't miss me. In a little while they'd forget I ever existed—al
except Lee. And I wonder whether Lee likes me. Maybe not." He doublec
his fists against his forehead. "Does Aron have to fight himself like this
I don't think so, but how do I know? I could ask him. He wouldn't say."

Cal's mind careened in anger at himself and in pity for himself. An(
then a new voice came into it, saying coolly and with contempt, "If you're
being honest—why not say you are enjoying this beating you're giving your
self? That would be the truth. Why not be just what you are and do jus
what you do?" Cal sat in shock from this thought. Enjoying?—of course. B
whipping himself he protected himself against whipping by someone else.
His mind tightened up. Give the money, but give it lightly. Don't depend
on anything. Don't foresee anything. Just give it and forget it. And forget
it now. Give—give. Give the day to Aron. Why not? He jumped up and
hurried out to the kitchen.

Aron was holding open the skin of the turkey while Lee forced stuffing
into the cavity. The oven cricked and snapped with growing heat.

Lee said, "Let's see, eighteen pounds, twenty minutes to the pound—
that's eighteen times twenty—that's three hundred and sixty minutes, six
hours even—eleven to twelve, twelve to one—" He counted on his fingers.

Cal said, "When you get through, Aron, let's take a walk."

"Where to?" Aron asked.

"Just around town. I want to ask you something."

Cal led his brother across the street to Berges and Garrisiere, who imported fine wines and liquors. Cal said, "I've got a little money, Aron. I
thought you might like to buy some wine for dinner. I'll give you the
money."

"What kind of wine?"

"Let's make a real celebration. Let's get champagne—it can be your
present."

Joe Garrisiere said, "You boys aren't old enough."

"For dinner? Sure we are."

"Can't sell it to you. I'm sorry."

Cal said, "I know what you can do. We can pay for it and you can send
it to our father."

"That I can do," Joe Garrisiere said. "We've got some Oeil de Perdrix—"
His lips pursed as though he were tasting it.

"What's that?" Cal asked.

"Champagne—but very pretty, same color as a partridge eye—pink but a little darker than pink, and dry too. Four-fifty a bottle."

"Isn't that high?" Aron asked.

"Sure it's high!" Cal laughed. "Send three bottles over, Joe." To Aron he said, "It's your present."

3

To Cal the day was endless. He wanted to leave the house and couldn't. At eleven o'clock Adam went to the closed draft-board office to brood over the records of a new batch of boys coming up.

Aron seemed perfectly calm. He sat in the living room, looking at cartoons in old numbers of the *Review of Reviews*. From the kitchen the odor of the bursting juices of roasting turkey began to fill the house.

Cal went into his room and took out his present and laid it on his desk. He tried to write a card to put on it. "To my father from Caleb"—"To Adam Trask from Caleb Trask." He tore the cards in tiny pieces and flushed them down the toilet.

He thought, Why give it to him today? Maybe tomorrow I could go to him quietly and say, This is for you, and then walk away. That would be easier. "No," he said aloud. "I want the others to see." It had to be that way. But his lungs were compressed and the palms of his hands were wet with stage fright. And then he thought of the morning when his father got him out of jail. The warmth and closeness—they were the things to remember—and his father's trust. Why, he had even said it. "I trust you." He felt much better then.

At about three o'clock he heard Adam come in and there was the low sound of voices conversing in the living room. Cal joined his father and Aron.

Adam was saying, "The times are changed. A boy must be a specialist or he will get nowhere. I guess that's why I'm so glad you're going to college."

Aron said, "I've been thinking about that, and I wonder."

"Well, don't think any more. Your first choice is right. Look at me. I know a little bit about a great many things and not enough about any one of them to make a living in these times."

Cal sat down quietly. Adam did not notice him. His face was concentrated on his thought.

"It's natural for a man to want his son to succeed," Adam went on. "And maybe I can see better than you can."

Lee looked in. "The kitchen scales must be way off," he said. "The turkey's going to be done earlier than the chart says. I'll bet that bird doesn't weigh eighteen pounds."

Adam said, "Well, you can keep it warm," and he continued, "Old Sam Hamilton saw this coming. He said there couldn't be any more universal philosophers. The weight of knowledge is too great for one mind to absorb. He saw a time when one man would know only one little fragment, but he would know it well."

"Yes," Lee said from the doorway, "and he deplored it. He hated it."

"Did he now?" Adam asked.

Lee came into the room. He held his big basting spoon in his right hand, and he cupped his left under the bowl for fear it would drip on the carpet. He came into the room and forgot and waved his spoon and drops of turkey fat fell to the floor. "Now you question it, I don't know," he said. "I don't know whether he hated it or I hate it for him."

"Don't get so excited," said Adam. "Seems to me we can't discuss anything any more but you take it as a personal insult."

"Maybe the knowledge is too great and maybe men are growing too small," said Lee. "Maybe, kneeling down to atoms, they're becoming atom-sized in their souls. Maybe a specialist is only a coward, afraid to look out of his little cage. And think what any specialist misses—the whole world over his fence."

"We're only talking about making a living."

"A living—or money," Lee said excitedly. "Money's easy to make if it's money you want. But with a few exceptions people don't want money. They want luxury and they want love and they want admiration."

"All right. But do you have any objection to college? That's what we're talking about."

"I'm sorry," said Lee. "You're right, I do seem to get too excited. No, if college is where a man can go to find his relation to his whole world, I don't object. Is it that? Is it that, Aron?"

"I don't know," said Aron.

A hissing sound came from the kitchen. Lee said, "The goddam giblets are boiling over," and he bolted through the door.

Adam gazed after him affectionately. "What a good man! What a good friend!"

Aron said, "I hope he lives to be a hundred."

His father chuckled. "How do you know he's not a hundred now?"

Cal asked, "How is the ice plant doing, Father?"

"Why, all right. Pays for itself and makes a little profit. Why?"

"I thought of a couple of things to make it really pay."

"Not today," said Adam quickly. "Monday, if you remember, but not today. You know," Adam said, "I don't remember when I've felt so good. I feel—well, you might call it fulfilled. Maybe it's only a good night's sleep and a good trip to the bathroom. And maybe it's because we're all together and at peace." He smiled at Aron. "We didn't know what we felt about you until you went away."

"I was homesick," Aron confessed. "The first few days I thought I'd die of it."

Abra came in with a little rush. Her cheeks were pink and she was happy. "Did you notice there's snow on Mount Toro?" she asked.

"Yes, I saw it," Adam said. "They say that means a good year to come. And we could use it."

"I just nibbled," said Abra. "I wanted to be hungry for here."

Lee apologized for the dinner like an old fool. He blamed the gas oven which didn't heat like a good wood stove. He blamed the new breed of turkeys which lacked a something turkeys used to have. But he laughed with them when they told him he was acting like an old woman fishing for compliments.

With the plum pudding Adam opened the champagne, and they treated it with ceremony. A courtliness settled over the table. They proposed toasts. Each one had his health drunk, and Adam made a little speech to Abra when he drank her health.

Her eyes were shining and under the table Aron held her hand. The wine dulled Cal's nervousness and he was not afraid about his present.

When Adam had finished his plum pudding he said, "I guess we never have had such a good Thanksgiving."

Cal reached in his jacket pocket, took out the red-ribboned package, and pushed it over in front of his father.

"What's this?" Adam asked.

"It's a present."

Adam was pleased. "Not even Christmas and we have presents. I wonder what it can be!"

"A handkerchief," said Abra.

Adam slipped off the grubby bow and unfolded the tissue paper. He stared down at the money.

Abra said, "What is it?" and stood up to look. Aron leaned forward. Lee, in the doorway, tried to keep the look of worry from his face. He darted a glance at Cal and saw the light of joy and triumph in his eyes.

Very slowly Adam moved his fingers and fanned the gold certificates. His voice seemed to come from far away. "What is it? What—" He stopped.

Cal swallowed. "It's—I made it—to give to you—to make up for losing the lettuce."

Adam raised his head slowly. "You made it? How?"

"Mr. Hamilton—we made it—on beans." He hurried on, "We bought futures at five cents and when the price jumped— It's for you, fifteen thousand dollars. It's for you."

Adam touched the new bills so that their edges came together, folded the tissue over them and turned the ends up. He looked helplessly at Lee. Cal caught a feeling—a feeling of calamity, of destruction in the air, and a weight of sickness overwhelmed him. He heard his father say, "You'll have to give it back."

Almost as remotely his own voice said, "Give it back? Give it back t who?"

"To the people you got it from."

"The British Purchasing Agency? They can't take it back. They're payin twelve and a half cents for beans all over the country."

"Then give it to the farmers you robbed."

"Robbed?" Cal cried. "Why, we paid them two cents a pound over th market. We didn't rob them." Cal felt suspended in space, and time seeme very slow.

His father took a long time to answer. There seemed to be long space between his words. "I send boys out," he said. "I sign my name and they g out. And some will die and some will lie helpless without arms and legs Not one will come back untorn. Son, do you think I could take a profit or that?"

"I did it for you," Cal said. "I wanted you to have the money to make up your loss."

"I don't want the money, Cal. And the lettuce—I don't think I did that for a profit. It was a kind of game to see if I could get the lettuce there, and I lost. I don't want the money."

Cal looked straight ahead. He could feel the eyes of Lee and Aron and Abra crawling on his cheeks. He kept his eyes on his father's lips.

"I like the idea of a present," Adam went on. "I thank you for the thought—"

"I'll put it away. I'll keep it for you," Cal broke in.

"No. I won't want it ever. I would have been so happy if you could have given me—well, what your brother has—pride in the thing he's doing, glad-ness in his progress. Money, even clean money, doesn't stack up with that." His eyes widened a little and he said, "Have I made you angry, son? Don't be angry. If you want to give me a present—give me a good life. That would be something I could value."

Cal felt that he was choking. His forehead streamed with perspiration and he tasted salt on his tongue. He stood up suddenly and his chair fell over. He ran from the room, holding his breath.

Adam called after him, "Don't be angry, son."

They let him alone. He sat in his room, his elbows on his desk. He thought he would cry but he did not. He tried to let weeping start but tears could not pass the hot iron in his head.

After a time his breathing steadied and he watched his brain go to work slyly, quietly. He fought the quiet hateful brain down and it slipped aside and went about its work. He fought it more weakly, for hate was seeping all through his body, poisoning every nerve. He could feel himself losing control.

Then there came a point where the control and the fear were gone and his brain cried out in an aching triumph. His hand went to a pencil and he drew tight little spirals one after another on his blotting pad. When Lee came in an hour later there were hundreds of spirals, and they had become smaller and smaller. He did not look up.

Lee closed the door gently. "I brought you some coffee," he said.

"I don't want it—yes, I do. Why, thank you, Lee. It's kind of you to think of it."

Lee said, "Stop it! Stop it, I tell you!"

"Stop what? What do you want me to stop?"

Lee said uneasily, "I told you once when you asked me that it was all in yourself. I told you you could control it—if you wanted."

"Control what? I don't know what you're talking about."

Lee said, "Can't you hear me? Can't I get through to you? Cal, don't you know what I'm saying?"

"I hear you, Lee. What are you saying?"

"He couldn't help it, Cal. That's his nature. It was the only way he knew. He didn't have any choice. But you have. Don't you hear me? You have a choice."

The spirals had become so small that the pencil lines ran together and the result was a shiny black dot.

Cal said quietly, "Aren't you making a fuss about nothing? You must be slipping. You'd think from your tone that I'd killed somebody. Come off it, Lee. Come off it."

It was silent in the room. After a moment Cal turned from his desk and the room was empty. A cup of coffee on the bureau top sent up a plume of vapor. Cal drank the coffee scalding as it was and went into the living room.

His father looked up apologetically at him.

Cal said, "I'm sorry, Father. I didn't know how you felt about it." He took the package of money from where it lay on the mantel and put it in the inside pocket of his coat where it had been before. "I'll see what I can do about this." He said casually, "Where are the others?"

"Oh, Abra had to go. Aron walked with her. Lee went out."

"I guess I'll go for a walk," said Cal.

4

The November night was well fallen. Cal opened the front door a crack and saw Lee's shoulders and head outlined against the white wall of the French Laundry across the street. Lee was sitting on the steps, and he looked lumpy in his heavy coat.

Cal closed the door quietly and went back through the living room. "Champagne makes you thirsty," he said. His father didn't look up.

Cal slipped out the kitchen door and moved through Lee's waning kitchen garden. He climbed the high fence, found the two-by-twelve plank that served as a bridge across the slough of dark water, and came out between Lang's Bakery and the tinsmith's shop on Castroville Street.

He walked to Stone Street where the Catholic church is and turned left, went past the Carriaga house, the Wilson house, the Zabala house, and turned left on Central Avenue at the Steinbeck house. Two blocks out Central he turned left past the West End School.

The poplar trees in front of the schoolyard were nearly bare, but in the evening wind a few yellowed leaves still twisted down.

Cal's mind was numb. He did not even know that the air was cold with frost slipping down from the mountains. Three blocks ahead he saw his brother cross under a streetlight, coming toward him. He knew it was his brother by stride and posture and because he knew it.

Cal slowed his steps, and when Aron was close he said, "Hi. I came looking for you."

Aron said, "I'm sorry about this afternoon."

"You couldn't help it—forget it." He turned and the two walked side by side. "I want you to come with me," Cal said. "I want to show you something."

"What is it?"

"Oh, it's a surprise. But it's very interesting. You'll be interested."

"Well, will it take long?"

"No, not very long. Not very long at all."

They walked past Central Avenue toward Castroville Street.

5

Sergeant Axel Dane ordinarily opened the San Jose recruiting office at eight o'clock, but if he was a little late Corporal Kemp opened it, and Kemp was not likely to complain. Axel was not an unusual case. A hitch in the U.S. Army in the time of peace between the Spanish war and the German war had unfitted him for the cold, unordered life of a civilian. One month between hitches convinced him of that. Two hitches in the peacetime army completely unfitted him for war, and he had learned enough method to get out of it. The San Jose recruiting station proved he knew his way about. He was dallying with the youngest Ricci girl and she lived in San Jose.

Kemp hadn't the time in, but he was learning the basic rule. Get along with the topkick and avoid all officers when possible. He didn't mind the gentle riding Sergeant Dane handed out.

At eight-thirty Dane entered the office to find Corporal Kemp asleep at his desk and a tired-looking kid sat waiting. Dane glanced at the boy and then went in back of the rail and put his hand on Kemp's shoulder.

"Darling," he said, "the skylarks are singing and a new dawn is here."

Kemp raised his head from his arms, wiped his nose on the back of his hand, and sneezed. "That's my sweet," the sergeant said. "Arise, we have a customer."

Kemp squinted his crusted eyes. "The war will wait," he said.

Dane looked more closely at the boy. "God! he's beautiful. I hope they take good care of him. Corporal, you may think that he wants to bear arms against the foe, but I think he's running away from love."

Kemp was relieved that the sergeant wasn't quite sober. "You think some dame hurt him?" He played any game his sergeant wished. "You think it's the Foreign Legion?"

"Maybe he's running away from himself."

Kemp said, "I saw that picture. There's one mean son of a bitch of a sergeant in it."

"I don't believe it," said Dane. "Step up, young man. Eighteen, aren't you?"

"Yes, sir."

Dane turned to his man. "What do you think?"

"Hell!" said Kemp. "I say if they're big enough, they're old enough."

The sergeant said, "Let's say you're eighteen. And we'll stick to it, shall we?"

"Yes, sir."

"You just take this form and fill it out. Now you figure out what year you were born, and you put it down right here, and you remember it."

FIFTY

Joe didn't like for Kate to sit still and stare straight ahead—hour after hour. That meant she was thinking, and since her face had no expression Joe had no access to her thoughts. It made him uneasy. He didn't want his first real good break to get away from him.

He had only one plan himself—and that was to keep her stirred up until she gave herself away. Then he could jump in any direction. But how about it if she sat looking at the wall? Was she stirred up or wasn't she?

Joe knew she hadn't been to bed, and when he asked whether or not she wanted breakfast she shook her head so slowly that it was hard to know whether she had heard him or not.

He advised himself cautiously, "Don't do nothing! Just stick around and keep your eyes and ears open." The girls in the house knew something had happened but no two of them had the same story, the goddam chicken-heads.

Kate was not thinking. Her mind drifted among impressions the way a bat drifts and swoops in the evening. She saw the face of the blond and

beautiful boy, his eyes mad with shock. She heard his ugly words aimed no
so much at her as at himself. And she saw his dark brother leaning agains
the door and laughing.

Kate had laughed too—the quickest and best self-protection. What woul
her son do? What had he done after he went quietly away?

She thought of Cal's eyes with their look of sluggish and fulfilled cruelty
peering at her as he slowly closed the door.

Why had he brought his brother? What did he want? What was he after?
If she knew she could take care of herself. But she didn't know.

The pain was creeping in her hands again and there was a new place. He
right hip ached angrily when she moved. She thought, So the pain will
move in toward the center, and sooner or later all the pains will meet in
the center and join like rats in a clot.

In spite of his advice to himself, Joe couldn't let it alone. He carried a
pot of tea to her door, knocked softly, opened the door, and went in. As
far as he could see she hadn't moved.

He said, "I brought you some tea, ma'am."

"Put it on the table," she said, and then as a second thought, "Thank you,
Joe."

"You don't feel good, ma'am?"

"The pain's back. The medicine fooled me."

"Anything I can do?"

She raised her hands. "Cut these off—at the wrists." She grimaced with
the extra pain lifting her hands had caused. "Makes you feel hopeless," she
said plaintively.

Joe had never heard a tone of weakness in her before and his instinct
told him it was time to move in. He said, "Maybe you don't want me to
bother you but I got some word about that other." He knew by the little
interval before she answered that she had tensed.

"What other?" she asked softly.

"That dame, ma'am."

"Oh! You mean Ethel?"

"Yes, ma'am."

"I'm getting tired of Ethel. What is it now?"

"Well, I'll tell you like it happened. I can't make nothing out of it. I'm
in Kellogg's cigar store and a fella come up to me. 'You're Joe?' he says,
an' I tell him, 'Who says?' 'You was lookin' for somebody,' he says. 'Tell
me about it,' I says. Never seen the guy before. So he says, 'That party tol'
me she wants to talk to you.' An' I told him, 'Well, why don't she?' He
gives me the long look an' he says, 'Maybe you forgot what the judge said.'
I guess he means about her coming back." He looked at Kate's face, still
and pale, the eyes looking straight ahead.

Kate said, "And then he asked you for some money?"

"No, ma'am. He didn't. He says something don't make no sense. He says, 'Does Faye mean anything to you?' 'Not a thing,' I tol' him. He says, 'Maybe you better talk to her.' 'Maybe,' I says, an' I come away. Don't make no sense to me. I figured I'd ask you."

Kate asked, "Does the name Faye mean anything to you?"

"Not a thing."

Her voice became very soft. "You mean you never heard that Faye used to own this house?"

Joe felt a sickening jolt in the pit of his stomach. What a goddam fool! Couldn't keep his mouth shut. His mind floundered. "Why—why come to think of it, I believe I did hear that—seemed like the name was like Faith."

The sudden alarm was good for Kate. It took the blond head and the pain from her. It gave her something to do. She responded to the challenge with something like pleasure.

She laughed softly. "Faith," she said under her breath. "Pour me some tea, Joe."

She did not appear to notice that his hand shook and that the teapot spout rattled against the cup. She did not look at him even when he set the cup before her and then stepped back out of range of her eyes. Joe was quaking with apprehension.

Kate said in a pleading voice, "Joe, do you think you could help me? If I gave you ten thousand dollars, do you think you could fix everything up?" She waited just a second, then swung around and looked full in his face.

His eyes were moist. She caught him licking his lips. And at her sudden move he stepped back as though she had struck at him. Her eyes would not let him go.

"Did I catch you out, Joe?"

"I don't know what you're getting at, ma'am."

"You go and figure it out—and then you come and tell me. You're good at figuring things out. And send Therese in, will you?"

He wanted to get out of this room where he was outpointed and out-fought. He'd made a mess of things. He wondered if he'd bollixed up the breaks. And then the bitch had the nerve to say, "Thank you for bringing tea. You're a nice boy."

He wanted to slam the door, but he didn't dare.

Kate got up stiffly, trying to avoid the pain of moving her hip. She went to her desk and slipped out a sheet of paper. Holding the pen was difficult.

She wrote, moving her whole arm. "Dear Ralph: Tell the sheriff it wouldn't do any harm to check on Joe Valery's fingerprints. You remember Joe. He works for me. Y'rs, Kate." She was folding the paper when Therese came in, looking frightened.

"You want me? Did I do something? I tried my best. Ma'am, I ain't been well."

"Come here," Kate said, and while the girl waited beside the desk Kate slowly addressed the envelope and stamped it. "I want you to run a little errand for me," she said. "Go to Bell's candy store and get a five-pound box of mixed chocolates and a one-pound box. The big one is for you girls. Stop at Krough's drugstore and get me two medium toothbrushes and a can of tooth powder—you know, that can with a spout?"

"Yes, ma'am." Therese was greatly relieved.

"You're a good girl," Kate went on. "I've had my eye on you. I'm not well, Therese. If I see that you do this well, I'll seriously consider putting you in charge when I go to the hospital."

"You will—are—are you going to the hospital?"

"I don't know yet, dear. But I'll need your help. Now here's some money for the candy. Medium toothbrushes—remember."

"Yes, ma'am. Thank you. Shall I go now?"

"Yes, and kind of creep out, will you? Don't let the other girls know what I told you."

"I'll go out the back way." She hurried toward the door.

Kate said, "I nearly forgot. Will you drop this in a mailbox?"

"Sure I will, ma'am. Sure I will. Anything else?"

"That's all, dear."

When the girl was gone Kate rested her arms and hands on the desk so that each crooked finger was supported. Here it was. Maybe she had always known. She must have—but there was no need to think of that now. She would come back to that. They would put Joe away, but there'd be someone else, and there was always Ethel. Sooner or later, sooner or later—but no need to think about that now. She tiptoed her mind around the whole subject and back to an elusive thing that peeped out and then withdrew. It was when she had been thinking of her yellow-haired son that the fragment had first come to her mind. His face—hurt, bewildered, despairing—had brought it. Then she remembered.

She was a very small girl with a face as lovely and fresh as her son's face —a very small girl. Most of the time she knew she was smarter and prettier than anyone else. But now and then a lonely fear would fall upon her so that she seemed surrounded by a tree-tall forest of enemies. Then every thought and word and look was aimed to hurt her, and she had no place to run and no place to hide. And she would cry in panic because there was no escape and no sanctuary. Then one day she was reading a book. She could read when she was five years old. She remembered the book—brown, with a silver title, and the cloth was broken and the boards thick. It was *Alice in Wonderland*.

Kate moved her hands slowly and lifted her weight a little from her arms. And she could see the drawings—Alice with long straight hair. But it was the bottle which said "Drink me" that had changed her life. Alice had taught her that.

When the forest of her enemies surrounded her she was prepared. In her pocket she had a bottle of sugar water and on its red-framed label she had written, "Drink me." She would take a sip from the bottle and she would grow smaller and smaller. Let her enemies look for her then! Cathy would be under a leaf or looking out of an ant-hole, laughing. They couldn't find her then. No door could close her out and no door could close her in. She could walk upright under a door.

And always there was Alice to play with, Alice to love her and trust her. Alice was her friend, always waiting to welcome her to tinyness.

All this so good—so good that it was almost worth while to be miserable. But good as it was, there was one more thing always held in reserve. It was her threat and her safety. She had only to drink the whole bottle and she would dwindle and disappear and cease to exist. And better than all, when she stopped being, she never would have been. This was her darling safety. Sometimes in her bed she would drink enough of "Drink me" so that she was a dot as small as the littlest gnat. But she had never gone clear out— never had to. That was her reserve—guarded from everyone.

Kate shook her head sadly, remembering the cut-off little girl. She wondered why she had forgotten that wonderful trick. It had saved her from so many disasters. The light filtering down at one through a cloverleaf was glorious. Cathy and Alice walked among towering grass, arms around each other—best friends. And Cathy never had to drink all of "Drink me" because she had Alice.

Kate put her head down on the blotter between her crooked hands. She was cold and desolate, alone and desolate. Whatever she had done, she had been driven to do. She was different—she had something more than other people. She raised her head and made no move to wipe her streaming eyes. That was true. She was smarter and stronger than other people. She had something they lacked.

And right in the middle of her thought, Cal's dark face hung in the air in front of her and his lips were smiling with cruelty. The weight pressed down on her, forcing her breath out.

They had something she lacked, and she didn't know what it was. Once she knew this, she was ready; and once ready, she knew she had been ready for a long time—perhaps all of her life. Her mind functioned like a wooden mind, her body moved crookedly like a badly operated marionette, but she went steadily about her business.

It was noon—she knew from the chatter of the girls in the dining room. The slugs had only just got up.

Kate had trouble with the doorknob and turned it finally by rolling it between her palms.

The girls choked in the middle of laughter and looked up at her. The cook came in from the kitchen.

Kate was a sick ghost, crooked and in some way horrible. She leaned against the dining-room wall and smiled at her girls, and her smile frightened them even more, for it was like the frame for a scream.

448

"Where's Joe?" Kate asked.

"He went out, ma'am."

"Listen," she said. "I've had no sleep for a long time. I'm going to take some medicine and sleep. I don't want to be disturbed, I don't want any supper. I'll sleep the clock around. Tell Joe I don't want anybody to come near me for anything until tomorrow morning. Do you understand?"

"Yes, ma'am," they said.

"Good night, then. It's afternoon but I mean good night."

"Good night, ma'am," they chorused obediently.

Kate turned and walked crabwise back to her room.

She closed her door and stood looking around, trying to form her simple procedure. She went back to her desk. This time she forced her hand, in spite of the pain, to write plainly. "I leave everything I have to my son Aron Trask." She dated the sheet and signed it "Catherine Trask." Her fingers dwelt on the page, and then she got up and left her will face upward on the desk.

At the center table she poured cold tea into her cup and carried the cup to the gray room in the lean-to and set it on the reading table. Then she went to her dressing table and combed her hair, rubbed a little rouge all over her face, covered it lightly with powder, and put on the pale lipstick she always used. Last she filed her nails and cleaned them.

When she closed the door to the gray room the outside light was cut off and only the reading lamp threw its cone on the table. She arranged the pillows, patted them up, and sat down. She leaned her head experimentally against the down pillow. She felt rather gay, as though she were going to a party. Gingerly she fished the chain out from her bodice, unscrewed the little tube, and shook the capsule into her hand. She smiled at it.

"Eat me," she said and put the capsule in her mouth.

She picked up the tea cup. "Drink me," she said and swallowed the bitter cold tea.

She forced her mind to stay on Alice—so tiny and waiting. Other faces peered in from the sides of her eyes—her father and mother, and Charles, and Adam, and Samuel Hamilton, and then Aron, and she could see Cal smiling at her.

He didn't have to speak. The glint of his eyes said, "You missed something. They had something and you missed it."

She thrust her mind back to Alice. In the gray wall opposite there was a nail hole. Alice would be in there. And she would put her arm around Cathy's waist, and Cathy would put her arm around Alice's waist, and they would walk away—best friends—and tiny as the head of a pin.

A warm numbness began to creep into her arms and legs. The pain was going from her hands. Her eyelids felt heavy—very heavy. She yawned.

She thought or said or thought, "Alice doesn't know. I'm going right on past."

Her eyes closed and a dizzy nausea shook her. She opened her eyes and stared about in terror. The gray room darkened and the cone of light flowed and rippled like water. And then her eyes closed again and her fingers curled as though they held small breasts. And her heart beat solemnly and her breathing slowed as she grew smaller and smaller and then disappeared —and she had never been.

2

When Kate dismissed him Joe went to the barbershop, as he always did when he was upset. He had his hair cut and an egg shampoo and tonic. He had a facial massage and a mud pack, and around the edges he had his nails manicured, and he had his shoes shined. Ordinarily this and a new necktie set Joe up, but he was still depressed when he left the barber with a fifty-cent tip.

Kate had trapped him like a rat—caught him with his pants down. Her fast thinking left him confused and helpless. The trick she had of leaving it to you whether she meant anything or not was no less confusing.

The night started dully, but then sixteen members and two pledges from Sigma Alpha Epsilon, Stanford chapter, came in hilarious from a pledge hazing in San Juan. They were full of horseplay.

Florence, who smoked the cigarette in the circus, had a hard cough. Every time she tried, she coughed and lost it. And the pony stallion had diarrhea.

The college boys shrieked and pounded each other in their amusement. And then they stole everything that wasn't nailed down.

After they had left, two of the girls got into a tired and monotonous quarrel, and Therese turned up with the first symptoms of the old Joe. Oh, Christ, what a night!

And down the hall that brooding dangerous thing was silent behind its closed door. Joe stood by the door before he went to bed and he could hear nothing. He closed the house at two-thirty and was in bed by three—but he couldn't sleep. He sat up in bed and read seven chapters of *The Winning of Barbara Worth*, and when it was daylight he went down to the silent kitchen and made a pot of coffee.

He rested his elbows on the table and held the coffee mug with both hands. Something had gone wrong and Joe couldn't figure what it was. Maybe she'd found out that Ethel was dead. He'd have to watch his step. And then he made up his mind, and made it up firmly. He would go in to see her at nine and he'd keep his ears open. Maybe he hadn't heard right. Best thing would be to lay it on the line and not be a hog. Just say he'd take a thousand bucks and get the hell out, and if she said no he'd get the hell out anyway. He was sick of working with dames. He could get a job dealing faro in Reno—regular hours and no dames. Maybe get himself an apartmen[t] and fix it up—big chairs and a davenport. No point in beating his brain[s] out in this lousy town. Better if he got out of the state anyway. He con[-] sidered going right now—just get up from this table, climb the stairs, tw[o] minutes to pack a suitcase, and gone. Three or four minutes at the most[.] Don't tell nobody nothing. The idea appealed to him. The breaks abou[t] Ethel might not be as good as he thought at first, but a thousand buck[s] was a stake. Better wait.

When the cook came in he was in a bad mood. He had a developing carbuncle on the back of his neck and the skin from the inside of an egg-shell stretched over it to draw it to a head. He didn't want anybody in his kitchen, feeling the way he did.

Joe went back to his room and read some more and then he packed his suitcase. He was going to get out any way it went.

At nine o'clock he knocked gently on Kate's door and pushed it open. Her bed had not been slept in. He set down the tray and went to the door of the lean-to and knocked and knocked again and then called. Finally he opened the door.

The cone of light fell on the reading stand. Kate's head was deeply cushioned in the pillow.

"You must have slept all night here," Joe said. He walked around in front of her, saw bloodless lips and eyes shining dully between half-closed lids, and he knew she was dead.

He moved his head from side to side and went quickly into the other room to make sure that the door to the hall was closed. With great speed he went through the dresser, drawer by drawer, opened her purses, the little box by her bed—and he stood still. She didn't have a goddam thing—not even a silver-backed hairbrush.

He crept to the lean-to and stood in front of her—not a ring, not a pin. Then he saw the little chain around her neck and lifted it clear and un-snapped the clasp—a small gold watch, a little tube, and two safe-deposit keys, numbers 27 and 29.

"So that's where you got it, you bitch," he said.

He slipped the watch off the thin chain and put it in his pocket. He wanted to punch her in the nose. Then he thought of her desk.

The two-line holograph will attracted him. Somebody might pay for that. He put it in his pocket. He took a handful of papers from a pigeon-hole—bills and receipts; next hole, insurance; next, a small book with records of every girl. He put that in his pocket too. He took the rubber band from a packet of brown envelopes, opened one, and pulled out a photograph. On the back of the picture, in Kate's neat, sharp handwriting, a name and address and a title.

Joe laughed aloud. This was the real breaks. He tried another envelope[.]

id another. A gold mine—guy could live for years on these. Look at that
it-ass councilman! He put the band back. In the top drawer eight ten-dollar
ills and a bunch of keys. He pocketed the money too. As he opened the
econd drawer enough to see that it held writing paper and sealing wax and
ik there was a knock on the door. He walked to it and opened it a crack.

The cook said, "Fella out here wants to see ya."

"Who is he?"

"How the hell do I know?"

Joe looked back at the room and then stepped out, took the key from
he inside, locked the door, and put the key in his pocket. He might have
verlooked something.

Oscar Noble was standing in the big front room, his gray hat on his
iead and his red mackinaw buttoned up tight around his throat. His eyes
vere pale gray—the same color as his stubble whiskers. The room was
n semidarkness. No one had raised the shades yet.

Joe came lightly along the hall, and Oscar asked, "You Joe?"

"Who's asking?"

"The sheriff wants to have a talk with you."

Joe felt ice creeping into his stomach. "Pinch?" he asked. "Got a warrant?"

"Hell, no," said Oscar. "We got nothing on you. Just checking up. Will
you come along?"

"Sure," said Joe. "Why not?"

They went out together. Joe shivered. "I should of got a coat."

"Want to go back for one?"

"I guess not," said Joe.

They walked toward Castroville Street. Oscar asked, "Ever been mugged
or printed?"

Joe was quiet for a time. "Yes," he said at last.

"What for?"

"Drunk," said Joe. "Hit a cop."

"Well, we'll soon find out," said Oscar and turned the corner.

Joe ran like a rabbit, across the street and over the track toward the stores
and alleys of Chinatown.

Oscar had to take a glove off and unbutton his mackinaw to get his gun
out. He tried a snap shot and missed.

Joe began to zigzag. He was fifty yards away by now and nearing an opening between two buildings.

Oscar stepped to a telephone pole at the curb, braced his left elbow
against it, gripped his right wrist with his left hand, and drew a bead on
the entrance to the little alley. He fired just as Joe touched the front sight.

Joe splashed forward on his face and skidded a foot.

Oscar went into a Filipino poolroom to phone, and when he came out
there was quite a crowd around the body.

FIFTY-ONE

In 1903 Horace Quinn beat Mr. R. Keef for the office of sheriff. He had been well trained as the chief deputy sheriff. Most of the voters figured that since Quinn was doing most of the work he might as well have the title. Sheriff Quinn held the office until 1919. He was sheriff so long that we growing up in Monterey County thought the words "Sheriff" and "Quinn" went together naturally. We could not imagine anyone else being sheriff. Quinn grew old in his office. He limped from an early injury. We knew he was intrepid, for he had held his own in various gunfights; besides, he looked like a sheriff—the only kind we knew about. His face was broad and pink, his white mustache shaped like the horns of a longhorn steer. He was broad of shoulder, and in his age he developed a portliness which only gave him more authority. He wore a fine Stetson hat, a Norfolk jacket, and in his later years carried his gun in a shoulder holster. His old belt holster tugged at his stomach too much. He had known his county in 1903 and he knew it and controlled it even better in 1917. He was an institution, as much a part of the Salinas Valley as its mountains.

In all the years since Adam's shooting Sheriff Quinn had kept track of Kate. When Faye died, he knew instinctively that Kate was probably responsible, but he also knew he hadn't much of any chance of convicting her, and a wise sheriff doesn't butt his head against the impossible. They were only a couple of whores, after all.

In the years that followed, Kate played fair with him and he gradually achieved a certain respect for her. Since there were going to be houses anyway, they had better be run by responsible people. Every so often Kate spotted a wanted man and turned him in. She ran a house which did not get into trouble. Sheriff Quinn and Kate got along together.

The Saturday after Thanksgiving, about noon, Sheriff Quinn looked through the papers from Joe Valery's pockets. The .38 slug had splashed off one side of Joe's heart and had flattened against the ribs and torn out a section as big as a fist. The manila envelopes were glued together with blackened blood. The sheriff dampened the papers with a wet handkerchief to get them apart. He read the will, which had been folded, so that the blood was on the outside. He laid it aside and inspected the photographs in the envelopes. He sighed deeply.

Every envelope contained a man's honor and peace of mind. Effectively used, these pictures could cause half a dozen suicides. Already Kate was on the table at Muller's with the formalin running into her veins, and her stomach was in a jar in the coroner's office.

When he had seen all of the pictures he called a number. He said into the phone, "Can you drop over to my office? Well, put your lunch off, will you? Yes, I think you'll see it's important. I'll wait for you."

A few minutes later when the nameless man stood beside his desk in the front office of the old red county jail behind the courthouse, Sheriff Quinn stuck the will out in front of him. "As a lawyer, would you say this is any good?"

His visitor read the two lines and breathed deep through his nose. "Is this who I think it is?"

"Yes."

"Well, if her name was Catherine Trask and this is her handwriting, and if Aron Trask is her son, this is as good as gold."

Quinn lifted the ends of his fine wide mustache with the back of his forefinger. "You knew her, didn't you?"

"Well, not to say know. I knew who she was."

Quinn put his elbows on his desk and leaned forward. "Sit down, I want to talk to you."

His visitor drew up a chair. His fingers picked at a coat button.

The sheriff asked, "Was Kate blackmailing you?"

"Certainly not. Why should she?"

"I'm asking you as a friend. You know she's dead. You can tell me."

"I don't know what you're getting at—nobody's blackmailing me."

Quinn slipped a photograph from its envelope, turned it like a playing card, and skidded it across the desk.

His visitor adjusted his glasses and the breath whistled in his nose. "Jesus Christ," he said softly.

"You didn't know she had it?"

"Oh, I knew it all right. She let me know. For Christ's sake, Horace—what are you going to do with this?"

Quinn took the picture from his hand.

"Horace, what are you going to do with it?"

"Burn it." The sheriff ruffled the edges of the envelopes with his thumb. "Here's a deck of hell," he said. "These could tear the county to pieces."

Quinn wrote a list of names on a sheet of paper. Then he hoisted himself up on his game leg and went to the iron stove against the north wall of his office. He crunched up the *Salinas Morning Journal* and lighted it and dropped it in the stove, and when it flared up he dropped the manila envelopes on the flame, set the damper, and closed the stove. The fire roared and the flames winked yellow behind the little isinglass windows in the front of the stove. Quinn brushed his hands together as though they were dirty. "The negatives were in there," he said. "I've been through her desk. There weren't any other prints."

His visitor tried to speak but his voice was a husky whisper. "Thank you, Horace."

The sheriff gimped to his desk and picked up his list. "I want you to do something for me. Here's a list. Tell everyone on this list I've burned the pictures. You know them all, God knows. And they could take it from you. Nobody's holy. Get each man alone and tell him exactly what happened. Look here!" He opened the stove door and poked the black sheets until they were reduced to powder. "Tell them that," he said.

His visitor looked at the sheriff, and Quinn knew that there was no power on earth that could keep this man from hating him. For the rest of their lives there would be a barrier between them, and neither one could ever admit it.

"Horace, I don't know how to thank you."

And the sheriff said in sorrow, "That's all right. It's what I'd want my friends to do for me."

"The goddam bitch," his visitor said softly, and Horace Quinn knew that part of the curse was for him.

And he knew he wouldn't be sheriff much longer. These guilt-feeling men could get him out, and they would have to. He sighed and sat down. "Go to your lunch now," he said. "I've got work to do."

At quarter of one Sheriff Quinn turned off Main Street on Central Avenue. At Reynaud's Bakery he bought a loaf of French bread, still warm and giving off its wonderful smell of fermented dough.

He used the hand rail to help himself up the steps of the Trask porch.

Lee answered the door, a dish towel tied around his middle. "He's not home," he said.

"Well, he's on his way. I called the draft board. I'll wait for him."

Lee moved aside and let him in and seated him in the living room. "You like a nice cup of hot coffee?" he asked.

"I don't mind if I do."

"Fresh made," said Lee and went into the kitchen.

Quinn looked around the comfortable sitting room. He felt that he didn't want his office much longer. He remembered hearing a doctor say, "I love to deliver a baby, because if I do my work well, there's joy at the end of it." The sheriff had thought often of that remark. It seemed to him that if he did his work well there was sorrow at the end of it for somebody. The fact that it was necessary was losing its weight with him. He would be retiring soon whether he wanted to or not.

Every man has a retirement picture in which he does those things he never had time to do—makes the journeys, reads the neglected books he always pretended to have read. For many years the sheriff dreamed of spending the shining time hunting and fishing—wandering in the Santa Lucia range, camping by half-remembered streams. And now that it was almost time he knew he didn't want to do it. Sleeping on the ground would make his leg ache. He remembered how heavy a deer is and how hard it is to carry the dangling limp body from the place of the kill. And, frankly, he didn't are for venison anyway. Madame Reynaud could soak it in wine and lace it with spice but, hell, an old shoe would taste good with that treatment.

Lee had bought a percolator. Quinn could hear the water spluttering against the glass dome, and his long-trained mind made the suggestion that Lee hadn't told the truth about having fresh-made coffee.

It was a good mind the old man had—sharpened in its work. He could bring up whole faces in his mind and inspect them, and also scenes and conversations. He could play them over like a record or a film. Thinking of venison, his mind had gone about cataloguing the sitting room and his mind nudged him, saying, "Hey, there's something wrong here—something strange."

The sheriff heeded the voice and looked at the room—flowered chintz, lace curtains, white drawn-work table cover, cushions on the couch covered with a bright and impudent print. It was a feminine room in a house where only men lived.

He thought of his own sitting room. Mrs. Quinn had chosen, bought, cleaned, every single thing in it except a pipestand. Come to think of it, she had bought the pipestand for him. There was a woman's room too. But this was a fake. It was too feminine—a woman's room designed by a man—and overdone, too feminine. That would be Lee. Adam wouldn't even see it, let alone put it together—no—Lee trying to make a home, and Adam not even seeing it.

Horace Quinn remembered questioning Adam so very long ago, remembered him as a man in agony. He could still see Adam's haunted and horrified eyes. He had thought then of Adam as a man of such honesty that he couldn't conceive anything else. And in the years he had seen much of Adam. They both belonged to the Masonic Order. They went through the chairs together. Horace followed Adam as Master of the Lodge and both of them wore their Past Master's pins. And Adam had been set apart—an invisible wall cut him off from the world. You couldn't get into him—he couldn't get out to you. But in that old agony there had been no wall.

In his wife Adam had touched the living world. Horace thought of her now, gray and washed, the needles in her throat and the rubber formalin tubes hanging down from the ceiling.

Adam could do no dishonesty. He didn't want anything. You had to crave something to be dishonest. The sheriff wondered what went on behind the wall, what pressures, what pleasures and achings.

He shifted his behind to ease the pressure on his leg. The house was still except for the bouncing coffee. Adam was long coming from the draft board. The amused thought came to the sheriff, I'm getting old, and I kind of like it.

Then he heard Adam at the front door. Lee heard him too and darted into the hall. "The sheriff's here," said Lee, to warn him perhaps.

Adam came in smiling and held out his hand. "Hello, Horace—have you got a warrant?" It was a damn good try at a joke.

"Howdy," Quinn said. "Your man is going to give me a cup of coffee."

Lee went to the kitchen and rattled dishes.

Adam said, "Anything wrong, Horace?"

"Everything's always wrong in my business. I'll wait till the coffee comes."

"Don't mind Lee. He listens anyway. He can hear through a closed door. I don't keep anything from him because I can't."

Lee came in with a tray. He was smiling remotely to himself, and when he had poured the coffee and gone out Adam asked again, "Is there anything wrong, Horace?"

"No, I don't think so. Adam, was that woman still married to you?"

Adam became rigid. "Yes," he said. "What's the matter?"

"She killed herself last night."

Adam's face contorted and his eyes swelled and glistened with tears. He fought his mouth and then he gave up and put his face down in his hands and wept. "Oh, my poor darling!" he said.

Quinn sat quietly and let him have it out, and after a time Adam's control came back and he raised his head. "Excuse me, Horace," he said.

Lee came in from the kitchen and put a damp towel in his hands, and Adam sponged his eyes and handed it back.

"I didn't expect that," Adam said, and his face was ashamed. "What shall I do? I'll claim her. I'll bury her."

"I wouldn't," said Horace. "That is, unless you feel you have to. That's not what I came about." He took the folded will from his pocket and held it out.

Adam shrank from it. "Is—is that her blood?"

"No, it's not. It's not her blood at all. Read it."

Adam read the two lines and went right on staring at the paper and beyond it. "He doesn't know—she is his mother."

"You never told him?"

"No."

"Jesus Christ!" said the sheriff.

Adam said earnestly, "I'm sure he wouldn't want anything of hers. Let's just tear it up and forget it. If he knew, I don't think Aron would want anything of hers."

"'Fraid you can't," Quinn said. "We do quite a few illegal things. She had a safe-deposit box. I don't have to tell you where I got the will or the key. I went to the bank. Didn't wait for a court order. Thought it might have a bearing." He didn't tell Adam he thought there might be more pictures. "Well, Old Bob let me open the box. We can always deny it. There's over a hundred thousand dollars in gold certificates. There's money in there in bales—and there isn't one goddam thing in there but money."

"Nothing?"

"One other thing—a marriage certificate."

Adam leaned back in his chair. The remoteness was coming down again, the soft protective folds between himself and the world. He saw his coffee and took a sip of it. "What do you think I ought to do?" he asked steadily and quietly.

"I can only tell you what I'd do," Sheriff Quinn said. "You don't have to take my advice. I'd have the boy in right now. I'd tell him everything—every single thing. I'd even tell him why you didn't tell him before. He's—how old?"

"Seventeen."

"He's a man. He's got to take it some time. Better if he gets the whole thing at once."

"Cal knows," said Adam. "I wonder why she made the will to Aron?"

"God knows. Well, what do you think?"

"I don't know, and so I'm going to do what you say. Will you stay with me?"

"Sure I will."

"Lee," Adam called, "tell Aron I want him. He has come home, hasn't he?"

Lee came to the doorway. His heavy lids closed for a moment and then opened. "Not yet. Maybe he went back to school."

"He would have told me. You know, Horace, we drank a lot of champagne on Thanksgiving. Where's Cal?"

"In his room," said Lee.

"Well, call him. Get him in. Cal will know."

Cal's face was tired and his shoulders sagged with exhaustion, but his face was pinched and closed and crafty and mean.

Adam asked, "Do you know where your brother is?"

"No, I don't," said Cal.

"Weren't you with him at all?"

"No."

"He hasn't been home for two nights. Where is he?"

"How do I know?" said Cal. "Am I supposed to look after him?"

Adam's head sank down, his body jarred, just a little quiver. In back of his eyes a tiny sharp incredibly bright blue light flashed. He said thickly, "Maybe he did go back to college." His lips seemed heavy and he murmured like a man talking in his sleep. "Don't you think he went back to college?"

Sheriff Quinn stood up. "Anything I got to do I can do later. You get a rest, Adam. You've had a shock."

Adam looked up at him. "Shock—oh, yes. Thank you, George. Thank you very much."

"George?"

"Thank you very much," said Adam.

When the sheriff had gone, Cal went to his room. Adam leaned back in

his chair, and very soon he went to sleep and his mouth dropped open and he
snored across his palate.

Lee watched him for a while before he went back to his kitchen. He
lifted the breadbox and took out a tiny volume bound in leather, and the
gold tooling was almost completely worn away—*The Meditations of Marcus
Aurelius* in English translation.

Lee wiped his steel-rimmed spectacles on a dish towel. He opened the
book and leafed through. And he smiled to himself, consciously searching
for reassurance.

He read slowly, moving his lips over the words. "Everything is only for a
day, both that which remembers and that which is remembered.

"Observe constantly that all things take place by change, and accustom
thyself to consider that the nature of the universe loves nothing so much as
to change things which are and to make new things like them. For everything that exists is in a manner the seed of that which will be."

Lee glanced down the page. "Thou wilt die soon and thou are not yet simple nor free from perturbations, nor without suspicion of being hurt by external things, nor kindly disposed towards all; nor dost thou yet place wisdom
only in acting justly."

Lee looked up from the page, and he answered the book as he would answer one of his ancient relatives. "That is true," he said. "It's very hard. I'm
sorry. But don't forget that you also say, 'Always run the short way and the
short way is the natural'—don't forget that." He let the pages slip past his
fingers to the fly leaf where was written with a broad carpenter's pencil,
"Sam'l Hamilton."

Suddenly Lee felt good. He wondered whether Sam'l Hamilton had ever
missed his book or known who stole it. It had seemed to Lee the only clean
pure way was to steal it. And he still felt good about it. His fingers caressed
the smooth leather of the binding as he took it back and slipped it under
the breadbox. He said to himself, "But of course he knew who took it.
Who else would have stolen *Marcus Aurelius*?" He went into the sitting
room and pulled a chair near to the sleeping Adam.

2

In his room Cal sat at his desk, elbows down, palms holding his aching head
together, hands pushing against the sides of his head. His stomach churned
and the sour-sweet smell of whisky was on him and in him, living in his
pores, in his clothing, beating sluggishly in his head.

Cal had never drunk before, had never needed to. But going to Kate's had
been no relief from pain and his revenge had been no triumph. His memory
was all swirling clouds and broken pieces of sound and sight and feeling.
What now was true and what was imagined he could not separate. Coming
out of Kate's he had touched his sobbing brother and Aron had cut him

down with a fist like a whip. Aron had stood over him in the dark and then suddenly turned and ran, screaming like a brokenhearted child. Cal could still hear the hoarse cries over running footsteps. Cal had lain still where he had fallen under the tall privet in Kate's front yard. He heard the engines puffing and snorting by the roundhouse and the crash of freight cars being assembled. Then he had closed his eyes and, hearing light steps and feeling a presence, he looked up. Someone was bending over him and he thought it was Kate. The figure moved quietly away.

After a while Cal had stood up and brushed himself and walked toward Main Street. He was surprised at how casual his feeling was. He sang softly under his breath, "There's a rose that grows in no man's land and 'tis wonderful to see—"

On Friday Cal brooded the whole day long. And in the evening Joe Laguna bought the quart of whisky for him. Cal was too young to purchase. Joe wanted to accompany Cal, but Joe was satisfied with the dollar Cal gave him and went back for a pint of grappa.

Cal went to the alley behind the Abbot House and found the shadow behind a post where he had sat the night he first saw his mother. He sat cross-legged on the ground, and then, in spite of revulsion and nausea, he forced the whisky into himself. Twice he vomited and then went on drinking until the earth tipped and swayed and the streetlight spun majestically in a circle.

The bottle slipped from his hand finally and Cal passed out, but even unconscious he still vomited weakly. A serious, short-haired dog-about-town with a curling tail sauntered into the alley, making his stations, but he smelled Cal and took a wide circle around him. Joe Laguna found him and smelled him too. Joe shook the bottle leaning against Cal's leg and Joe held it up to the streetlight and saw that it was one-third full. He looked for the cork and couldn't find it. He walked away, his thumb over the neck to keep the whisky from sloshing out.

When in the cold dawn a frost awakened Cal to a sick world he struggled home like a broken bug. He hadn't far to go, just to the alley mouth and then across the street.

Lee heard him at the door and smelled his nastiness as he bumped along the hall to his room and fell over on his bed. Cal's head shattered with pain and he was wide awake. He had no resistance against sorrow and no device to protect himself against shame. After a while he did the best he could. He bathed in icy water and scrubbed and scratched his body with a block of pumice stone, and the pain of his scraping seemed good to him.

He knew that he had to tell his guilt to his father and beg his forgiveness. And he had to humble himself to Aron, not only now but always. He could not live without that. And yet, when he was called out and stood in the room with Sheriff Quinn and his father, he was as raw and angry as a surly dog and his hatred of himself turned outward toward everyone—a vicious cur he was, unloved, unloving.

Then he was back in his room and his guilt assaulted him and he had no weapon to fight it off.

A panic for Aron arose in him. He might be injured, might be in trouble. It was Aron who couldn't take care of himself. Cal knew he had to bring Aron back, had to find him and build him back the way he had been. And this had to be done even though Cal sacrificed himself. And then the idea of sacrifice took hold of him the way it does with all guilty-feeling men. A sacrifice might reach Aron and bring him back.

Cal went to his bureau and got the flat package from under his handkerchiefs in his drawer. He looked around the room and brought a porcelain pin tray to his desk. He breathed deeply and found the cool air good tasting. He lifted one of the crisp bills, creased it in the middle so that it made an angle, and then he scratched a match under his desk and lighted the bill. The heavy paper curled and blackened, the flame ran upward, and only when the fire was about his fingertips did Cal drop the charred chip in the pin tray. He stripped off another bill and lighted it.

When six were burned Lee came in without knocking. "I smelled smoke," and then he saw what Cal was doing. "Oh!" he said.

Cal braced himself for intervention but none came. Lee folded his hands across his middle and he stood silently—waiting. Cal doggedly lighted bill after bill until all were burned, and then he crushed the black chips down to powder and waited for Lee to comment, but Lee did not speak or move.

At last Cal said, "Go ahead—you want to talk to me. Go ahead!"

"No," said Lee, "I don't. And if you have no need to talk to me—I'll stay a while and then I'll go away. I'll sit down here." He squatted in a chair, folded his hands, and waited. He smiled to himself, the expression that is called inscrutable.

Cal turned from him. "I can outsit you," he said.

"In a contest maybe," said Lee. "But in day to day, year to year—who knows?—century to century sitting—no, Cal. You'd lose."

After a few moments Cal said peevishly, "I wish you'd get on with your lecture."

"I don't have a lecture."

"What the hell are you doing here then? You know what I did, and I got drunk last night."

"I suspect the first and I can smell the second."

"Smell?"

"You still smell," said Lee.

"First time," said Cal. "I don't like it."

"I don't either," said Lee. "I've got a bad stomach for liquor. Besides it makes me playful, intellectual but playful."

"How do you mean, Lee?"

"I can only give you an example. In my younger days I played tennis. I liked it, and it was also a good thing for a servant to do. He could pick up his master's flubs at doubles and get no thanks but a few dollars for it. Once, I think it was sherry that time, I developed the theory that the fastest and most elusive animals in the world are bats. I was apprehended in the middle of the night in the bell tower of the Methodist Church in San Leandro. I had a racquet, and I seem to have explained to the arresting officer that I was improving my backhand on bats."

Cal laughed with such amusement that Lee almost wished he had done it.

Cal said, "I just sat behind a post and drank like a pig."

"Always animals—"

"I was afraid if I didn't get drunk I'd shoot myself," Cal interrupted.

"You'd never do that. You're too mean," said Lee. "By the way, where is Aron?"

"He ran away. I don't know where he went."

"He's not too mean," said Lee nervously.

"I know it. That's what I thought about. You don't think he would, do you, Lee?"

Lee said testily, "Goddam it, whenever a person wants reassurance he tells a friend to think what he wants to be true. It's like asking a waiter what's good tonight. How the hell do I know?"

Cal cried, "Why did I do it—why did I do it?"

"Don't make it complicated," Lee said. "You know why you did it. You were mad at him, and you were mad at him because your father hurt your feelings. That's not difficult. You were just mean."

"I guess that's what I wonder—why I'm mean. Lee, I don't want to be mean. Help me, Lee!"

"Just a second," Lee said. "I thought I heard your father." He darted out the door.

Cal heard voices for a moment and then Lee came back to the room. "He's going to the post office. We never get any mail in midafternoon. Nobody does. But every man in Salinas goes to the post office in the afternoon."

"Some get a drink on the way," said Cal.

"I guess it is a kind of a habit and a kind of a rest. They see their friends." And Lee said, "Cal—I don't like your father's looks. He's got a dazed look. Oh, I forgot. You don't know. Your mother committed suicide last night."

Cal said, "Did she?" and then he snarled, "I hope it hurt. No, I don't want to say that. I don't want to think that. There it is again. There it is! I don't —want it—like that."

Lee scratched a spot on his head, and that started his whole head to itching, and he scratched it all over, taking his time. It gave him the appearance of deep thought. He said, "Did burning the money give you much pleasure?"

"I—I guess so."

"And are you taking pleasure from this whipping you're giving yourself? Are you enjoying your despair?"

"Lee!"

"You're pretty full of yourself. You're marveling at the tragic spectacle of Caleb Trask—Caleb the magnificent, the unique. Caleb whose suffering should have its Homer. Did you ever think of yourself as a snot-nose kid—mean sometimes, incredibly generous sometimes? Dirty in your habits, and curiously pure in your mind. Maybe you have a little more energy than most, just energy, but outside of that you're very like all the other snot-nose kids. Are you trying to attract dignity and tragedy to yourself because your mother was a whore? And if anything should have happened to your brother, will you be able to sneak for yourself the eminence of being a murderer, snot-nose?"

Cal turned slowly back to his desk. Lee watched him, holding his breath the way a doctor watches for the reaction to a hypodermic. Lee could see the reactions flaring through Cal—the rage at insult, the belligerence, and the hurt feelings following behind and out of that—just the beginning of relief.

Lee sighed. He had worked so hard, so tenderly, and his work seemed to have succeeded. He said softly, "We're a violent people, Cal. Does it seem strange to you that I include myself? Maybe it's true that we are all descended from the restless, the nervous, the criminals, the arguers and brawlers, but also the brave and independent and generous. If our ancestors had not been that, they would have stayed in their home plots in the other world and starved over the squeezed-out soil."

Cal turned his head toward Lee, and his face had lost its tightness. He smiled, and Lee knew he had not fooled the boy entirely. Cal knew now it was a job—a well-done job—and he was grateful.

Lee went on, "That's why I include myself. We all have that heritage, no matter what old land our fathers left. All colors and blends of Americans have somewhat the same tendencies. It's a breed—selected out by accident. And so we're overbrave and overfearful—we're kind and cruel as children. We're overfriendly and at the same time frightened of strangers. We boast and are impressed. We're oversentimental and realistic. We are mundane and materialistic—and do you know of any other nation that acts for ideals? We eat too much. We have no taste, no sense of proportion. We throw our energy about like waste. In the old lands they say of us that we go from barbarism to decadence without an intervening culture. Can it be that our critics have not the key or the language of our culture? That's what we are, Cal—all of us. You aren't very different."

"Talk away," said Cal, and he smiled and repeated, "Talk away."

"I don't need to any more," said Lee. "I'm finished now. I wish your father would come back. He worries me." And Lee went nervously out.

In the hall just inside the front door he found Adam leaning against the wall, his hat low over his eyes and his shoulders slumped.

"Adam, what's the matter with you?"

"I don't know. Seem tired. Seem tired."

Lee took him by the arm, and it seemed that he had to guide him toward the living room. Adam fell heavily into his chair, and Lee took the hat from his head. Adam rubbed the back of his left hand with his right. His eyes were strange, very clear but unmoving. And his lips were dry and thickened and his speech had the sound of a dream talker, slow and coming from a distance. He rubbed his hand harshly. "Strange thing," he said, "I must have fainted—in the post office. I never faint. Mr. Pioda helped me up. Just for a second it was, I guess. I never faint."

Lee asked, "Was there any mail?"

"Yes—yes—I think there was mail." He put his left hand in his pocket and in a moment took it out. "My hand is kind of numb," he said apologetically and reached across with his right hand and brought out a yellow government postcard.

"Thought I read it," he said. "I must have read it." He held it up before his eyes and then dropped the card in his lap. "Lee, I guess I've got to get glasses. Never needed them in my life. Can't read it. Letters jump around."

"Shall I read it?"

"Funny—well, I'll go first thing for glasses. Yes, what does it say?"

And Lee read, " 'Dear Father, I'm in the army. I told them I was eighteen. I'll be all right. Don't worry about me. Aron.' "

"Funny," said Adam. "Seems like I read it. But I guess I didn't." He rubbed his hand.

FIFTY-TWO

That winter of 1917–1918 was a dark and frightened time. The Germans smashed everything in front of them. In three months the British suffered three hundred thousand casualties. Many units of the French army were mutinous. Russia was out of the war. The German east divisions, rested and re-equipped, were thrown at the western front. The war seemed hopeless.

It was May before we had as many as twelve divisions in the field, and summer had come before our troops began to move across the sea in numbers. The Allied generals were fighting each other. Submarines slaughtered the crossing ships.

We learned then that war was not a quick heroic charge but a slow, incredibly complicated matter. Our spirits sank in those winter months. We lost the flare of excitement and we had not yet put on the doggedness of a long war.

Ludendorff was unconquerable. Nothing stopped him. He mounted attack after attack on the broken armies of France and England. And it oc-

curred to us that we might be too late, that soon we might be standing alon
against the invincible Germans.

It was not uncommon for people to turn away from the war, some t
fantasy and some to vice and some to crazy gaiety. Fortunetellers were i
great demand, and saloons did a roaring business. But people also turne
inward to their private joys and tragedies to escape the pervasive fear an
despondency. Isn't it strange that today we have forgotten this? We remem
ber World War I as quick victory, with flags and bands, marching and horse
play and returning soldiers, fights in the barrooms with the goddam Limey
who thought they won the war. How quickly we forgot that in that winte
Ludendorff could not be beaten and that many people were preparing i
their minds and spirits for a lost war.

2

Adam Trask was more puzzled than sad. He didn't have to resign from the
draft board. He was given a leave of absence for ill health. He sat by the
hour rubbing the back of his left hand. He brushed it with a harsh brush
and soaked it in hot water.

"It's circulation," he said. "As soon as I get the circulation back it'll be
all right. It's my eyes that bother me. I never had trouble with my eyes.
Guess I'll have to get my eyes tested for glasses. Me with glasses! Be hard
to get used to. I'd go today but I feel a little dizzy."

He felt more dizzy than he would admit. He could not move about the
house without a hand brace against a wall. Lee often had to give him a
hand-up out of his chair or help him out of bed in the morning and tie his
shoes because he could not tie knots with his numb left hand.

Almost daily he came back to Aron. "I can understand why a young man
might want to enlist," he said. "If Aron had talked to me, I might have
tried to persuade him against it, but I wouldn't have forbidden it. You know
that, Lee."

"I know it."

"That's what I can't understand. Why did he sneak away? Why doesn't
he write? I thought I knew him better than that. Has he written to Abra?
He'd be sure to write to her."

"I'll ask her."

"You do that. Do that right away."

"The training is hard. That's what I've heard. Maybe they don't give
him time."

"It doesn't take any time to write a card."

"When you went in the army, did you write to your father?"

"Think you've got me there, don't you? No, I didn't, but I had a reason.
I didn't want to enlist. My father forced me. I was resentful. You see, I had
a good reason. But Aron—he was doing fine in college. Why, they've written,

asking about him. You read the letter. He didn't take any clothes. He didn't take the gold watch."

"He wouldn't need any clothes in the army, and they don't want gold watches there either. Everything's brown."

"I guess you're right. But I don't understand it. I've got to do something about my eyes. Can't ask you to read everything to me." His eyes really troubled him. "I can see a letter," he said. "But the words jumble all around." A dozen times a day he seized a paper or a book and stared at it and put it down.

Lee read the papers to him to keep him from getting restless, and often in the middle of the reading Adam went to sleep.

He would awaken and say, "Lee? Is that you, Cal? You know I never had any trouble with my eyes. I'll just go tomorrow and get my eyes tested."

About the middle of February Cal went into the kitchen and said, "Lee, he talks about it all the time. Let's get his eyes tested."

Lee was stewing apricots. He left the stove and closed the kitchen door and went back to the stove. "I don't want him to go," he said.

"Why not?"

"I don't think it's his eyes. Finding out might trouble him. Let him be for a while. He's had a bad shock. Let him get better. I'll read to him all he wants."

"What do you think it is?"

"I don't want to say. I've thought maybe Dr. Edwards might just come by for a friendly call—just to say hello."

"Have it your own way," said Cal.

Lee said, "Cal, have you seen Abra?"

"Sure, I see her. She walks away."

"Can't you catch her?"

"Sure—and I could throw her down and punch her in the face and make her talk to me. But I won't."

"Maybe if you'd just break the ice. Sometimes the barrier is so weak it just falls over when you touch it. Catch up with her. Tell her I want to see her."

"I won't do it."

"You feel awful guilty, don't you?"

Cal did not answer.

"Don't you like her?"

Cal did not answer.

"If you keep this up, you're going to feel worse, not better. You'd better open up. I'm warning you. You'd better open up."

Cal cried, "Do you want me to tell Father what I did? I'll do it if you tell me to."

"No, Cal. Not now. But when he gets well you'll have to. You'll have to for yourself. You can't carry this alone. It will kill you."

"Maybe I deserve to be killed."

466   EAST OF EDEN

"Stop that!" Lee said coldly. "That can be the cheapest kind of self-indulgence. You stop that!"

"How do you go about stopping it?" Cal asked.

Lee changed the subject. "I don't understand why Abra hasn't been here —not even once."

"No reason to come now."

"It's not like her. Something's wrong there. Have you seen her?"

Cal scowled. "I told you I have. You're getting crazy too. Tried to talk to her three times. She walked away."

"Something's wrong. She's a good woman—a real woman."

"She's a girl," said Cal. "It sounds funny you calling her a woman."

"No," Lee said softly. "A few are women from the moment they're born. Abra has the loveliness of woman, and the courage—and the strength—and the wisdom. She knows things and she accepts things. I would have bet she couldn't be small or mean or even vain except when it's pretty to be vain."

"You sure do think well of her."

"Well enough to think she wouldn't desert us." And he said, "I miss her. Ask her to come to see me."

"I told you she walked away from me."

"Well, chase her then. Tell her I want to see her. I miss her."

Cal asked, "Shall we go back to my father's eyes now?"

"No," said Lee.

"Shall we talk about Aron?"

"No."

3

Cal tried all the next day to find Abra alone, and it was only after school that he saw her ahead of him, walking home. He turned a corner and ran along the parallel street and then back, and he judged time and distance so that he turned in front of her as she strolled along.

"Hello," he said.

"Hello. I thought I saw you behind me."

"You did. I ran around the block to get in front of you. I want to talk to you."

She regarded him gravely. "You could have done that without running around the block."

"Well, I tried to talk to you in school. You walked away."

"You were mad. I didn't want to talk to you mad."

"How do you know I was?"

"I could see it in your face and the way you walked. You're not mad now."

"No, I'm not."

"Do you want to take my books?" She smiled.

A warmth fell on him. "Yes—yes, I do." He put her schoolbooks under his arm and walked beside her. "Lee wants to see you. He asked me to tell you."

She was pleased. "Does he? Tell him I'll come. How's your father?"

"Not very well. His eyes bother him."

They walked along in silence until Cal couldn't stand it any more. "You know about Aron?"

"Yes." She paused. "Open my binder and look next to the first page."

He shifted the books. A penny postcard was in the binder. "Dear Abra," it said. "I don't feel clean. I'm not fit for you. Don't be sorry. I'm in the army. Don't go near my father. Good-by, Aron."

Cal snapped the book shut. "The son of a bitch," he said under his breath.

"What?"

"Nothing."

"I heard what you said."

"Do you know why he went away?"

"No. I guess I could figure out—put two and two together. I don't want to. I'm not ready to—that is, unless you want to tell me."

Suddenly Cal said, "Abra—do you hate me?"

"No, Cal, but you hate me a little. Why is that?"

"I—I'm afraid of you."

"No need to be."

"I've hurt you more than you know. And you're my brother's girl."

"How have you hurt me? And I'm *not* your brother's girl."

"All right," he said bitterly, "I'll tell you—and I don't want you to forget you asked me to. Our mother was a whore. She ran a house here in town. I found out about it a long time ago. Thanksgiving night I took Aron down and showed her to him. I—"

Abra broke in excitedly, "What did he do?"

"He went mad—just crazy. He yelled at her. Outside he knocked me down and ran away. Our dear mother killed herself; my father—he's—there's something wrong with him. Now you know about me. Now you have some reason to walk away from me."

"Now I know about him," she said calmly.

"My brother?"

"Yes, your brother."

"He was good. Why did I say *was?* He *is* good. He's not mean or dirty like me."

They had been walking very slowly. Abra stopped and Cal stopped and she faced him.

"Cal," she said, "I've known about your mother for a long, long time."

"You have?"

"I heard my parents talking when they thought I was asleep. I want to tell you something, and it's hard to tell and it's good to tell."

"You want to?"

"I have to. It's not so terribly long ago that I grew up and I wasn't a little girl any more. Do you know what I mean?"

"Yes," said Cal.

"You sure you know?"

"Yes."

"All right then. It's hard to say now. I wish I'd said it then. I didn't love Aron any more."

"Why not?"

"I've tried to figure it out. When we were children we lived in a story that we made up. But when I grew up the story wasn't enough. I had to have something else, because the story wasn't true any more."

"Well—"

"Wait—let me get it all out. Aron didn't grow up. Maybe he never will. He wanted the story and he wanted it to come out his way. He couldn't stand to have it come out any other way."

"How about you?"

"I don't want to know how it comes out. I only want to be there while it's going on. And, Cal—we were kind of strangers. We kept it going because we were used to it. But I didn't believe the story any more."

"How about Aron?"

"He was going to have it come out his way if he had to tear the world up by the roots."

Cal stood looking at the ground.

Abra said, "Do you believe me?"

"I'm trying to study it out."

"When you're a child you're the center of everything. Everything happens for you. Other people? They're only ghosts furnished for you to talk to. But when you grow up you take your place and you're your own size and shape. Things go out of you to others and come in from other people. It's worse, but it's much better too. I'm glad you told me about Aron."

"Why?"

"Because now I know I didn't make it all up. He couldn't stand to know about his mother because that's not how he wanted the story to go—and he wouldn't have any other story. So he tore up the world. It's the same way he tore me up—Abra—when he wanted to be a priest."

Cal said, "I'll have to think."

"Give me my books," she said. "Tell Lee I'll come. I feel free now. I want to think too. I think I love you, Cal."

"I'm not good."

"Because you're not good."

Cal walked quickly home. "She'll come tomorrow," he told Lee.

"Why, you're excited," said Lee.

4

Once in the house Abra walked on her toes. In the hall she moved close to the wall where the floor did not creak. She put her foot on the lowest step of the carpeted stairs, changed her mind, and went to the kitchen.

"Here you are," her mother said. "You didn't come straight home."

"I had to stay after class. Is Father better?"

"I guess so."

"What does the doctor say?"

"Same thing he said at first—overwork. Just needs a rest."

"He hasn't seemed tired," said Abra.

Her mother opened a bin and took out three baking potatoes and carried them to the sink. "Your Father's very brave, dear. I should have known. He's been doing so much war work on top of his own work. The doctor says sometimes a man collapses all at once."

"Shall I go in and see him?"

"You know, Abra, I've got a feeling that he doesn't want to see anybody. Judge Knudsen phoned and your father said to tell him he was asleep."

"Can I help you?"

"Go change your dress, dear. You don't want to get your pretty dress soiled."

Abra tiptoed past her father's door and went to her own room. It was harsh bright with varnish, papered brightly. Framed photographs of her parents on the bureau, poems framed on the walls, and her closet—everything in its place, the floor varnished, and her shoes standing diligently side by side. Her mother did everything for her, insisted on it—planned for her, dressed her.

Abra had long ago given up having any private thing in her room, even any personal thing. This was of such long standing that Abra did not think of her room as a private place. Her privacies were of the mind. The few letters she kept were in the sitting room itself, filed among the pages of the two-volume Memoirs of Ulysses S. Grant, which to the best of her knowledge had never been opened by anyone but herself since it came off the press.

Abra felt pleased, and she did not inspect the reason. She knew certain things without question, and such things she did not speak about. For example, she knew that her father was not ill. He was hiding from something. Just as surely she knew that Adam Trask was ill, for she had seen him walking along the street. She wondered whether her mother knew her father was not ill.

Abra slipped off her dress and put on a cotton pinafore, which was understood to be for working around the house. She brushed her hair, tiptoed past her father's room, and went downstairs. At the foot of the stairs she opened her binder and took out Aron's postcard. In the sitting room she shook

Aron's letters out of Volume II of the *Memoirs*, folded them tightly, and, raising her skirt, tucked them under the elastic which held up her panties. The package made her a little lumpy. In the kitchen she put on a full apron to conceal the bulge.

"You can scrape the carrots," her mother said. "Is that water hot?"

"Just coming to a boil."

"Drop a bouillon cube in that cup, will you, dear? The doctor says it'll build your father up."

When her mother carried the steaming cup upstairs, Abra opened the incinerator end of the gas stove, put in the letters, and lighted them.

Her mother came back, saying, "I smell fire."

"I lit the trash. It was full."

"I wish you'd ask me when you want to do a thing like that," her mother said. "I was saving the trash to warm the kitchen in the morning."

"I'm sorry, Mother," Abra said. "I didn't think."

"You should try to think of these things. It seems to me you're getting very thoughtless lately."

"I'm sorry, Mother."

"Saved is earned," said her mother.

The telephone rang in the dining room. Her mother went to answer it. Abra heard her mother say, "No, you can't see him. It's doctor's orders. He can't see anyone—no, not anyone."

She came back to the kitchen. "Judge Knudsen again," she said.

FIFTY-THREE

All during school next day Abra felt good about going to see Lee. She met Cal in the hall between classes. "Did you tell him I was coming?"

"He's started some kind of tarts," said Cal. He was dressed in his uniform —choking high collar, ill-fitting tunic, and wrapped leggings.

"You've got drill," Abra said. "I'll get there first. What kind of tarts?"

"I don't know. But leave me a couple, will you? Smelled like strawberry. Just leave me two."

"Want to see a present I got for Lee? Look!" She opened a little cardboard box. "It's a new kind of potato peeler. Takes off just the skin. It's easy. I got it for Lee."

"There go my tarts," said Cal, and then, "If I'm a little late, don't go before I get there, will you?"

"Would you like to carry my books home?"

"Yes," said Cal.

She looked at him long, full in the eyes, until he wanted to drop his gaze, and then she walked away toward her class.

2

Adam had taken to sleeping late, or, rather, he had taken to sleeping very often—short sleeps during the night and during the day. Lee looked in on him several times before he found him awake.

"I feel fine this morning," Adam said.

"If you can call it morning. It's nearly eleven o'clock."

"Good Lord! I have to get up."

"What for?" Lee asked.

"What for? Yes, what for! But I feel good, Lee. I might walk down to the draft board. How is it outside?"

"Raw," said Lee.

He helped Adam get up. Buttons and shoelaces and getting things on frontways gave Adam trouble.

While Lee helped him Adam said, "I had a dream—very real. I dreamed about my father."

"A great old gentleman from all I hear," said Lee. "I read that portfolio of clippings your brother's lawyer sent. Must have been a great old gentleman."

Adam looked calmly at Lee. "Did you know he was a thief?"

"You must have had a dream," said Lee. "He's buried at Arlington. One clipping said the Vice-President was at his funeral, and the Secretary of War. You know the *Salinas Index* might like to do a piece about him—in wartime, you know. How would you like to go over the material?"

"He was a thief," said Adam. "I didn't think so once, but I do now. He stole from the G.A.R."

"I don't believe it," said Lee.

There were tears in Adam's eyes. Very often these days tears came suddenly to Adam. Lee said, "Now you sit right here and I'll bring you some breakfast. Do you know who's coming to see us this afternoon? Abra."

Adam said, "Abra?" and then, "Oh, sure, Abra. She's a nice girl."

"I love her," said Lee simply. He got Adam seated in front of the card table in his bedroom. "Would you like to work on the cutout puzzle while I get your breakfast?"

"No, thank you. Not this morning. I want to think about the dream before I forget it."

When Lee brought the breakfast tray Adam was asleep in his chair. Lee awakened him and read the *Salinas Journal* to him while he ate and then helped him to the toilet.

The kitchen was sweet with tarts, and some of the berries had boiled over in the oven and burned, making the sharp, bitter-sweet smell pleasant and astringent.

There was a quiet rising joy in Lee. It was the joy of change. Time's draw
ing down for Adam, he thought. Time must be drawing down for me, but I
don't feel it. I feel immortal. Once when I was very young I felt mortal—
but not any more. Death has receded. He wondered if this were a normal
way to feel.

And he wondered what Adam meant, saying his father was a thief. Part
of the dream, maybe. And then Lee's mind played on the way it often did.
Suppose it were true—Adam, the most rigidly honest man it was possible to
find, living all his life on stolen money. Lee laughed to himself—now this
second will, and Aron, whose purity was a little on the self-indulgent side,
living all his life on the profits from a whorehouse. Was this some kind of
joke or did things balance so that if one went too far in one direction an
automatic slide moved on the scale and the balance was re-established?

He thought of Sam Hamilton. He had knocked on so many doors. He had
the most schemes and plans, and no one would give him any money. But
of course—he had so much, he was so rich. You couldn't give him any more.
Riches seem to come to the poor in spirit, the poor in interest and joy. To
put it straight—the very rich are a poor bunch of bastards. He wondered if
that were true. They acted that way sometimes.

He thought of Cal burning the money to punish himself. And the punishment hadn't hurt him as badly as the crime. Lee said to himself, "If there
should happen to be a place where one day I'll come up with Sam Hamilton,
I'll have a lot of good stories to tell him," and his mind went on, "But so
will he!"

Lee went in to Adam and found him trying to open the box that held
the clippings about his father.

3

The wind blew cold that afternoon. Adam insisted on going to look in on
the draft board. Lee wrapped him up and started him off. "If you feel faint
at all, just sit down wherever you are," Lee said.

"I will," Adam agreed. "I haven't felt dizzy all day. Might stop in and have
Victor look at my eyes."

"You wait till tomorrow. I'll go with you."

"We'll see," said Adam, and he started out, swinging his arms with
bravado.

Abra came in with shining eyes and a red nose from the frosty wind, and
she brought such pleasure that Lee giggled softly when he saw her.

"Where are the tarts?" she demanded. "Let's hide them from Cal." She sat
down in the kitchen. "Oh, I'm so glad to be back."

Lee started to speak and choked and then what he wanted to say seemed
good to say—to say carefully. He hovered over her. "You know, I haven't

wished for many things in my life," he began. "I learned very early not to wish for things. Wishing just brought earned disappointment."

Abra said gaily, "But you wish for something now. What is it?"

He blurted out, "I wish you were my daughter—" He was shocked at himself. He went to the stove and turned out the gas under the teakettle, then lighted it again.

She said softly, "I wish you were my father."

He glanced quickly at her and away. "You do?"

"Yes, I do."

"Why?"

"Because I love you."

Lee went quickly out of the kitchen. He sat in his room, gripping his hands tightly together until he stopped choking. He got up and took a small carved ebony box from the top of his bureau. A dragon climbed toward heaven on the box. He carried the box to the kitchen and laid it on the table between Abra's hands. "This is for you," he said, and his tone had no inflection.

She opened the box and looked down on a small, dark green jade button, and carved on its surface was a human right hand, a lovely hand, the fingers curved and in repose. Abra lifted the button out and looked at it, and then she moistened it with the tip of her tongue and moved it gently over her full lips, and pressed the cool stone against her cheek.

Lee said, "That was my mother's only ornament."

Abra got up and put her arms around him and kissed him on the cheek, and it was the only time such a thing had ever happened in his whole life.

Lee laughed. "My Oriental calm seems to have deserted me," he said. "Let me make the tea, darling. I'll get hold of myself that way." From the stove he said, "I've never used that word—never once to anybody in the world."

Abra said, "I woke up with joy this morning."

"So did I," said Lee. "I know what made me feel happy. You were coming."

"I was glad about that too, but—"

"You are changed," said Lee. "You aren't any part a little girl any more. Can you tell me?"

"I burned all of Aron's letters."

"Did he do bad things to you?"

"No. I guess not. Lately I never felt good enough. I always wanted to explain to him that I was not good."

"And now that you don't have to be perfect, you can be good. Is that it?"

"I guess so. Maybe that's it."

"Do you know about the mother of the boys?"

"Yes. Do you know I haven't tasted a single one of the tarts?" Abra said. "My mouth is dry."

"Drink some tea, Abra. Do you like Cal?"

"Yes."

Lee said, "He's crammed full to the top with every good thing and every bad thing. I've thought that one single person could almost with the weight of a finger—"

Abra bowed her head over her tea. "He asked me to go to the Alisal when the wild azaleas bloom."

Lee put his hands on the table and leaned over. "I don't want to ask you whether you are going," he said.

"You don't have to," said Abra. "I'm going."

Lee sat opposite her at the table. "Don't stay away from this house for long," he said.

"My father and mother don't want me here."

"I only saw them once," Lee said cynically. "They seemed to be good people. Sometimes, Abra, the strangest medicines are effective. I wonder if it would help if they knew Aron has just inherited over a hundred thousand dollars."

Abra nodded gravely and fought to keep the corners of her mouth from turning up. "I think it would help," she said. "I wonder how I could get the news to them."

"My dear," said Lee, "if I heard such a piece of news I think my first impulse would be to telephone someone. Maybe you'd have a bad connection."

Abra nodded. "Would you tell her where the money came from?"

"That I would not," said Lee.

She looked at the alarm clock hung on a nail on the wall. "Nearly five," she said. "I'll have to go. My father isn't well. I thought Cal might get back from drill."

"Come back very soon," Lee said.

4

Cal was on the porch when she came out.

"Wait for me," he said, and he went into the house and dropped his books.

"Take good care of Abra's books," Lee called from the kitchen.

The winter night blew in with frosty wind, and the street lamps with their sputtering carbons swung restlessly and made the shadows dart back and forth like a runner trying to steal second base. Men coming home from work buried their chins in their overcoats and hurried toward warmth. In the still night the monotonous scattering music of the skating rink could be heard from many blocks away.

Cal said, "Will you take your books for a minute, Abra? I want to unhook this collar. It's cutting my head off." He worked the hooks out of the eyes and sighed with relief. "I'm all chafed," he said and took her books back. The

ranches of the big palm tree in Berges's front yard were lashing with a dry
latter, and a cat meowed over and over and over in front of some kitchen
oor closed against it.

Abra said, "I don't think you make much of a soldier. You're too inde-
endent."

"I could be," said Cal. "This drilling with old Krag-Jorgensens seems silly
o me. When the time comes, and I take an interest, I'll be good."

"The tarts were wonderful," said Abra. "I left one for you."

"Thanks. I'll bet Aron makes a good soldier."

"Yes, he will—and the best-looking soldier in the army. When are we gong for the azaleas?"

"Not until spring."

"Let's go early and take a lunch."

"It might be raining."

"Let's go anyway, rain or shine."

She took her books and went into her yard. "See you tomorrow," she said.

He did not turn toward home. He walked in the nervous night past the
high school and past the skating rink—a floor with a big tent over it, and a
mechanical orchestra clanging away. Not a soul was skating. The old man
who owned it sat miserably in his booth, flipping the end of a roll of tickets
against his forefinger.

Main Street was deserted. The wind skidded papers on the sidewalk. Tom
Meek, the constable, came out of Bell's candy store and fell into step with
Cal. "Better hook that tunic collar, soldier," he said softly.

"Hello, Tom. The damn thing's too tight."

"I don't see you around the town at night lately."

"No."

"Don't tell me you reformed."

"Maybe."

Tom prided himself on his ability to kid people and make it sound serious. He said, "Sounds like you got a girl."

Cal didn't answer.

"I hear your brother faked his age and joined the army. Are you picking
off his girl?"

"Oh, sure—sure," said Cal.

Tom's interest sharpened. "I nearly forgot," he said. "I hear Will Hamilton is telling around you made fifteen thousand dollars in beans. That true?"

"Oh, sure," said Cal.

"You're just a kid. What are you going to do with all that money?"

Cal grinned at him. "I burned it up."

"How do you mean?"

"Just set a match to it and burned it."

Tom looked into his face. "Oh, yeah! Sure. Good thing to do. Got to go in here. Good night." Tom Meek didn't like people to kid him. "The youn punk son of a bitch," he said to himself. "He's getting too smart for himself

Cal moved slowly along Main Street, looking in store windows. He wor dered where Kate was buried. If he could find out, he thought he migh take a bunch of flowers, and he laughed at himself for the impulse. Was good or was he fooling himself? The Salinas wind would blow away a toml stone, let alone a bunch of carnations. For some reason he remembered th Mexican name for carnations. Somebody must have told him when he was kid. They were called Nails of Love—and marigolds, the Nails of Death. I was a word like nails—*claveles*. Maybe he'd better put marigolds on hi mother's grave. "I'm beginning to think like Aron," he said to himself.

FIFTY-FOUR

The winter seemed reluctant to let go its bite. It hung on cold and wet and windy long after its time. And people repeated, "It's those damned bi, guns they're shooting off in France—spoiling the weather in the whole world."

The grain was slow coming up in the Salinas Valley, and the wildflowers came so late that some people thought they wouldn't come at all.

We knew—or at least we were confident—that on May Day, when all the Sunday School picnics took place in the Alisal, the wild azaleas that grew in the skirts of the stream would be in bloom. They were a part of May Day.

May Day was cold. The picnic was drenched out of existence by a freez ing rain, and there wasn't an open blossom on the azalea trees. Two weeks later they still weren't out.

Cal hadn't known it would be like this when he had made azaleas the signal for his picnic, but once the symbol was set it could not be violated.

The Ford sat in Windham's shed, its tires pumped up, and with two new dry cells to make it start easily on Bat. Lee was alerted to make sandwiches when the day came, and he got tired of waiting and stopped buying sand wich bread every two days.

"Why don't you just go anyway?" he said.

"I can't," said Cal. "I said azaleas."

"How will you know?"

"The Silacci boys live out there, and they come into school every day. They say it will be a week or ten days."

"Oh, Lord!" said Lee. "Don't overtrain your picnic."

Adam's health was slowly improving. The numbness was going from his hand. And he could read a little—a little more each day.

"It's only when I get tired that the letters jump," he said. "I'm glad I didn't get glasses to ruin my eyes. I knew my eyes were all right."

Lee nodded and was glad. He had gone to San Francisco for the books he needed and had written for a number of separates. He knew about as much as was known about the anatomy of the brain and the symptoms and severities of lesion and thrombus. He had studied and asked questions with the same unwavering intensity as when he had trapped and pelted and cured a Hebrew verb. Dr. H. C. Murphy had got to know Lee very well and had gone from a professional impatience with a Chinese servant to a genuine admiration for a scholar. Dr. Murphy had even borrowed some of Lee's news separates and reports on diagnosis and practice. He told Dr. Edwards, "That Chink knows more about the pathology of cerebral hemorrhage than I do, and I bet as much as you do." He spoke with a kind of affectionate anger that this should be so. The medical profession is unconsciously irritated by lay knowledge.

When Lee reported Adam's improvement he said, "It does seem to me that the absorption is continuing—"

"I had a patient," Dr. Murphy said, and he told a hopeful story.

"I'm always afraid of recurrence," said Lee.

"That you have to leave with the Almighty," said Dr. Murphy. "We can't patch an artery like an inner tube. By the way, how do you get him to let you take his blood pressure?"

"I bet on his and he bets on mine. It's better than horse racing."

"Who wins?"

"Well, I could," said Lee. "But I don't. That would spoil the game—and the chart."

"How do you keep him from getting excited?"

"It's my own invention," said Lee. "I call it conversational therapy."

"Must take all your time."

"It does," said Lee.

2

On May 28, 1918, American troops carried out their first important assignment of World War I. The First Division, General Bullard commanding, was ordered to capture the village of Cantigny. The village, on high ground, dominated the Avre River valley. It was defended by trenches, heavy machine guns, and artillery. The front was a little over a mile wide.

At 6:45 A.M., May 28, 1918, the attack was begun after one hour of artillery preparation. Troops involved were the 28th Infantry (Col. Ely), one battalion of the 18th Infantry (Parker), a company of the First Engineers, the divisional artillery (Summerall), and a support of French tanks and flame throwers.

The attack was a complete success. American troops entrenched on the new line and repulsed two powerful German counterattacks.

The First Division received the congratulations of Clemenceau, Foch, and Pétain.

3

It was the end of May before the Silacci boys brought the news that the salmon-pink blossoms of the azaleas were breaking free. It was on a Wednesday, as the nine o'clock bell was ringing, that they told him.

Cal rushed to the English classroom, and just as Miss Norris took her seat on the little stage he waved his handkerchief and blew his nose loudly. Then he went down to the boys' toilet and waited until he heard through the wall the flush of water on the girlside. He went out through the basement door, walked close to the red brick wall, slipped around the pepper tree, and, once out of sight of the school, walked slowly along until Abra caught up with him.

"When'd they come out?" she asked.

"This morning."

"Shall we wait till tomorrow?"

He looked up at the gay yellow sun, the first earth-warming sun of the year. "Do you want to wait?"

"No," she said.

"Neither do I."

They broke into a run—bought bread at Reynaud's and joggled Lee into action.

Adam heard loud voices and looked into the kitchen. "What's the hullabaloo?" he asked.

"We're going on a picnic," said Cal.

"Isn't it a school day?"

Abra said, "Sure it is. But it's a holiday too."

Adam smiled at her. "You're pink as a rose," he said.

Abra cried, "Why don't you come with us? We're going to the Alisal to get azaleas."

"Why, I'd like to," Adam said, and then, "No, I can't. I promised to go down to the ice plant. We're putting in some new tubing. It's a beautiful day."

"We'll bring you some azaleas," Abra said.

"I like them. Well, have a good time."

When he was gone Cal said, "Lee, why don't you come with us?"

Lee looked sharply at him. "I hadn't thought you were a fool," he said.

"Come on!" Abra cried.

"Don't be ridiculous," said Lee.

4

It's a pleasant little stream that gurgles through the Alisal against the Gabilan Mountains on the east of the Salinas Valley. The water bumbles over
round stones and washes the polished roots of the trees that hold it in.

The smell of azaleas and the sleepy smell of sun working with chlorophyll
filled the air. On the bank the Ford car sat, still breathing softly from its
overheating. The back seat was piled with azalea branches.

Cal and Abra sat on the bank among the luncheon papers. They dangled
their feet in the water.

"They always wilt before you get them home," said Cal.

"But they're such a good excuse, Cal," she said. "If you won't I guess
I'll have to—"

"What?"

She reached over and took his hand. "That," she said.

"I was afraid to."

"Why?"

"I don't know."

"I wasn't."

"I guess girls aren't afraid of near as many things."

"I guess not."

"Are you ever afraid?"

"Sure," she said. "I was afraid of you after you said I wet my pants."

"That was mean," he said. "I wonder why I did it," and suddenly he was
silent.

Her fingers tightened around his hand. "I know what you're thinking. I
don't want you to think about that."

Cal looked at the curling water and turned a round brown stone with his
toe.

Abra said, "You think you've got it all, don't you? You think you attract
bad things—"

"Well—"

"Well, I'm going to tell you something. My father's in trouble."

"How in trouble?"

"I haven't been listening at doors but I've heard enough. He's not sick.
He's scared. He's done something."

He turned his head. "What?"

"I think he's taken some money from his company. He doesn't know
whether his partners are going to put him in jail or let him try to pay it
back."

"How do you know?"

"I heard them shouting in his bedroom where he's sick. And my mother
started the phonograph to drown them out."

He said, "You aren't making it up?"

"No. I'm not making it up."

He shuffled near and put his head against her shoulder and his arm crept timidly around her waist.

"You see, you're not the only one—" She looked sideways at his face. "Now I'm afraid," she said weakly.

5

At three o'clock in the afternoon Lee was sitting at his desk, turning over the pages of a seed catalogue. The pictures of sweet peas were in color.

"Now these would look nice on the back fence. They'd screen off the slough. I wonder if there's enough sun." He looked up at the sound of his own voice and smiled to himself. More and more he caught himself speaking aloud when the house was empty.

"It's age," he said aloud. "The slowing thoughts and—" He stopped and grew rigid for a moment. "That's funny—listening for something. I wonder whether I left the teakettle on the gas. No—I remember." He listened again. "Thank heaven I'm not superstitious. I could hear ghosts walk if I'd let myself. I could—"

The front doorbell rang.

"There it is. That's what I was listening for. Let it ring. I'm not going to be led around by feelings. Let it ring."

But it did not ring again.

A black weariness fell on Lee, a hopelessness that pressed his shoulders down. He laughed at himself. "I can go and find it's an advertisement under the door or I can sit here and let my silly old mind tell me death is on the doorstep. Well, I want the advertisement."

Lee sat in the living room and looked at the envelope in his lap. And suddenly he spat at it. "All right," he said. "I'm coming—goddam you," and he ripped it open and in a moment laid it on the table and turned it over with the message down.

He stared between his knees at the floor. "No," he said, "that's not my right. Nobody has the right to remove any single experience from another. Life and death are promised. We have a right to pain."

His stomach contracted. "I haven't got the courage. I'm a cowardly yellow belly. I couldn't stand it."

He went into the bathroom and measured three teaspoons of elixir of bromide into a glass and added water until the red medicine was pink. He carried the glass to the living room and put it on the table. He folded the telegram and shoved it in his pocket. He said aloud, "I hate a coward! God, how I hate a coward!" His hands were shaking and a cold perspiration dampened his forehead.

At four o'clock he heard Adam fumbling at the doorknob. Lee licked his lips. He stood up and walked slowly to the hall. He carried the glass of pink fluid and his hand was steady.

FIFTY-FIVE

All of the lights were on in the Trask house. The door stood partly open, and the house was cold. In the sitting room Lee was shriveled up like a leaf in the chair beside the lamp. Adam's door was open and the sound of voices came from his room.

When Cal came in he asked, "What's going on?"

Lee looked at him and swung his head toward the table where the open telegram lay. "Your brother is dead," he said. "Your father has had a stroke."

Cal started down the hall.

Lee said, "Come back. Dr. Edwards and Dr. Murphy are in there. Let them alone."

Cal stood in front of him. "How bad? How bad, Lee, how bad?"

"I don't know." He spoke as though recalling an ancient thing. "He came home tired. But I had to read him the telegram. That was his right. For about five minutes he said it over and over to himself out loud. And then it seemed to get through into his brain and to explode there."

"Is he conscious?"

Lee said wearily, "Sit down and wait, Cal. Sit down and wait. Get used to it. I'm trying to."

Cal picked up the telegram and read its bleak and dignified announcement.

Dr. Edwards came out, carrying his bag. He nodded curtly, went out, and closed the door smartly behind him.

Dr. Murphy set his bag on the table and sat down. He sighed. "Dr. Edwards asked me to tell you."

"How is he?" Cal demanded.

"I'll tell you all we know. You're the head of the family now, Cal. Do you know what a stroke is?" He didn't wait for Cal to answer. "This one is a leakage of blood in the brain. Certain areas of the brain are affected. There have been earlier smaller leakages. Lee knows that."

"Yes," said Lee.

Dr. Murphy glanced at him and then back at Cal. "The left side is paralyzed. The right side partly. Probably there is no sight in the left eye, but we can't determine that. In other words, your father is nearly helpless."

"Can he talk?"

"A little—with difficulty. Don't tire him."

Cal struggled for words. "Can he get well?"

"I've heard of reabsorption cases this bad but I've never seen one."

"You mean he's going to die?"

"We don't know. He might live for a week, a month, a year, even two years. He might die tonight."

"Will he know me?"

"You'll have to find that out for yourself. I'll send a nurse tonight and then you'll have to get permanent nurses." He stood up. "I'm sorry, Cal. Bear up! You'll have to bear up." And he said, "It always surprises me how people bear up. They always do. Edwards will be in tomorrow. Good night." He put his hand out to touch Cal's shoulders, but Cal moved away and walked toward his father's room.

Adam's head was propped up on pillows. His face was calm, the skin pale; his mouth was straight, neither smiling nor disapproving. His eyes were open, and they had great depth and clarity, as though one could see deep into them and as though they could see deep into their surroundings. And the eyes were calm, aware but not interested. They turned slowly toward Cal as he entered the room, found his chest, and then rose to his face and stayed there.

Cal sat down in the straight chair beside the bed. He said, "I'm sorry, Father."

The eyes blinked slowly the way a frog blinks.

"Can you hear me, Father? Can you understand me?" The eyes did not change or move. "I did it," Cal cried. "I'm responsible for Aron's death and for your sickness. I took him to Kate's. I showed him his mother. That's why he went away. I don't want to do bad things—but I do them."

He put his head down on the side of the bed to escape the terrible eyes, and he could still see them. He knew they would be with him, a part of him, all of his life.

The doorbell rang. In a moment Lee came to the bedroom, followed by the nurse—a strong, broad woman with heavy black eyebrows. She opened breeziness as she opened her suitcase.

"Where's my patient! There he is! Why, you look fine! What am I doing here? Maybe you better get up and take care of me, you look good. Would you like to take care of me, big handsome man?" She thrust a muscular arm under Adam's shoulder and effortlessly hoisted him toward the head of the bed and held him up with her right arm while with her left she patted out the pillows and laid him back.

"Cool pillows," she said. "Don't you love cool pillows? Now, where's the bathroom? Have you got a duck and a bedpan? Can you put a cot in here for me?"

"Make a list," said Lee. "And if you need any help—with him—"

"Why would I need help? We'll get along just fine, won't we, sugar-sweetie?"

Lee and Cal retired to the kitchen. Lee said, "Before she came I was going to urge you to have some supper—you know, like the kind of person who uses food for any purpose good or bad? I bet she's that way. You can eat or not eat, just as you wish."

Cal grinned at him. "If you'd tried to make me, I'd have been sick. But since you put it that way, I think I'll make a sandwich."

"You can't have a sandwich."

"I want one."

"It all works out," said Lee, "true to outrageous form. It's kind of insulting that everyone reacts about the same way."

"I don't want a sandwich," Cal said. "Are there any tarts left?"

"Plenty—in the breadbox. They may be a little soaky."

"I like them soaky," Cal said. He brought the whole plate to the table and set it in front of him.

The nurse looked into the kitchen. "These look good," she said and took one, bit into it, and talked among her chewings. "Can I phone Krough's drugstore for the things I need? Where's the phone? Where do you keep the linen? Where's the cot you're going to bring in? Are you through with this paper? Where did you say the phone is?" She took another tart and retired.

Lee asked softly, "Did he speak to you?"

Cal shook his head back and forth as though he couldn't stop.

"It's going to be dreadful. But the doctor is right. You can stand anything. We're wonderful animals that way."

"I am not." Cal's voice was flat and dull. "I can't stand it. No, I can't stand it. I won't be able to. I'll have to—I'll have to—"

Lee gripped his wrist fiercely. "Why, you mouse—you nasty cur. With goodness all around you—don't you dare suggest a thing like that! Why is your sorrow more refined than my sorrow?"

"It's not sorrow. I told him what I did. I killed my brother. I'm a murderer. He knows it."

"Did he say it? Tell the truth—did he say it?"

"He didn't have to. It was in his eyes. He said it with his eyes. There's nowhere I can go to get away—there's no place."

Lee sighed and released his wrist. "Cal"—he spoke patiently—"listen to me. Adam's brain centers are affected. Anything you see in his eyes may be pressure on that part of his brain which governs his seeing. Don't you remember?—he couldn't read. That wasn't his eyes—that was pressure. You don't know he accused you. You don't know that."

"He accused me. I know it. He said I'm a murderer."

"Then he will forgive you. I promise."

The nurse stood in the doorway. "What are you promising, Charley? You promised me a cup of coffee."

"I'll make it now. How is he?"

"Sleeping like a baby. Have you got anything to read in this house?"

"What would you like?"

"Something to take my mind off my feet."

"I'll bring the coffee to you. I've got some dirty stories written by a French queen. They might be too—"

"You bring 'em with the coffee," she said. "Why don't you get some shut-eye, sonny? Me and Charley'll hold the fort. Don't forget the book, Charley."

Lee set the percolator on the gas jet. He came to the table and said, "Cal!"

"What do you want?"

"Go to Abra."

2

Cal stood on the neat porch and kept his finger on the bell until the harsh overlight flashed on and the night bolt rasped and Mrs. Bacon looked out. "I want to see Abra," Cal said.

Her mouth dropped open in amazement. "You want what?"

"I want to see Abra."

"You can't. Abra's gone to her room. Go away."

Cal shouted, "I tell you I want to see Abra."

"You go away or I'll call the police."

Mr. Bacon called, "What is it? Who is it?"

"Never you mind—go back to bed. You aren't well. I'll handle this."

She turned back to Cal. "Now you get off the porch. And if you ring the bell again I'll phone the police. Now, get!" The door slammed, the bolt scraped, and the hard overlight went off.

Cal stood smiling in the dark for he thought of Tom Meek lumbering up, saying, "Hello, Cal. What you up to?"

Mrs. Bacon shouted from inside. "I see you. Go on now! Get off the porch!"

He walked slowly down the walk and turned toward home, and he hadn't gone a block before Abra caught up with him. She was panting from her run. "Got out the back way," she said.

"They'll find you gone."

"I don't care."

"You don't?"

"No."

Cal said, "Abra, I've killed my brother and my father is paralyzed because of me."

She took his arm and clung to it with both hands.

Cal said, "Didn't you hear me?"

"I heard you."

"Abra, my mother was a whore."

"I know. You told me. My father is a thief."

"I've got her blood, Abra. Don't you understand?"

"I've got his," she said.

They walked along in silence while he tried to rebalance himself. The wind was cold, and they quickened their steps to keep warm. They passed the last streetlight on the very edge of Salinas, and blackness lay ahead of them and the road was unpaved and sticky with black 'dobe mud.

They had come to the end of the pavement, to the end of the street-lights. The road under their feet was slippery with spring mud, and the grass that brushed against their legs was wet with dew.

Abra asked, "Where are we going?"

"I wanted to run away from my father's eyes. They're right in front of me all the time. When I close my eyes I still see them. I'll always see them. My father is going to die, but his eyes will still be looking at me, telling me I killed my brother."

"You didn't."

"Yes, I did. And his eyes say I did."

"Don't talk like that. Where are we going?"

"A little farther. There's a ditch and a pump house—and a willow tree. Do you remember the willow tree?"

"I remember it."

He said, "The branches come down like a tent and their tips touch the ground."

"I know."

"In the afternoons—the sunny afternoons—you and Aron would part the branches and go inside—and no one could see you."

"You watched?"

"Oh, sure. I watched." And he said, "I want you to go inside the willow tree with me. That's what I want to do."

She stopped and her hand pulled him to a stop. "No," she said. "That's not right."

"Don't you want to go in with me?"

"Not if you're running away—no, I don't."

Cal said, "Then I don't know what to do. What shall I do? Tell me what to do."

"Will you listen?"

"I don't know."

"We're going back," she said.

"Back? Where?"

"To your father's house," said Abra.

3

The light of the kitchen poured down on them. Lee had lighted the oven to warm the chilly air.

"She made me come," said Cal.

"Of course she did. I knew she would."

Abra said, "He would have come by himself."

"We'll never know that," said Lee.

He left the kitchen and in a moment he returned. "He's still sleeping." Lee set a stone bottle and three little translucent porcelain cups on the table.

"I remember that," said Cal.

"You ought to." Lee poured the dark liquor. "Just sip it and let it run around your tongue."

Abra put her elbows on the kitchen table. "Help him," she said. "You can accept things, Lee. Help him."

"I don't know whether I can accept things or not," Lee said. "I've never had a chance to try. I've always found myself with some—not less uncertain but less able to take care of uncertainty. I've had to do my weeping—alone."

"Weeping? You?"

He said, "When Samuel Hamilton died the world went out like a candle. I relighted it to see his lovely creations, and I saw his children tossed and torn and destroyed as though some vengefulness was at work. Let the ng-ka-py run back on your tongue."

He went on, "I had to find out my stupidities for myself. These were my stupidities: I thought the good are destroyed while the evil survive and prosper.

"I thought that once an angry and disgusted God poured molten fire from a crucible to destroy or to purify his little handiwork of mud.

"I thought I had inherited both the scars of the fire and the impurities which made the fire necessary—all inherited, I thought. All inherited. Do you feel that way?"

"I think so," said Cal.

"I don't know," Abra said.

Lee shook his head. "That isn't good enough. That isn't good enough thinking. Maybe—" And he was silent.

Cal felt the heat of the liquor in his stomach. "Maybe what, Lee?"

"Maybe you'll come to know that every man in every generation is refired. Does a craftsman, even in his old age, lose his hunger to make a perfect cup —thin, strong, translucent?" He held his cup to the light. "All impurities burned out and ready for a glorious flux, and for that—more fire. And then either the slag heap or, perhaps what no one in the world ever quite gives up, perfection." He drained his cup and he said loudly, "Cal, listen to me. Can you think that whatever made us—would stop trying?"

"I can't take it in," Cal said. "Not now I can't."

The heavy steps of the nurse sounded in the living room. She billowed through the door and she looked at Abra, elbows on the table, holding her cheeks between her palms.

The nurse said, "Have you got a pitcher? They get thirsty. I like to keep a pitcher of water handy. You see," she explained, "they breathe through their mouths."

"Is he awake?" Lee asked. "There's a pitcher."

"Oh, yes, he's awake and rested. And I've washed his face and combed his hair. He's a good patient. He tried to smile at me."

Lee stood up. "Come along, Cal. I want you to come too, Abra. You'll have to come."

The nurse filled her pitcher at the sink and scurried ahead of them.

When they trooped into the bedroom Adam was propped high on his pillows. His white hands lay palms down on either side of him, and the sinews from knuckle to wrist were tight drawn. His face was waxen, and his sharp features were sharpened. He breathed slowly between pale lips. His blue eyes reflected back the night light focused on his head.

Lee and Cal and Abra stood at the foot of the bed, and Adam's eyes moved slowly from one face to the other, and his lips moved just a little in greeting.

The nurse said, "There he is. Doesn't he look nice? He's my darling. He's my sugar pie."

"Hush!" said Lee.

"I won't have you tiring my patient."

"Go out of the room," said Lee.

"I'll have to report this to the doctor."

Lee whirled toward her. "Go out of the room and close the door. Go and write your report."

"I'm not in the habit of taking orders from Chinks."

Cal said, "Go out now, and close the door."

She slammed the door just loud enough to register her anger. Adam blinked at the sound.

Lee said, "Adam!"

The blue wide eyes looked for the voice and finally found Lee's brown and shining eyes.

Lee said, "Adam, I don't know what you can hear or understand. When you had the numbness in your hand and your eyes refused to read, I found out everything I could. But some things no one but you can know. You may, behind your eyes, be alert and keen, or you may be living in a confused gray dream. You may, like a newborn child, perceive only light and movement.

"There's damage in your brain, and it may be that you are a new thing in the world. Your kindness may be meanness now, and your bleak honesty fretful and conniving. No one knows these things except you. Adam! Can you hear me?"

The blue eyes wavered, closed slowly, then opened.

Lee said, "Thank you Adam. I know how hard it is. I'm going to ask you to do a much harder thing. Here is your son—Caleb—your only son. Look at him, Adam!"

The pale eyes looked until they found Cal. Cal's mouth moved dryly and made no sound.

Lee's voice cut in, "I don't know how long you will live, Adam. Maybe a long time. Maybe an hour. But your son will live. He will marry and his children will be the only remnant left of you." Lee wiped his eyes with his fingers.

"He did a thing in anger, Adam, because he thought you had rejected him. The result of his anger is that his brother and your son is dead."

Cal said, "Lee—you can't."

"I have to," said Lee. "If it kills him I have to. I have the choice," and he smiled sadly and quoted, " 'If there's blame, it's my blame.' " Lee's shoulders straightened. He said sharply, "Your son is marked with guilt out of himself —out of himself—almost more than he can bear. Don't crush him with rejection. Don't crush him, Adam."

Lee's breath whistled in his throat. "Adam, give him your blessing. Don't leave him alone with his guilt. Adam, can you hear me? Give him your blessing!"

A terrible brightness shone in Adam's eyes and he closed them and kept them closed. A wrinkle formed between his brows.

Lee said, "Help him, Adam—help him. Give him his chance. Let him be free. That's all a man has over the beasts. Free him! Bless him!"

The whole bed seemed to shake under the concentration. Adam's breath came quick with his effort and then, slowly, his right hand lifted—lifted an inch and then fell back.

Lee's face was haggard. He moved to the head of the bed and wiped the sick man's damp face with the edge of the sheet. He looked down at the closed eyes. Lee whispered, "Thank you, Adam—thank you, my friend. Can you move your lips? Make your lips form his name."

Adam looked up with sick weariness. His lips parted and failed and tried again. Then his lungs filled. He expelled the air and his lips combed the rushing sigh. His whispered word seemed to hang in the air:

"Timshel!"

His eyes closed and he slept.

The Wayward Bus

I pray you all gyve audyence,
And here this mater with reverence,
By fygure a morall playe;
The somonynge of Everyman called it is,
That of our lyves and endynge shewes
How transytory we be all daye.

—EVERYMAN

For
GWYN

ONE

Forty-two miles below San Ysidro, on a great north-south highway in California, there is a crossroad which for eighty-odd years has been called Rebel Corners. From here a county road goes at right angles toward the west until, after forty-nine miles, it connects with another north-south highway that leads from San Francisco to Los Angeles and, of course, Hollywood. Anyone who wishes to go from the inland valley to the coast in this part of the state must take the road that begins at Rebel Corners and winds through hills and a little desert and through farmland and mountains until, at last, it comes to the coastal highway right in the middle of the town of San Juan de la Cruz.

Rebel Corners got its name in 1862. It is said that a family named Blanken kept a smithy at the crossroads. The Blankens and their sons-in-law were poor, ignorant, proud, and violent Kentuckians. Having no furniture and no property, they brought what they had with them from the East—their prejudices and their politics. Having no slaves, they were ready, nevertheless, to sell their lives for the free principle of slavery. When the war began, the Blankens discussed traveling back across the measureless West to fight for the Confederacy. But it was a long way and they had crossed once, and it was too far. Thus it was that in a California which was preponderantly for the North, the Blankens seceded a hundred and sixty acres and a blacksmith shop from the Union and joined Blanken Corners to the Confederacy. It is also said that they dug trenches and cut rifle slits in the blacksmith shop to defend this rebellious island from the hated Yankees. And the Yankees, who were mostly Mexicans and Germans and Irish and Chinese, far from attacking the Blankens, were rather proud of them. The Blankens had never lived so well, for the enemy brought chickens and eggs and pork sausage in slaughter time, because everyone thought that, regardless of the cause, such courage should be recognized. Their place took the name of Rebel Corners and has kept it to this day.

After the war the Blankens became lazy and quarrelsome and full of hatreds and complaints, as every defeated nation does, so that, pride in them having evaporated with the war, people stopped bringing their horses to be shoed and their plows for retipping. Finally, what the Union Armies

could not do by force of arms the First National Bank of San Ysidro did b
foreclosure.

Now, after eighty-odd years, no one remembers much about the Blanken
except that they were very proud and very unpleasant. In the followin;
years the land changed hands many times before it was incorporated int(
the empire of a newspaper king. The blacksmith shop burned down an(
was rebuilt and burned again, and what was left was converted into a garag(
with gas pumps and then into a store-restaurant-garage and service station
When Juan Chicoy and his wife bought it and got the franchise to run a
public conveyance between Rebel Corners and San Juan de la Cruz, it became all these and a bus station too. The rebel Blankens have, through
pride and a low threshold of insult which is the test of ignorance and laziness, disappeared from the face of the earth, and no one remembers what
they looked like. But Rebel Corners is well known and the Chicoys are well
liked.

There was a little lunchroom in back of the gas pumps, a lunchroom with
a counter and round, fixed stools, and three tables for those who wanted to
eat in some style. These were not used often for it was customary to tip
Mrs. Chicoy when she served you at a table and not to if she served you at
the counter. On the first shelf behind the counter were sweet rolls, snails,
doughnuts; on the second, canned soups, oranges, and bananas; on the third,
individual boxes of cornflakes, riceflakes, grapenuts, and other tortured
cereals. There was a grill at one end behind the counter and a sink beside it,
beer and soda spouts beside that, ice cream units beside those, and on the
counter itself, between the units of paper napkin containers, juke-box coin
slots, salt, pepper, and ketchup, the cakes were displayed under large plastic
covers. The walls, where there was room, were well decorated with calendars
and posters showing bright, improbable girls with pumped-up breasts and
no hips—blondes, brunettes and redheads, but always with this bust development, so that a visitor of another species might judge from the preoccupation of artist and audience that the seat of procreation lay in the
mammaries.

Alice Chicoy, Mrs. Juan Chicoy, that is, who worked among the shining
girls, was wide-hipped and sag-chested and she walked well back on her
heels. She was not in the least jealous of the calendar girls and the Coca-
Cola girls. She had never seen anyone like them and she didn't think anyone
else ever had. She fried her eggs and hamburgers, heated her canned soup,
drew beer, scooped ice cream, and toward evening her feet hurt and that
made her cross and snappish. And as the day went on the flat curl went out
of her hair so that it hung damp and stringy beside her face, and at first she
would brush it aside with her hand and finally she would blow it out of her
eyes.

Next to the lunchroom was a garage converted from the last blacksmith shop, its ceiling and beams still black from the soot of the old forge, and here Juan Chicoy presided when he was not driving the bus between Rebel Corners and San Juan de la Cruz. He was a fine, steady man, Juan Chicoy, part Mexican and part Irish, perhaps fifty years old, with clear black eyes, a good head of hair, and a dark and handsome face. Mrs. Chicoy was insanely in love with him and a little afraid of him too, because he was a man, and there aren't very many of them, as Alice Chicoy had found out. There aren't very many of them in the world, as everyone finds out sooner or later.

In the garage Juan Chicoy fixed flat tires, got the air locks out of gas lines, cleaned the diamond-hard dust from choked carburetors, put new diaphragms in tubercular gasoline pumps, and did all the little things that the motor-minded public knows nothing whatever about. These things he did except during the hours from ten-thirty until four. That was the time he drove the bus, carrying passengers who had been deposited at Rebel Corners by the big Greyhound busses to San Juan de la Cruz and bringing passengers back from San Juan de la Cruz to Rebel Corners, where they were picked up either by the Greyhound bus going north at four-fifty-six or by the Greyhound going south at five-seventeen.

While Mr. Chicoy was gone on his route his duties at the garage were carried out by a succession of overgrown boys or immature young men who were more or less apprentices. None of them lasted very long. Unwary customers with dirty carburetors could not know in advance the destruction these apprentices could heap on a carburetor, and while Juan Chicoy himself was a magnificent mechanic, his apprentices usually were cocky adolescents who spent their time between jobs putting slugs in the juke box in the lunchroom and quarreling mildly with Alice Chicoy. To these young men opportunity beckoned constantly, drawing them ever southward toward Los Angeles and, of course, Hollywood, where, eventually, all the adolescents in the world will be congregated.

Behind the garage were two little outhouses with trellises, one of which said "Men" and the other "Ladies." And to each one a little path led, one around the right-hand side of the garage and one around the left-hand side of the garage.

What defined the Corners and made it visible for miles among the cultivated fields were the great white oaks that grew around the garage and restaurant. Tall and graceful, with black trunks and limbs, bright green in summer, black and brooding in winter, these oaks were landmarks in the long, flat valley. No one knows whether the Blankens planted them or whether they merely settled near to them. The latter seems more logical; first, because the Blankens are not known to have planted anything they could not eat, and second, because the trees seemed more than eighty-five years old. They might be two hundred years old; on the other hand, they

498

might have their roots in some underground spring which would make them grow large quickly in this semidesert country.

These great trees shaded the station in summer so that travelers often pulled up under them and ate their lunches and cooled their overheated motors. The station itself was pleasant too, brightly painted green and red, a deep row of geraniums all around the restaurant, red geraniums and deep green leaves thick as a hedge. The white gravel in front and around the gas pumps was raked and sprinkled daily. In the restaurant and in the garage there was system and order. For instance, on the shelves in the restaurant the canned soup, the boxed cereals, even the grapefruits, were arranged in little pyramids, four on the bottom level, then three, then two, and one balanced on top. And the same was true of the cans of oil in the garage, and the fan belts hung neatly in their sizes on nails. It was a very well kept place. The windows of the restaurant were screened against flies, and the screen door banged shut after every entrance or exit. For Alice Chicoy hated flies. In a world that was not easy for Alice to bear or to understand, flies were the final and malicious burden laid upon her. She hated them with a cruel hatred, and the death of a fly by swatter, or slowly smothered in the goo of fly paper, gave her a flushed pleasure.

Just as Juan usually had a succession of young apprentices to help him in the garage, so Alice hired a succession of girls to help her in the lunchroom. These girls, gawky and romantic and homely—the pretty ones usually left with a customer within a few days—seemed to accomplish little in the way of work. They spread dirt about with damp cloths, they dreamed over movie magazines, they sighed into the juke box—and the most recent one had reddening eyes and a head cold and wrote long and passionate letters to Clark Gable. Alice Chicoy suspected every one of them of letting flies in. Norma, this most recent girl, had felt the weight of Alice Chicoy's tongue many times about flies.

The routine of the Corners in the morning was invariable. With the first daylight or, in the winter, even before, the lights came on in the lunchroom, and Alice steamed up the coffee urn (a great godlike silver effigy which may, in some future archaeological period, be displayed as an object of worship of the race of Amudkins, who preceded the Atomites, who, for some unknown reason, disappeared from the face of the earth). The restaurant was warm and cheerful when the first truck drivers pulled wearily in for their breakfast. Then came the salesmen, hurrying to the cities of the south in the dark so as to have a full day of business. Salesmen always spotted trucks and stopped, because it is generally believed that truck drivers are great connoisseurs of roadside coffee and food. By sun-up the first tourists in their own cars began to pull in for breakfast and road information.

The tourists from the north did not interest Norma much, but those from the south or those who came over the cutoff from San Juan de la Cruz and

ho might have been to Hollywood fascinated her. In four months Norma
ersonally met fifteen people who had been to Hollywood, five who had
een on a picture lot, and two who had seen Clark Gable face to face. In-
pired by these last two, who came in very close together, she wrote a twelve-
age letter which began, "Dear Mr. Gable," and ended, "Lovingly, A
riend." She often shuddered to think that Mr. Gable might find out that
he had written it.

Norma was a faithful girl. Let others, featherbrains, run after the upstarts
-the Sinatras, the Van Johnsons, the Sonny Tufts. Even during the war,
hen there had been no Gable pictures, Norma had remained faithful,
eeping her dream warm with a colored picture of Mr. Gable in a flying suit
ith two belts of 50-caliber ammunition on his shoulders.

She often sneered at Sonny Tufts. She liked older men with interesting
aces. Sometimes, wiping the damp cloth back and forth on the counter,
er dream-widened eyes centered on the screen door, her pale eyes flexed
nd then closed for a moment. Then you could know that in that secret
garden in her head, Gable had just entered the restaurant, had gasped when
he saw her, and had stood there, his lips slightly parted and in his eyes the
recognition that this was his woman. And around him the flies came in and
out with impunity.

It never went beyond that. Norma was too shy. And, besides, she didn't
know how such things were done. The actual love-making in her life had
been a series of wrestling matches, the aim of which was to keep her clothes
on in the back seat of a car. So far she had won by simple concentration.
She felt that Mr. Gable not only would not do things like that, but wouldn't
like them if he heard about them.

Norma wore the wash dresses featured by the National Dollar Stores,
though, of course, she had a sateen dress for parties. But if you looked
closely you could always find some little bit of beauty even on the wash
dresses. Her Mexican silver pin, a representation of the Aztec calendar stone,
was left to her in her aunt's will after Norma had nursed her for seven
months and really wanted the sealskin stole and the ring of baroque pearls
and turquoise. But these went to another branch of the family. Norma had
also a string of small amber beads from her mother. She never wore the
Mexican pin and the beads at the same time. In addition to these, Norma
possessed two pieces of jewelry which were pure crazy and which she knew
were pure crazy. Deep in her suitcase she had a gold-filled wedding ring
and a gigantic Brazilian-type diamond ring, the two of which had cost five
dollars. She wore them only when she went to bed. In the morning she took
them off and hid them in her suitcase. No one in the world knew that she
owned them. In bed she went to sleep twisting them on the third finger of
her left hand.

The sleeping arrangements at the Corners were simple. Directly behind the lunchroom there was a lean-to. A door at the end of the lunch counte opened into the Chicoys' bed-sitting room, which had a double bed with a afghan spread, a console radio, two overstuffed chairs and a davenport which group is called a suite—and a metal reading lamp with a marble green glass shade. Norma's room opened off this room, for it was Alice' theory that young girls should be watched a little and not let to run wild Norma had to come through the Chicoys' room to go to the bathroom—that or slip out the window, which she ordinarily did. The apprentice-mechanic' room was next to the Chicoys' on the other side, but he had an outside en trance and used the vine-covered cubicle marked "Men" behind the garage

It was a nice compact grouping of buildings, functional and pleasant. The Rebel Corners of the Blankens' time had been a miserable, dirty, and sus picious place, but the Chicoys flourished here. There was money in the bank and a degree of security and happiness.

This island covered by the huge trees could be seen for miles. No one ever had to look for road signs to find Rebel Corners and the road to San Juan de la Cruz. In the great valley the grain fields flattened away toward the east, to the foothills and to the high mountains, and toward the west they ended nearer in the rounded hills where the live oaks sat in black splotches. In the summer the yellow heat shimmered and burned and glared on the baking hills, and the shade of the great trees over the Corners was a thing to look forward to and to remember. In the winter when the heavy rains fell, the restaurant was a warm place of coffee and chili beans and pie.

In the deep spring when the grass was green on fields and foothills, when the lupines and poppies made a splendid blue and gold earth, when the great trees awakened in yellow-green young leaves, then there was no more lovely place in the world. It was no beauty you could ignore by being used to it. It caught you in the throat in the morning and made a pain of pleasure in the pit of your stomach when the sun went down over it. The sweet smell of the lupines and of the grass set you breathing nervously, set you panting almost sexually. And it was in this season of flowering and growth, though it was still before daylight, that Juan Chicoy came out to the bus carrying an electric lantern. Pimples Carson, his apprentice-mechanic, stumbled sleepily behind him.

The lunchroom windows were still dark. Against the eastern hills not even a grayness had begun to form. It was so much night that the owls were still shrieking over the fields. Juan Chicoy came near to the bus which stood in front of the garage. It looked, in the light of the lantern, like a large, silver-windowed balloon. Pimples Carson, still not really awake, stood with his hands in his pockets, shivering, not because it was cold but because he was very sleepy.

A little wind blew in over the fields and brought the smell of lupine and the smell of a quickening earth, frantic with production.

TWO

The electric lantern, with a flat downward reflector, lighted sharply only legs and feet and tires and tree trunks near to the ground. It bobbed and swung, and the little incandescent bulb was blindingly blue-white. Juan Chicoy carried his lantern to the garage, took a bunch of keys from his overalls pocket, found the one that unlocked the padlock, and opened the wide doors. He switched on the overhead light and turned off his lantern.

Juan picked a striped mechanic's cap from his workbench. He wore Headlight overalls with big brass buttons on bib and side latches, and over this he wore a black horsehide jacket with black knitted wristlets and neck. His shoes were round-toed and hard, with soles so thick that they seemed swollen. An old scar on his cheek beside his large nose showed as a shadow in the overhead light. He ran fingers through his thick, black hair to get it all in the mechanic's cap. His hands were short and wide and strong, with square fingers and nails flattened by work and grooved and twisted from having been hammered and hurt. The third finger of his left hand had lost the first joint, and the flesh was slightly mushroomed where the finger had been amputated. This little overhanging ball was shiny and of a different texture from the rest of the finger, as though the joint were trying to become a fingertip, and on this finger he wore a wide gold wedding ring, as though this finger was no good for work any more and might as well be used for ornament.

A pencil and a ruler and a tire pressure gauge protruded from a slot in his overalls bib. Juan was clean-shaven, but not since yesterday, and along the corners of his chin and on his neck the coming whiskers were grizzled and white like those of an old Airedale. This was the more apparent because the rest of his beard was so intensely black. His black eyes were squinting and humorous, the way a man's eyes squint when he is smoking and cannot take the cigarette from his mouth. And Juan's mouth was full and good, a relaxed mouth, the underlip slightly protruding—not in petulance but in humor and self-confidence—the upper lip well formed except left of center where a deep scar was almost white against the pink tissue. The lip must have been cut clear through at one time, and now this thin taut band of white was a strain on the fullness of the lip and made it bunch in tiny tucks on either side. His ears were not very large, but they stood out sharply from his head like seashells, or in the position a man would hold them with his hands if he wanted to hear more clearly. Juan seemed to be listening intently all the time, while his squinting eyes seemed to laugh at what he heard, and half of his mouth disapproved. His movements were sure even when he was not doing anything that required sureness. He walked as though he were going to some exact spot. His hands moved with speed and precision and never fiddled with matches or with nails. His teeth were long and the edges were framed with gold, which gave his smile a little fierceness.

At his workbench he picked tools from nails on the wall and laid them in a long, flat box—wrenches and pliers and several screwdrivers and a machine hammer and a punch. Beside him Pimples Carson, still heavy with sleep, rested his elbow on the oily wood of the bench. Pimples wore the tattered sweater of a motorcycle club and the crown of a felt hat cut in saw teeth around the edge. He was a lank and slender-waisted boy of seventeen, with narrow shoulders and a long foxy nose and eyes that were pale in the morning and became greenish-brown later in the day. A golden fuzz was on his cheeks, and his cheeks were rivuleted and rotted and eroded with acne. Among the old scars new pustules formed, purple and red, some rising and some waning. The skin was shiny with the medicines that were sold for this condition and which do no good whatever.

Pimples' blue jeans were tight, and so long that they were turned up ten inches on the bottoms. They were held to his narrow middle by a broad, beautifully tooled leather belt with a fat and engraved silver buckle in which four turquoises were set. Pimples kept his hands at his sides as much as he could, but in spite of himself his fingers would move to his pitted cheeks until he became conscious of what he was doing and put his hands down again. He wrote to every company that advertised an acne cure, and he had been to many doctors, who knew that they could not cure it but who also knew that it would probably go away in a few years. They nevertheless gave Pimples prescriptions for salves and lotions, and one had put him on a diet of green vegetables.

His eyes were long and narrow and slanted like the eyes of a sleepy wolf, and now in the early morning they were almost sealed shut with mucus. Pimples was a prodigious sleeper. Left to his own devices, he could sleep nearly all the time. His whole system and his soul were a particularly violent battleground of adolescence. His concupiscence was constant, and when it was not directly and openly sexual it would take to channels of melancholy, of deep and tearful sentiment, or of a strong and musky religiosity. His mind and his emotions were like his face, constantly erupting, constantly raw and irritated. He had times of violent purity when he howled at his own depravity, and these were usually followed by a melancholy laziness that all but prostrated him, and he went from the depression into sleep. It was opiatic and left him drugged and dull for a long time.

He wore pierced white and brown saddle oxfords on bare feet this morning, and his ankles, where they showed below the turned-up jeans, were streaked with dirt. In his periods of depression Pimples was so prostrated that he did not bathe nor even eat very much. The felt hat crown notched so evenly was not really for beauty but served to keep his long light brown hair out of his eyes and to keep the grease out of it when he worked under a car. Now he stood stupidly watching Juan Chicoy put the tools in his box while his mind rolled in great flannel clouds of sleepiness, almost nauseating in their power.

Juan said, "Get the work light on the long cord connected. Come on, Pimples. Come on now, wake up!"

Pimples seemed to shake himself like a dog. "Can't seem to come out of it," he explained.

"Well, get the light out there and take my back board out. We've got to get going."

Pimples picked up the hand light, basketed for protection of the globe, and began unwinding the heavy rubber-guarded cable from around its handle. He plugged the cord into an outlet near the door and the hand light leaped into brilliance. Juan lifted his toolbox and stepped out of the door and looked at the darkened sky. A change had come in the air. A little wind was stirring the young leaves of the oaks and whisking among the geraniums and it was an uncertain, wet wind. Juan smelled it as he would smell a flower.

"By God, if it rains," he said, "that would be one too many."

To the east the tops of the mountains were just becoming visible in outline with the dawn. Pimples came out carrying the lighted hand lamp and unkinking the cable behind him on the ground. The light made the great trees stand out, and it was reflected on the yellow-green of the new little oak leaves. Pimples took his light to the bus and went back to the garage for the long board with casters on the bottom on which a man could lie and wheel himself about when he worked under a car. He flung the board down beside the bus.

"Well, it's like to rain," he said. "Take nearly every year in California it rains this season."

Juan said, "I'm not complaining about the season, but with this ring gear out and the passengers waiting, and the ground is pulpy with rain—"

"Makes good feed," said Pimples.

Juan stopped and looked around at him. His eyes crinkled with amusement. "Sure," he said, "it sure does."

Pimples looked shyly away.

The bus was lighted by the hand lamp now and it looked strange and helpless, for where the rear wheels should have been were two heavy sawhorses, and instead of resting on axles the rear of the bus rested on a four-by-four which extended from one horse to the other.

It was an old bus, a four-cylinder, low-compression engine with a special patented extra gear shift which gave it five speeds ahead instead of three, two below the average ratio, and two speeds in reverse. The ballooning sides of the bus, heavy and shining with aluminum paint, showed nevertheless the bumps and bends, the wracks and scratches, of a long and violent career. A home paint job on an old automobile somehow makes it look even more ancient and disreputable than it would if left in honorable decay.

Inside, the bus was rebuilt too. The seats which had once been woven of cane were now upholstered in red oilcloth, and while the job was neatly done, it was not professionally done. There was the slightly sour smell of oilcloth in the air and the frankly penetrating odor of oil and gasoline. It was an old, old bus, and it had seen many trips and many difficulties. Its oaken floorboards were scooped and polished by the feet of passengers. Its sides were bent and straightened. Its windows could not be opened, for the whole body was slightly wracked out of shape. In the summer Juan removed the windows and in the winter put them back again.

The driver's seat was worn through to the springs, but in the worn place was a flowered chintz pillow which served the double purpose of protecting the driver and holding down the uncovered springs. Hanging from the top of the windshield were the penates: a baby's shoe—that's for protection, for the stumbling feet of a baby require the constant caution and aid of God; and a tiny boxing glove—and that's for power, the power of the fist on the driving forearm, the drive of the piston pushing its connecting rod, the power of person as responsible and proud individual. There hung also on the windshield a little plastic kewpie doll with a cerise and green ostrich-feather headdress and a provocative sarong. And this was for the pleasures of the flesh and of the eye, of the nose, of the ear. When the bus was in motion these hanging items spun and jerked and swayed in front of the driver's eye.

Where the windshield angled in the middle and the center of support went up, sitting on top of the dashboard was a small metal Virgin of Guadalupe painted in brilliant colors. Her rays were gold and her robe was blue and she stood on the new moon, which was supported by cherubs. This was Juan Chicoy's connection with eternity. It had little to do with religion as connected with the church and dogma, and much to do with religion as memory and feeling. This dark Virgin was his mother and the dim house where she, speaking Spanish with a little brogue, had nursed him. For his mother had made the Virgin of Guadalupe her own personal goddess. Out had gone St. Patrick and St. Bridget and the ten thousand pale virgins of the North, and into her had entered this dark one who had blood in her veins and a close connection with people.

His mother admired her Virgin, whose day is celebrated with exploding skyrockets, and, of course, Juan Chicoy's Mexican father didn't think of it one way or another. Skyrockets were by nature the way to celebrate Saints' Days. Who could think otherwise? The rising, hissing tube was obviously the spirit rising to Heaven, and the big, flashing bang at the top was the dramatic entrance to the throne room of Heaven. Juan Chicoy, while not a believer in an orthodox sense, now he was fifty, would nevertheless have been uneasy driving the bus without the Guadalupana to watch over him. His religion was practical.

Below the Virgin was a kind of converted glove box, and in it were a Smith & Wesson 45-caliber revolver, a roll of bandage, a bottle of iodine, a vial of lavender smelling salts, and an unopened pint of whisky. With this equipment Juan felt fairly confident that he could meet most situations.

The front bumpers of the bus had once borne the inscription, still barely readable, "*el Gran Poder de Jesus,*" "the great power of Jesus." But that had been painted on by a former owner. Now the simple word "Sweetheart" was boldly lettered on front and rear bumpers. And the bus was known as "Sweetheart" to all who knew her. Now she was immobilized, her rear wheels off, her end sticking up in the air and resting on a four-by-four set between two sawhorses.

Juan Chicoy had the new ring and pinion gears and he was rolling them carefully together. "Hold the light close," he said to Pimples, and he turned the pinion in the ring all the way around. "I remember once I put a new ring on an old pinion and she went out right away."

"Busted tooth sure makes a noise," said Pimples. "It sounds like it's coming through the floor at you. What do you suppose knocked that tooth out?"

Juan held the ring gear up sideways and in front of the light turned the pinion slowly, inspecting the fit of tooth against tooth as he went. "I don't know," he said. "There's lots nobody knows about metal and about engines too. Take Ford. He'll make a hundred cars and two or three of them will be no damn good. It's not just one thing that's bad, the whole car's bad. The springs and the motor and the water pump and the fan and the carburetor. It just breaks down little by little and there don't nobody know what makes them. And you'll take another car right off the line, you'd say it was just exactly the same as the others, but it's not. It's got something the others haven't got. It's got more power. It's almost like a guy with a lot of guts. It won't bust down no matter what you do."

"I had one of them," said Pimples. "Model A. I sold her. Bet she's still running. Had her three years and never spent a dime on her."

Juan laid his ring gear and pinion on the step of the bus and picked up the old ring from the ground. With his finger he traced the raw place where the tooth had broken out. "Metal's funny stuff," he said. "Sometimes it seems to get tired. You know, down in Mexico where I came from they used to have two or three butcher knives. They'd use one and stick the others in the ground. 'It rests the blade,' they said. I don't know if it's true, but I know those knifes would take a shaving edge. I guess nobody knows about metal, even the people that make it. Let's get this pinion on the shaft. Here, hold the light back here."

Juan put his little platform behind the bus and he lay on it on his back and scooted himself under with his feet. "Hold the light a little more to the left. No, higher. There. Now shove me my toolbox, will you?"

Juan's hands worked busily and a little oil dropped down on his cheek. He rubbed it off with the back of his hand. "This is a mean job," he said.

Pimples peered underneath the bus at him. "Maybe I could hook the light over that nut," he said.

"Oh, you'd just have to move it in a minute," said Juan.

Pimples said, "I sure hope you get her going today. I'd like to sleep in my own bed tonight. You don't get no rest in a chair."

Juan chuckled. "Did you ever see madder people in your life when we had to come back after that tooth broke out? You'd think I did it on purpose. They were so mad they gave Alice hell about the pie. I guess they thought she made it. When people are traveling they don't like anything to interrupt them."

"Well, they got our beds," Pimples observed. "I don't see what they got to squawk about. You and me and Alice and Norma were the ones slept in chairs. And them Pritchards was the worst. I don't mean Mildred, the girl, but her old man and old lady. They figure they've been getting gypped someway. He tells me a hundred times how he's a president or something and he's going to make somebody suffer for this. Outrage, he says it was. And him and his wife had your bed. Where'd Mildred sleep?" Pimples' eyes glowed a little.

"On the davenport, I guess," said Juan. "Or maybe with her father and mother. That fellow from the trick company got Norma's room."

"I kinda liked that guy," Pimples said. "He didn't say nothing much. He said he'd just as soon set up. He didn't say what line he was in. But them Pritchards made up for it, all except Mildred. You know where they're going, Mr. Chicoy? They're going on a trip down to Mexico. Mildred's been studying Spanish in college. She's going to interpret for them."

Juan drove a key pin into the shaft and pounded it gently into place. He pulled himself from under the bus. "Let's get that rear-end assembly now."

Light was creeping up the sky and over the mountains. The colorless dawn of grays and blacks moved in so that white and blue things were silver and red and dark green things were black. The new leaves on the big oaks were black and white, and the mountain rims were sharp. Lumpish, heavy clouds that rolled in the sky like dumplings were beginning to take on a faint rose-pink color on their eastern edges.

Suddenly the lights in the lunchroom sprang on and the geranium border around the building leaped into being. Juan glanced toward the lights. "Alice is up," he said. "Won't be long till the coffee's ready. Come on, let's move the rear end in now."

The two men worked together well. Each understood what was to be done. Each did his piece. Pimples lay on his back too, tightening the housing nuts, and in the teamwork a good feeling came to him.

Juan strained a tight forearm against a nut and his wrench slipped and he took skin and flesh off his knuckle. The blood ran thick and black out of his greasy hand. He put the knuckle in his mouth and sucked it and made a line of grease around his mouth.

"Hurt it bad?" Pimples asked.

"No, it's good luck, I guess. You can't finish a job without blood. That's what my old man used to say." He sucked the blood again and already the flow was lessening.

The warmth and pinkness of the dawn sneaked in about them so that the electric light seemed to lose some of its brilliance.

"I wonder how many will come in on the Greyhound," Pimples asked idly. And then a strong thought came to him out of the good feeling for Mr. Chicoy. It was a thought so sharp that it almost hurt him. "Mr. Chicoy," he began uncertainly, and his tone was fawning, craven, begging.

Juan stopped turning the nut and waited for the request for a day off, for a raise, for something. There was going to be a request. That was inherent in the tone, and to Juan it was trouble. Trouble always started this way.

Pimples was silent. He couldn't get the words.

"What do you want?" Juan asked guardedly.

"Mr. Chicoy, could we fix it—I mean—could you fix it so you don't call me Pimples any more?"

Juan took his wrench from the nut and turned his head sideways. The two were lying on their backs, their faces toward each other. Juan saw the craters of old scars and the coming eruptions and one prime, tight, yellow-headed pustule about to burst on the cheek. As he looked, Juan's eyes softened. He knew. It came on him suddenly, and he wondered why he had not known before.

"What's your name?" he asked roughly.

"Ed," said Pimples. "Ed Carson, distant relative of Kit Carson. Before I got these in grammar school, why, they used to call me Kit." His voice was studied and calm, but his chest rose and fell heavily and the air whistled in his nostrils.

Juan looked away from him and back at the bulbous lump of the rear-end housing. "O.K.," he said, "let's get the jacks underneath." He rolled out from under the bus. "Get the oil in there now."

Pimples went quickly into the garage and brought out the pressure gun, trailing the air hose behind him. He turned the petcock and the compressed air hissed into the gun behind the oil. The gun clicked as he filled the housing with the oil until a little ran thickly out. He screwed in the plug.

Juan said, "Kit, wipe your hands and see if Alice has got any coffee ready, will you?"

Pimples went toward the lunchroom. Near the door where one of the great oaks stood there was a patch of near darkness. He stood there for a moment, holding his breath. He was shaking all over in a kind of a chill.

THREE

When the rim of the sun cleared the mountains to the east, Juan Chicoy stood up from the ground and brushed the dirt from the legs and seat of his overalls. The sun flashed on the windows of the lunchroom and lay warm on the green grass that edged the garage. It blazed on the poppies in the flat fields and on the great islands of blue lupines.

Juan Chicoy went to the entrance door of the bus. He reached in, turned the ignition key, and pushed down the starter with the heel of his hand. For a while the starter whined rustily, and then the engine caught and roared for a moment until Juan throttled it down. He pushed down the clutch with his hand, put the gear in compound low, and let up the clutch. The rear wheels turned slowly in the air and Juan went around to the rear to listen to the action of the gears, to try to hear any uneven matching of the assembly.

Pimples was washing his hands in a flat pan of gasoline in the garage. The sun warmed a brown leaf left by the past year and blown into a corner of the garage doorframe. After a while a little night-laden fly crawled heavily out from under the leaf and stood in the clear sun. Its wings were muddily iridescent and it was sluggish with night cold. The fly rubbed its wings with its legs and then it rubbed its legs together and then it rubbed its face with its forelegs while the sun, slanting under the great puffed clouds, warmed its juices. Suddenly the fly took off, circled twice, fluttered under the oaks and crashed against the screen door of the lunchroom, fell on its back and buzzed against the ground, upside down for a second. Then it righted itself and flew up and took its position on the frame beside the lunchroom door.

Alice Chicoy, haggard from the night of sitting up, came to the door and looked out toward the bus. The screen door opened only a few inches, but the fly flung himself through the opening. Alice saw him come through and whacked at him with the dish towel she carried in her hand. The fly buzzed crazily for a moment and then settled under the edge of the counter. Alice watched the rear wheels of the bus idly turning in the air and then she went in back of the counter and turned off the steam valve of the coffee urn.

The brown fluid in the glass pipe on the side of the urn looked thin and pale. She ran her towel over the counter and in doing so noticed that the big white coconut cake in its transparent plastic cover was ragged on one edge with a "V" cut out of it. She took a knife from the silver tray, lifted cover, trimmed the cake's edge, and put the crumbs in her mouth. And just before the cover went back into place the fly lunged under the edge and flung himself on the coconut filling. He clung under a slight overhang so that he was not visible from above, and he dug and struggled hungrily into the sweet filling. He had a high, huge mountain of cake and he was very happy.

Pimples came in, smelling of gasoline and grease, and he took his place on one of the round stools. "Well, we got that done," he said.

"You and who else?" Alice asked satirically.

"Well, of course, Mr. Chicoy done the expert work. I'd like to have a cup of coffee and a piece of cake."

"You been in that cake already, before I got up." She brushed her hair out of her eyes with one hand. "You can't cover up," she said.

"Well, charge it to me," said Pimples. "I'm paying for my feed, ain't I?"

"What do you want to eat all that sweet stuff for?" Alice said. "You're at the candy tray all day long. You don't get hardly any pay. All goes for sweet stuff. I bet that's what makes all them pimples. Why don't you lay off for a while?"

Pimples looked shyly down at his hands. The nails were rimmed with black where the gasoline had not reached. "It's rich in food energy," he said. "Fellow's going to work, he needs food energy. Take about three o'clock in the afternoon when you get a let-down. Why, you need something rich in food energy."

"It's rich in lead in the pants," Alice observed. "You need food energy about as much as I need a—" and she left it in the air. Alice was a very profane woman but she never said the words, she only led up to them. She drew a cup of coffee from the spout—a thick, flat-bottom cup with no saucer —spurted in some milk and slipped the cup across the counter.

Pimples, looking hazily at the Coca-Cola girl who swung provocatively over the juke box, put in four spoonfuls of sugar and stirred the coffee around and around with the spoon straight up.

"I like to have a piece of cake," he repeated patiently.

"Well, it's your funeral. You're going to have a can on you like a balloon."

Pimples looked at Alice's well-formed behind and then quickly away. Alice took the knife from behind the counter and cut a wedge of coconut cake. The cliff of cake toppled on the fly and pressed him down. Alice shoveled the cake onto a saucer and slid it along the counter. Pimples went at it with his coffee spoon.

"Those folks didn't get up yet?" he asked.

"No, but I heard them stirring around. One of them must have used up all the hot water. I haven't got a bit in the lunchroom."

"That must be Mildred," said Pimples.

"Huh?"

"The girl. Maybe she took a bath."

Alice looked at him levelly. "You get to your food energy and keep your mind where it belongs," she said sharply.

"I never said nothing. Hey, there's a fly in this cake!"

Alice stiffened. "You had a fly in your soup yesterday. I think you carry flies in your pocket."

"No, look here. He's still kicking."

Alice came near. "Kill him," she cried. "Squash him! You want him to get loose?" She picked up a fork from behind the counter and mashed the fly and cake crumbs together and scraped the whole thing into the garbage can.

"How about my cake?" Pimples asked.

"You'll get another piece of cake. I don't know why you always get flies. Nobody else does."

"Just lucky, I guess," Pimples said softly.

"Huh?"

"I said I was—"

"I heard what you said." She was unrested and nervous. "You watch your mouth or you'll go out of here so fast you'll think you're on fire. I don't care if you are a mechanic. To me you're just a punk. A pimple-faced punk." Pimples had withered. His chin had settled lower and lower against his chest as her anger rose. And he didn't know that she was making him the depositary of a number of things.

"I didn't say nothing," he said. "Can't a guy even make a joke?"

Alice had reached a point where she had either to go on into a crazy, hysterical rage that tore the living daylights out of herself and everyone else around her, or she had to begin to taper off quickly, for she could feel the uncontrollable pressure rising in her chest and throat. In a second she appraised the situation. Things were tight. The bus had to get out. Juan had not rested either. The people who were using the beds would hear her rage and come out and Juan might hit her. He had once. Not hard, but accurately, and timed so perfectly that she imagined he had nearly killed her. And then the black fear that was always on the edge of her mind—Juan might leave her. He had left other women. How many she didn't know because he'd never spoken of it, but a man of his attractiveness must have left other women. All of this happened in a split second. Alice decided on no rage. She forced the pressure down in her chest. Woodenly she raised the plastic cake cover and cut an oversized wedge and put it on a saucer and she carried this down the counter and set it in front of Pimples.

"Everybody's nervous," she said.

Pimples looked up from his fingernails. He saw how the little lines of age were sneaking down her neck, and he noticed the thickness of her upper eyelids. He saw that her hands had lost the tightness of skin of young girls. He was very sorry for her. Unblessed with beauty as he was, he thought that youth was the only thing in the world worth having and that one who had lost youth was already dead. He had won a great victory this morning, and now when he saw the weakness and indecision in Alice he pressed for a second victory.

"Mr. Chicoy says he ain't going to call me Pimples no more," he said.

"Why not?"

"Well, I asked him not. My name's Edward. They used to call me Kit in school on account my last name's Carson."

"Is Juan calling you Kit?"

"Uh-huh."

Alice didn't really understand what it was about, and behind her in the bedroom there was movement, footsteps between the rugs and a little low talking. Now that she was aware of the strangers, Pimples became closer to her because he was not quite a stranger. "I'll see how it goes," she said.

The sun had been shining in through the front windows and the door, making five bright splashes on the wall, illuminating the grapenuts packages and the pyramids of oranges behind the counter. And now the bright squares dimmed and went out. There was a roll of thunder, and without warning the rain began. It whisked down on the roof.

Pimples went to the door and looked out. The rain sheeted down, obscuring the country, splashing high on the cement road. There was a steely look to the wet light. Pimples saw Juan Chicoy inside the bus for shelter. The back wheels were still turning around slowly. As he watched, Juan leaped to the ground and made a run for the lunchroom. Pimples held the door open for him and he bolted through, but even in the little run his overalls were dark with water and his shoes squidged sloppily on the floor.

"God Almighty," he said, "that's a real cloudburst."

The gray wall of water obscured the hills and there was a dark, metallic light with it. The heads of the lupines bent down, heavy with water. The petals of the poppies were beaten off and lay on the ground like gold coins. The already wet ground could absorb no more water, and little rivulets started immediately for the low places. The cloudburst roared on the roof of the lunchroom at Rebel Corners.

Juan Chicoy had taken one of the tables by the lunchroom window and he drank well-creamed coffee and chewed a doughnut and looked out at the downpour. Norma came in and began to wash the few dishes on the stainless steel sink behind the counter.

"Bring me another cup of coffee, will you?" Juan asked.

She came listlessly around the end of the counter. The cup was too full. A little stream of coffee dripped off the bottom of it. Juan pulled out a paper napkin and folded it as a blotter for the wet cup.

"Didn't get much rest, did you?" he asked.

Norma was drawn, and her dress was wrinkled. You could see now that she would be an old-looking woman long before she was old. Her skin was muddy and her thin hands were splotched. Many, many things gave Norma the hives.

"Didn't get any sleep at all," she said. "I tried the floor but I couldn't sleep."

"Well, we'll see it doesn't happen again," said Juan. "I should have gc a car to take them into San Ysidro."

"Giving them our beds!" Alice said derisively. "Now, where did you ge that idea? Where else do you suppose they could have got the owners' beds They don't have to work today. They could just as well of sat up."

"Slipped up on me, I guess," said Juan.

"You don't care if your wife sleeps in a chair," Alice said. "You'd giv away her bed any time." Again Alice could feel rage rising in her and i frightened her. She didn't want it to rise. She knew it would spoil things and she was afraid of it, but there it was, rising and boiling in her.

A sheet of rain whisked over the roof like a heavy broom and left silenc as it moved on, and almost immediately another flat of rain took its place The drip and gurgle of water from the roof eaves and from the drains wa. loud again. Juan had been looking reflectively at the floor, a small smile tightening his mouth against the white band of the scar on his lip. And thi was another thing Alice was frightened of. He had set her out to observe her. She knew that. All relations and all situations to Alice were person-to person things in which she and the other were huge and all others were removed from the world. There was no shading. When she talked to Juan, there were only the two of them. When she picked at Norma, the whole world disappeared, leaving only Norma and her in a gray universe of cloud.

But Juan, now, he could shut everything out and look at each thing in relation to the other. Things of various sizes and importance. He could see and judge and consider and enjoy. Juan could enjoy people. Alice could only love, like, dislike, and hate. She saw and felt no shading whatever.

Now she tucked her loosening hair back. Once a month she used a rinse on her hair which was guaranteed to give it the mysterious and glamorous glints that capture and keep men in slavery. Juan's eyes were distant and amused. This was a matter of horror to Alice. She knew he was seeing her, not as an angry woman who darkened the world, but as one of thousands of angry women to be studied, inspected, and, yes, even enjoyed. This was the cold, lonely horror to her. Juan blotted out the universe to her and she sensed that she blotted out nothing to him. He could see not only around her but through her to something else. The remembered terror of the one time he had hit her lay not in the blow—she had been hit before, and far from hating it had taken excitement and exuberance from it—but Juan had hit her as he would a bug. He hadn't cared about it much. He hadn't even been very angry, just irritated. And he had hit a noisy thing to shut it up. Alice had only been trying to attract his attention in one of the few ways she knew. She was trying to do the same thing now, and she knew from the changed focus in his eye that he had slipped away from her.

"I try to make a nice little home for us; nice, and with a carpet and a velveteen suite, and you got to give it away to strangers." Her voice was losing its certainty. "And you let your own wife sit up in a chair all night."

Juan looked up slowly. "Norma," he said, "bring me another cup of coffee, will you? Plenty of cream."

Alice braced herself for the rage she knew was coming, and then Juan looked slowly toward her. His dark eyes were amused and warm, the focus changed again, and he was looking at her and she knew that he saw her.

"It didn't hurt you any," he said. "Make you appreciate the bed tonight."

Her breath caught. A hot wave flooded over her. Rage was transmuted to hot desire. She smiled at him vacantly and licked her lips. "You bastard," she said very softly. And she took a huge, shuddering sigh of air. "Want some eggs?" she asked.

"Yeah. Two in the water, about four minutes."

"I know how you like them," she said. "Bacon on the side?"

"No. A piece of toast and a couple of doughnuts."

Alice went behind the counter. "I wish they'd come out of there," she said. "I'd like to use my own bathroom."

"They're stirring around," said Juan. "They'll be out in a little."

And they were stirring. There were footsteps in the bedroom. A door inside opened and a woman's voice said sharply, "Well, I think you could knock!" And a man replied, "I'm sorry, ma'am. The only other way was to go out the window."

Another man's voice with a brittle singsong of authority said, "Always a good idea to knock, my friend. Hurt your foot?"

"Yes."

The door at the end of the counter opened and a small man came out into the lunchroom. He was dressed in a double-breasted suit; his shirt was of that light brown color worn by traveling men and known as a thousand-miler because it does not show dirt. His suit was a neutral pepper-and-salt for the same reason, and he wore a knitted dark green tie. His face was sharp, like a puppy's face, and his eyes were bright and questioning, like a puppy's eyes. A small, carefully trimmed mustache rode his upper lip like a caterpillar, and when he talked it seemed to hump its back. His teeth were white and even except for the two front uppers, and these were glittering gold. He had a brushed look about him, as though he had cleaned the lint from his suit with his hairbrush; and his shirt had the strained appearance that comes from washing the collar in the hand basin and patting it flat on the dresser top to dry. There was a kind of shy confidence in his manner and a wincing quality in his face, as though he protected himself from insult with studied techniques.

"Morning, folks," he said. "I just wondered where you all slept. And I'll bet you sat up all night."

"Well, we did," Alice said sourly.

"It's all right," said Juan. "We'll get to bed early tonight."

"Get the bus fixed? Think we'll make it in this rain?"

"Oh, sure," said Juan.

The man limped around the end of the counter and sat painfully down at one of the little tables. Norma brought a glass of water and a handful of silver wrapped in a paper napkin.

"Eggs?"

"Fried, with their eyes open, crisp bacon, and buttered toast. Buttered —get it? Hardest thing in the world is to get buttered toast. Now you butter that toast, plenty of butter, and let it melt in so there's no yellow lumps showing and you'll get yourself a nice tip." He lifted his foot shod in a perforated and decorated brown oxford and looked at it and grunted with pain.

"Sprain your ankle?" Juan asked.

The door at the end of the counter opened and a medium-sized man came out. He looked like Truman and like the vice-presidents of companies and like certified public accountants. His glasses were squared off at the corners. His suit was gray and correct, and there was a little gray in his face too. He was a businessman, dressed like one, looked like one. In his lapel buttonhole there was a lodge pin so tiny that from four feet away you couldn't see what it was at all. His vest was unbuttoned one notch at the bottom. Indeed, this bottom button was not intended to be buttoned. A fine gold watch and key chain crossed this vest and ducked in and out of a buttonhole on the way.

He said, "Mrs. Pritchard will have scrambled eggs, moist if they're fresh, toast and marmalade. And Miss Pritchard only wants orange juice and coffee. I'll have grapenuts and cream, eggs turned over and well done—don't let the yolk be running—dry toast and Boston coffee—that's half milk. You can bring it all in on a tray."

Alice looked up with fury. "You better come out here," she said. "We haven't got tray service."

Mr. Pritchard looked at her coldly. "We got held up here," he said. "I've already lost one day of my vacation. It isn't my fault that the bus broke down. Now the least you can do is to bring that breakfast in. My wife isn't feeling so good. I'm not used to sitting on a stool and Mrs. Pritchard isn't either."

Alice lowered her head like an angry milk-cow. "Look, I want to go to the toilet and wash my face and you're holding up my bathroom."

Mr. Pritchard touched his glasses nervously. "Oh, I see." He turned his head toward Juan and the light reflected from his glasses so that there were two mirrors with no eyes behind them. His hand whipped his watch chain out of his vest pocket. He opened a little gold nail file and ran the point quickly under each nail. He looked about and a little shudder of uncertainty came over him. Mr. Pritchard was a businessman, president of a medium-sized corporation. He was never alone. His business was conducted by groups of men who worked alike, thought alike, and even looked alike. His lunches were with men like himself who joined together in clubs so that no foreign element or idea could enter. His religious life was again his lodge and his church, both of which were screened and protected. One night a week he played poker with men so exactly like himself that the game was fairly even, and from this fact his group was convinced that they were very fine poker players. Wherever he went he was not one man but a unit in a corporation, a unit in a club, in a lodge, in a church, in a political party. His thoughts and ideas were never subjected to criticism since he willingly associated only with people like himself. He read a newspaper written by and for his group. The books that came into his house were chosen by a committee which deleted material that might irritate him. He hated foreign countries and foreigners because it was difficult to find his counterpart in them. He did not want to stand out from his group. He would like to have risen to the top of it and be admired by it; but it would not occur to him to leave it. At occasional stags where naked girls danced on the tables and sat in great glasses of wine, Mr. Pritchard howled with laughter and drank the wine, but five hundred Mr. Pritchards were there with him.

And now, at the end of Alice's ugly statement about a toilet, he looked about the lunchroom and found that he was alone. There were no other Mr. Pritchards here. For a moment his glance rested on the little man in the business suit, but there was something queer about him. True, there was some kind of a pin in his buttonhole, a little blue enamel bar with white stars on it, but it was no club Mr. Pritchard recognized. He found himself hating these people and hating even his vacation. He wanted to go back to the bedroom and close the door, but here was this stout woman who wanted to go to the toilet. Mr. Pritchard cleaned his nails very rapidly with the gold nail file on his watch chain.

At bottom, and originally, Mr. Pritchard was not like this. He had once voted for Eugene Debs, but that had been a long time ago. It was just that the people in his group watched one another. Any variation from a code of conduct was first noted, then discussed. A man who varied was not a sound man, and if he persisted no one would do business with him. Protective coloring was truly protective. But there was no double life in Mr. Pritchard. He had given up his freedom and then had forgotten what it was like. He thought of it now as youthful folly. He put his vote for Eugene Debs alongside his visit to a parlor house when he was twenty. Both were things to be expected of growing boys. He even occasionally mentioned at a club luncheon his vote for Debs, to prove that he had been a spirited young man and that such things were, like a kid's acne, a part of the process of adolescence. But although he excused and even enjoyed his prank in voting for Debs, he was definitely worried about the activities of his daughter Mildred.

She was playing around with dangerous companions in her college, professors and certain people considered Red. Before the war she had picketed a scrap-iron ship bound for Japan, and she had gathered money for medical supplies for what Mr. Pritchard called the Reds in the Spanish war. He did not discuss these things with Mildred. She didn't want to talk it out with him. And he had a strong feeling that if everyone was quiet and controlled she would get over it. A husband and a baby would resolve Mildred's political uneasiness. She would then, he said, find her true values.

Mr. Pritchard's visit to the parlor house he did not remember very well. He had been twenty and drunk, and afterward he had had a withering sense of desecration and sorrow. He did remember the subsequent two weeks when he had waited in terror for symptoms to develop. He had even planned to kill himself if they did; to kill himself and make it look like an accident.

Now he was nervous. He was on a vacation he didn't really want to take. He was going to Mexico which, in spite of the posters, he considered a country not only dirty but dangerously radical. They had expropriated the oil; in other words, stolen private property. And how was that different from Russia? Russia, to Mr. Pritchard, took the place of the medieval devil as the source of all cunning and evil and terror. He was nervous this morning because he hadn't slept either. He liked his own bed. It took him a week to get used to a bed, and here he was in for three weeks of a different bed practically every night, and God knew how some of them would be populated. He was tired and his skin felt grainy. The water was hard here so that when he shaved he knew he would have a ring of ingrown hairs around his neck within three days.

He took a handkerchief from his breast pocket, removed his glasses and polished them. "I'll tell my wife and daughter," he said. "We didn't know we were discommoding you so."

Norma liked that word and she said it over under her breath. "Discommode—I wouldn't want to discommode you, Mr. Gable, but I think you should know . . ."

Mr. Pritchard had gone back into the bedroom. His voice was audible, explaining the situation, and women's voices were questioning.

The man with the mustache got up from his chair and limped painfully to the counter, groaning under his breath. He brought the sugar bowl back with him and sank, with grimaces, back into his chair.

"I would have got that for you," Norma said with concern.

He smiled at her. "I wouldn't want to trouble you," he explained bravely.

"It wouldn't discommode me none," said Norma.

Juan put down his coffee cup.

Pimples said, "I'd like to have a piece of that coconut cake."

Alice absently cut him a piece and slid the saucer down the counter and made a note on a pad.

"I guess there ain't never one on the house," said Pimples.

"I figure there's plenty on the house the house don't know about," Alice replied.

"Looks like a bad sprain you've got there," Juan observed to the little man.

"Crushed," he said, "toes crushed. Here, I'll show you."

Mr. Pritchard came out of the bedroom and took a seat at the remaining table.

The little man unlaced his oxford and took it off. He slipped his sock off and laid it carefully in the oxford. His foot was bandaged from the instep to the ends of the toes, and the bandage was spotted and soaked with bright red blood.

"You don't need to show us," Alice said quickly. Blood made her faint.

"I ought to change the bandage anyway," said the little man, and he unwound the gauze and exposed the foot. The big toe and the two next to it were horribly crushed, the nails blackened and the ends of the toes tattered and bloody and raw.

Juan had arisen. Pimples came close. Even Norma could not stay away.

"My God, that's an awful smash," Juan said. "Let me get some water and wash it. You ought to have some kind of salve. You'll get an infection. You might lose that foot."

Pimples whistled shrilly between his teeth to indicate interest and a kind of enthusiasm for the quality of the hurt. The little man was looking into Juan's face, his eyes shining with pleasure and anticipation.

"You think it's bad?" he demanded.

"You're damn right, it's bad," said Juan.

"You think I should get a doctor?"

"Well, I would if it was me."

The little man chuckled with delight. "That's all I wanted to hear," he said. He ran his thumbnail down his instep, and the top of his foot lifted off—the skin, the blood, the mashed toes—and underneath there was his foot whole and unhurt and his toes untouched. He put back his head and laughed with glee.

"Good, isn't it? Plastic. New product."

Mr. Pritchard had come close, a look of disgust on his face.

"It's the 'Little Wonder Artificial Sore Foot,'" the man said. He pulled a flat box from his side pocket and handed it to Juan. "You've been so nice to me, I want you to have one. Compliments of Ernest Horton representing the Little Wonder Company." His voice raced with his enthusiasm. "It comes in three sizes—one, two, or three crushed toes. This one I'm giving you is the three-toe number, just like the one you just saw. It's got bandage and a bottle of artificial blood to keep the bandage looking terrible. Instructions inside. You've got to soften it in warm water the first time you put it on. Then it fits like skin and nobody can tell. You can have a barrel of fun with it."

Mr. Pritchard leaned forward. Way in the back of his mind he could see himself taking off his sock at a board meeting. He could do it right after he got back from Mexico, tell some story about bandits first.

"What do you get for them?" he asked.

THE WAYWARD BUS

"Dollar and a half, but I hardly ever sell for retail," Ernest Horton said. "The trade snaps them up as fast as I can get them. I sold forty gross to the trade in two weeks."

"No?" said Mr. Pritchard. His eyes were wide with appreciation.

"Show you my order book if you don't believe it. It's the fastest selling novelty I've ever handled. Little Wonder is cleaning up with it."

"What is the mark-up?" Mr. Pritchard demanded.

"Well, I wouldn't like to say unless you're in the trade. Business ethics, you know."

Mr. Pritchard nodded. "Well, I'd like to try one at the retail price," he said.

"Get you one right after I eat. You got that buttered toast?" he asked Norma.

"Coming up," said Norma, and she went guiltily behind the counter and switched on the toaster.

"You see, it's the psychology that sells it," Ernest said exultantly. "We've stocked artificial cut fingers for years and they moved slow, but this—it's the psychology of taking off your shoe and sock. Nobody ever thinks you'd go to the trouble of doing that. The fellow that figured that out got himself a very nice fee."

"I guess you're making a little something out of it yourself," said Mr. Pritchard with admiration. He was feeling much better now.

"I do all right," said Ernest. "I got one or two other little things that might interest you in my sample case. Not for sale except to the trade, but I'll demonstrate them. It might give you a laugh."

"I'd like to take half a dozen of the sore feet," said Mr. Pritchard.

"All the three toes?"

Mr. Pritchard considered. He wanted them for gifts, but he didn't want competition. Charlie Johnson could sell the tricks better than Mr. Pritchard could. Charlie was a natural comic.

"Suppose you let me have one three-toe and three two-toe and two one-toe," he said. "That'd be about right for me, I guess."

The quality of the rain was changing. It came with great, gusty, drenching downpours and with short, drippy intervals between. Juan sat with his coffee by the window. Half a brown doughnut lay in the saucer.

"I think she's going to let up a little," said Juan. "I'd like to turn over that rear end some more before we start."

"I'd like to have a piece of that coconut cake," said Pimples.

"No you don't," Alice said. "I've got to keep a little cake for customers."

"Well, I'm a customer, ain't I?"

"I don't know if we'll get deliveries from San Ysidro today," said Alice. "I got to keep a little cake on hand."

At the very end of the counter there was a candy tray arranged like steps, with wrapped and packaged candy bars in it. Pimples got up from his stool

and stood in front of the display. He considered the bright little packages
a long time before he made his selections. Finally he picked out three bars
and put them in his pocket. "One Baby Ruth, one Love Nest, and one
Coconut Sweetheart," he said.

"Coconut Sweethearts are a dime. They got nuts," said Alice.

"I know," said Pimples.

Alice picked up her pad from behind the counter. "You're one jump ahead
of your pay now," she said.

FOUR

The moment the Pritchards came out of the bedroom Norma said quickly,
"I got to brush my hair and clean up a little bit." And she bolted for the
door. Alice was right behind her.

"After me in the bathroom," Alice said coldly. Norma went across the
bedroom of Mr. and Mrs. Chicoy and into her own bedroom. She closed the
door behind her and, as there was no key, she snapped the little catch beside the lock to secure her privacy. Her narrow iron Army cot was unmade,
and Ernest Horton's big sample case stood against the wall.

It was a very narrow room. A dresser with a bowl and pitcher stood against
one wall, a silken pillow top, fringed and shiny, was tacked up over the
dresser. It was pink and had a picture of crossed cannons in front of a bunch
of red roses. And printed on the pillow top was a poem called "A Soldier's
Prayer to His Mother."

> Midst shot and shell I think of you, Mother dear
> I hope your prayers will keep me clear
> And when the war is o'er and won,
> I will come back to you, my Number One.

Norma looked quickly at the window, murky with rainy light, and then
she reached inside the neck of her dress and turned back the material. On a
safety pin, fastened to the turned edge, was a small key. Norma unpinned it.
She pulled her suitcase from under the dresser, unlocked and opened it. A
shiny picture of Clark Gable in a silver frame lay on top, and it was signed
"With Best Regards—Clark Gable." She had bought the picture and frame
and signature in a gift shop in San Ysidro.

She ran her hand quickly to the bottom of the suitcase. Her fingers came
on a little square ring box. She pulled it out and jerked it open, saw that
the rings were there, and shoved the box back to the bottom of the suitcase.
She closed and locked the case, pushed it under the dresser, and pinned the
key back inside her dress. She opened the dresser drawer, lifted out a brush

and comb, and went to the window. On the wall beside the red-and-green-flowered cretonne drapes there was a framed mirror. Norma stood in front of it and looked at herself.

A lead-colored light came through the window and fell on her face. She widened her eyes with intensity and then she smiled, showing all her teeth, smiled vivaciously. She stood on her toes a little and waved to an immense crowd and smiled again. She ran the comb through her thin hair and tugged as the teeth caught in the marceled ends. She got a pencil from the dresser and worked the dull point through her pale eyebrows, accentuating the curve in the middle so that her face took on a surprised look. Then she began to brush her hair, ten strokes on one side and ten on the other. And while she brushed, she raised and flexed the muscles of one leg and then the other to develop the calves. It was a routine recommended by a picture star who had never willingly taken any exercise of any kind but who had beautiful legs.

Norma glanced quickly at the window as the light grew still dimmer. She would have hated to be observed in the grotesque dance. Norma was even more submerged than an iceberg. Only the tiniest part of Norma showed above the surface. For the greatest and best and most beautiful part of Norma lay behind her eyes, sealed and protected.

The doorknob of her bedroom turned and then there was pressure against the door. Norma stiffened and stood rigid. Only one hand moved, and it frantically rubbed at her eyebrows and succeeded in making gray smudges on her forehead. And now there came a knocking at the bedroom door. A light, courteous knocking. She put her brush on the dresser, smoothed down her dress, and went to the door. She pushed the catch and opened the door a crack. The face of Ernest Horton was looking in at her. His tight, hairy mustache arched over his mouth.

"I thought I'd take my sample case out of your way," he said.

Norma still held the door open only a crack.

"You folks have been so nice and all," he went on. "I don't want to be any more nuisance than I have to."

Norma slowly relaxed, but she was still breathing a little hard. She opened the door and stepped back. Ernest, with a smile of embarrassment, came into the room. He went to the bed.

"I should have made this bed," he said, and he drew the sheet and blanket up and began to pat the wrinkles out.

"No, I'll do that," said Norma.

"You didn't even wait for your tip I promised you," said Ernest. "But I've got it for you." He made the bed neatly, as though he had done it many times before.

"I could have done that just as well," said Norma.

"Well, it's done now," he said. He went to his big sample case. "Mind if I open this? I want to get some stuff out."

"Go ahead," said Norma. Her eyes filled with interest.

He laid the big sample case on her bed and snapped the catch and threw back the lid. There were wonderful things in the case. There were cardboard tubes and handkerchiefs that changed color. There were exploding cigars and stink-bombs. There were voice-throwers and horns and paper hats for parties and pennants and funny buttons. There were silken pillows like the one on the wall. Ernest was extracting six of the artificial sore feet in their flat packages, and Norma had moved close to look into the wonderful sample case. Her eyes had been caught by a series of photographs of picture stars. They were not like any she had ever seen. The pictures were pressed and molded into thick sheets of sheer plastic at least a quarter of an inch through. And there was another curious thing about them. The pictures did not look flat. By some trick of bending, or possibly of refracted light, the faces were rounded and had depth. They seemed to be three-dimensional, and the frames were eight by ten inches in size.

On top was a lifelike, smiling picture of James Stewart, and projecting from under that was a second picture of which she could only see the hair and a part of the forehead, but she knew that hair and that forehead. Her lips parted and a shine came into her eyes. Slowly her hand moved into the case and lifted James Stewart aside. And there he was, Clark Gable, looking round and full. It was a serious, intense pose, the chin out, the eyes level and intent. It was such a picture as she had never seen. She sighed deeply and tried to control her breath so that it could not be heard. She lifted the picture out and stared into the eyes, and her own were wide and hypnotized.

Ernest watched her and saw her interest. "Isn't that a knockout?" he said. "It's a new idea. Notice how it looks round, almost like a statue?"

Norma nodded, speechless.

"I make a prophecy," Ernest said. "I go down the line and lay my word on it. That little number is going to wipe every other kind of pictures right off the map. It's acid-proof, moisture-proof, lasts forever, won't ever turn brown. It's molded and baked right inside the frame. It'll last forever."

Norma's eyes never left the picture. Ernest reached for the picture and her fingers tightened on it like claws.

"How much?" Her voice came out a throaty, rasping growl.

"It's just a sample," said Ernest. "It's something to show to the trade. It's not for sale. You order them."

"How much?" Her fingers were white with pressure. Ernest looked at her closely. He saw her face intent and set, jaw muscles rigid and nostrils flaring a little with controlled breathing.

Ernest said, "They bring two bucks retail, but I said I was going to give you a nice tip. Would you rather have that than a nice tip?"

Norma's voice was hoarse. "Yes."

"Well, then, you can have it."

The whiteness went slowly out of her fingers. There was a light of glory in her eyes. She licked her lips. "Thanks," she said. "Oh, thanks, mister!" She turned the face of the picture toward her and pressed it against her. The plastic was not cold, like glass, but warm and soft-feeling.

"I guess I can get along with only one sample," Ernest said. "See, I'm swinging south. I won't go back to the head office for six weeks. I figured to spend two weeks in L. A. That's a great place for novelties."

Norma carried the picture to her dresser and opened the drawer and shoved the picture down under a pile of clothes and closed the drawer. "I suppose you'll get to Hollywood," she said.

"Oh, sure. That's even better than L. A. for novelties. Then, it's kind of like my vacation too. I've got a lot of friends there. I have my vacation and get around and see things and I see the trade too. Kills two birds. I don't lose any time. I got an Army friend works in a studio there. I always run around some with him. Last time we had a party it started out in the Melrose Grotto. That's over on Melrose, right next to RKO. And that really was a party! I wouldn't really like to tell you what we did do, but I never had so much fun in my life. And then my friend, of course, had to go back to work at the studio."

Norma had become as intent as a setter pup watching a bug. "Your friend works in a studio?" she asked casually. "Which one?"

"Metro-Goldwyn-Mayer," said Ernest. He was repacking his sample case and not looking up at her. He did not hear the rasp of breath in her throat or the unnatural tone that came into her voice.

"You go into the studio lots?"

"Yeah. Willie gets me a pass. I go and watch them shoot sometimes. Willie's a carpenter. Worked there before the war and now he's back there. I soldiered with him. Awful nice fellow. And what a guy at parties! He knows more dames, he's got more phone numbers than you ever saw. A big thick black book full of phone numbers. Even he can't remember who half the dames are he's got the phone numbers of."

Ernest was warming to his subject. He sat down on the little straight chair beside the wall. He chuckled. "Willie was stationed in Santa Ana first of the war, before I even knew him. Well, the officers got to know about his black book and they'd take Willie into Hollywood and he'd get dames for them and then Willie got a pass when he wanted it. He was making out good when they shipped his outfit out."

Norma's eyes took on a quick look of annoyance during this recital. Her fingers picked at her apron. Her voice became high and then low. "I wonder if it would discommode you to do a favor for me?"

"Sure," said Ernest. "What do you want?"

"Well, if I was to give you a letter and you was—er—were on the MGM lot and you happened to see Mr. Gable, why I wonder if you'd give it to him?"

"Who's Mr. Gable?"

"Mr. Clark Gable," said Norma sternly.

"Oh, him. You know him?"

"Yes," said Norma frostily, "I'm—I'm his cousin."

"Oh, I see. Well, sure I will. But maybe I don't go. Why don't you put it in the mail?"

Norma's eyes narrowed. "He don't get his mail," she said mysteriously. "There's a girl, a secretary like, that just takes it and burns it up."

"No!" said Ernest. "What for?"

Norma stopped to consider this. "They just don't want him to see it."

"Not even from his own relatives?"

"Not even from his cousin," said Norma.

"Did he tell you that?"

"Yes." Her eyes were wide and blank. "Yes. Course I'll go there pretty soon," she said. "I've had offers and once I was just about to go and my cousin—Mr. Gable, that is—he said, 'No, you've got to get experience,' he said. 'You're young. You're not in any hurry.' So I'm getting experience. You learn a lot about people in a lunchroom. I study them all the time."

Ernest looked at her a little skeptically. He knew the fantastic stories about waitresses who became dramatic stars overnight, but Norma didn't have the bubs for it, he thought, nor the legs. Norma's legs were like sticks. But, then, he knew about two or three picture stars who were so plain without make-up that no one would recognize them off the screen. He'd read about them. And Norma, even if she didn't look it—well, they could pad her out, and if her cousin was Clark Gable, why, that was an "in" you couldn't beat. That was the breaks.

"Well, I hadn't thought much about asking Willie to get me a pass this time," he said. "I've been out there quite a few times but—well, if you want me to I'll go right in, find him, and give him your letter. What do you suppose they throw away his mail for?"

"They just want to work him to death and then throw him away like an old shoe," said Norma passionately. Wave after wave of emotion swept over her. She was in an ecstasy, and at the same time panic was crowding up on her. Norma was not a liar. She had never done anything like this before. She was going out on a long teetering plank and she knew it. One question, one bit of knowledge on Ernest's part, would throw her off and hurtle her into a chasm, and yet she couldn't stop.

"He's a great man," she said, "a great gentleman. He don't like the parts they make him do because he isn't like that. Even Rhett Butler—he didn't like to play that because he's not a rat and he don't like to play rat parts."

Ernest had lowered his eyes and was studying Norma through his eyelashes. And Ernest was beginning to understand. The key to it was creeping into his brain. Norma was as pretty now as she was ever likely to be. There was dignity in her face, courage, and a truly great flow of love. There were only two things for Ernest to do—to laugh at her or play along. If there'd

been any other person in the room—another man, for instance—he probabl
would have laughed to protect himself from the other person's scorn, an
he would have been ashamed and more boisterous because he could see tha
it was a powerful, pure, and overwhelming thing shining in this girl. Thi
was the thing that kept the neophytes lying through the nights on th
stone floors in front of the altars. This was an outpouring of an attar of love
of a naked intensity that Ernest had never seen before in anyone.

"I'll take the letter," he said. "I'll tell him it's from his cousin."

A look of fright came on Norma's face. "No," she said, "I'd rather sur
prise him. Just tell him it's from a friend. Don't tell him a single othe
thing."

"When do you think you'll be going down there to take a job?" Ernest
asked.

"Well, Mr. Gable says I ought to wait another year. He says I'm young
and need experience studying people. I get pretty tired of it sometimes,
though. Sometimes I wish I was there in my own house with them—those—
big, thick curtains and a long couch, like, and I'd see all my friends—Bette
Davis and Ingrid Bergman and Joan Fontaine, because I don't mess around
with that other kind that's always getting divorced and things like that. We
just sit around and talk about serious things, and we study all the time because that's how you get ahead and be a great actress. And there's lots that
treat their fans mean; won't sign autographs and things like that, but not
us! Not our kind, I mean. We even have girls right off the streets sometimes
in for a cup of tea and talk and just like they were us because we know we
owe everything we got to the loyalty of our fans." She was quaking inside
with fear and she couldn't stop. She was getting far out on the plank and
she couldn't stop and it was about to throw her.

Ernest said, "I didn't understand at first. You've already been in pictures.
Are you a star already?"

"Yes," said Norma. "But you wouldn't know me by the name I'm using
here. I have another name I use in Hollywood."

"What is it?"

"I couldn't tell," said Norma. "You're the only person anywhere around
here that knows anything about me. Now, you won't tell, will you?"

Ernest was shaken. "No," he said, "I won't tell if you don't want me to."

"Keep my secret inviolate," said Norma.

"Sure," said Ernest. "Just give me the letter and I'll see he gets it."

"You'll see who gets what?" said Alice from the doorway. "What are you
two doing alone in a bedroom?" Her eyes roved suspiciously about for
evidence, skimmed over the sample case on the bed, stopped on the pillow,
inspected the spread, and then moved to Norma. Alice's eyes traveled up
her feet and legs, lingered a moment on her skirt, hesitated on her waist,
and then settled on her flaming face.

Norma was almost sick with embarrassment. Her cheeks were splotched with blood. Alice put her hands on her hips.

Ernest said placatingly, "I was just getting my sample case out of the way and she asked me to take a note to a cousin of hers in L. A."

"She's got no cousin in L. A."

"Yes, she has too," Ernest said angrily, "and I know her cousin."

And now the rage that had been trying to get out of Alice all morning burst from her. "You listen to me," she shouted. "I won't have you drummers diddling my hired girls."

"Nobody's touched her," Ernest said. "Nobody laid a hand on her."

"No? Well, then, what'cha doing in her bedroom? Take a look at her face." The hysteria boiled over in Alice. A heavy, throaty, screaming voice came from her throat. Her hair fell about her face and her eyes rolled and watered and her lips became cruel and tight, as a fighter's do when he is slugging a half-conscious opponent. "I won't have it. You think I want her knocked up? You think I want bastards all over the place? We give you our beds and our rooms!"

"I tell you nothing happened!" Ernest shouted at her. He was overwhelmed with hopelessness in the face of this craziness. His denials sounded in his ears almost like admissions. He didn't understand why she was doing it, and the injustice made him sick to his stomach and rage was rising in him too.

Norma's mouth was open and she was catching the microbe of hysteria. Whinnying cries came from her with every panting breath. Her hands fought in front of her as though they were trying to destroy each other.

Alice advanced on Norma and her right fist was doubled, not like a woman's fist, but with the fingers folded tightly and the knuckles up and outstuck, the thumb laid close against the first joints. Her words were thick and moist. "Get out of here! Get out of the whole place! Get out in the rain!" Alice descended on Norma and Norma backed away and a terrified scream came from her mouth.

There were quick steps in the doorway and Juan said sharply, "Alice!"

She stopped. Her mouth sagged open and her eyes grew afraid. Juan came slowly into the room. His thumbs were hooked in his overalls pockets. He moved toward her as lightly as a creeping cat. The gold ring on his amputated finger glimmered in the leaden light from the window. Alice's rage poured over into terror. She cringed away from him, passed the end of the bed and into the blind alley until she came up against the wall, and there she was stopped.

"Don't hit me," she whispered. "Oh, please don't hit me."

Juan came close to her and his right hand moved slowly to her arm just above the elbow. He was looking at her, not through her or around her. He swung her gently about and led her across the room and through the door and he closed the door on Norma and Ernest.

They stared at the closed door and hardly breathed. Juan led Alice to the double bed and turned her gently and she sagged down like a cripple and fell back, staring wildly up at him. He picked a pillow from the top of the bed and put it under her head. His left hand, the one with the stump finger and the wedding ring, stroked her cheek gently. "You'll be all right now," he said.

She crossed her arms over her face and her sobs were strangled and harsh and dry.

FIVE

Bernice Pritchard and her daughter Mildred and Mr. Pritchard sat at the small table to the right of the entrance door of the lunchroom. The little group had drawn closer together. The two older people because they felt that in some way they were under attack, and Mildred in a kind of protective sense toward them. She often wondered how her parents had survived in a naughty and ferocious world. She considered them naïve and unprotected little children, and to a certain extent she was right about her mother. But Mildred overlooked the indestructibility of the child and the stability, its pure perseverance to get its own way. And there was a kind of indestructibility about Bernice. She was rather pretty. Her nose was straight and she had for so long worn pince-nez that the surfaces between her eyes were shaped by the pressure. The high, gristly part of her nose was not only very thin from the glasses, but two red spots showed where the springs regularly pressed. Her eyes were violet colored and myopic, which gave her a sweet, inward look.

She was feminine and dainty and she dressed always with a hint of a passed period. She wore jabots occasionally and antique pins. Her shirtwaists had always some lace and some handwork, and the collars and cuffs were invariably immaculate. She used lavender toilet water so that her skin and her clothing and her purse smelled always of lavender, and of another, almost imperceptible, acid odor which was her own. She had pretty ankles and feet, on which she wore very expensive shoes, usually of kid and laced, with a little bow over the instep. Her mouth was rather wilted and childlike, soft, and without a great deal of character. She talked very little but had in her own group gained a reputation for goodness and for sagacity; the first by saying only nice things about people, even people she did not know, and the second by never expressing a general idea of any kind beyond perfumes or food. She met the ideas of other people with a quiet smile, almost as though she forgave them for having ideas. The truth was that she didn't listen.

There had been times when Mildred wept with rage at her mother's knowing, forgiving smile after one of Mildred's political or economic deliveries. It took the daughter a long time to discover that her mother never listened to any conversation that had not to do with people or places or material things. On the other hand, Bernice never forgot a detail about goods or colors or prices. She could remember exactly how much she had paid for black suede gloves seven years ago. She was fond of gloves and rings —any kind of rings. She had a rather large collection, but she wore with anything else, always, her small diamond engagement ring and her gold wedding band. These she removed only to bathe. She left them on when she washed her combs and brushes in ammonia water in the hand basin. The ammonia cleaned the rings and made the little diamonds shine brightly.

Her married life was fairly pleasant and she was fond of her husband. She thought she knew his weaknesses and his devices and his desires. She herself was handicapped by what is known as a nun's hood, which prevented her experiencing any sexual elation from her marriage; and she suffered from an acid condition which kept her from conceiving children without first artificially neutralizing her body acids. Both of these conditions she considered normal, and any variation of them abnormal and in bad taste. Women of lusty appetites she spoke of as "that kind of woman," and she was a little sorry for them as she was for dope fiends and alcoholics.

Her husband's beginning libido she had accepted and then gradually by faint but constant reluctance had first molded and then controlled and gradually strangled, so that his impulses for her became fewer and fewer and until he himself believed that he was reaching an age when such things did not matter.

In her way she was a very powerful woman. She ran an efficient, clean, comfortable house and served meals which were nourishing without being tasty. She did not believe in the use of spices, for she had been told long ago that they had an aphrodisiac effect on men. The three—Mr. Pritchard, Mildred, and herself—did not take on any weight, probably because of the dullness of the food. It did not stimulate any great appetite.

Bernice's friends knew her as one of the sweetest, most unselfish people you will ever meet, and they often referred to her as a saint. And she herself said often that she felt humbly lucky, for she had the finest, most loyal friends in the whole world. She loved flowers and planted and pinched and fertilized and cut them. She kept great bowls of flowers in her house always, so that her friends said it was like being in a florist's shop, and she arranged them herself so beautifully.

She did not take medicines and often suffered in silence from constipation until the accumulated pressure relieved her. She had never really been ill nor badly hurt, and consequently she had no measuring rod of pain. A stitch in her side, a backache, a gas pain under her heart, convinced her secretly that she was about to die. She had been sure she would die when she had borne

Mildred, and she had arranged her affairs so that everything would be easy for Mr. Pritchard. She had even written a letter to be opened after her death, advising him to marry again so that the child could have some kind of mother. She later destroyed this letter.

Her body and her mind were sluggish and lazy, and deep down she fought a tired envy of the people who, so she thought, experienced good things while she went through life a gray cloud in a gray room. Having few actual perceptions, she lived by rules. Education is good. Self-control is necessary. Everything in its time and place. Travel is broadening. And it was this last axiom which had forced her finally on the vacation to Mexico.

How she reached her conclusions not even she knew. It was a long, slow process built up of hints, suggestions, accidents, thousands of them, until finally, in their numbers, they forced the issue. The truth was that she didn't want to go to Mexico. She just wanted to come back to her friends having been to Mexico. He husband didn't want to go at all. He was doing it for his family and because he hoped it would do him good in a cultural way. And Mildred wanted to go, but not with her parents. She wanted to meet new and strange people and through such contacts to become new and strange herself. Mildred felt that she had great covered wells of emotion in her, and she probably had. Nearly everyone has.

Bernice Pritchard, while denying superstition, was nevertheless profoundly affected by signs. The bus breaking down so early in the trip frightened her, for it seemed to portend a series of accidents which would gradually ruin the trip. She was sensitive to Mr. Pritchard's unrest. Last night, lying sleepless in the Chicoys' double bed, listening to the sighing breaths of her husband, she had said, "This will turn into an adventure when it's over. I can almost hear you telling it. It will be funny."

"I suppose so," Mr. Pritchard answered.

There was a certain fondness between these two, almost a brother-and-sister relationship. Mr. Pritchard considered his wife's shortcomings as a woman the attributes of a lady. He never had to worry about her faithfulness. Unconsciously he knew that she was without reaction, and this was right in his mind. His nerves, his bad dreams, and the acrid pain that sometimes got into his upper abdomen he put down to too much coffee and not enough exercise.

He liked his wife's pretty hair, always waved and clean; he liked her spotless clothes; and he loved the compliments she got for her good housekeeping and her flowers. She was a wife to be proud of. She had raised a fine daughter, a fine, healthy girl.

Mildred was a fine girl; a tall girl, two inches taller than her father and five inches taller than her mother. Mildred had inherited her mother's violet eyes and the weakness that went with them. She wore glasses when she wanted to see anything clearly. She was well formed, with sturdy legs and strong, slender ankles. Her thighs and buttocks were hard and straight and smooth from much exercise. She played tennis well and was center on her college basketball team. Her breasts were large and firm and wide at the base. She had not inherited her mother's physiological accident, and she had experienced two consummated love affairs which gave her great satisfaction and a steady longing for a relationship that would be constant.

Mildred's chin was set and firm like her father's, but her mouth was full and soft and a little frightened. She wore heavy black-framed glasses, and these did give her a student look. It was always a surprise to new acquaintances to see Mildred at a dance without glasses. She danced well, if a little precisely, but she was a practicing athlete and perhaps she practiced dancing too carefully and without enough relaxation. She did have a slight tendency to lead, but that could be overcome by a partner with strong convictions.

Mildred's convictions were strong too, but they were variable. She had undertaken causes and usually good ones. She did not understand her father at all because he constantly confused her. Telling him something reasonable, logical, intelligent, she often found in him a dumb obtuseness, a complete lack of thinking ability that horrified her. And then he would say or do something so intelligent that she would leap to the other side. When she had him catalogued rather smugly as a caricature of a businessman, grasping, slavish, and cruel, he ruined her peace of conception by an act or a thought of kindliness and perception.

Of his emotional life she knew nothing whatever, just as he knew nothing of hers. Indeed, she thought that a man in middle age had no emotional life. Mildred, who was twenty-one, felt that the saps and juices were all dried up at fifty, and rightfully so, since neither men nor women were attractive at that age. A man or a woman in love at fifty would have been an obscene spectacle to her.

But if there was a chasm between Mildred and her father, there was a great gulf between Mildred and her mother. The woman who had no powerful desires to be satisfied could not ever come close to the girl who had. An early attempt on Mildred's part to share her strong ecstasies with her mother and to receive confirmation had met with a blankness, a failure to comprehend, which hurled Mildred back inside herself. For a long time she didn't try to confide in anyone, feeling that she was unique and that all other women were like her mother. At last, however, a big and muscular young woman who taught ice hockey and softball and archery at the university gained Mildred's confidence, her whole confidence, and then tried to go to bed with her. This shock was washed away only when a male engineering student with wiry hair and a soft voice did go to bed with her.

Now Mildred kept her own counsel, thought her own thoughts, and waited for the time when death, marriage, or accident would free her from her parents. But she loved her parents, and she would have been frightened at herself had it ever come to the surface of her mind that she wished them dead.

There had never been any close association among these three although they went through the forms. They were dear and darling and sweet, but Juan and Alice Chicoy regularly established a relationship which Mr. or Mrs. Pritchard could not have conceived. And Mildred's close and satisfying friendships were with people of whose existence her parents were completely ignorant. They had to be. It had to be. Her father considered the young women who danced naked at stags depraved, but it would never have occurred to him that he who watched and applauded and paid the girls was in any way associated with depravity.

Once or twice, on his wife's insistence, he had tried to warn Mildred against men just to teach her to protect herself. He hinted and believed that he had considerable knowledge of the world, and his complete knowledge, besides hearsay, was his one visit to the parlor house, the stags, and the dry, unresponding acquiescence of his wife.

This morning Mildred wore a sweater and pleated skirt and low, moccasin-like shoes. The three sat at the little table in the lunchroom. Mrs. Pritchard's three-quarter-length black fox coat hung on a hook beside Mr. Pritchard. It was his habit to shepherd this coat, to help his wife on with it and to take it from her, and to see that it was properly hung up and not just thrown down. He fluffed up the fur with his hand when it showed evidence of being crushed. He loved this coat, loved the fact that it was expensive, and he loved to see his wife in it and to hear other women speculate upon it. Black fox was comparatively rare, and it was also a valuable piece of property. Mr. Pritchard felt that it should be properly treated. He was always the first to suggest that it go into summer storage. He had suggested that it might be just as well not to take it to Mexico at all, first, because that was a tropical country, and second, because of bandits who might possibly steal it. Mrs. Pritchard held that it should be taken along, because, in the first place, they would be visiting Los Angeles and Hollywood where everyone wore fur coats, and second, because it was quite cold in Mexico City at night, so she had heard. Mr. Pritchard capitulated easily; to him, as well as to his wife, the coat was the badge of their position. It placed them as successful, conservative, and sound people. You get better treatment everywhere you go if you have a fur coat and nice luggage.

Now the coat hung beside Mr. Pritchard, and he ran his fingers deftly up through the hairs to clear the long guard hairs from the undercoat. Sitting at the table, they had heard through the bedroom door Alice's hoarse, screaming attack on Norma, and the animal vulgarity of it had shocked them deeply, had driven them as nearly close together as they could be. Mildred had lighted a cigarette, avoiding her mother's eye. She had done this only in the six months since she had turned twenty-one. After the initial blow-up the subject had never verbally come up again, but her mother disapproved with her face every time Mildred smoked in front of her.

The rain had stopped and only the drips from the white oaks fell on the roof. The land was soggy, water-beaten, sodden. The grain, fat and heavy with the damp, rich springtime, had lain heavily down under the last downpour, so that it stretched away in tired waves. The water trickled and ran and gurgled and rushed to find low places in the fields. The ditches beside the state highway were full, and in some places the water even invaded the raised road. Everywhere there was a whisper of water and a rush of water. The golden poppies were all stripped of their petals now, and the lupines lay down like the grain, too fat, too heavy, to hold up their heads.

The sky was beginning to clear. The clouds were tattering, and there were splashes of lovely clear sky with silks of cloud skittering across them. Up high a fierce wind blew, spreading and mixing and matting the clouds, but on the ground the air was perfectly still, and there was a smell of worms and wet grass and exposed roots.

From the area of the lunchroom and garage at Rebel Corners the water ran in shallow ditches to the large ditch beside the highway. The bus stood shining and clean in its aluminum paint, and the water still dripping from its sides and its windshield flecked with droplets. Inside the lunchroom it was a lttle overwarm.

Pimples was behind the counter, trying to help out, and this would never have occurred to him before today. Always, in other jobs, he had hated the work and automatically hated his employer. But the experience of the morning was still strong in him. He could still hear Juan's voice saying in his ears, "Kit, wipe your hands and see if Alice got the coffee ready yet." It was the sweetest-sounding sentence he had ever heard. He wanted to do something for Juan. He had squeezed orange juice for the Pritchards and carried coffee to them, and now he was trying to watch the toaster and scramble eggs at the same time.

Mr. Pritchard said, "Let's all have scrambled eggs. That'll make it easier. You can leave mine in the pan and get them good and dry."

"O.K.," said Pimples. His pan was too hot and the eggs were ticking and clicking and sending up an odor of wet chicken feathers that comes from too fast frying.

Mildred had crossed her legs and her skirt was caught under her knee, so that the side away from Pimples must be exposed. He wanted to get down that way and look. His darting, narrow eyes took innumerable quick glances at what he could see. He didn't want her to catch him looking at her legs. He planned it in his mind. If she didn't move he would serve the eggs and he would take a napkin over his arm. Then, after he set down their plates, he would pass their table and go on about ten feet and drop the napkin as though by accident. He would lean down and look back under his arm, and then he would be able to see Mildred's leg.

He had the napkin ready and he was mixing the eggs to get them done before she moved. He stirred the eggs. They were stuck by now so he scooped shallowly to leave the burned crust in the pan. The odor of burning eggs filled the lunchroom. Mildred looked up and saw the flash in Pimples' eye. She looked down, noticed how her skirt was caught, and pulled it clear. Pimples saw her without looking directly at her. He knew that he had been caught and his cheeks stung with blood.

A dark smoke rose from the egg pan and a blue smoke rose from the toaster. Juan came in quietly from the bedroom and sniffed.

"God Almighty," he said, "what are you doing, Kit?"

"Trying to help out," said Pimples uneasily.

Juan smiled. "Well, thanks, but I guess you'd better not help out with eggs." He came to the gas stove, took the hot pan of burned eggs, put the whole thing into the sink, and turned the water on. It hissed and bubbled for a moment and then subsided, complaining, in the water.

Juan said, "Kit, you go out and try to start the engine. Don't choke her if she won't start. That'll only flood her. If she doesn't start right away, take off the distributor head and dry the points. They may have got wet. When you get her started, put her in low for a few minutes and then shift her to high and let the wheels turn over. But be careful she doesn't shake herself off those sawhorses. Just let her idle."

Pimples wiped his hands. "Should I open the grease cock first and see if she's still full?"

"Yeah. You know your stuff. Yeah, take a look. That gudgeon grease was pretty thick this morning."

"It might of shook down," said Pimples. He had forgotten the last look at Mildred's leg. He glowed under Juan's praise.

"Kit, I don't figure anybody would steal her, but keep an eye on her." Pimples laughed in sycophantic amusement at the boss's joke and went out the door. Juan looked over the counter. "My wife's not feeling very well," he said, "What can I get for you folks? More coffee?"

"Yes," said Mr. Pritchard. "The boy was trying to scramble some eggs and he burned them up. My wife likes hers moist—"

"If they're fresh," Mrs. Pritchard interposed.

"If they're fresh," said Mr. Pritchard. "And I like mine dry."

"They're fresh, all right," said Juan. "Right fresh out of the ice."

"I don't think I could eat a cold-storage egg," said Mrs. Pritchard.

"Well, that's what they are, I wouldn't lie to you."

"I guess I'll just have a doughnut," said Mrs. Pritchard.

"Make mine the same," said Mr. Pritchard.

Juan looked frankly and with admiration at Mildred's legs. She looked up at him. Slowly his eyes rose from her legs, and his dark eyes were filled with so much pleasure, were so openly admiring, that Mildred blushed a little. She warmed up in the pit of her stomach. She felt an electric jar.

"Oh—!" She looked away from him. "More coffee, I guess. Well, maybe I'll take a doughnut too."

"Only two doughnuts left," said Juan. "I'll bring two doughnuts and a snail and you can fight over them."

The engine of the bus exploded into action outside and in a moment was throttled down to a purr.

"She sounds good," said Juan.

Ernest Horton came quietly, almost secretly, out of the bedroom door and closed it softly behind him. He walked over to Mr. Pritchard and laid the six thin packages on the table. "There you are," he said, "six of them."

Mr. Pritchard pulled out his billfold. "Got change for twenty?" he asked.

"No, I haven't."

"You got change for twenty?" Mr. Pritchard asked Juan.

Juan pushed the "No Sale" button on the cash register and raised the wheel weight on the bill compartment. "I can give you two tens."

"That will do," said Ernest Horton. "I've got a dollar bill or so. You owe me nine dollars." He took one of the tens and gave Mr. Pritchard a dollar.

"What are they?" Mrs. Pritchard asked. She picked one up but her husband snatched it out of her hand. "No you don't," he said mysteriously.

"But what are they?"

"That's for me to know," said Mr. Pritchard playfully. "You'll find out quick enough."

"Oh, a surprise?"

"That's right. Little girls better keep their noses out of what doesn't concern them." Mr. Pritchard always called his wife "little girl" when he was playful, and automatically she fell into his mood.

"When do iddle girls see pretty present?"

"You'll find out," he said, and he stuffed the flat packages in his side pocket. He wanted to come in limping when he got the chance. He had a variation on the trick. He would pretend that his foot was so sore that he couldn't take off his shoe and sock himself. He would get his wife to take off the sock for him. What a kick that would be to watch her face! She'd nearly die when she saw that sore foot on him.

"What is it, Elliott?" she asked a little peevishly.

"You'll find out, just keep your pretty hair on, little girl."

"Say," he went on to Ernest, "I just thought up a new wrinkle. Tell you about it later."

Ernest said, "Yup, that's what makes the world tick. You get a new wrinkle and you're fixed. You don't want to go radical. Just a wrinkle, like they call it in Hollywood, a switcheroo. That's with a story. You take a picture that's made dough and you work a switcheroo—not too much, just enough, and you've got something then."

"That makes sense," said Mr. Pritchard. "Yes, sir, that makes good sense."

"It's funny about new wrinkles," said Ernest. He sat down on a stool and crossed his legs. "Funny how you get a wrong idea. Now, I've got a kind of an invention and I figured I could sit back and count my money, but I was wrong. You see, there's lot of fellows like me traveling around living out of a suitcase. Well, maybe there's a convention or you've got a date that's pretty fancy. You'd like to have a tuxedo. Well, it takes a lot of room to pack a tuxedo and maybe you only use it twice on a whole trip. Well, that's when I got this idea. Suppose, I said, you've got a nice dark business suit —dark blue or almost black or oxford—and suppose you got little silk slip-covers like little lapels and silk stripes that just snap on the pants. In the afternoon you've got a nice dark suit and you slip on the silk covers to the lapels and snap on the strips and you've got a tuxedo. I even figured out a little bag to carry them in."

"Say!" cried Mr. Pritchard, "that's a wonderful idea! Say, why I've got to take up room in my suitcase right now for a tuxedo. I'd like to get in on a thing like that. If you get up a patent and put on a campaign, a big national advertising campaign, why, you might maybe get a big movie star to endorse it—"

Ernest held up his hand. "That's just the way I figured," he said. "And I was wrong and you're wrong. I drew it all out on paper and just how it would go on and how the trousers leg would have little tiny silk loops for the hooks for the stripes to go on, and then I had a friend who travels for a big clothes manufacturer"—Ernest chuckled—"he put me right mighty quick. 'You'd get every tailor and every big manufacturer right on your neck,' he said. 'They sell tuxedos anywhere from fifty to a hundred and fifty bucks and you come along with ideas to take that business away with a ten-dollar gadget. Why, they'd run you right out of the country,' he said."

Mr. Pritchard nodded gravely. "Yes, I can see the point. They have to protect themselves and their stockholders."

"He didn't make it sound too hopeful," said Ernest. "I figured I'd just sit and count the profits. I figured that a fellow, say, traveling by air—he's got the weight limitations. He's got the right to save room in his suitcase. It'd be like two suits for the weight of one. And then I figured maybe the jewelry companies might take it up. Set of studs and cuff links and my lapels and stripes all in a nice package. I haven't got around to that yet. Haven't asked anybody. Might still be something in it."

"You and I ought to get together for a good talk," said Mr. Pritchard. "Have you got it patented?"

"Well, no. I didn't want to go to the expense until I could see if anybody was interested."

"Oh," said Mr. Pritchard. "I guess maybe you're right. Patent attorneys and all, they cost quite a bit of money. Maybe you're right." Then he changed the subject. "What time can we get started?" he asked Juan.

"Well, the Greyhound gets in around ten. They bring regular freight and some passengers. We should get started at ten-thirty. That's the schedule. Can I get you folks anything else? Some more coffee?"

"Some more coffee," said Mr. Pritchard.

Juan brought it to him and looked out the window at the bus with its wheels turning over in the air. Mr. Pritchard looked at his watch.

"We've still got an hour," he said.

A tall, stooped old man came around the side of the building. The man who had slept in Pimples' bed. He opened the door to the lunchroom, came in, and sat down on a stool. He had his head bent permanently forward on the arthritic stalk of his neck so that the tip of his nose pointed straight at the ground. He was well over sixty, and his eyebrows overhung his eyes like those of a Skye terrier. His long, deeply channeled upper lip was raised over his teeth like the little trunk of a tapir. The point over his middle teeth seemed to be almost prehensile. His eyes were yellowish gold, so that he looked fierce.

"I don't like it," he said without preliminaries. "I didn't like it yesterday when you broke down, and I like it even less today."

"I've got the rear end fixed," said Juan. "Turning over right now."

"I think I'll cancel and go on back to San Ysidro on the Greyhound," said the man.

"Well, you can do that."

"I've got a feeling," said the man. "I just don't like it. Something's trying to give me a warning. I've had 'em before a couple of times. I didn't pay any mind to them once and I got into trouble."

"The bus is all right," said Juan, his voice rising a little in exasperation.

"I'm not talking about the bus," said the man. "I live in this county, native of it. The ground's full of water. San Ysidro River will be up. You know how the San Ysidro rises. Right under Pico Blanco it comes down that Lone Pine Canyon and makes a big loop. Ground gets full of water and every drop runs right off into the San Ysidro. She'll be raging right now."

Mrs. Pritchard began to look alarmed. "Do you think there's danger?" she asked.

"Now, dear," said Mr. Pritchard.

"I've got a feeling," said the man. "The old road used to go around that loop of the river and never cross it. Come thirty years ago Mr. Trask got himself made roadmaster of this county. The old road wasn't good enough for him. He put in two bridges and saved what? Twelve miles, that's what he saved. It cost the county twenty-seven thousand dollars. Mr. Trask was a crook."

He turned his stiff neck and surveyed the Pritchards. "A crook. Just about to indict him for another job when he died, three years ago. Died a rich man. Got two boys in the University of California right now living on the taxpayers' money." He stopped and his upper lip waggled from side to side over his long yellow teeth. "If those bridges get any real strain on them they'll go out. The concrete isn't stout enough. I'll just cancel and go back to San Ysidro."

"The river was all right day before yesterday," said Juan. "Hardly any water in it."

"You don't know the San Ysidro River. She can get up in a couple of hours. I've seen her half a mile wide and covered with dead cows and chickenhouses. No, once I get this kind of feeling I won't go. I'm not superstitious, either."

"You think the bus might go through the bridge?"

"I don't say what I think. I know Trask was a crook. Left an estate of thirty-six thousand five-hundred dollars. His boys are up at college spending it right now."

Juan came out from behind the counter and went to the wall phone. "Hello," he said. "Give me Breed's Service Station out on the San Juan road. I don't know the number." He waited a while and then he said, "Hello. Say, this is Chicoy down at the Corners. How's the river? Oh, yeah? Well, is the bridge all right? Yeah. Well, O.K., I'll see you pretty soon." Juan hung up. "The river is up pretty high," he explained. "They say the bridge is all right."

"That river can rise a foot an hour when Pine Canyon dumps a cloudburst into it. Time you get there the bridge might be gone."

Juan turned a little impatiently to him. "What do you want me to do? Not go?"

"You do just as you like. I only want to cancel and get back to San Ysidro. I'm not going to fool around with this kind of nonsense. Once I had a feeling like this and I didn't pay attention and I broke both legs. No, sir, I got that feeling when you broke down yesterday."

"Well, consider yourself canceled," said Juan.

"That's what I want, mister! You're not an old-timer here. You don't know what I know about Trask. Salary of fifteen hundred a year and he leaves thirty-six thousand five-hundred, and a clear title to a hundred and sixty acres of land. Tell me!"

Juan said, "Well, I'll see you get on the Greyhound."

"Well, I'm not telling you anything about Trask, I'm just telling you what happened. You figure it out for yourself. Thirty-six thousand five-hundred dollars."

Ernest Horton asked, "Suppose the bridge is out?"

"Then we won't go across it," said Juan.

"Then what'll we do? Turn around and come back?"

"Sure," said Juan. "We'll either do that or jump it."

The stooped man smiled about the room in triumph. "You see?" he said. "You'll come back here and there'll be no bus here for San Ysidro. You'll sit around here for how long? Months? Wait for them to build a new bridge? You know who the new roadmaster is? A college boy. Just out of college. All books and no practice. Oh, he can draw a bridge, but can he build one? We'll see."

Suddenly Juan laughed. "Fine," he said. "The old bridge isn't washed out yet and already you're having trouble with the new one that isn't built."

The man turned his aching neck sideways. "Are you getting lippy?" he demanded.

For a moment a dark red light seemed to glow in Juan's black eyes. "Yes," he said. "I'll get you on the Greyhound, don't you worry. I wouldn't want you on this run."

"Well, you can't kick me off, you're a common carrier."

"O.K.," said Juan wearily. "Sometimes I wonder why I keep the bus. Maybe I won't much longer. Just a headache. You've got a feeling! Nuts!"

Bernice had been following this conversation very closely. "I don't believe in these things," she said, "but they say it's the dry season down in Mexico. It's like autumn. Summer's when it rains."

"Mother," said Mildred, "Mr. Chicoy knows Mexico. He was born there."

"Oh, were you? Well, it's the dry season, isn't it?"

"Some places," said Juan. "I guess it is where you'll be going. Other places there isn't any dry season."

Mr. Pritchard cleared his throat. "We're going to Mexico City and to Puebla and then to Cuernavaca and Tasco, and we may take the trip to Acapulco and we'll go to the volcano if it's all right."

"You'll be all right," said Juan.

"You know those places?" Mr. Pritchard demanded.

"Sure."

"How are the hotels?" Mr. Pritchard asked. "You know how the travel agencies are—everything is wonderful. How are they really?"

"Wonderful," Juan said, smiling now. "They're great. Breakfast in bed every morning."

"I didn't mean to cause trouble this morning," said Mr. Pritchard.

"Sure, it's all right." He leaned his arms on the counter and spoke confidentially. "I get fed up a little sometimes. I drive that damn bus back and forth and back and forth. Sometime I'd like to take and just head for the hills. I read about a ferryboat captain in New York who just headed out to sea one day and they never heard from him again. Maybe he sunk and maybe he's tied up on an island some place. I understand that man."

A great red truck with a trailer slowed down on the highway outside. The driver looked in. Juan moved his hand rapidly from side to side. The truck went into second gear, gathered speed, and went away.

"I thought he was coming in," said Mr. Pritchard.

"He likes raspberry pie," said Juan. "He always stops when we got some. I just told him we haven't got any."

Mildred was looking at Juan, fascinated. There was something in this dark man with his strange warm eyes that moved her. She felt drawn to him. She wanted to attract his attention, his special attention, to herself. She had thrown back her shoulders so that her breasts were lifted.

"Why did you leave Mexico?" she asked, and she took off her glasses so that when he answered he would see her without them. She leaned on the table, and put her forefinger to the corner of her left eye, and pulled the skin and eyelid backward. This changed the focus of her eye. She could see his face more clearly that way. It also gave her eyes a long and languorous shape, and her eyes were beautiful.

"I don't know why I left," Juan said to her. His warm eyes seemed to surround her and to caress her. Mildred felt a little weak and sirupy in the pit of her stomach. "I'll have to stop this," she thought. "This is crazy." A quick and sexual picture had formed in her mind.

Juan said, "People down there, unless they're rich, have to work too hard and for too little money. I guess that's the main reason I left."

"You speak very good English," Bernice Pritchard said as though it were a compliment.

"Why not? My mother was Irish. I got both languages at once."

"Well, are you a Mexican citizen?" Mr. Pritchard asked.

"I guess so," said Juan. "I never did anything about it."

"It's a good idea to take out your first papers," said Mr. Pritchard.

"What for?"

"It's a good idea."

"It doesn't make any difference to the government," said Juan. "They can tax me and draft me."

"It's still a pretty good idea," said Mr. Pritchard.

Juan's eyes were playing with Mildred, touching her breasts and sliding down over her hips. He saw her sigh and arch her back a little, and deep in Juan an imp of hatred stirred. Not strongly because there wasn't much of it in him, but the Indian blood was there, and in the dark past lay the hatred for the *ojos claros*, the light eyes, the blonds. It was a hatred and a fear of a complexion. The light-eyed people who had for centuries taken the best land, the best horses, the best women. Juan felt the stirring like a little heat lightning, and he felt a glow of pleasure knowing that he could take this girl and twist her and outrage her if he wanted to. He could disturb her and seduce her mentally, and physically too, and then throw her away. The cruelty stirred and he let it mount in him. His voice grew softer and more rich. He spoke directly into Mildred's violet eyes.

"My country," he said, "even if I don't live there, it is in my heart." He laughed inside at this, but Mildred did not laugh. She leaned forward a little and pulled back the corners of both eyes so that she could see his face more clearly.

"I remember things," said Juan. "In the square of my town there were public letter-writers who did all the business for the people who couldn't read or write. They were good men. They had to be. The country people would know if they weren't. They know many things, those people of the hills. And I remember one morning when I was a little boy I was sitting on a bench. There was a fiesta in this town in honor of a saint. The church was full of flowers and there were candy stands and a ferris-wheel and a little merry-go-round. And all night the people shot off skyrockets to the saint. In the park an Indian came to the letter-writer and said, 'I want you to write a letter to my patron. I will tell you what to say and you will put it in good and beautiful form so he will not find me discourteous.' 'Is it a long letter?' the man asked. 'I don't know,' said the Indian. 'That will be one peso,' said the man. And the little Indian paid him, and he said, 'I want you to say to my patron that I cannot go back to my town and my fields for I have seen great beauty and I must stay behind. Tell him I am sorry and I do not wish to give him pain, nor my friends, either, but I could not go back. I am different and my friends would not know me. I would be unhappy in the field and restless. And because I would be different my friends would reject me and hate me. I have seen the stars. Tell him that. And tell him to give my chair to my friend brother and my pig with the two little ones to the old woman who sat with me in fever. My pots to my brother-in-law, and tell the patron to go with God, with loveliness. Tell him that.'"

Juan paused and saw that Mildred's lips were open a little, and he saw that she was taking his story as an allegory for herself.

"What had happened to him?" she asked.

"Why, he had seen the merry-go-round," said Juan. "He couldn't leave it. He slept beside it, and pretty soon his money was gone and he was starving, and then the owner let him turn the crank that ran the merry-go-round and fed him. He couldn't ever leave. He loved the merry-go-round. Maybe he's still there." Juan had become foreign in the telling. A trifle of accent had come into his speech.

Mildred sighed deeply. Mr. Pritchard said, "Let me get this straight. He gave away his land and all his property and he never went home because he saw a merry-go-round?"

"He didn't even own his land," said Juan. "Little Indians never own their land. But he gave away everything else he had."

Mildred glared at her father. This was one of the times when she found him stupid to the point of nausea. Why couldn't he see the beauty in this story? Her eyes went back to Juan to tell him silently that she understood, and she thought she saw something in his face that had not been there before. She thought there was a cruel, leering triumph in his face, but it was probably her eyes, she thought. Her damnable eyes that couldn't see very well. But what she saw was a shock to her. She looked quickly at her mother and then at her father to see whether they had noticed anything, but they were regarding Juan vacantly.

Her father was saying in his slow and, to Mildred, maddening way, "I can understand how he would think it was fine if he had never seen a merry-go-round before, but you get used to anything. A man would get used to a palace in a few days and then he'd want something else."

"It's just a story," Mildred said with so much fierceness that her father turned surprised eyes on her.

Mildred could almost feel Juan's fingers on her thighs. Her body tingled with desire, aroused and unsatisfied. She itched with a pure sexual longing, and her anger arose against her father as though she had been interrupted in the midst of connection. She put on her glasses, looked quickly at Juan and then away, for his eyes were veiled although he looked at all of them. He was enjoying a kind of triumph. He was laughing at her and also at the thing her father and mother did not know was happening. And suddenly her desire hardened into a knot in her stomach and her stomach ached and she felt a revulsion. She thought she would be sick.

Ernest Horton said, "I always intended to get down Mexico way. Thought I might ask the head office about it some time. Might make some pretty valuable contacts down there. Like these fiestas they have. They sell novelties, don't they?"

"Sure," said Juan. "They sell little rosaries and holy pictures and candles and things like that, candy and ice cream."

"Well, if a guy went down and got a line on that stuff, why, we could probably turn it out a lot cheaper than they can. We could stamp out those rosaries—well, nice ones—out of pot metal. And skyrockets. My company supplies some of the biggest celebrations, all kinds of fireworks. It's an idea. I think I'll write a letter."

Juan looked at the increasing pile of dirty dishes in the sink. He stared over his shoulder at the door to the bedroom and then he opened the door and looked in. The bed was empty. Alice had got up, but the bathroom door was shut. Juan came back and began to scrub the dirty dishes in the sink.

The sky was clearing fast now, and the clean yellow sun was shining on the washed land. The young leaves of the oaks were almost yellow in the new light. The green fields looked incredibly young.

Juan smiled shortly. He cut two slices of bread.

"I think I'll walk around a little bit," said Mr. Pritchard. "Want to come, dear?" he asked his wife. She looked quickly at the bedroom door.

"Pretty soon," she said, and he understood her.

"Well, I'll just go outside," he said.

SIX

After Juan left her Alice lay a long time on her back with her arms crossed over her face. Her sobbing stopped gradually, like a child's. She could hear the murmuring talk out in the lunchroom. The inside of her arm was warm and wet over her eyes. She was flooded with a kind of comfort, and the release from tension was as though a tight mesh had been loosened from her body. As she lay in relaxed comfort, her mind jumped back to what had happened. She didn't remember the woman who had screamed at Norma. The morning was beginning to be hazy to her. She had not yet found her own rationalization for her action. Now that she thought of it, she knew she had not really suspected Norma of misconduct, and if she had she really wouldn't have cared very much. She did not love Norma. She didn't care a thing for Norma. Poor little washed-out cat.

When Norma had come to work, Alice, of course, put her senses on the girl and on Juan like a stethoscope, and when she had found no reaction on Juan's part, no quickening, no little creeping and trailing with the eye, Alice had lost interest in Norma except as an organism for carrying coffee and washing dishes. Alice was not very aware of things or people if they did not in some way either augment or take away from her immediate life. And now, as she lay relaxed and warm and quiet, her mind began to work and terror came with her thoughts.

She went back over the scene. Her terror grew out of Juan's gentleness. He should have hit her. His failure to do so worried her. Maybe he didn't care about her any more. Casual kindness in a man she had found to be the preliminary to a brush-off. She tried to remember what the Pritchard women looked like, and she tried to remember whether Juan had looked with warmth on either of them. She knew Juan. His eyes heated up like a stove when his interest was aroused. Then, with a little shock, she remembered that he had given up their bed to the Pritchards. She could smell the lavender on the bedclothes right now. A hatred and a distaste for that odor came to her.

She listened to the murmur of voices through the door. Juan was feeding them. He wouldn't have done it if he hadn't been interested. Juan would say the hell with it and go on out to work on the bus. A restless fear arose in Alice. She had mistreated Norma. That was easy. With Norma's kind you showed weakness, and Norma would melt and run down over herself. Take a girl like that, why, she had so little love that even a stink of it on a wind would knock her ass over teacup. Alice was contemptuous of this starvation for love. She could not tie her own up with Norma's. Alice was big in herself and everyone else was very little, everyone, that is, except Juan. But, then, he was an extension of herself. She thought it might be just as well to put Norma on her feet before anything else. She needed Norma to run the lunchroom, because Alice intended to get drunk just as soon as Juan went away in the bus. She would tell him when he came back that she had a toothache that was killing her.

She didn't do it very often, but she looked forward to it now. And if she

was going to do it, she'd better begin covering her tracks. Juan didn't like
drunk women. She uncrossed her arms from over her face. Her eyes were
sunken from the pressure and it took a moment to get them to track. She
saw how the sun was flooding sweetly over the green plain behind the bedroom, and how it flowed over the rising hills far to the west. A sweet day.

She struggled her body upright and went to the bathroom. There she
dampened one end of a bath towel in cold water and patted it against her
face to take out the creases where her arms had pressed down against her
plump cheeks. She rubbed the end of the towel around her face and over
her nose and along the edge of her hairline. A brassière strap was broken.
She slipped open her dress and found that the little safety pin that held it
was still there, so she pinned the strap to the brassière again. It was a little
tight but she'd sew it after Juan had gone. She wouldn't, of course. When
enough of the strap was broken she'd buy a new brassière.

Alice brushed her hair and put on lipstick. Her eyes were still red. She
put some eyedrops in the corners with a medicine dropper and rubbed the
lids against her eyeballs with her fingers. For a moment she inspected herself in the medicine-chest mirror and then went out. She slipped off her
wrinkled dress and put on a clean print.

Quickly she crossed the bedroom to Norma's door and knocked softly.
There was no answer. She knocked again. From inside the room came a
rustling of paper. Norma came to the door and opened it. Her eyes were
glazed, and she seemed to have been just awakened. In her hand she held the
stub pencil she had used for the eyebrows earlier.

When she saw Alice a look of alarm came upon her face. "I didn't do
nothing wrong with that fellow," she said quickly.

Alice stepped into the room. She knew how to handle the Normas when
she had her wits. "I know you didn't, honey," Alice said. She cast down her
eyes as though she were ashamed. She knew how to handle girls.

"Well, you shouldn't of said it. Suppose somebody heard it and believed
it? I'm not that kind. I'm just trying to make my living and no trouble."
Her eyes suddenly swam in tears of self-pity.

Alice said, "I shouldn't of done it but I just felt so bad. It's my time of
the month. You know yourself how miserable you feel. Sometimes you go
kind of crazy."

Norma inspected her with interest. This was the first time she'd ever
found softness in Alice. This was the first time that Alice had ever needed
to enlist Norma. She didn't like women and girls. There was a streak of
cruelty in Alice toward other women, and when she saw Norma's eyes
brim with tears of sympathy she felt triumphant.

"You know how it is," Alice said. "You just get a little crazy."

"I know," said Norma. Soft tentacles of warmth stretched out from her.
She ached for love, for association, for some human being in the world to

be friendly with. "I know," she said again, and she felt older and stronger than Alice and a little protective too, which was what Alice wanted.

Alice had seen the pencil in her hand. "Maybe you had better come out now and help. Mr. Chicoy's doing it all alone."

"I will in just a moment," said Norma.

Alice closed the door and listened. There was a pause, a slipping sound, and then the sharp sound of the bureau drawer closing. Alice pushed back her hair with her hand and walked softly toward the door into the lunchroom. She felt fine. She had gathered a great deal of information about Norma. She knew how Norma felt about things. She knew where Norma had put the letter.

Alice had tried to get into Norma's suitcase before but it was always locked, and while she could have taken it apart with her fingers—it was only cardboard—the marks would have showed tampering. She would wait. Sooner or later, if she was careful, Norma would neglect to lock her suitcase. Alice was clever, but she didn't know that Norma was clever too. Norma had worked for Alices before. When Alice went through Norma's dresser drawers and looked at her things and read the letters from her sister, she didn't notice the paper match carelessly lying on the drawer's edge. Norma always put it there, and when it was displaced she knew someone had been going through her things. She knew it couldn't be Juan or Pimples, so it must be Alice.

Norma was not likely to leave her suitcase unlocked. For all her dreams Norma was not stupid. In a toothpaste box in her locked suitcase there was twenty-seven dollars. When she had fifty dollars Norma would go to Hollywood and get a job in a restaurant and wait her chance. The fifty dollars would rent her a room for two months. Food she would get where she worked. Her high, long-legged dreams were one thing, but she could take care of herself too. Norma was no fool. True, she didn't understand Alice's hatred of all women. She didn't know that this apology was a trick. But she would probably find it out in time to save herself. And while Norma believed that only the best and most noble thoughts and impulses resided in Clark Gable, she had a knowledge of and a lack of respect for the impulses of the people she met and came in contact with in everyday life.

When Pimples came scratching softly at her window at night she knew how to take care of that. She locked her window. He wouldn't dare make too much noise trying to get in for fear Juan in the next room would hear him. Norma was nobody's fool.

Now Alice stood in front of the door between the bedroom and the lunchroom. She ran her finger down either side of her nose and then she opened the door and went behind the counter as though nothing at all had happened.

SEVEN

The big and beautiful Greyhound bus was pulled in under the loading shed at San Ysidro. Helpers put gasoline into the tank and checked the oil and the tires automatically. The whole system worked smoothly. A colored man cleaned between the seats, brushing the cushions and picking up gum wrappers and matches and cigarette butts from the floor. He ran his fingers behind the last seat, which stretched across the rear. Sometimes he found coins or pocketknives behind this seat. Loose money he kept, but most other articles he turned in to the office. People made an awful stink about things they left, but not about small change. Sometimes the swamper managed as much as a couple of dollars behind that seat. Today he had dug out two dimes, a fifty-cent piece, and a hip-pocket wallet with a draft card, driver's license, and a Lions Club membership card.

He glanced inside the bill section. Two fifty-dollar bills and a certified check for five-hundred dollars. He put the wallet in his shirt pocket and brushed the seat with his whisk broom. He breathed a little hard. The money was easy. He could take it out and leave the wallet behind the seat for some other swamper to find down the line. The check would be left too. There was too much danger in checks. But those two sweet fifties—those sweet, sweet fifties! His throat was tight and would be until he got those sweet fifties out and the wallet behind the seat.

But he couldn't get to them because the punk kid was washing the outside of the windows where they were splashed with dirty mist from the highway. The swamper had to wait. If they caught him they'd put him away.

There was a little rip in the cuff of his blue serge trousers. He figured he would slip those two sweet fifties in there, inside the cuff, before he got off the bus. Then he'd get sick before he went off the job. He'd be sick, all right. Like enough he wouldn't be back for a week. If he got sick on the job and still stayed out the day till quitting time, they wouldn't figure anything if he didn't show up for a few days and it would save his job. He heard a step on the bus and stiffened a little. Louie, the driver, looked in.

"Hi, George," he said. "Say, did you find a wallet? Guy says he lost it."

George mumbled.

"Well, I'll come back and look," said Louie.

George swung around, still on his knees. "I found it," he said. "I was going to turn it in as soon as I finished."

"Yeah?" said Louie. He took the wallet from George's hand and opened it. The punk kid looked in through the window. Louie smiled sorrowfully at George and flicked his eyes toward the punk.

"Too bad, George," Louie said. "I guess they've got 'em stacked against us. Two fifties the guy said and two fifties it is." He pulled out the bills and the check so the punk looking through the window could see them. "Better luck next time, George," Louie said.

"Suppose the guy pays a reward," said George.

"You'll get half," said Louie. "If it's under a buck, you'll get it all."

Louie moved out of the bus and into the waiting room. He handed the wallet in at the desk.

"George found it. He was just bringing it in," said Louie. "That's a good nigger."

Louie knew the wallet's owner was right beside him so he said to the cashier, "If it was me that lost this, I'd give George a nice little present. Nothing don't turn a guy bad like no appreciation. I remember a guy found a grand and he turned it in and he didn't even get a thank-you. The next thing you know he robbed a bank and killed a coupla guards." Louie lied easily and without strain.

"How many going south?" Louie asked.

"You're full up," said the clerk. "You got one for Rebel Corners, and don't forget the pies like you did last week. I never had so much trouble with fifty pies in my life. Here's your wallet, sir. Will you inspect it to see if it's all right?"

The owner paid a five-dollar reward. Louie figured to give George a buck sometime. He knew George wouldn't believe him, but what the hell. It was a stinker's game and a muddy track. Everybody had to take his chance. Louie was big, a little on the stout side, but a dresser. His party friends called him "meat-face." He had a fast line and was smart and liked to be known as a horse player. He called race horses dogs and spoke of all situations as parlays. He would have liked to be Bob Hope or, better, Bing Crosby.

Louie saw George looking in from the loading platform doors. An impulse of generosity seized him. He walked over and gave George a dollar bill. "Cheap son of a bitch!" he said. "Here, you take the buck. Over five-hundred dollars he gets back and he puts out a buck!"

George looked into Louie's face, just one quick, brown flash of the eyes. He knew it was a lie and he knew there wasn't anything he could do about it. If Louie was mad at him he could make it tough. And George had wanted that drunk. He had almost felt the liquor take hold of him. If only that punk kid had kept his big nose out of it.

"Thanks," said George.

The kid went by with his bucket and sponge. George said, "You call those windows clean?" And Louie made it up to George. He said to the kid, "You want to get any place, you better get on the ball. Those windows stink. Do them again."

"I ain't taking orders from you. I'll wait till I get some kind of complaints from the super."

Louie and George exchanged glances. It was just a punk. In less than a week he'd be out on his ass if Louie thought of it.

The big Greyhounds came in and out of the covered loading shed heavy and high as houses. The drivers slipped them smoothly and beautifully into place. The station smelled of oil and diesel exhaust fumes and candy bars and a powerful floor cleaner that got in the nose.

Louie went back toward the front. His eyes had caught a girl coming in from the street. She was carrying a suitcase. All in one flash Louie caught her. A dish! A dish like that he wanted to ride in a seat just behind his own raised driver's chair. He could watch her in the rear-view mirror and find out about her. Maybe she lived somewhere on his route. Louie had plenty of adventures that started like this.

The light from the street was behind the girl so he couldn't see her face, but he knew she was a looker. And he didn't know how he knew it. There might have been fifty girls come in with a light behind them. But how did he know this one was a looker? He could see a nice figure and pretty legs. But in some subtle way this girl smelled of sex.

He saw that she had carried her suitcase over to the ticket window so he did not go directly toward her. He went into the washroom. And there he stood at the wash basin and dipped his hands in water and ran them through his hair. From his side pocket he took a little comb and combed his hair back smoothly and patted it behind where the suggestion of a duck tail stood out. And he combed his mustache, not that it needed combing for it was very short. He settled his gray corduroy jacket, tightened the belt, and pulled his stomach in a little bit.

He put the comb back in his pocket and inspected himself again in the mirror. He ran his hand over the sides of his hair. He felt behind to see that no strands were out and that the duck tail was lying down. He straightened his regulation black ready-made bow tie and he took a few grains of sen-sen out of his inner shirt pocket and threw them in his mouth. And then he seemed to shake himself down in his coat.

Just as his right hand went to the brass knob of the washroom door, Louie's left hand flipped fingers up and down his fly to be sure he was buttoned up. He put on his face a little crooked smile, half worldliness and half naïveté, an expression that had been successful with him. Louie had read someplace that if you looked directly into a girl's eyes and smiled it had an effect. You must look at her as though she were not only the most beautiful thing in the world, but you must keep looking into her eyes until she looked away. There was another trick too. If it bothered you to look into people's eyes, you should look at a point on the bridge of the nose right between the eyes. To the person looked at it appeared that you were

ooking into the eyes, only you weren't. Louie had found this a very successful approach.

Nearly all his waking hours Louie thought about girls. He liked to outrage them. He liked to have them fall in love with him and then walk
away. He called them pigs. "I'll get a pig," he would say, "and you get a
pig, and we'll go out on the town."

He stepped through the door of the washroom with a kind of lordliness,
and then had to back up because two men came down between the benches
carrying a long crate with slats to let air in. The side of the crate said in
large white letters MOTHER MAHONEY'S HOME-BAKED PIES. The two men went
in front of Louie and through to the loading platform.

The girl was sitting on a bench now, her suitcase beside her on the floor.
As he moved across the room Louie took a quick look at her legs and then
caught her eyes and held them as he walked. He smiled his crooked smile
and moved toward her. She looked back at him, unsmiling, and then
moved her eyes away.

Louie was disappointed. She hadn't been embarrassed as she should have
been. She had simply lost interest in him. And she was a looker too—fine
well-filled legs with rounded thighs and no stomach whatever and large
breasts which she made the most of. She was a blonde and her hair was
coarse and a little broken at the ends from a too-hot iron, but well-brushed
hair that had good lights in it and a long, curling bob that Louie liked. Her
eyes were made up with blue eyeshadow and some cold cream on the eyelids
and plenty of mascara on the lashes. No rouge, but a splash of lipstick that
was put on to make her mouth look square, like some of the picture stars.
She wore a suit, a tight skirt and a jacket with a round collar. Her shoes
were tan saddle-leather with white stitching. Not only a looker but a dresser.
And the stuff looked good.

Louie studied her face as he walked. He had a feeling that he had seen
her someplace before. But then, she might look like someone he knew, or
he might have seen her in a movie. That had happened. Her eyes were
wide set, almost abnormally wide-set, and they were blue with little brown
specks in them and with strongly marked dark lines from the pupil to the
outer edge of the iris. Her eyebrows were plucked and penciled in a high
arch so that she looked a little surprised. Louie noticed that her gloved
hands were not restless. She was not impatient nor nervous, and this
bothered him. He was afraid of self-possession, and he did feel that he had
seen her somewhere. Her knees were well-covered with flesh, not bony, and
she kept her skirt down without pulling at it.

As he strolled by Louie punished her for looking away from his eyes by
staring at her legs. This usually had the effect of making a girl pull down
her skirt, even if it was not too high, but it hadn't any effect on this girl.
Her failure to react to his art made him uneasy. Probably a hustler, he said

to himself. Probably a two-dollar hustler. And then he laughed at himself. Not two dollars with that stuff she's wearing.

Louie went on to the ticket window and smiled his sardonic smile at Edgar, the ticket clerk. Edgar admired Louie. He wished he could be like him.

"Where's the pig going?" Louie asked.

"Pig?"

"Yeah. The broad. The blonde."

"Oh, yes." Edgar exchanged a secret man-look with Louie. "South," he said.

"In my wagon?"

"Yeah."

Louie tapped the counter with his fingers. He had let the little fingernail on his left hand grow very long. It was curved, like half a tube, and sanded to a shallow point. Louie didn't know why he did this, but he was gratified to notice that some of the other bus drivers were letting their little fingernails grow too. Louie was setting a style and he felt good about it. There was that cab driver who had tied a raccoon's tail on his radiator cap and right overnight everybody had to have a piece of fur flapping in the breeze. Furriers made artificial fox tails, and high-school kids wouldn't be seen in a car without a tail whipping around. And that cab driver could sit back and have the satisfaction of knowing he had started the whole thing. Louie had been letting his little fingernail grow for five months and already he'd seen five or six other people doing it. It might sweep the country, and Louie would have started the whole thing.

He tapped the counter with the long, curved nail, but gently, because when a nail gets that long it breaks easily. Edgar looked at the nail. He kept his left hand below the counter. He was growing one too, but it wasn't very long yet, and he didn't want Louie to see it until it was much longer. Edgar's nails were brittle, and he had to put colorless nail polish on his to keep it from breaking right off. Even in bed it broke once. Edgar glanced toward the girl.

"Figure to make some time with the—pig?"

"No harm trying," said Louie. "Probably a hustler."

"Well, what's wrong with a good hustler?" Edgar's eyes flicked up. The girl had recrossed her legs.

"Louie," he said apologetically, "before I forget, you'd better see to the loading of that crate of pies yourself. We had a complaint last week. Someplace along the line somebody dropped the crate and a raspberry pie got all mixed up with a lemon pie and there was raisins all over hell. We had to pay the claim."

"It never happened on my run," said Louie truculently. "It goes to San Juan, don't it? That jerk line from Rebel Corners done it."

"Well, we paid the claim," said Edgar. "Just kind of check it, will you?"

"There wasn't no pies dropped on my run," Louie said dangerously.

"I know. I know you didn't. But the front office told me to tell you to check it."

"Why don't they come to me?" Louie demanded. "They got complaints, why don't they call me up instead of sending messages?" He tended his anger as he would a fire. But he was angry at the blonde. The god-damned hustler. He looked up at the big clock on the wall. A hand two feet long jerked seconds around the dial, and in the reflection of the glass Louie could see the girl sitting with crossed legs. Although he couldn't be sure because of the curve of the glass, he thought she was looking at the back of his head. His anger melted away.

"I'll check the pies," he said. "Tell them there won't be any raspberries in the lemon pie. I guess I'll make a little time with the pig." He saw the admiration in Edgar's eyes as he turned slowly and faced the waiting room.

He was right. She had been looking at the back of his head, and when he was turned she was looking in his face. There was no interest, no nothing, in her glance. But she had beautiful eyes, he thought. God-damn, she was a looker! Louie had read in a magazine that wide-set eyes meant sexiness, and there was no doubt that this girl put out a strong, strong feeling of sex. She was the kind of girl everybody watched walk by. Why, she walked in a place and everybody turned and looked at her. You could see their heads turn, like watching a horse race. It was something about her, and it wasn't make-up and it wasn't the way she walked, although that was part of it too. Whatever it was, it projected all around her. Louie had felt it when she came in from the street and the light was behind her so he couldn't really see her then. And now she was looking in Louie's face, not smiling, not putting out anything, just looking, and he still felt it. A tightness came into his throat and a little flush rose out of his collar. He knew that in a moment his glance would slide away. Edgar was waiting, and Edgar had faith in Louie.

There were a few lies in Louie's reputation but actually he did have a way, he did make time with pigs. Only now he wasn't easy. This pig was getting him down. He wanted to slap her face with his open hand. His breath was rising painfully in his chest. The moment was going to be over unless he did something. He could see the dark raylike lines in her irises and the fullness of her jowls. He put on his embracing look. His eyes widened a little and he smiled as though he had suddenly recognized her. At the same time he moved toward her.

Carefully he made his smile a little respectful. Her eyes held onto his, and a little of the coldness went out of them. He stepped near to her. "Man says you're going south on my bus, ma'am," he said. He almost laughed at that "ma'am," but it usually worked. It worked with this girl. She smiled a little.

"I'll take care of your bag," Louie went on. "We leave in about three minutes."

"Thanks," said the girl. Her voice was throaty and sexy, Louie thought.

"Let me take your suitcase. I'll put it on now and then you'll have a seat."

"It's heavy," said the girl.

"I ain't exactly a midget," said Louie. He picked up her suitcase and walked quickly out to the loading platform. He climbed into the bus and put the suitcase down in front of the seat that was right behind his seat. He could watch the girl in his mirror and he could talk to her some when they got rolling. He came out of the bus and saw the punk and another swamper putting the crate of pies on top of the bus.

"Careful of that stuff," Louie said loudly. "You bastards dropped one last week and I got the beef."

"I never dropped nothing," said the punk.

"The hell you didn't," said Louie. "You watch your step." He went through the swinging doors to the waiting room.

"What's eating him?" the other swamper asked.

"Oh, I sort of jammed him up," said the punk. "The nigger found a wallet and I seen it, so they figured they got to turn it in. It was a big roll of jack too. They're both sore at me 'cause I seen it. Louie and that nigger was gonna split them up a coupla half centuries and I guess I jammed it for 'em. Course they had to turn it in when they seen I saw 'em."

"I could use some of that," said the swamper.

"Who couldn't," said the punk.

"I can take me a century and I can go out and I can get very nice stuff for that there." They went on for a time with ritual talk.

In the waiting room there was a little burst of activity. The crowd for the southbound bus was beginning to collect. Edgar was busy behind his counter, but not too busy to keep his eye on the girl. "A pig," he said under his breath. It was a new word to him. From now on he would use it. He glanced at the little fingernail on his left hand. It would be long before he would have as good a one as Louie's. But why kid himself? He couldn't make time like Louie anyway. He always ended up by going down the line.

There was a last-minute flurry of customers at the candy counter, at the peanut vending machines, at the gum dispensers. A Chinaman bought copies of Time and Newsweek and rolled them carefully together and put them in his black broadcloth overcoat pocket. And old lady restlessly turned over magazines on the newsstand without any intention of buying one. Two Hindus with gleaming white turbans and shining black curly beards stood side by side at the ticket window. They glanced fiercely about as they tried to make themselves understood.

Louie stood by the entrance to the loading platform and glanced continually at the girl. He noticed that every man in the room was doing the same thing. All of them were watching her secretly, and they didn't want to get caught at it. He turned and looked through the swinging glass doors and saw that the punk and the swamper had got the crate of pies safely on top of the bus and the tarpaulin pulled down over it. The light in the waiting room dimmed to dusk. A cloud must have covered the sun. And then the light rose again as though controlled by a rheostat. The big bell over the glass doors clamored. Louie looked at his watch and went through the door to his big bus. And the passengers in the waiting room got up and shuffled toward the door.

Edgar was still trying to make out where the Hindus wanted to go. "The god-damned rag heads," he said to himself. "Why'nt they learn English before they start running around?"

Louie climbed into the high seat enclosed by a stainless steel bar and glanced at the tickets as the passengers got on. The Chinaman in the dark coat went directly to the back seat, took off his coat, and laid the *Time* and *Newsweek* in his lap. The old lady clambered breathlessly up the step and sat down in the seat directly behind Louie.

He said, "I'm sorry, ma'am, that seat's taken."

"What do you mean, taken?" she said belligerently. "There aren't any reserved seats."

"That seat's taken, ma'am," Louie repeated. "Don't you see the suitcase beside it?" He hated old women. They frightened him. There was a smell about them that gave him the willies. They were fierce and they had no pride. They never gave a damn about making a scene. They got what they wanted. Louie's grandmother had been a tyrant. She had got whatever she wanted by being fierce. From the corners of his eyes he saw the girl on the lower step of the bus, waiting behind the Hindus to get in. He was pushed into a spot. Suddenly he was angry.

"Ma'am," he said, "I'm the boss on my bus. There's plenty of good seats. Now will you move back?"

The old woman set her chin and scowled at him. She switched her behind a little, settling into the seat. "You've got that girl in this seat, that's what you've got," she said. "I've got a mind to report you to the management."

Louie blew up. "All right, ma'am. You just get out and report me. The company's got lots of passengers, but it hasn't got many good drivers." He saw that the girl was listening, and he felt pretty good about it.

The old woman saw that he was angry. "I'm going to report you," she said.

"Well, report me then. You can get off the bus," Louie said loudly, "but you're not going to sit in that seat. The passenger in that seat got a doctor's order."

It was an out, and the old woman took it. "Why didn't you say so?" she said. "I'm not unreasonable. But I'm still going to report you for discourtesy."

"All right, ma'am," Louie said wearily. "That I'm used to."

The old woman moved back one seat.

"Going to hang out her big ear and catch me off base," Louie thought. "Well, let her. We got more passengers than drivers." The girl was beside him now, holding out her ticket. Involuntarily Louie said, "You only going as far as the Corners?"

"I know, I've got to change," said the girl. She smiled at his tone of disappointment.

"That's your seat right there," he said. He watched the mirror while she sat down and crossed her legs and pulled down her skirt and put her purse beside her. She straightened her shoulders and fixed the collar of her suit.

She knew Louie was watching every move. It had always been that way with her. She knew she was different from other girls, but she didn't quite know how. In some ways it was nice always to get the best seat, to have your lunches bought for you, to have a hand on your arm crossing the street. Men couldn't keep their hands off her. But there was always the trouble. She had to argue or cajole or insult or fight her way out. All men wanted the same thing from her, and that was just the way it was. She took it for granted and it was true.

When she'd been young she'd suffered from it. There had been a sense of guilt and of nastiness. But now she was older she just accepted it and developed her techniques. Sometimes she gave in and sometimes she got money or clothes. She knew most of the approaches. She could probably have foretold everything Louie would do or say in the next half hour. By anticipating, she could sometimes stave off unpleasantness. Older men wanted to help her, put her in school or on the stage. Some young men wanted to marry her or protect her. And a few, a very few, openly and honestly simply wanted to go to bed with her and told her so.

These were the easiest because she could say yes or no and get it over with. What she hated most about her gift, or her failing, was the fighting that went on. Men fought each other viciously when she was about. They fought like terriers, and she sometimes wished that women could like her, but they didn't. And she was intelligent. She knew why, but there wasn't anything she could do about it. What she really wanted was a nice house in a nice town, two children, and a stairway to stand on. She would be nicely dressed and people would be coming to dinner. She'd have a husband, of course, but she couldn't see him in her picture because the advertising in the women's magazines from which her dream came never included a man. Just a lovely woman in nice clothes coming down the stairs and guests in the dining room and candles and a dark wood dining table and clean children to kiss good night. That's what she really wanted. And she knew as well as anything that that was not what she would ever get.

There was a great deal of sadness in her. She wondered about other women. Were they different in bed than she was? She knew from watching that men didn't react to most women the way they did to her. Her sexual impulses were not terribly strong nor very constant, but she didn't know about other women. They never discussed this kind of thing with her. They didn't like her. Once the young doctor to whom she had gone to try to have the pain of her periods relaxed had made a pass at her, and when she had talked him out of that he had told her, "You just put it out in the air. I don't know how, but you do it. Some women are like that," he said. "Thank God there aren't many of them or a man would go nuts."

She tried wearing severe clothes, but that didn't help much. She couldn't keep an ordinary job. She learned to type, but offices went to pieces when she was hired. And now she had a racket. It paid well and it didn't get her in much trouble. She took off her clothes at stags. A regular agency handled her. She didn't understand stags or what satisfaction the men got out of them, but there they were, and she made fifty dollars for taking off her clothes and that was better than having them torn off in an office. She'd even read up on nymphomania, enough, anyway, to know that she didn't have it. She almost wished she had. Sometimes she thought she'd just go into a house and make a pile of dough and retire to the country—that, or marry an elderly man she could control. It would be the easiest way. Young men who were attractive to her had a way of turning nasty. They always suspected her of cheating them. They either sulked or tried to beat her up or they got furious and threw her out.

She'd tried being kept and that was the way it ended. But an old man with some money—that might be the way. And she would be good to him. She'd really make it worth his money and his time. She had only two girl friends, and both of them were house girls. They seemed to be the only kind who weren't jealous of her and who didn't resent her. But one was out of the country now. She didn't know where. She followed troops somewhere. And the other was living with an advertising man and didn't want her around.

That was Loraine. They had had an apartment together. Loraine didn't care much about men; still, she didn't go for women. But then Loraine got caught short with this advertising man and asked her to move out. Loraine explained everything when she told her not to come around.

Loraine was working in a house and this advertising man fell for her. Well, Loraine had got gonorrhea, and before she even had a symptom she gave it to this advertising man. He was a nervous type and he blew his top and lost his job and came bellyaching to Loraine. She felt responsible in a way so she took him in and fed him while they both got cured. That was before the new treatment, and it had been pretty rough.

And then this advertising man went on a sleeping-pill pitch. She'd find him passed out and he was pretty vague, and his temper was bad unless he had his pills, and he took more and more of them. Twice Loraine had to have him pumped out.

Loraine was a really good girl and things were hard because she couldn't work in the house until she was cleared up. She didn't want to infect anybody she knew, and still she had to have money for doctor's bills and rent and food. She had to work the streets in Glendale to make it, and she wasn't feeling good herself. And then, with everything else, the advertising man turned jealous and didn't want her to work at all in spite of the fact that he didn't have a job. It would be nice if the whole thing had blown over by now and she and Loraine could have the apartment together. They had been a good pair together. They had had fun, good, quiet fun.

There had been a whole series of conventions in Chicago and she had saved some money from the stags. She was taking busses back to Los Angeles to save money. She wanted to live quietly a while. She hadn't heard from Loraine for a long time. The last letter said this advertising man was reading her mail so not to write.

The last passengers were coming through the doors and getting into the bus.

Louie had his legs crossed. He was a little timid with this girl. "I see you're going to L. A.," he said. "Do you live there?"

"Part of the time."

"I like to try and figure people out," he said. "A guy like me sees so many people."

The motor of the bus breathed softly. The old woman was glaring at Louie. He could see her in the mirror. She would probably write a letter to the company.

"Well," Louie said to himself, "the hell with the company." He could always get a job. The company didn't pay much attention to old ladies' letters anyway. He glanced back down the bus. It looked like the two Hindus were holding hands. The Chinaman had both *Time* and *Newsweek* open on his lap and he was comparing stories. His head swung from one magazine to the other, and a puzzled wrinkle marked his nose between his brows. The dispatcher waved at Louie.

Louie swung the lever that closed the door. He eased his gear into compound-reverse and crept out of the concrete slip, then swung delicately and wide so that his front fender cleared the north wall by a part of an inch. He swung wide again in compound-low and cleared the other side of the alley by a fraction of an inch. At the entrance to the street from the alley he stopped and saw that the street was clear for him. He turned the bus and it took him over to the other side of the street. Louie was a good driver with a perfect record. The bus moved down the main street of San Ysidro and came to the outskirts and to the open highway.

The sky and the sun were washed and clean. The colors were sharp. The ditches ran full of water; and in some places, where the ditches were clogged, the water extended out onto the highway. The bus hit this water with a great swish, and Louie could feel the tug at the wheel. The grass was matted down from the force of the rain, but now the warmth of the sun was putting strength into the rich grass and it was beginning to rise up again on the high places.

Louie glanced in the rear-view mirror at the girl again. She was looking at the back of his head. But something made her look up at the mirror and right into Louie's eyes, and the eyes with their dark lines and the straight, pretty nose and the mouth painted on square photographed permanently in Louie's brain. When she looked into his eyes she smiled as though she felt good.

Louie knew that his throat was closing, and a rising pressure was in his chest. He thought he must be nuts. He knew he was shy, but mostly he convinced himself that he was not, and he was going through all the symptoms of a sixteen-year-old. His eyes flicked from road to mirror, back and forth. He could see that his cheeks were red. "What the hell is this?" he said to himself. "Am I going to go ga-ga over a chippie?" He looked at her more closely to find some thought to save himself, and then he saw deep forceps marks along her jaws. That made him feel more comfortable. She wouldn't be so god-damned confident if she knew he saw the forceps marks. Forty-two miles. The figures came into his head. She'd get off in forty-two miles. Louie would have to make time. He couldn't waste a minute if he wanted to throw a line over this little hustler. And when he tried to speak his voice was hoarse.

She leaned close behind him. "I couldn't hear you," she said.

Louie coughed. "I said the country looks nice after the rain."

"Yes, it does."

He tried to get back to his usual opening. He noticed in the mirror that she was still leaning forward to listen.

"Like I said," he began, "I try to figure people out. I'd say you was in the movies or on the stage."

"No," said the girl. "You'd be wrong."

"Aren't you in show business?"

"No."

"Well, do you work?"

She laughed, and her face was very charming when she laughed. But Louie noticed that one of her upper front teeth was crooked. It leaned over and interfered with its neighbor. Her laughter stopped and her upper lip covered the tooth. "Conscious of it," Louie thought.

She was ahead of him. She knew what he was going to say. It had happened so many times before. He was going to try to find out where she lived. He wanted her telephone number. It was simple. She didn't live

anywhere. She had a trunk stored with Loraine with some books in it—
Captain Hornblower, and a *Life of Beethoven,* and some paper books of
the short stories of Saroyan, and some old evening dresses to be made over.
She knew Louie was having trouble. She knew that blush that rose out of a
man's collar and the thickness of labored speech. She saw Louie glance apprehensively in the mirror at the rear of the bus.

The Hindus were smiling a little at each other. The Chinaman was
staring up in the air, trying to work up in his mind some discrepancy in
the stories he had been reading. A Greek in the rear seat was cutting an
Italian cigar in two with a pocketknife. He put one piece in his mouth and
thoughtfully placed the other half in his breast pocket. The old woman was
working herself up into a rage at Louie. She directed an iron look at the
back of his head, and her chin quivered with fury and her lips were white
with the tension of their compression.

The girl leaned forward again. "I'll save you time," she said. "I'm a dental
nurse. You know, I do all those things in a dentist's office." She often used
this. She didn't know why. Perhaps because it stopped speculation and
there were never any more questions after she said it. People didn't want to
talk much about dentistry.

Louie digested this. The bus came to a railroad crossing. Automatically
Louie set his air brakes and stopped. The brakes hissed as he released them
and went through the gears to cruising speed again. He sensed that things
were closing in on him. The old bitch was going to start trouble any minute
now. He didn't have forty-two miles at all. Once the old bitch put in her
oar the thing would be over. He wanted to make time while he could, but
it was too soon according to Louie's methods. He shouldn't make a play
for a good half hour, but the old bitch was going to force his hand.

"Sometimes I get into L. A.," he said. "Is there someplace I could call you
and maybe we could—have dinner and go to a show?"

She was friendly about it. There wasn't anything mean or bitchy about
her. She said, "I don't know. You see, I haven't any place to live now. I've
been away. I want to get an apartment as soon as I can."

"But you work someplace," said Louie. "Maybe I could call you there."

The old woman was squirming and twitching in her seat. She was mad
because Louie had kicked her out of the front seat.

"Well, no," said the girl. "You see, I haven't got a job. Of course, I'll get
one right away because you can always get a job in my profession."

"This isn't a brush-off?" Louie asked.

"No."

"Well, maybe you could drop me a line when you get settled."

"Maybe."

"Because I'd like to know someone to take out in L. A."

And now here it came, the voice as shrill as a whetstone. "There's a state
law about talking to passengers. You watch the road." The old woman ad-

dressed the whole bus. "This driver's putting our lives in danger. I'm going to ask to get off if he can't keep his attention on his driving."

Louie closed up. This was serious. She really could make trouble. He looked in the mirror and found the girl's eyes. With his lips he said, "The god-damned dried up old bitch!"

The girl smiled and put her fingers to her lips. In a way she was relieved and in another she was sorry. She knew that sooner or later she would have trouble with Louie. But she also knew that in many ways he was a nice guy and one she could handle up to a certain point. She knew from his blush that she could probably stop him by hurting his feelings.

But it was over and Louie knew it. The girl wasn't going to get herself in a mess. He had to make time while the bus was rolling. He knew that. Once you got to a station the passengers wanted out as quick as possible. Now he'd lost out. At Rebel Corners he would stop only long enough to let her off and unload that god-damned crates of pies. He hunched over the wheel. The girl had folded her hands in her lap and her eyes would not raise to meet his in the mirror. There were lots of girls prettier than this one. Those forceps scars were damned ugly. They'd give a guy the shivers. Of course, she wore her hair long and forward to cover them. A girl like that couldn't wear her hair up. Louie liked hair up and, Jesus! suppose you woke up in bed and saw those scars. There were plenty of pigs in the world and Louie could get along. But in his chest and his stomach there was a weight of sorrow. He fought at it and picked at it but it wouldn't move. He wanted this girl more than he had ever wanted anyone, and in a different way. He felt a dry and grainy sense of loss. He didn't even know her name, and now he wouldn't get to know her. He could see Edgar's eager eyes questioning him when he came back to San Ysidro. Louie wondered if he would lie to Edgar.

The great tires sang on the road, a high, twanging song, and the motor throbbed with a heavy beat. There were big, wet, floppy clouds in the sky, dark as soot in the middle and white and shining on the edges. One of them was creeping up on the sun now. Already, ahead on the highway, Louie could see the shadow of it rushing toward the bus, and far ahead on the highway he could see the towering green mound of the oaks that grew about the lunchroom at Rebel Corners. He was filled with disappointment.

Juan Chicoy came to the side of the bus as it pulled in.

"What you got for me?" he asked as the door opened.

"One passenger and a flock of pies," said Louie. He got up from his seat, reached around, and lifted the girl's suitcase. He climbed down to the ground and held up his hands, and the girl put her hands on his arms and stepped down. They walked toward the lunchroom.

"Good-by," she said.

"Good-by," said Louie. He watched her go through the door, her little behind bobbing up and down.

Juan and Pimples had the crate of pies off the top of the bus. Louie climbed back into the bus.

"So long," said Juan.

The old woman had moved up into the front seat. Louie levered the door shut. He went into gear and moved away. When he was in cruising speed and the tires were ringing on the highway, he looked in the mirror. The old woman wore a look of mean triumph.

"You killed it," Louie said to himself. "Oh, you murdered it."

The woman looked up and caught his eyes in the mirror. Deliberately Louie made silent words with his lips. "You god-damned old bitch!" He saw her lips grow tight and white. She knew what he meant.

The highway sang along ahead of the bus.

EIGHT

Juan and Pimples carried the crate of Mother Mahoney's Home-Baked Pies near to the door of the lunchroom and set it down on the ground. Both of them watched the blonde go through the door. Pimples whistled a low gurgling note. The palms of his hands turned suddenly sweaty. Juan's eyes had lowered until only a little glint of light shone between his lashes. He licked his lips quickly and nervously.

"I know what you mean," said Juan. "Want to take time out and go over and lift your leg on a tree?"

"God Almighty," said Pimples. "Whew!"

"Yeah," said Juan. He bent over, turned the latch on the crate, and raised the hinged side. "I'll take a small bet, Kit."

"What's that?" Pimples asked.

"I bet," said Juan, "I bet two to one you already got in your mind the idea that you didn't have a day off for two weeks and you'd like to take today and ride over to San Juan with me. Maybe it would even help if the bus breaks down again."

Pimples started to blush around his eruptions. He raised his eyes uneasily and looked at Juan, and there was so much humor without poison in Juan's eyes that Pimples felt better. "God damn!" he thought, "there is a man. Why'd I ever work for anybody else?"

"Well," Pimples said aloud, and he felt he was talking to a man. Juan understood how a guy looked at things. When a cookie went by, Juan knew how a guy felt. "Well," he said again.

"Well," Juan mimicked him, "and who's gonna take care of the gas pumps and fix the flats?"

"Who done it before?" Pimples asked.

"Nobody," said Juan. "We used to just put a sign on the garage—Closed For Repairs. Alice can pump gas." He slapped Pimples on the shoulder.

"What a guy," Pimples thought. "What a guy!"

The pies were held by little traylike slots which gripped the edges of the pans and left each pie separate from all the others. There were four stacks of twelve pies—forty-eight pies.

"Let's see," said Juan, "we get six raspberry, four lemon cream, four raisin, and two caramel custard cream." He pulled out the pies as he spoke and laid them on top of the crate. "Take them in, Pim—Kit, I mean."

Pimples took a pie in each hand and went into the lunchroom. The blonde was sitting on a stool drinking a cup of coffee. He couldn't see her face but he felt the electricity or whatever it was she had. He put the pies on the counter.

As he turned to go out again he felt the silence in the room.

Mr. Pritchard and the crabby old guy and the young fellow, Horton, were entranced. Their eyes rose and washed the blonde and fell away. Miss Pritchard and her mother looked pointedly at the piles of bran in back of the counter. Alice was not there, but Norma was in front of the blonde, wiping the counter with her rag.

"Like to have a snail?" Norma asked.

Pimples paused. He had to hear the tone of the blonde's voice.

"Yes, I guess so," she said. A quick spasm kinked Pimples' stomach at the throaty tone. He hurried outside and gathered up more pies.

"Get moving," Juan said. "You can look at her all the way over to San Juan, unless you'd rather drive."

Pimples rushed the pies in. Sixteen pies out. That left thirty-two. Juan closed the side of the crate and turned the catch. When Pimples came out the last time he helped Juan put the pie crate in the big black trunk of "Sweetheart," the bus. She was ready now. Ready to go. Juan stood back and looked at her. She was no Greyhound but she wasn't bad. Around the windows a little rust showed through the aluminum paint. He would have to touch that up. And the hub caps could take a new coat too.

"Let's get going," he said to Pimples. "Lock the garage doors. Right between the benches under the radiator hose connections you'll find the sign to put on the door. Jump now if you want to get your clothes changed."

Pimples leaped for the garage door. Juan straightened up and stretched his arms from his sides and moved toward the lunchroom.

Mr. Pritchard's right leg was crossed over his left and his suspended toe made little convulsive jumps. He had glanced into the blonde's face when she came in and now there was a pleasant excitement in him. But he was puzzled. Somewhere, he thought, he had seen this girl. Maybe she'd worked in one of his plants, maybe a secretary, maybe in some friend's office. But he'd seen her. He felt sure he had. He truly believed that he never forgot a face, when the truth was that he rarely remembered one. He didn't look closely at any face unless he planned to do business with its owner. He wondered about the sense of sin he got out of the recognition. Where could he have seen this girl?

His wife was looking secretly at his swinging foot. Ernest Horton was frankly gazing at the blonde's legs. Norma liked the girl. In one respect Norma was like Loraine. She didn't love anyone—well, except one—so she had nothing to be taken away, nothing to lose. And this girl was nice. She was pleasant-spoken and polite. Actually the girl felt good toward Norma too, sensing that this girl could like her.

Just before the Greyhound came in Alice had said to Norma, "Watch the counter, will you? I'll be right back." And then the bus and the blonde and getting the coffee had taken up Norma's thoughts. But now a certain knowledge struck her, made her turn cold and nauseous inside. She knew what was happening as though she could see it. She knew, and knowing, many calculations came into her head around her sick anger. The little roll of money in small bills. That could be used until she could get a job. And why couldn't she go now? She was going to sometime. She opened the cabinets beneath the shelves in back of the lunch counter and shoved the pies in, all except one of each kind. One raspberry, one raisin, one lemon cream, and one caramel custard cream she lined up on the counter, and the smell of them made her sicker. She still didn't quite know what to do.

Juan came through the front door and stood looking at the back of the blonde's head.

Norma said, "Will you watch the counter a minute, Mr. Chicoy?"

"Where's Alice?" Juan asked.

"I don't know," said Norma. She could see Alice in her mind. Alice's eyes weren't so good. She would take the letter to the window and hold it up to the light. She wasn't really interested. It was a casual, vague kind of curiosity. She would lean sideways to the light and her hair would fall in her eyes so she would blow it, and her fingers would scrabble through the pages. Norma shivered. She saw herself hurtling into the room. She saw herself snatch the letter, and her fingers flexed. She felt Alice's skin against her fingernails and her nails striking and clawing for Alice's eyes, those horrible, wet, juicy eyes. Alice would fall on her back and Norma would come down on that great, soft stomach with her knees, and she'd scratch and tear at Alice's face and the blood would run in the scratches.

Juan, looking at Norma, said, "What's the matter? Are you sick?"

"Yes," said Norma.

"Go ahead before you get sick here."

Norma edged down the counter and opened the bedroom door softly. The door to her own room was open just a crack. She closed the door into the lunchroom and moved silently toward her own door. She was cold now and shivering. Cold as ice. Noiselessly she pushed her door open. And there it was—Alice, by the window, holding the letter to Clark Gable up to her eyes and blowing her hair sideways.

Alice blew her hair and looked up and saw Norma standing in the doorway. Her mouth was open, her face avid. She couldn't change her expression. Norma took a step into the room. Her chin was set so hard that the lines receded from her mouth. Alice stupidly held the letter out to her. Norma took it, folded it carefully, and tucked it in her bodice. And then Norma went to her bureau. She drew her suitcase from underneath. She unpinned the key from the inside of her dress and unlocked the suitcase. Heavily she began to pack. She emptied the bureau drawers into the suitcase and pressed the mound of clothes down with her fist. From the closet she dragged out her three dresses and her coat with the rabbit collar and she laid the coat on the bed and rolled the dresses up around the hangers and poked them in the suitcase too.

Alice couldn't move. She watched Norma, her head swinging as the girl passed back and forth. In Norma's brain there was a silent scream of triumph. She was on top. After a life of being pushed around, she was on top and she was silent. She felt good about that. Not one word did she say and not one word would she say. She threw two pairs of shoes into the suitcase and put the lid firmly down and locked it.

"You going right now?" Alice asked.

Norma didn't answer. She wouldn't break her triumph. Nothing could force her.

"I didn't mean to do anything wrong," Alice said.

Norma didn't look up.

"You'd better not tell or I'll fix you," Alice suggested uneasily. Still Norma did not speak. She went to the bed and got her black coat with the rabbit collar. Then she picked up her suitcase and walked out of the room. Her breath was whistling in her nose. She went in back of the lunch counter and pushed the "No Sale" button on the cash register. Norma took out ten dollars, a five and four ones and a half and two quarters. She shoved the money in the side pocket of her black coat. Her weak mouth was set in a hard line.

Juan said, "What's going on here?"

"I'm going to San Juan with you," said Norma.

"You've got to help Alice," said Juan. "She can't stay here alone."

"I've quit," said Norma. She saw that the blonde watched her as she came around the edge of the counter. Norma went out the screen door. She carried her suitcase to the bus and she climbed in and took a seat toward the rear. She stood her suitcase up on its end beside her. She sat very straight.

Juan watched her go out of the door. He shrugged his shoulders. "What do you suppose that was?" he asked of no one in particular.

Ernest Horton was scowling. He hated Alice Chicoy. He said, "What time you think we'll get started?"

"Ten-thirty," said Juan. "It's ten-ten now." He glanced at the Pritchards. "Look, I've got to change my clothes. If you folks want coffee or anything, just come back here and get it."

He went into the bedroom. He slipped the shoulder straps of his overalls and let the pants fall down around his shoes. He had on shorts with narrow blue stripes. He peeled his blue chambray shirt over his head and kicked off his moccasins and stepped out of the overalls, leaving shoes and socks and overalls in a pile on the floor. His body was hard and brown, colored not by the sun but by brown ancestry. He moved over to the bathroom and knocked on the door. Alice flushed the toilet and opened the door. She had been washing her face again and a wet strand of hair was plastered to her cheek. Her mouth was lax and her eyes were swollen and red.

"What's going on?" Juan asked. "You're having one hell of a time for yourself, aren't you?"

"I've got a toothache," Alice said. "I can't help it. I've got a jumping pain right here."

"What's the matter with Norma?" Juan asked.

"Let her go," Alice said. "I knew I'd catch up with her sometimes."

"Well, what did she do?"

"She's just a little light-fingered," said Alice.

"What did she take?"

"Just thought I'd see. Remember that bottle of Bellodgia you gave me for Christmas? Well, it was gone and I found it in her suitcase. She came in when I found it and she got huffy and I told her she could go."

Juan's eyes veiled. He knew it was a lie, but he didn't much care what the truth was. Women fights didn't interest him at all. He got in the tub and pulled the shower curtain about him.

"You've been a mess all morning," he said. "What's the matter with you?"

"Well, it's my time," said Alice, "and then this toothache."

Juan knew the first was not true. But he only suspected the second could be false. "Take yourself a slug of liquor when we go. That'll be good for both ends," he said.

Alice was pleased. She wanted him to suggest it.

"You've got to take care of everything," Juan went on. "Pimples is going along with me today."

Excitement surged in Alice. She would be alone, all by herself. But she couldn't let Juan know that was what she wanted. "What's Pimples going for?" she asked.

"He wants to get some things over in San Juan. Say, why don't we close up the place? You can go to the dentist in San Juan."

"No," Alice said. "It's not a good idea. I'll go in to San Ysidro tomorrow or the next day. It's not a good idea to close the lunchroom."

"O.K. It's your tooth," said Juan, and he turned on the water. He poked his head out of the curtain. "Go on out there and take care of the passengers."

Ernest Horton had moved in on the blonde when Alice came into the lunchroom.

"Now, let's have a couple of cups of coffee," he said. And to the blonde, "You rather have a coke?"

"No. Coffee. Cokes make me fat."

Ernest had been making time. He had asked her name and the blonde had said it was Camille Oaks. It wasn't, of course. It was a quick grouping of a Camel advertisement on the wall—another blonde on a poster with balloon-like breasts—and a tree she could see through the window. But Camille Oaks she was from now on, for this trip at least.

"I heard that name recently some place," Ernest said. He passed the sugar dispenser politely to her.

Mr. Pritchard's foot was swinging in little jerks and Mrs. Pritchard was watching. She knew Mr. Pritchard was getting irritable at something, but she didn't know why. She had no experience with this kind of thing. Her women friends were not of a kind to put Mr. Pritchard's foot swinging. And she knew nothing about his life outside of her own social movements.

He uncrossed his legs, stood up, and went to the counter. "You're thinking of the Oakes murder trial," he said to Ernest. "I'm sure this young lady wasn't murdered or vice versa," he chuckled. "A little more coffee," he said gallantly to Alice.

His daughter pulled her right eye sideways to look at him. There was a quality in his voice she had never heard before. And there was a little grandeur in his tone. He was broadening his "a" and putting an unnatural formality into his speech. It shocked his daughter. She peered at the girl and suddenly she knew what it was. Mr. Pritchard was reacting to Camille Oaks. He was making a play—a kind of fatherly play. His daughter didn't like it.

Mr. Pritchard said, "I have an impression I have met you. Could that be?"

In her head Mildred paraphrased it, "Ain't I seen you somewheres?"

Camille looked at Mr. Pritchard's face and her eyes flicked to the club button on his lapel. She knew where he had seen her. When she took off her clothes and sat in the bowl of wine she very carefully didn't look at the men's faces. There was something in their wet, bulging eyes and limp, half-smiling mouths that frightened her. She had a feeling that if she looked directly at one he might leap on her. To her, her audiences were blobs of pink faces and hundreds of white collars and neat four-in-hand ties. The Two Fifty—Three Thousand Clubs usually wore tuxedos.

She said, "I don't remember."

"Ever been in the Middle West?" Mr. Pritchard insisted.

"I've been working in Chicago," said Camille.

"Where?" Mr. Pritchard asked. "The impression is very strong."

"I'm a dental nurse," said Camille.

Mr. Pritchard's eyes brightened behind his glasses. "Say, I'll bet that's it. Dr. Horace Liebholtz, he's my dentist in Chicago."

"No," said Camille, "no, I never worked for him. Dr. T. S. Chesterfield, that was my last job." She got that from a poster too and it wasn't clever. She hoped he wouldn't notice right over his shoulder the sign, "Chesterfields —They Satisfy."

Mr. Pritchard said gaily, to his daughter's disgust, "Well, I'll remember sooner or later. I never forget a face."

Mrs. Pritchard had caught her daughter's eyes and she saw the distaste in Mildred's expression. She glanced at her husband again. He was acting queerly. "Elliott," she said, "will you bring me a little coffee?"

Mr. Pritchard seemed to shake himself into reality. "Oh, yes—sure," he said, and his voice returned to normal. But he was irritated again.

The screen door opened and banged shut. Pimples Carson entered, but a Pimples transformed. His face was heavily powdered in an attempt to cover up the eruptions, and this succeeded in turning their redness to a rich purple. His hair was slicked back and stuck with pomade. He wore a shirt with a very tight collar, a green tie with a small knot, and the shirt collar was pinned under the knot with a gold collar pin. Pimples seemed to be strangling a little, so tight was his collar. Shirt and tie rose and fell slightly when he swallowed. His suit was a chocolate brown, a hairy material, and on the sides of the trousers were the almost indistinguishable prints of bedsprings. He wore white shoes with brown saddles and woolen socks of red and green plaid.

Alice looked up at him in astonishment. "Well, will you look what just come in!" she said.

Pimples hated her. He sat on a stool in the place Mr. Pritchard had only just vacated to take coffee to his wife. "I'd like to have a piece of that new raspberry pie," he said. He glanced nervously at Camille and his voice strangled a little. "Miss, you ought to have a piece of that pie."

Camille looked at him and her eyes grew warm. She knew when a man was having trouble. "No thanks," she said kindly. "I had breakfast in San Ysidro."

"It's on me," said Pimples frantically.

"No, really, thanks. I couldn't."

"Well, he could," said Alice. "He could eat pies standing on his head in a washtub of flat beer on Palm Sunday." She whirled a pie and got out a knife.

"Double, please," said Pimples.

"I don't think you got any pay coming," said Alice cruelly. "You've eaten yourself right through your salary this week."

Pimples winced. God, how he hated Alice! Alice was watching the blonde. She'd caught it. Every man in the room was alert, his senses feeling toward this girl. Alice was nervous about it. She would know when Juan came in. A moment ago she had wanted the bus to be on its way so she could have a good big drunk. But now, now she was getting nervous.

Ernest Horton said, "If I can get to my sample case I'll show you some cute gadgets I'm selling. New stuff. Very cute."

Camille said, "How long you been out of the Army?"

"Five months," said Ernest.

She dropped her eyes to his lapel with the blue bar and white stars. "That's a nice one," she said. "That's the real big one, isn't it?"

"That's what they tell me," said Ernest. "It don't buy any groceries, though." They laughed together.

"Did the big boss pin it on you?"

"Yeah," said Ernest.

Mr. Pritchard leaned forward. It bothered him that he didn't know what was happening.

Pimples said, "You ought to try some of this raspberry pie."

"I couldn't," said Camille.

Alice said, "You find a fly in that and I'll let you have the rest of the pie right in the kisser."

Camille knew the symptoms. This woman was getting ready to hate her. She glanced uneasily at the other two women in the room. Mrs. Pritchard wouldn't bother her. But the girl, there, who was trying to go without her glasses. Camille just hoped she didn't cross with her. That could be a tough babe. She cried in her mind, "Oh, Jesus, Loraine, get rid of that jerk and let's live in the apartment again." She had a dreadful sense of loneliness and weariness. She wondered how it would be to be married to Mr. Pritchard. He was something like the man she had in mind. It was probably not very hard being married to him. His wife didn't look as though he gave her much trouble.

Bernice Pritchard was in the dark. She didn't hate Camille. Vaguely she knew that some change had come over the room, but she didn't know what was. "I guess we'd better get our things together," she said brightly to Mildred. And this in spite of the fact that their things were together.

Now Juan came out of the bedroom. He was dressed in clean corduroy trousers, a clean blue shirt, and a leather windbreaker. His thick hair was combed straight back and his face was shiny from shaving.

"All ready, folks?" he said.

Alice watched him as he walked around the end of the lunch counter. He didn't look at Camille at all. Alice felt a stir of alarm. Juan looked at all girls. If he didn't there was something wrong. Alice didn't like it.

Mr. Van Brunt, the old gentleman with the stiff neck, came in from outside and held the screen door open a little. "Looks like more rain," he said.

Juan addressed him shortly. "You'll get on the next Greyhound north," he said.

"I changed my mind," said Van Brunt. "I'm going along with you. I want to see that bridge. But it's going to rain more, I tell you that."

"I thought you didn't want to go."

"I can change my mind, can't I? Why don't you call up again about that bridge?"

"They said it was all right."

"That was some time ago," said Van Brunt. "You're a stranger here. You don't know how fast the San Ysidro can rise. I've seen it come up a foot an hour when the hills dump into her. You better call up."

Juan was exasperated. "Look," he said, "I drive the bus. I've been doing it for some time. Would you mind? You just ride and take a chance on me, or don't, but let me drive it."

Van Brunt turned his face up sideways and stared at Juan coldly. "I don't know whether I'll go with you or not. I might even write a note to the railroad commission. You're a common carrier, you know. Don't forget that."

"Let's go, folks," said Juan.

Alice kept secret eyes on him, and he didn't look at Camille, didn't offer to carry her suitcase. That was bad. Alice didn't like it. It wasn't like Juan.

Camille picked up her suitcase and scuttled out of the door. She didn't want to sit with any of the men. She was tired. Quickly her mind had gone over the possibilities. Mildred Pritchard was unattached and already Mildred didn't like her. But the girl who had quit was out there in the bus. Camille hurried out the door and climbed in. As quickly as they could, Ernest Horton and Mr. Pritchard followed, but Camille was in the bus. Norma sat quite still. Her eyes were hostile and her nose red and shiny. Norma was very much frightened at what she had done.

Camille said, "Would you mind if I sit with you, honey?"

Norma turned her head stiffly and regarded the blonde. "There's plenty of seats," she said.

"Would you mind? I'll tell you why later."

"Suit your own convenience," said Norma grandly. She could tell that this girl was expensively dressed. It didn't make sense. People didn't want to sit with Norma. But there was a reason. Maybe a mysterious reason. Norma knew her movies. Things like this could turn into nine reels of pure delight. She moved over near the window and made room.

"How far are you going?" Norma asked.

"To L. A."

"Why, I'm going there too! Do you live there?"

"Off and on," said Camille. She noticed that the men who had come piling out of the lunchroom had seen her sit down with Norma. Their drive slowed down. There was going to be no competition. They clustered around the rear end of the bus to have the bags put in the luggage compartment.

Juan lingered at the lunchroom door with Alice looking through the screen at him. "Take it easy," he said. "Had a god-damn mess all morning. Try to get it cleared up before I get home."

A sharpness came on Alice's face. She was about to answer.

Juan went on, "Or one of these days I won't get home."

Her breath caught. "I just don't feel good," she whined.

"Well, start feeling good, then, and don't run it into the ground. Nobody likes sick people very long. Nobody. Get that straight." His eyes were not looking at her but around her and through her, and panic came over Alice. Juan turned away and walked toward the bus.

Alice leaned her elbows on the cross piece of the screen door. Big soft tears filled her eyes. "I'm fat," she said quietly, "and I'm old. Oh, Jesus, I'm old!" The tears ran into her nose. She snorted them back. She said, "You can get young girls, but what can I get? Nothing. An old slob." She sniffled quietly behind the screen.

Mr. Pritchard would have liked to have sat behind the blonde to watch her, but Mrs. Pritchard took a seat near the front and he had to sit down beside her. Mildred sat alone on the other side and behind them. Pimples climbed on and he got the seat Mr. Pritchard wanted, and Ernest Horton sat with him.

Juan noticed with dismay that Van Brunt took the seat directly behind the driver's seat. Juan was nervous. He hadn't had much sleep and some kind of hell had been popping since early morning. He got the bags neatly stacked in the rear trunk, pulled the canvas cover down, and closed the door of the trunk. He waved his hand at Alice leaning inside the screen door. He knew from her posture that she was crying and he intended that she should. She'd got out of hand. He wondered why he stayed with her. Just pure laziness, he guessed. He didn't want to go through the emotional turmoil of leaving her. In spite of himself he'd worry about her and it was too much trouble. He'd need another woman right away and that took a lot of talking and arguing and persuading. It was different just to lay a girl but he would need a woman around, and that was the difference. You got used to one and it was less trouble. Besides Alice was the only woman he had ever found outside of Mexico who could cook beans. A funny thing. Every little Indian in Mexico could cook beans properly and no one up here except Alice—just enough juice, just the right flavor of the bean without another flavor mixed up with it. Here they put tomatoes and chili and garlic and such things in the beans, and a bean should be cooked for itself, with itself, alone. Juan chuckled. "Because she can cook beans," he said to himself.

But there was another reason too. She loved him. She really did. And he knew it. And you can't leave a thing like that. It's a structure and it has an architecture, and you can't leave it without tearing off a piece of yourself. So if you want to remain whole you stay no matter how much you may dislike staying. Juan was not a man who fooled himself very much.

He was almost to the bus when he turned back and walked quickly to the screen door. "Take care of yourself," he said. His eyes were warm. "Get a slug of liquor for that tooth." He turned away and walked back to the bus. She'd be drunker than a skunk when he got back, but maybe that would blow out her tubes and she'd feel better. He would sleep in Norma's bed if Alice passed out. He couldn't stand the smell of her when she was drunk. She had an acid, bitter smell.

Juan glanced up at the sky. The air was still but up high a wind was blowing, bringing legions of new clouds over the mountains, and these clouds were flat and they were joining together and moving in on one another as they hurried across the sky. The big oaks still dripped water from the morning rain and the geranium leaves held shining drops in the centers. There was a hush on the land and a great activity.

Much as he hated to give Van Brunt any credit, Juan was afraid it was going to rain some more, and soon. He climbed up the steps of the bus. Van Brunt caught him before he even sat down.

"Know where that wind's coming from? Southwest. Know where those clouds are coming from? Southwest. You know where our rain comes from?" he demanded triumphantly. "Southwest."

"O.K., and we're all gonna die sometime," said Juan. "Some of us pretty horribly. You might get run over by a tractor. Ever seen a man run over by a tractor?"

"How do you figure that?" Van Brunt demanded.

"Let it rain," said Juan.

"I don't own a tractor," said Van Brunt. "I got four pair of the best horses in this state. How do you figure that tractor?"

Juan stepped on the starter. It had a high, thin, scratchy sound, but almost immediately his motor started and it sounded good. It sounded smooth and nice. Juan turned in his seat.

"Kit," he called, "keep listening to that rear end."

"O.K.," said Pimples. He felt good about Juan's confidence.

Juan waved his hand to Alice and closed the bus door with his lever. He couldn't see what she was doing through the screen. She would let him get out of sight before she brought out a bottle. He hoped she wouldn't get into any trouble.

Juan drove around the front of the lunchroom and turned right into the black-top road that led to San Juan de la Cruz. It wasn't a very wide road but it was fairly smooth and the crown had a high arch so that it shed the water nicely. The valley and the hills were splashed with gouts of sunlight, and they were fenced with the moving shadows of clouds rushing across the sky. The sun spots and the shadows were somber gray, threatening and sad.

"Sweetheart" bumped along at forty. She was a good bus and the rear end sounded good too.

"I never liked tractors," said Mr. Van Brunt.

"I don't either," Juan agreed. He felt fine all of a sudden.

Van Brunt couldn't let it alone. Juan had succeeded beyond his hopes. Van Brunt turned his head sideways on his stiff neck. "Say, you're not one of these fortunetellers or anything like that?"

"No," said Juan.

"Because I don't believe any stuff like that," said Van Brunt.

"Neither do I," said Juan.

"I wouldn't have a tractor on the place."

Juan was about to say "I had a brother who was kicked to death by a horse," but he thought, "Aw, nuts, the guy's a pushover. I wonder what he's scared of."

NINE

The highway to San Juan de la Cruz was a black-top road. In the twenties hundreds of miles of concrete highway had been laid down in California, and people had sat back and said, "There, that's permanent. That will last as long as the Roman roads and longer, because no grass can grow up through the concrete to break it." But it wasn't so. The rubber-shod trucks, the pounding automobiles, beat the concrete, and after a while the life went out of it and it began to crumble. Then a side broke off and a hole crushed through and a crack developed and a little ice in the winter spread the crack, so the resisting concrete could not stand the beating of rubber and broke down.

Then the county maintenance crews poured tar in the cracks to keep the water out, and that didn't work, and finally they capped the roads with an asphalt and gravel mixture. That did survive, because it offered no stern face to the pounding tires. It gave a little and came back a little. It softened in the summer and hardened in the winter. And gradually all the roads were capped with shining black that looked silver in the distance.

The San Juan road ran straight for a long way through level fields, and the fields were not fenced because cattle didn't wander any more. The land was too valuable for grazing. The fields were open to the highway. They terminated in ditches beside the road. And in the ditches the wild mustard grew rankly and the wild turnip with its little purple flowers. The ditches were lined with blue lupines. The poppies were tightly rolled, for the open flowers had been beaten off by the rain.

The road ran straight toward the little foothills of the first range—rounded, woman-like hills, soft and sexual as flesh. And the green clinging grass had the bloom of young skin. The hills were rich and lovely with water, and along the smooth and beautiful road "Sweetheart" rolled. Her washed and shining sides reflected in the water of the ditches. The little tokens swung against the windshield—the tiny boxing gloves, the baby's shoe. The Virgir of Guadalupe on her crescent moon on top of the instrument board looked benignly back at the passengers.

There was no rough or ill sound from the rear end, just the curious whine of the transmission. Juan settled back in his seat prepared to enjoy the trip. He had a big mirror in front of him so that he could watch the passengers, and he had a long mirror out the window in which he could see the road behind. The road was deserted. Only a few cars passed, and none came from the direction of San Juan. At first this puzzeld him unconsciously, and then he began to worry actively. Perhaps the bridge was out. Well, if it was he would have to come back. He'd take the whole crowd of passengers into San Ysidro and turn them loose there. If the bridge was out, there would be no bus line until it was in again. He noticed in his mirror that Ernest Horton had got his samples case open and was showing Pimples some kind of gadget that whirled and flashed and disappeared. And he noticed that Norma and the blonde had their heads together and were talking. He increased his speed a little.

He didn't think he was going to do anything about the blonde. There wasn't any possible way to get at her. And Juan was old enough not to suffer from something that was out of possibility. Given the opportunity there wasn't any question about what he would do. He had felt a wrench in the pit of his stomach when he first saw the blonde.

Norma had been stiff with Camille so far. She was so frozen up it took her some time to thaw. But Camille needed Norma as a kind of a shield, and they had their destination in common.

"I've never been in L. A. or Hollywood," Norma confided softly so that Ernest could not hear. "I won't know where to go or anything."

"What are you going to do?" Camille asked.

"Get a job, I guess. Waitress or something. I'd like to get in pictures."

Camille's mouth tightened in a smile. "You get a job waitressing first," she said. "Pictures are a very tough racket."

"Are you an actress?" Norma asked. "You look like you might be an actress."

"No," said Camille. "I work for dentists. I'm a dental nurse."

"Well, do you live in a hotel, or a room, or a house?"

"I don't have any place to live," said Camille. "I used to have an apartment with a girl friend before I went to Chicago to work."

Norma's eyes grew eager. "I've got a little money put away," she said. "Maybe we could get an apartment together. Say, if I got a job in a restaurant it wouldn't cost hardly anything for food. I could bring stuff home." A hunger was growing in Norma's eyes. "Why, maybe sharing the rent it wouldn't be much. I could make good tips, maybe."

Camille felt a warmth for the girl. She looked at the red nose and the dull complexion, the small pale eyes. "We'll see how it goes," she said.

Norma leaned close. "I know your hair's natural," she said. "But maybe you could show me how to kind of touch mine up. My hair's mousy. Just mousy."

Camille laughed. "You'd be surprised if you knew what color my hair is," she said. "Hold still a minute." She studied Norma's face, trying to visualize what cold cream and powder and mascara could do for her, and she thought of the hair shining and waved, and the eyes made a little larger with eyeshadow, and the mouth reshaped with lipstick. Camille hadn't any illusions about beauty. Loraine was a washed-out little rat without make-up but Loraine did all right. It would be fun and company to make this girl over and to give her some confidence. It might even be better than Loraine.

"Let's think about it," she said. "This is pretty country. I'd like to live in the country some time." A picture had projected itself on her mind, the pattern of what would happen. She would fix Norma up. She could be kind of pretty if she was careful. And then Norma would meet a boy and naturally she'd bring him home to show him off and the boy would make passes at Camille and Norma would hate her. That's the way it would happen. That's the way it had happened. But what the hell! it would be fun before it happened. And maybe she could anticipate it and never be in when Norma brought a boy home.

She felt warm and friendly. "Let's think about it," she said.

On the highway ahead Juan saw a crushed jackrabbit. Lots of people liked to run over things like that, but Juan didn't. He moved his steering wheel so that the flattened carcass passed between the wheels and there was no crunching under the tires. He had the bus at forty-five. The big highway busses sometimes went sixty miles an hour, but Juan had plenty of time. The road was straight for another two miles before it began wandering into the soft foothills. Juan took one hand off the wheel and stretched.

Mildred Pritchard felt the telegraph poles whipping by as little blows on her eyes. She had her glasses on again. She watched Juan's face in the mirror. She could see little more than a profile from her angle. She noticed that he raised his head to look back at the blonde every minute or so, and she felt a bitter anger. She was confused about what had happened that morning. No one knew, of course, unless Juan Chicoy had guessed. She was still a little swollen and itchy from the thing. A sentence kept repeating itself in her mind. She's not a blonde and she's not a nurse and her name is not Camille Oaks. The sentence went on, over and over. And then she chuckled at herself inwardly. "I'm trying to destroy her," she thought. "I'm doing a stupid thing. Why not admit I'm jealous? I'm jealous. All right. Does admitting it make me any less jealous? No, it does not. But she forced my father to make a fool of himself. All right. Do I care whether my father is a fool? No, I do not— if I'm not with him. I don't want people to think I'm his daughter, that's all. No, that's not true either. I don't want to go to Mexico with him. I can hear everything he'll say." She was uncomfortable and the movement of the bus was not helping. "Basketball," she thought, "that's the stuff." She flexed the muscles of her thighs and thought about the engineering studen' with the crew-cut hair. She pictured her affair with him.

Mr. Pritchard was bored and tired. He could be very irritating when he was bored. He twitched. "This looks like rich country," he said to his wife. "California raises most of the vegetables for the United States, you know."

Mrs. Pritchard could hear herself talking after she got home. "Then we drove through miles and miles of green fields with poppies and lupines, just like a garden. There was a blond girl got on at a funny little place and the men made fools of themselves, even Elliott. I joshed him about it for a week afterward." She'd write it in a letter. "And I'm pretty sure the poor little painted thing was just as nice and sweet as could be. She said she was a nurse, but I think she was probably an actress—little parts, you know. There are so many of them in Hollywood. Thirty-eight thousand listed. They've got a big casting agency. Thirty-eight thousand." Her head nodded a little. Bernice was sleepy and hungry. "I wonder what adventures we'll have now," she thought.

When his wife slipped into her daydream Mr. Pritchard knew it. He had been married to her long enough to know when she wasn't listening to him, and ordinarily he went right on talking. He often clarified his thinking about business or politics by telling his thoughts to Bernice when she wasn't listening. He had a trained memory for figures and for bits of information. He knew approximately how many tons of sugar beets were produced in the Salinas valley. He had read it and retained it in spite of the fact that he had no use whatever for the information. He felt that such information was good to know and he had never questioned its value or why it might be good to know. But now he had no inclination toward knowledge. A powerful influence was battering at him from the rear of the bus. He wanted to turn around and look at the blonde. He wanted to sit where he could watch her. Horton and Pimples were behind him. He couldn't just sit opposite and look at her.

Mrs. Pritchard asked, "How old do you think she is?" And the question shocked him because he had been wondering the same thing.

"How old who is?" he asked.

"The young woman. The blond young woman."

"Oh, her. How should I know?" His answer was so rough that his wife looked a little bewildered and hurt. He saw it and tried to cover his mistake. "Little girls know more about little girls," he said. "You could tell better than I could."

"Why? I don't know. Well, with that make-up and the hair tint it's hard to tell. I just wondered. Somewhere between twenty-five and thirty, I guess."

"I wouldn't know about that," said Mr. Pritchard. He looked out the window at the approaching foothills. His palms were a little damp and the magnet drew at him from the rear of the bus. He wanted to look around. "I don't know about that," said Mr. Pritchard. "But I'm interested in that young Horton. He's young, and he's got lots of get-up, and he's got ideas. He really caught my fancy. You know, I might find a place for a man like that in the organization." This was business.

Bernice too could draw a magic circle around herself, with motherhood, or say, menstruation, a subject like that, and no man could or would try to get in. Business was her husband's magic circle. She had no right to go near him when it was business. She had no knowledge nor interest in business. It was his privacy and she respected it.

"He seems a nice young man," she said. "His grammar and his back-ground—"

"My God, Bernice!" he cried irritably. "Business isn't background and grammar. It's what you can produce. Business is the most democratic thing in the world. It's what you can do that counts."

He was trying to remember what the blonde's lips looked like. He believed that full-lipped women were voluptuous. "I'd like to have a little talk with Horton before he gets away," Mr. Pritchard said.

Bernice knew that he was restless.

"Why don't you talk to him now?" she suggested.

"Oh, I don't know. He's sitting with that boy."

"Well, I'm sure that boy will move if you ask him nicely." She was con-vinced that anyone would do anything if nicely asked. And in her case she was right. She claimed and got the most outrageous favors from strangers simply by asking nicely. She would ask a bellboy to carry her bags four blocks to the station because it was too close, really, to get a cab, and then thank him nicely and give him a dime.

Now she knew she was helping her husband to do something he wanted to do. What it was she didn't quite know. She wanted to get back to writing the imaginary letter about their trip. "Elliott is so interested in everything. He had long talks with everyone. I guess that's why he's so successful. He takes such an interest. And he's so thoughtful. There was a boy with big pimples and Elliott didn't want to disturb him, but I told him just to ask nicely. People do love nice manners."

Mr. Pritchard was cleaning his nails again with the gold appliance he wore on his watch chain.

Pimples' eyes were on the back of Camille's head. But first when he had sat down he made sure that he couldn't see her legs under the seat, not even her ankles. Now and then she turned to look out of the window, and he could see her profile, the long, darkened eyelashes which curled upward, the straight, powdered nose, nostrils a little coated with tobacco smoke and the dust of traveling. Her upper lip curved upward to a sharp line before it pillowed out in its heavy red petal, and Pimples could see the downy hair on her upper lip. For some reason this aroused him agonizingly. When her head was turned straight ahead he could see one of her ears where the hair parted a little and exposed it. He could see the heavy lobe and the crease behind her ear where it fitted so close to her head. The edge of her ear was fluted. As he stared at the ear she almost seemed to be conscious of his look, for she raised her chin and shook her head from side to side so that the part in her hair fell together and concealed the ear. She got a comb from her purse because the backward shake had uncovered the deep forceps scars along her jaw. Now Pimples saw the ugly scars for the first time. He had to lean sideways to see them, and a stab of pain entered his chest. He felt a deep and unreasoning sorrow, but the sorrow was sexual too. He imagined himself holding her head in his arms and stroking the poor scars with his finger. He swallowed several times.

Camille was saying softly to Norma, "Then there's this Wee Kirk i' the Heather. I guess that's the prettiest cemetery in the world. You know, you have to get a ticket to get in. I like just to walk around in there. It's so beautiful and the organ plays nearly all the time and you find people buried there that you've seen in pictures. I always said I'd like to be buried there."

"I don't like to talk about things like that," said Norma. "It's bad luck."

Pimples had been vaguely discussing the Army with Ernest Horton. "They say you can learn a trade and travel all over. I don't know. I'm taking a course in radar engineering. It starts next week by mail. I guess radar is going to be pretty hot stuff. But you can get a real good course in radar in the Army."

Ernest said, "I don't know how it would be in peacetime. You can have it when there's a war."

"Did you get to do some real fighting?"

"I didn't ask for it but I got it."

"Where were you?" Pimples asked.

"All over hell," said Ernest.

"Maybe I could get a good line and get in selling, like you," Pimples suggested.

"Oh, that's just plain starvation till you get your contacts," Ernest said. "It took me five years to build up my contacts and then I got drafted. I'm just getting back on my feet now. You can't just step into it and you've got to work at it. It doesn't look like work but it is. If I was to start over again I'd learn a trade so I could have a home. Pretty nice to have a wife and a couple of kids." Ernest always said this. When he was drunk he believed it. He didn't want a home. He loved moving around and seeing different people. He would run away from a home immediately. Once he had been married, and the second day he had walked out, leaving a thoroughly frightened and angry wife, and he never saw her again, nor wrote to her. But he saw her picture once. She was picked up for marrying five men and drawing Army allotments from each one. What a dame. A real hustler. Ernest almost admired her. There was hustling that paid dividends.

"Why don't you go back to school?" he asked Pimples.

"I don't want no fancy stuff," said Pimples. "Them college boys are just a bunch of nances. I want a man's life."

Camille had leaned close to Norma and was whispering in her ear. The two girls were shaking with laughter. The bus surged around the bend and entered the hill country. The road cut between high banks, and the soil of the cuts was dark and dripping with water. Little goldy-backed ferns clung to the gravel and dripped with rain. Juan put his right hand on the wheel and let his elbows hang free. There would be fifteen minutes of twisting hill road now with no straight stretches at all. He glanced in his rear-view mirror at the blonde. Her eyes were puckered with laughter and she'd covered her mouth with spread fingers the way little girls do.

Mr. Pritchard, going back, was not careful, and when the bus took a curve he was flung sideways. He clutched at the seat-back, missed it, and fell sprawling on Camille's lap. His right hand reaching to break his fall whipped her short skirt up and his arm went between her knees. Her skirt was slightly torn. She helped him disengage himself and she pulled down her skirt. Mr. Pritchard was blushing violently.

"I'm very sorry," he said.

"Oh, it's all right."

"But I've torn your skirt."

"I can mend it."

"But I must pay to have it mended."

"I'll just patch it up myself. It isn't bad." She looked at his face and knew that he was prolonging the affair as much as he could. "He'll want to know what address to send the money to," she thought.

Mrs. Pritchard called, "Elliott, are you trying to sit in that lady's lap?"

Even Juan laughed then. Everyone laughed. And suddenly the bus was not full of strangers. Some chemical association was formed. Norma laughed hysterically. All the tension of the morning came out in her laughter.

Mr. Pritchard said, "I must say, you take it very well. I didn't come back here to sit in your lap. I wanted to have a few words with this gentleman. Son," he said to Pimples, "would you mind moving for just a little while. I have some business I'd like to talk over with Mr.—I don't think I heard your name."

"Horton," said Ernest, "Ernest Horton."

Mr. Pritchard had a whole series of tactics for getting on with people. He never forgot the name of a man richer or more powerful than he, and he never knew the name of a man less powerful. He had found that to make a man mention his own name would put that man at a slight disadvantage. For a man to speak his own name made him a little naked and unprotected.

Camille was looking at her torn skirt and talking softly to Norma. "I always wanted to live on a hill," she said. "I love hills. I love to walk in hills."

"It's all right after you're rich and famous," Norma said firmly. "I know people in pictures that every chance they get, why, they go hunting and fishing and wear old clothes and smoke a pipe."

Camille was bringing Norma out. She had never in her whole life felt so excited and free. She could say anything she wanted. She giggled a little.

"It's nicer to wear old dirty clothes if you've got a closet full of nice fresh clean ones," she said. "Old clothes are the only kind I've got and I'm god-damned sick of it." She glanced at Camille to see how she'd react to such candor.

Camille nodded. "You aren't kidding, sister." Something very strong and sympathetic was growing up between these two. Mr. Pritchard tried to hear the conversation but he couldn't.

The ditches beside the highway ran full with water descending toward the valley. The heavy clouds were massing for a new attack.

"It's coming on to rain," Van Brunt said happily.

Juan grunted. "I had a brother-in-law kicked to death by a horse," he observed.

"Couldn't have used any sense," said Van Brunt. "Horse kicks a man, it's usually the man's fault."

"Killed him anyway," said Juan, and he settled into silence.

The bus was nearing the top of the grade and the turns were becoming tighter all the time.

"I was very much interested in our little talk this morning, Mr. Horton. It's a pleasure to talk with a man with some get-up and go. I'm always on the look-out for men like that for my organization."

"Thanks," said Ernest.

"We're having trouble right now with these returning veterans," said Mr. Pritchard. "Good men, you understand. And I think everything should be done for them—everything. But they've been out of the run. They're rusty. In business you've got to keep up every minute. A man that has kept up is twice as valuable as a man that has been out of the mill, so to speak." He looked at Ernest for approval. Instead he saw a kind of hard, satiric look come into Ernest's eyes.

"I see your point," Ernest said. "I was four years in the Army."

"Oh!" said Mr. Pritchard. "Oh, yes—you're not wearing your discharge button, I see."

"I've *got* a job," Ernest said.

Mr. Pritchard fumbled with his thoughts. He had made a bad mistake. He wondered what the thing was in Ernest's lapel button. It looked familiar. He should know. "Well, they're a fine bunch of boys," he said, "and I only hope we can put in an administration that will take care of them."

"Like after the last war?" Ernest asked. It was a double brush, and Mr. Pritchard began to wonder if he'd been right about Horton. There was a kind of a brutality about Horton. He had a kind of swagger and a headlong quality so many ex-soldiers had. The doctors said they would get over it just as soon as they lived a good normal life for a while. They were out of line. Something would have to be done.

"I'm the first one to come to the defense of our veterans," Mr. Pritchard said. He wished to God he could get off the subject. Ernest was looking at him with a slightly crooked smile that he was beginning to recognize in applicants for jobs. "I just thought I'd like to interview a man with your get-up and go," Mr. Pritchard said uneasily. "When I get back from my vacation I'd be very glad to have you call on me. We can always make room for a man who's got it."

"Well, sir," said Ernest, "I get very sick of running around the country all the time. I often thought I'd like to have a home and a wife and a couple of kids. That's the real way to live. Come home at night and lock the whole world outside, and a boy and a girl, maybe. This sleeping in hotels isn't living."

Mr. Pritchard nodded. "You're four-square right," he said, and he was very much relieved. "I'm just the right man to say that to. Twenty-one years married and I wouldn't have it any other way."

"You've been lucky," said Ernest. "Your wife's a fine-looking woman."

"And she's a fine woman," said Mr. Pritchard. "The most thoughtful person in the world. I often wonder what I'd do without her."

"I was married once," said Ernest. "My wife died." His face was sad.

"I'm sorry," said Mr. Pritchard. "And this may sound silly. Time does heal wounds. And maybe some day—well, I wouldn't give up hope."

"Oh, I don't."

"I didn't mean to pry into your affairs," said Mr. Pritchard, "but I've been thinking about your idea for those lapel slipcovers for a dark suit to convert into a tuxedo. If you're not tied up with anyone I thought we might—well, talk about doing a little business."

"Well," said Ernest, "it's like I told you. Clothes manufacturers won't want something that will rule out some of their business. I just don't see the angle right now."

Mr. Pritchard said, "I forget whether you said you had applied for a patent."

"Well, no. I told you. I just registered the idea."

"How do you mean, registered?"

"Well, I wrote out a description and made some drawings and put it in an envelope and mailed it to myself, registered mail. That proves when I did it because that envelope is sealed."

"I see," said Mr. Pritchard, and he wondered whether such a method would have any standing in court. He didn't know. But it was always better to take the inventor in on a percentage. Only the really big fellows could afford to lift an invention whole. The big fellows could afford a long fight.

They figured it was cheaper than cutting in an inventor and the figures proved they were right. But Mr. Pritchard's firm wasn't big enough and, besides, he always thought that generosity paid off.

"I've got an idea or two that might work out," he said. "Course, it'll take some organization. Now, suppose you and I could make a deal. This is just a supposition, you understand. I'd handle the organization and we would take a percentage of profit after expenses."

"But they don't want it," Ernest said. "I've asked around."

Mr. Pritchard laid a hand on Ernest's knee. He had a hollow feeling that he ought to shut up, but he remembered the satiric look in Ernest's eyes and he wanted Ernest to admire him and to like him. He couldn't shut up.

"Suppose we formed a company and we protected the idea?" he said. "Patent it, I mean. Now we organize to manufacture this product, a national advertising campaign—"

"Just a moment," Ernest broke in.

But Mr. Pritchard was carried away. "Now suppose these layouts just happened to fall into the hands of, say, oh, Hart, Schaffner and Marx or some big manufacturer like that, or maybe the association. They'd get ahold of it by accident, of course. Well, maybe they'd like to buy us out."

Ernest began to look interested. "Buy the patent?"

"Buy not only the patent but the whole company."

"But if they bought the patent then they could kill it," Ernest said.

Mr. Pritchard's eyes were slitted and his pupils shone through his glasses and a little smile lay on the corners of his mouth. For the first time since she had got off the bus from San Ysidro he had forgotten Camille. "Look ahead a little further," he said. "When we sell and dissolve the company we only pay a capital gain tax on the profits."

"That's smart," said Ernest excitedly. "Yes, sir, that's very smart. That's blackmail and a very high-class blackmail. Yes, sir, nobody could touch us."

The smile vanished from Mr. Pritchard's mouth. "What do you mean, blackmail? We would intend to go ahead and manufacture. We could even order machinery."

"That's what I mean," said Ernest. "It's very high class. It's all wrapped up. You're a smart man."

Mr. Pritchard said, "I hope you don't think it's dishonest. I've been in business thirty-five years and I've climbed to the head of my company. I can be proud of my record."

"I'm not criticizing you," Ernest said. "I think you've got a very sound idea there. I'm for it, only—"

"Only what?" said Mr. Pritchard.

"I'm kind of low on dough," said Ernest, "and I'm gonna need a quick buck. Oh, well, I can borrow it, I guess."

"What do you need money for? Maybe I could advance—"

"No," said Ernest, "I'll get it myself."

"Is it some new wrinkle you figured out?" Mr. Pritchard asked.

"Yes," said Ernest. "I gotta get this idea into the patent office by carrier pigeon."

"You don't think for one minute—"

"Of course not," said Ernest. "Certainly not. But I'm gonna be happier when that envelope gets to Washington alone."

Mr. Pritchard leaned back in his seat and smiled. The highway whirled and twisted ahead, and between two great abutments was the pass into the next valley.

"You'll be all right, son. I think we can do business. I don't want you to think I'd take advantage though. My record speaks for itself."

"Oh, I don't," said Ernest. "I don't." He looked secretly at Mr. Pritchard. "It's just that I've got a couple of very luscious dames in L. A. and I don't want to get in that apartment and forget everything." He saw the reaction he wanted.

"I'm going to be two days in Hollywood," Mr. Pritchard said. "Maybe we could talk a little business."

"Like in these dames' apartment?"

"Well, a man needs some kind of relaxation. I'm going to be at the Beverly Wilshire. You could call me there."

"I sure will," said Ernest. "What color dame you like best?"

"Don't misunderstand me," said Mr. Pritchard. "I like to sit and have a scotch and soda but I've got a position, you know. I don't want you to misunderstand."

"Oh, I don't," said Ernest. "I could maybe pick up the blonde ahead here, if you want."

"Don't be silly," said Mr. Pritchard.

Pimples had moved forward in the bus. On the underside of his jaw he felt an itching burn and he knew an eruption was forming. He sat down in the seat across from Mildred Pritchard. He didn't want to touch the new place but he was powerless over his hands. His right hand moved upward and his forefinger rubbed the lump under the chin. It was a very sore lump. This one was going to be a devil. He knew already what it would look like. He wanted to squeeze it, to scratch it, to rip it out. His nerves were on edge. He forced his hand into his coat pocket and clenched his fist there.

Mildred was staring vacantly out of the window.

"I wish I could go to Mexico," Pimples said.

Mildred looked around at him in surprise. Her glasses caught the light from his window and glared blindly at him.

Pimples swallowed. "I never been there," he said weakly.

"Neither have I," said Mildred.

"Yeah, but you're going."

She nodded. She didn't want to look at him because she couldn't keep her eyes from his eczema and that embarrassed him. "Maybe you can go soon," she said uneasily.

"Oh, I'll go," said Pimples. "I'll go everywhere. I'm a great traveler. I'd rather travel than anything. You get experience that way."

She nodded again and took off her glasses in protection against him. Now she couldn't see him so clearly.

"I thought maybe I'd be a missionary like Spencer Tracy and go to China and cure them of all those diseases. You ever been to China?"

"No," said Mildred. She was fascinated by his thinking.

Pimples took most of his ideas from moving pictures and the rest from the radio. "It's very poor people there in China," he said, "some of them so poor they just starve to death right outside your window if some missionary don't come along and help them. And if you help them, why, they love you, and let any Jap come around and make trouble and they stick a knife right in him." He nodded solemnly. "I think they're just as good as you and me," he said. "Spencer Tracy just came along and he cured them up and they loved him—and you know what he done? He found his own soul. And there was this girl and he didn't know whether he ought to marry her because she had a past. Of course, it came out it wasn't her fault and it wasn't even true, but this old dame told lies about her." Pimples' eyes glowed with pity and enthusiasm. "But Spencer Tracy didn't believe those lies and he lived in an old palace that had secret passages and tunnels and —well, then the Japs come."

"I saw the picture," Mildred said.

The bus went into second gear for the last climb. Now it was in the gap at the top and then it emerged and turned sharp left, and below was the valley gloomy with gray clouds, and the great loop of the San Ysidro River gleamed like dark steel under the glowering light. Juan eased the bus into high gear and began the descent.

TEN

The San Ysidro River runs through the San Juan valley, turning and twisting until it discharges sluggishly into Black Rock Bay under the protection of Bat Point. The valley itself is long and not very wide, and the San Ysidro River, having not very far to run, makes the most of what distance it has by moving from one side of the level stretch to the other. Here it cuts under a cliff, against a mountain, and then it spreads thinly out on sandbanks. During a good part of the year there is no surface water at all, and the sandy bed grows full of willows which stretch their roots down toward underground water.

Rabbits and raccoons and small foxes and coyotes make their homes in the willows of the river bottom when the water is down. At the head of the valley to the north and east the river rises, not as one head, but in many little branches, so that the source on a map looks like a tree with small, leafless branches. The dry and stony hills with shoulders and gullies and canyons do not supply water to the river during all the year, but when the rains fall in the late winter and spring the rocky shoulders absorb a little of the water and cast the rest in black torrents to the little streams that tumble out of the creases, and the streamlets combine and join larger creeks and the creeks come together at the northern end of the valley.

So it is that in the late spring, when the hills have digested as much rain as they can, a heavy storm may swell the San Ysidro River to a raging flood in a very few hours. Then the foamy yellow water cuts at the banks and great hunks of farmland cave into the river. Then the bodies of cows and sheep go tumbling and rolling in the yellow flood. It is an unstable and precocious river; dead during part of the year and deadly during another part.

In the middle of the valley, which is on a direct line between Rebel Corners and San Juan de la Cruz, the river makes a great loop, ranging from side to side of the level valley, casting its coil against the mountain on the eastern edge and moving away to cross the fields and farmlands. In the old times the road followed the loop of the river and crawled up the side of the hill to avoid crossing. But with the coming of engineers and steel and concrete, two bridges had been thrown over the river, and these cut out twelve miles of the San Ysidro's playfulness.

They were wooden bridges, backed and suspended by steel rods, and each one was supported in the middle and at the ends by concrete piers. The wood was painted dark red and the iron was dark with rust. On the river side of each bridge backwaters of piles and braided, mattressed willow deflected the water toward the spans and kept the gnawing current from undermining the bridgeheads.

These bridges were not very old, but they had been built at a time when the tax rate was not only low, but much of it uncollectable because of what was called "hard times." The county engineer had found it necessary to build within a budget that allowed only the simplest construction. His timber should have been heavier and his struts more numerous, but he had to build a bridge within a certain cost and he did. And every year the farmers of the middle valley watched the river with cynical apprehension. They knew that some time there would be a quick and overwhelming flood that would take the bridges out. Every year they petitioned the county to replace the wooden bridges, but there weren't enough votes in the rural section to make the petitions mandatory. The large towns, which had not only the votes but the taxable assets, got the improvements. People were not moving to the medium-rich farmlands. A good service-station corner in

San Juan had a higher assessed valuation than a hundred acres of grainland in the valley. The farmers knew that it was only a question of time before the bridges were destroyed and then, they said, the county would god-damned well come to its senses.

A hundred yards from the first bridge toward Rebel Corners there was a little general store on the highway. It stocked the groceries, the tires, the hardware a man bought on Saturday afternoon or when he didn't have time to drive either to San Juan de la Cruz or to San Ysidro over the range. This was Breed's General Store. And of late years it had, as did all country stores, added gas pumps and a stock of automobile accessories.

Mr. and Mrs. Breed were unofficial custodians of the bridge, and at flood time their phone rang constantly and they supplied information about the river's rise. They were used to this. Their one great fear was that some day the bridge would go out and the new one might be a quarter of a mile down the river, and then they would have to move their store or build a new one near the new bridge.

At least half of their trade nowadays was in soft drinks, sandwiches, gasoline, and candy bought by travelers on the highway. Even the bus be-tween Rebel Corners and San Juan invariably stopped there. It brought express packages, and the passengers drank soft drinks. Juan Chicoy and the Breeds were old and good friends.

And now the river was up, and not only up, but, as Mr. Breed said to his wife, "there's a backwash cutting in under the piles above the bridge, and if it cuts a channel in back, there goes your ball game." He had made half a dozen trips to the bridgehead since daylight. This was a bad one and Mr. Breed knew it. Thin-lipped and unshaven, he had stood on the bridge at eight o'clock this morning and watched the tumbling yellow water laced with yellow foam and dotted with uprooted scrub oak and cottonwood. And he had seen a few planks of planed lumber come twisting down, and then a piece of roof with shingles still on, and then the drowned, bobbing body of McElroy's black Angus bull, square and short-legged. As it went under the bridge it rolled over on its back, and Breed could see the wild upturned eyes and the flapping tongue. It made Breed sick to his stomach.

Everyone knew McElroy's barn was too close to the bank and that bull cost eighteen hundred dollars. McElroy didn't have that kind of money to throw away. He didn't see any of the rest of the herd come down, but the bull would be enough. Mac had put a lot of faith in that bull.

Breed walked farther out on the bridge. The water was only three feet below the timbers now and Breed could feel the plunging water plaguing the caissons to protest under his feet. He rubbed his unshaven chin with his fingers and walked back to the store. He didn't tell his wife about McElroy's black Angus. It would only make her sad.

When Juan Chicoy called up about the bridge Breed told him the truth. The bridge was still in, but God knew for how long. The water was still rising. The bare, stony hills were still emptying their freshets into the river, and it was clouding up again.

At nine o'clock the lower timbers cleared the flood only by eighteen inches. Once the pressure came on those struts and braces and a few up-rooted trees banged into the bridge, it was only a question of time. Breed stood inside his screen door and drummed his fingers on the wire.

"Let me fix you some breakfast," his wife said. "You'd think you owned the bridge."

"I guess I do in a way," said Breed. "If it went out they'd say it was my fault. I've called the supervisor's office and I've called the county engineer. They're both closed. If that channel gets back of the pier, there goes your ball game."

"You'd better eat some breakfast. I'll make you some wheat cakes."

"All right," Breed said. "Don't make them too thick."

"I never make them thick," said Mrs. Breed. "Want an egg on top?"

"Sure," said Breed. "I don't know whether Juan is going to make it or not. He's not due for more than an hour yet and, Jesus! how the water is coming up!"

"No reason to swear," said Mrs. Breed.

Her husband looked around at her. "I'd say this was one of the times when there's every reason to swear. I'm going to take a drink."

"Before breakfast?"

"Before anything."

She didn't know about the black bull, of course. He went to the wall phone and rang McElroy's, a three-two ring, and he kept it up until Pine-dale, two miles this side of McElroy's, answered.

"I've been trying to get him too," Pinedale said. "His line's dead. I'm going to ride up and see if he's all right."

"I wish you would," said Breed. "His new bull went under the bridge this morning."

Mrs. Breed raised frightened eyes. "Walter!" she cried.

"Well, it's true. I didn't want you to fret."

"Walter! Oh, my God!" said Mrs. Breed.

ELEVEN

Alice Chicoy stood inside the screen door and watched the bus pull away. She let the tears dry on her cheeks.

When the bus passed beyond her view from the door she went to the side window from which she could see the county road. The bus ran into a patch of sunlight and gleamed for a moment, and then she couldn't see it any more. Alice drew a great breath and released it in a luxurious sigh. It was her day! She was alone. She felt happy and secret, and she felt sinful too. Slowly she smoothed her dress down over her hips and caressed her thighs. She looked at her nails. No, later for that.

She looked slowly around the lunchroom. She could still smell cigarette smoke. There were things to be done, yet it was her day and she went about them slowly. First she got from the cupboard a cardboard sign that said "Closed" in large letters. She went outside and hung the sign on a nail on the edge of the screen door. Then she went inside and closed and latched the screen door. And she pulled the inner door and turned the key in it. Next she went from window to window and let down the Venetian blinds and pulled the slats downward so no one could see in.

The lunchroom was dusky and very quiet. Alice worked deliberately. She washed and put away the dirty coffee cups and she washed the lunch counter and the tabletops. The pies she put out of sight under the counter. Then she brought a broom from the bedroom and swept the floor and put the dust and the mud and the cigarette butts in the garbage can. The counter gleamed a little in the dusky light and the tabletops looked white and clean.

Alice came around the counter and sat on one of the stools. It was her day! She felt silly and giddy. "Well, why not?" she said aloud. "I don't have much fun. Bring me," she said, "bring me a double whisky and hurry it up."

She put her hands on the counter and looked at them carefully. "Poor work-ruined hands," she whispered, "dear hands." Then in a shout, "Where the hell is that whisky?" And she answered herself, "Yes, ma'am, it's coming right up, ma'am."

"Well, that's better," said Alice. "I just want you to know who you're talking to. Don't put on any lip because you can't get away with it. I've got my eye on you."

"Yes, ma'am," she answered herself. And she got up and went in back of the counter.

At the far end and low to the floor there was a small cabinet. Alice bent over, opened the door, and reached blindly in and brought out a fifth of Old Grandad bourbon. She picked a water glass from the rack and carried the bottle and the glass to the counter in front of the stool where she had been sitting.

"Here you are, ma'am."

"Take it over to that table. Do you think I look like someone that stands up at bars?"

"No, ma'am."

"And bring another glass. And a bottle of cold beer."

"Yes, ma'am."

She carried all these things to the table beside the door and laid them out. "You can go now," she said, and answered, "Yes, ma'am."

"But don't go far, I might want something."

As she poured out the beer she giggled to herself. If anybody heard me they'd think I was crazy. Well, maybe I am. She poured out a fine shot in the other glass. "Alice," she said, "ready, set, go!" She waved the glass and drank slowly. She did not toss it. She let the hot, straight whisky ease and burn and flow over her tongue and in back of her tongue, and she swallowed slowly and felt the bite on her palate, and the warmth of the whisky went into her chest and into her stomach. Even after she had emptied the glass she still held it to her lips. She put down the glass and she said, "Ah!" and breathed outward harshly.

She could taste the sweet whisky again on her returning breath. Now she reached for the tumbler of beer. She crossed her legs and drank very slowly until the glass was empty.

"God!" she said.

It seemed to Alice she had never realized how utterly comfortable and charming the lunchroom was, the light glimmering down between the slanting blinds. She heard a truck go by on the highway and it disturbed her. Suppose something happened to interfere with her day? Well, they'd have to break the door down. She wouldn't let anyone in. She poured two fingers of whisky in one glass and four fingers of beer in the other glass.

"There's more than one way to skin a drink," she said, and she tossed the whisky in and tossed the beer right in after it. Now, there's an idea. It doesn't taste the same. The way you drink changes the taste. Why had no one else ever found that out, only Alice. Somebody should write that down—"The way you drink makes the taste." There was a little tension in her right eyelid, and a curious but pleasant pain ran down the veins of her arms.

"Nobody has time to find out things," she said solemnly. "No time." She poured half a glass of beer and filled the glass with whisky. "I wonder if anybody ever tried this before?"

The metal paper-napkin holder was in front of her and she could see her face in it. "Hello, kid," she said. She waved the glass, and it was as distorted in the shining metal as her face. "Here's a go, kid. Your health, kid." And she drank the beer and the whisky the way a thirsty man drinks milk. "Ah," she said, "that's not so god-damned bad. No sir. I think I've got something there. That's good."

She adjusted the paper-napkin holder so that she could see herself better. But a bend in the metal surface made her nose look broken at the top and fat and bulbous at the bottom. She got up and went around the counter and into the bedroom, and she brought a round hand mirror back to the table and propped it against the sugar dispenser. She settled herself and crossed her legs. "Now there! I'd like to invite you for a drink." She poured whisky in each glass. "No beer," she said. "All out of beer. Well, we'll fix that."

She went to the icebox and brought another bottle of beer. "Now, you see," she said to the mirror, "we first put a little whisky—not too much—not too little—and we add just the right amount of beer. And there you are." She pushed one glass toward the mirror and drained the other one. "Some people are afraid to take a drink," she said. "They can't handle it."

"Oh, you don't want it? Well, that's your privilege. I'm not going to make you take it. I'm not going to let it go to waste, either." And she drank off the other glass. Her cheeks were tingling now as though a frost were stinging the surface. She brought the mirror close and inspected herself. Her eyes were damp and shiny. She whipped back a strand of loose hair.

"No reason to let yourself run down just because you're having a good time." And without warning a vision flipped into place in her head and she turned the mirror face down. The vision struck so hard and so quickly that it was like a blow. Perhaps it was the darkened room. Alice cried, "I don't want to think about that. I hate to think about that."

But the thought and vision were in. A darkened room and a white bed and her mother paralyzed, rigid, unmoving, the eyes staring straight up, and then the white hand rising from the counterpane in a gesture of despair, a gesture for help. Alice could creep in, no matter how stealthily, and that hand would rise in frightful helplessness, and Alice would hold it for a moment and then put it gently down and go out. Every time she came into that room she would beg the hand not to rise, to lie still, to be dead, like the rest of the body.

"I don't want to think about that," she cried. "How did that get in?" Her hand shook and the bottle rattled against the glass. She poured an enormous drink and drained it, and it caught in her throat so that she coughed, and she just saved herself from being sick. "That'll fix you," she said. "I want to think about something else."

She imagined herself in bed with Juan, but her mind slipped on past that. "I could have had any man I wanted," she boasted. "Enough made passes at me, God knows, and I didn't give in much." Her lips writhed away from her teeth a little salaciously. "Maybe I should of while I could. I'm getting along— That's a god-damned lie," she shouted, "I'm as good as I ever was. I'm better! Who the hell wants a skinny bitch that don't know what to do? No real man wants stuff like that. I could go right out now and pick them off like flies."

The bottle was a little less than half full now. She spilled some in pouring and giggled at herself. "I do believe I'm getting a little drunk," she said.

There came a great knocking at the screen door and Alice froze and sat silent. The knocking came again. A man's voice called, "Nobody here. I thought I heard talking."

"Well, try it again. They might be in back," a woman's voice answered.

Alice picked up the hand mirror gently and looked at herself. She nodded her head and closed one eye in a large wink. The knocking came again.

"I tell you there's nobody here."

"Well, try the door."

Alice heard the rattling of the screen door.

"It's locked up," the man said, and the woman replied, "It's locked on the inside. They must be in there."

The man laughed and his feet scraped on gravel. "Well, if they're in there they want to be alone. Don't you ever want to be alone, baby? With me, I mean."

"Oh, shut up," said the woman. "I want a sandwich."

"For that you'll have to wait."

Alice wondered why she hadn't heard the car or the footsteps on the gravel before the knock. "I'll bet I'm plastered," she thought. She could hear the car drive away all right.

"Can't take 'no' for an answer," Alice said aloud. "Just because a person wants to take a day to rest and get pulled together, why, they've got to have a god-damned sandwich."

She held up the bottle and squinted judiciously through the glass. "Not a lot left." She became frightened. Suppose she should run out before she was ready? And then she nodded and smiled to herself. There were two bottles of port wine right in the back of that cabinet. They gave her a sense of security and she poured herself a big drink and sipped at it. Juan didn't like to be around women when they were drinking. He said their faces got crooked and he hated that. Well, Alice would just show him. She drank half the whisky in her glass and stood up heavily.

"Now, you just stay here and wait for me," she said politely to the glass. Turning the edge of the counter she swayed a little, and the corner bit into her side just above the hip. "That's going to be black and blue," she said. She crossed the bedroom and went into the bathroom.

She dampened the washcloth and rubbed soap into it till she had a thick paste and then she scrubbed her face. She scrubbed hard beside her nose and in the little crease that crossed her chin. She put the cloth over her little finger and twisted it into her nostrils and she washed her ears. Then, with her eyes squinted shut, she rinsed the soap off and looked at herself in the mirror over the basin. Her face seemed very red and her eyes were a little bloodshot. For a long time she worked on her face. Cream, and then that rubbed off on a towel. She inspected the towel for dirt and found it. She worked at her eyebrows with a brown eyebrow pencil. The lipstick gave her some trouble. She got a blob of carmine red too low on her under lip and had to wipe it all off on the towel and start again. She made her lips very full and then put them together and rolled one against the other, and she looked at her teeth and rubbed some lipstick off with her towel. She should have washed her teeth before she put on the lipstick. Now powder.

That would take the redness out of her face. Then she brushed her hair. She had never liked her hair. Holding it this way and that for effect, she began to lose interest.

In the bedroom she dug out a close-fitting black felt hat with a kind of a visor. She pushed her hair up inside the hat and angled the brim rakishly. "Now," she said, "now we'll see how a woman's face gets crooked. I wish Juan would come home right now. He'd change his tune."

In the bedroom she got the bottle of Bellodgia from her dresser drawer and put perfume on her bosom and on the lobes of her ears and at her hair line. And she patted a little on her upper lip. "I like to smell it too," she said.

She walked back to the lunchroom, carefully avoiding the corner that had struck her before. It was even darker than it had been, for the clouds were getting thick and very little light was coming through. Alice sat down at her table and adjusted her hand mirror. "Pretty," she said, "you're kind of pretty. What are you doing this evening? Would you like to go dancing?"

She poured off the drink in her glass. Suppose that driver for the Red Arrow Line should come by and knock on the door. She'd let him in. He was a greater kidder. She'd give him a drink or two and then she'd show him a thing or two.

"Red," she'd say, "you set yourself up as a great kidder but I'm going to show you something. There's some kidding on the level." She let her mind dwell on his narrow waist and heavy muscled forearms. He wore a broad belt around his blue jeans, and the jeans—well, the guy was O.K. Something about thinking of those jeans. There was a copper rivet at the bottom where the fly started. And something about that rivet brought sorrow to Alice. Bud had had one. A copper rivet just there. She tried to evade this vision too, and failing, gathered it—gathered it to her mind. He had begged her over and over again. And finally they walked four miles out to the picnic grounds. Bud carried the lunch—hard-boiled eggs and ham sandwiches and an apple pie. Alice bought the pie but she told Bud she made it. And he didn't even wait for the lunch.

He hurt her. And after, she said, "Where are you going?"

"I've got work to do," Bud said.

"You said you love me."

"Did I?"

"You aren't going to leave me, Bud?"

"Listen, sister, you got laid, that's all. I didn't sign no long-term contract."

"But it's the first time, Bud."

"There's got to be a first time for everybody," he said.

Alice was crying over herself now. "It's no damn good!" she shouted at herself in the mirror. "None of it's any damn good." She blubbered while she drank off another whisky and poured the last of the bottle into her glass.

All the others were no damn good, either, and what had she now? A stinking job with bed privileges and no pay. That's what. And married to a stinking greaser, that's what. Married to him! Too far out in the country to go to the movies. Got to sit in a stinking lunchroom.

She put her head down on her arms and cried brokenheartedly. And a second Alice could hear her crying. A second Alice stood at her shoulder and watched her. Got to walk on eggs all the time to keep him happy. She raised her head and looked in the mirror. The lipstick was smeared all over her upper lip. Her eyes were red and her nose was running. She reached for the napkin container, pulled out two paper napkins, and blew her nose. She balled up the paper and threw it on the floor.

What did she want to keep this joint clean for? Who cared? Who gave a damn about her? Nobody! But she could take care of herself. Nobody was going to kick Alice around and get away with it. She emptied the last of the whisky.

Getting out the port wine was a job. She staggered and fell against the sink. There was hot pressure against the inside of her nose and her breath whistled in her nostrils. She stood the bottle of port wine on the counter and got a corkscrew. The bottle fell over when she tried to get the corkscrew into it, and the second time the cork broke into small pieces. She pushed the rest of it into the bottle with her thumb and lunged back to the table.

"Soda pop," she said. She filled her glass full of the dark red wine. "Wish there was some more whisky." Her mouth was dry. She drank half the tumbler of wine thirstily. "Why, that's good," she giggled. Maybe she'd always have whisky first to give flavor to the wine.

She drew the mirror close to her. "You're an old bag," she said bitterly. "You're a dirty drunken old bag. No wonder nobody wants you. I wouldn't have you myself."

The image in the mirror was not double but it had double outlines, and at the outside of her range of vision Alice could feel the room begin to rock and sway. She drank the rest of the glass and choked and sputtered and the red wine ran out of the corners of her mouth. She missed the glass and poured wine over the tabletop before she got her glass filled. Her heart was pounding. She could hear it, and she could feel it beat in her arms and shoulders and in the veins on her breasts. She drank solemnly.

I'm gonna pass out, and a damn good thing. I wish I would never come to. I wish that would be the end of it—the end of it—the end of it— Show these bastards I don't have to live if I don't want to. I'll show 'em.

And then she saw the fly. He wasn't an ordinary housefly but a newborn bluebottle, and his body shone with an iridescent blue sheen. He had come to the table and was standing on the edge of the pool of wine. He dipped his proboscis and went back to cleaning himself.

Alice sat perfectly still. Her flesh crawled with hatred. All her unhappiness, all her resentments, centered in the fly. With an effort of will she forced the two images of the fly to be one image. "You son of a bitch," she said softly. "You think I'm drunk. I'll show you."

Her eyes were wary and smart. Slowly, slowly, she slipped sideways from the table and crouched low to the floor, supporting herself with her hand. She kept her eyes on the fly. He had not moved. She crept over to the counter and went behind it. A dish towel was lying on the stainless steel sink. She took it in her right hand and folded it carefully. It was too light. She dampened it under the tap and squeezed out the excess water. "I'll show the son of a bitch," she said, and she moved catlike along the counter. The fly was still there, still shining.

Alice raised her hand and let the towel fall back on her shoulder. Step by careful step she moved close, her hand raised and flexed. She struck. Bottle and glasses and sugar dispenser and napkin holder all crashed to the floor. The fly zoomed and circled. Alice stood still, following him with her eyes. He landed on the lunch counter. She lunged, striking at him, and when he rose again she flailed the air with the towel.

"That's not the way," she said to herself. "Creep up on him. Creep up on him." The floor tilted under her feet. She put out her hand and supported herself on the stool. Where was he now? She could hear the buzz. The angry, sickening whine of his wings. He's got to land sometime, somewhere. She felt sickness rising in her throat.

The fly made a series of loops and eights and circles and then settled down to low, swooping flights from one end of the room to the other. Alice waited. There was darkness crowding in on the edges of her vision. The fly landed with a little plop on the box of cornflakes on the top of the great pyramid of dry cereals on the shelf behind the counter. He landed on the "C" of "corn" and moved restlessly over to the "O." He stood very still. Alice snuffled.

The room was rocking and whirling but with will power the fly and the area around him were unblurred. Her left hand reached back to the counter and her fingers crept across it. She moved silently, slowly, around the end of the counter. She raised her right hand very, very carefully. The fly sprang forward a step and paused again. He was ready to take off. Alice sensed it. She sensed his rise before he rose. She swung with all the weight of her body. The wet towel smashed against the pyramid of cardboard boxes and followed through. Boxes and a row of glasses and a bowl of oranges crashed to the floor behind the counter and Alice fell on top.

The room rushed in on her with red and blue lights. Under her cheek a broken box spilled out its cornflakes. She raised her head once and then put it down again and a rolling darkness dropped over her.

The lunchroom was dusky and very quiet. The fly moved to the edge of the drying pool of wine on the white tabletop. For a moment he sensed in all directions for danger, and then deliberately he dipped his flat proboscis into the sweet, sticky wine.

TWELVE

The clouds piled in gray threat on threat and a blue darkness settled on the land. In the San Juan valley the darker greens seemed black and the lighter green of grass, a chilling wet blue. "Sweetheart" came rolling heavily along the highway and the aluminum paint on her gleamed with the evil of a gun. Away to the south a bank of dark cloud fringed off into rain and the curtain of it descended slowly.

The bus pulled in close to the gas pumps in front of Breed's store and stopped. The little boxing gloves, the baby shoe, swung back and forth in little pendulum jerks. Juan sat in the seat after the bus had stopped. He raced the motor for a moment, listening to it, and then he sighed and turned the key and the engine stopped.

"How long are you going to wait here?" Van Brunt asked.

"I'm going to take a look at the bridge," said Juan.

"It's still there," Van Brunt said.

"So are we," said Juan. He pulled the lever to open the door.

Breed came out of his screen door and walked toward the bus. He shook hands with Juan. "Aren't you a little late?"

"I don't think so," said Juan, "unless my watch is off."

Pimples climbed down and stood beside them. He wanted to be ahead so he could see the blonde get off the bus.

"Got any coke?" he asked.

"No," said Breed. "Few bottles of Pepsi-Cola. Haven't had any coke for a month. It's the same stuff. You can't tell them apart."

"How's the bridge?" Juan asked.

Mr. Breed shook his head. "I think here goes your ball game. Take a look for yourself. I don't like it."

"There's no break yet?" Juan asked.

"She could go like that," said Breed, and he sideswiped the palms of his hands together. "She's got a strain on her that makes her cry like a baby. Let's take a look."

Mr. Pritchard and Ernest climbed down from the bus and then Mildred and Camille, with Norma behind her. Camille was expert. Pimples didn't see anything.

"They got some Pepsi-Cola," Pimples said. "You like to have one?"

Camille turned to Norma. She was beginning to see how Norma could be valuable. "Like a drink?" she asked.

"Well, I wouldn't mind," said Norma.

Pimples tried not to show his disappointment. Breed and Juan strolled down the highway toward the river. "Going to look at the bridge," Juan called over his shoulder.

Mrs. Pritchard called from the step, "Dear, do you think you could get me a cold drink? Just water if there isn't anything else. And ask where the 'you-know-what' is."

"It's around back," said Norma.

Breed fell into step beside Juan as they strode toward the bridge. "I've been expecting her to go out every year," he said. "I wish we'd get a bridge so when a big rain came I could sleep at night. I just lay in bed and hear the rain on the roof, but I'm listening for the bridge to go out. And I don't even know what kinda sound she'll make when she goes."

Juan grinned at him. "I know how that is. I remember in Torreón when I was a little kid. We used to listen at night for the popping that meant fighting. We kinda liked the fighting, but it always meant my old man would go away for a while. And at last he went away and he didn't come back. I guess we always knew that would happen."

"What became of him?" Breed asked.

"I don't know. Somebody got him, I guess. He couldn't stay home when there was any fighting. He had to get in it. I don't think he much cared what they were fighting about. When he came home he was full of stories every time." Juan chuckled. "He used to tell one about Pancho Villa. He said a poor woman came to Villa and said, 'You have shot my husband and now I and the little ones will starve.' Well, Villa had plenty of money then. He had the presses and he was printing his own. He turned to his treasurer and said, 'Roll out five kilos of twenty-peso bills for this poor woman.' He wasn't even counting it, he had so much. So they did and they tied the bills together with wire and that woman went out. Well, then a sergeant said to Villa, 'There was a mistake, my general. We did not shoot that woman's husband. He got drunk and we put him in jail.' Then Pancho said, 'Go immediately and shoot him. We cannot disappoint that poor woman.'"

Breed said, "It don't make any sense."

Juan laughed. "I know, that's what I like about it. God, that river is eating around the back of the breakwater."

"I know. I tried to phone and tell them," said Breed. "I can't get anybody on the phone."

They walked together out on the wooden bridge. And the moment Juan stepped on the flooring he could feel the thrumming vibration of the water. The bridge shivered and trembled. And there was a deep hum in the timbers that was louder than the rush of the water. Juan looked over the side of the bridge. The supporting timbers were under water and the river foamed and bubbled under it. And the whole bridge trembled and panted, and there were little strained cries from the timbers where the iron turnbolts went through. As they watched, a great old live oak tree came rolling heavily down the stream. When it struck the bridge and turned, the whole structure cried out and seemed to brace itself. The tree caught in the submerged underpinning and there came a shrill, ripping sound from under the bridge. The two men moved quickly back off the bridgehead.

"How fast is she coming up?" Juan asked.

"Ten inches in the last hour. Of course, she might start to go down now. Might have reached flood."

Juan looked at the side of the supporting streamers. His eye found a brown bolthead on the edge of the water and he kept his eyes on it. "I guess I could make it all right," he said. "I could make a run for it. Or I could get the passengers to walk across and I could drive over and pick them up on the other side. How's the other bridge?"

"I don't know," said Breed. "I tried to phone and find out but I can't get anybody. And suppose you cross this one and the other one's out, and you come back and this one's out? You'd be trapped in the bend. You'd have some mighty sore passengers."

"I'm going to have some mighty sore passengers anyway," said Juan. "I've got one—no, two—that are going to raise hell no matter what happens. I know the signs. You know a man named Van Brunt?"

"Oh, that old fart! Yes, I know him. He owes me thirty-seven dollars. I sold him some alfalfa seed and he claimed it was no good. Wouldn't pay for it. He's got bills all over the county. Nothing he buys is any good. I wouldn't sell him a candy bar on credit. He'd claim it wasn't sweet. So you got him along?"

"I got him," said Juan. "And I got a man from Chicago. Big business bug. He's going to be pretty sore if things don't come out the way he wants them to."

"Well," said Breed, "you got to make up your own mind."

Juan looked at the threatening sky. "I guess it's going to rain, all right. And with the hills full up it'll all dump right into the river. I could get over all right, but about what chance have I got to get back?"

"About ten per cent," said Breed. "How's your wife?"

"Not too good," said Juan. "She's got a toothache."

"It pays to keep your teeth up," said Breed. "Should go to the dentist every six months."

Juan laughed. "I know. Are you acquainted with anybody that does?"

"No," said Breed. He liked Juan. He didn't even consider him a foreigner.

"I don't either," said Juan. "Well, there's one other way to stay out of trouble with the passengers."

"What's that?"

"Let them decide. This is a democracy, isn't it?"

"They'll just get to fighting."

"Well, what's wrong with that if they fight each other?" said Juan.

"You've got something there," Breed said. "But I'll tell you one thing. Whatever side everybody else is on, Van Brunt is gonna be on the other side. There's a fellow wouldn't vote for the second coming of Christ if it was a popular measure."

"He's all right," said Juan. "You just gotta know how to handle him. I had a horse once that was so ornery that if you reined left he'd turn right. I fooled him. I did everything opposite and he thought he was getting his own way. You could get Van Brunt to do almost anything by disagreeing with him."

"I'm going to forbid him to pay that thirty-seven dollars," said Breed.

"It might work at that," Juan said. "Well, the river isn't at flood. That bolthead is covered. I'm going to see what the passengers want to do."

Back in the store Pimples felt a little cheated. He had been maneuvered into buying both Norma and Camille a Pepsi-Cola. Try as he would, he couldn't separate Camille from Norma. And it wasn't Norma's fault. Camille was using her.

Norma was flushed with pleasure. She had never been so happy in her life. This beautiful creature was nice to her. They were friends. And she didn't say they'd live together. She said she'd see how things worked out. For some reason this gave Norma a great deal of confidence. People had not been nice to Norma. They had said "yes" to things and then wormed out of them. But this girl, who looked like everything Norma wanted to be, said "she'd see." In her mind Norma could see the apartment they would get. It would have a velvet davenport and a coffee table in front of it. And the drapes would be wine-colored velvet. They'd have a radio and phonograph combination, of course, and plenty of records. She didn't like to think past that. It was almost like spoiling her luck to think past that. There was a kind of an electric blue for the davenport.

She raised her glass of Pepsi-Cola and let the sweet, biting drink run down her throat, and in the middle of the swallow despair settled down on her like a heavy gas. "It won't ever happen," her mind cried. "It'll get away! It'll be just like always and I'll be alone again." She squeezed her eyes shut and wiped the back of her hand across them. When she opened her eyes again she was all right. "I'll save it," she thought. "Little by little I'll make the apartment, and then if it doesn't happen I'll still have it." A hardness came over her and an acceptance. "If any of it comes through it'll just be gravy. But I can't expect it, I can't let myself expect it. That will take it away from me."

Pimples said, "I've got plenty of plans. I'm studying radar. That's going to be a very important job. Fellow that knows radar is going to be fixed pretty nice. I think a person's got to look ahead, don't you? You take some people, they don't look ahead into the future and they end up right where they started." A little smile was fixed on Camille's lips.

"You've got something there," she said. She wished she could get away from this kid. He was a nice kid, but she just wished she could get away from him. She could practically smell him. "Thank you very much for the drink," she said. "I think I'll just go and freshen up a little. You want to come, Norma?"

A look of devotion came on Norma's face. "Oh, yes," she said, "I guess I ought to freshen up too." Everything Camille said was right, was dainty and fine. "Oh, Jesus Christ, let it happen!" Norma cried in her mind.

Mrs. Pritchard was sipping a lemonade. It had taken a little time to get it because they didn't serve lemonade. But when Mrs. Pritchard had pointed out the lemons in the grocery section and had even offered to squeeze them herself—well, there was nothing Mrs. Breed could do, and she'd made it.

"I just can't drink old bottled things," Mrs. Pritchard explained. "I like just the pure fruit juice." Mrs. Breed resentfully went down under this wave of sweetness. Mrs. Pritchard sipped her lemonade and looked through a rack of postcards on the novelty counter. There were pictures of the courthouse in San Juan de la Cruz and of the hotel in San Ysidro which was built over a hot spring of epsom salts. A fine old hotel much frequented by rheumatic people who bathed in the strong waters. The hotel was called a Spa on the postcards. There were other items on the novelty counter. Painted plaster dogs and glass pistols full of colored candy and bright kewpie dolls and fancy redwood boxes of glacée California fruits. And there were lamps whose shades turned when the lights were on so that the forest fires and ships under full sail moved and shone in a very lifelike manner.

Ernest Horton stood at the counter too and looked at the display with a certain amount of contempt. He said to Mr. Pritchard, "Sometimes I think I ought to open a novelty store with all new stuff. Some of this old stuff's been on the market for years and nobody buys it. Now my company has nothing but up-and-coming stock, all new."

Mr. Pritchard nodded. "Gives a man confidence to work for a firm he knows is on its toes," he said. "That's why I think you might like to work for us. You could be sure we're on our toes every hour of the day."

Ernest said, "Excuse me, I'm going to get my case. I've got an item that really isn't before the public yet but it's gone like hot cakes to the trade already, just to the trade. I'd like to place a few here, maybe."

He went out quickly and lugged his sample case in. He opened it and brought out a cardboard box. "Plain wrapping, you see. That's for the surprise." He opened the box and took out a perfect little high tank toilet twelve inches high. There was the box and a little chain with a brass knob on the bottom, and the toilet bowl was white. And it even had a little seat cover colored to look like wood.

Mrs. Breed had moved down in back of the counter. "My husband does all the buying," she said. "You'll have to see him."

"I know," said Ernest. "I just want you to look at this item. It sells itself."

"What's it for?" Mr. Pritchard asked.

"You just watch," said Ernest. He pulled the little chain and immediately the toilet bowl flushed with a brown fluid. Ernest lifted the toilet seat right out of the bowl and it was a small glass. "That's one ounce," he said triumphantly. "If you want a double shot, say for a highball, you pull the chain twice."

"Whisky!" cried Mr. Pritchard.

"Or brandy, or rum," said Ernest. "Anything you want. See, here in the tank is the place you fill it, and the tank is guaranteed plastic. It knocks 'em cold. I've got orders for eighteen hundred of this little item already. It's a knockout. It gets a laugh every time."

"By George, that's clever," Mr. Pritchard said. "Who thinks these things up?"

"Well," Ernest explained, "we've got an idea department. Everybody puts ideas in. This item was suggested by our salesman in the Great Lakes area. He'll make himself a nice bonus. Our company gives two per cent of the profits to any employee who sends in a workable idea."

"It's clever," Mr. Pritchard repeated. In his mind he could see Charlie Johnson when he first saw it. Charlie would want to rush right out and get one for himself. "What do you get for them?" Mr. Pritchard asked.

"Well, this one retails for five dollars. But if you don't mind my making the suggestion, we have a model that sells for twenty-seven fifty."

Mr. Pritchard pursed his lips.

"But look what you get," Ernest went on. "This one is plastic. The better item is—well, the box is oak and is made of old whisky barrels so that it'll take the liquor fine. The chain is real silver and it has a Brazilian diamond for a knob. The bowl is porcelain, real toilet quality porcelain, and the seat is hand-carved mahogany. And on the box there's a little silver plate for, if, like you wanted to present it to a lodge or a club, your name goes on that."

"It sounds like a good value," Mr. Pritchard said. His mind was made up. He knew how he would get the better of Charlie Johnson now. He would give one of the toilets to Charlie. But on the plate he would put "Presented to Charlie Johnson, the all-American soandso, by Elliott Pritchard," and then let Charlie show off all he wanted to. Everybody would know who had the idea first.

"You haven't got one with you, have you?" he asked.

"No, you have to order."

Mrs. Pritchard spoke up. She had moved close, quietly. "Elliott, you're not going to get one of those. Elliott, they're vulgar."

"I wouldn't have it around if there were ladies, of course," said Mr. Pritchard. "No, little girl. Know what I'm going to do? I'm gonna send one of them to Charlie Johnson. That'll get back at him for sending me that stuffed skunk. Yes, sir, I'll fix him."

Mrs. Pritchard explained. "Charlie Johnson was Mr. Pritchard's roommate in college. They have the wildest jokes. They're like little boys when they get together."

"Now," said Mr. Pritchard seriously, "if I ordered one, could you have it sent to an address I'll give you? And could you have it engraved? I'll write what I want you to put on the plate."

"What are you going to say?" Bernice asked.

"Little girls keep their noses out of big man's business," said Mr. Pritchard.

"I'll bet it'll be awful," said Bernice.

Mildred was in the dumps. She felt heavy and tired and she wasn't interested in anything. She was sitting in a twisted wire candy-store chair all by herself at the end of the counter. Cynically she had watched Pimples trying to get the blonde alone. The trip had let her down. She was disgusted with herself and what had happened. What kind of a girl was she if a bus driver could set her off? She shivered a little with distaste. Where was he now? Why didn't he come back? She smothered her impulse to get up and go look for him. Van Brunt's voice sounded beside her so that she jumped.

"Young lady," he said, "your skirt shows. I thought you'd like to know."

"Oh, yes. Thank you very much."

"You might have gone all day thinking you were all fixed up if somebody didn't tell you," he said.

"Oh, yes, thank you." She stood up and, leaning backward, pushed her skirt against her legs so that she could see. There was an inch of slip showing behind.

"I think it's better to be told things like that," Van Brunt said.

"Oh, it is. I guess I broke a shoulder strap."

"I don't care to hear about your underwear," he said coldly. "My only remark is—and I repeat it—your skirt shows. I don't want you to think I had any other motive."

"I don't," said Mildred helplessly.

Van Brunt went on, "Too many young girls get self-conscious of their legs. They think everybody is looking at them."

Suddenly Mildred was laughing wildly like a sick woman.

"What's so funny?" Van Brunt demanded angrily.

"Nothing," said Mildred. "I just thought of a joke." She had remembered that Van Brunt had never missed any show of legs all morning.

"Well, if it's that funny, tell it," he said.

"Oh, no. It's a personal joke. I'll go out and fix my strap." She looked at him and then, deliberately, she said, "You see, there are two straps on each shoulder. One is for the slip and the other supports the brassière and the brassière holds the breasts up firmly." She saw Van Brunt's color come up out of his collar. "There isn't anything below that until the panties, if I wore panties, which I don't."

Van Brunt turned and walked away quickly and Mildred felt better. Now the old fool wouldn't have a comfortable moment. She could watch him and maybe later trick him and catch him in the act. She got up, laughing to herself, and went out around the back of the store to the lean-to marked "Ladies."

A lattice covered the door and the morning glory was beginning to climb up. Mildred stood in front of the closed door. She could hear Norma talking to the blonde inside. She listened. Maybe this would make the trip worth while, just listening to people talk. Mildred liked to eavesdrop on people. Sometimes her liking to bothered her. She could listen to inanities with interest. But of all the listening, the best was in women's rest rooms. The freedom of women in any room where there was a toilet, a mirror, and a washbowl had interested her for a long time. She had once written a paper in college, which had been considered daring, in which she had maintained that women lost their inhibitions when their skirts were up.

It must be either that, she thought, or the certainty that man, the enemy, could never invade this territory. It was the one place in the world where women could be certain there would be no men. And so they relaxed and became outwardly the people they were inwardly. She had thought a great deal about it. Women were more friendly or more vicious to one another in public toilets, but on personal terms. Perhaps that was because there were no men. Because, where there were no men, there was no competition, and their poses dropped from them.

Mildred wondered whether it was the same in men's toilets. She just didn't think it was likely, because men had many competitions besides women, while most of women's insecurities had to do with men. Her paper on the subject had been returned marked "Not carefully thought out." She planned to do it over again.

Out in the store she had not been friendly toward Camille. She just didn't like her. But she knew her dislike would not carry into the rest room. She thought, "Isn't it strange that women will compete for men they don't even want?"

Norma and Camille were talking on and on. Mildred put her hand on the door and pushed it open. In the small room were a toilet stall and a washbowl with a square mirror over it. A dispenser of paper seatcovers was on one wall, and paper towels beside the basin. A slot machine for sanitary pads was on the wall beside the frosted glass window. The concrete floor was painted dark red and the walls were thick with layers of white paint. There was a sharp smell of perfumed disinfectant in the air.

Camille was seated on the toilet and Norma stood in front of the mirror. They both looked at Mildred as she came in.

"Want to get in here?" Camille asked.

"No," said Mildred. "I've got a drooping strap on my slip."

Camille looked down at the skirt. "You have all right. No, not that way," she said to Norma. "You see the way your hair line goes? Well, make the eyebrows go up a little on the outside, just a little. Wait, honey. Wait a minute and I'll show you."

She stood up and moved to Norma. "Turn around so I can see you. There, now. And there, now look at yourself. See how it kind of brings down your hairline a little bit? Your forehead's high so you try to bring it down. Now look, close your eyes." She took the eyebrow pencil from Norma and rubbed it gently on the lower lids just below the lashes, making the line a little darker as it passed the outside corners.

"You've got the mascara on too thick, honey," she said. "See how the lashes stick together? Use more water and take a little more time. Wait a minute." She brought out of her purse a little plastic case of eyeshadow. "Now you go careful with this stuff." She dipped her finger into the blue paste, rubbed a little on each of Norma's upper eyelids, making it heavier toward the outside corners. "Now, let me see." She inspected her work. "Look, honey, you keep your eyes too wide, like a rabbit. Let your upper lids down a little bit. No, and don't squint. Just let your upper lids droop down a little bit. There, like that. Now look at yourself. See the difference?"

"My God, I look different," Norma said. Her voice was awed.

"Sure you do. Now, you've got the lipstick on all wrong. Look, honey, your lower lip is too thin. So is mine. Bring the lipstick down a little bit here, and a little here."

Norma stood still like a good child and let her work.

"See? Heavier in the corners," Camille said. "Now your lower lip looks fuller."

Mildred said, "You're good. I could use some advice too."

"Oh, well," said Camille. "It's pretty simple."

"That's theatrical make-up," Mildred said. "I mean it's a kind of theatrical type make-up."

"Well, you know, dealing with the public—dentists use their nurses almost like receptionists."

"Oh, damn it!" Mildred exclaimed. "This strap isn't loose, it's broken." She peeled her dress off her shoulder and she had a little silken string in her hand.

"You'll have to pin it," Camille said.

"But I haven't got a pin and my needle and thread's in one of the suitcases!"

Camille opened her purse again, and in the lining were half a dozen tiny safety pins. "Here," said Camille, "I always go heeled." She unfastened one of the pins. "You want me to fix it for you?"

"If you don't mind. My damned eyes. I can't see anything."

Camille pulled the loose slip up, folded the end of the strap, and pinned it firmly to the edge of the slip. "That's hardly all right, but at least it doesn't show. It's still a pin job. You always been shortsighted, honey?"

"No," said Mildred. "I was all right until—well, right when I was about fourteen. One doctor said it had to do with puberty. He said some girls get their eyesight back when they have their first baby."

"That's tough," said Camille.

"It's a damn nuisance," Mildred said. "I don't care how much they make new shapes of glasses. They still aren't very good looking."

"Ever heard of that kind that fit right down against the eyes?"

"I've thought about it and I haven't done anything about it. I guess I'm scared to have anything touch my eyes."

Norma was still regarding herself with wonder in the mirror. Her eyes had suddenly become larger and her lips fuller and softer and the wet rat look had gone from her face.

"Isn't she wonderful?" Norma said to no one. "Isn't she just wonderful?"

Camille said, "She's gonna be a pretty kid when she learns a few tricks and gets some confidence. We'll touch up that hair, honey, as soon as we get in."

"You mean you've thought it over?" Norma cried. "You mean we'll get the apartment?" She whirled on Mildred. "We're going to have an apartment," she said breathlessly. "We're going to have a davenport and Sunday morning we'll wash and set our hair—"

"We'll see," Camille broke in. "We'll just have to see how things work out. Here's the two of us without jobs and already she's got a duplex rented. Hold your horses, honey."

"It's a funny trip," Mildred said. "We're on our way to Mexico. Everything's gone wrong from the start. My father wanted to see the country. He thinks we might settle in California some time. So he wanted to take the bus to Los Angeles. He thought he could see the country better."

"Well, he can," said Camille.

"He can see too much of it maybe," Mildred said. "But did you ever see such a collection of people as we've got?"

"They're all about the same," said Camille.

"I like Mr. Chicoy," said Mildred. "He's part Mexican, you know. But that boy! I've got a feeling he'd climb all over you if you weren't careful."

"Oh, he's all right," Camille said. "He's just a little goaty. Most kids are like that. He'll probably get over it."

"Or maybe he won't," said Mildred. "Did you take a good look at that old fellow, Van Brunt? He didn't get over it. It just ingrew. That's a pretty filthy man in his mind."

Camille smiled. "He's pretty old," she said.

Mildred went into the little cubicle and sat down. "There's something I wanted to ask you," she said. "My father thinks he's seen you somewhere. He's got a pretty good memory. Did you ever see him?"

For a second Mildred saw the hostility in Camille's eyes, saw the tightened mouth, and she knew she'd touched something sore. And instantly Camille's face was placid again.

"I think I must look like somebody else," she said. "This time he's made a mistake unless he saw me in the street somewhere."

"On the level?" Mildred asked. "I'm not trying to catch you now. I just wondered."

The friendliness, the companionship, the relaxation, slipped from the room. It was as though a man had entered. Camille's eyes stabbed at Mildred. "He made a mistake," she said coldly. "You can take that any way you want."

The door opened and Mrs. Pritchard came in. "Oh, there you are," she said to Mildred. "I thought you'd wandered off."

"Oh, I broke a strap on my slip," said Mildred.

"Well, hurry up. Mr. Chicoy's back and there's quite an argument going on— Thank you, dear," she said to Norma, who had moved away from the basin to make room for her. "I'll just moisten my handkerchief and take a little of the dust off— Why don't you have a lemonade?" she said to Mildred. "That nice woman doesn't mind making them at all. I told her she'd be quite famous if she just served pure fruit juices."

Suddenly Camille said, "I wish we could get something to eat. I'm getting hungry. I'd like something good."

"So would I," said Mrs. Pritchard.

"I'd like a cold cracked crab with mayonnaise and a bottle of beer," Camille said.

"Well, I've never had crab that way," said Mrs. Pritchard, "but I wish you could have tasted the way my mother fried butterfish. She used to take an old-fashioned cast-iron skillet—and the fish, it had to be very fresh and very carefully trimmed. She'd make a batter with brown toasted crumbs—bread crumbs, not cracker crumbs—and she'd put a whole tablespoon—no, two tablespoonfuls—of Worcestershire sauce in a beaten egg. I think that was the secret."

"Mother," said Mildred, "don't start on the butterfish recipe."

"You'd better have a lemonade," said Mrs. Pritchard. "It'd clean up your skin. A good long trip makes a person blotchy."

"I wish we'd get moving," Mildred said. "We can get lunch in the next town. What's its name?"

"San Juan de la Cruz," said Norma.

"San Juan de la Cruz," Mrs. Pritchard repeated softly. "I think the Spanish names are so pretty."

Norma took a long, astonished look at herself in the mirror before they went out. She drooped her eyes. It was going to take practice to remember to do that all the time, but it changed her whole appearance and she liked it.

THIRTEEN

Juan sat on a stool drinking a Pepsi-Cola and rubbing the shiny end of his amputated finger over the corduroy ridges of his trousers. When the women came around from the back and entered the store he looked up at them and the rubbing of his finger became a tapping.

"Is everybody here?" he asked. "No, there's one missing. Where's Mr. Van Brunt?"

"I'm over here." He spoke from behind the counter on the grocery side, where, concealed by a stacked wall of canned coffee, he was inspecting the shelves idly.

Mr. Pritchard said, "I want to know when we can get started. I have connections to make."

"I know," Juan said gently, "and that's what I want to talk about. The bridge is not safe. I can probably get across it. But there's another bridge and it may be out, or it may go out. We can't get any news about it. If we get into the bend of the river with both bridges out, we'd be caught, and nobody could make any connections. Now, I'm willing to take a vote and do anything the majority of the passengers want to do. I'll make a run for it and take a chance, or I'll take you back and you can make other plans. It's up to you. But when you make up your minds I want you to stick to the verdict."

He raised the bottle and drank the Pepsi-Cola.

"I haven't the time," Mr. Pritchard said loudly. "Look, my friend. I've had no vacation since the war started. I've been making the implements of war that gave us the victory, and this is my first vacation. I just haven't the time to go gallivanting all over the country. I need a rest. I only have a few weeks and this is eating them up."

Juan said, "I'm sorry. I'm not doing it on purpose, you know, and if you got caught in the bend of the river you might lose a lot more time and I might lose the bus getting it across. The bridge is strained to the breaking point. It may come down any minute. The only other choice is to go back."

Van Brunt came from behind the stack of coffee. He had a two-and-a-half pound can of sliced peaches in his hand. He crossed the store to Mrs. Breed. "How much?" he asked.

"Forty-seven cents."

"My God! For a can of peaches?"

"The profit hasn't changed," she said. "We've just got to pay more for them."

Van Brunt threw a half-dollar violently down on the counter. "Open 'em up," he said. "Forty-seven cents for a mean little can of peaches!"

Mrs. Breed put the can in a wall opener, turned the crank, and stopped just as the edge raised. She passed the can over the counter to Van Brunt. He drank off part of the juice first, then reached in and picked out a yellow slice with his fingers. He held it over the open can to drip.

"Now I heard what you said," he observed. "You think you can waste our time. I've got to get in to the courthouse and I've got to get in this afternoon. And it's up to you to get me through. You're a common carrier, subject to the rules of the railroad commission."

"That's what I'm trying to do," said Juan. "And one of the rules of the commission is don't kill the passengers."

"It comes of not knowing the country," Van Brunt went on. "There ought to be a strict law that you've got to know the country before you can drive a bus." He waved a slice of peach and flipped it into his mouth and picked up another slice between his thumb and forefinger. He was enjoying himself.

"You said there was only two things to do. Well, there's three. You don't know about the old road that was there before they put in those damn-fool bridges. It goes right around the outside of the bend. The stagecoaches used to use it."

Juan looked questioningly at Mr. Breed. "I heard about it, but what condition is it in?"

"Stages used it for over a hundred years," said Van Brunt.

Mr. Breed said, "I know it's all right for a couple of miles, but I don't know it beyond that. It goes up the side of the mountain to the east, there. It might be washed out. I haven't been over it since way before the rains."

"You've got your choice," Van Brunt said. He waved his piece of peach, flung it into his mouth, and talked around it. "I told you it was going to rain. I told you the river would be up, and now, when you're stuck, I tell you how to get out of it. Do I have to drive your god-damned bus too?"

Juan bawled, "Keep your pants on and watch your language. There's ladies here."

Van Brunt tilted the can and drank the rest of the juice, straining the peaches out with his teeth. The thick juice ran down his chin and he wiped it off with his sleeve. "God, what a trip!" he said. "Right from the beginning."

Juan turned and faced the other passengers. "Well, there it is. My franchise says I'm supposed to go on the highway. I don't know the old road. I don't know if I could get through or not. It's up to you to decide what you want to do. If we get hung up I don't want to be to blame."

Mr. Pritchard said, "I like to see things get done. Now, I've got to get to Los Angeles, man. I've got airplane tickets for Mexico City. Do you know what they cost? And the planes are booked solid. We've got to get through. Let's get some action on this. You think the bridge is dangerous?"

"I know it's dangerous," said Juan.

"Well," said Mr. Pritchard, "you say you don't know whether you can get through on the old road?"

"That's right," said Juan.

"So you've got two gambles and one sure thing. And the sure thing don't get you through either. Hmmmm," said Mr. Pritchard.

"What do you think, dear?" Mrs. Pritchard said. "We've got to do something. I haven't had a good bath for three days. Dear, we've got to do something."

Mildred said, "Let's try the old road. It might be interesting." She glanced at Juan to see how he would take this attitude, but already his eyes had moved from her to Camille.

Something about the recent association made Camille say, "I vote for the old road. I'm so tired and dirty now, nothing would make much difference to me."

Juan looked down and his eyes sharpened when he saw Norma's face. She didn't look like the same girl. And Norma knew he had noticed. "I say the old road," she said breathlessly.

Ernest Horton found a chair, the one Mrs. Breed ordinarily used when her legs swelled up in the afternoons. He had been watching the counting of noses.

"I don't much care," he said. "Of course, I'd like to get to L. A., but it don't make much difference. I'll stick with the others, whatever they say."

Van Brunt put the can down loudly on the counter. "It's going to rain," he said. "That back road can get awful slippery. You might not make it up over the hill, to the eastward. It's steep and slick. If you mired down there I don't know how you'd ever get out."

"But you're the one that suggested it," Mildred said.

"I'm just getting all the objections down," Van Brunt said. "Just getting them in order."

"How would you vote?" Juan asked.

"Oh, I won't vote. That's the silliest thing I ever heard of. Seems to me the driver ought to make the decisions, like a captain of a ship."

Pimples went to the candy counter. He laid down a dime and picked up two Baby Ruths. He put one in his side pocket to give to Camille when he could get her alone, and the other he unwrapped slowly. A wild, exciting thought had just popped into his mind. Suppose they went over the bridge and right in the middle the span broke and the bus fell into the river? Pimples would be thrown clear, but the blonde would be trapped in the bus. And Pimples dived and dived and he was nearly dead, but at last he broke a window and pulled Camille out and he swam ashore and laid her, unconscious, on the green grass and he rubbed her legs to get the circulation started. But better, he turned her over and he put his hands under her breasts and gave her artificial respiration.

But suppose they took the old road and the bus mired down? Then they'd be there all night, with maybe a fire going, and they'd be together and sit together in front of the fire with a light on their faces and maybe a blanket thrown over the two of them.

Pimples said, "I think we'd better try the old road." Juan looked at him and grinned.

"You've got real Kit Carson blood in you, haven't you, Kit?" And Pimples knew it was a joke, but it wasn't a mean joke.

"Well, I guess that's everybody but one, and he won't vote. What's the matter? Do you want to be able to sue?"

Van Brunt swung around to the others. "You're all being crazy," he said. "Know what he's doing? He's pulling out from under. If anything should happen he won't get the blame because he could say he only did what you told him to. No, he's not going to trap me that way."

Mr. Pritchard cleaned his glasses on his white linen handkerchief. "It's an idea," he said. "I hadn't thought of it quite that way. We're really giving up our rights."

Juan's eyes glowed with rage. His mouth grew thin and tight. "Get in the bus," he said. "I'm taking you back to San Ysidro and dumping you. I'm trying to get you through and you act as though I were trying to murder you. Come on, get in the bus. I'm sick of it. Since last night I've had my life turned upside down for your comfort and I'm tired of it. So come on. We're going back."

Mr. Pritchard walked over to him. "No, I didn't mean that," he said. "I appreciate what you've done. We all do. I was just trying to think clearly on all sides of the subject. That's what I do in business. Don't do anything until you've thought it through."

"I'm sick of it," Juan said again. "You had my bed last night. I just want to get rid of you."

Van Brunt said, "Don't forget, it was your bus that broke down. It wasn't our fault."

Juan said evenly, "Mostly, I think, I want to get rid of you."

"Watch yourself," Van Brunt said. "Don't forget, you're a common carrier with a franchise. After this example it wouldn't be hard to get the franchise removed."

Juan changed suddenly. He laughed. "Boy, that would be a relief. I'd be free of people like you, and I can think where I would put that franchise, rolled up and tied with barbed wire."

Camille laughed aloud and Ernest Horton giggled happily. "I've got to remember that," he said, "yes, sir. Look, Mr. Chicoy, these two men have been talking. The rest of us want to go. We'll take our chance. Why don't you just draw a line and anybody over the line wants to go, the rest stay here. That's fair enough."

Mildred said, "Mr. Chicoy, I want to go."

"O.K.," said Juan. "That big crack there in the floor. Everybody that don't

THE WAYWARD BUS

want me to take the back road get over on the other side with the vegetables."

Nobody moved. Juan looked carefully into each face.

"It isn't legal," Van Brunt said. "It won't hold in any court."

"What won't hold?"

"What you're doing."

"It isn't in any court."

"It may be," said Van Brunt.

"You can't come even if you want to," said Juan.

"You just try to keep me off. I've got a ticket and I've got a right to go on the bus. You just try to keep me off and I'll have you up so fast it'll make your head spin."

Juan hunched his shoulders. "And you would too," he said. "O.K., let's get started." He turned to Mr. Breed. "Could you lend me a few tools? I'll bring them right back."

"What kind of tools?"

"Oh, a pick and shovel."

"Oh, sure. You mean in case you get stuck?"

"Yeah, and have you got a block and tackle?"

"Not a very good one. The blocks are all right, but there's just some old half-inch line on them. I don't know how much strain it would take. That's a pretty heavy bus."

"Well, it would be better than nothing," Juan said. "Haven't got any new line I could buy here, have you?"

"I haven't had a new piece of Manila line since the war started," said Breed. "But you're welcome to what I have got. Come along. Pick up what you want."

Juan said, "Come along, Kit, and give me a hand, will you?" The three went out of the store and around to the back.

Ernest said to Camille, "I wouldn't have missed this. I wouldn't for anything."

"I just wish I wasn't so tired," she said. "I've been riding busses for five days. I want to get out of my clothes and get some real sleep for a couple of days."

"Why didn't you take the train? Chicago, you said?"

"Yes, Chicago."

"Well, you coulda got on the Super Chief and slept all the way to L. A. That's a nice train."

"Saving pennies," said Camille. "I've got a little piece of change and I want to lay around for a few weeks before I got to work. And I'd rather do it in a double bed than a berth."

"Did I catch you right?" he asked.

"You did not," said Camille.

"O.K., you're the boss."

"Look, let's not play," Camille said. "I'm too damn tired to play guessing games with you."

"O.K., sister, O.K. I'll play any way you want."

"Well, then, let's just sit this one out. Do you mind?"

"You know? I like you," Ernest said. "I'd like to take you out when you get rested up."

"Well, we'll see how it goes," Camille said. She liked him. She could talk to him. He knew a few answers and that was a relief.

Norma had been watching them, listening. She was full of admiration for Camille. She wanted to learn just how it was done. Suddenly she realized that her eyes were wide open as a rabbit's and she drooped the upper lids.

Mrs. Pritchard said, "I hope I'm not going to get a headache. Elliott, see if they have any aspirins, will you?"

Mrs. Breed tore a cellophane bag off a big cardboard display. "You want one of them? That's a nickel."

"We better have half a dozen," Mr. Pritchard said.

"That'll be twenty-six cents with tax."

"You needn't have got so many, Elliott," Mrs. Pritchard said. "I have a bottle of five hundred in my bag."

"It's best to be prepared," he answered. He knew her headaches and they were dreadful. They twisted her face and reduced her to a panting, sweating, grinning, quivering blob of pain. They filled a room and a house. They got into everyone around her. Mr. Pritchard could feel one of her headaches through walls. He could feel it all over his body, and the doctor said there was nothing to do about it. They injected calcium and they gave her sedatives. The headaches usually came when she was nervous and when things, through no fault of her own, were not going well.

Her husband would have liked to protect her. They seemed to be selfish, these headaches, and yet they were not. The pain was real. No one could simulate such agonizing pain. Mr. Pritchard dreaded them more than anything in the world. A good one could make the whole house vibrate with horror. And they were a little like conscience. Try as he would, Mr. Pritchard could never lose the feeling that they were in some way his fault. Not that Mrs. Pritchard ever said anything or indicated that this might be so. In fact she was very brave. She tried to muffle her screams with a pillow.

Mr. Pritchard didn't bother her much in bed—very seldom, in fact. But in a curious way he tied up his occasional lust and his loss of self-control with her headaches. It was planted deep in his mind that this was so, and he didn't know how it had got planted. But he did have a conscience about it. His bestiality, his lust, his lack of self-control, were the cause. And he didn't have any means of saving himself. Sometimes he found himself hating his wife very deeply because he was unhappy. He stayed in his office overtime when she had a headache, and sometimes he just sat at his desk for hours, staring at the brown paneling, his body throbbing with his wife's pain.

In the middle of one of her worst spells she would try to save him. "Go to a movie," she would moan. "Go over to Charlie Johnson's. Take some whisky. Get drunk. Don't stay here. Go to a movie." But it was impossible. He couldn't.

He put the six little transparent bags into his coat pocket. "Would you like to take a couple now, just in case?" he asked.

"No," she said. "I think I'm going to be all right." She smiled her brave, sweet smile.

Mildred, when she heard the first mention of aspirin, went to the grocery side and studied the OPA price-ceiling chart on the wall. Her mouth pinched tight and her throat was convulsed. "Oh, Jesus Christ," she said softly under her breath. "Oh, Christ, is she going to start that already?" Mildred didn't quite believe the headaches. She'd never had a bad headache herself, only mild periodic ones and a few hangover headaches at school. She called her mother's psychosomatic and psychotic, and she dreaded them even more than her father did. As a little girl she had run from them and gone to earth in the cellar or in the space behind the cabinet in the sewing room. And usually she was pulled out and taken in to her mother because when mother had a headache she needed love and she needed to be petted. Mildred thought of the headaches as a curse. She hated them. And she hated her mother when she had them.

For a time Mildred had thought them pure sham, and even now, when through reading she knew the pain was real, Mildred still considered the headaches a weapon her mother used with complete cunning, with complete brutality. The headaches were pain to her mother, truly, but they governed and punished the family too. They brought the family to heel. Certain things her mother didn't like were never done because they brought on a headache. And when she was at home, Mildred knew that her fear about getting into the house not later than one in the morning was caused by the almost certainty that her mother would get a headache if she didn't.

Between headaches you forgot how devastating they were. Mildred thought that a psychiatrist was what her mother needed. And Bernice would have done anything. She wanted to do anything. It was Mr. Pritchard who put his foot down. He didn't believe in psychiatrists, he said. But actually he did believe in them, so much that he was afraid of them. For Mr. Pritchard had gradually come to depend on the headaches. They were in a way a justification to him. They were a punishment on him and they gave him sins to be atoned for. Mr. Pritchard needed sins. There were none in his business life, for the cruelties there were defined and pigeonholed as necessity and responsibility to the stockholders. And Mr. Pritchard needed personal sins and personal atonement. He denounced the idea of a psychiatrist angrily.

Mildred forced herself to turn around and go back to her mother. "Are you all right, dear?"

"Yes," Bernice said brightly.

"No headache?"

Bernice was apologetic. "I just had a twinge and it frightened me," she said. "I could never forgive myself if I had one of those horrible things and ruined papa's trip."

Mildred felt a little shiver of fear at this woman who was her mother—at her power and her ruthlessness. It must be unconscious. It had to be. Mildred had seen and heard the engineering of this trip to Mexico. Her father hadn't wanted to go. He would have liked to take a vacation by just staying home from the office, which would mean that he would go to the office every day; but by going at odd hours and returning, not by the clock but by his feeling, he would have had a sense of vacation and rest.

But the trip to Mexico had been planted. When and how? Mildred didn't know and her father didn't know. But gradually he became convinced not only that it was his idea, but that he was forcing his family with him. And this gave him a fine sense of being boss in his own home. He had walked through closing door after closing door in the maze. It was rather like a trap nest. A hen finds a hole, looks in, sees there is a bit of grain, steps through the door—the door closes. Well, here is a nest. It's dark and quiet. Why not lay an egg? It'd be a good joke on whoever left that door open.

Her father had almost forgotten that he didn't want to go to Mexico. Both Mr. and Mrs. Pritchard were doing it for Mildred. That was really the safe thing. She was studying Spanish in college, a language she was incapable of understanding, just as her instructors were. Mexico would be just the place to practice up. Her mother said there was no way of learning a language like having to use it.

Mildred, looking at her mother's sweet, relaxed face, simply could not believe that this woman could engineer a thing and then destroy it. Why? And she would do it. She had planted the idea. Sure as hell she was going to have a headache. But she would wait until she was out of touch with doctors, until her headache would cause the greatest possible impression. It was hard to believe. Mildred didn't think her mother really knew what she was doing. But there was a doughy lump in Mildred's chest and it weighed down on her stomach. The headache was coming. She knew it.

She envied Camille. Camille was a tramp, Mildred thought. And things were so much easier for a tramp. There was no conscience, no sense of loss, nothing but a wonderful, relaxed, stretching-cat selfishness. She could go to bed with anyone she wanted to and never see him again and have no feeling of loss or insecurity about it. That was the way Mildred thought it was with Camille. She wished she could be that way, and she knew she couldn't. Couldn't because of her mother. And the unbidden thought entered her mind—if her mother were only dead Mildred's life would be so much simpler. She could have a secret little place to live somewhere. Almost fiercely, she brushed the thought away. "What a foul thing to think," she said to herself ceremoniously. But it was a dream she often had.

She looked out the front window. Pimples had helped to put the block and tackle into the bus, and the Manila line had grease on it and the grease had got on Pimples' chocolate brown trousers. He was trying to rub out the spot with a handkerchief. "Poor kid," Mildred thought, "that's probably his only suit." She was going to tell him not to touch it when she saw him go to the gasoline pump and put a little of the gas on his handkerchief and go to work expertly on the spot.

And there was Juan calling, "Come on, you folks."

FOURTEEN

The back road around the San Ysidro River bend was a very old road, no one knew how old. It was true that the stage coaches had used it, and men on horseback. In the dry seasons the cattle had been driven over it to the river, where they could lie in the willows during the heat of the day and drink from holes dug in the river bed. The old road was simply a slice of country, uncultivated to start, marked only by wheel ruts and pounded by horses' hoofs. In the summer a heavy cloud of dust arose from its surface when a wagon went by, and in winter, pastelike mud spurted from under horses' feet. Gradually the road became scooped out so that it was lower than the fields through which it traveled, and this made it a long lake of standing water in the winter, sometimes very deep.

Then it was that men with plows made ditches on either side, with the embankments toward the road. And then cultivation came in and the cattle became so valuable that the owners of the property along the road put up fences to keep their cattle in and other people's cattle out.

The fences were split redwood posts set in the ground with one-by-six planks nailed halfway up connecting them. And along the top of the posts was old-fashioned barbed wire, a strip of twisted metal with sharpened spikes. The fences weathered in the sun and rain, the redwood planks and the posts turned light gray and gray-green, and lichens grew on the wood and moss formed on the shady sides of the posts.

Walking men burning with messages came by and painted their messages on the planks. "Repent, for the Kingdom of Heaven is at hand"—"Sinner, come to God"—"It is late"—"Wherefore shall it profit a man . . ."—"Come to Jesus." And other men put other signs on the fence with stencils. "Jay's Drugs"—"Cyrus Noble—The Doctors' Whisky"—"San Ysidro Bicycle Shop." These signs were all weathered and dimmed now.

As the fields were used less for grazing and more for wheat and oats and barley, the farmers began to remove from their fields the weeds, the field turnip, the yellow mustard, the poppies and thistles and milkweeds, and these refugees found a haven in the ditches beside the road. The mustard stood seven feet high in the late spring, and red-winged blackbirds built their nests under the yellow flowers. And in the damp ditches the water cress grew.

The ditches beside the road under the high growth of weeds became the home of weasels and bright-colored water snakes, and the drinking places for birds in the evening. The meadow larks sat all morning on the old fences in the spring and whistled their yodeling song. And the wild doves sat on the barbed wire in the evening in the fall, shoulder to shoulder for miles, and their call rang down the miles in a sustained note. At evening the night hawks coursed along the ditches, looking for meat, and in the dark the barn owls searched for rabbits. And when a cow was sick the great ugly turkey buzzards sat on the old fence waiting for death.

The road was well-nigh abandoned. Only a few families who had farms that could not be reached in any other way ever used it any more. Once there had been many little holdings here, with a man living close to his acres and his farm behind him and his vegetable patch under the parlor window. But now the land stretched away, untenanted, and the little houses and the old barns stood windowless and gray and unpainted.

As noon came on the clouds hurried in from the southwest and bunched together. It is the rule that the longer the clouds prepare, the longer the rain will continue. But it was not ready yet. There were still some patches of blue sky and now and then a blinding flash of sun struck the ground. Once a tall cloud cut sun streaks into long, straight ribbons.

Juan had to drive back a little along the highway to reach the entrance to the old road. Before he turned into it he stopped the bus and got down and walked ahead. He felt the greaselike mud under his feet. And Juan knew a sense of joy. He had been trying to push his carload of cattle bodily about their business in which he had no interest. There was almost a feeling of malice in him now. They had elected this road, and it might be all right. He had a happy vacation-feeling. They wanted it, now let them take it. He would see what they would do if the bus stalled. He dug his toe into the mixed mud and gravel before he turned back. He wondered what Alice was doing. He knew damn well what Alice was doing. And if he wrecked the bus—well, he might just walk away from it, just walk away and never come back. It was a very happy vacation-feeling he had. His face was glowing with pleasure when he climbed into the bus.

"I don't know whether we'll make it or not," he said happily. And the passengers were a little nervous at his exuberance.

The passengers were seated in a bunch, as far forward as they could get. Every one of them felt that Juan was their only contact with the normal,

and if they had known what was in his mind they would have been very
much frightened. There was a high glee in Juan. He closed the door of the
bus and he put his foot twice on the throttle to race his engine before he set
the bus in low gear and turned it into the muddy country road.

The clouds were almost prepared for the stroke now. He knew that. In
the west he could see one cloud fraying down. There it was starting, and it
would move over the valley in another spring downpour. The light had
turned metallic again with a washed, telescopic quality that meant only
violent rain.

Van Brunt said brightly, "The rain's coming."

"Looks like," said Juan, and he turned his bus into the road. He had good
tread on his tires, but as he left the blacktop he could feel the rubber slip
a little on the greasy mud and the rear end swing in a small arc. But there
was a bottom to it, and the bus lumbered over the road. Juan put it in
second gear. He would keep it there probably for the whole distance.

Mr. Pritchard called above the beat of the motor, "How long is this
detour?"

"I don't know," said Juan. "I've never been over it. They say thirteen or
fifteen miles—something like that." He hunched over the wheel and his eyes
lifted from the road and glanced at the Virgin of Guadalupe in her little
shrine on top of his instrument board.

Juan was not a deeply religious man. He believed in the Virgin's power
as little children believe in the power of their uncles. She was a doll and a
goddess and a good-luck piece and a relative. His mother—that Irish woman
—had married into the Virgin's family and had accepted her as she had
accepted her husband's mother and grandmother. The Guadalupana became
her family and her goddess.

Juan had grown up with this Lady of the wide skirts standing on the new
moon. She had been everywhere when he was little—over his bed to super-
vise his dreams, in the kitchen to watch over the cooking, in the hall to
check him in and out of the house, and on the *zaguán* door to hear him
playing in the street. She was in her own fine chapel in the church, in the
classroom in school, and, as if that wasn't ubiquitous enough, he wore her
on a little gold medal on a golden chain about his neck. He could get away
from the eyes of his mother or his father or his brothers, but the dark
Virgin was always with him. While his other relatives could be fooled or
misled and tricked and lied to, the Guadalupana knew everything anyway.
He confessed things to her, but that was only a form because she knew them
anyway. It was more a recounting of your motives in doing a certain thing
than a breaking of the news that you had done it. And that was silly too,
because she knew the motives. Then, too, there was an expression on her
face, a half smile, as though she were about to break out into laughter.
She not only understood, she was also a little amused. The awful crimes
of childhood didn't seem to merit hell, if her expression meant anything.

Thus Juan as a child had loved her very deeply and had trusted her, and his father had told him that she was the one set aside especially to watch over Mexicans. When he saw German or Gringo children in the streets he knew that his Virgin didn't give a damn about them because they were not Mexicans.

When you add to this the fact that Juan did not believe in her with his mind and did with every sense, you have his attitude toward Our Lady of Guadalupe.

The bus slithered along the muddy road, moving very slowly and leaving deep ruts behind. Juan flicked his eyes to the Virgin and he said in his mind, "You know that I have not been happy and also that out of a sense of duty that is not natural to me I have stayed in the traps that have been set for me. And now I am about to put a decision in your hands. I cannot take the responsibility for running away from my wife and my little business. When I was younger I could have done it, but I am soft now and weak in my decisions. And I am putting this in your hands. I am on this road not of my own volition. I have been forced here by the wills of these people who do not care anything for me or for my safety or happiness, but only for their own plans. I think they have not even seen me. I'm an engine to get them where they are going. I offered to take them back. You heard me. So I am leaving it to you, and I will know your will. If the bus mires down so that ordinary work will let me get it out and proceed, I will get it out. If ordinary precaution will keep the bus safe and on the road, I will take that precaution. But if you, in your wisdom, wish to give me a sign by dropping the bus into the mud up to the axles, or sliding it off the road into a ditch where I couldn't do anything about it, I will know you approve of what I want to do. Then I will walk away. Then these people can take care of themselves. I will walk away and disappear. I will never go back to Alice. I will take off my old life like a suit of underwear. It is up to you."

He nodded and smiled at the Virgin, and she had the little smile on her face too. She knew what was going to happen, but, of course, there was no way of finding that out. He couldn't run away without sanction. He had to have the approval of the Virgin. It was directly up to her. If she felt strongly about his going back to Alice, she would smooth the road and get the bus through, and he would know that he was set for life with what he had.

He breathed high in his lungs with excitement and his eyes shone. Mildred could see his face in the rear-view mirror. She wondered what terrible joy there was in his mind to make his face light up. This was a man, she thought, a man of complete manness. This was the kind of a man that a pure woman would want to have because he wouldn't even want to be part woman. He would be content with his own sex. He wouldn't ever try to understand women and that would be a relief. He would just take what he wanted from them. Her disgust for herself passed, and she felt pretty good again.

Her mother was writing another letter in her mind. "There we were on that muddy road, miles from any place. And even the driver didn't know the road. Well, just anything could happen. Anything. There wasn't a house in sight and the rain was starting."

The rain was starting. Not like the gusts and spurts of the morning, but a heavy, driving, drumming, businesslike rain that delivered so many gallons an hour in a given area. And there was no wind. This was downpour, pure, straight rainfall. The bus hissed and splashed over the level road, and Juan, when he turned the front wheels a little, could feel the rear end slide.

"You got any chains?" Van Brunt called.

"No," said Juan happily. "Haven't been able to get chains since before the war."

"I don't think you're going to make it," said Van Brunt. "You're all right on the level but you've got to start going uphill pretty soon." He motioned to the east and the mountains toward which they were crawling. "The river cuts right up against a bluff," he shouted to the other passengers. "The road goes up over that bluff. I don't think we're going to make it."

To Pimples it had been a morning of conflicts and stresses. There weren't many relaxed moments in his life anyway, but this day had been particularly tearing. His body burned with excitements. Pimples was loaded with the concupiscent juices of adolescence. His waking and his sleeping hours were preoccupied with the one goal. But so variable was the reaction to the single stimulus that he found himself one moment as lustful as a puppy on a curtain, the next floundering in thick and idealistic sentiment, and the next howling with self-condemnation. He felt then that he was alone, that he, alone, was the great sinner of the world. He looked with fawning adoration at the self-control of Juan and other men he knew.

Since she had come into his sight all of his body and his brain yearned toward Camille, and his yearning went from lustful pictures of himself and her to visions of himself married to her and settled down with her. One moment he felt almost forward enough to just out and out ask her, and the next, her glance in his direction forced a quivering embarrassment on him.

Again he had tried to get a seat where he could watch her without being noticed, and again he had failed. He could see the back of her head, but he could see Norma's profile. So it was that only at this late time did Pimples notice the change in Norma and, noticing, he drew a deep breath. She was not the same. He knew that it was only make-up, for he could see the eyebrow pencil and the lipstick from where he sat, but that wasn't what sent his blood coursing hotly in his stomach. She was changed. There was a conscious girlness about her that had not been there before, and Pimples' wild juices whispered to him. If, as he really knew deep in his heart, he couldn't have Camille, he might maybe get Norma. He wasn't as frightened of her as he was of the goddess Camille. Unconsciously he began to make plans for trapping Norma, overwhelming her. A new pustule was forming right in front of his left ear. Automatically he scratched it, and the angry red of his tainted flesh spread outward on his cheek. He looked secretly at the fingernail that had done the business and put it in his pocket and cleaned it. He had made his cheek bleed. He took out his handkerchief and held it to his face.

Mr. Pritchard was worried about getting through and making his connection. There was a gnawing in him that would not let him rest or relax. He had tried to laugh it off to himself. He had used all the ordinary methods for throwing out unpleasant thoughts, and they didn't work.

Ernest Horton had said Mr. Pritchard's plan was blackmail, and Ernest had almost indicated that he thought Elliott Pritchard would steal his slipcover for a dark suit if he wasn't watched. This had at first outraged Mr. Pritchard—a man of his reputation and standing. And then he had thought, "Yes, I have standing and reputation in my own community, but here I have nothing. I am alone. This man thinks I am a crook. I can't send him to Charlie Johnson so he can get an idea of how wrong he is." This bothered Mr. Pritchard very much. Ernest had gone even further. He had indicated that he thought Mr. Pritchard was the kind of man who would go to an apartment with blondes. He had never done that in his life. He had to prove to Ernest Horton that his judgment had been wrong. But how could he do it?

Mr. Pritchard's arm was over the back of the seat, and Ernest was sitting alone in the seat behind him. The engine of the bus, traveling in second gear, was loud, and the old body vibrated noisily. There was only one way— to offer Ernest Horton something, something open and honest, so that he would see that Mr. Pritchard was not a crook.

A vague thought came back to him. He turned in his seat. "I was interested in what you said about what your company does with ideas that come in."

Ernest looked at him with amusement. The guy wanted something. He suspected the old boy wanted to get in on a party or two. Ernest's boss was that way. He wanted conferences at night and always ended up in a whorehouse and was always surprised at how he got there.

"We've got a very nice relationship," Ernest said.

"This idea is nothing much that I had," Mr. Pritchard said. "It's just something that came to me. You can have it if you want it and if it'll do you any good."

Ernest waited without comment.

"You take cuff links," Mr. Pritchard said. "Now, I always wear French cuffs and cuff links, and once you get the links in—well, you've got to take them out before you can take off the shirt. And if you want to push up your sleeves to wash your hands you've got to take out the cuff links. It's easy to put in cuff links before you put on the shirt, but you can't get your hands through. When you've got the shirt on it's hard to get the cuff links in. See what I mean?"

"There's that kind that clicks together," Ernest said.

"Yes, but they aren't popular. You're always mislaying or losing part."

The bus stopped. Juan put the bus in low gear and moved quickly on. There was a jar as he hit a hole and a second jar as the rear wheels went through it, and the bus moved slowly on. The rain drummed heavily on the roof. The windshield wiper squeaked on the glass.

Mr. Pritchard leaned back farther in his seat and pulled up his sleeve so that his plain gold cuff links showed. "Now, suppose," he said, "instead of links or a bar, there was a spring. When you put the cuff on over your hand the spring would give and you could push the cuff up your arm to wash, and then the spring would go right back into place." He watched Ernest's face closely.

Ernest's eyes were half closed in thought. "But how would it look? It would have to be a steel spring or it wouldn't last."

Mr. Pritchard said eagerly, "I thought that through. On the cheaper ones you could gold-plate the spring or silverplate it. But on the expensive ones, like pure gold or platinum—the quality ones—why, instead of a bar it's a tube, and when the cuff is at your wrist, why, the little spring has disappeared right into the tube."

Ernest nodded slowly. "Yes," he said. "Yes, sir. Sounds pretty good."

"You can have it," said Mr. Pritchard. "It's yours to make anything you want out of it."

Ernest said, "My company goes in for a different kind of novelties, but maybe—maybe I could talk them into it. The best-selling things in the world—for men, that is—are razors or razor gadgets, pens and pencils, and personal jewelry. The fellow that don't write five lines a year will buy a tricky fountain pen for fifteen dollars any day. And jewelry? Yes, sir, it might work out. What would you want out of it if they thought it was a good idea?"

"Nothing," Mr. Pritchard said. "Absolutely nothing. It's yours. I like to help an up-and-coming young fellow." He was beginning to feel good again. But suppose the thing worked out, this idea he'd cooked up. Suppose it made a million dollars. Suppose—but he had said it and his word was good. His word was his bond. If Ernest wanted to show appreciation, that was up to him. "I don't want a single thing," he repeated.

"Well, that's mighty nice of you." Ernest took a notebook from his pocket, made an entry, and tore out the page. "Of course, in a thing like that I'd have to get an assignment," he said. "If you've got a moment while you're in Hollywood, maybe you could give me a call and we'll talk some business. We might be able to do business." His left eye drooped a little as he said it, and then his eyes turned and rested a moment on Mrs.

Pritchard. He passed the slip to Mr. Pritchard and said, "Aloha Arms, Hempstead 3255, apartment 12B."

Mr. Pritchard colored a little, took out his wallet and put the paper in it, and he pushed the paper down in the back of the slot. He didn't really need to keep it. He could throw it away the first chance he got, for his memory was good. It would be years before he would forget that phone number. The system had clicked in his head, his old system. Three and two are five and repeat. And Hempstead. Hemp is rope. Yellow hemp, and you can't use anything instead of hemp. He used hundreds of memory tricks like that. Yellow hemp, blond hemp. His fingers itched to throw the paper away. Sometimes Bernice looked in his wallet for some change. He told her to. But he felt danger in his stomach—the miserable feeling of having been called a thief.

He said to his wife, "You feel all right, little girl?"

"Yes," she said. "I think I fought it off. I just said to myself, 'I won't let it come. I won't let it interfere with my darling's vacation.'"

"I'm glad," said Mr. Pritchard.

"And, dear," she went on, "how do you men get such ideas?"

"Oh, they just come to you," he said. "That new shirt with the small buttonholes is the cause of this one. I got caught in it a few days ago and nearly had to call for help."

She smiled. "I think you're very nice," she said. And he reached over and put his hand on her knee and squeezed her leg. She slapped his hand playfully and in a moment he took it away.

Norma had her head turned so that her mouth was close to Camille's ear. She spoke as softly as she could because she knew that Pimples was trying to listen. She was conscious of his gaze, and in a way she was gratified. She had never been so confident in her life as she was now.

"I haven't really got any family, like you'd call a family," she said. She was tumbling herself out in front of Camille. She was explaining and pouring out her life. She wanted Camille to know all about her, the way she was before this morning and the way she was now, and that would make Camille her family and would tie this beautiful and sure creature to her.

"When you're alone you do such funny things," she said. "I used to lie to people. I'd pretend things to myself. I would—well, do things like the things I was pretending were true. You know what I'd do? I'd picture like a certain movie star was—well, was my husband."

It had jumped out. She hadn't intended to go so far. She blushed. She shouldn't have told that. It was kind of like letting Mr. Gable down. But she inspected this and found it wasn't so. She didn't feel quite the same about Mr. Gable as she had. Her feeling had moved on to Camille. It was a shock to realize it. She wondered if she were being inconstant.

"It's when you don't have any family and no friends," she explained. "I guess you just make them up if you haven't got them. But now, well, if we could get an apartment I wouldn't have to make up anything."

Camille turned her face away so she couldn't see the nakedness in Norma's eyes, the complete defenselessness. "Oh, brother!" Camille thought. "What have I let myself in for now? I've got a baby. I've gone and got caught in something. How did this happen? I'm going to have to make her over and live her life and in a little while it'll probably bore the hell out of me and I'll be in too deep to get out of it. If Loraine's shucked off that advertising man and we can go back together, what am I going to do with this? How did it start? How the hell did I get into it?"

She turned to Norma. "Listen, honey," she said crisply. "I didn't say we could do it. I said we'd have to see how it worked out. There's a lot you don't know about me. For one thing, I'm engaged to be married, and my boy friend, he thinks it might be pretty soon. So you see, if he wants to now, why I couldn't go along with you."

Camille saw the despair come into Norma's eyes, like a cold horror, and the sagging of her cheeks and mouth and how the muscles of her shoulders and arms collapsed. Camille said to herself, "I can get a room in the next town and hide out till she gets lost. I can run out on her. I can—oh, Jesus, how did I let myself in for this? I'm too tired. I need a hot bath."

Aloud she said, "Don't take it so hard, honey. Maybe he isn't ready. Maybe —oh, look, honey, maybe it will work out. Maybe it will. Really. We'll just see how it goes."

Norma compressed her lips tightly and squinted her eyes. Her head jiggled with the vibration of the bus. Camille didn't want to look at her. After a time Norma got herself under control. She said quietly, "Maybe you're ashamed of me, and I wouldn't blame you. I can only be a waitress, but if you'd show me I could maybe get to be a dental nurse like you. I'd study nights and I'd work as a waitress in the daytime. But I'd do it, and then you wouldn't have to be ashamed of me. It wouldn't be so hard with you to help me."

Camille felt a rolling wave of nausea in her stomach. "Oh, God Almighty! Now I'm really trapped. What do I say? Tell her another lie? Would it be better to tell this girl exactly what I do for a living? Or would that make it worse? That might shock her so she wouldn't want me for a friend. Maybe that'd be the best thing. No, it would be best just to lose her in a crowd, I guess."

Norma was saying, "I'd like to have what you'd call a profession that had some dignity to it, like you."

Camille said in despair, "Look, honey, I'm awful tired. I'm too tired to think. I've been traveling for days. I'm too worn out to think about anything. Let's just let it lay for a while. We'll just see how it goes then."

"I'm sorry," Norma said. "I got excited and I forgot. I won't talk about it any more. We'll just see how it goes, huh?"

"Yes, we'll see how it goes," said Camille.

The bus jerked to a stop. They were coming near to the foothills now and the green billows of land were dimly visible through the rain. Juan half stood up to look down at the roadbed. There was a hole in the road, a hole full of water, no telling how deep. It might drop the bus clear out of sight. He glanced quickly at the Virgin. "Shall I take a chance?" he said under his breath. His front wheels were on the edge of the pool. He grinned, put the bus in reverse, and backed up twenty feet.

Van Brunt said, "You going to try a run for it? You'll get stuck."

Juan's lips moved silently. "My dear little friend, if you only knew," he whispered. "If all of the rest of you only knew." He put the bus in first gear and ran at the hole. The water splashed away with a rushing hiss. The rear wheels went into the hole. The bus slipped and floundered. The rear wheels spun and the motor roared and the spinning wheels edged the bumbling body slowly across and slithered it out on the other side. Juan slipped the gears to second and crawled on.

"Must have been a little gravel mixed in with that," he said over his shoulder to Van Brunt.

"Well, you wait till you start up the hill," Van Brunt said ominously.

"You know, for a man that wants to get through you put more things in the way," Juan said.

The road began to climb and the water did not stand any more. The ditches along the side were running full. The driving wheels of the bus slipped and churned in the ruts. Juan suddenly knew what he was going to do if the bus piled up. He hadn't known. He had thought he might go to Los Angeles and get a job driving a truck, but he wouldn't do that. He had fifty dollars in his pocket. He always carried that much for repair emergencies, and that would be enough too. He would walk away, but not far. He'd get under cover and wait until the rain stopped. He might even sleep some place. For food he would grab one of those pies. Then, when he was rested, he would walk over to the highway, bum a ride, just wait at a service station until someone picked him up. He would thumb his way to San Diego and then he'd go across the border to Tijuana. It would be nice there, and he might just lie on the beach for two or three days. The border wouldn't bother him. On this side he'd say he was American. On the other side he'd be Mexican. Then, when he was ready, he'd go out of town, maybe catch a ride or maybe just walk over the hills and by the little streams, perhaps as far as Santo Tomás, and there he'd wait for the mail carrier. He would buy a lot of wine in Santo Tomás, and he'd pay the mail carrier, and then down the peninsula he would go, through San Quintin, past Ballenas Bay. It might take two weeks through the rocks and the prickly desert and then across to La Paz. He would see that he had some money left. At La Paz he would catch a boat across the gulf to Guaymas or Mazatlán, maybe even to Acapulco, and in any of those places he would find tourists. More at Acapulco than at Guaymas or Mazatlán. And where there were tourists floundering around with the Spanish language in a strange country Juan would be all right. Gradually he'd work his way up to Mexico City and there were really tourists. He could conduct tours, and there were plenty of ways of getting money. He wouldn't need much.

He chuckled to himself. Why in God's name had he stuck to this as long as he had? He was free. He could do whatever he wanted to. Let them look for him. He might even see a note about it in the L. A. papers. They'd think he was dead and they'd look for his body. Alice would raise hell for a while. It would give her a great sense of importance. Plenty of people could cook beans in Mexico. He might lay up with one of those American women in Mexico City who lived down there to beat the taxes. With a few good suits of clothes Juan knew he was presentable enough. Why in hell hadn't he gone back before?

He could smell Mexico in his nose. He couldn't think why he hadn't done it before. And the passengers? Let them take care of themselves. They weren't very far out. They'd got so used to throwing their troubles on other people they had forgotten how to take care of themselves. It would be good for them. Juan could take care of himself and he was going to start doing it too. He'd been living a silly kind of life, worrying about getting pies from one town to the next. Well, that was over.

He glanced up with secret eyes at the Guadalupana. "Oh, I'll keep my word," he said under his breath. "I'll get them through if you want me to. But even then I'm not so sure I won't walk away."

His mind plunged with pictures of the sun-beaten hills of Lower California and the biting heat of Sonora, the chill morning air on the plateau of Mexico with the smell of pine knots in the huts and the popcorn smell of toasting tortillas. And a homesickness fell on him like a sweet excitement. The taste of fresh oranges and the bite of chili. What was he doing in this country anyway? He didn't belong here.

The curtain of the years rolled back, and superimposed on the muddy country road he saw and heard and smelled Mexico, the chattering voices of the market, the squawking parrot in the garden, the quarreling pigs in the street, the flowers and fish and the little modest dark girls in blue *rebozos*. How strange that he had forgotten for so long. He yearned toward the south. He wondered what crazy trap could have kept him here. Suddenly he was impatient to be away. Why couldn't he just slam on the brakes and open the door and walk away through the rain? He could see their stupid faces looking after him and hear their outraged comments.

He glanced again at the Virgin. "I'll keep my word," he whispered. "I'll get through if I can." He felt the wheels slip in the mud and he grinned at the Virgin of Guadalupe.

The river cut in close to the hills now, bringing its border of willows with it. And the road dodged sideways, away from it. The rain was thinning out, and from the road they could see the light yellow water whirling in the broad basin of the river and dragging lines of dirty foam in twisting streaks. Ahead the road climbed up the hill, and at the top there was a yellow cut, a kind of cliff, and the road ran in front of it. At the very top of the yellow cliff, in great faint letters, was the single word REPENT. It must have been a long and dangerous job for some wild creature to put it there with black paint, and it was nearly gone now.

In the cliff of sandstone there were erosion caves cut by the wind and dug out by animals. The caves looked like dark eyes peering out of the yellow cliff.

The fences were fairly strong here, and in the upland grass red cows stood dark and wet and some of them had already borne their spring calves. The red cows turned their heads slowly and watched the bus as it ground by, and one old fool of a cow became panic-stricken and ran away, kicking and bucking as though that would remove the bus.

The roadbed had changed. The gravel gave the bus better footing. The body bumped and jarred over the rain-rutted gravel, but the wheels did not slip. Juan looked suspiciously at the Virgin. Was she tricking him? Would she get him through and force him to make his own decision? That would be a dirty trick. With no sign from Heaven Juan didn't know what he would do. The road took a long loop around an old farm and then climbed toward the cliff in earnest.

Juan had the bus in low gear again and a wisp of steam came out of the overflow pipe and curled up in front of the radiator. The high point of the road was right in front of the cliff with its dark caves. Almost angrily Juan speeded his motor. The wheels threw gravel. There was a place where the ditch was plugged and water and topsoil flowed across the road. Juan raced at the dark streak. The front wheels crossed it and the back wheels spun in the greasy mud. The rear end swung around and the wheels spun and the hind end of the bus settled heavily into the ditch.

Juan's face had a fierce grin. He raced his motor and the wheels dug deeper and deeper. He reversed his direction and spun his wheels, and the spinning tires dug holes for themselves and settled into the holes, and the differential rested on the ground. Juan idled his motor. In the rear-view mirror he could see Pimples looking at him in amazement.

Juan had forgotten that Pimples would know. Pimples' mouth was open. Juan knew better than that. When you come to a soft place you don't spin the wheels. Juan could see the questions in Pimples' eyes. Why had he done it? He wasn't that stupid. He caught Pimples' eye in the mirror and all he could think to do was to wink secretly. But he saw relief come over Pimples' face. If it was a plan it was O.K. If there was something in back of it Pimples would go along. And then a horrible thought crossed Pimples' mind. Suppose it was Camille. If Juan wanted her Pimples wouldn't have a chance. He couldn't compete with Juan.

The angle of the bus was sharp. The rear wheels were buried and the front end stood high up on the road. "Sweetheart" looked like a crippled bug. Now Van Brunt's face cut out Pimples' reflection in the mirror. Van Brunt was red and angry and his bony finger cut the air under Juan's nose.

"So you did it," he cried. "So you tied us up. I knew you'd do it. By God, I knew you would! How am I going to get into the courthouse now? How are you going to get us out of this?"

Juan knocked the finger aside with the back of his hand. "Take your finger out of my face," he said. "I'm sick of you. Now get back to your seat."

Van Brunt's angry eyes wavered. He suddenly realized that this man was out of control. He wasn't afraid of the railroad commission or anybody. Van Brunt backed up a little and sat down on the angled seat.

Juan turned off the ignition and his motor died. The rain pattered on the roof of the bus. He tapped his palms on the steering wheel for a moment and then he turned in his seat and faced his passengers. "Well," he said. "That does it."

They stared back at him, shocked at the situation. Mr. Pritchard said softly, "Can't you get us out?"

"I haven't looked yet," said Juan.

"But it seems to me like we're in pretty deep. What are you going to do?"

"I don't know," said Juan. He wanted to see Ernest Horton's face, to see if he knew the thing had been deliberate, but Ernest was hidden behind Norma. Camille showed no effect at all. She had waited too long to be impatient.

"Sit tight," Juan said. He pulled himself upright against the angled bus and pushed the door lever. The lock clicked but the door was sprung. It did not open. Juan stood up and put his foot against the door and pushed it open. They could hear the hiss of rain on the road and on the grass. Juan stepped out into the rain and walked around to the back of the bus. The slanting rain felt cold on his head.

He had done a good job. It would probably take a wrecking car or maybe even a tractor to get it out. He leaned down and looked underneath to verify something he already knew. The axles and the differential were resting on the ground. Through the windows the passengers were looking out, their faces distorted by the wet glass. Juan straightened up and climbed back into the bus.

"Well, folks, I guess you'll just have to wait. I'm sorry, but don't forget you all wanted to come this way."

"I didn't," Van Brunt said.

Juan whirled on him. "God damn it, keep out of this! Don't get me mad because I'm right on the point of getting mad."

Van Brunt saw that he meant it. He looked down at his hands, pinched up the loose skin on his knuckles, and rubbed his left hand with his right

Juan sat sideways in the driver's seat. His eyes flicked over the Virgin. "All right, all right," he thought to her, "so I cheated a little bit. Not much, but a little. I guess you're justified now in making it pretty uncomfortable for me." Aloud he said, "I'll just have to walk on ahead and phone for a wrecking car. I'll tell them to send out a taxi for you folks. That shouldn't take very long."

Van Brunt spoke with restraint. "There isn't a place in four miles. The old Hawkins place is about a mile, but it's standing empty since the Bank of America took it over. You'll have to go to the county road and that's a good four miles."

"Well, if I have to go, I have to go," said Juan. "I can only get just so wet."

Pimples had a rush of friendliness. "I'll go," he said. "You stay here and let me go."

"No," said Juan, "this is your day off." He laughed. "You just enjoy it, Kit." He reached over to the instrument board, unlocked the glove box, and opened the little door. "There's some emergency whisky here," he said.

He paused. Should he take the pistol—a good Smith & Wesson 45-caliber revolver with a 6-inch barrel? It would be a shame to leave it. But it would be a nuisance to have it too. If he got into any kind of trouble the gun would go against him. He decided to leave it. If he was going to leave his wife, he could surely leave his gun too. He said lightly, "If you get jumped by tigers, there's a gun in here."

"I'm hungry," Camille said.

Juan smiled at her. "You take these keys and open up the back. There's a lot of pies there." He grinned at Pimples. "Don't eat 'em all, son. Now, you can stay in the bus or you can get out the tarpaulin from the back and put it on the ground up in those caves if you want. You might even build a fire in there if you can find any dry wood. I'll get a car sent out to you soon as I can."

"I'd like to go instead of you," Pimples said.

"No, you stick around and look after things," said Juan, and he saw a flash of pleasure on Pimples' face. Juan buttoned his jacket tightly over his chest. "Just sit tight," he said, and he stepped down out of the bus.

Pimples clambered down after him. He followed Juan a few steps until Juan turned and waited for him. "Mr. Chicoy," he said softly, "what is it you got on your mind?"

"On my mind?"

"Yeah. You see—well, you spun them wheels."

Juan put his hand on Pimples' shoulder. "Look, Kit, I'll tell you sometime. You just hold on for me, will you?"

"Well, sure, Mr. Chicoy, only—I'd just like to know."

"I'll tell you all about it when we get a minute alone," Juan said. "You just keep these folks from killing each other for a little while, will you?"

"Well, sure," Pimples said uneasily. "How long you think it'll be before you get back?"

"I don't know," Juan said impatiently. "How can I tell? You do like I say."

"Sure. Oh, sure," said Pimples.

"And eat all the pie you want," said Juan.

"But we'll have to pay for it, Mr. Chicoy!"

"Sure," said Juan, and he strode away along the road in the rain. He knew that Pimples was looking after him and he knew that Pimples sensed something. Pimples knew he was running out. Juan didn't feel good about it now. Not the way he thought he would. It didn't seem as good or as pleasant or as free. He stopped and looked back. Pimples was just getting into the bus.

The road went past the cliff with its eroded stone caves. Juan turned off the road and went into the shelter for a moment. The caves and their overhang were larger than they looked from outside and they were fairly dry too. In front of the entrance to the largest cave there were three fire-blackened stones and a battered tin can. Juan stepped back to the road and walked on.

The rain was thinning out. To his right, down the hill, he could see the great bend of the river and how it turned and headed back across the valley through the sodden green fields. The country was too wet. There was an odor of decay in the air, the fat green stems fermenting. The road ahead was rain-beaten and rotted by water, but not by wheels. Nothing had been over it for a long time.

Juan bowed his head into the rain and walked faster. It wasn't so good. He tried to remember the sunny sharpness of Mexico and the little girls in blue *rebozos* and the smell of cooking beans, and instead Alice came into his head. Alice, looking out of the screen door. And he thought of the bedroom with its flowered curtains. She liked things nice. She liked pretty things. The bedspread, now, a giant afghan she had knitted herself in little squares, and no two the same color. She said she could get over a hundred dollars for it. And she had knitted every bit of it herself.

And he thought of the big trees, and how nice it was to lie in a tub full of hot water in the bathroom, the first real bathroom he had ever had outside of hotels. And there was always a bar of sweet-smelling soap. "It's just a god-damned habit," he said to himself. "It's a damned trap. You get used to a thing and so you think you like it. I'll get over it the way I'd get over a cold. Sure, it'll be painful. I'll worry about Alice. I'll be sorry. I'll accuse myself, and it might be I won't sleep good. But I'll get over it. After a while I won't think about it. It's just a damned trap." And Pimples' face, trusting and warm, came up before him. "I'll tell you later. I'll tell you all about it, Kit Carson." Not many people had trusted Juan that way.

He tried to think of the lake at Chapala, and over its pale smooth water he saw "Sweetheart," the bus, sagged down in the mud.

Ahead and down the hill to the left, in an indentation of the foothills, he saw a house and a barn and a windmill with the blades broken and hanging. That would be the old Hawkins place. Just the set-up he'd been thinking about. He would go in there, maybe in the house, but more likely in the barn. An old barn is usually cleaner than an old house. There was bound to be a little hay or straw in the barn. Juan would crawl in there and sleep. He wouldn't think about anything. He would sleep until maybe this time tomorrow, and then he'd walk on to the county road and pick up a ride. What difference did it make to him about the passengers? "They can't starve. It won't hurt them at all. It'll be good for them. It isn't any business of mine."

He hurried his steps down the hill toward the old Hawkins place. They'd look for him. Alice would think he was murdered and she'd call in a sheriff. Nobody ever thought he'd run off like this. That's what made it such a good joke. Nobody thought he could do it. Well, he'd show them. Get to San Diego, cross the border, pick up the mail truck to La Paz. Alice would have the cops out.

He stopped and looked back at the road. His footprints were clear enough, but the rain would probably wash them out, and he could cover his tracks if he wanted to. He turned in off the road toward the Hawkins place.

The old house had gone to pieces very quickly once it was abandoned. A few wandering boys broke out the windows and stole the lead pipe and the plumbing, and the doors soon banged themselves silly and fell off their hinges. The old dark wallpaper, pulled down under wind-driven rain, revealed under-sheets made from old newspapers with old cartoons—"Foxy Grandpa" and "Little Nemo" and "Happy Hooligan" and "Buster Brown." Tramps had been there and had left their litter and burned the door casings in the old black fireplace. The smell of desertion and damp and sourness was in the house. Juan looked in the doorway, walked through and smelled the odor of the vacant house, and went out the back door toward the barn.

The corral fence was down and the big door off, but inside the barn smelled fresh. The stalls were polished where the horses had rubbed against the wood. The corners were cobwebbed. Between the manure windows were still the candleboxes with the worn brushes and rusty currycombs. And an old collar and hames and a set of tugs hung on a rack beside the door. The leather of the collar was split and the padding stuck out.

The barn had no loft. The whole central part had been used to store hay. Juan walked around the end of the last stall. It was dusky inside and the light of the sky lanced through broken shakes in the roof. The floor was covered with short straw, dark with age, and with a slightly musty smell. Standing still in the entrance, Juan could hear the squeaking of mice and he could smell the colonies of mice too. From a rafter two cream-colored barn owls looked down at him and then closed their yellow eyes again.

The rain had diminished so that there was only a faint puttering on the roof. Juan went to a corner and with his foot kicked aside a layer of the dusty top straw. He sat down and then lay back and thrust his hands behind his head. The barn was alive with secret little sounds, but Juan was very tired. His nerves itched and he felt mean. He thought perhaps if he slept he would feel better.

Back in the bus he had felt, in anticipation, a bursting, orgasmic delight of freedom. But it was not so. He felt miserable. His shoulders ached, and now that he was relaxed and stretched out he wasn't sleepy. He wondered, "Won't I ever be happy? Isn't there anything to do?" He tried to remember old times when it seemed to him that he was happy, when he had felt pure joy, and little pictures came into his mind. There was a very early morning with chill air and the sun was coming up behind the mountains and in a muddy road little gray birds were hopping. There wasn't any reason for joy, but it had been there.

And another. It was evening and a shining horse was rubbing his lovely neck on a fence and the quail were calling and there was a sound of dropping water somewhere. His breath came short with excitement just remembering it.

And another. He rode in an old cart with a girl cousin. She was older than he—he couldn't remember what she looked like. The horse shied at a piece of paper and she fell against him, and to right herself she put out her hand and touched his leg, and delight bloomed in his stomach and his brain ached with delight.

And another. Standing at midnight in a great, dim cathedral with a sharp, barbaric smell of copal smarting his nose. He held a skinny little candle with a white silk bow tied about it halfway up. And like a dream, the sweet murmur of the mass came from far away at the high altar and the drowsy loveliness drew down over him.

Juan's muscles relaxed and he slept in the straw of the deserted barn. And the timid mice sensed his sleep and came out from under the straw and played busily and the rain whispered quietly on the barn roof.

FIFTEEN

The passengers watched Juan walk away and disappear over the brow of the hill. They didn't speak, not even when Pimples climbed back into the bus and took his place in the driver's seat. The seats were tilted and each passenger tried to get comfortable.

At last Mr. Pritchard asked, generally, "How long do you suppose it'll take him to get a car out here?"

Van Brunt rubbed his left hand nervously. "Can't possibly expect it under three hours. He's got a four-mile walk. Even if he can get a car to come out, it'll take them an hour to get started and an hour to get here. That is, if they'll come out at all. I'm not sure anybody will come over this road. We should have walked in with him and caught a ride at the county road."

"We couldn't," said Mr. Pritchard. "We've got all our baggage."

Mrs. Pritchard said, "I didn't want to say anything when you got this crazy idea, Elliott. After all, it is your vacation."

She had been wanting to explain to the other passengers how people of the obvious position of the Pritchards should come to find themselves on a bus—should put themselves in the way of this kind of thing. They must have been wondering, she thought. Now she turned and addressed them. "We came out on a train, a nice train—the City of San Francisco, a very comfortable extra-fare train. And then my funny husband had this crazy idea of coming down on a bus. He thought he would see the country better that way."

"Well, we're seeing it, little girl," he said bitterly.

She went on, "My husband said he had been out of touch. He wanted to see what the people, the real people, were talking about." A delicate malice was creeping into her voice. "I thought it was silly but it's his vacation. He's the one who's worked so hard for the war effort. The wives didn't have much to do, just trying to make out with rationing and all, and no food in the stores. Why, once for two months we didn't taste beef. Nothing but chicken."

Mr. Pritchard looked at his wife in some surprise. It was not a common thing for this edge to come into her voice and it had a strange effect on him. Suddenly he found himself getting angry, getting wildly, unreasonably angry. It was her tone that did it. "I wish we'd never come," he said. "I didn't want to come anyway. I'd have had a real rest playing a little golf and sleeping in my own bed. I never wanted to come."

The other passengers watched with curiosity and interest. They were bored. This might be good. The anger of these two was beginning to fill the bus.

Mildred said, "Mother, Dad, cut it out."

"You stay out of this," Mr. Pritchard said. "I didn't want to come. I didn't want to at all. I hate foreign countries, particularly dirty ones."

Mrs. Pritchard's mouth pinched white and her eyes were cold. "This is a fine time to tell me about it," she said. "Who made all the plans for it and bought all the tickets? Who got us on this bus, stalled in the middle of nowhere? Who did all that? Did I?"

"Mother!" Mildred cried. She had never heard this tone in her mother's voice before.

"And it seems a strange thing"—Mrs. Pritchard's voice broke a little—"I try so hard. This trip, when you get it all paid for, is going to cost three or four thousand dollars. If you didn't want to come I could have built the little orchid house I've wanted so long, just a little, tiny orchid house. You said it wouldn't be a good example, getting it during war, but the war is over now and we take a trip you didn't want to take. Well, you spoiled it for me now too. I won't enjoy it. You spoil everything. Everything!" She covered her eyes with her hand.

Mildred stood up. "Mother, stop it. Mother, stop this right now!"

Mrs. Pritchard moaned a little.

"If you don't stop it I'm going to walk away," Mildred said.

"Go away," said Mrs. Pritchard. "Oh, go away. You don't understand anything."

Mildred's face set. She picked up her gabardine topcoat and put it on. "I'm going to walk to the county road," she said.

"That's four miles," Van Brunt said. "You'll spoil your shoes."

"I'm a good walker," said Mildred. She had to get out, her hatred for her mother was rising in her and making her sick.

Mrs. Pritchard's handkerchief was out and the scent of lavender filled the bus.

"Pull yourself together," Mildred said harshly. "I know what you're going to do. You're going to get a headache and punish us. I know you. One of your fake headaches," she said viciously. "I'm not going to sit around and see you get away with it."

Pimples watched, fascinated. He was breathing through his mouth.

Mrs. Pritchard looked up at her daughter with horror. "Dear! You don't believe that!"

"I'm beginning to," said Mildred. "Those headaches come too opportunely."

Mr. Pritchard said, "Mildred, stop it."

"I'm going on."

"Mildred, I forbid it!"

His daughter whirled on him. "Forbid and be damned!" She buttoned her coat over her chest.

Mr. Pritchard put out his hand. "Mildred, please, dear."

"I've had enough," she said. "I need the exercise." She stepped out of the bus and walked rapidly away.

"Elliott," Mrs. Pritchard cried. "Elliott, stop her. Don't let her go."

He patted her arm. "Now, little girl, she'll be all right. We're just irritable. All of us."

"Oh, Elliott," she groaned, "if only I could lie down. If only I could get some rest. She thinks my headaches aren't true. Elliott, I'll kill myself if she believes that. Oh, if I only could stretch out."

Pimples said, "Ma'am, we got some tarpaulins in the back end. We use 'em to cover the baggage when we carry it on top. If your husband would take one of them up in that cave, why, you could lay down there."

"Why, that's a wonderful idea," said Mr. Pritchard.

"Lie on the old damp ground?" she demanded. "No."

"No, on a canvas. I could fix you a sweet little bed for a sweet little girl."

"Well, I don't know," she said.

"Look, dear," he insisted. "Look, I'm going to roll up my topcoat. Now you just put your head down there, like that. Now, in a little while I'll come and get you and take you to your own little bed."

She whimpered.

"And rest your head on the pillow and close your eyes."

Pimples said, "Mr. Chicoy told me to bring out the pies if anybody got hungry. There's four flavors and they're pretty good too. I could eat a piece right now."

"Let's get that tarpaulin first," Mr. Pritchard said. "My wife is exhausted. She's about at the end of her strength. You help me fix her a bed, will you?"

"O.K.," said Pimples. He felt that he was doing all right in Juan's absence. He felt fine and jaunty. His posture showed his mood for his shoulders were back and his pale wolf eyes were bright and confident. There was only one worry in Pimples. He wished he had had sense enough to throw an old pair of shoes into the bus. His two-toned oxfords were likely to take a beating from the mud, and that would mean a long job with a toothbrush to clean them up again. And he couldn't appear to protect his shoes for that would indicate to Camille that he was not a devil-may-care fellow. She wouldn't be impressed by a man who was careful of his shoes even if they were new white and brown oxfords.

Ernest said, "I'm going to have a look at those caves," and he got up and climbed to the door of the bus. Van Brunt grumbled and followed.

Mrs. Pritchard nestled her cheek in Mr. Pritchard's coat and closed her eyes. She was filled with dismay. How could she have fought with him in public—with her own husband? It had never happened before. When it was necessary to quarrel she always managed that they should be alone. Not even Mildred was permitted to hear a quarrel. She felt it was vulgar to fight when people could hear, and, besides, it broke a pattern she had been years building, the story that because of her sweetness her marriage was ideal. Everyone she knew believed that. She believed it herself. Through her own efforts she had built a beautiful marriage and now she had slipped. She had quarreled. She had let it get out about the little orchid house.

For a number of years she had wanted such a house. Ever since, in fact, she had seen an article in *Harper's Bazaar* about a Mrs. William O. MacKenzie who had one. The pictures had been lovely. People would say of Mrs. Pritchard that she had the darlingest little orchid house. It was precious and valuable. It was better than jewelry or furs. People she didn't even know would hear about her little orchid house. Secretly she had learned a great deal about such projects. She had studied plans. She knew costs of heating systems and humidifiers. She knew where the original stock was bought and how much it cost. She had studied books on propagation. And all of this very secretly because she knew that if and when the time came that she could have it Mr. Pritchard would want to find out these things and tell her. It was the only way. She didn't even resent it. That was simply a way of life, the way she had made her marriage successful. She would be impressed with his knowledge and she would ask his advice about everything.

But she was worried because she had let the thing slip in anger. Such a mistake might set her back six months or more. She had planned to have him suggest it, and by careful reluctance cause him to overcome her opposition. But now the subject had been mentioned in anger and he would have a block against it. Unless she was very careful in the future he might never come around. It had been stupid of her and vulgar of her.

She could hear Norma and Camille talking softly behind her. Her eyes were closed and she looked so little and so ill that they couldn't imagine she was listening.

Norma was saying, "One of the things I'd like to have you show me is how you handle—well, fellas."

Camille laughed shortly. "What do you mean?" she asked.

"Well, you take Pimples. I can see how he's been—trying, and he can't get to first base with you, and at the same time you don't even seem like you're doing it. And you take that other fella. That salesman. Well, he's pretty clever and you handled him just like nothing. I wish I knew how you did it."

Camille was pleased. Much as she might be worried by this incipient millstone, it was pleasant to have admiration. Now was the time to tell Norma she wasn't a dental nurse, to tell her about the giant wine glass and the stags, and yet she couldn't. She didn't really want to shock Norma. She wanted to be admired.

"Thing I like is you never are mean or nasty about it and still they never lay a finger on you," Norma continued.

"I never noticed," Camille said. "I guess it's kind of like an instinct." She chuckled. "I've got a girl friend that can really handle men. She just don't give a hoot and she's kind of mean with men anyway. Well, Loraine —that's her name—was—well, she was kind of engaged to this fellow and he had a good job and so he wasn't any trouble. Loraine wanted a fur coat. Of course, she had a short wolf jacket and she had a couple of white fox furs because Loraine is a very popular girl. She's pretty and little and when she's with girls she'll keep you laughing all the time. So Loraine wanted a mink coat, not a short one, but a real full-length one, and they cost three, four thousand dollars."

Norma whistled between her teeth. "Jesus God!" she said.

"Well, one afternoon Loraine said, 'I guess I'll get my fur coat now.' And I said, 'You're kidding.'

"'You think I'm kidding? Eddie's going to give it to me.'

"'When did he tell you?' I asked her.

"Loraine just laughed. 'He didn't tell me. He don't even know it yet.'

"'Well,' I said. 'Look, you're nuts.'

"'You wanna bet?' Loraine will take a bet on anything.

"I don't bet on things so I said, 'How are you going to go about it?'

"'If I tell you, will you keep it to yourself?' she said. 'It's easy. I know Eddie. I'm gonna needle him tonight and keep needling him till he gets mad. And I'm gonna keep right on until he throws a punch at me. I may even have to step into one because when Eddie's a little drunk he misses pretty bad. Well, then I'm gonna let Eddie stew in his own juice. I know Eddie. He'll get to feeling mean and sorry. You want to take that bet?' she said. 'I'll even lay down a time. I'll bet you I have that coat by tomorrow night.'

"Well, I don't bet anything, so I said, 'Two bits you don't.'"

Norma's mouth was open with excitement, and a gleam of reflected light came from between Mrs. Pritchard's closed lashes.

"Did she get it?" Norma demanded.

"Well, I went over to her place Sunday morning. Loraine had a mouse all right, a real blue shiner, and she had a patch over it and her nose was cut up too."

"Well, did she get the coat?"

"She got the coat all right," Camille said. There was a frown on her face, a puzzled look. "She got the coat and it was a beauty. Well, then she took off all her clothes. There were just two of us there. She turned that coat inside out and she put it right on next her skin with the hair next her skin. And then she rolled and rolled on the floor and she laughed and giggled like she was crazy."

Norma's held breath exhaled slowly. "God," she said, "why did she do that?"

"I don't know," said Camille. "It was like she—well, it was like she was a little crazy, kinda nuts."

Mrs. Pritchard's face was glowing. She breathed very rapidly. Her skin tingled, and there was an aching, itching feeling in her legs and stomach she had never felt before, and there was an excitement in her that she had had only once in her life and that was on horseback a long time ago.

Norma said judiciously, "I don't think it was nice. If she really loved Eddie and he was going to marry her, I don't think it was a nice thing to do."

"I don't either," said Camille. "It kind of bothered me about Loraine and I told her so, but she said, 'Well, some girls just take the longer way around. I wanted it quick. It'll be the same thing in the end, anyway. Somebody was gonna work Eddie over.'"

"And did she marry him?"

"Well, no. She didn't."

"I'll bet maybe she never loved him at all," Norma said heatedly. "I'll bet she just gold-dug Eddie."

"Maybe," said Camille, "but she's been my girl friend for a long time, and if I ever needed anything she was right there. One time when I had pneumonia she sat up with me for three days and nights, and I was broke and she paid the doctor."

"I guess you just can't tell," Norma said.

"No, I guess not," said Camille. "Anyway, you asked me about how to handle men."

Mrs. Pritchard was beating herself with words. Her reaction had frightened her. She said to herself, even whispering the words, "What a horrible, vulgar story. What animals those young girls are. So this is what Elliott means by 'getting down to the people.' Oh, that's horrible. We just forget how people are, how nasty they can be. Dear Ellen," she wrote frantically, and the excitement was still tingling on the insides of her legs. "Dear Ellen, the trip was terrible between San Ysidro and San Juan de la Cruz. The bus went into a ditch and we just sat and waited for hours. My Elliott was very sweet and made me a bed in a funny cave. You said I would have adventures. Remember? You said I always would have adventures. Well, I did. There were two vulgar, illiterate girls on the bus, one of them a waitress and the other was rather pretty. She was a you-know-what. I was resting and I guess they thought I was asleep and they went right on talking. I couldn't put in a letter what they said. I'm still blushing. Gentle people just don't know how these little things live. It's incredible. I always think it's ignorance. If we only had better schools and if—well, if you want the truth—if we who should be examples were just better examples, I'm sure the whole picture might change, gradually, but certainly."

Ellen would read the letter over and over to people. "I just had a letter from Bernice. She's having the most exciting adventures. You know, she always does. Why, I want you to hear what she says. I've never known anyone who could see the good sides of people the way Bernice can."

Norma was saying, "If I liked a fella I wouldn't think of doing a thing like that to him. If he wanted to give me a present he'd have to think of it himself."

"Well, that's the way I feel about it too," said Camille. "But I haven't got a fur coat, not even a chubby. And Loraine's got three."

"Well, I don't think it's fair," said Norma. "I don't think I'd like Loraine."

"God Almighty!" Camille cried in her mind. "You don't know if you'd like Loraine. I wonder if you've got any idea what Loraine would think of you?" No, she thought, that isn't true. Loraine would probably take this girl and fix her up and help her. Whatever you could say about Loraine, nobody could say she wasn't a good scout.

SIXTEEN

Mildred put her head down to keep the rain from misting her glasses. The gravelly road felt good under her feet and the exercise made her draw her breath deeply. It seemed to her that the day was getting darker. It couldn't be very late, and still an evening light was creeping in, making light things, such as pieces of quartz and limestone, seem lighter, and dark things, such as the fence posts, seem black.

Mildred walked quickly, her feet stabbing at the ground and her heels striking into the gravel. She was trying to push the quarrel out of her mind. She did not remember having seen her mother and father fight before. But this had been a practiced thing with a routine-like quality that indicated it was a far from uncommon process. Her mother must maneuver the quarrels into the bedroom where no one could hear them. She had built up and maintained a story of the perfect marriage. This time the tension had got to a breaking point and there was no bedroom to retire to. There had been mean little drops of yellow venom in the quarrel that disturbed Mildred. It was a poison that seeped subtly in, not an open, honest rage but rather a secret, creeping anger that struck with a thin, keen blade and then concealed the weapon quickly.

And there was this endless trip to Mexico ahead. Suppose Mildred didn't come back? Suppose she walked on and caught a ride and disappeared—rented a room someplace, perhaps on the coast by the sea, and spent the time on the rocks or on the beach? The idea was very pleasant to her. She could cook for herself and get to know other people on the beach. The idea was ridiculous. She hadn't any money. Her father was very generous —but not with cash. She could charge her clothes and sign checks in restaurants, but her actual money was always very short. Her father was generous but very curious. He wanted to know what she bought and where she ate, and he could find these things out on the monthly bills.

Of course, she could go to work. She would pretty soon anyway, but not right yet. No, she had to weather it out. She had to stumble through this horrible Mexican trip, which could be so wonderful if she were alone, and then go back to college. It wouldn't be long until she would go to work, and her father would approve of that. He would say to Charlie Johnson, "I'd give her anything she wants, but no, sir, she's got too much get-up-and-go."

634	THE WAYWARD BUS

She's making her own living." And he would say it with pride, as though some virtue of his own was involved, and he would never know that she was working for the sake of privacy, so she could have her own apartment and some spending money, for things he didn't know about.

At home, for instance, she was free to go to the liquor cabinet any time she wanted, but she knew that her father had in his memory the exact level of liquid in every bottle, that if she took three drinks he would know it immediately. He was a very curious man.

She took off her glasses and wiped them on the lining of her coat and put them on again. In the road she could see Juan's tracks, long strides. There were places where his foot had slipped on a rock, and there were muddy stretches where the whole prints of his feet were visible, with the line broken by the drives of his toes. Mildred tried to walk in his tracks, but his step was too long for her, and she felt the pull on her thighs after she had kept it up for a while.

He was a strange, compelling man, she thought. She was glad she had got out of that crazy experience of the morning. No sense in it, she knew. Irritation and functioning glands interplaying—she knew all that. And she also knew herself to be a girl of strong sexual potential. There would come a time in the not far future when she would either have to get married or make some kind of permanent arrangement. Her times of restlessness and need were growing more frequent. She thought of Juan's dark face and shining eyes and she was not affected. But there was warmth in him and honesty. She liked him.

As she cleared the hill she saw the deserted farm below and was fascinated. She could feel the despondency of the place. She knew she couldn't pass the house without looking through it. Her steps quickened. All her interest was aroused.

"Bank foreclosed," Van Brunt had said, "and the family had to move, and the bank wouldn't be interested in an old house. It was the land they were taking."

Her strides were almost as long as Juan's now. She came swinging down to the foot of the hill to the muddy entrance of the farm and suddenly she stopped. Juan's tracks turned in. She walked along the road a little to find whether they emerged and continued, but she could find no other footsteps ahead.

"He must still be in there," she said to herself. "But why? He was going out to the county road. There couldn't be a telephone here." She grew cautious as she realized she didn't know what was going on, and she didn't know much about this man. She walked slowly into the entrance and moved out on the grass so that her feet would not make a rasping sound on the gravel.

There was something dangerous about the deserted house. She recalled old newspaper stories of murders in places like this. Her throat tightened

with fear. "Well," she consoled herself, "I can turn right around and go
out. Nobody's stopping me. Nobody's pushing me in, but I know I must.
I know I won't leave. Maybe those murdered girls could have got away too.
Maybe they were asking for it."

She saw a vision of herself lying on the floor of one of the rooms, strangled
or stabbed, and there was something in the vision that made her laugh—her
glasses were still on. And what did she know about Juan? He had a wife and
a business. Then there was a headline she remembered. "Father of three
in sadist murder. Parson murders choir singer." Why are so many choir singers
and organists murdered, she wondered. There seems to be a high occupa-
tional hazard about choir singing. Choristers are always being found choked
behind the organ. She laughed. She knew she was going into this house.
Should she just clump on in or should she steal in and catch Juan Chicoy at
whatever he was doing? Maybe he was just going to the toilet.

She put a careful foot on the step and paused when the floorboard creaked
under her weight. She went through the house opening cupboards. There
was an overturned pepper can in the kitchen and a coat hanger in the closet
of the bedroom. She turned her head sideways to look at the old comic
pages under the peeled wallpaper. She read a strip of "Happy Hooligan."
The mule, Maud, drew back her legs and kicked and Cy sailed through the
air, and on the seat of Cy's pants were the imprints of the mule's hoofs.

She straightened her head. Why hadn't she thought of the barn before?
Mildred crept back to the front porch and looked closely at the boards. She
could see the wet track of Juan's shoes. She followed the track to the living
room and lost it. Then she went to the open back door and looked out. What
a fool she had been, creeping about! There were the footprints going out,
headed, in fact, for the barn.

She went down the broken steps and followed the trail across the lot and
passed the old windmill. She entered the barn and stood listening. There
was no sound. She thought of calling out and gave it up. Slowly she moved
down the line of stalls and around the end stall. It had taken a little while
for her eyes to adjust to the light. She stood in the entrance to the central
part. All the little mice flicked out of sight. Then she saw Juan lying on his
back, his hands cupped behind his head. His eyes were closed and he
was breathing evenly.

"I can go away," Mildred said. "Nobody's keeping me. It will be my fault.
I just want to remember that. He's minding his own business. Oh, what's
this nonsense?"

She took off her glasses and put them in her pocket. The outline of the
man was fuzzy to her now, to her unfocused eyes, but she could still see
him. She walked slowly, carefully, across the straw-covered floor and when
she was beside him she crossed her ankles and let herself down and sat on
her crossed feet. The scar on his lip was white and he breathed shallowly

and evenly. "He was just tired," she said to herself. "He lay down to rest a moment and he fell asleep. I shouldn't wake him up."

She thought of the people back in the bus—suppose neither she nor Juan ever came back. What would they do? Her mother would collapse. Her father would wire the governor—two or three governors. He would call the FBI. There would be hell to pay. Yet what could they do? She was twenty-one. When they caught up with her she could say, "I'm twenty-one and doing what I want to do. Whose business is it?" And suppose she went to Mexico with Juan? That would be quite a different story, quite a different thing.

And now little irrelevancies invaded her mind. If he's an Indian or has Indian blood, how is it someone can creep up on him? She held her eye corners back to bring his face into focus. It was a scarred, leathery face, but it was a good face, she thought. The lips were full and humorous, but they were kind. He would be gentle while he was with a woman. He might not stay with her for very long, but he would be nice to her. But he had that wife, that horrid wife, and he stayed with her. God knows how long. She must have been pretty when he married her, but she was ugly now. What had happened there? How did that horrid woman hold him? Maybe he was just like everyone else, like her father. Maybe he was just held in line by fears and by habit. Mildred didn't see how it could happen to anyone, but she knew it did. When people got old they grew frightened of smaller and smaller things. Her father was frightened of a strange bed or a foreign language or a political party he didn't belong to. Her father truly believed that the Democratic party was a subversive organization whose design would destroy the United States and put it in the hands of bearded communists. He was afraid of his friends and his friends were afraid of him. A rat race, she thought.

She moved her eyes down over Juan's body, a tough, stringy body that would get tougher and stringier as he got older. His trousers were a little wet from the rain and they hugged close to his legs. There was a neatness about him—a neatness of a mechanic who has just washed up. She looked at his flat stomach and at his broad chest. She saw no change in his breathing, no muscular change, but his eyes were open and he was looking at her. And his eyes were not sleep-heavy, but bright.

Mildred started. Perhaps he hadn't been asleep at all. He might have watched her come into the barn. She found herself explaining, "I needed exercise. You know, I've been sitting a long time. I thought I'd walk to the county road and pick up the car there. And then I saw this old place. I like old places."

Her feet were going to sleep. She leaned sideways and, supporting herself with one hand, moved her legs and feet to one side and covered her knee carefully with her skirt. Her feet buzzed and burned with returning blood.

Juan did not answer. His eyes were on her face. Slowly he rolled on his side and supported his head with a hand under his ear. A dark gleam came into his eyes, and his mouth curled up a little at the corners. His face was hard, she thought. No way of getting past the eyes into the head. It was either all on the surface or else it was too completely protected ever to get at.

"What are you doing here?" she asked.

His lips parted a little. "What are you doing here?"

"I told you, I needed exercise. I told you."

"Yes, you told me."

"But what are you doing here?"

He didn't seem really awake. "Me? Oh, I sat down to rest. I went to sleep. No sleep last night."

"Yes, I remember," she said. She had to go on talking. She was wound up. "I wondered about you. You don't belong here. I mean, driving a bus. You belong someplace else."

"Like where?" he asked playfully. His eyes dropped to where the lapels of her coat crossed.

"Well," she said uneasily, "I had a funny kind of a thought while I was walking. I thought maybe you wouldn't come back. You might just keep going and maybe go back to Mexico. I could see how I might do that if I were you."

His eyes squinted and he peered into her face. "Are you nuts? What made you think that?"

"Well, it was just something that came to me. Your life, driving the bus, I mean, must be pretty dull after—well, after Mexico."

"You haven't been in Mexico?"

"No."

"Then you don't know how dull it is there."

"No."

He raised his head and straightened his arm and put his head down on his arm. "What do you think would happen to those people back there?"

"Oh, they'd get back somehow," she said. "It isn't far. They wouldn't starve."

"And what do you think would happen to my wife?"

"Well—" She was confused. "I hadn't thought of that."

"Yes, you did," said Juan. "You don't like her. I'll tell you something. Nobody likes her except me. One of the reasons I like her is because nobody likes her." He grinned. "What a liar," he said to himself.

"It was just a crazy thought I had," she said. "I even thought I might run away too. I thought I would disappear and live by myself and—well, never see anyone again that I knew." She rose up on her knees and sat down again on the other side.

Juan looked at her knee. He put out his hand and pulled her skirt down over it. She flinched when his hand came toward her and then relaxed uneasily.

"I don't want you to think I followed you in here," she said.

"You don't want me to think it, but you did," said Juan.

"Well, what if I did?"

His hand came out again and rested on her covered knee and fire raced through her.

"It's not you," she said. Her throat was dry. "I don't want you to think it's you. It's me. I know what I want. I don't even like you. You smell like a goat." Her voice staggered along. "You don't know the kind of life I lead. I'm all alone. I can't tell anyone anything."

His eyes were hot and shiny and they seemed to bathe her in heat.

"Maybe I'm not like anyone else," she went on. "How do I know? But it's not you. I don't even like you."

"You give yourself a hell of an argument, don't you?" said Juan.

"Look, what are you going to do about the bus?" she demanded. "Are you going to the road?"

The weight of his hand on her knee increased and then he took his hand away. "I'm going back and pull the bus out, pull those people through," he said.

"Then why did you come here?"

"Something went haywire," he said. "Something I figured out went haywire."

"When are you going back?"

"Pretty soon."

She looked at his hand, relaxed on the straw in front of her, its skin dark and shiny and a little wrinkled. "Aren't you going to make a pass at me?"

Juan smiled and it was a good, open smile. "Yes, I guess so. After you get through arguing with yourself. You're on both sides now. Maybe pretty soon you'll decide whether you're for or against and I'll have something to work on."

"Don't you—don't you want me?"

"Sure," said Juan. "Sure."

"Is it that you know I'll fall into your lap anyway, so you won't have to take any trouble?"

"Don't get me into your argument," said Juan. "I'm older than you are. I like this thing very much. I like it so much that I can wait. I can even go without for a while."

"I could dislike you very much," she said. "You don't give me any pride. You don't give me any violence to fall back on later."

"I thought you'd have more pride to be left to make up your own mind."

"Well, I don't."

"I guess not," he said. "The women in my country are like that too. They have to be begged or forced. Then they feel good about it."

"Well, are you always this way?"

"No," said Juan, "only with you. You came here for something. You said yourself it didn't have anything to do with me."

She looked at her fingers. "It's funny," she said. "I'm what you'd call an intellectual girl. I read things. I'm not a virgin. I know thousands of case histories, but I can't make the advances." She smiled quickly and warmly. "Can't you force me a little?"

His arms stretched out and she fell into place beside him in the straw.

"You won't hurry me?"

"We've got all day," he said.

"Will you despise me or laugh at me?"

"What do you care?"

"Well, I do, whether I want to or not."

"You talk too much," he said. "You just talk too much."

"I know it and it goes on all the time. Will you take me away? Maybe to Mexico?"

"No," said Juan. "Let's see if you can shut up for a little while."

SEVENTEEN

Pimples took the keys from the ignition lock on the instrument board and went to the rear of the bus. He unlocked the padlock which defended the luggage and threw up the lid. The smell of pies came sweetly to his nose. Mr. Pritchard looked in over his shoulder. The luggage was stacked tightly in the compartment.

"I guess I'll have to take it all out to get those tarps," said Pimples, and he began to pull at the wedged suitcases.

"Wait," said Mr. Pritchard. "Let me lift and you pull and we can leave them all in." He stood on the bumper and strained upward at the bottom suitcase while Pimples yanked at the heavy fold of canvas. Pimples worked it from side to side and gradually it came free from under the luggage.

"Maybe we'd better get a couple of pies while we got it open," Pimples said. "There's raspberry and lemon cream and raisin and caramel custard cream. A piece of caramel custard cream would go pretty good now."

"Later," said Mr. Pritchard. "Let's get my wife settled first." He took one side of the heavy cloth and Pimples the other and they proceeded toward the cliff with its caves.

It was a fairly common formation. The side of the little hill had dropped away in some old time, leaving a smooth surface of soft limestone. Gradually wind and rain cut under from below, while the top of the cliff was held in place by topsoil and grass roots. And over the ages several caves were formed under the overhanging cliff. Here a coyote littered her pups, and here, in the old days when there were such things, a grizzly bear came to sleep. And in the higher caves the owls sat during the day.

Three deep, dark caves developed at the bottom of the cliff and a few small ones higher up. All the cave entrances were now protected from the rain by the high overhang of the cliff itself. The caves were not entirely the inventions of nature, for bands of Indians hunting antelopes had rested here and lived here, and had even fought forgotten battles here. Later it became a stopping place for white men riding through the country, and the men had enlarged the caves and built their fires under the overhang.

The smoke stains on the sandstone were old and some fairly new, and the floors of the caves were comparatively dry, for this little hill, one side of which had dropped away, did not receive the drainage from other, higher hills. A few initials had been scratched on the sandstone cliff, but the surface was so soft that they soon became illegible. Only the large, weathering word "Repent" was still clear. The wandering preacher had let himself down with a rope to put up that great word in black paint, and he had gone away rejoicing at how he was spreading God's word in a sinful world.

Mr. Pritchard, carrying his end of the tarpaulin, looked up at the word "Repent." "Somebody went to a lot of trouble," he said, "a lot of trouble." And he wondered who had financed such a venture. Some missionary, he thought.

He and Pimples dropped the tarpaulin under the cliff's overhang while they went to inspect the caves. The shallow holes were nearly alike, about five feet high and eight or nine feet wide and ten or twelve feet deep. Mr. Pritchard chose the cave the farthest toward the right because it seemed to be drier and because it was a little darker inside. He thought the darkness would be good for his wife's coming headache. Pimples helped him spread the tarpaulin.

"I wish we could get some pine boughs or some straw to put underneath the canvas," Mr. Pritchard said.

"Grass is too wet," said Pimples, "and there ain't a pine tree in fifty miles."

Mr. Pritchard rubbed the canvas with the butt of his hand to see whether the cloth was dirty. "She can lie on my overcoat," he said, "and she can put her fur coat over her."

Ernest and Van Brunt came in to look at the cave.

"We could stay here for weeks if we had anything to eat," Ernest said.

"Well, we may be quite a time at that," said Van Brunt. "If that bus driver isn't back by tomorrow morning I'm going to walk in. I've had about all the nonsense I can take."

Pimples said, "I can break out a couple of pies if you folks want."

"That might be a good idea," said Ernest.

"What kind you like?" Pimples asked.

"Oh, any kind."

"The caramel custard cream is nice. It's got graham crackers instead of crust."

"That'll be fine," said Ernest.

Mr. Pritchard went back to the bus for his wife. He was feeling ashamed about his anger of a little time ago. He had the hard knot in his stomach he got when things were not going well, a fistlike knot. Charlie Johnson said he must have an ulcer, and Charlie was pretty funny about it. He said no one under twenty-five thousand dollars a year got an ulcer. It was a symptom of a bank account, Charlie said. And unconsciously Mr. Pritchard was a little proud of the pain in his stomach.

When he climbed into the bus, Mrs. Pritchard's eyes were closed.

"We've got your little bed all fixed," Mr. Pritchard said.

Her eyes opened and she stared wildly about.

"Oh!"

"Were you asleep?" he said. "I shoudn't have wakened you. I'm sorry."

"No, dear. It's all right. I was just dozing."

He helped her to her feet. "You can lie on my overcoat and put your little fur coat over you."

She smiled weakly at his tone.

He helped her down the steps. "I'm sorry I was rude, little girl," he said.

"It's all right. You're just tired. I know you didn't mean it."

"Well, I'm going to buy you a great big dinner in Hollywood to make up for it, maybe at Romanoff's, with champagne. Would you like that?"

"You can't be trusted with money," she said playfully. "It's all forgotten now. You were just tired."–"Dear Ellen, we had the nicest dinner at Romanoff's and you'll never guess who was at the next table."–"Why, it's hardly raining at all," she said.

"No, and I want my little girl to get some sleep so she'll be well and strong."

"Are you sure it's not damp and there aren't any snakes?"

"No, we looked around."

"And no spiders?"

"Well, there weren't any spider webs."

"But how about big, hairy tarantulas? They don't have webs."

"We can look around some more," he said. "The walls are smooth. There's no place for them to hide." He conducted her to the little cave. "See how nice? And you can lie with your head up this way so you can look out if you want to."

He spread his coat and she sat down on it.

"Now, lie down and I'll cover you up."

She was very docile.

"How's my girl's head?"

"Well, it's not as bad as I was afraid it would be."

"That's good," he said. "You get a little nap. Are you comfy?"

She made a little moan of comfort.

"If you want anything just call out. I'll be near."

Pimples came to the cave entrance. His mouth was full and he carried a pie tin in his hand. "You like to have a piece of pie, ma'am?"

Mrs. Pritchard raised her head and then she shivered and put her head down. "No, thank you," she said. "It was nice of you to think of me, but I couldn't eat pie."—"Elliott just treated me like a queen, Ellen. How many people can say that after they've been married twenty-three years? I just feel lucky all the time."

Mr. Pritchard looked down at her. Her eyes were closed and there was a small smile on her lips. He felt the sudden lonely sorrow that came so often. He remembered, really remembered, the first time it had happened. He had been five when his little sister was born, and suddenly there were doors closed against him and he couldn't go into the nursery and he couldn't touch the baby and the feeling came on him that he was always a little dirty and noisy and unworthy and his mother was always busy. And then the cold loneliness had fallen on him, the cold loneliness that still came to him sometimes, that came to him now. The little smile meant that Bernice had retired from the world into her own room, and he couldn't follow her.

He took his gold nail pick from his pocket and opened it and cleaned his nails as he walked away. He saw Ernest Horton sitting against the cliff on the other side of the overhang. The high cave was over his head. Ernest was sitting on some newspapers and as Mr. Pritchard approached he slipped a double sheet of paper from under him and held it out.

"Most useful things in the world," he said. "You can do anything with them except read them."

Mr. Pritchard chuckled, took the paper, and sat down on it beside Ernest. "If you read it in the paper it isn't true," he said, quoting Charlie Johnson. "Well, here we are. Two days ago I was in a suite in the Hotel Oakland and now we're in a cave. It just shows, you can't make plans."

He stared at the bus. Through the window he could see that Pimples was in there with the two girls and they were eating pie. He felt a strong urge to join them. He could eat a piece of pie.

Ernest said, "Everything goes to show something. I have to laugh sometimes. You know, we're supposed to be a mechanical people. Everybody drives a car and has an icebox and a radio. I suppose people really think they are mechanical minded, but let a little dirt get in the carburetor and—well, a car has to stand there until a mechanic comes and takes out the screen. Let a light go off, and an electrician has to come and put in a new fuse. Let an elevator stop, and there's a panic."

"Well, I don't know," said Mr. Pritchard. "Americans are pretty mechanical people all in all. Our ancestors did pretty well for themselves."

"Sure, they did. So could we if we had to. Can you set the timer on your car?"

"Well, I—"

"Go further," said Ernest. "Suppose you had to stay out here two weeks. Could you keep from starving to death? Or would you get pneumonia and die?"

"Well," said Mr. Pritchard, "you see, people specialize now."

"Could you kill a cow?" Ernest insisted. "Could you cut it up and cook it?"

Mr. Pritchard found that he was getting impatient with this young man. "There's a kind of cynicism running around the country," he said sharply. "It seems to me young people have lost their faith in America. Our ancestors had faith."

"They had to eat," Ernest said. "They didn't have time for faith. People don't work much any more. They've got time for faith."

"But they haven't any faith," Mr. Pritchard cried. "What's got into them?"

"I wonder," Ernest said. "I've even tried to figure it out. My old man had two faiths. One was that honesty got rewarded some way or other. He thought that if a man was honest he somehow got along, and he thought if a man worked hard and saved he could pile up a little money and feel safe. Teapot Dome and a lot of stuff like that fixed him on the first, and nineteen-thirty fixed him on the other. He found out that the most admired people weren't honest at all. And he died wondering, a kind of an awful wondering, because the two things he believed in didn't work out—honesty and thrift. It kind of struck me that nobody has put anything in place of those two."

Mr. Pritchard shook this out of his head. "You can't be thrifty because of taxes," he said. "There was a time when a man could build up an estate, but now he can't. Taxes take it all. You're just working for the government. I tell you, it knocks initiative on the head. No one has any ambition any more."

"It don't make a lot of difference who you work for if you believe in it," said Ernest. "The government or anybody else."

Mr. Pritchard interrupted him. "The returning soldiers," he said, "they're the ones I'm worrying about. They don't want to settle down and go to work. They think the government owes them a living for life and we can't afford it."

Ernest's forehead was beaded with perspiration now, and there was a white line around his mouth and a sick look in his eyes. "I was in it," he said softly. "No, no, don't worry. I'm not going to tell you about it. I wouldn't do that. I don't want to."

Mr. Pritchard said, "Of course, I've got the greatest respect for our soldiers, and I think they should have a voice."

Ernest's fingers crept to his lapel buttonhole. "Sure," he said, "sure, I know." He spoke as though he addressed a child. "I read in the papers about our best men. They must be our best men 'cause they got the biggest jobs.

I read what they say and do, and I've got a lot of friends that you might call bums, and there's awful little difference between them. I've heard some of the bums get off stuff that sounded even better than the stuff that the Secretary of State gets off— Oh, what the hell!" He laughed. "I've got an invention, and it's a rubber drum that you beat with a sponge. It's for the drunks that want to play traps in the orchestra. I'm going to take a little walk."

"You're nervous," said Mr. Pritchard.

"Yeah, I'm nervous," Ernest said. "Everybody's nervous. And I'll tell you something. If we've got to fight somebody again, you know what's the most awful thing? I'll go too. That's the most awful thing." And he got up and walked away, back in the direction from which the bus had come.

His head was down and his hands were in his pockets and his feet beat against the gravel of the road and he was holding his mouth very tight and he couldn't stop. "I'm nervous," he said, "I'm just nervous. That's all it is."

Mr. Pritchard stared after him and then he lowered his eyes to his hands and got out his nail file again and cleaned his nails. Mr. Pritchard was shaken and he didn't know why. With all Mr. Pritchard's pessimism about government interference with business, there was always in the back of his mind a great hopefulness. Somewhere there was a man like Coolidge or like Hoover, who would come along and take the government out of the hands of these fools in the administration, and then everything would be all right. The strikes would stop and everybody would make money and be happy. It was just around the corner. Mr. Pritchard believed it. He had no idea that the world had changed. It has just made a few mistakes and the right man would come along—say, Bob Taft—and everything would get on an even keel again and these damned experiments would stop.

But this young man bothered him because this was a bright young man, and he had a feeling of hopelessness. Although he hadn't said it, Mr. Pritchard knew that Ernest Horton wouldn't even vote for Bob Taft if he were nominated. And Mr. Pritchard, like most of his associates, believed in miracles, but he was deeply shaken. Horton hadn't attacked Mr. Pritchard directly but—now, about the carburetor. Mr. Pritchard let his mind create the shape of a carburetor. Could he take it apart? Vaguely he knew that there was a little float in a carburetor, and in his mind he could see the brass screen and the gaskets.

But he had more important things to think about, he told himself. Horton had said "if the lights went out"—and Mr. Pritchard tried to think where the fuse boxes were in his house, and he didn't know. Horton had been attacking him. Horton didn't like him. Suppose they were stranded as the young man had said.

Mr. Pritchard closed his eyes and he was standing in the aisle of the bus. "Don't worry," he said to the other passengers, "I'm going to take care of everything. I haven't built a big business organization without some ability,

you know. Let's reason this out," he said. "We need food first. There's
some cows in that field back there." And Horton had said he didn't
know how to kill a cow. Well, he'd show him. Probably Horton didn't
know there was a pistol in the compartment on the instrument board. But
Mr. Pritchard knew.

Mr. Pritchard took out the pistol. He got out of the bus and walked
away toward the field and climbed a fence. He held the big black pistol in
his hand. Mr. Pritchard had been to a great many movies. His mind unconsciously made a dissolve. He didn't see himself kill the cow or cut it up,
but he saw himself come to the overhang again with a great slab of red
meat. "There's food for you," he said. "Now for a fire." And again he dissolved, and the fire was leaping and a big piece of meat hung on a stick
over the blaze.

And Camille said, "But what about that animal? It belongs to someone."

Mr. Pritchard answered, "Expediency knows no law. The law of survival
comes first. Nobody could expect me to let you people starve."

And suddenly he dissolved again and he shook his head and opened his
eyes. "Stay off that," he whispered to himself. "Keep away from that." Where
had he seen her? If he could just talk to her a little while he ought to be
able to place it. He knew he wasn't wrong because her face had given him
a clutching sensation in his chest. He must not only have seen her, but
something must have happened. He looked toward the bus. Pimples and
the two girls were still inside.

He got to his feet and brushed the seat of his trousers as though the paper
had not protected him from dust. The rain was only misting a little now,
and in the west there were patches of blue sky. Everything was going to
be all right. He walked over to the bus and climbed the steps. Van Brunt
was stretched out on the seat at the rear which went across the width of
the bus. Van Brunt seemed to be asleep. Pimples and the girls were talking
softly so that they wouldn't disturb him.

"What I want in a wife is to be true," Pimples said.

"How about you?" Camille asked. "You figure to be true too?"

"Sure," said Pimples, "if she's the right kind of wife I will."

"Well, suppose she isn't?"

"Well, then I'll show her a thing or two. I'll show her two can play that
game, like Cary Grant done in that movie."

An empty pie tin and another with only a quarter of a pie left were on
the seat across from the group. The two girls sat together and Pimples,
sitting sideways on the seat ahead of them, dropped his arm over the back.

They all looked up as Mr. Pritchard came in. "You mind if I sit in?" he
said.

"Sure, come on in," said Pimples. "You like to have a piece of pie? Here's
a piece right here." And he handed the pie to Mr. Pritchard and moved the
empty tins so he could sit down.

"Have you got a girl now?" Camille continued.

"Well, kind of a one. But she's—er—well, she's kind of silly."

"Is she true to you?"

"Sure," said Pimples.

"How do you know?"

"Well, I never could—I mean—yeah, I'm sure."

"I guess you'll be getting married pretty soon," Mr. Pritchard said playfully, "and going in business for yourself."

"No, not for a while," said Pimples, "I'm studying by mail. There's a big future in radar. Make up to seventy-five dollars a week inside of a year."

"You don't say?"

"There's fellas that took that course that wrote in and said that's what they're making," said Pimples. "One of them is a district manager already, after one year."

"District manager of what?" Mr. Pritchard asked.

"Just district manager. That's what he said in his letter, and it's printed right in the ad."

Mr. Pritchard was beginning to feel good again. Here was ambition. Not everybody was cynical.

Camille said, "When do you think you'll get married?"

"Oh, not right yet," said Pimples. "I think a fella ought to see the world a little before he settles down. He ought to get around some. I might get on a ship. If you know radar, why, you know radio too. I thought I might get on a ship and be a radio operator for a while."

"But when are you going to finish your course?" Mr. Pritchard asked.

"Well, the lessons are going to start pretty soon now. I've got the coupon all made out and I'm saving up for the down payment. I took a test and they say I got plenty of talent. I had three or four letters from them."

Camille's eyes were very weary. Mr. Pritchard looked at her face. He knew his eyes were shielded by his glasses. He thought she had a fine face when you looked at it closely. Her lips were so full and friendly now, and only her eyes were tired. All the way from Chicago on a bus, he thought. She didn't look strong enough. He could see the fullness of her breasts under her suit and the suit was wrinkled. She had turned the French cuffs of her shirt inside out so that the edges would be clean. Mr. Pritchard noticed this. It meant neatness to him. He studied little details.

He felt this girl almost like a perfume. He felt an excitement and a hunger. It's just that you don't often see a girl like this, so attractive and so nice, he told himself. And then he heard himself talking and he hadn't even known he was going to talk.

"Miss Oaks," he said, "I've been thinking, and it occurred to me that you might like to listen to a little business idea I had. I'm president of quite a large corporation and I thought—well, I'm sure these young people would excuse us for a little while if you'd care to hear my ideas. Would you step over to the cliff there? I have some newspapers to sit on." He was astonished at his own words.

"Oh, Jesus!" Camille said to herself. "Here it comes."

Mr. Pritchard got down first and gallantly helped Camille off the bus. He held her elbow as she stepped across the ditch and he guided her gently to the spread newspapers where he and Ernest had sat. He pointed downward.

"Oh, I don't know," Camille said. "I've been sitting a long time."

"Well, maybe the change in position will rest you," said Mr. Pritchard. "You know, when I'm working long hours at my desk I change the height of my chair about every hour, and I find it keeps me fresh." He helped her to sit down on the newspapers. She covered her knees with her skirt and sat hugging her knees against her breast.

Mr. Pritchard sat down beside her. He took off his glasses. "I've been thinking," he said. "You know, a man in my position has to look ahead and plan. Now, technically, I'm on a vacation." He smiled. "Vacation—I wonder what a real vacation would be like."

Camille smiled. The ground felt very hard. She wondered how long this was going to take.

"Now the main raw product of a successful company is human beings," Mr. Pritchard said. "I'm always looking for human beings. You can get steel and rubber any time, but brains, talent, beauty, ambition—that's the difficult product."

"Look, mister," Camille said, "I'm awful tired."

"I know, my dear, and I'll come to the point. I want to employ you. That's as simply as I can say it."

"As what?"

"As a receptionist. It's quite a specialized job, and from there you could become—well, you might even become my personal secretary."

Camille was played out. She looked toward the cave entrance where Mrs. Pritchard was. She couldn't see anything. "What'll your wife have to say about that?"

"Well, what's she got to do with it? She doesn't run my business."

"Mister, like I said, I'm tired. We don't have to go through all that. I'd like to be married. I'd be a good wife, and with a settlement so I wouldn't have to worry for a while, why, I could even be good to a man."

"I don't see what you're getting at," Mr. Pritchard said.

"Yes, you do," said Camille. "You won't like me because I don't play it your way. You'd like to take months to get around to it and surprise me with it, but I'm nearly broke. You say your wife doesn't run your business, but I say she does. You and your business and everything about you. I'm trying to be nice but I'm tired. She probably picks your secretaries and you don't even know it. That's a tough woman."

"I don't know what you're talking about."

"Yes, you do," Camille said. "Who bought your tie?"

"Well—"

"She would know about me in a minute. She would. Now let me talk a little bit. You couldn't ask a girl outright. You'd have to go round about. But there's only two ways, mister. You either fall in love or you make a business proposition. If you'd said, 'Here's the way it is. So much for an apartment and so much for clothes,' why, I could have thought it out and I could have come to a conclusion, and it might have worked. But I'm not going to be nibbled to death by ducks. Did you want to surprise me after two, three months of me sitting at a desk? I'm getting too old to play."

Mr. Pritchard's chin stuck out. "My wife does not run my business," he said. "I don't know where you got that idea."

"Oh, skip it," said Camille. "But I'd just as soon come up against a nest of rattlesnakes as your wife if she didn't like me."

"I'm a little surprised at your attitude," Mr. Pritchard said. "I hadn't thought of any of these things. I was just trying to offer you a job. You can take it or leave it."

"Oh, brother!" said Camille. "If you can kid yourself into believing that, God help any girl you get. She'll never know where she stands."

Mr. Pritchard smiled at her. "You're just tired," he said. "Maybe when you get rested you'll think it over."

The enthusiasm was gone out of his voice and Camille was relieved. She thought maybe she had made a mistake because he'd be very easy to handle, a real sucker. Loraine could have taken his shirt in one day.

Mr. Pritchard saw her face differently now. He saw hardness in it and defiance, and now that he was this close he saw the make-up and how it was put on, and he felt naked before this girl. It bothered him to have her talk this way. He had thought if everything worked out—well, he would —well—but the trouble was that she knew. Only he wouldn't have called it—well, there was such a thing as being a lady about such things.

He was confused, and in his confusion he was getting angry again. Twice in one day to be angry was unusual with him. His neck was getting red with anger. He had to cover up. He had to for his own sake. He said crisply, "I simply offered you a job. You don't want it—all right. There's no reason to be vulgar about it. There's such a thing as being a lady."

An edge came into her voice. "Look, Mac," she said, "I can play rough too. This lady business does it. I'm going to tell you something. You thought you recognized me. Now, do you belong to any clubs like The Octagon International or The Birds of the World or The Two Fifty—Three Thousand Club?"

"I'm an Octagon," Mr. Pritchard said stiffly.

"You remember the girl that sits in the wine glass? I've seen what you boys look like. I don't know what you get out of it and I don't want to know. But I know it isn't pretty, mister. And maybe you'd know a lady if you saw one. I don't know." Her voice came in little breaks and there was almost a hysteria of weariness in her. She jumped to her feet. "I'm going to take a stroll now, Mac. Don't give me any trouble because I know you, and I know your wife."

She walked away quickly. Mr. Pritchard watched her go. His eyes were wide and there was a heavy weight in his chest, a kind of played-out, physical horror. He watched her pretty body swaying as she went, and he saw her pretty legs, and his mind took her clothes off, and she was standing beside the huge glass and the wine was running down in red streams over her stomach and thighs and buttocks.

Mr. Pritchard's mouth was open and his neck was very red. He looked away from her and studied his hands. He took out his gold nail file and put it back in his pocket again. A dizziness came over him. He stood up uncertainly and walked down under the cliff to the little cave where Mrs. Pritchard lay.

She opened her eyes and smiled as he entered. Mr. Pritchard lay down beside her quickly. He pulled up her coat and crawled under it.

"Dear, you're tired," she said. "Elliott! what are you doing? Elliott!"

"Shut up," he said. "You hear me? Shut up! You're my wife, aren't you? Hasn't a man got any rights with his wife?"

"Elliott, you're mad! Someone'll—someone'll see you." She fought him in panic. "I don't know you," she said. "Elliott, you're tearing my dress."

"I bought it, didn't I? I'm tired of being treated like a sick cat."

Bernice cried softly in fear and in horror.

When he left her she cried with her face nestled close to her fur coat. Gradually her crying stopped and she sat up and looked out the cave entrance. Her eyes were ferocious. She raised her hand and set her nails against her cheek. She drew them down experimentally once and then she bit her lower lip and slashed downward with her fingernails. She could feel the blood oozing from the scratches. She put out her hand and dirtied it on the cave floor and rubbed the dirt into her bleeding cheek. The blood flowed down through the dirt and down her neck to the collar of her waist.

EIGHTEEN

Mildred and Juan came out of the barn and she said, "Look, the rain has stopped. Look at the sun on the mountains. It's going to be beautiful."

Juan grinned.

"You know, I feel wonderful," she said. "I feel wonderful."

"Sure," said Juan.

"Do you feel wonderful enough to hold my mirror? I couldn't see in there." She took a little square mirror from her purse. "Here. No, a little higher." She combed her hair quickly and patted some powder on her cheeks and put on lipstick. She peered very closely in the mirror because she could see only at short range. "Do you think I'm flippant for a violated girl?"

"You're all right," he said. "I like you."

"But just that? No more?"

"Do you want me to lie?"

She laughed. "I guess I do a little. No, I don't. And you won't take me to Mexico?"

"No."

"This is the end then? There isn't any more?"

"How do I know?" Juan asked.

She put the mirror and the lipstick back in her purse and smoothed the lipstick on, one lip over the other. "Brush the straw off my coat, will you?"

She turned as he brushed her coat with his hand. "Because," she went on, "my father and mother don't know about these things. I'm sure I was conceived immaculately. My mother planted me, a number one bulb, before the snow came and covered me with soil and sand and manure." She was giddy. "Can't go to Mexico. What do we do now?"

"Go back and dig out the bus and drive to San Juan." He walked toward the entrance gate of the old farm.

"Can I take your hand just for a little?"

He looked at the hand with the amputated finger and started to move to the other side to give her his whole hand.

"No," she said, "I like that one." She took his hand and rubbed her finger over the smooth skin of the amputation.

"Don't do that," he said. "It makes me nervous."

She clutched his hand tightly. "I won't have to put on my glasses," she said.

The ranges to the east of them were glowing and gold with the setting sun. Juan and Mildred turned to the right and started up the hill toward the bus.

"Will you tell me something as—well, as a payment for my whoring?" Juan laughed. "What do you want?"

"Why did you come down here? Did you think I'd follow you?"

"You want the truth or do you want to play games?" he asked.

"Well, I'd like both. But no—er—I guess I want the truth first."

"Well, I was running away," said Juan. "I was going to beat my way back to Mexico and disappear and let the passengers take care of themeslves."

"Oh, and why don't you?"

"I don't know," he said. "It went sour. The Virgin of Guadalupe let me down. I thought I fooled her. She doesn't like fooling. She cut the heart out of it."

"You don't believe that," she said seriously. "I don't believe it either. What was the real reason?"

"For what?"

"For you coming down to that old place?"

Juan walked along and his face broke into a wide smile and the scar on his lip made the smile off-center. He looked down at her and his black eyes were warm. "I came down here because I hoped you would go for a walk, and then I thought I might—I might even get you."

She wrapped her arm around his arm and pulled her cheek hard against the sleeve of his jacket. "I wish it could go on a little more," she said, "but I know it can't. Good-by, Juan."

"Good-by," he said. And they walked slowly back toward the bus.

NINETEEN

Van Brunt lay outstretched on the back seat of the bus. His eyes were closed but he was not sleeping. His head rested on his right arm and the weight of his head cut off the full flow of blood to his right hand.

When Camille and Mr. Pritchard left the bus Pimples and Norma were silent for a while.

Van Brunt listened to age creeping in his veins. He could almost feel the rustle of blood in his papery arteries, and he could hear his heart beat with a creaking whistle in it. His right hand was going to sleep, but it was his left hand that worried him. There wasn't much feeling in his left hand. The skin was insensitive, as though it were a thick rubber. He rubbed and massaged his hand when he was alone to bring the circulation back, and he really knew what was the matter although he hardly admitted it even to himself.

A few months ago he had fainted, just for a moment, and the doctor had read his blood pressure and told him to take it easy and he'd be all right. And two weeks ago another thing had happened. There had been an electric flash in his head behind his eyes, a feeling like a blinding blue-white glare for a second, and now he couldn't read any more. It wasn't that he couldn't see. He saw clearly enough, but the words on a page swam and ran together and squirmed like snakes, and he couldn't make out what they said.

He knew very well he had had two little strokes, but it was a secret he kept from his wife and she kept from him and the doctor kept from both. And he waited, waited for another one, the one that would flash in his mind, would flash through his body, and if it didn't kill him, it would numb out all feeling. Knowing it had made him angry, angry at everyone. Physical hatred of everyone around him crowded in his throat.

He tried on all possible glasses. He used magnifying glasses on the newspapers because he himself, with half of his mind, was trying to keep his condition secret from himself. His angers had a habit now of bursting from him without warning, but the real horror to him was that he cried, uncontrollably sometimes, and couldn't stop. Recently he had awakened early in the morning saying to himself, "Why should I wait for it?"

His father had died of the same thing, but before he died he had lain like a gray, helpless worm in a bed for eleven months, and all the money he had saved for his old age was spent on doctor bills. Van Brunt knew that if the same thing happened to him the eight thousand dollars he had in the bank would be gone, and his old wife would have nothing after she buried him.

As soon as the drugstores opened that day, he went in to see his friend Milton Boston of the Boston Drug Store.

"I've got to poison some squirrels, Milton," he said. "Give me a little cyanide, will you?"

"That's damn dangerous stuff," Milton said. "I kinda hate to sell it. Let me give you some strychnine. It'll do the job just as well."

"No," Van Brunt said, "I've got a government bulletin with a new formula and it calls for cyanide."

Milton said, "Well, all right. You'll have to sign the poison book, of course. But look out for that stuff, Van. Look out for it. Don't leave it around."

They'd been friends for many years. They'd gone in the Blue Lodge together and had been through the Chairs, and in succeeding years they had been Worshipful Master of the San Ysidro Lodge, and then Milton went into the Royal Arch and the Scottish Rite and Van Brunt never went beyond the third degree. But they had remained friends.

"How much of the stuff do you want?"

"About an ounce, I guess."

"That's an awful lot, Van."

"I'll bring back what I don't use."

Milton was worried. "Don't touch it at all with your hands, will you?"

"I know how to handle it," Van Brunt said.

Then he went into his office in the basement of his house, and with a sharp pocketknife he pricked the back of his hand. When there was a little blood coming out, he opened the glass tube of crystals. And then he stopped. He couldn't do it. He just couldn't tip the crystals into the cut.

After an hour he took the tube to the bank and put it in his safety-deposit box along with his will and his insurance policies. He thought of buying a little ampule to wear around his neck. Then, if the big one came, he could maybe get it to his mouth the way those people in Europe did. But he couldn't take it now. Maybe it wouldn't happen.

There was a weight of disappointment on him, and there was anger in him too. All the people around him who weren't going to die angered him. And there was another thing that bothered him. The stroke had knocked the cap off one set of his inhibitions. He had suddenly reachieved powerful desires. He was pantingly drawn toward young women, even little girls. He couldn't keep his eyes and his thought from them, and in the midst of his sick desires he would burst into tears. He was afraid, as a child is afraid of a strange house.

He was too old to accommodate the personality change of his stroke and the new nature it gave him. He had never been a reader, but now that he could not read he was famished for reading. And his temper grew sharper and more violent all the time until people he had known for years began to avoid him.

He listened to time passing in his veins and he wanted death to come and he was afraid of it. Through half-shut eyes he saw the golden light of the sunset come into the bus. His lips moved a little and he said, "Evening, evening, evening." The word was very beautiful, and he could hear the whistling in his heart. A fullness of feeling came on him, swelled in his chest, swelled in his throat, pulsed in his head. He thought he was going to cry again. He tried to clench his right hand, but it was asleep and it wouldn't clench.

And then he became rigid with tension. His body seemed distended, like a blown-up rubber glove. The evening light blazed in. In back of his eyes a terrible flickering flash came. He felt himself tumbling and tumbling toward grayness and toward darkness and into black, black. . . .

The sun touched the western hills and flattened itself, and its light was yellow and clear. The saturated valley glittered under the level light. The clean, washed air was crisp. In the fields the flattened grain and the thick, torpid stems of the wild oats tightened themselves, and the sheathed petals of the golden poppies loosened a little. The yellow river boiled and swirled and cut viciously at the banks. In the back seat of the bus Van Brunt snored hoarsely against his palate. His forehead was wet. His mouth was open and so were his eyes.

TWENTY

Pimples moved into the seat beside Norma and she gathered her skirts daintily against her and slid a little toward the window.

"What do you suppose that old guy wants with that girl?" he asked suspiciously.

"I don't know," said Norma. "But I tell you one thing. She can handle him. She's a wonderful girl."

Pimples said, "Oh, I don't know. There's other wonderful girls."

Norma flared up. "Like who?" she said, derisively.

"Like you," said Pimples.

"Oh!" She hadn't expected this. She put her head down and stared at her laced fingers, trying to regain her balance.

"What did you have to go and quit for?" Pimples said.

"Well, Mrs. Chicoy wasn't nice to me."

"I know. She isn't nice to anybody. But I wish you didn't quit. We could have got together, maybe."

Norma didn't answer. Pimples said, "If you say the word I'll get out one of the raisin pies. They're pretty nice."

"No. No, thanks. I couldn't eat anything."

"You sick?"

"No."

"Well, if you'd only come back to work at the Corners we could maybe go into San Ysidro Saturday nights and dance and stuff like that."

"You didn't think of that before," she said.

"I didn't think you liked me."

She became a little arch now. This was a delightful game. "What makes you think I like you now?" she said.

"Well, you're different now. You kinda changed. I like the way you done your hair."

"Oh, that," she said. "Well, there wasn't any reason to kinda fix myself up back at the lunchroom. Who'd see me?"

"I would," Pimples said gallantly. "Come on back. They'll give you your job again. I guarantee that."

She shook her head. "No, when I quit, I quit. I don't go crawling back. Besides, there's a future. We've got plans."

"What kind of plans?"

Norma wondered whether she ought to tell. In some ways it was bad luck, but she found she couldn't help herself. "We're going to get a little apartment with a nice davenport and a radio. And we're going to have a stove and an icebox and I'm going to study to be a dental nurse." Her eyes were shining.

"Who's 'we'?"

"Me and Miss Camille Oaks, that's who. When I'm a dental nurse I can dress good and we'll go to shows and maybe give little dinners."

"Nuts," he said. "You won't never do that."

"What makes you say that?"

"You just won't. Now, why don't you come back to the Corners? I'm studying radar and we'll go out together sometimes and you can't tell—we might get together. You take a girl—she's gonna want to get married. I'm a young guy. It's—er—it's good for a young guy to have a wife. It gives him kind of—ambition."

Norma looked into his face, a level, questioning look, to see whether he was making fun of her. And there was something so direct in her look that Pimples misinterpreted it and glanced away in embarrassment.

"I know," he said bitterly. "You think you couldn't go with a guy that's got these things. I done everything. I spent over a hundred dollars going to doctors and for stuff at the drugstore. But it don't do no good. There was one doctor says they won't last. He says they'll go away in a couple more years. But I don't know if that's the truth. Go ahead," he said fiercely. "Get your damn apartment. Maybe I got ways of having fun you never heard of. I don't have to take no guff from nobody." His voice was completely miserable and he stared down into his lap.

Norma looked at him in amazement. She had never known this kind of abject pain in anyone but herself. No one ever needed Norma for sympathy or reassurance. A bubble of warmth burst in her and a kind of gratefulness.

She said, "Don't you think like that. You don't have to, because if a girl cared for you she wouldn't think like that. The doctor knew what he was talking about. I knew three other young fellows, and them things went away after a while."

Pimples kept his head down. There was still misery in him but an imp was stirring too. He felt the advantage coming to his side and he began to use it, and it was a new thing to him, a new discovery. Always he had blustered with girls and bragged, and this was so easy. A sly imp began to operate.

"Well, it just gets so you can't stand it," he said. "Sometimes I think I'll just kill myself." He forced a half sob.

"Now don't you say like that," said Norma. This was a new function for her too, but one she fitted into probably better than any other.

"Nobody likes me," Pimples said. "Nobody won't have nothing to do with me."

"Don't you say like that," Norma repeated. "It's not true. I always liked you."

"No, you never."

"I did too." She laid her hand on his arm in reassurance.

Blindly he reached up and held her hand against his arm. And then his hand clasped hers and he squeezed her fingers and automatically she squeezed back. He turned in his seat and flung his arms about her and pushed his face into hers.

"Don't!" she cried. "Stop that!"

He gripped her more tightly.

"Stop it," she said. "Stop it. That old man back there."

Pimples whispered, "Listen to the old bastard snore. He's pounding his ear. Come on, come on."

She wedged her elbows against his chest to hold him away. His hands began plucking at her skirt. "Stop," she whispered. "You just stop." She knew now that she had been tricked. "Stop it! Let me get out of here!"

"Come on," he said frantically. "Please come on." Pimples' eyes were glazed and he was fighting with her skirt.

"Stop it, please stop. Suppose—suppose Camille came in? Suppose she saw what you're—"

Pimples' eyes cleared for a moment. He looked at her evilly. "Suppose she did. What do you care what that god-damned tramp sees?"

Norma's mouth fell open and her muscles relaxed. She looked at him in unbelief. She looked at him as though she hadn't heard what he said. Then her rage was cold and murderous. Her work-hardened muscles set rigidly. She tore her hand free and hit him in the mouth. She leaped to her feet and swung at him with both her fists, and he was so startled that he covered his face with his hands to protect himself.

She was spitting at him like a cat. "You skunk!" she said. "Oh, you dirty little skunk." And she kicked and shoved and pushed him out into the aisle, and she ran up the aisle and out of the bus. His feet were tangled in the stanchions of the seats and he tried to roll over.

A sickness and a weakness came over Norma. Her lips were quivering and her eyes were streaming. "Oh, the dirty skunk," she cried. "The filthy, dirty skunk."

She crossed the ditch and flung herself down in the grass and put her head down on her arms. Pimples got to his feet and peeked out the window. He didn't know what in the world to do.

Camille, walking slowly back along the road, saw Norma lying face down in the grass. She stepped across the ditch and leaned over her. "What's the matter? Did you fall down? What's the matter with you?"

Norma raised her tearful face. "I'm all right," she said.

"Get up," said Camille shortly. "Get up out of that wet grass." She reached down and jerked Norma to her feet and led her under the cliff and sat her down on the folded newspapers. "Now, what in the hell is the matter with you?"

Norma wiped her wet face with her sleeve and destroyed the last of her lipstick. "I don't want to talk about it."

"Well, that's your business," said Camille.

"That Pimples. He grabbed me."

"Well, can't you take care of yourself? Do you have to pull a nosedive?"

"That wasn't why."

"Well, what was why?" Camille wasn't really interested. She had her own troubles.

Norma rubbed her red eyes with her fingers. "I hit him," she said. "I hit him because he said you was a tramp."

Camille looked quickly away. She stared across the valley where the last of the sun was disappearing behind the mountains and she rubbed her cheek with her hand. Her eyes were dull. And then she forced them to take on life and she forced them to smile and she gave the smile to Norma.

"Look, kid," she said. "You'll just have to believe this until you find it out for yourself—everybody's a tramp some time or other. Everybody. And the worst tramps of all are the ones that call it something else."

"But you aren't."

"Let it lay," said Camille. "Just let it lay. Come on, let's try to do something with your face. New lipstick isn't as good as a bath but it's better than nothing."

Camille opened her purse and dug into it and got out a comb.

TWENTY-ONE

Juan quickened his footsteps so that Mildred had trouble keeping up with him.

"Do we have to run?" she asked.

"It'll be a lot easier digging the bus out while it's still light than floundering around in the dark."

She trotted along beside him. "Do you think you can get it out?"

"Yes."

"Well, why didn't you do that in the first place instead of walking away?"

He slowed his footsteps for a moment. "I told you," he said. "I told you twice."

"Oh, yes. You really meant that, then."

"I really mean everything," said Juan.

They came to the bus after the sun had slipped below the range. But the high clouds were lighted with rose and they threw a rose transparency over the land and the hills.

Pimples skulked out from behind the bus when Juan approached. There was a hostile cringing about him. "When are they coming out?" he asked.

"I can't get anyone," Juan said shortly. "We'll have to do it ourselves. We're going to need help. Where the hell is everybody?"

"Scattered around," said Pimples.

"Well, get out the tarpaulin."

"That lady's got it laying down up there."

"Well, get her up. I want rocks if you can find any and I want planks or some posts. We may have to tear down some fence. But leave the barbed wire up so the stock won't get out. And, Pimples—"

Pimples' mouth dropped open and his shoulders sagged. "You said—"

658

"Get all the men. I'm going to need help. I'll get the big jack out from under the back seat."

Juan climbed into the bus. It was a little dark in the bus now. He saw Van Brunt lying on the seat. "You'll have to move so I can get the jack," he said.

Suddenly Juan leaned close. The eyes of the old man were open and rolled up, and a harsh, labored snoring came from his mouth, and there was spittle around the corners of his mouth. Juan turned him over on his back and his tongue fell into his throat and his in-breathing was plugged. Juan reached into the open mouth with his fingers and pushed the tongue down and forward. He shouted, "Pimples! Pimples!" and with his free hand he knocked on the window with his gold wedding ring.

Pimples climbed into the bus.

"This man's sick, goddammit. Call some help. Blow the horn."

It was Mr. Pritchard who took over Van Brunt. He hated it and yet he had to do it. Juan cut a little piece of stick and showed him how to hold down the tongue and wedge the stick against the roof of the mouth so that the old man could breathe. Mr. Pritchard was revolted by the look of the man, and the sour odor that came from the laboring chest sickened him. But he had to do it. He didn't want to think about anything. His mind wanted to stop. A series of chilling agonies ran through him. His wife came into the bus and saw him and took the first seat inside the door, as far from him as possible. And even in the dusky light he could see the scratches and the blood on her collar. She didn't speak to him.

He said in his mind, "I must have been crazy. I don't know how I could have done it. Dear, can't you just think I was sick, out of my head?" He said it in his head. He would give her the little orchid house, and not such a little one. He'd build her the finest orchid house money could buy. But he couldn't even mention it for a long time. And the Mexican trip—they would have to go through with it. It would be horrible, but they would have to go through with it. How long would it be before the look would go out of her eyes, the reproach, the hurt, the accusation? she wouldn't speak for several days, he knew, or when she did it would be with perfect politeness; short replies and a sweet voice, and her eyes would not meet his. "Oh, God," he thought, "how do I get into these things? Why can't it be me here, dying, instead of this old man? He's never going to have to go through anything again."

He felt the men working under him on the bus. He heard the shovel bite and the suck of mud and he heard the stone thrown under the wheels. His wife sat stiffly and her lips were set in a tolerant smile. He didn't know yet how she was going to handle the situation, but it would come to her.

She was sad and she said to herself, "I must think no evil. Just because Elliott went down under a brutishness is no reason for me to lose beauty and toleration." There was a flicker of triumph in her. "I have conquered anger," she whispered, "and I have conquered disgust. I can forgive him, I know I can. But for his own sake it must not be too soon—for his own good. I'll have to wait." Her face was full of dignity and hurt.

Outside, Pimples was performing miracles of muscle and fortitude. His two-toned oxfords were destroyed with mud. Almost purposely he destroyed them. There was a layer of mud on his chocolate trousers. He violated his fine clothes. He drove his shovel into the earth and dug down behind the wheels and underneath the sides and he threw the mud out. He got down on his knees in the mud to use his hands. His wolf eyes glittered with effort and the sweat stood out on his forehead. Out of the corner of his eye he watched Juan. Juan had forgotten, and just at a time when Pimples needed him most. Pimples drove his shovel into the ground with gusty bursts of strength.

Ernest Horton took a pickax and crossed the ditch. He picked away the turf and roots and topsoil until he found what he wanted. The broken stone from the ancient crash of the hill. He lifted the stones out and piled them on the grass beside his hole.

Camille came over to him. "I'll help you carry some of these down."

"You'll get all dirty," said Ernest.

"You think I can get any dirtier than I am?" she asked.

He rested the pick head on the ground. "You wouldn't like to give me your phone number? I'd take you out."

"That was the truth," said Camille. "I don't live any place yet. I haven't got a number."

"Have it your own way," said Ernest.

"No, this is straight. Where are you going to stay?"

"Hollywood Plaza," said Ernest.

"Well, if you're in the lobby about seven o'clock day after tomorrow, I might come by."

"Fair enough," said Ernest. "I'll take you to Musso-Franck's for dinner."

"I didn't say I would," she said. "I said I might. I don't know how I'm going to feel. If I don't show up, don't drop your watch. I'm too pooped to figure anything out."

"Fair enough," said Ernest. "I'll stick around till seven-thirty."

"You're a good guy," said Camille.

"I'm just another sucker," said Ernest. "Don't take those big ones. I'll bring those. You take the little ones."

She picked a rock up in each hand and walked toward the bus.

Juan went to the old fence and tore the posts out of the earth. He tore down eight of them, but alternate posts, so that the barbed wire would not fall down. He carried the posts down and went back for more.

The rose afterglow was turning pale pink and a duskiness settled on the valley. Juan set his jack against a post and under the flange of the wheel rim, and he lifted one side of the bus. As the wheel rose, Pimples filled the hole under the tires with rocks.

Juan took another bite and lifted again, and gradually one side of the bus rose out of the mud. Juan moved his jack to the other side and raised the other wheel.

Camille and Norma were carrying rocks to fill the holes, while Ernest dug them out.

Mildred asked, "What can I do?"

"Steady this post while I get a new pinch," said Juan. He was working furiously against the coming dark. His forehead was glistening with sweat. Pimples, on his knees in the mud, packed rocks under the wheels, and the other side of the bus rose out of the mud.

"Let's get it extra high," said Juan, "so we won't have to do it all over again. I'd like to have these posts in under the wheels."

It was almost dark when they were ready. Juan said, "I want everybody to give a push when I start. If we can just make three feet we'll be all right."

"How's the road ahead?" Pimples asked.

"It looked all right to me. God! You raised hell with your clothes."

Pimples' face was sick with disappointment. "It don't amount to nothing," he said. "What good is clothes?" His tone was so despondent that Juan stared at him in the half darkness.

A tight smile raised Juan's lips. "You'll have to take charge back here, Kit, while I drive. Make them throw their weight on it when I go ahead. You know how. You take charge back here, Kit."

Pimples threw down his shovel. "Come on, everybody," he shouted. "Come on, snap into it! I'll take the right side. Girls too. Everybody got to shove." He marshaled his people at the back of the bus. For a second he looked hungrily at Mrs. Pritchard sitting inside. "She'd just be in the way, I guess," he said.

Juan climbed into the bus. "Get out and give a shove," he said to Mr. Pritchard.

The engine started easily enough. Juan let it turn over for a moment. He eased it into compound-low and then he knocked twice on the side of the bus and heard Pimples knock back twice on the rear wall. He speeded his engine a little and let his clutch in. The wheels caught, slipped, groaned, and caught, and "Sweetheart" waddled drunkenly over the bed of rocks and climbed out onto the road. Juan pulled ahead out of the mud on the road and then he set his hand brake. He stood up and looked out the doorway.

"Just pile the tools in here on the floor," he said. "Come on, let's get moving."

He turned on his lights and the beam lighted the gravel road as far as the top of the little hill.

TWENTY-TWO

Juan took the bus very slowly over the hill and down the water-scarred gravel road past the deserted house. As he turned, his headlights picked out the eyeless house and the broken windmill and the barn.

The night was very black, but a new breeze had come up, bearing the semenous smell of grass and the spice of lupine. The headlights tunneled the night over the road and an owl flew flashing in and out of the light. Far ahead a rabbit crossing the road looked into the lights so that its eyes glowed red, and then it hopped clear into the ditch.

Juan kept the bus in second gear and missed the waterscored ruts with his wheels. The inside of the bus was dark except for the dash lights. Juan let his eyes dart to the Virgin. "I ask only one thing," he said in his mind. "I gave up the other, but it would be nice if you could make it so she was sober when I get back."

Mrs. Pritchard was not rigid any more. Her head swayed with the movement of the bus and she was dreaming. She was dressed in—what—what would she have on? Something light. It would have to be white. And she was taking Ellen through her little orchid house. "You wonder why I keep a few purple orchids?" she asked Ellen. "Well, everybody has relatives who like purple ones. Even you have, Ellen, you know that. But look over here. These are just coming—the lovely browns and greens. Elliott ordered those from Brazil. They came from a thousand miles up the Amazon."

On the floor of the bus the pickax clinked against the shovel.

Pimples leaned close to Juan's ear. "I could take her over, Mr. Chicoy. You're tired out. I'll drive if you want."

"No, thanks, Kit, you've had enough."

"But I ain't tired."

"It's all right," said Juan.

Mildred could see Juan's profile against the lighted road. "I wonder how long I can make the day last. Like a peppermint stick. I'll have to hold onto today until I can get another one as good."

Over the banging and the bouncing of the bus Mr. Pritchard listened for the breathing of Van Brunt. He could just barely see the face against the seat. He found that he hated this man because he was dying. He inspected his hatred in amazement. He felt that he could strangle this man easily and get it over with. "What kind of a thing am I?" he cried. "What makes these horrible things in me? Am I going crazy? Maybe I've been working too hard. Maybe this is a nervous breakdown."

He leaned close to make sure that the breathing of the sick man was not cut off. There would be a bad bruise in the roof of his mouth where the stick was wedged. He heard a little stir and saw that Ernest Horton had come back and taken the next seat.

"You want me to take over?"

"No," said Mr. Pritchard. "I guess everything's all right. What do you suppose it is?"

"It's a stroke," said Ernest. "I didn't mean to blast you today. I was just nervous."

"Just one of those days," said Mr. Pritchard. "When things are pretty bad my wife says, 'It'll be funny some time.'"

"Well, that's a good way to look at it if you can do it," said Ernest. "I'll be at the Hollywood Plaza if you want to give me a call. Or try that apartment some night—that number I gave you."

"I'm going to be all tied up, I'm afraid," said Mr. Pritchard. "I wish you'd look in at the plant some time, though. We might do business yet."

"We might at that," said Ernest.

Norma sat next to the window now and Camille was by her side. Norma leaned her elbow on the window sill and looked out at the fluttering dark. There was a little rim of lighter sky around the edge of a great dark cloud over the western mountains, and then as the cloud lifted the evening star shone out of it, clear and washed and steady.

"Star light, star bright, first star I see tonight, wish I may, wish I might, get the wish I wish tonight."

Camille turned her head sleepily. "What did you say?"

Norma was silent for a moment. Then she asked softly, "We'll see how it goes?"

"Yeah, we'll see how it goes," said Camille.

Far ahead and a little to the left a cluster of lights came into view—little lights winking with distance, lost and lonely in the night, remote and cold and winking, strung on chains.

Juan looked at them and called, "That's San Juan up ahead."